# True Blue At Heart

## Tori Hernandez

*For...*

*My greatest love, music.*
*This is a love letter to all the songs that got me here & continue to inspire, nurture,*
*and shape me.*

*1*

A slightly overweight officiant sweats bullets as he stares past the sitting crowd into the afternoon sun. He dabs his forehead briefly with a crumpled hanky as he clears his throat.

"You may now kiss the bride," he breathes into the mic.

Lips move toward me. I completely still.

*Do I want this?*

I gulp. *It's too late now.*

I close one eye and hold my breath, preparing for this moment. I open my eye briefly, hesitating for a second, as I contemplate my choice before peering through the viewfinder of my camera. Do I want a close up or a slightly wider shot? Wider, I decide. I quickly swing the focal dial on the lens, pulling out from the couple's beaming faces, going slightly wider to include their shoulders as they move in for the "big" kiss.

*Snap!* My shutter rolls off a few captures. Erring on the side of caution, it's better to have too many photos than to miss a moment. I look away from my camera's viewfinder and see the bride and groom giggling at each other as they turn to face their seated guests. The officiant, who looks slightly relieved the ceremony is over, addresses the crowd.

"Please rise as I introduce Mr. and Mrs. Wares!" he commands jubilantly.

The crowd stands and cheers. The new married couple, who by the way look like they're straight out of a professional wedding magazine, happily make their way down the aisle, beaming as they pass me. I twist as I awkwardly chase after them onto the next round of events. After family photos, bridal party pictures, and shots of the couple, my adrenaline is pumping. It's always a game trying to wedge in the different combinations of shots within such a short time constraint.

I glance at my watch, it's only 7PM... three more hours to go.

Following the bride and groom into the reception for the grand entrance, I nudge my way between two chairs and squat to get the right angle. They slowly dance and sway in the middle of the dance floor. Every eye in the large venue stares at them. As I snap photos of them twirling, the crowd "oohs" and "aahs." For many, this scene is a dream. For me, this is my worst nightmare... all that attention, not to mention all the money spent for just one night.

A flurry of bells tinker and chime, prompting the couple to go in for a kiss, which means more photos.

Damn my back is killing me lugging around almost twenty-five pounds of gear all day. Glancing at my watch, I realize it's only been five minutes since I last checked. I swear it's been at least a half hour... Time always seems to stand still once the reception starts. For guests, it's usually a moment of refreshment, rest and reflection, but for a photographer, it's "go-time."

I catch my watch again. I try not to, but I can't help myself. It reads 9:45PM. *Hallelujah! We're almost there, Nina.*

The bride pulls me aside. She's pretty tipsy and reeks of champagne. After these past twelve hours I could use a glass, I muse.

"Nina Esquivel, I can't thank you enough," she leans in, and breathily giggles. "You made this whole day so much fun and special. You really have a knack for this."

I smile shyly and nervously laugh. I hate talking about myself, even with clients, *especially* with clients.

"Thank *you* for planning such a special day, *Mrs.* Wares," I reply, aiming for a slight deflection.

She lights up at hearing her new name and rushes off to find her newly minted husband.

A few minutes drag on, but I'm in the home stretch now. The wedding planner passes out the jumbo sparklers and organizes the guests into two lines, forming an aisle for the grand departure. One sparkler ignites into a thousand micro sparks, blazing beautiful trails of light against the darkened night. One guest lights another's and within a couple of minutes, a gorgeous array of light bursts create a volcanic tunnel. Hand in hand, the bride and groom run through the lit archway, while the guests all whistle and wish them well. Another successful wedding in the books. Another night of cheerful smiles, laughter and love.

*So why do I feel so hollow inside?*

As I make my way down the dark highway on the long drive home from San Diego to San Clemente, I reflect on some of the key moments from the day, reliving them in my mind's eye.

I look across the room at the reception and see the cutest DJ dressed in black. I scope him out. He's pretty tall, probably 6'2" with a really great smile. At one point during the reception, he waves at me. Little butterflies leave me breathless like I've just gone down a rollercoaster. Could this be the start of something?

*You're a terrible flirt, Nina.*

I shake the thought away.

The DJ glances up as I cross the venue towards him. *Wow*, up close, his smile really lights up his whole face; his straight white teeth are practically glowing. A bright, silver ring shines from his nose in the twinkle light. A septum piercing is not really my bag, but whatever, I can't afford to be choosy.

About twenty feet away, I glance quickly down at my all black ensemble. I suck in my belly, but don't want to push my already robust boobs out too far to attract unwarranted attention from guests. I stand up straight before regaining a casual, nonchalant composure. Adjusting my smile, I want to give him my best one that doesn't scream overeagerness. The DJ walks up to me, and just as I think he's about to stop and talk to me, he brushes by and engages with the bride behind me, letting her know the toasts are coming up in five minutes. Awkwardly, I do my best to shake off this miscommunication on my behalf, and pat down my frizzy hair. My sister, Maria, always insists on straightening it for wedding days, but this morning, I was in too much of a rush.

At best my hair is a wonderful mane of thick, chocolate ringlets with little strands of sun kissed gold woven throughout. At worst, my hair looks like Hagrid from *Harry Potter*, a giant frizzy mess that cannot be contained. On the daily it tends to fall more on the Hagrid side of the spectrum, sometimes hitting the upper echelon of Tarzan after he's had a tussle with the apes. Today it's braided back to maximize my eyesight, while maintaining professionalism.

I shrug off yet another micro rejection and refocus my efforts on my job. Assuming my stealthy position for the toasts, this means squatting for at least twenty minutes, possibly longer. The physical discomfort all depends on whether the best man and maid of honor are Chatty Kathies or not… based on my current position kneeling on a slab of hard, cold concrete, I pray for short and sweet well wishes.

Forty minutes later, as the DJ grabs the mic from the father of the bride, I prep to stand. *Praise be!* My lower half might as well be gone. I have no feeling left in my legs or feet. Thanking the heavens the speeches are finally over, I shake my head, preparing to make my first movement. I wiggle my toes in my sneakers. Pins and needles flood my body, like a thousand knives jabbing my lower limbs. I stagger over behind a pillar to hide while I regain feeling and collect myself. I lean my head on my arm that's resting up on the pillar as Steely Dan's "Dirty Work" plays softly in the background. *Finally, a wedding with a decent setlist.* I swear, every single wedding this year has the same exact playlist, they just shuffle the order.

Trying not to dwell on the thousands of pictures I need to upload and sort through tomorrow, I think about the happy Mr. and Mrs. Wares. They are only twenty-four years old and they just made one of the biggest life choices you can make, that is if you're lucky enough to make it.

I used to think I'd be married with kids by twenty-five, like my parents. *"I'd be a young mom,"* I would always say... but apparently time has something different in store for me. Lately, it seems like time is flying by without a thought or care. I'm twenty-nine years old - or years young as I like to think - but damn, thirty is right around the corner... like a few months around the corner. I have zero romantic prospects, I live at my sister's house, and I barely have enough savings to buy a new camera.

I'm twenty-nine and a half(ish) and my life is at best a seven. Don't get me wrong, I live a wonderful life. I have a family most people would dream of; they're the kind of friends you would choose as your family, but I don't have to because they already are mine. However, being so close, we are up in each other's business about EVERYTHING, and I mean *every* thing.

They'll definitely want to hear all about tonight, and being a house full of night owls, they might expect a call, but I don't know if I have it in me to recap the day by the time I get home.

Coming back to reality, I get off the freeway and make my way through the neighborhoods. I have to text my sister when I arrive past 7PM because Javi, my one-year-old nephew, is asleep in bed, and their dog usually barks at my arrival, waking him up. Once he's up, he's up for the night.

I pull up to the curb, turn off the ignition, and just fall back into my seat, waiting for the green light to go inside. Closing my eyes, I exhale deeply, and listen to the sounds of Monster Rally's "Big Surf" as it serenades me. It's 10:45PM on a Saturday night and I can't wait to shower, get in my bed, and throw on an episode of *Bates Motel*. Hmm, maybe tonight I'm more in the mood for *I Dream of Jeannie*. I wish I could say my partying days were behind me, but they were never there to begin with.

My phone chirps, alerting me of a new text message. I look down and see a new message from my sister, Maria, the baby of the family at twenty-three years old. It's a video of her at the local bar surrounded by a bunch of friends raising shots together. A club beat rages on in the background as a bunch of colored lights pulse off their faces. She yells in the video for me to come join them.

A new text from her reads: *Come on, hunnay, live a little.*

The thought of getting dressed and hanging out with a bunch of twenty year olds terrifies me, but I appreciate the effort on Maria's part to ask.

I text her back: *Still on my way home from that wedding. Maybe next time. Love ya!*

A little thumbs down icon appears on my text just as the poop emoji pops up below it, followed by a blue heart icon.

I see the driveway light flicker on and off, signaling me that it's okay to come in. Like a cat burglar, I tiptoe inside, trying not to make a peep. I artfully close the door behind me without a sound, and plop down on my bed with keys, camera and all. I really should shower, but the whole process sounds odious and energy draining. Deciding I want to watch something light, I flip on *I Dream of Jeannie*. It's the one where Tony's jealous of Jeannie's fictitious Tony Millionaire. As I laugh at the screen, I feel my eyelids grow heavier by the second and before I realize it, I'm drifting off into dreamland.

The sun is out, the skies are clear. It's a beautiful day. After a little coastal drive, I pull up in front of my parents' house. Did I mention they live next door to my sister? Yeah, it's like one big compound. Parking out front, I stay in my car, *my sanctuary*. I drive a 1989 blue Land Cruiser, named Gloria. She's my heart and soul. She's a vibe. I get more stares and smiles and the occasional shakas thrown my way, sometimes even free valet parking, and it's all attributed to Gloria and her cool factor. *I am not that cool.* If I was driving any other car, I'd be paying for parking and people would easily be cutting me off while somehow blaming me for it.

The Beach Boys' "Kokomo" plays loudly from my epic sound system. I always listen to music on high decibels, no exception, even to my neighbors' dismay. It drives my mother insane. She's constantly reminding me that I'm going to lose my hearing someday. I lean my head back against my leather seat and close my eyes.

*"Aruba, Jamaica... Bermuda, Bahamas, come on pretty mama,"* the boys croon over the stereo.

*Ahhh* white sands, shady palms, crystal clear pools of water... a nice piña colada with a side of SPF 50 sunscreen mist. *Bliss.*

"Hmmmm, yes please," I mumble to myself, drumming up quite a visual of me relaxing under a coconut tree, taking in all the rays a warmer climate has to offer.

My daydream develops into an even clearer picture; the salty ocean mist breezes through my curls as I sit in my beach chair, alone... *ummm, this is a fantasy, Nina, you don't have to be alone.* Okay. Now there's a second beach chair next to mine, but it's empty. *Who shall sit beside me? Henry Cavill?* Just as I'm scanning through my potential fantasy partners, a giant rattling *bang!* hits the glass right next to my face. I jump in my seat.

A hand hysterically motions for me to roll down the window or open the car door. I don't even need to look to know who demands my attention.

"Nina, what are you doing out here?" my mother, Lucy, yells through the glass. My mom's piercing blue eyes look brighter - if possible - as her eyebrows lift almost all the way up to her strawberry blonde hairline. She has a bigger forehead, which is more prominent now as she's growing out her bangs. She energetically knocks on the window again with an exasperated look in her eyes. "Nina, turn that off. I can't hear myself think."

That's exactly why I listen to my music loudly, so I get lost in the melodies and lyrics and don't have to think about anything.

I can't totally hear Mom but I know the gist of her meaning. She repeatedly points a finger down, motioning for me to turn the music to a more "acceptable" volume. She won't relent. If us Esquivels know how to do one thing, it's holding our ground. I know she won't back down, so as per usual, I'm the one in the family who gives in.

Sighing, I turn the dial down slightly, and then surrender and just turn off the truck's ignition. All noise evaporates.

"Finally," Mom whines, somewhat pleased. "Come inside, quickly." She's off like a bee, making her way up to the front door and entryway into the house. When I don't follow quickly enough, she turns around and yells, "Nina, it's an emergency!"

What?! Why didn't she just say that at the beginning. My first thought is Abuela. *Is she okay??* I hasten into the house on the heels of my mom, still stiff from the wedding two nights ago. My heart drops like lead in the pit of my stomach. Mentally preparing for a major blow, I gather my emotions. A small part in the back of my mind is questioning whether I need to jump to such a devastating conclusion.

Mom sits down at the barstool and braces her hands on the countertop. She looks at me, full of apprehension and distress.

"C'mon, Mama, what is it?" I beg.

"Nina, it's your sister..." she informs me. "She might be getting back together with Jesse."

*Oh!* I immediately relax in relief.

"Geez, Mom, you gotta stop doing this," I plead. "I thought something seriously was wrong... I thought something happened to Abuela!"

She waves a hand all nonchalantly, shaking her head and giving me one of her signature hair tosses.

"Oh, Nina, stop being such a worrywart," she retorts. "It's nothing like that, but this is disastrous. She can't get back together with him... he's still in school for heaven's sake. I mean he's still in community college." I make a look that tells her to tread lightly; local community college is often underrated. Justifying her judgement, she elaborates, "After *six* years, you'd think he'd either finish or move on or have a masters by now."

I roll my eyes. Maria and her on-again, off-again boyfriend have been dancing around a committed relationship going on five years now. This is not only unsurprising, but half-expected.

"Mom, Ria's a big girl. She can make her own decisions, and there's nothing wrong with community college, in fact it's the smarter way to go; far more affordable," I inform her in a tone that implies her parental rights are minimal at best now that Maria is a grown human being.

"No, she can't!" she wails. "You remember the last time, she spiraled so hard she practically had to be committed."

"Maybe they'll finally realize they can't make it work, or they won't," I compromise. "We can only hope for the best for Ria, and you can't walk around saying that kind of stuff, Mom."

"He just has zero ambition, no prospective career, and no trust fund, and you know your sister and her lifestyle," she says, laying it all out there.

Here it comes. You know Mrs. Bennet from *Pride and Prejudice*? Well that's Mom, only an Irish American version meets Lucy Ricardo from *I Love Lucy*.

She slouches and pinches her forehead with her fingers.

Rumblings from my stomach below remind me I need food stat. I glance at the clock; it reads: 4PM. How did it get so late already? I walk over to the fridge and open the door. I might as well start on dinner.

"Mom, stop meddling," I say defensively on Maria's behalf, "she's only twenty-three. She's got a while to figure things out."

A package of ground beef catches my attention. Grabbing that and a pack of mushrooms, I place my items on the counter.

"Exactly, she's already twenty-three, Nina," Mom states matter-of-factly. "She's wasted so much time already. She only has a few good years left. We all can't sit around waiting for someone to walk through the front door, now can we?" Knowing where she's headed, I shut the fridge door with intended intensity. "Do you expect to marry the UPS man, honey," she says, "because unless you leave the house, that's your only option."

She raises an eyebrow at me.

*Shots fired*.

Two can play this game, Mom. I glare at her, arming myself for battle.

"Well, he's already married, Mom. Sorry to break it to you, and we're not talking about me, remember?"

She drops her face into her hands in defeat.

I pull open the cupboard drawer and grab a large dish, then I make my way through the back kitchen door into the backyard.

"Nina, don't run away from this conversation! Not this time," she bellows, as I walk towards my vegetable garden.

I root around for some ripe looking zucchini. A big, dark green one catches my eye. I grab it, twisting the stem clean off the vine. Some yellow squash also look ripe for the picking. I pull those as well. I take a deep breath, trying to focus on my veggies. *Gosh, Mother.* As much as I love my mom, sometimes she's just too all up in it. I know she means well, but she constantly reminds me of my life's current shortcomings. She's always comparing me to the next door neighbor's daughters or my own sister, Selena. Selena has it all together. She's married to a wonderful guy, Ray, has a perfect baby, Javi, and owns a house - in southern Orange County this is a big deal. Did I mention she's my younger sister... yep, I'm the oldest of three daughters.

I'm the "talented" sister, the sister who keeps to herself, and has only two friends - one of which is a dog, and the other lives across the state whom I haven't seen since college, who's now married and filed under the "Can't Relate" folder of my life. I get it. I truly do. Everyone wants me to find a husband and be happy. Something I desperately want for myself, but damn, the constant reminder of how alone I am is rough.

"Nina!"

Growing up in a small house, I'm in tune with all its tiny little noises. My mom's voice is one of those that I could pick out of a packed theme park on a hot sunny day. Hearing my name from across the house is no exception, even through closed doors.

Dreading facing the music that awaits me inside, I reluctantly check my garden. When I feel down, I focus my efforts and my energy on the small things that make me happy. I stare at all the tiny budding fruit. I feel better already. There's nothing more satisfying than growing your own food and cooking it up, savoring the taste. With a pile of squash in hand, I make my way inside to make some bulgogi bowls for the family.

*Australia.* White sandy beaches. Red earth. Marine life. That wonderful accent. Koala bears and kangaroos. It's beckoning me, calling my name. Australia's been on my mind lately. Not lately actually, but for about six years now. Do you ever have something that follows you around, drawing you towards it, like a magnet? This is me with the land Down Under.

The universe throws me signs all the time, pointing me to it, basically flashing in neon lights. I randomly received a travel magazine without ever having bought, signed up, or requested it and it focused on the Kimberley Coast; an entire publication dedicated to the beauty of the west coast. When I go on instagram, every targeted ad hails from the land of Oz. All of the beautiful creatives who inspire me artistically, and as human beings, happen to also be Aussie. One hint after another - from actors I love to umbrella and bathing suit brands - all point to Australia. I feel it calling me, whispering to me like a song, simmering along in the background. *Ninaaaa.*

Sitting at my computer desk, I finish editing the last photos from the Wares wedding. It's 2AM and I open up my email. The header "Flights So Hot: Australia" jumps out at me amongst the unread subject lines. Next thing I know I'm down the rabbit hole searching for cheap flights to Sydney.

*"Thirty years old,"* my mom's voice echoes in my head. I don't want to turn thirty having never left the country. I have dreams and ambitions and I'm tired of just thinking about doing it! My whole life I've vowed not to be a pipe dreamer and that is exactly what I have become.

Hmm, I do have some saved up miles on my travel credit card... like $850 worth towards a flight... Oooh, there's a Quantas flight to Brisbane with a layover in Honolulu and another quick one in Sydney... I could travel the coast and then fly back out of Sydney in three weeks. *Should I do it?* The possibility alone makes my heart flutter.

"¿Que piensas, Cos, am I crazy?" I ask, glancing down at Cosmo, my family dog - a miniature dachshund.

Before I know it, I'm clicking on the purchase button, entering my credit card info, and receiving an email confirmation reiterating the fact that I just bought a ticket to the Gold Coast. I'm not a planner at all, but I didn't even consult with my family first. I just did it, and it feels AMAZINGLY satisfying.

"You *WHAT?"* My mom and sister exclaim in unison.

"I bought a ticket to Australia," I clarify for the tenth time. "I just got my tourist visa approved. I'm leaving tomorrow morning."

"But, Neens, you can't go to Australia," Maria states, completely baffled, shaking her head. "It's hot there. There are sharks everywhere and the bugs are the size of hamsters."

Hmmm, I didn't really think about those things, but it doesn't matter. I've been wanting to do this for years. Now is my time.

"So it'll be good for me," I answer, almost as a question.

"You hate bugs," Maria reminds me. "You get spooked when I accidentally bump into you in the hallway. You're the biggest scaredy-cat I know."

"Thanks," I mutter sardonically.

"You know what I mean," she explains. "You can't go alone."

"Maybe Ria can go with you?" Mom asks, looking from me to Maria with more hope than before.

Maria frowns slightly, thinking. She runs her hand through her bleached blonde, curly bob.

"No, I wish I could, but I can't," she says sadly, and sighs. "I'm doing all the hair for that wedding next weekend, and I can't cancel, especially on such short notice."

"It's fine. You need to do that," I reply, looking at Maria, then redirect my gaze towards Mom and look her straight in the eyes. This is important, I need her to hear me. "I am going, Mom. I'm tired of talking about my dreams. Like you've been dramatically telling me for the past five years, I'll be thirty soon. I'm tired of being a pipe dreamer. I need to do this."

"But you can't go now," Mom mutters, giving a sideways glance at Maria, looking for backup support. She continues, grasping at straws, "You know Selena's been having a rough time juggling work and Javi. She needs your help."

"I know, guys," I nod, smiling, "but I'm only going on a little trip. I need to do this for me, and besides, I'll be back before you know it. You won't even miss me. Promise."

The car carousels around the airport terminal. As usual, it's a whole family affair to send me off on my way. Abuela even tried to come, but we told her to stay behind.

"Do you have your rape whistle?" Mom asks, for the fifth time in the last ten minutes.

"Yes," I reassure her again.

"You can never be too careful. Remember girls, ten—."

"Steps of rape!" Maria and I finish off the Lucy mantra we've been hearing since we were nine.

My dad, Papi, pulls over at the unloading dock. He jumps out and unloads my small carry-on, and wheels it over to me.

"I'll miss you, Mija. Llámame if you need anything or just wanna talk," he mutters, pulling me in for a crushing hug. "Be safe. Te quiero mucho."

"Love you too, Papi," I mumble into his arms.

I'm a homebody. As much as I want to go and need to do this, I also really hate the act of leaving and saying goodbye, even if I know it's only for twenty-two days. The morbid back part of my brain always imagines a goodbye as a final one. I don't hate flying, but it's definitely not one of my favorite things to do. I would love nothing more to teleport straight there than being trapped in a box in the sky. *Stop it,* Nina. There it is again, the fear gene spreading like wildfire. Before I can dwell too much on worst case scenarios, Mom and Maria clutch me into a bone crushing group hug, kissing my cheeks in turn.

"Love you so much, Neens. Wish I was going with you," Maria says. "Send me pictures of any hot Aussies, especially ones at the beach showing some skin."

"Yeah, okay, I'll be sure to ask the ones with the six packs, Ria," I reply sarcastically, laughing into her hair.

"You know, it's not too late to cancel," Mom butts in.

I shake my head, rolling my eyes, and step away from their dual embrace. I gather my backpack, printed ticket, and carry-on bag. Mom hands me my passport, and starts sniffling as she gives me a last minute once over.

"Oh, Mama, I'll miss you most," I whisper, "but I'll be back in three weeks, and it'll be like I never left. Call me if you forget your passwords." Standing on the curb, I face the three of them as they all gather in front of the car, smiling at me. "Love you guys! I gotta go. Getting my camera and drone through security takes forever."

"Okay, okay. Fly safe, and please call us when you land in Honolulu, and again in Australia," Mom fiercely pleads. "No matter the time or the cost. You hear me?"

I nod my head and turn, shuffling towards the entrance, trying to straighten out the wheels of my little carry-on.

"Yes! Love you guys!" I shout over my shoulder.

I look up and see "Arrivals This Way" with an arrow and hastily make my way towards security.

# 2

Wheels down. After twenty-three hours of airport lounging or being stuck in the middle seat, three seasons of *Absentia* binge watched, I make it. Touchdown. *Praise be. Hallelujah.*

I smile hugely. Adventure awaits.

I barely notice the lingering wait to get off the plane in Brisbane as I retrieve my carry-on from the overhead bin with the biggest grin. Aside from the amazing feeling of finally stretching my legs, I feel like I'm on Cloud Nine. After maneuvering through the large airport, I make my way outside to the car rental agency.

"Ya sure ya can drive manual?" the employee asks, confirming.

I smile wider. That Aussie accent is pure gold, and it's just the rental agent asking me a simple question.

"Of course," I hastily say, and nod, overcompensating a tad, not wanting to get caught in my white lie.

I may have some experience driving stick shift from when I was learning to drive, but it's been a few years... like fourteen years in fact.

It's significantly cheaper to rent a manual car for three weeks than an automatic. Plus, booking on such short notice, all the automatics were already reserved. Besides, how hard can it be? I just need to brush up on it. It'll be like riding a bike.

The agent has me sign the bill, the insurance disclaimer, and hands me my credit card along with the keys.

"Safe travels, 'n rememba ya can return the car to any of our locations throughout Australia," they inform me.

"Great, thanks. Have a good one," I respond, and head towards the parking lot.

Having the time of my life, ten days in Australia fly by in the blink of an eye. Living up to the dream and then some, this trip has been one of the best decisions I've ever made. From visiting Steve Irwin's zoo to droning one beautiful beach after the next, I've never seen so much beauty in one place, nor felt so free. Brisbane. Byron Bay. Sydney. Canberra. Every stop along my road trip has not disappointed. I'm currently in Melbourne, Victoria en route to Adelaide, South Australia.

*Like seriously where has the time gone?*

I stand at the entrance of a local airport hanger full of smaller planes. Seeing the tarmac reminds me I only have a little over a week left in this beautiful country before I board my flight back home.

So far my trip has been nothing short of marvelous. I don't say that word enough, but it's true. From sun bathing until sunset to eating dessert for breakfast, I do whatever I want to do 24/7. I really haven't missed the constant nagging or judgement regarding how I want to spend my time or what I want to eat. Every time I FaceTime, I'm reminded of what awaits me at home. That's not to say I don't miss my family, because I do, *a lot*, but I also have been reveling in my own agenda, or lack thereof.

I met someone. *Not* a man, but a gal pal. She's become my travel companion. I'm already dreading the thought of not seeing her back home. I don't have tons of friends, but the pair of us really hit it off. As I board the small plane, I think back to how we met, which makes me smile as I relive the memory in my mind like a movie.

I end up abandoning and returning the rental car in Byron Bay. The stick shift is too much. It takes me over five hours to drive 165 kilometers, something that should apparently take me maybe two hours… and I realize my priority is to see Australia, not the dashboard of my rental car. So after I return it, I walk to the nearest "watering hole" as I'm thirsty and hungry as hell, plus I need to figure out an alternative method of getting to Sydney.

I enter the pub, and being the solo traveler I am, bee-line straight to a booth in the corner. I've learned Aussies are way more inviting than what I'm used to, but old habits of social retreat die hard. It's perfectly dark over here. I'll go unnoticed and won't be bothered.

Checking out the menu, I feel the seat cushion swell and look up. A woman in her early thirties, looking almost like a bohemian vagabond with style, and with one of the friendliest smiles I've ever seen, plops down across from me. Sporting a loose ponytail, and wearing what looks like a burgundy unitard under cream linen pants, her large, round hazel eyes loom up at me.

"Just orda the chips," she commands, snatching up the menu. "It's by far the best thing they've got."

Chips? I was wanting something more substantial than that.

"Okay," I mutter, waiting for this woman to introduce herself.

I look at her with anticipation in my eyes. Taking the hint, her eyes widen in realization and she jumps slightly, extending her hand out across the table.

"Hey, I'm Mel, like Mel Gibson," she brightly introduces herself.

I reach out and she grabs my palm and shakes my hand fiercely. I smile, mouth closed.

"Nina. Just Nina," I reply simply.

A minute goes by and I half expect Mel to get up and walk away, but she doesn't. Instead, she reaches up, yanks out the rubber band and pulls her ashy brown hair back into a top knot before settling into the booth. She turns towards the bartender.

"Oy, I'm takin' my tea here," she yells across the room.

She twists back and faces me.

"Tea?" I ask, amused since it feels hot as Hades outside.

"Yeah, nah, sorry, dinna," she informs me, snorting.

*Hmm.* Tea means dinner? *That's a new one.* Good thing I'm from SoCal where we abbreviate a lot, but even home pales in comparison to this place. It's hard to keep up with all the sayings.

"So yar a Yank?" she asks, already knowing the answer, but I nod anyway. "Ya alone?" she persists. "Me too. Sorry to barge in, but this bloke wouldn't leave me alone at the bar. Ya came in just in the knick a time."

Silence.

The bartender comes over and just as I'm about to speak up, Mel butts in and orders, "Chips for this one, Love, oh 'n two throw downs, thanks." Not knowing what that means, I simply resign and recline back into the booth as the bartender departs back to the kitchen. Mel leans in and grabs a napkin, wiping down a dirty bit of leftover food off the table. "Ya stayin' at the hostel down the street?"

I pause. I don't know her. Do I divulge this information to a complete stranger? I look her over again, trying to be stealthy. She seems harmless and her smile feels very genuine, plus it's second nature for Aussies to be welcoming and hospitable, so I decide to take the leap of faith.

"Yeah, I am. Just for another night. I'm trying to find my way down south, but don't have a car anymore. The rental agency said to try back tomorrow... I need an automatic—."

"Ya don't anymore," she waives me off. "Ya can come with me. I'm making my way down to Adelaide 'n I welcome the company."

Again, unsure and assessing the risk of basically downright hitchhiking, I pause. My mom would kill me if she was here. She always instilled the fear of God when it came to Stranger Danger with us Esquivel girls.

"I see yar sussing me out," Mel says, narrowing her eyes in a smile. "Smart. But, I promise I'm not here to nap ya or anythin'. Think of it as gettin' a special tour, but betta 'cause it's free 'n it's me." I eye her, trying to make up my mind. "Come on," she quips, waving her hand casually, "we'll have heaps of fun. Live like a local for a little, Nina."

When she puts it like that, it does sound like a once in a lifetime opportunity. I waiver for a second. *You came here to live, so live. Take a chance.* Barry Manilow's "Ready to Take A Chance Again" plays in my head.

"What are ya hummin'?" Mel curiously asks, smiling.

"I didn't realize I was, sorry," I muse, snorting in embarrassment. "It's from one of my favorite movies, *Foul Play*, with Goldie Hawn and Chevy Chase."

She nods, not getting the reference; most people my age don't as the movie's from the 1970s and is only available on DVD.

Sitting here, my palms are getting a little sweaty. That usually means I'm nervous but also slightly excited. I let out a deep breath, and nod aggressively, committing; my head bobs quickly up and down the more I confirm my choice.

"You know what, yeah, let's do it!" I shout, louder than intended.

Mel excitedly claps in her seat as the bartender arrives with my fish 'n chips and two small tiny beer bottles.

"Enjoy, eh," he mumbles, lacking all enthusiasm.

I've never been a big drinker, but relieved I ended up with an actual meal, I go with the mood of the moment, grab the glass of beer, and slam it back. *Ugh, it's disgusting*. Warmth rushes down my throat and through my body as the heavy carbonated drink makes its way into my bloodstream. Mel laughs and takes the shot, not fazed in the slightest as she swallows.

"Mel Gibson, huh? Parents big fans of *Mad Max*?" I ask.

Chuckling, and grabbing a bite of the battered fish, she explains through a mouthful, "'Course, 'n *Tim* too."

Laughing, I pop a couple chips in my mouth.

Well, my gamble with Mel pays off. We take to the open highway, falling into an easy rhythm of travel. We quickly discover we have loads of common interests, nature being one of them. Mel has relatives that live in Adelaide, so once a year she takes a holiday and tours the coast, usually with her boyfriend of the season, but she informs me she broke it off with the latest one two months prior. She talks in detail about how even when she knows a relationship won't last, she stays in it out of complacency before jumping into a new one.

"Maybe you should take a time-out for some me-time," I casually suggest.

Her giant eyes widen slightly as if she's having an epiphany. She reflects quietly for a minute.

"So, Neens, what was yar last relationship like?" she asks, leaning over with a nudge, digging for some scoop.

I chuckle, trying to mask the sad truth, but remain silent. She keeps glancing at me every couple of seconds; clearly, she's waiting for either an answer or an explanation.

"Um, well, there's not a whole lot to tell," I squeeze out vaguely, and nervously smile.

"C'mon, out with it then!" she urges with the click of a suspicious tongue.

"Fine..." I admit defensively, surrendering. I take a deep breath. "So I'm kind of a homebody and uber shy, okay? To start, there's only ever been one 'relationship' — if that's what you even want to call it — it was with this guy in college. I actually knew him from home."

"Go on," she persists.

"Well," I continue, rolling my eyes, "we kind of hung out for a while, just as friends. He was pretty much the only friend I had there, then one night we were in his room, and well..."

Blood rises up my cheeks. Suddenly it's two hundred degrees in here.

"'N ya copped a root," Mel finishes for me.

"Does that mean what I think it does?" I ask, cringing at the nasty sounding expression.

"If ya mean do the naughty, have *sex*, then yeah," she explains in humor.

"Well then," I nod, laughing into my hands before admitting, "yeah, but just barely. Mel, it was so bad. Like so incredibly awkward and fast."

I realize this is the first time I've ever discussed this "occurrence" out loud to anyone.

"Then what happened?"

"Then nada. *Nothing*. The minute after it happened, he wanted nothing to do with me ever again. Turns out he just wanted to get his first time over with, and mine too apparently."

Mel looks hurt on my behalf.

Taking a deep breath, I have my defense on the tip of my tongue, but am unsure how to phrase it without looking like a creeper spinster who lives with a thousand cats in her mother's basement.

"But really," I stumble, "I was fine. I didn't let it bug me. In fact, I ended up finishing university early because I focused on school. And then I moved back home and basically became a hermit."

"So it did affect ya then," Mel states, looking over at me with a wince.

I lean back and stare out the window at the passing road. I've never looked at it that way before. I'm not one to dwell on the "what could have beens" because that game never gets you anywhere.

"I mean, maybe if something had come of it, things might have turned out differently," I realize aloud, "but I guess I'll never know." Mel focuses on the wheel in front of her, deep in thought. Masking my embarrassment, I jokingly mutter, "You probably don't know too many almost thirty year olds who are basically monks."

We sit to ourselves for a moment before she looks over at me, with a flood of warmth in her smile, and says sweetly, "Yeah, nah, Neens, but I reckon that just makes ya extra special."

Afterwards, Mel and I are thick as thieves. Honestly, there's not a whole lot of people I can travel with so freely or openly. Usually, I feel like I have to compromise as I'm not a planner. I have the rare gift of not suffering from jet lag, and I like to mosey about and see where the open road takes me. My sisters and Mom always joke that Papi and I could stare at a twig for eight hours straight. As we drive down the open highway, a smile forms on my lips when I think of Papi. He would love it here - the endless ocean, miles of unknown ground ahead, and a carefree atmosphere that stops me in my tracks.

Mel and I stretch the most out of our freedom before we hit Adelaide. We're about to hit hour six of being on the road for the day. Mel's just as bad as I am when it comes to getting easily distracted. All it takes is an enticing road sign or a hot guy to pull us off the road and onto a beach somewhere. Mel longboards so when we do chase down waves, I sit and watch her from the shoreline. She tries to get me out there surfing beside her, but I keep thinking of an excuse to refuse. For one, my bathing suit is a struggle to keep on even when I take a quick dip to cool off. When you don't weigh 125 pounds, bathing suits fit a little differently, as in they're usually too small. Secondly, I'm kind of scared to go out too far in case of a close encounter with a shark.

Waiting for Mel to paddle in, I walk along the beach looking for shells then lie down on my thin Turkish towel. After a thirty minute session, she comes in beaming.

"So stoked right now," she hollers. "What a banga last wave! Neens, we gotta get ya out there. No more excuses." I nod automatically, already trying to think up a new one as she looks me over, and notes, "Yar finally gettin' tan from all the lying about."

"It's my Mexi blood," I explain, smiling. While Mom's ancestry hails from Ireland, Papi's whole side comes from Mexico. While I might not get as tan as Selena with the olive skin, I can brown up to a nice dark golden pigment after being exposed to a high UV index. Mel points to a spot on my side. I look down and wince as my nail scratches a burnt spot. "And that's my Irish blood."

I look over and see some dolphins swimming by as the sun begins its descent. I exclaim in excitement and pull out my drone from my backpack. I unfold it and start up the battery. It comes to life with a couple of beeping sounds. Mel looks from the drone back to me with interest.

"I know ya told me ya drone," she remarks, with a hint of surprise, "but I kinda forgot until just now."

Smiling, I launch the drone into the sky from the palm of my hand. A small burst of wind blows from its tiny propellers, "props," as it zips up a few feet into the air.

"I call him The Great Khal Drono," I tell her proudly.

A huge snorting laugh bubbles up as Mel follows the drone with her gaze as it maneuvers across the air over the ocean.

"Good one," she jests, getting the *Game of Thrones* reference.

"It sounds like...?" she fumbles for the right word.

Having heard the sound of The Khal countless times, I surmise it sounds exactly like a bustling bee swarm.

I say so, and she exclaims in awe, "Nah, yeah, that's exactly right!" I take a few photos and record one long clip of the dolphins before bringing it back and landing it on my palm with steady precision. She shakes her head, impressed. "Now, I'm genuinely chuffed, Neens."

Taking that as a compliment, I nestle The Khal back in his resting place in my pack.

The sun is almost down, and the gold glow of its rays shines through the van's windshield, lighting my tawny hair a bright sienna.

Driving, Mel grabs the bottom of a russet curl and says in her best Kit Harrington accent, "Kissed by fire." She snorts at her poor imitation. "Nah, ya really do have the most beautiful hair. It's not even frizzy."

"Thanks," I mutter, patting my hair self-consciously. "It must be all the swimming or salt water. Normally it's out to here."

I place my hands about a foot away from my head on each side and laugh. She swerves a little and I reach over to the wheel, forcing her to pay attention to the road in front of us. I glance around. It feels like we're in the middle of nowhere. I don't even want to imagine how hopeless we would be if we crashed. Besides, I don't want to talk about me anymore. Uncomfortable, I pull out the rubber band in my hair and tidy up all my curls before defaulting back to my go-to hairdo. Tying a giant bun on top of my head, I look back at Mel. I want to change the subject.

"So, like how many 'blokes' have you been with?" I ask casually.

A little holler escapes through her lips before she throws her mouth wide open, laughing.

"I don't really keep track, but I reckon in the high teens most like," she states confidently.

My jaw drops. At my reaction, she raises an eyebrow.

"No, sorry," I quickly explain, backpedalling. "I'm not judging you. Honestly. I'm just now realizing how ridiculous you must think I am since I basically have *very* limited experience."

"Neens, here's the thing, yar a strong, beautiful lady," she states, clearly taking this opportunity to give me her personal TED talk. "Don't let anyone, and I mean *anyone* get ya down. So what if you're a little different than most? Ya just march to the beat of yar own drum." She nudges me, giving me a crooked smile. "I mean ya bloody drone."

"I need you back home," I say wistfully, elbowing her back. "It's easy to forget there. Most people don't have that mindset. I guess I've always been kind of a loner. And where I come from, either you have loads of friends, you're married to some great guy with kids by now, or there's 'something wrong with you.' It's just easier to stay in my bubble in category number three. I tried to explain before, but everyone I know - and it's not many - would laugh seeing me here with you because I don't do things like this. *Ever.* I can't tell you how many times guys walk right past me at home without giving me a single glance. They're always drawn to the leggy blondes with the perfect backsides."

"That's asinine," she exclaims, snorting, while shaking her head. "Most real women aren't leggy nor blonde." She winks. "Except my sista." She looks around us and whips her VW van, Nigel, to the left, pulling us off the road. The van screeches to a halt as Mel slams on the brakes. "Come on, Love, sun's almost down. Let's get ya a good shot."

After about an hour of sunset and droning, Mel and I sit side by side, quietly enjoying the cascading light of the blue hour. The water barely reaches our feet, the temperature fleeting with the tide.

"You, my friend, are a pearl," she states, "'n don't forget it. Someday, the right guy will come along 'n he'll just inherently know how special you are."

I nudge her at a loss for words. That's one of the nicest things anyone has ever said to me and is such a gift from a girl I barely know but who clearly sees me for who I am. I close my eyes, savoring this moment with this gem of a human being.

# 3

I look at the map lying on my AirB&B's bed. Pen marks and black circles fill the coastline. There's so much more I want to see and do, and time is running out.

I say a hard goodbye to Mel. She has to spend a week with her cousins in Adelaide and assures me her "rellos" are not the kind of people I should "waste my precious last few days with."

As a parting gift, she coordinates the last leg of my trip to the west coast. She has me flying into a tiny airport further north, but she's flown into it several times to go home. It will require a bit of a drive back down to Perth, but she tells me that's even more of a reason to go, so I can see as much of the country as I can before departing back across the globe. Mel even calls ahead and reserves an automatic car for me. She assures me its well worth the small hassle of extra travel.

As she drops me off at Adelaide Airport, I reluctantly wave goodbye to her and Nigel, and embrace the last chapter of my Aussie adventure.

<hr/>

Wheels down. I've landed. Another flight in the books. *Barely*. Catching a jumper plane from Perth, I only white knuckled it a couple of times as we hit major turbulence through a storm, but I made it in one piece. I better not tell Mom about this one; she's better off not knowing things like this.

I spot a tiny outpost at the micro terminal. I look around... *wow*, there's nothing for miles except endless red dirt and the "bush." Well there's no going back to

Sydney, not until my return ticket leaves in four days time out of Perth. Arriving at the kiosk, I see it's empty, and so is the rest of this makeshift terminal. "Terminal" is a generous term as this "airport" consists of a single red strip of dirt road that stretches next to an oversized shed that I presume is the hanger.

"Hello," I cry out, "anyone there?"

Nothing. *Damn, it's hot.* I look at the horizon, and a blurry, almost liquified mirage dances in the distance. I'm sweating bullets. It must be at least in the nineties, and there's no tree or shade to be found anywhere. I only have one water bottle with me and who knows where my AirB&B is... just as I'm contemplating that this endeavor might have been a bit bold for me to do on my own, a man walks out of the hanger and approaches me with a grin.

"Sorry 'bout that," he calls out, picking up the pace.

"No worries at all," I say with a polite smile.

"Ah, an American," he remarks, sounding surprised. "Alright, Dolly, what's yar name?"

"Nina Esquivel," I answer. "My friend called yesterday about my rental — the *automatic* car."

The breath catches in his throat.

"Oh, sorry, Love," he explains, through gritted teeth. "I'm afraid I just gave away our last auto this mornin', 'n next one's not due for anotha week..." Dread must cloud my eyes and face, because he frantically offers, "I can give ya a lift or ya can have a manual one for half price..."

I stand in a hesitating pause, debating my options. This guy seems harmless, nice even, but the thought of not having wheels and depending upon strangers for the next four days is a big drag. I did get some stick practice in once with Mel. It didn't go that well, but it wasn't necessarily horrible either. I could probably get by as a last resort.

"I don't know if this helps or not," the man says, smiling apologetically, "but ya dun have to worry about poppin' the clutch 'round here or stallin' out. It's pretty remote territory. No one to bump into ya."

"That's what I'm afraid of..." I admit; the thought of no assistance seems daunting and downright impossible.

Feeling so terrible, Kiosk Man awards me with complimentary vehicle insurance at his insistence. He assures me I can't inflict too much damage out here as long as I don't go off roading. With my current skill level, that shouldn't be a problem. I'll be sticking to the paved roads.

Twenty minutes later, after an impromptu shifting lesson, I'm equipped in a somewhat dodgy, albeit functional rental car, waving off to Kiosk Man as I harshly shift into second gear. It's a bit noisy sounding as I shift, but, hey, I'm moving forward.

An hour or so passes by on a straight strip of road, so I only have to shift a couple of times. I haltingly make my way down a longer decline, trying to juggle the task of changing gears and fiddling with the radio, all while simultaneously enjoying the awesome views to my right. It's bizarrely strange driving on the other side of the road, and now I realize I've drifted to the right side out of sheer habit.

I make it about a hundred kilometers, "kilometres," - even their spelling's slightly off - from the "airport" and am starting to get the hang of this stick thing. The sun begins its descent and the visibility drops little by little as the road begins to curve back and forth like a long unwinding snake as the highway circumvents more difficult sections of coastline. A longer, downhill turn approaches. I glance at the speedometer, it's gaining momentum quickly. I'm moving much faster than I'm comfortable going. In an automatic, speed is rarely a factor for me, but I don't want to try and burn through multiple gears all of a sudden to stop if the need arises.

Reaching up to push my loose hair out of my face, I realize I'm still wearing my sunglasses. I pull them back and rest them on top of my head. Scanning my surroundings, I surmise that night is falling upon me quickly. I should probably turn on my headlights. I reach down and roll the switch, but the lighting conditions lie in the funky in-between - when it's dark enough to need light, but also light enough where you can't quite see it.

INXS's "Shine Like It Does" blares on the radio, catching my attention, breaking up my thought.

"These speakers ain't bad," I happily assess to myself. I'm on a straightaway again so I begin to relax, releasing my grip on the steering wheel. I sing along at the top of my lungs, imagining a duet with Michael Hutchence's sultry voice. My favorite part of the whole song approaches. "*This is the story... since tiiiiime began,*" I belt out. I share with my imaginary passenger, "Oooh, yes, I LOVE that part."

I laugh out loud. I feel so amped. I'm cruising down a desert highway, soaking up my bit of freedom, enjoying the dying light. The breeze comes through the open windows, lifting the hair off my sweaty neck.

Suddenly, the song cuts out and static shredding noises fill the car as I look down and see my iPod screen fading to black; the battery must have finally died. I look down, trying to find my charging cord. I spot it on the floorboard of the passenger side. Shifting my attention from the road to the cord and back, I reach down, trying to locate it with my fingers. I can just feel the knobby end in my hand. I peek up and realize I'm hauling down a long dip in the highway, unable to see what's on the other end, while simultaneously veering off the side of the road. I lightly turn the wheel and regain my straight direction along the asphalt.

All in slow motion, but flying in high speed, I catapult over the top of the hill and a wallaby sits, parked in the middle of the road. She turns towards me, full deer in the headlights and I see another smaller pair of eyes staring at me in fear below. To avoid hitting the mother and joey, I sharply spin the wheel, barely skimming by them, but it's too fast and too late. My tires have a mind of their own, and I go barreling off the highway, through some bush, crossing a dirt path that parallels the beach. Looking straight in front of me, all I see is a giant sandy boulder growing bigger and bigger. In the mere seconds it takes me to collide with the giant formation, random memories flash in my mind:

*Rolling out masa, making sopapillas with Abuela Jovita as an eight-year-old.*
*Javi, smiling, playing with my music speaker.*
*Cosmo's wiry hair standing up straight between his ears.*
*Visions of me standing up, surfing for the first time.*

In the one nano second before I crash, I realize the last one is something I want to do. *I still have so much I want to do!* I pray, *God, please allow me the chance to try.*

Breathless in anticipation, I pull the steering wheel hard to avoid directly hitting the large rock, but end up careening straight into a ravine of sorts. A giant, washed up tree trunk impales my driver side door as I make impact. Feeling an immense amount of pressure and warmth in my right leg, I scream out in agony. The car then slides halfway into the crevasse, spiraling on the way down, crushing against one side of the chasm. The engine dies.

Momentary blackness.

Completely still, I notice a flat line ringing in my ears. Like in the movies, I swear I hear the sound of tires spinning endlessly. Dazed, and slightly confused, I realize that this is not what Kiosk Man had in mind when he offered the insurance policy at no cost.

Stiffness and agonizing pain well up. My chest heaves, trying to catch my breath, but it hurts to exhale. The rusty taste of blood fills my mouth. I must have badly bitten down on my tongue during the crash, but it feels okay as I move it around, trying to pinpoint the tender spot. I've never been in a car wreck before. Assessing myself first before any damage to the car, I touch my head instinctively and look down at my hand. More blood. *Damn.* Hopefully it's nothing major. I don't know a lot about human anatomy other than what I've learned from *Bones*, but I do know a head injury is never good. I glance in the review mirror. It's completely bent over, but angling towards me.

Seeing a trail of blood oozing down my temple, I frantically search my face for cuts. I find no signs of any gash on my forehead, thank goodness, only some minor surface abrasions. Probing around my skull, I come across a very tender spot on my right parietal lobe, at least that's what I think the front part of my brain is called. I probably whacked it against the door frame as I jolted against the unforgiving earth. I cautiously touch it again and *yep!* it hurts. Little white lights swirl around the edges of my vision.

I focus my efforts downward.

My right leg has gone numb. *Great.* I attempt to move it, but honestly am unsure if it's functional or not. I'm willing with all my might and strength to wiggle my foot, but nothing happens.

*Nothing.*

Exhaustion hits me like a tidal wave, and now I'm getting downright frustrated. Draining the last of my energy reserves, I have to stop. I slump in my seat, feeling absolutely defeated. Sitting still, the truth of my situation hits me.

*How am I going to get myself out of here?* I realize I don't even know exactly where I am... my phone, where's my phone?

A spark of hope ignites.

At first minimal glance, I don't see it anywhere. My range of motion is severely limited as the seat belt locks tight against me in heavy restraint. Starting to panic, I do my best to loosen the belt, but it won't budge. The tree log pushes the door against me, pinning me so I'm completely stuck.

Fear settles over me like a blanket of clouds descending on a sunny day. *Where the hell is my phone?!* Trying not to freak out over the thought of potential paralysis or dehydration or head trauma, I frantically search for my yellow phone case. I can't find it anywhere. No trace of color against the gray carpeted seats or floorboards. Without turning my head, with just the shift of my eyes towards the passenger door, I remember all the windows were down during the crash. Hopefully my phone didn't go flying out during the fall.

I send up a silent prayer to the Man Upstairs.

My vision slightly blurs. This seatbelt feels like it's gauging a hole in my neck and chest, it's so constricting.

"Don't lose it, Nina," I say aloud. "You can do this."

I need to talk myself through this and stay awake. *Just breathe. As long as you're breathing, there's a chance.*

Licking my lips, I'm parched. Sand and grit line my dry mouth, further emphasizing and adding to my discomfort. My vision blurs again. Tears well up. My head feels like it weighs a hundred pounds. Frizzy strands of hair stick to the sides of my sweaty and bloody cheeks.

I shut my eyes tightly and focus, praying out loud, "God, if you're listening, please help me. Send someone, anyone, or allow me to move my leg. I'm so thankful to be alive. I promise to pray more if you help me get out of this one. Amen."

I open my eyes and look straight out through the cracked windshield at the glassiest shoreline I've ever seen. The violet waters rolling onto the white sand look like something straight out of a travel postcard at moonlight. Well if I die, at least I'll die staring at an epic view.

Will someone even find my body out here? And when? Will my remains be found digesting in the belly of a crocodile? Will I be bones they have to identify, prolonging the whole identification process? Wait, no, they'll find my passport eventually and then contact home.

I breathe in sharply. *Home. My family.* What will they think? They'll all be so worried. I need to get out of here.

*I HAVE TO.*

A sob breaks out. I feel myself spiraling in grief and terror.

*Pull it together, Nina Esquivel.*

Some feeling starts to return, more like more pain emerges as I sit here helplessly. My leg sears below, while something else is lodging its way into my backside. I reach behind my back, trying not to breathe deeply to avoid physical torment, and feel a rounded object. I move my hand slowly up the foreign shape and tighten my finger tips around a hard plastic circle. *My water bottle!* At least this decreases the chances of me dying of thirst first. Shaking from lack of strength, I sluggishly pull it out from behind my back, but not without considerable energy spent. By the time I free it and pull it in front of me, I'm out of breath, completely winded.

Getting my breathing under control, I delicately untwist the cap from the bottle and slowly raise the opening to my cracked lips. I gently tip it towards my mouth and allow a trickle to playfully rest on my lips before swallowing. I think this is the best feeling I've ever felt in my entire life. I take another drink.

*Don't get carried away, Nina. Conserve your water.*

Reluctantly, I close the lid back on the bottle and set it down next to me, resting it on the shifter for safe keeping.

I strain to hear if there are any sounds coming from any direction. Nothing. Not a sound for miles, except the soft crashing of waves out on the reef.

Just when I begin to calm down momentarily, a twig snaps. My eyes snap towards the direction of the noise, out into the light shining from the high beams. I hear another snap. Suddenly it dawns on me that I've crash landed in the Australian bush. Who knows what kinds of animals or reptiles are out here.

My vision blurs again and this time the light swirls return. I rest my head back against the seat. I don't know that much about head injury, but I do know you don't want to fall asleep right after cranial trauma. I hear the lulling tide again in front of me.

Sleep sounds so appealing right now.

*Don't you dare fall asleep.*

My eyelids feel like lead. I am defeated. The more I think about it, the more my lids want to close and stay closed. It would be easy to just let go.

*Open your eyes, Nina.*

They close.

*Open your eyes, Nina!*

They flutter but stay shut. I feel myself drifting, despite fighting with all my might to stay conscious.

"Hmmm, sleep good," I slur, and nod off, allowing the darkness to envelope me as I embrace it with open arms.

It's freezing. My skin feels like a popsicle wrapped up in freezer burn. I shiver convulsively.

*Where am I?*

My eyelids flutter and the devastating event of this evening comes crashing back as fragments of memory. It's pitch black out. I can't make out any shapes or see even inches in front of me. The car battery must have finally died. I crane my neck and look out the window to see stars blazing bright against the desolate landscape.

I wheeze, still unable to move. I'm even more tired now than I was before, if that's possible.

*Why fight it?*

Darkness comes again. Surrendering, I drift off into its sea.

Flickers of light, beautiful hues of oranges, pinks and reds dance through my eyelids.

I let out a small groan.

"Fuck me dead, yar alive," exclaims a textured Aussie accent, so thick that if I wasn't so unconscious I might want to marry it based on the iconic sound alone.

A giant moan whistles through my lips. I try to lift my head, but it collapses and bobs forward. My neck cannot support itself. *Damnit.* I scurry to find the strength and try once more. A combination of strangled and muffled sounds ooze out of me.

"You real?" I manage to croak.

A pair of hands appear warmly on my stiff cold shoulders. The heated touch sets my icy body ablaze, and I immediately begin to relax in mirth.

"Bloody hell, yar frozen. Ya must be in shock. Here, lemme try 'n loosen—," the voice drops off, as the effort to free me impedes his thought.

Grunting, the man saws with a knife at what I assume is the seatbelt.

I nod off again.

"Stay with me, ya hear?" he yells, panicking as he attempts to catch my head.

He lightly slaps my cheeks, trying to keep me awake. I try my best, but the absence of his warm touch sends me back to my frozen escape. The unconscious void looms and swirls inside my head.

I hear the voice grow frustrated as he commands, "Stella, get back in the ute. Get!"

*Stella, who is this Stella person?*

I don't have time to find out the answers. I fall forward, feeling like I'm jumping off a tightrope at the end of a deep canyon, and the blackness encompasses me yet again.

# 4

Florescent lights. Blues. Purples. Whites.

I try to open my eyes, but they're not cooperating. Instead I focus on the sounds around me: beeping, a ticking of some sort, a small shuffling noise. Something warm lifts my hand up, applying pressure around my wrist. It releases my wrist and my arm drops suddenly, landing with a slight *thud* on a blanket.

"Ah, she's comin' 'round," a nice sounding soprano declares next to me, as I mumble and groan.

My eyelids flicker open; my vision blurs and I can only make out general shapes as I try to lift my head, but it falls back instantly. Staring through the blur, waiting for my eyes to adjust and focus on the grooves in the ceiling, I numbly feel my way around. Cloth, fabric? I move my swollen fingers a couple of inches before encountering something hard and cold. The cold repels my touch. I lift my arm briefly and carry it towards my head, feeling a piece of gauze wrapped around my temple. My arm falls quickly away, too weak. This is so frustrating. My breathing deepens. Finally my eyes flicker open as they adjust to my surroundings, and I wake up, realizing I'm in a stale hospital room. Not the fanciest, nor the most state-of-the-art room, but hey, beggars can't be choosers. The bed next to me lies vacant.

I attempt to sit up, but collapse instantly. From my peripheral, I see another hand grab a remote and aim it at the bed. Slowly, the bed rises to a slight incline. I glance around the room again. I see a pair of feet in molasses colored flip flops belonging to a sitting figure slumping in a chair at the opposite side of the room. My eyes trail upward over this person who sits before me, looking absolutely wiped out themselves. I realize it's a man in his mid-thirties with dark, sun kissed, clipped curly hair. Eyes closed, he rests his head in his tan hands, propped up on the chair's armrests. I notice his eyelids are white against his golden face.

Another man, old enough to be my grandpa, sits in the seat beside the younger guy. This man is dressed in a worn flannel and Levis. He's awake. His face is flooded with concern, his eyes clouded with worry. He catches me eying him, and darts up pretty spryly for a man of his age.

"Oh, Sweetheart, yar alive 'n yar whole," he says, seeming to want to reassure me of this fact.

Geez, how bad am I? I knew it couldn't be great, but the way this man is consoling me makes me reconsider the extent of my injuries. I look down at my leg. I still can't feel it or move it. I discover it's wrapped up in a white hard cast. My puffy toes protrude out at the bottom.

"What happened?" I choke out.

At the sound of my mangled voice, the younger man bounces up, dropping his hands down, and wipes his eyes gently awake.

"Is she okay?" he mutters groggily to the nurse. "Any brain damage?"

"*Brain damage?*" I croak.

"Sheila, do ya know who you are?" the old man asks me.

"Of course I do," I reply in confusion, "I'm Nina. Nina Esquivel."

"My friend here found ya on the outskirts of town," the elderly man nods towards his companion.

"I saw yar high beams in the distance, but they went out shortly afta 'n it took me a while to find ya," the young man explains. "Ya flipped yar car. Ya were in bad shape, so I called him, 'n togetha we brought ya here. Just in time it would seem."

"Thank you...?" I leave a question in the air, not knowing the names of my rescuers. It's a wobbly reply and super lackluster. I wish I could find the words for more. "I don't know how to thank you both enough, I..."

I'm trying to find the words, but my head feels so foggy and cloudy. The old man must see the struggle on my face because he pats my good foot.

"Best rest, Sweetheart," he reassures me calmly. "The name's Mick, 'n ya can thank us in the mornin'."

I redirect my gaze to the younger one. Fit and sun kissed, his face almost looks sunburnt. He stands in trunks and a gray hoodie. He returns my stare. *Dang, he's cute.* What must I look like to him right now? I can't make out his expression.

"I reckon we can head back now," he suggests, nudging Mick.

"That was mighty kind of ya, Brodie, to come all this way to pick him up," the nurse says.

They both smile. Brodie bumps Mick's arm, and Mick reluctantly nods. Together they leave the room as the nurse returns to check on my vitals.

"Dearie, ya had a bad wreck to say the least," she smiles warmly. "The docta will be in to explain soon."

I sit up intensely, but not without painful effort.

"Wait, I need to call my parents and let them know," I persist. "Do you know where my phone is?"

"All in due time," she hushes me, clicking on a button next to the IV. "Ya need yar rest. I'll bring the phone in afta."

I feel a wave of fatigue like no other and succumb to the enticing arms of sleep. Just as swiftly as I fell asleep, I wake up to the news. *I hate the news.* It only amplifies my already active anxieties. Reports of that novel corona virus, Covid-19, seem to be popping up more and more these days. Mom was so worried about it when I left, but I assured her it was reported mainly in China.

"*Australia's east coast hit with an astounding wave of new cases. As of tomorrow, international travel is prohibited, and the border will be closed to all non-residents,*" a news anchor informs the camera.

Tomorrow?? Wait, what day is it?

I stare annoyingly at my useless leg. I use all my might to wiggle my toes - still nothing... The nurse enters my room, this time attended by a man wearing an ID badge and a long, white overcoat.

"This is Docta Mills, Dearie," she says, gesturing to the man, "the surgeon who helped stitch ya back togetha, so to speak."

I look bewildered at the good "docta." He smiles at me and waves both hands around the air as he informs me that aside from my head contusion, my right leg was broken badly in two places, one being a compound fracture. He had to perform emergency surgery so they wouldn't be forced to amputate from all the blood loss. I gulp down a little bile that rises in my throat. I zone out a little, but understand his gesticulations as an explanation.

"I reckon yar lucky to be alive," he offers. "Nurse Gail here is yar attendin'. She'll inform ya on the next step in terms of recovery 'n the rehab regime yull need to pursue if ya want to walk normally again." Panic crosses my face. He pats my arm to reassure me, but I don't feel comforted. "Nina, yar gonna be right," he states confidently. "In time ya will regain yar mobility. Ya just need to rest 'n focus on gettin' those sutures healed up. Yar nerves are very fragile right now, but I assure you, ya will regain feeling if ya follow the proper path to recovery. I reckon it'll take only a few weeks before ya can get a jump start on that."

"*A few weeks?*" I ask, gobsmacked. "But I needed to be on a plane home, like yesterday. I just saw the border is shutting down—."

"Nina, Dearie," the nurse gently spells it out for me, "ya already missed yar flight. Ya've experienced somethin' very traumatic, bein' left alone in shock overnight. The bent door frame applied enough pressure like a tourniquet to yar leg or ya woulda bled out. Ya've been in 'n out of a medically induced coma for the past four days to allow the swelling of yar brain to come down... Yar in no shape - whatsoeva - to get in a car, let alone board a plane, all the way to The States."

"If ya insist on going home, 'n fly, ya run the risk of brain hemorrhaging," the doctor clarifies, pausing a moment. "I'm afraid it would be too much too soon, far too risky *and* yar leg injuries would assuredly open back up." I balk at this piece of information. Literally, I have no words. The doctor expresses deep sympathy in his eyes. "This is unfortunate timing indeed."

*That's the biggest understatement of my life.*

"I've taken the liberty of filing a medical visa, allowing ya to stay in the country if lockdown is to take effect, which we're gettin' word that even our domestic borders are closin' at midnight," he explains. "Yull need to remain here in hospital for at least the next fortnight or so, 'n if that goes swimmingly, then yull be transported to Recovery Centre."

Stunned, a single tear rolls down my face.

*I just want to be in my bed eating Mom's albondigas soup.*

"Do you have that phone I could borrow?" I finally ask. "I need to discuss this with my family first."

"'Course," the doctor agrees, gesturing to the nurse to take over.

He receives a beep on his pager, glances at it, and smiles at me before exiting the room. Nurse Gail walks up to my bed and leans over, mustering up her practiced maternal instinct. It works, but she's still not Mom. And boy, do I want Mom... and my sisters and Papi right now. There's nothing in my life I've ever wanted more: *I want to go home.*

"Well, if it had to be right now, Dearie, at least it happened up here," Nurse Gail shares, trying to cheer me up. "It's remote territory, not much should reach us here in terms of that contagion. 'Course we'll be wearing masks I reckon until the dust settles, so don't be alarmed next time ya see us."

I don't know if she means that to be reassuring, but it's not much. I hastily nod, not wanting to make her feel bad and settle back in my bed. Clearly, I'm going nowhere.

"Who were those two men?" I ask her, as she motions to walk out the door. "Have they been here the whole time?"

"Poor Mick's been mighty worried 'bout ya, glued to yar room since they brought ya in," she replies, "'n the younga spunk's been back 'n forth. I reckon it's not been a bed of roses for them either."

I nestle back into my hospital bed. The IV pulses, throbbing as it pinches the back of my hand, drawing my skin tight. I realize that this is the least of my problems.

After much debate regarding my long departure home, the family agrees that it's too soon to travel and not worth the risk, despite how they desperately wish I was home with them.

Two weeks in the hospital drudge along like a bottomless hour glass. Each day feels like a year. Most of the time, I sit staring out the window at the surrounding bush, feeling desperately alone. I just want to be at home in my bed... in America.

I think of Mel. I wish I could get ahold of her; she's the one person I know in this country, but I have no way of tracking her down. I don't know her number and she's not on social media.

Kindly enough, my older savior, Mick, checks in on me every couple of days, and even gives Nurse Gail a pleasant surprise to pass along to me. While my phone was never recovered, thankfully my backpack was in the trunk, more or less unscathed, and my iPod shockingly was found on the floorboards with only one big crack across the front. I don't have a charging cord, but at least my entire music library with all of my well selected playlists I've made throughout the years is in intact, and knowing that gives me a small spark of joy.

As I open my backpack, I'm elated to find my laptop. There's a new, considerable dent in the corner, and occasionally the screen flickers, but overall it appears to be in working order. *There are small miracles.* Having my computer allows me to burn hours editing some landscape shots, and FaceTime with my family, that is when the drastic fifteen hour time difference works out. They've all been so incredibly worried. Mom, ready to hop on the next flight over, feels helpless being half a world away and forbidden to come. She iMessages me constantly, even when she should be sleeping. Poor Nurse Gail deals with her millions of questions every day, but is as patient as Mother Theresa.

My parents check in every single day. While usually exhausting to answer the same question regarding my wellbeing, I can finally share that this morning, my doctor informed me my latest cranial scan shows the swelling is gone and everything appears as it should. My parents are delighted as am I. However, the doctor also said the feeling in my leg should be returning by now, which it isn't, so one step forward, two steps back.

I awkwardly curl on my left side, accommodating my giant casted right leg. I lean my laptop against my stomach and scroll through Instagram. It's been weeks since I've logged on. I haven't been able to bring myself to see my family's and friends' posts; the more I see them the more I miss home. Nurse Gail worries it's not great for my mental health. As I scroll down, I see it's Covid post after Covid post. *Maybe I don't want to be on here…* I keep thumbing through, hoping it'll be different. Clicking through everyone's "stories," I discover that apparently toilet paper is nowhere to be found? What an odd hot commodity.

When I'm not being prodded or examined, I'm mostly isolated, alone with my thoughts. I feel myself slipping away into melancholia. As the days seem to blur together, life begins to resemble normalcy. While Covid-19 cases seem to skyrocket worldwide, borders everywhere shut down, including domestic ones here. Thankfully Nurse Gail was right. Western Australia hasn't been hit hardly at all, with no cases around here period… it's too remote, so the hospital allows me masked visitors. While I think this is a moot point since I'm a foreigner, I'm genuinely happy and surprised to learn I get one frequent visitor: Mick.

He's a retired medical doctor, which is why he was called upon for help on that fateful night a few weeks back. He always visits me at the same time each day - mid morning. He sits in my room, and we small talk this and that. He regales me of his time in the Australian army, and shares his experiences traveling all over the world as a Doctor Without Borders consultant many years ago. I don't know if it's the name, but he actually kind of resembles Mick from *Rocky* meets Mick "Croc" Dundee. I feel as if I've known him my whole life and believes he feels the same. I also get the feeling he has no one else, but decide to wait until he brings it up instead. I look forward to his visits like no other as they are my only ray of hope.

Today, he sits on the side of my hospital bed with a backgammon board wedged in between us. He brings cards with him sometimes, but mostly backgammon, and we enjoy a game or two. In fact, we're pretty evenly matched, which makes it pretty darn fun. The more time I spend with him, the more he reminds me of my late grandpa, who was a real "man's man" but with a great sense of humor and just the biggest, sweetest heart.

Mick picks up his blue dice and shakes them swiftly between his closed palms. He drops them and two "sixes" face upward.

"No!!" I exclaim, in genuine wonder. "Why do you always come in clutch with the doubles, Mick?"

"Scout's secret," he smiles bashfully, humbly shrugging.

There's a celebratory atmosphere today. Any minute now I'm to be transported to Recovery Campus. There, I'm told, is where the hard work begins. *Like it could get any harder.*

As if reading my mind, Mick grabs my hand and squeezes it.

"Sheila, smooth that worry line off that pretty face of yars," he soothes. "Yull be right. Just be happy yar moving onto the next step."

"I know. Thanks, Mick," I reply, smiling. "Honestly, I'm excited to be getting out of here."

A knock on the door informs me my ride's here, so I gather my things. Apparently, the recovery campus is nearby. From my general ever growing knowledge, I'm learning more about the town in bits and pieces. This town offers two supermarkets, three pubs, two major eateries, a hospital and a recovery center. To us Southern Californians this might seem remote, but to its local residents, this place is a thriving metropolis. As Mick packs up the gammon board, he informs me that he lives in another smaller town, about sixty-five kilometers away on the outskirts of this big town, which he calls a "city." Point proven.

Leaning down, he plants a kiss on the top of my head, promising me he'll see me tomorrow. He scoots out of the room with a little wave behind his back. Before I realize it, I'm being loaded up in a van and setting off towards the next leg of my journey, no pun intended.

Just as promised, Mick arrives at breakfast at the new campus. Not much has changed in terms of scenery, but they have me walking more and doing a more hardcore regime of exercise therapy. I urge the physical therapist to push me in that department. I've already gained some movement, but I want it to be more. I *need* it to be more, but the woman assures me I should be happy with how I'm currently progressing, even if it feels slow. Some times, like right now, I can't help but feel slightly frustrated. This process seems never ending some days. *Will I ever*

*walk normally again?* I was never one for exercise, but now that it's been stripped of me, I want it more than anything. Unfortunately, it hurts more than I could ever have imagined, yet I'm quite determined to do what it takes to get back up on my feet sooner rather than later.

The thought of my bleeding international medical bills leaves my stomach constantly in knots and is one of my biggest motivators. One less day here can only be beneficial in that regard. My parents set up a GoFund Me back at home. When news of my accident and situation spread through their spheres, people have been more than generous. The exchange rate also helps, but it's not going to be nearly enough. Not to mention, I hate asking people for money, like absolutely despise it, but I can't control it. All I can do is be eternally grateful, and make something good come of it. By a small miracle, I did buy traveler's insurance which covers bodily injury, but that process will apparently take months to sort out as I'm still in the throws of it all. Assuming it's even covered, the deductible alone makes me want to vomit. Nothing short of getting out of this place will help me at the moment, so I put my head down and go pedal to the metal to do my part.

Forty-five degrees. *You can do this, Nina.* Sweat beads down my neck. I lift my right leg up in the air, holding it for thirty second intervals at that forty-five degree angle. I count down aloud.

Mick enters my room, carting a small cardboard box.

"I don't reckon why they make us still wear these things," he blurts out in slight frustration, folding up his mask. "It's been long enough 'n no one here has contracted it. I'm a docta for heaven's sake. I reckon I know how to sanitize. They should be movin' towards the re-opening phase, at least here anyway." He looks over as I'm about to drop in exhaustion from trying to maintain my exercise those last few seconds. "Oh, sorry, Sweetheart, didn't realize ya were in the middle of that."

"Four, three, two, one," I exhale, almost out of breath.

Mick sits down at my little table in the corner of my room, sliding the box across the wooden top next to a backgammon board he left here last week.

"How ya feelin' today, Sheila?" he asks. "Four weeks down, eight more to go."

I groan at the math, *eight* weeks… it seems like a year from now, yet scarily not enough at the same time. I have a lot to do in two months.

Reflections of light dance off the room's ceiling from the pool water outside the window. I would love to just get in the water. I can't until all the wounds heal and stitches are removed. That'll be a couple more weeks at best.

"I'm doing okay, Mick. If it wasn't for you, I think they might admit me to the psych ward, but every day gets slightly better."

I gesture towards my leg; the hard cast was taken off when I arrived here, and a giant black brace now squeezes my leg in its place. Mick bends over my leg to inspect the stitches, and carefully assesses the wound.

"The sutures are healin' up nicely," he points out. "I'd say they can come out in a week actually. No signs of infection."

"Really?" I exclaim. "I can't wait to get back in the water."

"Soon. I rememba'd ya fancy mystery thrillas 'n I had a few lyin' around," he says, gesturing to the box, "'n reckoned ya could dust 'em off, ya know, have somethin' to distract ya." Excited to pour my bored heart into something, I accept them gladly. Going off of Mick's recommendations, I start with the Oliver Gideon series. Mick eagerly opens the gammon board. "Fancy a quick game?"

I rub my hands together in a mock-sinister way, and he hands me the white dice. He blows into his hands, wishing his blue dice good fortune.

"Ya seem extra determined today, exercisin' on yar own time, eh," Mick notes, impressed.

"I want to get out of here… I mean, I guess it doesn't matter too much seeing as how I can't leave Australia anyway, but I need to get off campus, Mick, the medical bills alone!"

"Dun worry, Sweetheart, those things always have a habit of sortin' themselves out," he says, waiving my worry away with the shake of his head, typical of his laid back demeanor. "The docta informs me yull still be too fragile to fly, if a flight were to magically appear, mind ya. Yar immune system is seriously compromised after yar surgeries. With the medical visa, yar not bein' forced out for at least the year, so don't worry yar pretty little head about it just now."

My mouth twitches. I know this, but I still don't like it. I laugh internally. In The States, Mick's last line would be taken, picked apart, and branded as misogynistic, but with Mick, he genuinely thinks I'm pretty and really wants me not to worry. People here seem much more genuine and have kind intentions, at least all the ones I've come across. Mick stands up, stretching out his back.

"Yar safe here with us in town," he reiterates his point, "but ya get out there in the world, 'n it's not good, Sweetheart."

I've literally been avoiding the topic of Covid-19, but that's all anyone wants to talk about when I FaceTime those back home. It's gone full scale lockdown, and apparently toilet paper still has higher value than gold. Changing the subject, I suggest we watch a movie next time Mick visits.

"Sounds lovely, Sheila. Just not tomorrow. I can't come in."

"Hmm, okay," I say, trying to disguise my disappointment.

Mick hasn't missed one single visit yet and is my only connection to the outside world. Curiosity builds... why can't he tomorrow? Where is he going? Is he hanging out with that Brodie guy? But I decide not to press further. He'll tell me if he feels comfortable enough. He picks up the empty cardboard box and bends down to kiss my hairline.

"I'll be seeing ya, Sweetheart," he mutters sweetly.

This has become his little endearing farewell to me. It makes my heart happy to hear. I nod and wave goodbye. Bracing to lift myself and return to bed, I actually do another rep of leg lifts. *Eight more weeks* repeats itself in my head.

Today is the day. I'm finally free, twelve weeks later. After extreme physical exercise regimes, I have regained most mobility, just as the doctor predicted I would. Filled with extra determination to leave this place in the best possible shape, I've poured my heart and soul into willing my leg to heal and recover. It's funny. I was kind of a couch potato before coming to Australia. Never one to exercise regularly, I now find that notion laughable. These days, I move constantly from cycling on the stationary bike to swimming daily, and find I have more strength than when I first started this ridiculous journey.

Mick graciously offers me to come live with him while I finish my final stint at a more local physical therapy office, and since my current housing prospects are bleak, I take him up on his more than generous offer. Mom and Papi insist on "meeting" Mick through FaceTime, more like vetting him before I move in, so we quickly sit down before my discharge goes through. By the end of the call, they are cracking jokes and expressing serious thanks to him. Mom mentions they mailed me a care package for my birthday, which is in a little over a month, but with Covid delays, they hope I'll receive it on time if at all. It's something to look forward to at least. Speaking of something to look forward to, Mick informs me they found my carry-on. It's back at his house.

I take a good look around at my little barren room that I've called home for the last seventy-five days, and leave Recovery Campus for good. Crazy to think that three-and-a-half months ago, I could not sit up, let alone walk, and now I'm practically skipping to the exit. Just goes to show you what hard work and a dedicated mindset can accomplish.

Mick waits for me in the car port, leaning against his Trooper. It reminds me of Gloria. I can't think about home too much because the fear of missing out envelopes me and leads me down a dark spiral of depression. I push the thought far away and choose to focus on what's in front of me as Mick reaches over and opens up the passenger door. He beams a radiating smile at me, a smile that warms my heart and melts my homesickness away.

# 5

My new roommate and I ride for a good while. I keep thinking the turnoff will come up, but we keep driving past many small clusters of homesteads. I look over at Mick in surprise. He's been driving this commute to visit me every single day.

Something dark and moving catches my attention out the window. I turn and see a pack of emus running, a trail of rust tinted dust kicking up in their wake. *Wild*. Being inside for months, it's easy to forget that I've been in the Australian Outback.

Not long after, the ute slows as we turn off and pull down a red dirt road that leads up to a little house. There is nothing around his property other than open land for miles. His land sits on the east side of the highway, while the coastline faces it a couple hundred feet away. In Southern California I'm accustomed to seeing houses and buildings blanket every square inch of available space, sometimes trampling other houses. All space is practically deemed buildable, so combined with the smoggy haze, it's a constant choking feeling of congestion. Here, on the other hand, there is more open land than dwellings or towns. It's so breathtaking in its vastness. Mick tells me most people live on the coast as the land inland isn't inhabitable nor sustainable. Also, due to its remoteness, houses or plots are still spread out rather widely, so you're kind of out here on your own.

I notice the home in front of me is older, but it's immaculately clean and tidy. Mick pulls the ute right up next to the adjoining, enclosed deck. He gets out and comes around and opens the door for me.

"Why, thank you, kind sir," I say in my most corniest British accent, graciously accepting his gentlemanly gesture.

He's slow, but sure footed. After I cautiously take the deck steps, he opens the front slider and we enter. Cozy, warm, happy thoughts come to mind. Shaggy green carpet lines the family room floor, while the rest of the floor that stretches into the adjacent kitchen is an old polished, hardwood. Framed photographs line the floral wallpapered walls. It's a small place, as I soon discover - two bedrooms, two bathrooms, single story. There's a small kitchen with original 1950s appliances, all looking like they were freshly purchased and installed.

"Well, Sheila, welcome home," Mick quips, smiling bashfully. "She might not look like much from the looks of her, but she's yars for as long as ya need her."

"Thanks, Mick," I mumble, "I truly can't thank you enough."

"Anytime, Sweetheart," he chuckles, and pats my arm affectionately. He then leads me down the little hallway and opens the door on the right, motioning me inside. "This room is yars. Mine is just down the hall if ya need anything. Toilet's down to the right."

I nod and smile. Mick heads back down the hallway.

My carry-on, while a little tattered, sits on my bed. I immediately cross the room straight to my bag and unzip it. Everything is intact just as I left it in the trunk. It's not much considering I now live here. I open my backpack and pull out a crumpled brown paper bag from the hospital. Unfolding the opening, I pull out the only jacket I brought. Not only is it tattered and shredded in places, but it's mostly covered in dried blood. I've been avoiding looking at it until now, with good reason. My tongue sticks to the roof of my dry mouth.

*I'm so lucky to be alive.*

Setting the non-salvageable jacket down, I scan the rest of my belongings. Originally only coming here for three weeks, I packed light. One pair of denim shorts, one jean skirt, one white dress, two tops, two tank tops, and an overnight sleep shirt are all I brought in terms of clothing, besides undies and a couple pairs of socks. I always pack plenty of undies; "*You can never have enough underwear,*" Mom always says.

*Mom, I miss you desperately.*

I unearth my drone, buried in the middle of my clothes for general padding. Holding my breath, I inspect it for damage. Spectacularly, there's not even a scratch on it. This reminds me, I need to give the luggage and backpack companies five star reviews for the protection alone. Double checking the propellers, I notice only one is a little bent, but that's what backups are for and I have three extra pairs with me.

"You've fought and conquered a tough battle, Khal," I whisper sincerely. "*Thank you.*"

Hope and excitement bloom in my tummy and I feel a little lighter. At least if I'm stuck in this country I might as well pursue some creative endeavors while endless gorgeous landscapes are at my disposal. I just need to get a new phone to fly it first.

By uncovering my drone, I find my two bathing suits. My fingers pry apart the wrinkled suits, squashed tightly together. One is a high wasted, aqua blue two-piece, and the other is a green and white, flower power one-piece. Still in awe that somehow my belongings are in tact, I pull out my toiletry bag… something must have burst on impact because there's dried whiteish fluid over everything. But all of this is salvageable or replaceable, so it's no big deal. I lay my backpack down and pull out my laptop and camera. The camera body seems okay with a small dent on the base, but the lens is completely smashed. Hopefully, I can borrow one or find one cheap around here to replace it.

Everything I own on this continent is displayed in front of me on the bed. Grabbing a pile of my undies and socks, I open a drawer in a wooden dresser that stands against the wall across from the bed. The top drawer is empty. I place my items in there; there's plenty of room to spare. Curiously, I open the second drawer and find stacks of women's clothes perfectly preserved. I lightly glide a hand over the vintage material. Despite my peaked curiosity, I slowly close the drawer.

Mick knocks lightly on the door a few minutes later, leaning in.

"Sheila, ya gettin' hungry? Wanna bevvie?" he asks. "We can go into town 'n get some tucker at the rubbidy, er pub, if that's alright with ya?"

Central and northern Western Australia are fully back open in terms of Covid lockdown. All my family and friends back in The States are jealous. While the virus rages on over there, life here feels normal, well as normal as it can be for an American marooned in Australia.

"Sounds great," I reply, finishing the last of my tidying up.

I'm along for the ride and the long haul, and honestly, I've been cooped up for months so I'm very eager and open for any type of excursion.

"Good," he says. "I reckon some of the folk in town will wanna see ya now that yar feelin' betta."

I give him a quizzical scowl.

"Mick, what do you mean people in town will want to see me?"

"I just mean they've been worried about ya. Ya've been the talk of town the last coupla months." My mouth goes dry. *Cool, cool.* "Dun worry, Sweetheart," Mick says, sensing my discomfort. "Pay 'em no heed. They're only a group of hearsay vultures. Let 'em babble on."

I nod my head, trying to channel Mick's confident demeanor and look down at my wardrobe options. Boy it's blazing hot out here in the bush, and Mick informs me that we're slowly approaching the *winter* season. I decide on wearing my coolest option: a basic white tank tucked into my vintage denim skirt, cut just above the knee. I particularly love the wooden buttons that line down the front of the lighter wash. Maria gifted it to me for Christmas. Just having it on reminds me of her, which makes me feel better instantly. She's here with me in some small way.

We leave the house and make our way to town, and park in front of the only bar around. I adjust the belt I'm borrowing from Mick. When I put on the skirt, instead of being snug at my waist, it dropped a little, catching at my curvy hips. Apparently monitored hospital food - which is not to be desired - and regular exercise really impact one's physicality. *Who would have thought?* I stifle a laugh. I've lost about twenty pounds, maybe more. Wearing baggy sweats every day is one way to obstruct noticeable change. I tinker with the tank straps and smooth out my skirt, glancing down at my caramel colored sandals. One of the straps was torn so Mick reinforced it tightly with duct tape, but I'm hoping no one will notice. I brush some stray frizzy strands away from my temple.

"Stop fidgeting. Ya look fine," Mick reassures me, as we make our way to the door of the pub. "No one will be payin' attention to what yar wearin'."

*Okay...* I don't know if that makes me feel better or disappointed. Sometimes I can be a downright typical female.

Mick opens the pub's door and motions for me to enter first. I swear every head inside turns up in unison, staring at us, well me. The room is dimly lit by a few old fashioned sconces. The bar runs along one side of the pub, and booths line the walls all the way around the other side. Two billiard tables encompass the middle of the room. Some classic 80s rock song plays in the background. I think it's Men At Work. Mick guides me to the bar and we sit down on a couple of old alligator covered barstools. People resume their activities, with only the occasional stare in my direction from some cackling lady hens.

"Usual for me, Billy," Mick taps the bar, flagging the bartender.

He nods towards me, eyebrows raised, waiting for my order.

"A Shirley Temple?" I reply, half in question, and look at Mick. "I'm still weaning off those pain meds. Don't think I should mix them with booze just yet." I wink. "Right, Doc?"

"Shirley for the lady, Bill," he confirms, nodding to Billy.

The bartender acknowledges the order and gets to work mixing our drinks. I catch sight of the other women. They keep glancing at me while snickering amongst themselves. I supposed I'm fresh meat for the *"hearsay vultures."* A beautiful pink, carbonated Shirley Temple sits right before me. No ice though. That's weird. I feel it and it feels cool, but definitely could be colder. I motion to Billy. He looks up from his other task with a glossed over expression and raises his eyebrows at me.

"Excuse me," I nervously ask, pushing the Shirley back towards him, clearing my throat, "is it possible to add ice?" Clearly put out at the small inconvenience, Billy lets out an exaggerated sigh and grabs my cup. He pulls out a spoonful of ice and dumps a couple of cubes into the cup. The Shirley splashes up and over the brim. I don't know if that's enough to cut it. Cautiously, I ask, "Maybe a few more?"

With a big huff, he digs deeply into the ice bucket, dumping a large handful of cubes in my drink. *Much better* my smile beams. I mutter a heartfelt thanks, but Billy literally just turns his back to me and resumes his previous task. I stare down at my fizzy drink. *Ice, I've missed you.* Recovery Centre wasn't big on ice either, and I've been dreaming of the day I would finally get my hands on a chilled drink of some sort. I take a giant swig and let the carbonation bubble up in my throat. It burns so good and leaves my eyes watering.

Catching whiffs of fries and burnt meat, saliva gathers in my mouth. I'm practically ready to start drooling. Recovery Centre wasn't known for its raving cuisine either. Even though all of this sounds amazing, I remember to try and order something light off the menu. I really don't want to upset my stomach with an overload of greasy food. Plus, in the past, I've been described as very chunky. Now I'd say I'm a healthier, fitter chunk, which accents my natural curves. I'd like to keep it that way.

As I take a sip from my drink, I catch the prying eyes of strangers, men aged eighteen to eighty, looking me over... *that's a first.* I'm always the girl men skip right over in a crowded room. While I'm pretty in my own way, my sisters are the real beauties of the family. At 5'7", both of them tower over me by a good three to four inches.

One young man, practically a boy, slides down the bar towards us. I naturally tense. Mick notices and gently pats my arm, all the while maintaining eye contact with this stranger.

"He's harmless, dun worry," he whispers out of the corner of his mouth to me, and I relax slightly.

"Buy ya some liquid gold?" the boy offers, raising his glass to me.

"Piss off, Andy," Mick playfully butts in. "I just sprang Nina from Recovery Centa. We're just here to grab some grub."

"Alright, alright, Mick," he says amenably, jokingly acting wounded, and backs off, giving me a wink as he does.

Suddenly, a door bursts open behind us. Light fills the dim, thick atmosphere. No one looks up this time. Apparently now that I've arrived, they don't really care who comes or goes.

I glance over my shoulder and see a dog, a mutt of some type, almost like a Goldendoodle. She's beautiful and has the most amazing, butter colored shaggy coat. At least I think it's a she - it doesn't have a collar on. The pup and its owner sit down at a booth, next to some pretty blonde chick. I recognize the man almost instantly. It's that attractive guy Brodie, Mick's friend from when I woke up at the hospital. Mick catches me staring inquisitively and whirls around to see what's going on. He eyes him and leans towards me.

"That's the bloke who found ya," he whispers. *Like I could forget.* Mick sits up a little straighter and smiles towards him and bellows, "Pryce!"

I lightly jab Mick's side, trying to be casual, but he already attracts Brodie's attention. He motions for him to come over. I sit up straight, trying to low-key smooth out my skirt. Brodie looks like he'd rather not engage, but goes along with it out of respect for Mick. He shuffles over to the bar and stands in front of us.

Upon closer inspection, and not dosed up on sedatives, I see his chiseled chin is lined with a light layer of dark scruff... not quite a beard, more like a five o'clock shadow, as if a painter took some charcoal and lightly dusted around his chin and cheeks. Dark, full lashes line his deep green eyes, hidden even more by his furrowed, thick eyebrows. The whites in his eyes contrast more prominently against his dark features and tanned skin.

Politely smiling, he avoids any eye contact.

"Day for it," he mumbles, acknowledging Billy, who reciprocates.

"Pryce, ya rememba Nina, don't ya?" Mick exclaims. "Nina, this is Brodie Pryce, yar knight 'n shinin' arma."

"More like my rescuers from Down Under," I happily tell the pair of them, giving homage to one of my favorite kid movies.

Still looking down at the floor, Brodie tightly smiles.

"I wouldn't put it that way," he modestly explains. "I reckon I just happened to be at the right place at the right time is all."

Hearing him speak somehow makes him more real and less of a clouded hallucination from my trauma memory. He's real, I have to remind myself. Suddenly, I'm very shy.

I realize I never got to properly thank him for finding me. Wishing I could at least buy him a drink, but with what money, I awkwardly and stupidly extend my hand out, wanting to shake his in the most underrated thanks imaginable. He shakes his head a little, refusing the gesture.

"Well, whatever you want to call it, I'm super grateful you were there," I offer, full of gratitude, before dropping my hand.

He shrugs, clearly uncomfortable. He's not looking for heroic praise. Refreshing.

"It's nice to see ya," he says, "...up." *And alive* his tone implies.

The cute, moving fur ball fiercely sniffs me up and down. I can barely see her eyes underneath all the shaggy strands. She then jumps up on her hind legs, smothering me in kisses, almost knocking me off the barstool in the process. I laugh. I miss my dog, Cosmo, though this dog is easily five times the size of Cos. Brodie intercedes and tries to pry the pup off me. She must weigh a good forty pounds I note. I catch him glancing at my mangled right leg. He pries his eyes away abashedly, and returns his attention to his fur baby.

"Sorry 'bout that," he mutters in apology. "She can be a little overzealous doggo sometimes."

"It's okay, puppy," I shake my head, reassuring the mutt. To show Brodie I'm not some broken porcelain doll, I hop off the stool and bend down so my eyes are level with his dog. I hide my wince as I hold the squat, and though I'm starting to shake, my leg feels strong overall. I'm making the classic overly lovey-dove sounds people make when talking to fur creatures. "Wow, you're beautiful," I croon. "Oh, more kisses? Thank you. And you're sweet too, huh? Yeah, yes, you are, sweet girl."

The pup sits with her tail wagging profusely, stealing little licks and kisses when she can. They don't bother me one bit. Out of the corner of my eye, I notice the local girls whispering as they stare in my direction from the booth. Brodie clears his throat. I forget it's not just me and the dog. Taking one more chance to thank him, I look at him, trying to catch his eye.

"Brodie, it's nice to meet you consciously and sober. I truly can't thank you enough," I say genuinely. When he just sheepishly smiles, I add, "Do you know where Stella is so I can thank her as well?"

Waiting for Brodie's response, Mick chuckles softly. I look at him, not understanding what's so comical.

"Well I'm sure she'd be keen if ya hadn't already done so," Brodie says, cracking a grin.

"I don't get it," I reiterate, feeling more confused. "Can you please tell her for me?"

"Sure, but," he nods and looks at his dog and declares, "tell her yarself." I follow his gaze to the mutt, as he says in a laugh, "Stel, someone wants to thank ya."

It dawns on me and I suppress a bubbling giggle. *Duh, Nina!*

Stella's ears move, fixating on the sound of her name. She tilts her head as if waiting for a biscuit. I know the look well. Regaining my composure, I look down at her with the utmost sincerity. I kneel down, wincing slightly as my right leg bends again so soon after my squat, and push back the hair covering her eyes. Little white edges pop out around her irises, reminding me of a sea lion's eyes. Her gaze jumps from me to Brodie and back.

"Stella, thank you for saving my life," I say, mustering up my most genuine tone. "I owe you a thousand biscuits and a thorough head scratching someday."

As if she understands English, which I think dogs sometimes can, she jumps up and wraps her paws around my neck. I almost fall backwards on the floor. I try to regain my stance, but my right leg gives way and I fall back. Brodie catches me before I land smack dab on my butt. He smells of salt, maybe rust, sweat and...fish? I notice his hair is clipped shorter, with traces of curls forming at the top. His strong arm comes around my shoulder and he gently props me up. His touch is hot and electrifying. I glance at him sharply in surprise. *Does he feel it too?*

"Stel, take it easy, she's fragile," he beseechers her, as he helps me up. He peers back over at me. "Again, sorry 'bout that."

"I'm okay, really," I mutter, chuckling softly.

I sit back on the barstool and Stella jumps up again, attempting to attack me with slobbery kisses. Brodie intercepts and tries to pry her off me one more time.

"Don't know what her deal is!" he snickers, more to himself.

"Pryce," Mick says in an ordering yet playful tone, as he cocks an eyebrow at Brodie before sardonically smiling at me, "maybe ya can take Nina out on the boat sometime. She's dying to get out on the wata."

*What's Mick up to?*

"Nah, yeah, sure," Brodie shrugs. "Tomorrow? No wait, I have the Carmichael family... hmmm, sorry, it's a bit busy. What about arvo afta next?"

Just as I'm about to ask what "arvo" means, Mick leans over, and points to Brodie with his thumb.

"Brodie's one of our local boat chartas," he informs me.

"I don't want to intrude or impose," I hastily exclaim.

The thought of being on a boat out in the middle of the ocean with some guy I just met is a little daunting. I've been alone for so long, I don't know how to handle any solo interactions or the attention. It makes me pretty uncomfortable.

*Exactly why you need to go. Come out of your shell.*

"No wucka's," Brodie shakes his head, waiving off my concern.

"Okay, then..." I say, in agreement, taken aback by his willingness. "I don't have much of a schedule these days, so just let Mick know and he can drop me off?"

"It's settled then," Mick states, looking back and forth between us.

Brodie clicks his tongue and Stella falls to his side. Billy brings out a paper bag and hands it to him.

"Cheers, mate," Brodie gently chimes to the bartender. He peers back to the booth and nods, smiling to the blonde, who grins eagerly back at him. He looks to Mick and me. "Well, be seein' ya then. Come on, girl, let's go."

With the click of his tongue, Brodie takes off through the door with Stella in tow. The bartender brings out our dinners. Mick must have ordered while I was knee deep in my love fest with Stella. I don't even care what's in store for me or my stomach anymore. As if in agreement, it growls fiercely. I'm famished. Mick slides over a juicy burger, with a good bun by the looks of it. Steam rises. I don't hesitate. I dig in and moan in delight. Mick laughs and bites into his steak.

"Are you sure he said today, Mick?" I ask, as we sit parked in front of a makeshift dock at a tiny, dirt launching ramp in the middle of nowhere.

"Yep," Mick confirms, checking his watch. "He musta got held up. It's not like Brodie to forget."

I can't help but feel a tad disappointed. I woke up early to perform my therapy exercises in time, and I was really looking forward to getting out on the water.

"It's fine," I say, perking up for Mick's sake. "We can do it some other time."

Just then an engine noise roars to life in the distance. We look up towards the sound, and a ute similar to Mick's, but white and newer, careens around the road, towing a twenty-five foot fishing boat. In letters on the side it reads: *Salty Stel*.

Mick visibly relaxes in relief. He gets out and rounds the truck to open the door for me. I don't even try to open it anymore as it just invites an argument and lecture on the lack of modern chivalry. I smile at him as I slide out of the seat to the ground.

Brodie begins backing in the trailer towards the water, but pauses as he pulls up beside Mick. Stella sits in the passenger seat with perfect posture, almost human-like. Her owner looks over and politely nods to Mick.

"Sorry 'bout that, Mick," he offers in apology, "got held up."

"Dun worry," Mick yells, waving us goodbye as he climbs up into his Trooper's cab. He catches my attention. "Have fun, Sheila, 'n Brodie, take care of her, eh."

"Yeah, mate, sure thing," Brodie calls back. "I'll have her back two fingers from the sun at the earliest."

Mick nods and drives off. I can feel the awkwardness begin to creep in. Brodie is a complete stranger! At least we have Stella to break the ice.

Standing by the shoreline, I stretch my leg a couple of times, loosening it up for the ride, while Brodie maneuvers the boat into the water. Ocean surrounds the sides of the boat, coming up around the back sides of the ute as it reverses deeper. He stops just as the ute's front doors are nearing the water line. As Brodie jumps out of the truck, Stella flings out, running around the loading ramp as she waits to board. Her master runs around the back of the trailer and unhooks the boat. He then acrobatically makes his way onto the deck and backs it up, steering it sideways towards the little dock. Once he expertly lines up alongside the small pier, he ties a rope around a wooden beam. All of this is accomplished in minutes while I stand here uselessly waiting. Stella runs up the dock and jumps over the rails and assumes what I gather is her normal spot on the bow.

"Can I move the ute?" I ask, trying to offer some service.

"Well no offense, Nina," he jokes, tying a knot, "but the last time ya tried to drive, it didn't end so hot, 'n I'm ratha fond of my ute."

I fold my arms, brushing off the small dig. *Touché.*

Brodie runs back to the ute, jumps in and drives forward. The wet trailer leaves a trail of fresh muddy tire tracks as the heavy drips of water hit the red earth.

I wear my faded, yellow billowy tank today paired with my denim high-wasted shorts, and taped together flip flops. The sun beats high and bright at this hour. The water bounces tiny, illuminated diamonds of light onto any nearby surface, including my face. I raise my arm to shield my eyes as much as I can. *I miss my sunglasses* - one of the biggest losses from the wreck.

Brodie parks the ute and trailer up the road a bit. He casually jogs past me back to the boat.

"Ready when ya are," he says, passing me.

That's my cue. I grab my backpack and canteen and follow suit down the little, rickety old dock. I awkwardly clamor over the railing into the boat, and lose my footing. I land with a wavering thud. Slight pain travels up my leg, but stretching it immediately relieves the pressure. I gather myself comfortably on one of the seats, choosing to focus on the excitement ahead. Brodie aptly jumps in and starts the engine, igniting the large exhaust, which bursts with noise, but it soon dies down to a light constant purring. He unties us and pushes us off. We slowly gain distance from the shore, and the ute shrinks smaller by the minute until it disappears altogether as an orange, silky mirage engulfs the shoreline.

I turn around and face forward towards Brodie, who commands the captain's chair. Stella, his co-captain, braces herself on the seat beside him. He reaches over and turns on the stereo. Linkin Park's "Papercut" blasts out of the boat speakers. I frown a little as he instantly drops the volume. The song reminds me of high school, and I smile as I remember spending lunch time in Selena's VW Squareback. *Selena, I miss you.*

Brodie motions to change the song, but I yell, "No, leave it. I forgot about this tune."

He shrugs, and lowers his hand.

"Turn it up?" I hesitantly ask. He reaches over and does so a little, but it's still pretty low. A little wary to bother him again, but also slightly irked that I can't hear it properly, I try again. "Sorry, but a little more, please?"

He reaches over, starting to get annoyed himself, and twists the knob. It only rises a couple of decibels. *Don't push it, Nina.* I decide to sit back in my chair and sing along in my everyday, naturally boisterous volume. It's probably louder than the actual song, because suddenly the music thunders around me. *Sweet, just how I like it.*

"That's perfect, thanks!" I twist back, hollering.

I can't tell if he's pleasantly surprised or annoyingly shocked. I see his lips move, but I can't hear or make out what he says. We ride for a while unspeaking as the music rolls loudly through Incubus, Evanescence and some Eminem.

The hair wispies around my temples dance widely, swirling in and out of my eyes, but I don't even care. The wind, the open ocean, the smell of sea salt, and the slight tickling of mist hitting my skin is the best thing I've felt in a long, long time. I close my eyes, open my mouth, ecstatically smiling. I even let out a little scream in elation at one point. The volume of the engine combining with the waves hitting the boat is so raucous I don't think Brodie hears my small outburst of happiness, at least I hope not. As I'm constantly wiping the hair from my face, I wish I had my sunglasses. *R.I.P.* I really need to go to town and find another pair or a hat, but hats never fit my large head with all my hair.

Abruptly, the boat stops and the engine dies. I open my eyes and look around eagerly. There's nothing for as far as the eye can see. Little lapping sounds of water roll through the utter quiet. I don't think I've ever seen anything so peaceful.

"It's beautiful," I admire aloud.

"Day for it," Brodie agrees, walking over to the side rail, glancing down. His face lights up in a giant radiating smile, and quite frankly, it blows me away. White shining teeth, pretty straight but still with some character, glisten as he chuckles. Stella peers over the edge, her giant ears like an alarm bell to pay attention. Seated, I glance over but don't see anything but shades of manganese holding my own reflection. My eyes dart back to Brodie, eyeing him dubiously. Clearly I'm missing something... *again*. He strips his shirt off and flings it on the seat next to me. I jump a little startled. He laughs. "Oh, sorry, Nina. Almost forgot yar here."

He motions for me to come over to the side of the rail, next to him. I get up and stand beside him, our shoulders almost touching, and peer over the edge. At first I don't see anything but clear, dark blue water. We're out pretty far. The soft current tosses the boat slightly, tilting us back and forth as we bob in tandem with the tide. I think of Mom, even rocking Javi to sleep turns her a pukey colored green. Thankfully I inherited Papi's sea legs.

"See it?" Brodie asks.

Shaking my head, he places a hand lightly on my back and gently urges me over more, pointing with his other hand close to my face so I can see the direction. I follow the trajectory of his moving finger until I spot something very large and dark near the surface. It's heading towards the boat. I jerk upright and let out a squeal as I see two more incoming shapes. I can make out their flapping wings and long thin tails. They're rays!

"Oh my gosh!" I exclaim.

Stella runs around the deck trying to find a better view of our massive party crashers. She even seems excited.

"Come on, they won't bite," Brodie tells me. "It's only a few mantas."

Scared, but insanely fascinated, I inch my way closer to the railing and firmly plant both hands on the smooth chrome. I look over the edge and see the magnificent beasts pass by only a few feet away. *I can't believe it.* The creatures swim with agile weightlessness, gliding through the water in an almost unconcerned and lackadaisical manner. They each must be at least ten feet across in length, maybe more. Brodie grabs a mask and snorkel and hands them to me, expecting me to put them on. Stella jumps up, wanting in on the action.

"You're not getting in there with those things are you?" I ask incredulously.

Stella wags her way to the back swim step.

"Stel, stay here, wait for Dad," he commands authoritatively, narrowing his eyes at her, and then resumes attaching his snorkel. Stella halts and returns to her position overlooking the edge, while Brodie snorts at me. "'N we're both hoppin' in the drink, Nina."

"The hell I am," I counter, in complete disbelief.

He stops spitting into his mask and looks at me with a look that screams *are you serious?!*

"Ya told me ya wanted to go out on the boat 'n get in the wata—."

"*No,*" I reiterate, "I said I wanted to get out *on* the water, and I love swimming, but pretty much in the shallows where I can escape to dry land if need be." I look out at the giant aliens and gulp. "And those are massive rays, look at their tails."

"It's not that deep," Brodie sighs, getting annoyed. "Only about thirty metres, 'n manta rays are crazy docile. They don't barb ya like a sting ray, aye. Look, ya've no idea what yar missin' out on. Do ya reckon how many people would kill to free dive with one of these pearlas? Or pay to?" He huffs as I simply raise my eyebrows and pinch my mouth shut. *I'm not budging on this one.* Shaking his head, he laughs. "We coulda just gone down to the local kiddie pool, eh."

Annoyed by his sarcastic remark, I deeply exhale. I want to swim, just *not* in the open water this far from shore. I rub my leg to emphasize my injury, or at least imply it.

*Stop using your leg as a crutch, Nina. You're perfectly capable, especially in the water.*

"Fine, yar loss," he says, in a tone that implies *more for me.* He sits on the edge, pulling on his mask and fins. "Suit yarself then."

He dives off the side and I peer over the edge, following his fins. I find him almost instantly with the amazing visibility. I rush to the other side of the boat trying to locate the rays. After a few seconds, I find them sunning themselves near the surface about fifteen feet away.

Thinking back to my fifth grade marine biology camp, I rack my brain for any information on manta rays. You never hear about them attacking people or hurting people, but I've never seen an animal so big up close before. It's easily twelve feet in circumference, not including its tail.

I refocus on locating Brodie, but can't find him. Whirling around, I check the perimeter of the boat. No rays. No Brodie. Stella makes her way around, but seems more interested in the occasional flash of bait fish that swim by than the vitality of her "dad." Cool, if left alone, I would have no idea how to captain this vessel back to shore. In fact, I don't even know which direction points to shore. I flip my head back and forth for any sign of outside life. There's only utter stillness.

I hear a big gasp and a release of air as Brodie pops out from under the surface towards the stern. He swims over to the swim step.

"Are you okay?!" I exclaim in panic, walking over.

I try to reign in my worry. Clearly he's not concerned as he floats in the water. He reaches for his mask, pulling it off his face with force. It emits a *pop!* as his face frees itself of the suction. Giant red rings line his forehead, cheeks and mouth.

"It's okay, Nina, the bloody giant was just cruisin'. I was completely fine the entire time, dun worry. She lemme get close before switchin' direction on me," he explains, with enthusiasm. "There's heaps of fish circlin' right below. I'm gonna take the gun out. I was just doin' a lesson this mornin' with a local ankle bita."

He nods to his spear gun and immediately educates me on spear gunning and free diving basics, informing me you should never go out alone, but he's not going to dive deep, just skim the surface so I can oversee from the boat.

From the water, he instructs me to carefully pick up the long wooden gun and bring it to him. In such a rush to meet Mick and me, he forgot to unfasten the coiled bands from the lesson with the boy, but he assures me the safety's on. He advises me to release the rubber bands and I try, but it's double banded and I can't muster up the upper body strength. I give up and walk towards Brodie with caution. I rub my hand along the shaft, up next to the trigger, admiring the craftsmanship. As he stresses again that I'm not to mess with the safety, *ever*, I bump something and freeze. *Did I just undo the safety?* I don't remember what it looked like in the first place... I think, and hope, it's okay. *Fingers crossed.* Just to be safe, I aim it away from either of us. Wondering why I've stilled, Brodie climbs up onto the swim deck, removing his fins. He then advances towards me at the exact same moment I step forward and trip over my backpack, slamming against the railing. I land partially on the gun. The spear shoots out, missing Brodie's head by inches and impales the back seat next to him.

*Shit.*

I see his eyes practically pop out of his head. Livid, he whirls around from me to the speargun shooting out of his vinyl seat, then back to me as I stand in shock. Dropping everything, I cover my open mouth with both quivering hands.

"I'm so sorry," I plead. "So so so so sorry!"

"Ya coulda killed me!" he roars, throwing his mask, snorkel, and fins onto the deck in anger.

I just keep repeating how sorry I am as he storms up and forcefully grabs the gun from my feet and inspects the damage to his boat before tediously plucking the spear out of his cushion. A dark hole the size of a nickel stands out against the white vinyl.

Shaking from adrenaline and guilt, tears flood my vision. I could have killed him in one accidental swoop, an accident, but manslaughter nonetheless. I try to wipe away my tearful eyes without his attention, but he catches me anyway. He squares his shoulders and walks up beside me, pulling the gun up close, right in my face.

"Here," he states, loudly and bluntly, pointing to the silver switch, "is the safety. *Always* make sure it stays pulled back like this or ya might kill a poor bloody bastard." I sink down on the vinyl seat, wincing, about ready to throw up as he walks off back towards the swim step. "I need to get back in the drink 'n cool off for a tick."

After a few minutes I look back to see if he's still out there, and find him floating next to the back swim step. I walk over to apologize once again. I lean down to literally extend my arm as an olive branch and help him up when I notice something slither up his back. I jump back a good four feet.

"I'm starting to get the notion that we have a scaredy-cat here, mate," he says very calmly to his constricting friend.

He patiently waits as the snake slithers around his shoulder. Poised, Brodie seems awfully careful not to make any alarming movements, but also looks somewhat familiar with this encounter.

In utter disbelief, I ask, "Is that a... a—?"

"Sea snake," he finishes, then joyfully cries out, "'n would ya look at her! What a beauty!" Slowly the snake dislodges itself from Brodie's shoulder and swims slowly off in a slithering liquid dance. Brodie hoists himself up onto the deck, super jazzed and pumped. Rubbing excess water away from his eyes, he laughs in happiness. "Man, that was bloody rippa!! One minute I go from almost bein' a dead man to rubbin' elbows with that pearla." My eyes round largely in surprise. *You're the crazy one, mate.* Seeing my look, he explains, "Ya just let 'em do their thing 'n neva interrupt 'em. Curious creatures, sea snakes are. Best leave 'em to investigate 'n then they'll move along. Otherwise they might bite ya 'n if that happens ya'd be dead by the time we'd reach the beach."

"And you just let something that venomous climb all over you?!" I gulp. "You're nuts. Absolutely nuts."

"Nina, how do ya reckon yar supposed to live if ya keep yarself hauled away in a tiny box of fear?" he soberly points out, toweling off and slipping his glasses back on. He fires up the engine, but instead of accelerating gears, he leans back and grabs a drink of water from his canteen. He takes a few big gulps. "Look, I'm not tryna tell ya what to do, I don't even know ya. I just reckon ya should live a little. Take it from some bloke ya almost just killed."

I like how he's already throwing the speargun accident in my face. I feel *awful* about it. Avoiding his direction, I turn my back to him in shame.

"You're the one who shouldn't have left the gun loaded," I whisper to myself, trying to justify it in my mind.

"Excuse me?" Brodie exclaims in disbelief, from behind me.

Did he hear that? *Shit.* I always forget how loud I am. I look back and raise my eyebrows, feigning not having said anything.

"Nothing," I mumble.

"No, I heard ya," he says, narrowing an eye at me. "Ya said *I* shouldn't have left the gun loaded." Unable to downright lie, I shrug and sigh, wishing to move onto a different topic, but his expression tells me he won't let it go. "Yar the one who bloody shot at me!"

"It was an accident!" I wail defensively. I want to go hide in a deep cave and never resurface. "Maybe we should just go back."

His eyebrows shoot up far past his oversized sunglasses.

"Yar jokin', right?" he spits out, stunned. "After I just took the time outta my busy schedule to give ya a free trip out here."

"I'm happy to pay you," I offer, if money's his concern.

"Pay me? Nah, I did this as a favour—."

*"'A favor?'* I don't want to be anyone's *'favor,'*" I interrupt, growing annoyed. "It just seems like neither of us is enjoying this, at least I'm not right now."

"Wow," he edges out, shaking his head. "Ya could just suck it up—."

*"'Suck it up?!' Really?* Some captain you are."

I exhale in an agitated guffaw as my blood starts to boil.

"Why ya ungrateful little..." he mumbles, searching for the word.

I raise my eyebrows, waiting for his choice word. I never imagined the day taking such a sour detour. *How did we end up here?* I curl my body inwardly, trying to shrink my presence, and give him my back. *Just ignore him, Nina.*

"Well if yar so bloody miserable in my company," he bellows dramatically over the engine, "I'll take ya back then."

"I think that'd be best," I retort, firmly crossing my arms.

"Aces!" he huffs in a gruff.

"Great!"

Brodie shakes his head in frustration and punches the gear. The boat jerks forward, and I emit a small howl as I topple back, catching myself on the bench seat. He reaches over to the stereo dial and cranks it. It's Switchfoot's "Meant to Live." I can barely make out the melody over the impacts of the waves and the revving engine. I look over my shoulder and see Brodie bobbing his head madly to the beat. We seem to be hitting every wave dead on. Audible sounds of fiberglass pelting through water rattle off with every thud. White caps begin to litter the open sea.

*Ram! Bam! Bam!* My neck is getting a work out. Hopefully, I'm not too sore from this tomorrow. And if that's not enough, darkening storm clouds gather as we approach land.

Mick is nowhere. It must be too early for it to be *"two fingers from the sun"* or whatever the heck that means. *Ugh, Brodie.* You could probably cut the awkward tension with a knife. I look over at him out of the corner of my sneering eye. He's off retrieving the ute. Standing on the dock waiting, I look over and see him backing in the trailer. Feeling miffed after our uncomfortable exchange, I want to get as far away as possible. I don't have a phone currently, but I will *not* ask him for a favor, no matter how desperate I am.

"*A favor?*" I repeat under my breath, flabbergasted.

There's little to no service here and Mick only operates via a landline so I have no immediate way to contact him. But I can't just sit here either. Annoyance and short temper filter the air so thickly I can practically hear them. While Brodie deals with the boat and gets that squared away, I start walking on foot from the dock towards the dirt road to the highway. Mick's place is only a couple of miles. I'm pretty sure my leg can handle it. The exercise might be good for me.

"Thanks, and sorry again," I mutter, walking away.

"Where ya off to?" he yells in amusement and exasperation, cranking the trailer hook from a good twenty feet behind me.

"I'm headed back to Mick's."

"*On foot?!*"

"It's not that far."

Slinging my backpack over my shoulder, I situate myself as I dig into the hard, red earth, trying to gain as much distance between the two of us. The engine revs to life, and after a couple of minutes, I hear the truck pull up beside me. I look over as Brodie cranks his window open.

"Look, Nina, Mick's place is about fifteen kilometres from here, in the *otha* direction, 'n it's 'bout to start pissin' down."

*Fifteen kilometers*?! Ugh! I can't remember if a mile is longer or shorter than a kilometer. Either way, it sounds far.

"I'm good, really, thanks," I heartily reply, with resolve I didn't know I was capable of having, despite my internal protests.

I spin around in the other direction while keeping my current pace. A few steps later, I hear the ute turning back around as it pulls up once again beside me, except now the driver side butts up right next to me. Brodie tries once more.

"Don't be so stubborn," he says, softly at first before exasperation returns. "I'm not here to fuck spidas. Hop in 'n I'll give ya a lift."

"No really, I'm good."

*Why, Nina?! He's trying here. Take the damn ride!*

"Ahhh, ya give me the shits," he spits out uncontrollably, boiling with irritation as he exhales in deep frustration.

Moisture gathers in the air and the tips of my long curls start to bounce up. He's right, it's about to rain any second. Monstrous precipitation clouds loom overhead. The sky seems to grow darker and angrier with each step I take. Clearly running out of patience, Brodie grabs the shifter, looking like he's about to punch on the gas.

"Wait!" I yell, surrendering.

He brakes. Begrudgingly, I walk around to the passenger side. I open the door and hoist my short legs up and in. I causally inspect my poor leg. Radiating heat pulses from the impact site, and overall it's slightly swollen from my hasty walk through the thick bush. *That's what you get for acting like a six year old, Nina.* I wince as it begins to throb and a small hiss escapes my lips as I lightly prod the vulnerable and inflamed area. Brodie turns sharply at my intake of breath and glances down at my leg. I put my backpack over my knee to avert his attention.

"Ya should ice that when ya get to Mick's," he states, frowning. "It's not lookin' too good."

"Yeah, thanks for the update," I remark sarcastically.

*What's my problem?!* I never act this way. I mean, sure, I have my hissy moments, I'm only human, but I'm never downright snarky and mean to someone willingly, let alone a complete stranger who saved my life.

We ride in silence for a little while. I stare out the window at the never ending burnt orange terrain. Apparently picking up on the current tension inside the ute, Mother Earth mimics us. The ocean now looks like angry black oil as white streaks of waves swirl fiercely all over the surface. Rain comes down as if someone left the tap on and forgot to switch it off. I've never seen such heavy downpour.

Clearly not hitting it off with Brodie, all I want is to blink myself back at Mick's, or anywhere but here.

*I miss California. I miss home badly. I wish this had never happened and I was snug in bed watching a corny movie with Mom and Ria.*

My eyes well up with tears at the thought of home.

*No, Nina, don't let this man see you cry. Stop being such a blubbering mess.*

Reaching up to push my sunglasses back out of sheer habit, I realize I don't even have them to mask my tears. This makes me want to cry even more. Thankfully, just as I'm feeling really down in the dumps, I recognize the turn off to Mick's. We're almost there.

The windshield wipers work overtime sloshing water, trying to clear a path of visibility. I have no idea how Brodie knows where he's going, but clearly he does. We pull up to Mick's and as soon as the ute haltingly stops, I mumble a tiny thanks and jump at my chance of escape. The rain pelts me as drops the size of ping pong balls drown me like I just fell into a dunk tank. I run quickly to Mick's covered deck, trying not to slip. Out of the rain, and away from Brodie, I instantly feel better.

Mick relaxes on the deck with a book in his hands, his reading glasses down his nose. He looks up far too happy for my current mood, and I don't want to worry him. I look back to extend a formal wave of thanks to Brodie, but he's already driving off down the path.

"Yar back early," Mick states, surprised. "Suppose the weatha had otha ideas. Get a wriggle on outta those clothes, ya don't wanna catch a chill." At the mention of a chill, my body shivers slightly. Mick looks me up and down. "Have a nice time?"

I muster the biggest smile I can, walk closer to him, and congenially agree, "Yep, it was beautiful out there. Saw some manta rays, and some scary creatures too."

I think about the sea snake, and the other monster, the captain, but hold my tongue.

"Just wondaful, Sweetheart. Glad ya had a nice time, sorry the weatha mucked it up early for ya," Mick remarks, opening his book and he continues to read before turning the page.

Happy to blame it on the weather, I gently squeeze his shoulder in passing, and walk straight into my room and plop down on my bed, completely drenched, facing upward towards the popcorn ceiling. Thoughts of Brodie Pryce loom over me like the stormy clouds loom in the sky above. I only pray Storm Pryce is as fleeting.

# 6

The monsoon rages on for four more days.

There's no WiFi at Mick's, but he has an older TV with tons of old VHS tapes, and a record player with shelves of old LPs. One channel comes in on the television, and luckily they rerun old syndicated *Jeopardy!* episodes. Mick laughs as I spit out random answers at the screen.

We spend the rainy days listening to music, discussing various bands in Australian and American pop culture, and watching old reruns of *I Dream of Jeannie*. We're watching the episode where Tony and Jeannie go to Hawaii and wind up on a yacht, so naturally, Mick asks how it felt to be back in the ocean after my long absence. I figuratively dive right in and recount my awkward encounter with Brodie. He laughs, while I reiterate how bad it ended up getting between the two of us.

"Trust me, Sheila," he assures me between chuckles, "Brodie's one of the good ones."

On the morning of the fifth day, the storm rages on so badly I opt to cancel my local physical therapy. I don't want Mick driving in this. We don't need another bad wreck. Good thing, because right after I call, the power goes out. By candlelight, Mick and I conduct a small backgammon tournament with the loser making dinner. Despite the mellow downtime, we enjoy each other's company. I mention to Mick that I used to paint, so he pulls out some paper and a few pencils. We pick random topics and do speed round drawings. I quickly learn that Mick has a talent for drawing, especially horses and koala bears.

Finally on the morning of the sixth day, the sun peeks through the dissipating clouds. I hear music playing from outside my room; our electricity must be restored.

Despite the strong weather, it's still warm outside. The local climate has been cooling off little by little as we approach the fall and winter months. Overall, it's still moderately hot out here in WA, with this winter apparently being unusually warmer than most. Not only do they drive on the other side of the road over here, but the seasons are flipped as well. My mind and body are naturally prepping for an upcoming summer season, so while it's a bit odd for me to think winter is coming, the fall temperatures feel like a California August.

After I dress and do my leg exercises, Mick states he's taking me into town so I can buy a phone. Not having WiFi makes the whole iPhone thing kind of pointless, but I prefer familiarity and more than that, I want to fly The Khal again; unfortunately I can't do that without a smartphone. The mere thought of flying my drone has my chest bubbling in mirth. Plus, I'll be able to FaceTime my family more regularly, that is when I have WiFi.

As we drive into town, I reflect on how time moves pretty slowly out here. I heard that from a lot of travelers in The States, but living it firsthand is kind of bizarre. Not only can the days drag on, but sometimes it feels like I'm in a time warp. I notice how locals aren't glued to their phones nor do they allow their phones and their busy work schedules to dictate their lives. I find that lifestyle incredibly refreshing and inspiring.

After picking up my phone from the general store, Mick runs an errand while I walk to the internet cafe, Lotte's, so I can check in with the family. We've been primarily communicating through email when I come into town, but today we are "seeing" each other for the first time since I've been at Mick's. I practically skip into Lotte's. Nestled into a leather chair, I make myself comfortable as the dial reaches all the way across the world. Maria answers, screaming when she sees my face. We catch up for a while before she models her new bikini. Back home, summer is in full swing. Despite Covid, the sun still shines and people want to get outside to breathe and relax, and enjoy one of their only freedoms.

While I have her attention, I have her water my plants. I'm surprised to see how many plants are surviving's Ria's care. She's not one born with a green thumb, and that's putting it generously. I request that she go outside and start Gloria's engine and she does just as Mom and Papi boot her out of the screen, holding Javi between them. He's already growing up so much. He looks like a little boy. My heart breaks a little knowing I'm missing out on this precious toddler time we'll never get back. I try to get him to wave to me through the screen, and for a second he seems to recognize me and smiles, but then gets bored easily and whines. Selena wedges into the frame, and she and Mom attribute his behavior to hunger and typical baby needs. I know they're just trying to make me feel better. Truthfully, I think Javi's starting to forget me.

They ask about me, my recovery, what I've been doing, and I give them the scoop. I share my encounter with the manta rays, leaving out the part where I almost impaled Brodie. They'll want to know every little detail and I'm trying to forget about it. I'd rather soak up the time I have with them hearing about home. I gather that life, while different, is still moving forward. Papi works full time from his satellite garage office so everyone's together all the time. I instantly get the sense that it's a blessing and a curse to be stuck together 24/7 for months straight with no end in sight.

I see Mom making albondigas soup with Abuela in the background as Cosmo yips for a piece of meatball at their heels. Everyone talks over each other so they can be heard. It's little moments like these that make me miss home *a lot*. It's chaotic and overwhelming to most, but to me, it's home, and home is *home*.

After my paid hour of WiFi is almost up and after many goodbyes and "I love you's," we sign off. The fifteen hour time difference really makes it challenging to connect. Either party is usually exhausted from it being either too early in the morning, or too late at night. While it's amazing to feel like I'm home for an hour, there's an ache in my chest burning a hole through my heart because I miss them so much.

Pocketing my fresh phone, I wave goodbye to Lotte and walk towards the hardware store to find Mick.

Back at Mick's house, I think he can detect my dampening mood. I try hard to hide it, but lately the homesickness squeezes me like a vice, unwilling to relent. Memories keep flooding my head of long walks with Cosmo, blasting music in Gloria as I hit the PCH, and my favorite blended mocha from JC Beans; I even miss Papi's snoring through the Dodger games. I feel like one of those vintage cartoon characters on TV, the ones where an animated cloud hovers directly above them as raindrops fall overhead like a magnet as they move around.

Mick's been wonderful and more than generous with me, so I feel guilty knowing he's aware I'm homesick. Making breakfast for us one morning, he reads his book while I place the hash browns and eggs on our plates. I arrange the two poached eggs to look like eyes, and shape the shredded potatoes into a smile. It's something Papi always does when making Sunday breakfast. My shoulders sink at the memory, but I muster up a smile. *Fake it until you make it, Nina.* Mick laughs at the face and digs in. Out of the blue, he asks me to name my top ten favorite songs. I bite my lip as my eyebrows jump. This question is always the hardest thing someone could ask me, but Mick gets what he wants, for me to be distracted. Before I know it, I'm debating between U2 and John Mayer, an impossible task! I come to the conclusion that I can't decide definitively between bands, let alone songs.

Mick shakes his head in mock disappointment before tidying up the plates and depositing them in the sink. I stand up and stretch before joining him in cleanup. He nudges my elbow to stop me and instead suggests we take the Trooper out for a driving lesson. I'm a bit hesitant after the accident, but he insists we need to do it, especially *because* of the accident.

"Dun worry, Sweetheart," he assures me. "I'll be with ya this time."

He throws me the keys and we walk outside to the ute where he opens the door for me. I climb my way into the driver's seat and notice my toes are feet away from the pedals, so with a little force, we nudge the seat closer. I don't think the seat has been moved in decades by the feel of it. He closes the door swiftly behind me, then hoists himself up into the passenger side and settles in. I look down at the keys, fumbling them around in my fingers.

"Are ya gonna keep an old man waitin' all day, Sheila?" Mick says, laughing.

"Where to?" I ask, looking around the dashboard and the floorboards; there's so much more going on down there than I remember.

"How 'bout we start by firin' up the old girl," he instructs simply, as I take hold of the shifter with my left hand, position my left foot on the clutch with my right foot on the brake. With the twist of the ignition, the engine fires right away. We sit, shaking to the engine vibration. He demonstrates all the different gears and when to shift. "Trust me, Sheila, yull get a feel for it," he coaxes, leaning over. "Now, to the post we go."

He grins a nice reassuring smile. I feel more at ease seeing it. He knows this trick works like magic and constantly uses it whenever I'm feeling the least bit nervous. I lower the emergency brake and the ute sways softly into an idling position. It waits for me to take command. Slowly, I take my foot off the brake. The clutch pretty much holds the ute in gear. Then reluctantly, I release pressure from the clutch as smoothly as my faulty leg allows. As this happens, I gently press on the gas.

Mick hollers in excitement as the gear transitions smoothly.

"Bloody rippa, Sheila, sweet as. Now try second into third, but first, chuck a u-ey here," he points, directing me.

After making a u-turn, I take a deep breath and press on the accelerator while also trying to feather the clutch. Mick motions the shifting pattern in his hand to remind me. I hear and feel the engine rev beneath me until it sounds like a tight wheeze in dire need of exhaling. Instinctively, I press down on the clutch and quickly repeat the same motion as earlier, but all at a much faster pace so I don't pop the clutch. It transitions rather well, maybe not as smooth as going from first to second, but much better than I anticipated. We drive to the post office, and I pull into a front parking spot. Mick quickly grabs his mail.

"Oh gosh, I have to backup now," I say dreadfully on his return.

"Pish posh, ya got this," he says matter-of-factly.

I haltingly make it out of the congested parking lot and feel much better once the tires return to the main road. We drive around practicing for about an hour before we decide to head back. When we reach the house, he makes me specifically practice reversing again to get more familiar with the feeling. My leg tires quickly and quivers from all the action of the day. I can't feather the clutch smoothly and now it catches when I put it in reverse. I release an exasperated cry on our fourth try and slam my hands against the steering wheel.

"It's alright, Sweetheart," Mick proudly says, patting me on the back. "Ya were downright marvelous today. We'll keep tryin' 'til yar a pro."

And tomorrow comes and we do keep trying again, and the day after, and the day after that, on and off for another week and a half. By the end of the following week, I have the clutch wired. Well maybe that's a generous description, but it's fair to say I can handle myself behind the wheel now.

After building up a sweat establishing our little vegetable garden, I take the ute for a spin and drive to town, wanting a cold treat. Mick decides to stay home today and rest. He's tired from not getting a good night's sleep. Queen shuffles loudly from the stereo, accompanying me to the one and only ice cream shop in town. It's a hot day today in the territory, despite it being an Australian July. A nice ice cream ought to do the trick. Glancing at the small bill Mick lent me, I remember I really need to get a job, and soon. Mick keeps lending me cash, and I insist on paying every cent back; I just need to get a job first. Not really knowing anyone here is a little daunting and I'm not the best at going out of my way to make friends or network much. I'm under the assumption that they also prefer to employ locals before a washed up foreigner. At least I have a small wedding coming up, so I'll have a little cashflow soon. One of Mick's old Army buddy's granddaughter is getting married and asked if I would shoot the small, intimate ceremony. I'm sure it's because Mick asked him for a favor, but Mick assures me my talent speaks for itself.

Pushing work thoughts aside, I glide the ute into a parking slot in front of the marina, pull the hand brake, leave the keys and jump out. My leg is feeling much better these days. Mick wants me to return to full strength so he still holds me accountable and has me doing my therapy regime nightly before bed, on top of my professional therapy. I only have a few of those appointments left, but the old Doc is right, my supplemental effort is helping tremendously.

A sign reading "Shaved Ice" catches my attention. I walk towards the tiny shack, buzzing with locals. It must be dessert hour or something, I muse, sensing a few more people arriving behind me. I try to read the list of flavors while reserving a spot in line. Moving forward as people order, I turn to look up, realizing it's my turn next. I motion to advance in front of the window, but haltingly freeze mid step trying to read the last written flavor on the menu behind me. Oh, it's grape. *My favorite.*

A body collides with mine. I turn around. It's Brodie.

*Wonderful.*

"Oh, it's you," I remark, in a mixture of relief and annoyance.

He doesn't seem too thrilled to see me either. He politely tips his hat off to me, greeting me with the classic, "Day for it."

I offer a half smile back, with the other half bubbling in edginess right below the surface.

*Focus on your shaved ice, Nina. It's a new day.*

I'm about to turn back to the window when I see a leggy blonde walk up out of nowhere, wearing a tank dress over a string bikini. The woman saunters over to Brodie clearly "sussing" me out. She rakes over my denim shorts, my white tank top, and my sweaty, frizzy hairline. She must deem me a non-threat because she smiles demurely at me. I don't know if her motive is to illustrate her prowess, but she stands directly next to me, highlighting our height difference. She towers over me by at least a crushing seven, maybe eight inches and probably weighs a total of one hundred pounds wet.

*She could use a steak dinner.*

She leans back into Brodie. Dang, this girl is tall. Brodie's a taller guy at around 6'2" or 6'3" and she's up there, just below his eye-line.

"Brodie, ya know each otha?" she addresses him, before looking to me, waiting to be introduced.

Brodie pinches his fingers between his eyes as he sighs politely, "This is Nina… the girl I told you about in the ravine."

Cool. *The girl in the ravine.* That's a new one. Better than girl who tried to spear me. Mentally, I push that nightmare of a day behind a locked door in my mind's eye.

"Hey there, I'm Nina. Nice to meet you," I smile at her awkwardly, and give her a wave as I refocus on the line, and notice the people in front of me grab their wallets.

"Woah, yar an American," Leggy Blonde lights up, casting accusatory eyes at Brodie. "Brodie neva mentioned that."

*Okay, then.*

I give a half-assed, polite smile and turn back to the open window. I notice the shaved ice employee is that interested boy from the pub. He must be in his late teens. He's got a nerdish vibe about him, but that's softened by his nice blonde wavy hair. His name tag reminds me of his name, "Andy."

Andy gives me the eye. He can't be more than eighteen, I assess, so it's more uncomfortable than flattering. I don't know if it's my history of my arrival here or the fact that I'm an American or just an excuse to gossip, but some townsfolk act fascinated around me. I find it quite disorienting and rather nerve wracking, so I try to act normally.

"I'll take a piña colada and grape shaved ice please," I order.

"That must be a Yank flavour thing, eh?" Andy questions, looking oddly at me. "Trifle bit weird combo."

"Nope, it's a Nina thing, I guess. My American friends think it's kind of weird too," I shrug, and raise my shoulders a little in apology. *Sorry, not sorry. I like what I like.* Remembering my favorite part, I speak up in haste. "Oh, and can you add a scoop of vanilla ice cream at the bottom, please?" Leggy Blonde laughs behind me, so I tell them, "Now *that's* an American thing, from Hawai'i actually."

I hear the word "loud" amongst the snickering line behind me and roll my eyes before noticing Andy. He looks me up and down, like he just won a prize. I let out a small, nervous laugh, and awkwardly smile.

"Ya have a bloody rippa accent, Nina," he swoons.

"No, you have it backwards, Andy, you're the one with the cool accent," I say, trying to reverse the attention. Without remorse, he zones out on my torso, so I pull out my cash, trying to break up his stare. "What's the total if you don't mind?" He snaps back into focus. Leggy Blonde seems totally enraptured by this cringe worthy encounter and stifles a snort, while Brodie sighs. I hand Andy my Australian dollars as he hands me my cup of shaved ice. "Thanks, and keep the change."

I walk over to a bench a couple feet away and sit down.

Brodie approaches the window, ready to order. Andy's gaze follows me, the tip still clutched in his upheld hand. Brodie snaps his fingers, breaking the boy's trance.

"Oy, mate, can I orda or what?" he impatiently snaps.

"Nah, yeah, sorry," Andy concedes.

My snow cone starts to melt almost instantly. Dang, I've barely been able to enjoy it in its original state. The heat is melting this thing faster than a snowman straddling a volcano. Once it begins the melting process, I jam the rest of the ice down into the juicy and creamy concoction, creating a purple ice cream slushy.

Leggy Blonde comes over and sits down next to me. I notice her hands are empty.

"You didn't get anything...?" I say, in between spoonfuls, realizing I don't know her name.

I tilt my head in her direction, searching for her name with questioning eyes. She laughs, and playfully informs me that she never gets dessert.

"It interferes with my digestion," she explains seriously. "'N by the way, I'm Margot."

"Nice to officially meet you, and that's too bad about desserts. But more power to ya," I state in a combination of jealousy and pity.

"Well aren't ya cute. Andy's right, it's the accent."

I smile and badly wish this girl would leave me and my tasty treat alone in peace. I'm approaching the end and I'd like to savor it, not be distracted. I should have ordered the bigger size.

Brodie brings over his vanilla ice cream cone and stands, waiting for Margot so they can leave. Margot, however, ignores him and stays put.

"Funny how Brodie neva mentioned ya being a wanka," she brings it up again. "No offense, he barely mentioned ya altogetha."

I realize Brodie must not have shared our failed boating excursion with her. Maybe he wants to forget it ever happened, like I do.

I nod in reaction to her remark, and fake smile.

"Well the last time he saw me was when I was *in the ravine,*" I reply with masked testiness. I offer up a look that says *thanks for that moniker.* "It's not like I was in a very talkative state."

I slurp up the last spoonful of ice cream juice before swallowing the last of it away.

"Rippa, now that that's all settled," Brodie turns from Margot to me, purses his lips. "Nina, as eva, this has been most... fun."

He gently pulls Margot by the shoulder, softly dragging her towards the car park.

"See ya around, Nina from America," she hollers in a slightly condescending tone, and turns, chuckling as she bounces against Brodie's side in jest.

He walks off without so much as a glance back in my direction.

# 7

Sitting on the couch in front of the open screened window, I listen to Patsy Cline croon from the record player. I hear a crashing *bang!* outside. I drop my phone on the couch, and curiously look out the window. A six foot kangaroo stands over a fallen rake in my garden, out a few feet from the deck. Built like a bodybuilder, the Australian icon's muscles pulsate from exertion. His look of superior strength downright terrifies me.

I glance over at my veggies and see them scattered in every which way under his giant feet as they lie limp around the raised bed. After weeks of nurturing them from seedlings to heftier sprouts on the kitchen windowsill, I find myself seeing red.

"Hey, shoo!" I yell, running out to the deck, throwing most of my self-preservation out the window to defend my veggie babies.

Clearly I don't sound that threatening because it has little to no effect. Instead the animal grabs a handful of my lettuce leaves and chomps down, as if it's deliberately throwing shade at me. Pieces of my beautiful, fluffy green little loves are being bit and shredded between its giant square teeth. Saliva pools and drips down the side of its mouth. *That's it.*

I run back inside and grab a pot and ladle from the kitchen cabinet. *This'll do.* I bang the two together, creating cantankerous, obnoxious sounds and run out in the direction of the garden. The kangaroo looks more annoyed than anything else, but something must warn it that I mean business because it hops off, leaving giant divots and gauges in the pathetic looking rows of my trampled garden. I bend over and assess the damage. It completely uprooted and squashed all of my weeks of hard work. I close my eyes in frustration and let out a scream in anger. It's a good thing Mick just left for town because I can fully embrace my livid mood without thought or care of upsetting him.

Already feeling better, I open Mick's shed, and grab the wheelbarrow. Pushing it to the raised bed, I set it by my veggie massacre, and pile in the sad, dying sprouts. Raking away the rows, the thought of tracking down the seeds again sounds like more work than I'm willing to give. As it is, I already bought the last seed packs in our little town. Living on the outskirts of a small town that sits on the outskirts of another town, the effort seems futile. If I happen to see some seeds, I'll give it another try, but at the moment I feel too disheartened.

After I dump my seedling carcasses behind a bush, I decide to clean Mick's shed, his "Shed of Wonder" as I sometimes like to call it. When I feel frustrated, nothing soothes me more than tackling a side project. His house is super clean and organized, but his shed looks like an atomic bomb landed there one day and the site was never recovered.

Extending the broom towards the corner of the ceiling to wipe away a giant cobweb, something big, fuzzy and brown catches my peripheral. I jump away just in time as a hairy, long limbed spider, the size of my fist, spins down towards my head. Scared out of my mind, I jump another five feet back, flinging the broom across the shed. It lands in a giant, heaping pile of wrenches. Clattering, rumbling noises thunder off the tin walls in every direction. The bold and blaring sounds of metal on concrete reverb off the aluminum roof, but have nothing on my screams and wails as I screech in horror. I put my head down between my legs to lower my heart rate, all the while remaining acutely aware that a sixteen legged monster the size of a baseball chills in very close proximity. I exhale deeply and the pulsing in my ears slows.

Something brushes my arm and I jump three feet in the air like a rabid animal. I whirl around on my "attacker" hoping it's not the kangaroo wanting to come back for a tussle, and see a startled Brodie holding both arms up and eyes wide open in disbelief. He looks like a criminal who's been caught red handed, only his shoulders shake quickly up and down as he cracks up in amusement. He even lets out a snort as his big boisterous laughs bellow over the dying clangs of metal.

I lay my hand on my chest and take another deep breath, trying to reign in my shot of adrenaline.

"Don't shoot, just me," he claims, lightly wiggling his raised fingers before doubling over, laughing.

"I'm so sorry... you caught me in a..." I fumble for the right word, "compromising position."

"I reckon so, ya got dirt all ova ya," he remarks, amused, and gestures to my face.

I reach up and feel dried dirt patches on my cheek and chin, and mumble, "Damn kangaroo."

His eyebrows shoot up a little, all whilst keeping a wary expression, looking like he's dealing with a feral creature who might pounce at any second.

"I'm like a horse," I explain, my voice emerging into a bubbling guffaw. Even I can't hold back at the hilarious scene, and besides, laughing always eases my nerves. He looks at me like he has no idea what I've just said, his giggling ebbing away as he waits for further explanation. "I'm like a horse," I repeat. "I spook real easily, but if I know the threat is there ahead of time, I can handle it better."

He still eyes me cautiously, but I see a smile start to creep up on his face again and I find myself smiling too.

"So yar sayin' ya have to suss out every sitch then," he states. "That's a bit rough, eh?"

The smile falters on my lips.

"Well no," I reply defensively, "I'm not saying—."

"But ya just said ya basically need to be aware of everythin' beforehand. Isn't plannin' every minute of yar life exhaustin'?"

He's misinterpreting my meaning, he's pegging me all wrong which irks my tempered mood even more.

"No, I love spontaneity, in fact, I abhor plans," I counter. "I'm just saying when it comes to fear specifically, I'm better suited if I see it coming."

"Well life doesn't work that way," he quips in a slightly condescending tone, like he's eager for a debate. "In the real world, we have to deal with fear in all shapes 'n sizes whether we know what's comin' or not."

"Look, I'm not really in the mood to have a philosophical debate at the moment. Let's just agree to disagree on this one. The weirdest part is I think we actually believe the same thing." Scratching my head, I hastily add, "But let's not rehash it."

"No, let's not," he agrees matter-of-factly.

"Great," I echo back in sarcasm. We stand in charged silence for a minute. Finally, I concede. "You looking for Mick? Or are you just here to scare the crap out of me?"

Smirking, he holds up his elbow so I can see it more clearly. He has a red gash that oozes blood down his forearm.

"I busted my arm 'n was wonderin' if Old Mick would glue it back togetha," he explains.

"Geez, no, you just missed him."

"I reckon I could do it myself, but I can't reach, 'n the bloody thing won't stop bleedin'. Just tell him I'm lookin' for him when he gets back this arvo," he adds, disappointed as he walks away.

"Don't these people have phones?" I ask the universe, but find myself yelling after Brodie to wait. He reluctantly turns on his heels and faces me. I ask him against my better judgement, "Got that glue?"

He squints his eyes, clearly making up his mind. Sighing, he bridges the gap back to the shed and sits down on a little stool.

"Red toolbox on the top shelf," he advises me. Following his directions, I open the lid and peer down to find a few tubes of superglue amongst a general first aid kit. Looking to see if there's a specific tube of glue, Brodie informs me, "Any'll do."

I grab the bottle of rubbing alcohol and a couple of gauze pads, and one red tube of glue. Laying out my supplies on the workbench next to Brodie, I raise his arm up to get a better angle. Taking the gauze pad, I pour some alcohol on it and gently clean the wound, wiping away blood crustees around the site.

"So I take it Mick's cleaned you up before?" I note.

"More than a few I reckon," he shares in a laugh.

I untwist the superglue cap, careful to not get it anywhere else.

"I've never done this so bear with me," I confess to my patient.

Pinching his skin together along the gash, I debate my method of application. Do you just literally glue along the open cut? How much pressure do you apply to the tube?

"Don't ovathink it," he suggests impatiently. "Just do what feels right."

As soon as I have the cut pinched together, my finger slips.

"Damnit," I exclaim, sighing. Brodie stands up, but I push him back down, and state with a hint of sass, trying to make light of my incompetence, "Unless you want to cover yourself completely in blood, you're stuck with me. Plus, Mick won't be back until tonight."

Begrudgingly, he sits back, and following his advice, I grab the skin together and instinctively glue the two sides of flesh as one. I take the second gauze pad and carefully clean the blood trail off his arm. I lean down to blow on the glue, hoping it will dry a little faster, when Brodie looks at me with his big green eyes. He stares at me for a long second, before abruptly shrugging me out of the way, standing up.

*Okay, then... sorry I was just trying to help.*

He mutters a small thanks and bounds back to his ute.

The next couple of weeks pass by without any major hiccups, well there is one that I'd like to forget, but I can't quit reliving it in my head. So Mick and I attend the wedding of his friend as guest and photographer respectively. Everything goes well. Another happy day in the books, and best part is I get paid. After several attempts of thrusting money into Mick's hands, he denies me every time, vehemently insisting I put it towards a fun experience.

"Ya already help me out heaps 'round the house, Sweetheart," he reveals after my latest attempt. "Truthfully, if I needed or wanted it, I'd tell ya. Go do somethin' fun with it."

Following the whole Brodie boat and spider debacles, I've decided to work on facing my fears. *It's not like you owe him anything, Nina.* I don't need to prove him wrong, but what he said really irked me to the core. I decide to play tourist for the day and set up a jet-ski tour of a blowhole. Internet cafe Lotte hooks me up with the local price since her cousin runs it. I've always wanted to rent a jet-ski so it should be really fun.

On the phone, the man tells me to meet him at the first dock, so here I am waiting at the area reserved for smaller sea craft. I huddle in front of a pair of SeaDoos that I assume we'll board. Admiring the view of all the docked boats, I realize I've yet to be actually down on the marina until now. It's a lot bigger than it looks from the road. I suppose it makes sense since the community's largest attraction is the harbor, with almost everyone owning a boat either for work or pleasure or both. Footsteps grow louder and the dock bobs up and down below my feet as someone approaches. I whirl around to encounter a shorter man in his late fifties with shoulder length hair brushed back into a low pony, accenting his receding hairline. He wears neon green trunks so low on his hips it reveals almost *all* of his copper toned, leather skin.

"Nina," he croons, reaching out and grabbing my hand against my will. "Big Al here. Ready to ski?"

"Big Al, nice to meet you. Thanks so much for squeezing me in. I'm super excited," I say cheerfully, gesturing towards the SeaDoos.

He jumps on the nearest one, skillfully balancing as the ski rocks back and forth from the disturbance of weight. He reaches out a hand to help me aboard and I can see my perfect reflection in his bright, rainbow reflective lenses. I stifle a giggle. He helps me onto his SeaDoo where he pats the seat for me to sit down. He shows me the ropes and basic commands from over my shoulder. Just as we're about to start the engine, a woman clambers right up to the side of Big Al's jet-ski. She wears the most sour expression on her middle-aged face.

"Oy, I've been tryin' to reach ya, ya bloody dipstick," she half screams over me to Big Al.

"Midge, I got a payin' customer, eh," he snickers out of the corner of his mouth, nervously laughing to hide his embarrassment, but this does little to assuage her anger.

Things escalate. Literally stuck in the middle of a boiling disagreement, I carefully stand up to not rock the "boat." *Good one, Nina*. Reaching for anything to free me from this argument, I hastily grab a PVC pipe sticking out from the dock, and jump across the gap. I land with such forward momentum that I almost launch off the other side of the dock into the water. I let out a holler as I come to a crashing halt merely inches away. A few fisherman watch me curiously. Looking back, Big Al's deep in it with Midge and it doesn't appear to be ending any time soon. Good thing I didn't pay him until it was over. Still, I'm bummed. I was really looking forward to getting on the water... hmm, there's got to be something else. I return to the dock's entrance where a few advertisements litter the notice board. I scan the posted sheets searching for something fitting my interests.

"Sorry about that, Nina," I hear a ragged breath come from behind me, and I turn to find Big Al, looking abashed as he carries his gear over his shoulder.

"Don't worry about it. I hope everything... works out for you guys."

"Sorry to bail fat, but I just rang a mate 'n he said he can take ya out, easy. He's perfect for ya, super friendly, easy on beginners, real cracker of a bloke. Everyone loves the guy. Dock three."

"Okay, great! I appreciate that."

"Slip twenty-three, eh, 'n again, sorry."

He points in the general direction of the slip and heads off towards the parked cars, his plumber's crack widening with each hurried step. I look away quickly to dispel the visual.

Okay, so change of plans, no biggie. I take it as a sign that this will mean something better awaits me.

"Slip twenty-three," I repeat aloud, making my way down the third dock, paying attention to the slip numbers as I go. If I can't jet-ski, I really hope I can go snorkeling, the other activity that looks fun and will hopefully test my theory. My theory is if I do enough things outside of my comfort zone, then I'll hopefully desensitize myself to the majestic creatures of the deep and therefore grow as a person. Entering the twenties, I repeat, "Twenty-three."

I see slip twenty-one and two spaces over is twenty-five. Looking in between the two, a bunch of buoys hide the number of the slip in front of me, but this has to be it. A beautiful, white fishing boat about twenty-five feet long floats soundly in front of me. Feelings of excitement mingled with trepidation swirl in my tummy. I walk up to the side of the bow. A burst of color pops against the white as an aqua towel hangs over the side rail. Oddly, this feels familiar. I don't see a name on the vessel and Big Al didn't give me one either.

"Hello?" I cry out, searching for the captain.

"Out in two shakes," a male voice cries out, from a small compartment towards the cockpit.

I see the boat rock slightly, and hear feet landing on the deck. A hand grabs a railing as the guy jumps over the side, landing in front of me. We both gasp as I realize it's Brodie and he realizes it's me.

"So you're the captain who comes so highly recommended?" I mutter, laughing in disbelief.

"'N yar the sweet girl who wants to snorkel 'n go swimmin' with sharks?" he counters, just as shocked.

"Not with you."

"Well, I reckon the kiddie pool at the local aquarium should do nicely for ya, eh."

Seriously offended, I scoff aloud and fold my arms across my chest. Turning on my heels, I walk back towards the marina's parking lot. Brodie breaks into a run behind me and catches up in seconds. He passes me, then spins around in front of me, forcing me to stop.

"Look, let's start ova, eh?" he says in surrender, looking down at his hands. "Today we don't know each otha. I'm just a charta captain, 'n yar my hire. Deal?"

He holds out his hand as a peace offering. Staring at his outstretched arm, I smirk, questioning his dubious intentions. I decide to concede and bury the hatchet. Mick seems to think highly of him, so if Brodie can make an effort, so can I.

"Deal," I agree, accepting his hand in mine.

When I go to let go, he holds onto it in his warm grasp, and adds boisterously, "G'day, miss. The name's Brodie. I'm the captain here."

He shakes my hand up and down in mock introduction.

"Hi Brodie, I'm Nina," I answer, playing along as my shoulders relax. "I'm really excited to get out there."

"Bet ya are," Brodie snorts sarcastically.

"Really?" I sassily quip, scoffing, and begin to walk away when Andy, the boy from the shaved-ice shack, waves at me from the slip across in his own nice looking boat.

"Day for it," he hollers, motioning me over. "Ya lookin' to charter or?"

Well if Brodie wants to play that game, then two can play.

"Nah, mate," Brodie yells, at the same time I happily cheer, "Yes!"

I glance back and see Brodie staring at us. He puts both hands up in mock surrender. I turn back and Andy walks over to the rail and offers me a hand in.

"How much?" I ask.

I should have clarified this before agreeing to come aboard, but it's too late now. Hopefully it'll be within my budget.

"For ya, Miss Nina, first one's free," he exclaims, winking.

"Oh, that's really kind of you," I reply, taken aback at the generous offer. "Are you sure? I'm happy to pay."

He nods his head enthusiastically and starts the boat.

A very tiny part in the pit of my stomach feels bad for abandoning Brodie, but one glance back and he's already on his boat with Two Door Cinema Club playing. Apparently I didn't wound him too badly or even bruise him. Facing back forward, I admire my new surroundings. This boat is different than Brodie's. For one, it feels a lot smaller. While *Salty Stel* has ample deck space and a big roof shade overhead, Andy's boat has little deck space. Most of the hangout space is inside, I note with slight disappointment. Personally, I believe that if you have a boat, you'd want to spend all your time up on deck watching for wildlife and being right in on the action. Plus, being inside a cabin without windows can be downright nauseating.

Andy opens the cabin door and proudly gives me the tour. He shares a couple of his favorite stories that mostly involve his own big catches or the "famous" people he's had aboard. Finally, he pulls the boat out and away we go. We travel up shore a few miles and end up snorkeling around the shallow reef for a while. I'm right in my element, but that defeats the whole purpose. It seems a bit tame for what I originally had in mind, but I chalk it up to a beautiful day, and luckily, it's free.

As I snorkel around the surface and approach a cluster of giant coral reefs, an eel slithers out about ten feet in front of me. For a moment I panic, but it swims in the opposite direction, clearly disinterested. I kick forward while keeping an eye on it until it's completely out of sight.

We climb out of the water up into the boat and I dry off next to Andy. After, he walks up to me and sits beside me on the bench seat, a little too close for my own personal comfort level.

"Nina," he says, "I think yar crackin'. Wanna mess around for a bit?"

He lightly puts one hand on my leg and I still.

Gently nudging his hand off, but utterly shocked at his forthright proposal, I come up with the quickest answer I can think of, which is, "Andy, I'm sorry, but there's someone else."

His posture drops immediately. He looks at me with a quizzical brow, wanting an explanation.

Stumbling to find the words to my made-up story, I ramble a little, trying to let him down easy as I lie, "He's waiting for me when I get back."

"Well he's not here now. We can just root around a little. I won't tell anyone."

He's really close to me now. His slight underbite seems considerable from this closer angle. I also notice acne litters his greasy face. While I appreciate his confidence, he's just a boy!

"You're really sweet, Andy, but..." I say, "...it's really new and I can't take the risk."

Wow, this is hard. I've never had to turn down advances before, let alone blatantly lie to someone's face. Finally taking the hint, he smiles brightly and hops up from the seat, and takes the wheel. We head back towards the marina. When we arrive, he helps me out onto the dock. I give him a little nudge on the arm, thanking him again for the fun afternoon. His face lights up as I do and I walk back towards the harbor entrance. I glance back at slip twenty-three to find it empty.

# 8

Mick has made it his personal mission to have me master the stick shift. He'll use any excuse to get us in the ute to have a lesson or "pop quiz." Mick is by far better at this than my parents ever were. Maybe because I'm not actually related to him or maybe because he's the most patient man on the planet, these lessons are going really well. In the beginning, it was easy to pop the clutch, but now I find myself enjoying the feeling of the transmission sliding in and out of gear. Back home, I used to love driving, but ever since my accident I've found it nerve-racking and more of a chore. Lately, the vehicle feels more a part of me, and I never realized how much I could love driving again until now. I've taken back the power and actually find it really freeing and fun. Days spent driving are some of my favorite ones. I don't even hesitate hopping into the driver's seat anymore when Mick's around. He expresses so much faith in my ability, he even graciously allows me to take the Trooper for rides on the sand, along the beach, or to run into town.

Only having sixty pages left of his current page-turner, Mick stays back at the house while I pick up dinner tonight at the pub.

I haven't told a soul here in Australia, but today is my thirtieth birthday. Staying at Mick's all day, I haven't been able to FaceTime my family, much to their dismay. I'm sure the next time I'm on WiFi, the messages and texts will pour in, but for now I'm enjoying the low key nature of such a life marker. *I am thirty years old.* I don't really feel that different. I'm sure Mick would love to celebrate, but I'm reveling in no one knowing here.

It's a beautiful evening. On the way back from town, I meander a bit. There's only one highway out here, and thankfully it mirrors the rugged coastline. Right before the turn off to Mick's, I find myself on a dirt road that leads to the beach. I recently discovered this spot and have been coming here whenever I get the chance. I'd love to see the water before calling it a night on my birthday. I drive down towards the shore, almost to the median tide line. Being born and raised in regulated Southern California, it's beyond liberating to have the freedom to pull straight up to the ocean, let alone drive on the beach. I could sleep here if I want or build a bonfire with friends, *if I had any.* This is easily one of my favorite aspects so far about this country.

I note the tide is out far tonight, revealing a sandy floor mixed with tide pools. I bet it would look really cool from the sky and the drone's POV. I park on the coarse, compact sand and get out, surveying the climate and conditions. I haven't droned since the accident and honestly am a tad nervous about flying since it's been so long. I glance at my backpack in the passenger seat of the Trooper. *Do it!* Reaching over, I pull it out and unfold my drone's arms and props, clip in the battery and attach the remote to my phone. Standing out on the sand, using my car seat as a table, I turn on the remote controller and the drone. Both roar to life with their usual beeping noises. While those warm up and connect to the closest satellites, I check the wind. Not even a ripple disrupts the ocean tonight, it's so glassy. Double checking my surroundings, I laugh out loud in eagerness and excitement.

I guess there's nothing around to worry about colliding into, other than the water. My whole life, I've always felt this sense of nervous anxiety before performing anything work related, like weddings or photoshoots, but droning has always felt like an extension of my arm, something I don't have to think about when operating. Right before take off, I perform one final scan of any obstacles out of habit. There are no trees to avoid, no houses, not even people to worry about. The western landscapes provide ideal droning conditions. I hit the lift off button and The Khal hovers in the air as I command it higher with the press of the control stick. The familiar buzzing sound zooms around overhead. *It's like riding a bike.* All my hesitations melt away. I don't even have to think about the mechanics of maneuverability. My fingers take over on instinct, operating on muscle memory.

Not even fifty feet into the air, and I'm already flabbergasted at the perspective. Reefs and crystal clear water envelope my screen, and it's almost dark. Imagine the colors and marine life daylight has to offer!? I am *so* coming back here in the morning. I snap some captures of the romantic scene: the fading light kisses the water farewell until dawn.

A motor screams in the distance and it growls louder, interrupting my zen moment. Where is it coming from? I glance around. Nothing behind the ute... I look out on the water but can't make anything out. I spin the camera around 360 degrees, but don't see anything. I'm about 385 feet high in the air so anything small at ground level is harder to track at this time of day. Erring on the side of caution and not wanting to piss off any locals on the off chance they show up, I bring the drone back down. It always takes longer to descend. Even in sport mode, I find myself wishing it could operate at a faster speed. Finally, it's right above me and I land it in my open palm without having to take a single step in any direction.

The battery display tells me I could have kept flying for another twenty minutes, but it's growing dark and it was just enough to get my feet wet again. I pack the drone and look back, admiring the amazing vista before me. The sun fades just now, yellows and oranges melting into one blur of color as the last light dips into night. Thin and wispy cirrus clouds line the horizon, disappearing like a long drawn out breath into the dark cobalt above. Tiny little stars begin to dance their way into view.

Wearing a baggy oversized flannel of Mick's, I step out and walk to the front of the ute and lean back on its hood. The quiet peace is unlike anything I've ever experienced. It's just me and the sea and everything else can just be.

Micro waves hit the shore, and the little lapping sounds suddenly get swallowed up by that impending motor noise. I forgot all about it, but there it is again. I shrug off this slight annoyance, assuming it will pass in a few seconds, but it only grows louder and louder until I realize it's headed right at me. Using the moonlight, I squint out into the darkness, hoping my eyes will adjust quickly. I think it's a SeaDoo. Who's the rider? It's almost dark and I'm out here on a remote beach, totally alone...

The SeaDoo pulls right up to shore and the engine dies. It's just one dark blob against the almost finished light. A smaller, blurry figure hastily jumps off and runs in my direction. I tense momentarily before making out the shape to be Stella, Brodie's dog. She bounds across the sand and jumps up, paws hitting my stomach, smothering me in sandy kisses. Laughing, I scratch her ears and praise her with affectionate crooning noises. If she's here, he must be here too. My mind's eye replays our last icy encounter on the docks like a poorly scripted telenovela.

It's dark enough that I don't even try to hide the fact that I look for his shadowy figure, which I see hop off the SeaDoo and run towards the beach. Bright headlights abruptly beam from his ute a few feet down the beach, obscured by a crevice. My eyes adapt to the harsh light against the darkness. Brodie slowly backs in a small trailer a couple of feet into the ocean before jumping out and making his way to the SeaDoo.

"How'd ya find out about this place?" he asks, then laughs to himself. "Mick's place, ya galah."

No "hi" or "hello." Honestly, I'm not sure how he knows it's even me. Maybe he can tell it's Mick's ute, and clearly I'm not Mick.

"Hi, there," I say politely, trying to get off to a better start than how our previous encounter ended. He merely nods at me, curtly smiling. Trying to tread lightly and keep it cordial, I ask, "Is this like your spot or something?"

"Yeah, actually, my property's just there," he notes, pointing behind us, "'n covers these few dozen acres, so yeah, I guess it is my spot."

Wow! A few dozen acres... on the beach. That's actually impressive.

While Brodie loads the SeaDoo onto the trailer, Stella sits still like a perfect statue at my side, glancing at me, eagerly waiting for me to scratch her ears.

"Fine then, Stella," I tell her, in a dog-friendly voice as I give her a pet, "looks like my happy place is already taken." I return her licks with some kisses. "But this place is the prettiest, isn't it? Like you are, Lella."

Brodie lingers by the door, not climbing in just yet. I catch sight of his taught muscles as he holds onto the frame of the truck, and quickly avert my eyes back to the sunset.

While temps have soared lately despite the calendar month, I guess tonight decided to finally feel like winter. Goosebumps break out on my arms. I shake off a running shiver and rub my forearms with my hands before promptly gathering myself tighter in Mick's flannel. Brodie jumps down and rummages around for something in his back seat. Stella looks rather curious, peering around my legs as he walks over to me. He outstretches his arm, offering me a familiar gray hoodie. It's the same one he was wearing in the hospital; it has a spearfishing brand's emblem on the front. He tosses it at me and it lands on my face. I slowly pull it off and my frizzy hair clings to my eyes.

"Sorry 'bout the other day on the dock," he says genuinely, as I look at the sweatshirt like it's a Trojan horse. He laughs. "It won't bite, eh. C'mon, just put it on, Nina."

"Thanks," I reply, accepting his olive branch by pulling it up and over my head. My stiff, cold body immediately relaxes as the warmth embraces me. It smells like Brodie: faint whiffs of manly sweat, ocean and salt. It even has little dried sand and salt crustees on the ribbed cuffs. Oddly, it's comforting. I melt in mirth. "Ahh."

I can't tell in the dark, but I think Brodie's smiling at me.

"Ya stayin' out here much longa?" he asks curiously.

"I can't seem to tear myself away from it. It's just so beautiful."

"I reckon I know what ya mean. I could stare at her for hours, n' when I'm not starin', I'm in her fishin', swimmin, somethin' of the like."

I look up at the starry sky, and for a moment I'm so lost in its vastness that I don't even realize I've said aloud, "Ah, man, Javi would love this place so much... they all would."

"Who?"

Embarrassed by my external internal monologue, I quickly mutter, full of yearning and longing I can't contain, "Sorry, just my nephew and my sisters... they would be freaking out, well, really my whole family would be."

"Sounds like ya miss 'em terribly," he says, with a hint of compassion I haven't heard from him before.

We stand there staring out into the night for a couple more minutes before Brodie opens his car door, and motions with the snap of a neck and a click of the tongue for Stella to hop in.

"Wait!" I yell after him, before he climbs in. He stops and stares at me. My eyes are fully adjusted now, so I can see his face clearly. "I just wanted to say I'm sorry too, for in general I mean, especially about the whole speargun... *incident.*"

"Ya mean where ya almost killed me?" he clarifies boldly, with a hint of jest.

I look at my hands, feeling terrible. Frowning, I reach down and caress Stella's head some more, avoiding him. Brodie sighs again, and stands a little straighter, looking at me.

"Look, it wasn't totally all yar fault... Ya were right," he says calmly, and softly, "I shouldna left it rigged... 'n as far as the other day goes, like I said, sorry."

He must truly mean it because I see his mouth brighten into a brilliant, flashing smile from across the ute. It blows me away. Biting my lip, I look at Stella, then finally up at him and give him a genuine smile in return. Brodie grabs the frame of the door and motions again for Stella to jump in, but she holds her ground by my side.

"Stella, come, girl," he warns her lightly as I laugh at her rebellious outburst. I've seen Brodie with Stella. It's amazing. They're almost two halves of one spirit. She must really be digging this head scratch. Waiting for her, I see Brodie's shoulders drop. He looks back at me and grins. "'N Stella would like ya to know yar free to come here wheneva ya'd like."

As if she speaks human, Stella understands this exchange and runs off into the ute's seat before settling herself into the passenger side, clearly pleased with her skills of persuasion. Brodie pauses, poised up on his running board, and stares at the water. I follow his gaze and smile out at the horizon, letting the little breeze kiss my neck. *This is a wonderful life.*

"You know, I think this is the best birthday I've ever had," I whisper.

He breaks from his reverie and turns to me in complete surprise.

"Today's yar birthday?" he asks, flabbergasted. "Whaddaya doin' here?"

"No one here knows, well I suppose you do now," I shrug, and explain, "but today I turned thirty... thirty years *young."* I sigh with a chuckle. Most people throw giant vacation parties or ragers for their thirtieths, but I chose to spend it with an eighty-six-year-old doing crossword puzzles and listening to Jim Croce. And you know what? I actually wouldn't have it any other way at the moment, because right now, I'm standing across the world in this gorgeous place and for once am at peace with getting older. *You're growing older, but never growing up, Nina.* Feeling deeply full of gratitude, I say more to myself, "Maybe it was my near brush with death, but hell I'm just happy to be here."

He furrows his brow, thinking about something.

"Hold on a tick," he mumbles, and darts off to the trunk or "boot" of his ute, rooting around for something. He returns holding a bottle of clear booze. He untwists the cap and cheerfully hands it to me. "I reckon that deserves a skull." Smiling in thanks, I take the bottle and tilt it back, taking one big gulp of gin. I wince as it slides down my throat, and Brodie chuckles. I quickly hand the bottle back to him and he does the same. After he swallows, he declares, "Happy Birthday, Nina."

Never in my wildest dreams did I imagine sharing a birthday toast with Brodie Pryce of all people, but if I'm being honest, I'm glad he's here. He actually made it feel real for the first time today. We sit quietly, neither one of us wanting to be the one to bring an end to such a peaceful moment, but suddenly my stomach rumbles.

"Shoot, dinner!" I remember, jumping up as Brodie laughs. I gasp, "I completely forgot about dinner. Mick!"

"Poor Old Boy, 'n to think he's been waitin' on ya this whole time," Brodie adds, rubbing it in. I scramble, trying to take off the hoodie hastily. "Yeah, nah, keep it," Brodie interjects, "ya can give it back to me lata."

"Thanks a million!" I call over my shoulder, rushing inside the ute.

"Dun worry," he hollers back, "and many happy returns!"

"¡Adiós, Stel, hasta luego!" I call out through the window, starting up the engine.

She cocks her head and barks farewell.

I throw the truck into first gear and away I go home to Mick's. Hopefully, our dinner's not too soggy. Fingers crossed. Glancing back in the rear view mirror, my thoughts linger on those headlights sparking up in the distance.

Mick and I head into town. He's meeting a friend, Gus, at the pub for breakfast, "brekky," and I'm going to the internet cafe to FaceTime with Selena. Mick's quick to invite me for breakfast but I think they'd have more fun without a girl third wheeling. We agree that I'll arrive at the start to meet Gus and then be on my way. I don't tell him this, but I can't miss this FaceTime meeting as my family is adamant about wanting to wish me a belated happy birthday. After Mick introduces us and the boys get settled in their booth, I bid them a fun brekky and make my way for Lotte's. Syncing up with Selena is a small miracle these days. She's the one person who can't jump online as much since she's trying to keep a toddler alive, which I totally understand, but it makes it harder for us to find the time to connect. However, lately she's up all night while Javi teethes, so she might as well make the most of it. I couldn't be happier. I miss my sister so much.

Almost to the cafe, I see Brodie walking in my direction. *Boy does he look great in blue.* While my first instinct is to run and hide, I remember the other night and how we seemed to have turned a corner towards civility. I glance at the time on my phone. I'm set to call Selena in ten minutes so I can't really get distracted. Looking to see if I can duck and cover somewhere, he spots me. *Too late now.* I stand up a little straighter and attempt to walk nonchalantly. Thinking we're just going to pass each other, I politely grin at him, not wanting to be totally rude and ignore him, but instead, he slows and confronts me.

"Brodie," I mutter pleasantly.

"Nina," he counters, smiling.

We stand in silence for a beat. I rub my hands lightly together, waiting for a reason why he's stopped me if none other than to say hello. The silence lingers.

"Sorry, but I'm late…" I explain apologetically, tilting my head. My curls spring to one side. "Do you need something or…?"

"Look," he says, "I saw ya 'n reckoned maybe we could—."

Suddenly, I see Andy coming across the street, waving at me obnoxiously, trying to get my attention. I *really* don't have time to deal with him either. Plus, if he keeps up with such persistence he's going to catch wind of my lie. Startling Brodie and myself, I grab his arm and pull it around me. He tries to shake it off in protest and confusion.

"Please, just go with it, I beg you," I plead quickly and quietly, as Andy walks right up to us. I plaster a fake, loving smile on my face, gazing overzealously at Brodie. I say lovingly, hoping he plays along, "Oh, Brodie, stop."

"G'day, Nina," Andy shouts excitedly.

"Andy!" I cry out.

Anyone who actually knows me would die laughing at my horrible attempt at subtlety.

Andy then looks at Brodie and nods more hesitantly, "Day for it, mate."

"Day for it. Doesn't my Nina look heatha today?" Brodie says, overly enthusiastically, turning in my direction.

He pulls me in for a second and buries his lips in my hair. *He smells good.* My eyes widen in surprise and a nervous laugh escapes me as I feel Brodie's nose rooting around my neck. Andy seems just as taken aback as I am, and his eyes pop open wide.

"Wait, Pryce is the bloke ya told me about?" he clarifies.

"Uhh, yeah, that's him," I mutter, nodding in exaggeration.

Andy scratches his head, while Brodie looks at me and playfully chomps his jaw at my face. I jump back, startled from the close proximity, but laugh loudly to cover it up.

"Yep, I'm the lucky fella," Brodie quips. "Can't quite believe it myself just yet, eh."

I nudge him in the side, widening my plastered smile.

Andy nods, looking a bit discouraged, which is good, that means this horrible charade is working.

"How long ya two been togetha?" he asks.

"Remember, I told you it's new. Like really new," I reiterate at the same time as Brodie mutters, "A while."

Andy looks confused.

"Feels like a blink of an eye with this one," I blurt out, squeezing Brodie's side.

Brodie pulls at my hair behind my back, and I twist to free it from his grasp. I bend into his side and apparently make some crude position because suddenly Andy gawks, and scrambles off.

"Lata, Nina," he yells over his shoulder.

The second he's around the corner, I step away from Brodie, who bends over, slapping his knee in laughter.

"What the hell was that all about?" he asks, between wheezes.

"It's a long story, well not that long actually. He wanted to *ya know*," I say suggestively, "and I felt bad for rejecting him, so I invented a mystery man and then you just happened to be in the wrong place at the right time."

I go to pieces laughing as I relive some of those moments in a sequence of replays in my head.

"Nina, ya owe me huge," he jokes, "no ya owe me for life."

"Can we just pretend it never happened?" I plead, chuckling.

"One day, I'm gonna call in a fava," he says, biting his lip and raising his brows.

"Thanks will have to suffice."

"Should I call him back here?" he says, gesturing with his thumb back towards the direction in which Andy left. "Sounds like ya don't really appreciate my efforts. Let's tell Andy we broke up already... or maybe tell him it's a lie."

My eyes almost pop out of my head, as I yell, "No!"

"Andy!" he hollers loudly, as I take a step towards him. Shushing him, I reach for his mouth, but he quiets, shaking in amusement. Pulling back, I stand there with my arms folded. Brodie looks at me, his face softening only a small fragment. "Look, what I was tryin' to say before that whole Andy... debacle, is maybe we can be friends?"

Just when I'm about to answer, Margot runs down the sidewalk towards us, well to Brodie, jumping on his side.

"Hey, lover," she snarls into his ear, not even giving me a glance.

Clearly the outsider in the dynamic, I look at my phone and realize I only have one minute until I need to be phoning Selena. Brodie looks like he wants to say something, but I don't have time to give him the chance.

"Sorry, gotta run," I say, holding up my phone and hightailing it out of there to Lotte's, not even glancing back at Brodie and his stage five cling-on.

Wearing headphones, Lotte bobs her head when she sees me entering the cafe. She smiles and waves. I point to the chair in the corner by the window and she gives me a thumbs up in approval. Pulling out my phone, I nestle in the cozy chair. Panting from my mini run, I bring up my Favorites list and scroll down a couple of names, looking for "Marci." It's our inside joke. Selena's real name is Marcelina, after my great grandma who came from México. Growing up in a less diverse part of SoCal, Marcelina chose to adopt Selena when many of her elementary classmates couldn't pronounce her true name. But I love it, and therefore it's my pet name for her. She picks up after two dial tones.

"¡Feliz cumple!" she beams with excitement.

Breathing heavily, I match her enthusiasm with a "¡Herrro, mi hermana!"

We both reach for each other's screens, arms outstretched towards the cameras, giving each other virtual hugs.

"I miss you, Marci," I blubber, as my breathing evens out.

Tears begin to form. When it comes to my family, I always go straight to pieces and to tears.

"Not as much as I miss you, Neens," she counters, then her forehead creases. "Wait, why are you panting?"

"I'll explain later. ¿Primero, dondé está mi sobrino? Is he awake? I miss him so much, Marci, it hurts."

She looks around and Ray, who's looks like a zombie, walks in carrying Javi, who's super alert and active, squirming all over.

"Javi, can you wave to your Auntie Nina?" Selena instructs him, picking up his arm and waving it up and down towards the screen.

Javi's full head of hair has lightened so much and grown about five inches, and his eyelashes are crazy long and dark. He has two little ringlets for sideburns and he's so chunky and solid for a baby. Sadly, I realize that he's officially not a baby anymore, but a toddler. I reach for the screen "touching" his sweet face.

"Baby, I miss you!" I say wistfully. "How's my baby boy? Gosh, you're getting so big. Auntie Neens loves you so much, little man, remember how much I love you."

Javi attempts to grab the phone and drops it with a thunk. The camera points up at a ceiling fan before Selena recovers it. Javi yawns, and Ray looks at Selena and she nods back. Ray brings Javi closer to the camera for a goodbye "kiss."

"Besos," I coo at his face. "Muchos besos por mi Javier."

It's our little thing, the "besos" bit, or it used to be. He shyly twists the other way and buries his face into Ray's shirt.

"It's his new thing he's been doing, even with Mom," Selena explains.

I laugh at him, trying to hide the despair growing like a weed in the pit of my heart. One of my deepest fears has come to pass: *we're losing our connection*.

"Besos from Auntie Nina," she mutters, smiling at him and steals a little kiss on his cheek. "Say night, night, Tia. Buenos noches."

"Te quiero mi amor. I love you!" I say affectionately, but also with some urgency. Ray smiles at me as he exits the frame with Javi. I express in alarm, "Selena, what if he forgets all about me? I'm missing so much. I'm basically missing his little life."

"We'll all still be here when you get back," she reassures me, "and the best part is he won't even remember you being away. In the meantime let's change the subject. How was your birthday? What'd you do? Have you made any friends or met anyone since we last talked?"

I shrug. There's not lots to tell. When you're not with someone on the day-to-day, life creates a divide. During the in-between time when you're out on your own, you feel like so much happens all the time. Yet, when you go to recap that period to someone else on the outside, it always falls mega flat. With us sisters it's different because there's no option of falling out. Wherever we are in the world, literally, we'll always have each other when we come back.

I tell her how I kept my birthday low-key, in which she rolls her eyes and shakes her head with an expectant smile.

"Neens, you can't shut yourself out from the world," she says. "Use this opportunity to be whoever you want to be. Do whatever you want to do. In a way, I'm a tad jealous."

"What? Why would you be jealous? Everyone loves you. You live the dream. You've got a dream husband, an angel baby—."

"No, I mean, it must be so liberating to be surrounded by new people who don't know you, don't know your fears or your awkward teenage horror stories, who don't have one single expectation from you. And you don't have Mom nagging you every hour to do something or find a husband. You really have ultimate freedom. Enjoy it while it's yours for the taking."

Selena has always been the brightest of us three, more wise than I could ever hope to be, so what she says, I always take to heart.

"I'm not a total lost cause yet," I offer lamely. "I've met some people."

"Oh, yeah, and who are these 'people'?" she asks, throwing up air quotation marks with raised eyebrows.

I tell her about Andy, but even she laughs, saying that doesn't really count. Smirking at her dubiety, I tell her all about Brodie and Leggy Blonde Margot, going all the way back to Big Al, the failed jet ski tour guide. She laughs at most of it.

"Sounds like this Brodie guy really gets under your skin," she says somewhat suspiciously, playfully smiling.

"Well, I did almost impale him with a spear," I add, knowing where her tone is headed. "And no, it's not like that, Marci. He has a girlfriend I'm pretty sure, 'Leggy Blonde.' Besides, it could never work out between us. We pretty much despise each other."

I recount our most recent encounter in my head and reconsider while Selena looks like she's going to say something, but holds her tongue.

"Okay, whatever you say, Neens," she says, backing off.

We chat for another half hour and she fills me in on some funny stories regarding the family. There's one story about Ria and her waxing lady that has me almost peeing my pants. Due to the statewide Covid shutdown of all salons, her waxing lady sent out a graphic "How to Bikini Wax Yourself" instructional video to her clients. Selena's detailed description of the lady naked on the floor has me doubled up on the floor in front of the chair, crying and wheezing from laughter. Selena also bursts into tears, laughing so hysterically, when suddenly Javi shrieks in the background. Our laughter quickly abates.

"Well, that's my cue," she says, wiping her eyes.

I hate when our chats have to end. They all get to go back to each other while I face the loneliness. At least I have Mick. Without him, I don't know what I'd do.

"Ok," I say, unable to mask the sadness in my voice.

"I love you so much, Neens. Tell Mick we say hi."

"I will. I love you lots and lots and lots. Thanks for making this happen. I really needed to just sit and talk to you and feel normal for a little while."

"I'm proud of you," she declares, blowing me a kiss.

I pretend to catch it like I did when we were kids.

"Chat soon. Love you," I say, trying to detach myself. "Okay, bye."

She reaches down and the screen goes black. I sit back in my chair letting all the emotions from the past hour settle. Just as the quiet creeps in, I see the video chat request notification pop up, indicating the rest of my family is awaiting me. Smiling, I accept it and the screen opens to rowdy roars and cheers.

About an hour later, and still reeling from a touch of homesickness mixed with laughter, I lethargically make my way towards the pub. Nowhere to be just yet, I shuffle my feet and take my time. I'd bet eighty-five-year-olds could do laps around me. The visual of the wax lady sending her lady bits to her clients starts my shoulders shaking all over again. After every time I call home, my feelings are always so volatile. One second I feel happy, jovial even, recalling their stories, and then the next moment I feel the tears forming thinking about Javi and all that I'm missing. I'm not quite ready to go sit in a pub and act like everything's coming up roses. I spot a little bench in front of the post office and sit down. After catching up with Mom and her worries about the ticking clock on my ovaries, I question everything all over again. *Where am I even going? What am I even doing with my life?*

Selena comes to mind and I hear her say, "*Make the most of this opportunity. Be whoever you want to be.*"

"You're right!" I exclaim, stamping my foot down on the sidewalk.

A man looks at me strangely for talking to myself. I stand up a little straighter, straighten my top, fix my hair as best I can, and am off at a much more energetic rate and positive note. If I could have a soundtrack playing over my life at this exact moment I envision Blind Melon's "No Rain" loudly playing. I practically skip across the street and am half trotting, half running around the corner of main street when I hear, "Neens!?!"

*No, it can't be.* I stop in my tracks and whirl around. Mel comes barreling into me, practically knocking me down onto the floor, enveloping me in a bone crushing hug.

"Neens, what the blazes are ya doin' here?" she shouts, pinching me a couple of times to make sure she's not hallucinating.

I laugh at her while wincing from her nails. We hold onto each others' outstretched arms. I shake my head, trying to figure out where to start.

"Um, long story...?" I say, completely gobsmacked. She stands there, eagerly waiting for an explanation. I take a deep breath. "Short story is I got in a really bad accident, lost my phone, and ended up getting stuck here for the duration. *Covid.*"

"I want the long story, 'n I can already tell we're gonna need some schooners for this one," she states, bewildered as she turns me back on my heels and drags me towards the bar.

Minutes later, we enter the pub. Mick is still engrossed with his friend. I wave to him when Mel and I enter. She notices and looks at me somewhat oddly. After a few pints of amber fluid, I more or less inform Mel of my long journey of physical recovery and my friendship with Mick. I start to get into it about Brodie, without naming names.

"Doesn't matter," I mutter, settling the matter. "I barely see the guy."

"Wow, what a stunner, Neens," she belatedly says, then takes a long sip of her beer after being speechless for my whole story.

"I know, right?" I agree, taking a big gulp of Shirley Temple.

"Well, no wonder I neva heard from ya again!" she projects with a tone of realization.

I look at Mel and smile. I've missed her. It dawns on me.

"Wait, why are *you* here?" I ask quizzically.

She laughs and shrugs. That's so like Mel, so mellow, so chill. She waves her hand all casual like.

"I grew up here, Neens," she snorts. "Rememba, I told ya 'bout my sista, well she still lives here 'n so does Mum 'n Dad. I finally got through the borda 'n made it home. Covid shut down the southern borders for quite a while so my whole trip was prolonged indefinitely 'n I was stuck at my rellie's dodgy house for way too long, until I was allowed to come back." She shudders, trying to forget the memory. "Wild, eh, we'd wind up togetha months lata in the same town in the middle of nowhere."

"You have no idea how happy I am that you're here. Like no idea," I announce in a mixture of jest and desperation. "I could really use a friend."

Billy, the bartender, walks over and picks up our empty bottles. Mick's friend stands up, and the two shake hands, smiling. He looks back at me and waves. I wave back. Out of nowhere, Margot saunters inside and comes up to our table.

I'm about to say hi when Mel starts first, "Oy, I'm glad yar here. I was just about to text ya."

"Nina from America?" Margot says broadly, realizing I'm at the table. She looks back and forth between Mel and me. She leans down and half whispers, "Mel, I see ya met the one the whole town's been wafflin' on about. Isn't she cute?" She speaks out of the corner of her mouth, "We think it's the accent."

Mel laughs and informs Margot of our backstory, explaining that I'm the new friend she thought long gone, back in America. These two seem to have a short hand. I start to get the impression that I'm missing something.

"Wait, so how do you two know each other?" I ask them.

They freeze and look at each other before a smile erupts on Mel's face.

"Margot's my sista, Neens," she states with humor. "Sorry should have started with that."

I lift my head up in enlightenment and nod. *Ohhhh.* I do vaguely remember Mel saying something about a sister who is blonde and leggy. *Cool. Cool.*

Margot loses interest quickly and shakes the car keys as a reminder for Mel to get going. Mel gathers her things and stands, pulling out some cash for the drinks.

"Oh, Neens, I almost forgot, a few of us are going campin' this weekend since I'm back. Ya should totally come!" she happily invites me, while her sister looks less than thrilled.

"'Course ya should come," Margot says, as Mel jabs her side.

The thought of camping with Leggy Blonde doesn't exactly excite me, but Selena's *"make the most of this opportunity"* sounds off in my head again like a siren.

"Sure. Love to!" I accept exuberantly.

"Brilliant! 'N bring yar Khal," Mel echoes my energy.

Margot merely turns on her heels and leaves without so much as a goodbye.

# 9

It's well before sunrise and Mel is picking me up soon. Mick has a sleeping bag and a swag, a single man mini tent, rolled up, sitting next to a hot thermos of coffee for the long road trip. He thinks it's wonderful that I'm going, reiterating how it'll be good for me make some "nice young mates." Wearing his old flannel robe, he combs his hair. I tell him to go back to bed, but he insists on seeing me off.

"Let 'em see yar true self, Sheila," he says sweetly. "They'll be linin' up at the door."

I inform him that there are a couple of pre-made meals in the fridge and to not let them go to waste. I can't help but worry about him knowing I'm heading on a trip a good distance away, about twenty hours away in fact.

Before I can dwell on that too much, headlights fill the drive. Mel comes into view in her yellow bus, Nigel. The site of it alone makes me so happy. Mel pops out in her usual exuberant manner, and skips over to me. She tells Mick she already packed a tent, so the swag's not needed. Mick tosses my sleeping back to her.

"Have fun, yous," Mick says, smiling at us, then directly looks at me. "I'll be seein' ya, Sweetheart."

He hands me the thermos. I beam at him, bounce over and plant a soft kiss on his cheek as I take the warm jug.

"I'll be back before you know it," I lean in and quickly whisper.

He chuckles as I turn and open the bus's passenger door, lightly tossing in my backpack.

"Thanks, Mick!" Mel yells from the driver side window.

He tips his head to us and we make our way down the drive. I twist in my seat, smudging the cold glass with my fingers as I wave goodbye through the window. His shrinking figure disappears amongst the house's lights as we turn onto the highway. We drive and drive and drive. The endless dark void in front of us has me nodding off, and before I know it I jump wide awake, head snapping back into place.

"Day for it," Mel lightly announces.

"Morning," I mumble. "How long was I asleep for?"

I stretch a little in the front seat, and wipe a bit of drool off my lips.

"A while," she answers in humor. "At least a few hours."

I peer out the window. The sun still sleeps, but the moon dips towards the horizon about to set. Small shreds of light begin to emerge. It looks like the birth of a new day is upon us. I'm usually asleep for sunrise, unless for special occasions such as road trips or planned photoshoots, so witnessing one is always something special for me.

I yawn something big, and reach for the thermos. I need caffeine. Light begins to fill the bus. Mel has her driving glasses on, accenting and magnifying her already giant hazel eyes. I untwist the cap and two tiny stacked cups pop off with it. I pour a small cup and extend it to Mel. She takes is gladly.

"Careful, I think it's still pretty hot," I inform her, seeing the steam rise off the top of the mocha colored coffee.

She cautiously takes a tiny sip, then returns for a longer one.

"Mmmm, yeah, nah, it's perfect actually," she responds.

Handling the second little cup, I pour myself a glass and pull it towards my nose, and inhale deeply, "I love that smell."

"God, that's good. What's in this?" she asks, enjoying it.

I lightly chuckle. Mick has been trying to win me over to the "black coffee only crowd" since day one. I take a little sip, smiling as I swish it around lightly, tasting the splash of coffee creamer and oat milk Mick added.

"I'm not the biggest fan of black coffee, remember?" I laugh. "Looks like Mick finally gave in and made me the Nina Special."

"He's so good with ya. At first I thought it was a bit odd, him takin' care of ya, but Old Mick really is the sweetest. He's been through hell 'n back so I'm happy he's got ya, Neens."

My eyebrows turn down. *Hell and back?* I never did ask Mick about the woman's clothes in the dresser, and while I'd love to know, I never want to pry, especially with how wonderful he's been towards me. *But* I'm also super curious and finding out indirectly couldn't hurt, could it?

"What do you mean, hell and back?" I press slightly further.

Mel takes a sip of her coffee before answering, "Oh ya know, all that with his wife 'n child some years ago. Poor Old Boy, finally gets home from enlistment 'n comes home to that."

Now, I'm not only curious, but slightly concerned. *Child?* Poor Mick. I'm almost certain he's not in touch with any kids.

"Wait, what—," I ask, but my voice drops off.

The sun peeks out from above the shadowed horizon.

"It's gonna be a stunna," Mel gasps.

I set my cup down in the holder and dig through my backpack, hunting for my camera. Knowing I was coming camping, I had Mick put out the word I was looking for a lens, and sure enough, there was an old lady a few homesteads over that had one she hasn't used in years. It's a little older, but it works and is still in clean condition. I got a good deal on it too. I hold up my camera kit and instead of taking a photo of the sunrise, I angle it towards Mel's face. I snap a photo as she drives with the cotton candy pink light glowing through her glasses' frames and her ashy hair. She laughs at me, glances back and forth between the road, the sunrise, and the camera. I love that about Mel. She never ducks away from the camera, nor shies away from who she is, and I deeply admire that about her.

A few more hours pass. Mel tells me all about how she took my advice and has been single ever since breaking up with her ex over seven months ago. She blames me and the pandemic for her decision, but admits she's the happiest she's ever been. I congratulate her on her special feat. I rest my barefoot ankles out of the open window, stretching my legs, wiggling my toes in the breeze. Temps are up again and it's not even mid day yet. We are headed further north, so the days will grow hotter and more unforgiving.

"Oh, I forgot," Mel says, glancing at my moving toes, "I brought ya somethin'." She reaches her right arm behind my seat while continuing to steer, and moves her right hand around in search of something. She feels her way under a blanket and then pulls out a pair of old Blundstone hiking boots. "These oughtta do the trick, Neens."

"You know I only have like two pairs of shoes, including sandals," I explain in a laugh, glancing at my discarded sneakers on the floorboards.

"I remba'd that last night when I was packin', 'n remba'd we're 'bout the same size, so here, take 'em," she says, dumping the boots in my lap. "'N dun worry, they're older, *pre-China*."

While Australia is synonymous with Blundstone boots, many of the locals aren't pleased with the quality ever since pushing domestic production overseas. I grab the pair of socks from inside my sneakers and toss them on, and wiggle my feet into the ankle high, tobacco leather boots. A perfect fit, and I don't even have to break them in.

"Awesome, I can't thank you enough," I say, smiling from her to my newly rugged, yet stylish feet.

"Keep 'em," she declares. "Now yar one of us, eh."

I reach over, nodding, and turn up the volume. Spacey Jane's "Booster Seat" fills Nigel's cabin. Mel introduced me to this awesome band during our first roadtrip months ago. We both grin remembering, and yell the chorus together as we make our way down the boundless highway.

Finally after a full day and night of driving and twelve albums later, we reach the state park. Having been in the same locale for the past five months, we're both happy to explore some new territory, especially any pushing north. The earth is so red, it feels like another planet. It's rich, rust colored, sandy clay reflects pink onto the fraying clouds overhead. Random little green tufts of bush occasionally pop up through the desolate landscape. Giant boulders of red, sedimentary rock formations create clusters of soft outlines reaching for the heavens. The contrast of blue sky is quite striking. Aside from the coastline, I don't think I've ever seen a scene so breathtakingly outer worldly, yet so gorgeous and vast. Suddenly in this moment, I feel small. Not in a sad way, but quite the opposite, in a way where the world seems infinite and full of possibilities.

*I, Nina, am standing here.* How many others can say the same? What have these mystical, enchanted lands born witness to?

As the first light of the day hits, we make our way closer to the larger formations along a bumpy dirt path. The path curves to the side, mirroring the foundation's contour along the rocks. The whole scene feels like a moving painting as the shortening distance bears new perspective with each passing kilometer. After following the path for a little while longer, we pull down another dirt road and stop. This new trail is far skinnier and more run down, clearly a path less chosen. Mel turns off the ignition and Nigel's engine slowly dies away into the quiet.

"They'll be here shortly," she says, gathering her overnight bag and sleeping bag out of the backseat.

I grab my backpack and sleeping bag, and look around at our surroundings. I don't hear any engine noises or see any chalky dust trails from tires treading along red dirt.

"How much time do we have, you think?" I ask her, continuing my scan of the horizon.

"Hmm, hard to say exactly, but we all agreed sunrise, so should be any time, I reckon," she says, wincing as she pulls out the tent, buried underneath the seat.

I love how Aussies rely on the light of day for a lot of their time keeping. It adds to the rugged, primitive character of this land.

I think I have enough time to pop The Khal up in the sky. I might as well make the most of this desolate, beautiful landscape. I power on the battery. It roars to life with its customary beeps which seem extra amplified against the stark juxtaposition of untouched nature. Waves of guilt wash over me. I'm disturbing the land's quiet and peaceful splendor, but the artist and documentarian in me is salivating at the potential landscape photos I have at my fingertips. As a lover of the earth, and one who inherently wants to protect it, I frequently find myself the subject of an internal conflict. I agree on a compromise amongst myself, and vow to not wander too far so I don't disrupt anything major. Launching The Great Khal Drono into the air, it whizzes up in a little burst. The most breathtaking aerial shot fills my screen and I let out a small, yet high pitched squeal. Mel laughs, sitting on a log nearby, and watches The Khal do his thing.

"Mel, you've got to see this. It's insane. I feel like a kid on Christmas morning!" I gush. I video for a little, then hit the shutter button continuously. I can't contain my excitement. "I mean the colors alone, not to mention that formation."

Another squeal erupts as I nod to the distance in front of me.

"Alright, lemme see," she quips, as she hops up and walks over, peering over my shoulder. She takes off her sunglasses to see through the glare, and her eyes round wide. She shakes her head looking back and forth between the screen and our ground level view. "Remarkable, Neens. A bloody rippa if I eva saw one."

I hear an engine looming in the distance, and begin The Khal's descent back towards land, pausing to snap some pics along the way. Within a minute, I'm catching it in my hand, powering him down. I definitely need to preserve some battery. I can tell this place is magical for a photographer. I'll have to scope and get a feel for when the time is right again. I grab my pack and sleeping bag, and almost trip. These new boots are already saving my feet from rock shards and clumsiness. This outback territory is no joke.

Red dust clouds form above the bushes, alerting us to an impending visitor. Mel playfully sticks her arm out with a thumbs up, mimicking a hitch hiker. Two utes pull up right beside her.

One silver truck is filled with three guys, all in their late twenties to mid thirties from the looks of them. One is pretty cute - golden skin, tall, blonde, muscular; his eyes are hidden by giant black sunglasses. The other two aren't shabby looking either, especially the bigger one of Aborigine descent. With dark features, he's jacked; his muscles look like they could easily rip his shirt open or destroy any opponent in the heaviest weight class. The third guy is a lanky, shorter brunette with long, shaggy hair. All three are kind of rugged outdoorsmen meets surfer vibes, but each in their unique ways. I see the linebacker guy clean off his flashy reflective sunglasses.

Speaking of sunglasses, my eyes are dying out here with all the bright, unobstructed light. I put my hand over my brows to provide some form of shade. Meanwhile, Mel starts loading up her things in the boot of their truck as the three men stretch their legs a little. The big guy with the flashy sunglasses catches my eye. His face lights up into a giant smile. It's so genuine and pure, I can't help but smile back immediately.

"G'Day, 'n who do we have here?" he says appreciatively, looking me up and down.

The shorter lanky man just casually waves, friendly, but keeping his distance. The tall blonde walks up next to the smiley guy. He looks from Mel to me, extending his hand outwardly for a handshake.

"Ya must be Nina," he says smoothly.

I smile a tad awkwardly, but grip his nice firm hand.

"Yep, that's me," I say, a trifle bit taken aback that he knows my name.

I glance at Mel. They've been talking about me I see.

"She's American," Margot declares, rounding behind the ute.

*Has this become her new tagline?*

The guys nod their heads, making little comments of approval as they stare at me. I'm finding it extremely unnerving. As Mel locks up Nigel, I pivot, avoiding their stares, and see Brodie coming up behind Margot, followed by another girl I don't know. I assumed he would be here with Margot coming, but seeing him sends a jolt through my system. He walks right up to the guys, powerfully slapping their backs with a few claps of his hand.

"What's up, boys?" he hollers. "How was yar trip?"

This happy-go-lucky Brodie takes me by pleasant surprise.

The three men turn to him and start laughing, giving high fives and "bro hugs." Afterwards, they turn and hug the girls, extra happy to see Mel. Clearly they're all good friends. I stand here awkwardly, living that third wheel life to the fullest. The new girl sees me and waves, perhaps sensing my self-ostracizing nature. She smiles at me with so much sincerity, I can already tell I'm going to get along with her really well. There are some people you jive with right away, and within this small moment, I already know she's one of them.

"Sorry, I'm Jacinda," she says apologetically, "but everyone calls me Jaz. 'N you are?"

"I'm Nina," I declare, super friendly.

At the sound of my voice, Stella sticks her head out of Brodie's truck and barks. With one look from Brodie, she obediently waits in the car. I raise my eyes back to the boys. Jaz picks up on this.

"So the lads here - I'm guessin' they didn't tell ya their names - they're actually on their way back from anotha campin' trip up north. The one on the far end, the shorter one, is Shane, 'Shayno,' as well call him," she offers, introducing us.

"*Shorter one?*" Shayno repeats, in mock disappointment.

"Ya know what I mean," Jaz amends, rolling her eyes at him as she gestures to the tall, blonde guy. "That one's Jordan or Jordo."

"We met," says Jordan, smiling at me broadly as he takes off his black sunglasses, showing a twinkle in his eye.

*Jordan, eh, you have really nice baby blues.*

"That's Adoni," Jaz sings, turning to the ripped, dark haired man, "which is Aboriginal for 'sunset.' Isn't that just beautiful? But we call him Donnie for short."

"Nice to meet you guys," I mutter, looking at the three of them.

Jaz then points to Brodie and Margot, and I interrupt her, informing her that the three of us are well acquainted. She nods happily. Brodie catches my eye, just barely, but I look away, noticing how Margot watches him like a hawk. Jordan walks towards me and reaches for my sleeping bag.

"Where's yar bags?" he says, waiting to take them to the truck.

"This is it, right here," I say proudly, patting my backpack.

"While she may seem like an American wanka, she's actually True Blue at heart," Mel says fondly.

They all hesitate, and I get the feeling they feel like time will tell on that one.

"Here, I'll load that on top of the esky in my ute, Nina," Brodie offers, grabbing my sleeping bag from Jordan. Jordan looks slightly accosted, but nods as Brodie explains to his friend, "I've got heaps more room."

"Well, we could all just go wafflin' on," Margot pipes up, "but camp's not gonna make itself."

The group snickers in agreement and hastily jumps into action. Mel tells me we're to ride with the boys in their ute. I nod and turn to see Brodie, looking eager to get moving, hopping into the drivers seat behind us. Jaz, Shayno, and Margot both climb into the backseat while Stella commands the front, sticking her head out the window. Doors shut loudly in all directions. Donnie drives our truck and punches the vehicle into a nice steady pace down the narrow trail. We have to avoid bigger rocks and super uneven spots, but on the whole, it's really enjoyable and rough, but in a fun, adventurous way. A memory of the Indiana Jones ride at Disneyland comes to mind, but this is so much better.

It's officially morning now. The light is shifting so shadows fall heavily in the wake of the giant rock cluster. I snap furiously away on my camera, documenting the road, the car ride, the boisterous and happy company, and even turn around, sticking my head out the window to capture Brodie's ute in front of us. Before I know it, I'm laughing my head off and even joining in on the conversation and discussions. We pass some rivers, and drive through some rivers, the trucks handling the stream crossings without a hitch or hesitation. It feels like something out of a movie. I'm giddy with adventurous delight. No wonder we couldn't bring Nigel on this leg of the journey.

While we drive for another hour to our camp site, Mel informs me that the guys all live scattered about forty minutes to an hour apart back home, so they try and do camping trips or day trips often to hang out. Donnie's an electrician, Shayno an engineer, and Jordan's a real estate agent. Jordan lives more towards the bigger town, but grew up with Brodie and is his oldest friend.

Mel is uber bubbly and outgoing, more than normal. I forgot how flirty she can be, especially with undivided male attention. I laugh internally. I wish I could be more like that. *Nina, you're a terrible flirt.* I roll my eyes at myself, but it's true. I'm the worst flirt in history of flirts. I don't even know how to do it, I'm that bad.

Mel tried to give me lessons back in Melbourne, and although she started quite determined and optimistic, she genuinely became impressed with how bad I am. She has taken it as her personal mission to improve my flirtatious and seductive ways. As if she can read my mind, she nudges me and winks.

"Watch this," she mouths, leaning forward, playfully resting her hand on Donnie's toned arm. She lets it linger for a second too long, and even rubs it, just slightly. Donnie turns his head back, clearly interested. "Oh, Don," Mel asks in a cutesy tone, "do ya think ya can pass me the canteen... I'm awfully thirsty."

"Sure, Mel, hold on a sec," he quickly says, reaching for the water.

As he hands it back to her, she lays her hand on his bicep.

"Thanks, Love," she says puckishly, giggling. "Cheers."

Slowly and methodically, she drinks from the canteen. Small drips of water flow down her neck. She's actually successful because it comes off like one of those sexy marketing commercials. If I tried that, I'd end up needing mouth to mouth from dry drowning. She takes some more sips. How does she do it? *It's a canteen for crying out loud.* Donnie and Jordan both stare at her; Donnie practically drools through the rear view mirror, while Jordan audibly swallows next to her. I stifle a snorting laugh. Mel glances at me out of the corner of her eye and winks again, pleased with her efforts. I'm trying so hard not to laugh. We can't meet each others' eyes or we'll both lose it. And I really need to pee, badly.

Just when I think I'm going to burst, Jordan yells, "Oy, we've arrived cobbers. I reckon that's a new record for us."

He laughs and shouts excitedly as Donnie backs in the ute next to a giant bush and parks. Doors open, and feet hit the barren earth. Grabbing my backpack and camera, I stumble out of the truck. Brodie parks about twenty feet away. Stella's first out, speeding around, sniffing every square inch of dirt. Her dad and his passengers climb out too.

The most beautiful swimming hole, surrounded by red earth, sits idyllically nestled amongst the red rocks and green plants. The camp sits at the base of the massive rock formation. Old bonfire wood and ashes line the shoreline.

"You guys come here often?" I ask, looking around as they unload.

"We've been trekkin' out here, since what, we were fifteen, sixteen years old?" Brodie asks Jordan, Jaz, and Mel, who nod and gruff in confirmation.

Stella explores thoroughly. Brodie doesn't even need to keep an eye on her. She's a dog of the land. She respects it, and she respects him. Seeing me, she runs over, and wags her tail excitedly. She kisses my leg along my long purple scar, leaving large slobber marks running from my shin and up my knee to the hem of my denim shorts. I walk over to Brodie's ute to grab my sleeping bag and find him unloading a couple of duffels from the floorboards of the back seat.

"Do you know where my sleeping bag is?" I politely ask him.

Maybe we can try that friend thing he suggested.

He stops and looks up at me. The canteen strap dangles between his front teeth.

"In the boot, on top of the esky," he squeezes out.

He says the last part with a bit of annoyance. What did I do? I hoped maybe we could have a fresh start. *Maybe he just can't talk right now, Nina.* I hate it when my subconscious plays devils advocate against itself.

I walk around the back and glance around, trying to pinpoint the ice chest. There it is! It's wedged in between a few other bags of tents and sleep sacks. I pull hard, trying to counterbalance the resistance with my sheer strength. I literally have a leg up on the trunk's frame, but with my leg not at one hundred percent, it's not really working. Swiftly, the bag rips free, and I stagger back into Brodie's arm. He pushes me back upright while also holding onto the sleeping bag.

"Thanks, got it," I say a bit breathlessly and defensively, grabbing it from his hand, trying not to come off weak.

"Okay, then," he quips.

Jaz rounds the open trunk door and sees us together, side by side. She gives Brodie some inquisitive eyes, but I catch him shake his head in dismissal and a smile. He nudges her in the side as he passes her.

An hour passes, and after a major group effort of establishing tents and setting up the stove cooker, we are ready to enjoy the afternoon and night and all they have to offer. Admittedly, I don't contribute very much. These people are pros. Again, coming from California, while we do have beautiful state parks, my family only camps maybe once a year. Instead of physically helping out, I settle for being the trip documentarian.

Tired, we all sit in our camping chairs as Mel passes coldies around to us all. In charge of our "bevvies" for the trip, she went to the Bottle-O. Not really a beer drinker, unless as a last resort, I gave Mel some money for some hard seltzers. She passes me one of my drinks with a wink.

As everyone sits and bullshits around in a circle, dusk slowly approaches, and Brodie starts to gather all the supplies for dinner.

"It's gonna be a banga sunset, I reckon," Donnie declares, looking up at the sky.

I glance up and smile, nodding in total agreement. The light has already begun its downward spiral into darkness. Neon pinks and purples fill the vast skyline.

"Neens, why don't you take the dronie up?" Mel shouts from inside our tent.

"Dronie?" Jaz asks eagerly. "Ya've got a drone?"

"Possibly," I say, downplaying it.

Mel walks out of the tent, a little sweaty, and ties up her hair.

"You lot should see her work," she says proudly. "Truly remarkable."

Brodie glances up from the stove at me, curious and maybe a tad impressed. I avoid his inquisitive stare.

"Well, I don't know about that," I counter the group's prying eyes. "It doesn't take much when you have amazing scenery at your fingertips."

I gesture to the stunning rock plateaus, and the exquisite and saturated sunset unfolding right before our eyes.

"Come on, then, bust it out!" Donnie yells.

Caving to peer pressure, and not wanting to miss such a glorious capture, I reach in my backpack and pull out The Great Khal, readying him for his debut.

"Wow, that thing's smol," Jaz says, genuinely intrigued, peering at The Khal and my backpack. "'N ya keep yar gear in there too? Where da yar clothes go?"

"Wearing most of them," I announce, with a hint of satisfaction, "and the rest are rolled up under my camera."

I've always been a light packer with a somewhat minimalist mindset, but I still get happy to hear the occasional praise for it.

I start the remote controller first, then unfold the drone, place the base between my right hand's fingers, and fire it up. The beeps sounds off, alerting everyone it's awake, and the props twist slightly, testing themselves before take off.

"Fuck me dead," states Donnie, looking at The Khal like it's going to beam us to an alien planet.

The rest of my audience shrieks and laughs in excitement. While drone life is very normal for me, I have to remind myself that it's not typical for everyone.

"Here we go," I declare, building up the lift off.

I raise my arm away from my face and angle the controller toggle up, and away it flies into the air. Its buzzing trail leaves everyone in awe. The entire group follows it as it flies away out of earshot. Even Margot looks mildly fascinated.

"How far's it go?" she asks, biting away at her fingertips.

I explain some details, including his name, general distance capabilities, communication... some basic drone knowledge, and they all eat it up, even Brodie. I hover the drone down closer, above our heads, and tilt my head up.

"Okay, everyone look up and wave," I command, raising a free arm up. "I'm doing a video."

Everyone follows suit. I quickly glance around and everyone's laughing up to the sky in total awe. Even I have to admit, nestled against the rock formation with a drone, the contrast against this amazing, barren landscape feels bizarre and uber alien. Remembering my internal conflict, I don't want to be up in the air for very long, so I tell them I'm going to land it and offer one of them the chance to catch it in their bare hands. That really throws them all into a tizzy.

"Whaddabout yar fingers?" Margot asks dubiously.

"It's easy," I assure them, backing away a couple feet from them. "Look, I'll show you."

In one swift movement, I fly The Khal with extreme precision right in front of me. It hovers next to my head and I reach out and grab the body, underneath the spinning propellers. I angle the toggle stick downwards with my thumb and the engine dies in seconds. The propellers come to an abrupt stop.

The group cheers, hoots and hollers.

"Ya make that look like a piece of piss," Donnie chimes in, very much interested.

Jordan scrambles next to Donnie, and yells, "I'm gonna catch it first thing tomorrow."

The whole group bursts into a boisterous guffaw. I gather it must be an inside joke. My face must reflects some curiosity because Brodie leans over and provides some clarity.

"Jordo's always first cab off the rank," he explains.

I'm partially distracted by the way his mouth moves. *He has nice lips.* Why am I just now noticing them? Shaking my internal thoughts away, I then question this saying. While I've heard loads of Aussie expressions and abbreviations — *they abbreviate everything!* — this is a new one. I continue making another face, showing my misunderstanding.

"He's always the first one to do anythin'," Brodie further clarifies with emphasis.

"Ah, got it, thanks," I say, mentally tucking it away for later.

I pack up the drone and fit it neatly back into my backpack. I go back to the ute and stow away my bag for safe keeping; wouldn't want any accidents to befall it. I think I already used up my nine lives all in one swoop with my car crash. I return and see Brodie dicing up some onions, zucchini and lettuce. He pulls out a tub of fresh white fish from the esky and seasons it. He shakes the tub, letting it all mix and marinate together before tossing it straight on the grill. Within minutes, I'm salivating from the stellar smells coming from the tiny barbecue.

Jaz comes up and nudges Brodie's arm. *Are they a thing? I thought he's maybe with Margot...* I'm a little confused. To add to my confusion, Jaz rests her head on his shoulder and takes a giant whiff.

"Agh, it's the best. Brodie's always been a top notch cook," she informs me, squeezing his arm affectionately.

He looks down at her and smiles sweetly.

"Well, ya'd be the one to know," he declares sarcastically.

"How long have you two known each other," I casually ask, fishing for more information, but trying not to come off too nosy.

They both start laughing. Brodie stirs his concoction around in the pan. It's starting to smell even more amazing.

"Our whole lives," he answers, starting to pull off some of the veggies. "She's my numba one. Yeah, nah, Stella is actually."

Jaz laughs and grins back, nudging him, and playfully responds, "What? A doggo outranks yar own sista?"

*Sister!*

I smile nodding at this key piece of information. Now knowing, I look at the pair of them standing side by side. I can make out the resemblance. Jaz is shorter than Brodie, standing slightly taller than average for a girl at around 5′7″. They both have the same green eyes and brow. Jaz's hair is slightly lighter in color than Brodie's and not curly at all.

Suddenly, lanterns come to life around us. Brodie pulls the fish filets off the grill and places them on some bread with cabbage. He's really into the complete presentation apparently as he dishes everyone up. I must say I'm impressed. I don't know many guys who cook, let alone take pride in it.

Beers, AKA "tinnies," "coldies," "frothies," "stubbies," and "throw downs," amongst about a hundred other names, are handed to everyone. They each line up, taking their sandwiches, AKA "sangers," and relax by the firewood. Shayno and Donnie have been trying to build a fire for a while now. Jaz butts in and ignites one in two minutes. Clapping her hands clean, she smugly returns to her food.

After we eat, feeling full and a little tipsy, I lounge on a towel. My head rests on Mel's legs behind me as she sits in a camp chair. She strokes my head and I emit small sounds of mirth. It feels heavenly. My mom and sisters used to do this all the time when we'd pile on the couch with each other. *I miss you guys so much it hurts.* I push the thought of them away because tonight, I feel the best I've felt in ages. Tonight, I feel like maybe, hopefully, I've found my groove. Jordan sits next to me, a little closer than I'd prefer being as we just met a few hours ago, but he is awfully cute, and if he hasn't found my lack of charm repelling by now, maybe he won't. He hears me moan slightly, enjoying my head massage, and looks over in my direction, raising an eyebrow. He smiles, his eyes smoldering.

Brodie casually leans back in his chair, watching Jordan. Margot sits inches next to Brodie. She even rests her head on his arm at one point, and he seems unbothered by it. Directing my gaze elsewhere, I look into the flames in front of me. Beautiful, burning bright wisps of color form shapes that appear, disappear then reappear in an endless cycle. Hearing a big crack in the close distance, I jump in reflex. Brodie snorts and shakes his head as I relax back into my makeshift chair.

"Whaddaya reckon? Should we tell her 'bout the Drop Bear?" Brodie asks the group before his eyes settle back on me.

Their eyes shoot up in a collective smile.

"What's a drop bear?" I ask nervously, glancing around.

Donnie clears his throat, ready to tell me.

"Only the scariest creature in all a Straya, Nina," he declares.

"Where do these animals live?" I ask, feeling threatened.

I've never heard of such a creature.

"Try not to be too devo, but the last attack was reported only a few kilometres from here," Brodie informs me, with raised wary brows.

Jaz gawks at her brother in shock.

"It's a rello of the koala bear," Donnie further educates me, "but unlike its docile cuz, it jumps outta trees attackin' unsuspecting blokes, mainly tourists 'cause they don't know to watch out for 'em, eh."

"Somethin' fierce, Drop Bears are," Brodie reiterates seriously.

Gulping, I huddle closer to Mel, peering over my shoulder every time I hear so much as a crack, creak, or shuffle.

"Brotha," Jaz scolds him.

Suddenly, Brodie, Donnie, and the gang all bust out in mutual laughter. I look around, not getting the joke.

"Wowser," Jordan grimaces to Jaz.

"Well, they almost took it too far," she sneers, with a hint of humor.

"They were yankin' yar chain, Neens," Mel says, leaning down in my ear. "The Drop Bear is just some urban lej."

Shaking my head as the butt of the joke, I joke in my best Aussie accent, "Good on ya, mates."

Hearing me actually use an Australian colloquialism correctly, but in a quasi British accent, they roar in laughter even more.

"Alright, alright," Mel says, and they die down a little, refocusing on the raging fire in the middle of us.

"I gotta go find the dunny," Jaz announces, standing before she exits our circle.

"Do you guys do s'mores here?" I ask, looking up at the contented faces around me.

"Yeah, the thing with the mallows 'n chokkie?" Donnie asks.

"Chocolate," Mel translates in my ear.

I nod. I got that one.

"Yep. First you spear a mallow and roast it on a mini spic. Then you pry the mallow off the spic and in-between two graham crackers lined with a sliver of chocolate, *chokkie*," I amend. "And bob's your uncle!"

They all laugh, especially since I used another Aussie colloquialism correctly. I find out no one brought any s'mores supplies as it's not a very popular camping treat like in the US. I'll have to remember to bring the goods one time in the future.

Margot glances around the campfire clearly waiting for her turn to speak.

"Well, why that does sound *intriguin'*, Nina," she mocks me in a slight belittling tone, as she leans forward, "I propose a round of skinny dippin'!"

She gets up and races a couple of paces towards the shore to the swimming hole, all while pulling off her shirt. She flings it back in the air, then her shoes, and lastly her shorts. Arms outstretched to the moon, she screams as she dances freely, about to pull off her underwear. The boys immediately spring up, shedding clothes, hats, and shoes.

"Neens, come on, live a little!" Mel screams over her shoulder, as she runs down toward the shoreline, undressing.

*Why does she have to always put it like that?* I groan audibly.

Brodie smiles and laughs. I don't see him acting like his pants are on fire. We stare at each other a moment, unsure if the other one will commit. After a beat, I stand and strip off my shoes and socks. I slowly make my way to shore. The others jump around in the dark, moonlit water, splashing and dunking each other. Hardly anyone pays attention to us. Mel unclips her bra, letting herself go *a la natural*. She peels off her thong undies too. In the dim light, you can pretty much only make out silhouettes, *thankfully*.

"Nina, ya HAVE to join in," she wheezes, sprinting to the others as she pants with excitement.

*Live a little, Nina.*

I compromise and undress down to my undies and bra, but keep them on. I had no idea I'd be parading around in front of people in my intimates. I catch Jordan staring from the water. My bra's way more revealing than I'm generally comfortable with so I cross my arms over my chest, trying to obscure as much as possible. Brodie looks, but tries to avoid staring, and instead strips his shirt off. I take a second to admire his abs in the moonlight. We both lock eyes. It's so intense that my brain scrambles and before I know it, my body has a mind of its own and I'm running and smashing into the water next to Mel and Margot. Brodie dives in, leaving his trunks on and wrestles with the guys.

Did he wear his trunks out of modesty as we're just getting to know each other, or did he do it so I wouldn't be singled out amongst all these free spirits? The thought slips away as we all swim around, enjoying the cool water, the beautiful warm night, and mainly the roaring laughter, which rings like freedom in the air.

# 10

The sun rises. Another day lies before us, and I can't wait to see what's in store. The crew wakes up one by one. Everyone emerges from their respective tents, swags and ute beds, looking a tad worse for wear, but happy nonetheless. Jaz, Mel, and Jordan all suffer from a little case of bedhead, but secretly I've always loved the bedhead look. I think sometimes a person's most natural state is prettiest. Donnie has a nice clipped cut so no whacky hair there, and Shayno's still asleep.

"Woah, Nina," Jordan mutters, taking a step back as his eyes settle on me.

I raise my hand and try to gather my curls. Being thirty years old, I don't need a mirror to know the current state of my bedhead. With a light graze, I can feel frizz and curls spiraling all around my head, and pretty far out too. Swimming and letting my hair air dry always results in some crazy and voluminous spiral curls. I pat it a little, but it's no use. It's either up in a top knot or like this, and right now, I'm actually feeling this.

"Morning," I offer, shrugging.

Brodie smiles to himself as he pulls on his boots. His natural curls look a little smashed on top of his head, but overall he looks the same. I don't see any crustees around his eyes either. Must be an early riser. Mel and Jaz announce they're heading "to use the dunny" and Donnie hops up, following them. I squint, looking after them, but it's too bright. I close my eyes for a second. Stella sits next to me, her head in my lap as I stroke her ears. Brodie jumps up and runs to his ute. Stella's ears perk up, always on high alert when her dad steps away, but she stays put. He's back in just a minute.

"Here," I hear him say, behind my shoulder.

Feeling something small nudging my arm, I twist my head back and look over. In his hand is a pair of sunglasses. I reach out in disbelief and he lets them fall into my open palms. I sit, staring at them for a minute. I look up at him, completely touched.

"Brodie, I don't know how to thank you..." I mutter in genuine gratitude, my eyes softening. "But won't you need them?"

I motion to hand them back to him, but he pushes them back on me, shaking his head in outright refusal.

"Nah, I've got anotha pair," he urges, "'n seein' ya squint like that reminded me of yar crushed ones."

His voice drops, not naming the unspoken elephant in the room: my accident. It's not something we generally discuss for reasons I don't really know other than neither of us prefers to relive any of the horrible details.

I unfold the sunnies before me. They're big, circular frames in a cool 1970s fashion, with corners that tip out in a little cat-eye. The frames are honey colored, and I am in love. I actually prefer them to my original pair. *Hopefully he doesn't want them back.* I laugh at my internal admission and try them on for size. The immediate relief from the light and the familiarity almost makes me want to cry in happiness.

"How do I look?" I ask.

Glasses usually go one of two ways with my round face shape: I either look decent or terrible. The default conclusion is usually the latter.

"Heaps betta than on me," he responds casually. "They suit ya. Keep 'em."

"You sure?" I double check.

He nods and puts on the black, large framed squarish pair he wears regularly as the bathroom gang arrives back to camp. Shayno enters the communal space, and Margot also emerges. Her blonde hair looks like it just got blown out by a professional, and her skin's all dewy too. I swear she wears mascara, but jury's still out on that little detail. I glance back at the group. Jordan smiles at me.

"So what do we do today?" I ask them in anticipation.

They all laugh and snicker.

"Just ya wait, Nina," I hear one of them tease.

"Wahooo!" I howl at the top of my lungs.

*Oh my goodness, this is the best feeling ever.*

I holler again and hold on tight on the back of Jordan's dirt bike. Since I'm the newbie, I was offered first dibs to sit behind him as we lead the caravan's way on our desert riding excursion. I didn't even notice this beast hitched on the back of Donnie's ute. Pretty wary at first, I decline almost instantly. I'm still a little sketched from my accident and absently rub my leg just thinking about it. However, I hear tons of support from everyone, except Brodie, urging me to "give it a red hot go." Before I know it, I'm situated up on the back of the bike, holding on for dear life.

My face crashes into Jordan's back as our speed adjusts to the terrain's demands. I hold on tight, squeezing his ribs, hopefully not too hard. He laughs, not seeming to mind too much, and revs the engine more, shifting gears. Not wanting to scratch my new sunnies, I left them behind in Brodie's ute. I'm wearing motocross goggles now, an extra pair Jordan had lying around. Good thing too, because it's like a mini sand storm out here as red dirt fills my vision. We slash through bush branches, slide out in the clay and avoid fallen rocks in our path. While I'm a bit nervous at times, I'm also attempting to let loose a bit. Feeling comfortable, I even take my hand off Jordan's torso and raise it up, enjoying the wind resistance surge through my fingertips. I glance behind us and see Brodie's white ute trailing us, not too far behind.

"This is amazing!" I yell over the roaring engine.

"It's fuckin' banga!" Jordan screams in agreement.

I feel his muscles tense as he commands the bike. Feeling a little cocky, he steers us up an embankment. The bike stalls out, barely making it. I latch on tightly again.

*Hold on a second, this feels sketchy...*

Just as the thought comes, we're back on the trail, and all is right.

*Phew.*

A minute or two passes. Jordan steers us towards another embankment, this one steeper and bigger. I tense, and before I can cry out "no" in fear, he zips us up the side. I scream as the bike's tires wobble and teeter towards the top as it turns back towards the path.

"Jordo, we're going to fall," I yell.

Feeling a bit helpless, I look back behind me, wishing I was seated cozy next to Mel or Jaz in the confines of the truck.

"Nah, we're fine," Jordan exclaims over the high pitch squeal of the engine.

As if he's trying to impress me, he does another trick and this time I almost fall off the back. *I'm not impressed!*

"Stop!" I scream, pleading. "Jordan, stop! I want off!"

He continues raging on. I glance back again at the trailing utes, trying to signal them, but I don't want to let go of my strong grip.

*Hold it together, Nina.*

We reach a hillside that overlooks a large ravine. Flashbacks of my car accident litter my mind: *hitting the side of the embankment, shivering in the cold, blood trickling down my face.*

*I need to get off now!*

I pinch my companion's torso, trying to get his attention. We harshly scrape through a bush and my arm starts burning. I can feel the air escaping out of my lungs. I'm on the brink of a panic attack.

"Jordan, enough!" I wail. "Please let me the fuck off!!"

I never say that word, in fact, I'm shocked to hear it slip out, but the circumstance warrants it I guess. I look back at Brodie's ute, and it pulls off the trail. Apparently Jordan notices too because he slows down and turns us around to see what's going on. *Hallelujah.*

Brodie parks and Donnie pulls up next to him in the silver ute. Jordan pulls right up to the back of Brodie's truck and as soon as the engine cuts out, I fling myself off, panting with adrenaline and shaking with fear. I rip off my helmet and goggles, and the rubber piece sticks to my tangled hair. I'm covered in chalk and look a little worse for wear, but I don't even care. Coughing, I step away, looking for relief and refuge.

Mel comes running back, followed by Brodie and the gang.

"Ya alright, Love?" she asks slowly, with worry, putting her arm around my shoulder.

I wince as she grazes a tender spot.

"She'll be right," Jordan says casually.

"When were ya gonna quit, ya dipstick?" Mel says, holding up my bleeding arm.

"Mate, I told ya to take it easy with her," Brodie shouts, looking from my bloody arm back to Jordan.

Margot and Jaz stand awkwardly in the middle, looking around at the commotion.

"I'm fine, really. Just got a little too dicey there for a second," I say, downplaying my feelings as my breathing returns to normal.

I don't want Jordan to feel bad. We were, after all, having a great time before things got out of hand.

"Did ya think about her accident?" Brodie asks Jordan.

I didn't think Jordan knew about it, but he drops his head, not wanting to meet Brodie's eyes. How could he know the extent of my wreck anyway?

"Brodie, I'm okay, really," I assure him, nudging him. I redirect my gaze towards Jordan and muster up the best smile I can make. "Really, I'm fine."

"Hey, why don't we go for a spin on the bike to shake things up?" Margot asks Brodie, coming up behind him.

Without looking at her, Brodie replies, "Yeah, nah, sorry Mar, but I reckon I'm not in the mood just now."

She looks at me with daggers. I hastily look anywhere else. Margot walks right up to Jordan and pulls his shirt.

"Fine," she declares, "Jordo, you can take me."

"Let's go," he agrees, perking up.

"Brotha, we should turn back towards camp," Jaz says, assessing my injured arm. "Nina's arm's bleedin' pretty good 'n needs to be cleaned, 'n honestly, I'm cooked."

Margot and Jordan mumble something in annoyance, saddle on the bike and whiz away. The rest of us climb back into our respective vehicles and make our way back to camp. It's about a thirty minute drive. As Reuben Fillies' "Sincerity" plays through the speakers, I sit up front, holding a towel wrapped around my forearm with Stella on my lap. Her head's out the window, in all her glory. Her ears flap down around her neck, and her crimped, shiny hair billows as it surfs the wind. Feeling better and in a more stable environment, my body relaxes and I close my eyes for a second, enjoying the music. Dozens of slobbery kisses pull me from my daze as I sit up a little straighter. Stella mops my face with her long tongue. She breaks away and resumes her stance out the window. I giggle at her as she maintains heavy focus on the road. Occasionally, she breaks away and glances back at us. Going with the wind, her hair blows back, covering her eyes and nose, emphasizing her scruffy face.

"This never gets old, does it?" I yell, laughing at her.

Brodie looks over and pauses for a minute, admiring his floppy pride and joy.

"Well, who's the bloody beauty, Stel?" he beams.

Jaz laughs in the backseat.

"Oy, can we get some volume back here?" Mel requests.

Brodie reaches over and turns the dial up just as the song changes to AC/DC's "Thunderstruck."

"Oh, no!" I playfully exclaim, hearing the high intensity guitar and shrieking vocals. "You don't like this song do you?"

Mustering up his dignity, Brodie chides, "I'll have ya know Accaddacca is one of the best rock bands of all time."

"I know, but so overplayed," I counter.

"Here we go," Mel mutters to Jaz.

"'*Here we go*,' what?" Jaz asks, confused.

"Nina is a music fiend," Mel informs the car. "Once she starts debatin' music, we could be here all arvo."

To prove her wrong, I decide to let it go. *For now.*

We ride for a little. The dried blood stiffens my arm, so as soon as we pull back up to camp, I jump straight into the swimming hole to wash off. Today

I was careful to wear a bathing suit underneath my clothes in case of another skinny dipping incident were to happen in broad daylight. Night offers way more forgiveness in that regard. While I inspect my arm, the others eat lunch. The road rash scratches really aren't bad. They'll heal up in no time. I've had worse. Jaz helps me pour some antiseptic on the area and I leave it to the fresh air to begin the healing process.

While we eat, some of the others prepare to go for a little hike around the rock clusters. Jaz and I scarf down our food so we can catch up with them. Just as we're all suited up with canteens in hand, Donnie comes racing from the ute, hollering in concern.

"What's wrong, D-Man?" Jaz asks, worrying.

"There's been an accident back home," Donnie pants.

Apparently he heard over the CB radio that Mel's dad got in a bad accident at work, and Jordan's dad has been involved as well. Mel, Margot and Jordan all decide to head back home now while there's still a lot of light left. Hugs go all around. I tell Mel we'll be on our way tomorrow after we break down camp, and we'll check in first thing when we regain cell signal. They each urge us to stay longer and make the most of the rest of the trip, especially considering the distance it took to get here. Packing up quickly, they take off in Donnie's ute.

I realize now we only have the two person tent and one ute to shelter us for the evening, and there's five of us sleeping here tonight. Thank heavens Jaz is still here. I'll share the ute with her. The boys can squeeze in the tent. It's decided then.

After a little hike, which was great strengthening exercise for my leg, we all gather back at camp and Brodie begins to make dinner. I ask him if I can chop anything, but looking at my scabbed arm, he shrugs the notion away.

Once the fish is ready, our chef serves us, and we eat in merriment, and some of us get a little too hammered. I only have one drink and one shot so I'm mostly sober... well maybe a little tipsy, but Jaz and Shayno keep slamming them back. As the night goes on, they keep getting more and more handsy and touchy feely towards one another. Brodie chooses to ignore them, while I can't help but laugh at them. Once the last piece of wood drops in the fire, turning into ash, Jaz and Shayno walk off hand in hand around the bush, stopping occasionally to make out and then drunkenly continue on. Donnie's passed out cold in his sleeping bag, propped up on the chair by the fire's glowing embers.

"Mozzies will eat him for tucker," Brodie whispers.

He walks up with a mosquito net and places it around Donnie's upper body, shielding him. Donnie doesn't even flinch or move a muscle. He's clearly in a deep sleep.

Little fits of laughter burst through the camp as Jaz and Shayno stumble through, clumsily trying to unzip the tent as they shower the other in kisses. One of them manages to open it, and they clamor in, falling on a pile of sleeping bags. They burst into a snort of giggle fits. A few minutes pass and slowly, the tent starts to shake back and forth. I look away, a bit scandalized, and yawn.

"I'm beat," I manage to squeeze out.

"I'm knacka'd myself," Brodie breathes, yawning too. Glancing briefly at the tent, he says quickly, "I'll arrange the Troopy. Be ready in two shakes."

He walks off and it dawns on me that Brodie and I will be sharing the trunk space of the ute. *Together.* Another couple of minutes pass, and as I hear Brodie's footsteps approaching, I also hear small grunts coming from the tent. Wanting to spare Brodie, I turn and make my way for the truck instead. Seeing me, he stalls and waits by the tailgate. Two sleeping bags lie flat, side by side. A lantern sits in between them. Pillows are fluffed, butted up against the front seats as the backseat lays flat under a blanket of coziness. Our canteens rest picturesquely next to our pillows.

*He sure thinks of everything.* I smile at the thought.

I place both hands on the trunk's tailgate, prepping to hoist myself up. I jump up, but not high enough, and slide back down. As I'm struggling to climb up the second time, Brodie extends a hand. I take it, pulling myself up with more ease, but crash land face first into the sleeping bags. I break out in a fit of laughter. While I'm face down, I kick off my boots. They fall to the dirt below.

"'Help me, I've fallen and I can't get up,'" I quote, in the midst of my hilarity.

I'm too tired to move, so I lie face down for a minute or two, letting my tired laughter bubble up and get the best of me.

"Gotta get ya a stool for the boot," Brodie says playfully.

Leaving my face smashed against the sleeping bag, I arrange my arms around my sides to lift up my body. Feeling like I'm moving in slow motion, I grunt as I lift my weight, but just plop over on my side and collapse again.

"Nice, Nina," Brodie snorts, somewhere behind me.

"They call me Grace," I reply sarcastically, stifling another laugh.

Crawling on my hands and knees, I haltingly and slowly move up to my side of the bed. Stella jumps up too, waiting for her designated space.

"Sorry, we're a package deal, I'm afraid," Brodie states, gesturing to her hairy face.

"Oh, I don't mind one bit," I smile at her. "I miss sleeping with my puppy, Cosmo. It'll make me sleep better knowing she's there."

I turn to take off my pants. He's already seen me in my undies, and I tend to be a hot sleeper. I just know I'll be up all night sweating if I wear these bottoms. And sleep comes first. I pull my sweatshirt off too, but keep my loose tank top on. I slide in-between my sleeping bag. My whole body relaxes as I let go of all the tension I didn't realize I've been carrying during the day. It's remarkable what the human body holds onto subconsciously. Brodie takes off his shirt, sleeping in just his boardies. He grabs the mosquito netting and pins it across the back of the open ute before lying down next to me. He adjusts himself in his sleeping bag too. Stella scratches on the soft, plaid fabric, nestling into her bed for the night. She plants herself in the small gap directly between our legs. I pull out my arms and hands, resting them on the fluffy sleeping bag. It's surprisingly quite comfy in here.

"Lights out?" he asks me.

"Yep," I answer. "Night."

He awkwardly strains his arm, trying to reach the bottom of the lantern, before finally finding the switch. It clicks off, and the florescent light instantly dies. Brodie shuffles a little before stilling, finding the sweet spot of comfort like his dog. I lay on my back and look out the ute's windows and see stars like never before.

"Ahh," I quietly gasp, perking up as the amazement brings a new wave of energy.

The sky feels enormous. Swirls of nebula and granulated colors join the tiny twinkling stars, composing a masterpiece for the ages. Astonished, I silently laugh in mirth. Brodie must feel the slight movements of my laughter because he turns towards me and points over my shoulder, putting his pointed hand directly in my line of sight.

"Look, there," he whispers towards my ear, and directs my eyes to a wondrous cluster of stars. They form a slanted pattern. "'N there," he informs me, slowly shifting his hand as he points to a bigger ball of light, "is Venus rising."

I let out a giant breath of excitement, like a soft chuckle.

"I can't believe my eyes. Literally, it's stunning. I've never seen anything quite like this," I say serenely, resting my head on the pillow, emitting blissful "mmhmms" every time I discover a new cluster.

I softly grab his hand in mine and guide it to another constellation I have my eye on.

"What's that one?" I whisper. "It's beautiful."

He shuffles closer and peers behind my head to line up his sight with his hand. The close proximity oddly feels really comfortable and familiar, but also makes me hyper aware of his handsome face just inches from mine.

"Ah, that's one of my favourites. It's the Southern Cross. It's hardly visible back home, but out woop woop," he pauses to clarify, "*out here* - towards the Northern Territory - offers one of the best 'n most visible views." His tone is full of admiration and appreciation. "It's the stars on our nation's flag, so it's rather special in a way."

"That's why it looks so familiar," I realize, nodding slightly. "And is that the Milky Way?"

I gesture to the looming swirl, and he nods. It's so peaceful. I shake my head a little, blown away. Abruptly, I yawn hugely. It must be pushing early morning. It's been a big day. Stretching, I murmur an "ouch" as I lean on my scabbed arm.

"How is it?" I hear him mumble in the dark.

"Fine. Honestly I forgot about it until right now," I answer, stifling another yawn.

Brodie leans back and adjusts himself again in his bed. I lean back myself and face the headliner of the ute. It's so quiet. No freeways, no loud engines, no jet stream. There's just pure outback, full of raw, rugged nature, and I absolutely love it. The only noises I occasionally hear are small croaks of lizards or frogs, a slight breeze through the bush, and some laughter coming from the nearby tent, followed by hushing snorts. I find myself succumbing to the oblivion of sleep.

"Brodie?" I ask aloud, almost in a whisper, half delirious. No answer. Maybe he's fallen asleep already. "Thanks for looking out for me today. Despite all that's happened, I'm glad you were there."

Maybe it's for the best he doesn't hear me, but a small part of me smiles knowing maybe we can be friends.

I drift off and allow sleep to take me to my dreams.

Morning light blares through the side window of the ute. Bright warm light shines through my closed lids. I stretch a little, moving my arms and spreading my legs around, and I realize where I am. My eyelids flicker open, adjusting to the brightness. Looking over to the sleeping bag next to me, I find it empty; it's just me. My sleeping companion must be up and at 'em already. Two days in a row; he's definitely an early bird then.

Somehow during my slumber, I kicked off the top layer of the sleeping bag, hanging a leg out. *Oh gosh! And I'm pant-less...* I sit up, and catch my reflection in the window; my hair stands on end, like a lopsided bird's nest. My shorts from yesterday sit on top of my backpack, and I grab them and my bikini, changing while I have a moment of privacy. Dressed, I jump out of the tailgate, landing softly. I roll up my sleeping bag and neatly pile my things in the corner. I don't want to be a burden for anyone, especially a certain someone. I hear small voices towards the bonfire area of camp and walk over. Brodie and Donnie are up and alert. Brodie mans the stove again, while Stella sits at his feet, patiently waiting for any morsel of food.

"Mornin', Sunshine," Brodie cheerfully greets me, grabbing his set of tongs that sit on the pop-up table.

He's so chipper in the morning, I note.

"Buenos días," I say back hoarsely, my voice dry and rough from sleep as I wipe crustees out of the corners of my eyes.

"Is that Spanish?" Donnie asks, half asleep himself.

"Claro que sí," I nod, chuckling. "Mi apellido es Esquivel. Mi gente es de México y por eso hablo español." Both mens' eyebrows shoot up not expecting that, so I further explain. "Irish mother, hence my whiteness."

"Cool," Donnie mutters, then adds with a raised eyebrow, "Chica."

As I laugh, Stella whimpers.

"Now, Stel, be a good girl," Brodie orders. "No whingin'."

She cocks her head in anticipation. I walk over to her and rub her head playfully. Her fur flops around, like a mop. I realize we have similar hair at the moment and laugh a little at that.

"Stel, you beauty, you," I coo. "Seems I'm not the only one with some bedhead around here."

Brodie quietly snorts and flips something in front of him. The lid of the stove stands open, blocking our tasty smelling brekky from sight.

"Wanna pikelet?" he asks me, then turns to Donnie, extending the question.

"A what?" I ask. "You know, I speak English and Spanish, and I still can't understand you Aussies half the time."

His arms move around behind the stove, and he places something round and slightly fluffy on a plate. He hands it to me, letting the pancake speak for itself. Smiling, I click my tongue in understanding.

"We say pancakes too," says Donnie, laughing.

"Oh, we do, eh?" I counter in my best Australian accent.

Brodie laughs and hands us each our pancakes covered in syrup and a little butter. It smells mouth watering good. I dive in as Jaz and Shayno unzip their tent and make their way to the table. Brodie glances at them, then back at the grill.

"Why if it isn't the lovebirds?" he jests, hassling them. "I knew the smell of bacon 'n pancakes would eventually draw ya out."

"Shut up, brotha," Jaz dishes back, wincing away from the bright morning light.

"Wait, there's bacon?" I ask a little too eagerly, and they all laugh.

Brodie grabs a nice, dark crunchy piece and extends it out to me, but before I can take it, he tosses it to Stella, who catches it midair.

"Sorry, my numba one calls first dibs, always," he sappily assures his puppy.

I shrug. Fair enough. As we eat, the five of us decide to start the route back home earlier than planned. Brodie suggests we stop at some places along the way to do a little sightseeing for me, the foreigner, AKA "the blow in." Plus, we can check in with Mel when we reach the nearest town. While I'm definitely anxious to hear how Mel's dad is doing, I'm also thinking, depending on how bad he is, who knows when the next time I'll be back here. So why not take our time getting back?

We pack up camp pretty quickly before it gets too hot, and the boys load the ute while Jaz and I cover the fire and pick up any stray trash. Always leave a place better than when you found it. The classic park mantra applies to all parts of the world. As the two of us conduct our little clean up, I learn Jaz is a marine biologist and works for a conservation group, being so close to Ningaloo Reef. She says she might have some droning work for me as they track the migratory patterns of whale sharks, amongst other species in the area.

Before piling into the ute, we all take one last good look around. Brodie drives, Donnie rides shotgun, while I sit directly behind the driver seat next to Jaz and Shayno. We drive for a while, making the occasional pit stop to stretch our legs, mainly mine. A few hours south, Brodie gets in touch with Jordan. The text is short, but bottom line is their dads are going to be okay. As we continue driving, a feeling of relief hovers in the air amidst the good news. Stella straddles the center console, leaning into the turns and twists of the road. The desolate, dry landscape of deep red earth slowly fills up with more bush as we make our way closer to the coast. My metaphoric gills must be flapping, because suddenly we see our familiar terrain of coastline again. The ocean is exquisitely crystal clear up here. Myriads of light glint off the surface, refracting into endless bright shapes, dancing along the sandy bottom.

We stop a few different times, the crew urging me to bust out the dronie and get some shots. On the third flight up with Khal, I see a hammerhead swimming swiftly near the surface and very close to shore. My eyes bulge with excitement.

"Shark!" I cry out. "'There's a shark in the pond!'"

The boys perk up as Jaz laughs. Brodie jogs over behind me and peers over my shoulder. I screech in delight and point to it on screen. I press record and video the creature as it moves with incredible sleekness. It looks prehistoric contrasting against the clear water along the shallows. Its dorsal fin slices through the water like a knife through liquid butter. Brodie looks back and forth between the screen and the ocean, searching for the shark's current position.

"Get this," Brodie yells. Pulling off his shirt, he runs off towards the shore in the direction of the shark. He yells back to the boys, "Come on, lads!" Stella follows him, barking at his heels until he jumps in. She tries to go in after him, but he yells at her to stop. "No, Stel, wait for Dad on the beach."

She obeys but keeps a watchful eye on him. He dunks under the surface. The guys follow Brodie, but not in due haste. They seem slightly more hesitant and wary than their eager friend. I look down at the screen and bring The Khal slightly closer, dropping it down to get a nice, clear shot. Donnie and Shayno wade knee deep in the shallows at apparently a depth they're more comfortable with. Brodie swims alongside the hammer from a respectful distance. It's massive. It's easily a few feet longer than him. Its giant dorsal fin sticks out a good two to three feet out of the water.

"He's crazy!" I shout aloud, completely baffled.

"He's been bloody fearless his whole life," Jaz exclaims, shaking her head, not the least bit surprised.

"Does he have a death wish?" I gasp. The shark turns towards Brodie, and advances a couple of feet closer to him. "Oh my gosh!"

I'm the one on land and my heart is about to beat out of my chest. *What must Brodie be thinking?*

Jaz puts her hand over her brows, scanning the beach for the commotion. Feeling spooked, the hammerhead suddenly pivots quickly away and swims at a much faster speed into deeper depths.

My heart rate normalizes as Brodie emerges. Standing in the shallows, he bellows at the top of his lungs on the empty beach. He releases some ear piercing screams and hollers as he slams his fists into the water. He comes running up to his pals, and gives them giant high fives, his muscles popping and pumping full of adrenaline. Clearly, he's amped on life. All of us on the beach yell out in shock, admiration and excitement. I land the drone and catch it in my hands.

"Did ya get that?!" Brodie advances towards me, clearly eager and hopeful that I did.

"You're nuts!" I yell, nodding. "For a second there I thought you were gonna be his dinner!"

"Me too!" he laughs, bursting with joy. "Aw, man, this is the life. This is living, folks."

He leans over Stella and shakes his head like a dog, letting the tiny rivulets of water splash her in the face. He then rubs down his head, squeezing the water out of his curls through his fingers.

After all that excitement on the beach, everyone rides in cheerful spirits for the duration of the drive home. Close to a bigger town, we turn on the radio and Elton John's "Tiny Dancer" captures our attention. Donnie leans forward and turns the dial to the right. No one sings at first, but I can't help myself. We catch the song at the very beginning - a rare treat. The beginning melody is my favorite part.

I start singing, at first a little softly, "*Blue jean baby... L.A. lady, seamstress for the band.*"

They all smile and laugh, bobbing their heads to the catchy tune.

"*Pretty eyes... pirate smile... yull marry the music man,*" Shayno chimes in.

"Ooh, Shayno!" cries Donnie, impressed at his participation.

Brodie jumps in loudly, "*Ballerina, ya musta seen her... dancin' in the sand.*"

This next line, I pipe up, projecting loudly, well more loudly than normal, "*And now she's in me... always with me... tiny dancer in my hand.*"

Jaz and Donnie take turns for the next couple of lines, each of us laughing, wondering who will take the next one. Spirits in the ute are skyrocketing as the chorus approaches. I'm having full flashbacks to *Almost Famous*, when we all erupt, "*Hold me closer, tiny dancer!*"

"I love this song!" Donnie shouts.

Laughing, I stick my head out the window. I can see Brodie in his side mirror, looking back at me, beaming. The fever of Elton John catches on quick. We all bellow the rest of the song at the top of our lungs, giggling and hollering nonsense as it winds down. I snap some pictures and take some videos - Brodie smiling in the side mirror, Stella looking back from Donnie's lap, Shayno looking like he's about to explode as he cranes his head back to the roof of the car, while Jaz laughs her head off beside him. By this point in the day, the sun begins to droop. Beautiful flares of orange and yellow tint the ambiance of the car and everything in it. Jaz grabs my camera and captures a quick still of me. My hair flies everywhere around my face. Small squiggles of curls dance in the light around my new sunnies. Brodie announces we're all going out on the boat next weekend to swim, dive, and spearfish. We all roar in cheerful, contagious agreement.

Dropping Donnie and Shayno off at their place, Brodie, Jaz and I drive the last hour towards home. I call Mick and let him know I'll be home soon.

"I'll drop ya first," Brodie says to Jaz, who nods.

"Oh, you can drop me first that way you don't have to circle back," I offer, trying to make it easier for everyone.

"No need," Jaz informs me, "I'm on the way to Brodie's."

*Oh, so they don't live together then.* Does he live alone?

About twenty minutes outside of town, Brodie pulls off the highway onto a dirt road. As we ride the stretch, Jaz leans over the seat and gathers her things. We pull up to the front of a modest looking single story home. It's pretty isolated, but right on the beach. Brodie kills the engine and hops out. Opening the tailgate, he gathers Jaz's luggage, sleeping bag and chair. He hauls it all off to the shed on her behalf, while she rummages in the front seat, looking for her phone. She finds it, holding it up in triumph, and jumps out. Brodie comes back and rearranges the trunk.

"Neens, why don't ya come in real quick, 'n meet the 'rents," he urges.

"Really?" I ask, looking down at myself; I'm a mess and not very presentable.

"Ya look great, Neens, not to worry, eh," Brodie assures me.

Shrugging, I exit the ute and walk around towards the front deck. Brodie's parents have already made their way outside towards us. They give Jaz and Brodie each big squeezes, full of smiles and hearty laughter.

"How was the trip?" Brodie's dad inquires genially.

"Wondaful," Brodie exclaims.

"He swam with a big hamma earlier today, so ya know, good day for brotha," Jaz jumps in.

His parents nod, beaming. Again, they aren't shocked at this revelation.

"Was she a pearla?" his dad asks, full of excitement.

"Ya shoulda seen her, Old Boy, at least three metres," Brodie exclaims, gesticulating.

I smile shyly off to the side of this happy family reunion. Seeing them all close with one another reminds me of home and my family and how much I wish I could give them a hug. Brodie looks over at me, and catches my eye with a giant smile on his face. He remembers I'm here and waves me over to them.

"This, Mum 'n Old Boy, is Nina," he introduces us kindly.

"Hi, there," I say, smiling, and give a little wave.

Their mom walks over and envelopes me in a big, warm hug.

"Hi, Nina, I'm Sue, 'n that's Jim, otherwise known as Mum 'n Old Boy," she says, nodding to her husband as she pulls away.

"G'day, Nina," Jim grins.

"It's so nice to meet you," I say sweetly and genuinely.

Sue stands tall, a few inches over me, her light, gray hair flying in tendrils around her face. She's no fuss, no frills. Old Boy has a thick, full head of hair. His hair is surprisingly dark for a man of at least sixty; only speckles of white spin through his curls.

*So that's where Brodie gets his curls from.*

"Ya wanna come in 'n have a bevvie?" Old Boy asks us.

I'm about to politely refuse, when Brodie interjects, "Ah, wish we could Old Boy, but Nina needs to get back. Old Man Mick's up waitin' for her."

"Oh, so yar the blow in staying with Mick," Old Boy says, the news dawning on him.

"Yep, that's me. Raincheck on the drinks. It sounds lovely, but I don't want to keep Mick waiting all night," I say truthfully. "He's too old for that and needs his sleep."

"That's sweet," Sue mutters, smiling.

"I'm buggered. Alrighty then, we're off," Brodie yawns, clasping Old Boy's shoulder with his hand, then a quick hug to Sue, who both turn and smile at me.

"Lovely to meet ya, Nina," Sue hollers.

"You too," I agree with a grin.

"See ya, Nina. Brotha!" Jaz shouts, as we get in the ute.

Brodie waves and smiles as he starts the car.

Almost out of earshot, I hear Jaz say, "I know, she's great, right?"

Smiling to myself, I buckle my seatbelt and we take off down the highway.

Mick has been exceptionally attentive and present the last few days since my return. He must have really missed me when I was away. I hate to think of me leaving back *home* home and him here all by himself, but I push the thought away quickly.

"Here ya go, Sweetheart," he says affectionately, setting down my plate in front of me, full of biscuits and gravy.

"Yum," I exclaim, my mouth watering.

As soon as he sits down, I spear a biscuit with my fork and push it around, trying to absorb as much gravy as possible. I close my eyes for a second. Mick's biscuits and gravy are definitely up there on my list of favorite foods. They're never dry, and the gravy flavor is out of this world tasty. As I eat in delightful bliss, he asks all about the trip. I recount Brodie's hammerhead encounter for the fifth time since I've been back. I'm sure to leave out the dirt bike story. In fact, I've been wearing Mick's long flannel so he can't see the healing scab on my arm.

"I feel like I'm finally meeting people and making some friends," I declare, finishing my last bite, wiping some gravy and crumbs from the corners of my mouth. "Brodie invited us all out on his boat on Saturday."

"That's terrific, Sheila," Mick agrees, and takes a swig of his orange juice. He chuckles and winks at me. "Hopefully it goes betta than the last time."

The clock seems to stop every time I glance at it. It's only Wednesday. I'm literally counting down the minutes until the weekend. Everyone's busy, working their various jobs. Even Brodie, who's schedule is flexible, is full this week. Not so busy myself, I walk around town at lunchtime, trying to drum up work. Luckily, last week I firmed up another local girl's spur of the moment wedding. Oddly it's a weekday wedding, which is actually kind of great; my weekend schedule seems to be filling up quickly these days. Best part is it's this Friday, so in two days.

On Mick's recommendation, I stop in at the local real estate office to see if any photography or aerials are needed, and meet the agent in charge, Mr. Fairchild, who works with Jordan. We get to talking, and he's in dire need of some drone work for some listings. He normally has to pay an aerial photographer to come all the way from Perth, and foot the bill for them to stay in a nearby motel, so he is more than happy I'm local. He states the price and his budget, which happens to be substantially more than what I would have quoted him. We coordinate a test shoot for tomorrow.

Thrilled, I leave the office with some newfound hope. I can finally start paying Mick back for real and maybe even save a little for all these fun outings so I can start contributing more. I feel like a giant mooch and it's not who I'm comfortable being. My hospital bills are never far from my mind, even with the GoFund Me money covering a big chunk of the deductible amount. I just received an email from the travel insurance's company saying they are processing my claim, so that's some news. At least it's heading in the right direction.

I drive back to Mick's and tell him the good news about my new business relationship. He's over the moon, saying he knew I'd find something. We put on *Jeopardy!* while we have dinner. I take a stab at each question, answering a substantial amount of guesses not even in the ballpark. Tonight, I manage to get a fifth of them right, while Mick gets more than half.

Sitting at Lotte's after my recent real estate drone trial, I finish editing the photos and email the link to Mr. Fairchild. All goes smoothly, and he's super happy with the finished images. He stops by Lotte's and pays me in cash. He's so pleased with the experience, he pays me upfront and sends me back out to drone another three listings in the neighboring "town," well more like scattered properties on the outskirts.

I race back home and tell Mick, who offers to come along with me to keep me company. I know it's also because he wants to make sure I arrive at the correct destinations.

"Some of these locations can be a bit... remote, Sheila," he warns, grabbing the keys.

After these past few months, I don't doubt him.

With my pockets feeling figuratively heavier with coin, I wake up today feeling great, full of creative confidence. Today is my first full wedding since the accident. I can't lie, I'm a little nervous.

People don't realize how much physical work goes into photographing and shooting a wedding. One, it's an all day affair, and two, you have to be on your A-game the *entire* time. I'm mostly worried about my leg. True, it's been feeling infinitely better these past couple of months, but for a wedding, the photographer is constantly squatting. Trying to scale the weight down, I keep my camera kit basic. Thankfully, I always shoot in natural light, even at night, hence my gnarlier, capable camera with high ISO settings, so I won't have a big flash to cart around on top of everything else.

Gearing up, I wear my token dress - a white tunic with embroidered florals along the hems in beautifully vibrant colored threads. It has characteristics of a huipil, but is slightly more modern and billowy. I pair it with my newer boots from Mel; the combo looks cute while functional as well. I loosely braid my hair back and roll it up into a casual cute messy bun. I can't have any stray frizz obstructing a shot or distracting me, and sadly I don't have Ria around to straighten it for me. My outfit is slightly too casual for fitting in as a guest, at least by American standards, and is not totally work professional being a shorter dress, but it's all I have.

Mick drops me off an hour before the ceremony starts and I walk around the grounds, getting a lay of the land. It's going to be a small wedding, with only twenty guests, which makes my life all the easier. I meet up with the bride, Millie, as she gets ready, finishing the last of her hair before adorning her white dress. I immediately start snapping away with my camera. Thirty minutes go by like they were one. Millie's mom runs around reminding everyone that the ceremony is about to start. The last guests come trickling in. I'm very surprised to see Jordan burst through the open patio walkway, straightening his collar. He almost bumps into me as I stand in position, waiting for the bridal party to make their way down the aisle. I admit it's nice to see a familiar face. It usually brightens up a long day like this. There's something shared in a long joint experience, especially a wedding.

"G'day, Nina," he exclaims in surprise, realizing it's me.

"Hey," I whisper, smiling. "Better find your seat. It's about to begin."

He nods and runs to his chair.

The rest of the day goes well and smoothly. It helps when the couple is very adorable and extremely happy like Millie and her new husband. By the time we reach the intimate reception, we all act like we've known each other for years.

Out of the corner of my eye, I note Jordan watching me work and I find the attention slightly disconcerting. I'm totally one of those people who doesn't like anyone to watch them during the creative process. Trying to be friendly, I smile at him when I catch his eye, but I also have a job to do. No distractions or I might miss a kiss or something crucial. A moment's break comes and I tuck myself away in a small alcove around the corner from the reception area. I glance at the clock. Two hours left. Mick's picking me up out front at 10PM on the dot. While people say I have a knack for this line of work, I don't necessarily enjoy it. I see it for what it is - a job. Don't get me wrong, I'm very thankful to have work again, but I'm out of practice, and I forgot how intense it is in the moment... all the responsibility.

Jordan takes this opportunity to come over and greet me.

"Nina, ya must be cooked," he surmises.

"Yeah, you could say that again," I reply, sighing into a laugh.

"Here," he confidently says, walking behind me and placing his hands on my upper back and neck.

Kind of taken aback at his forthrightness, I stifle my emerging protest as he pushes down on my skin with the balls of his thumbs, releasing tension, and gently massages my shoulders and neck. Thanking the heavens the alcove is hidden behind a barrier, I can't help but let out a small moan. *This feels amazing.* I better step away now or I'll never want to leave. *It feels so good though.* One of the cater waiters walks by, turning his head towards us, and raises an eyebrow in question. Catching this, I pull away, shaking off the terrific feeling. *Back to work.*

Another hour into the reception and I've documented everything I can think of: all customs and traditions captured, all dances, rituals, and toasts. Especially with smaller weddings, unless something unexpectedly happens, there's only so much you can photograph without repeating yourself. It's 9:07PM at night and the guests are a bit hammered so they all sway and dance obnoxiously on the dance floor. I hold up my camera, peer through the viewfinder, and pretend to take pictures for the guests' and clients' sake. It might sound awful, but it'll save me hours of having to sort through today's thousands of photos, and no one's the wiser. Besides I already have about two hundred dancing shots logged in my memory card.

Finally, guests start to depart and the party winds down for good. I look at the clock and it reads 9:38PM. Having been paid, I walk out to the front of the venue, smiling with pleasure that I survived a whole day up and down on my leg. While it's starting to throb, it held up way longer than I anticipated. Most of the remaining guests depart to their cars and smile goodnight to me as I stand, waiting for Mick. I take out the envelope and count my earnings. Not bad, I muse. I keep counting. *Wow!* They gave me a more than generous tip. Hearing footsteps behind me, I stash the envelope back in my backpack and turn to find Jordan advancing towards me.

"Lovely day, wasn't it?" I say rhetorically.

I glance down the road, hoping headlights will appear. Even if Mick's early, he still won't be here for a few minutes. The wedding cut about twenty minutes shorter than they originally said.

Jordan looks around the car port and back at me.

"Need a lift?" he asks casually, maybe with a hint of hopefulness.

"No, thanks so much though," I reply, shaking my head. "My ride should be here any minute."

He looks a little disappointed. He walks up close behind me and removes my backpack in one swift motion. Before I can resist, his hands are back on my shoulders as he begins to massage me again. I sway a little on my feet as the evasive touch of his fingers traces the side of my neck down to my shoulder. Little chills travel up my spine; it tickles. He grips my shoulders and strongly massages them as he pulls me around. Like a rag doll, my muscles go limp. I want to stop him, but I can't help it. After over ten hours of holding my rig and standing all day, I just go with it. The devil may care, but I don't.

"So I heard yar dronin' for Gary, Mr. Fairchild," Jordan mutters, putting more pressure on my shoulder blades. A muffled groan escapes me, but this time there's no one around to eavesdrop. Jordan laughs. "Ya know, I've heaps of work ya can do for me. Give me yar numba, 'n we can work somethin' out."

Slowly he moves lower, working his way down towards my lower back. When his momentum starts to reach my tailbone, I stiffen slightly at the intimate proximity. *You can work your way back up now, Jordo.*

"Relax, Nina," he whispers, feeling me tense.

His soft voice on my neck makes me shiver. I inhale sharply in surprise when he grazes my tailbone and moves lower. My eyes pop open. The spell breaks. *Okay, buddy, that's a little too far.* To my relief, he moves back up to my shoulders, but his hands slide under the hem of my neckline, stroking skin on skin across my trap. Slowly, he moves over, and slyly slides my bra strap down my shoulder. *Hold up.* I'm trying to figure a way out of this nicely and passively when headlights appear. From the engine sound alone, I know it's Mick.

"Thanks so much for the uh... massage. See ya later!" I holler as I jump up, adjust my strap, grab my backpack, and run towards the truck. "Oh, and I'll be in touch. I could really use the work."

Jordan stands on the curb, looking a little speechless.

Mick gets out, opens the door for me, and gives Jordan a quick assessment. I jump in and he closes the door behind me in true gentlemanly fashion. I politely wave goodbye to Jordan, and we take off down the road.

"Thank you, perfect timing," I mutter in relief to Mick.

"Yar way too good for him, Sheila."

"Do you even know who that is?"

"Doesn't matta," Mick shrugs. "Whoeva he is, he's neva gonna be good enough for ya."

I lean over and grab Mick's hand and squeeze it three times.

# 11

Finally, it's Saturday and the crew's back at it again. Brodie offers to pick me up, being we're neighbors and all. Physically sore from yesterday's wedding, I drag myself out of my comfy bed, waiting until the last minute. Mick hollers that Brodie's just pulled up to the house. Scrambling to gather my charged drone batteries and backpack, I reach for my toothbrush, brush away my morning breath, and head towards the bathroom. After, I stand in the open front doorway as I grab and pull on my sandals rather clumsily. I lose my balance and almost face plant out the deck, letting out a little shriek. Mick and Brodie casually glance at me.

"I'm alright," I holler. "Be there in a second!"

When I stumble out of the house, still half asleep, I see Mick leaning on Brodie's passenger door as they exchange pleasantries. My new sunnies help my eyes adjust immediately to the bright light, and the best part is they mask the dark bags under my eyes. Bumbling down the little walkway with my tank top in hand, my denim shorts unbuttoned over my suit, and my frizzy hair seriously disheveled, I hear Brodie chuckle.

"Mornin', Sunshine, or should I say Sleepyhead?" he jokes through the open window.

I roll my eyes and clamor into the passenger seat as Mick holds open the door for me, per usual. He grabs my backpack and hands it to me gently through the window.

"I'll have her back not too late, Mick, dun worry," Brodie emphasizes.

"If anythin' changes, just call," Mick nods approvingly. "I'll be here all night." He softly, yet thoroughly, closes the door tight. He leans in and whispers encouragingly, "Have fun. I'll be seein' ya, Sweetheart."

"See ya later, Old Man," I hoarsely mumble, mid yawn, giving him a wink and he laughs. As we start to pull away down the long driveway, I lean out. "Don't miss me too much!"

Mick heads towards the house as we make our way down to the highway. Listening to the hushed, mellow tones of Joshua Radin's *Rock and the Tide* album, Brodie and I ride for about ten to fifteen minutes until we pull up to the launching ramp.

"Remember the last time we were here?" I remind Brodie, laughing.

"Geezus," he gasps, twisting his body around to get eyes on the trailer as he reverses into the water. "Don't remind me or I might ditch ya right here n' now."

He laughs as I playfully punch his arm. Today he wears black boardies, a loose white t-shirt, a black baseball cap, and his usual sunglasses. As he skillfully positions the trailer, I watch as his toned arm muscles flex. His neck muscles tense as he maneuvers the steering wheel, aligning the trailer in the right angle. I'm realizing, it's a lot harder than it looks. Before submerging the ute too deep in the water, Brodie motions for me to hop out. He jumps out too and unlocks the trailer's locking mechanism. As I get out, Stella follows me then lifts her head, alerting me to a new arrival. I turn to see Donnie and Margot pull up. They park and get out, and walk towards us.

"Day for it, Chica," Donnie says nicely, winking at me.

"Morning, Donnie," I reply, smiling to him first, then at Margot.

She avoids direct eye contact with me, and folds her arms as she stands tall, dwarfing me yet again. After a moment, she smiles politely with a touch of coolness. She eyes Brodie and runs towards the trailer, offering help.

"Yeah, nah, I reckon I've got it," he tells her.

A minute later, when the boat is fully submerged and floating, he steers the boat back, guiding it over towards the dock and leaps out, tying it off on the cleats. Working overtime, he then runs to the ute and drives the trailer forward, parking it up the road a little, next to Donnie's car. He locks it and then trots his way back to us. Stella and I advance towards the boat as Donnie climbs aboard, carrying a slab under his arm. Boy do these Aussies enjoy their beer. We walk along the dock casually and once we're next to the vessel, Stella leaps over the edge like a polo pony and lands on the cushy, vinyl seat.

Remembering the last time I so eloquently "hopped" in, my leg swelled up for days. As I hesitantly assess my best entry point, Margot jogs up beside me, illustrating her gracefulness and athleticism - something I clearly lack. With her long giraffe-like limbs, she bounces over in a heartbeat, looking like a cat landing light as a feather after a twenty foot drop. I look down in front of me at the chrome railing. This is as good a place as any to swing my leg over. I'm about to climb over, when Brodie appears at my side, reaches over and grabs my hand, anchoring my weight as I stretch my short legs over the rail. I land on my feet rather fluidly. He vaults over the edge with ease and familiarity after me.

"Much better," I mumble more to myself, then look at him. "Thanks."

"Don't mention it," he replies nicely, taking my backpack from me and stowing it in a white cabinet by the open cockpit. "It'll be nice 'n safe in there 'til yar ready to use it."

I settle myself on the white bench seat and relax.

"God, where are they?" Margot asks impatiently, glancing at her phone. "I reckon we go without 'em."

"Being as how I'm the cap'n, 'n we're waitin' on my sista 'n half the crew, we're not goin' anywhere just yet," Brodie counters, more firmly.

That puts an end to it. Bruised, Margot sneers at his chastising tone and twirls her back to him, giving him the cold shoulder. Abruptly, she stands and huffs, climbing into the small hidey-hole cabin located between the two pilot chairs.

Brodie checks the sun then scans the shore, searching for a sign of a car. Despite his comment, he seems a little antsy to get going as well. A purring engine sound materializes as Nigel comes careening around the bend and parks. Mel, Jaz, and Shayno get out. Mel runs towards the boat with a cold bag of food in her arms. Shayno and Jaz walk a tad slower, smiling at one another in conversation. Mel hops on board, hands Brodie the bag, and crashes down next to me, jostling me as the seat expands under her added weight.

"Hey, Neens," she exhales happily, pulling me into a giant hug.

"Hey, back," I reply. "Mel, I'm so relieved your dad is alright."

"I know, me too," she explains. "Aside from a few bruises 'n a couple of ribs outta socket, he's on the mend now."

"I wasn't sure if you'd come today with all that going on."

"Bulldust, he's fine," she waives off my concern, "'n besides, Mum's there."

"Well, I'm glad," I say kindly, "And Jordo's dad?"

"He's good, it was a complete misunderstandin'. He was neva injured, thank God."

"Speaking of Jordo, where is he?" I ask, looking around towards the dirt road, hoping he's not joining us.

After the whole tailbone rubdown, I'm not totally sure how to act around him. He seems way more experienced, but then again pretty much everyone is more experienced than me.

"He's gonna meet up with us in a bit," Mel informs me.

I sigh in relief and she catches it. I hope she doesn't think it's out of longing or disappointment.

Brodie opens and closes all the little doors, securing the cabinets. Margot sulks alone in the hidey-hole, and Shayno, Jaz, and Donnie sit opposite Mel and me. Donnie sees the hole from the speargun accident in the back cushion and asks about it. Blush swells inside my cheeks as I glance from the visible mark to Brodie, waiting for him to tell the group the awful and embarrassing story. Biting his lip, he stifles a big smile.

"Accident, mate," he merely states. He catches my eye for a fraction of a second and raises his eyebrows playfully before I look away, relieved he kept our story in confidence. Stella assumes the co-captain seat next to him. He walks past us for a second, double checking the bungee strap on the esky before heading back to take the helm. He fires the engine and rubs his palms together in happy anticipation. "Alrighty then."

He reverses the boat away from the dock and directs the steering wheel towards the open ocean. We ride for a few minutes. The sandy bottom slips slowly away under the bow as we make our way into deeper depths. As the boat gains more momentum, I stand and wobble over to Brodie. Trying not to lose my balance, I grasp his chair, pulling myself behind him.

"Before we really get going, can we turn on some tunes?" I yell boisterously over the wind, water, and noisy engine.

Grinning, he tilts his head towards me, while keeping his eyes forward facing, and hollers out of the corner of his mouth, "Whaddaya want?"

"Iration's brand new album *Coastin',*" I reply loudly in his ear. "It's bomb. Start from the top."

Instead of putting it on, he just hands me his phone hooked up to the stereo and I unplug it, replacing it with mine. I scroll to the top of my library and click on the album artwork. The title track starts to play, but we definitely need it louder. I reach over Brodie's shoulder and ask him if I can turn it up with a look. He nods and I crank the dial far to the right. While Brodie glances at me, chuckling, I happily bob my head up and down to the much improved volume. We hit a bigger wave and land with a heavier *thud* and I lose my balance. I reach for anything so I don't fall, and grab onto Brodie's shoulder, gripping hard as we push through this rough patch. As it smooths, I release my iron grip and slowly return to my seat by Mel.

I can hear the music with greater clarity now that the sea seems calmer. The idyllic album is the perfect trip companion. Brodie keeps turning around, smiling at me as we listen to the first few songs, nodding his head to the keyboards. "Daylight Saving" comes on, one of my favorites so far, and everyone on board starts grooving to its catchy cadence. Brodie seems particularly into this one. I am too because I love its more traditional reggae vibe with the amazing timbales and keyboard rhythms. I sing aloud at the top of my lungs, enjoying the flow of this adventurous record as we journey out to sea.

Our captain really picks up the pace, pushing the knots higher as we speed along. I can feel the force of the knots pulling my body backwards. Those of us sitting can't help but lean back into the person directly next to us. Luckily Mel's beside me and we have the whole bench to ourselves so we can spread out more than the others. One of the best parts about having a little extra room is I can keep my hair down to experience complete liberation and lightness. Normally, whoever sits behind me eats my long curls as they blow back off my face. I close my eyes, absorbing the feeling of mist lightly greeting my skin, my wind blown hair, and the eager anticipation of endless direction. I let out a yell in elation, and the rest of the crew chimes in. Brodie glances back, smiling ear to ear.

The boat surges on for a good fifty kilometers before Brodie lowers the engine's speed and we begin to slow down. The rocking picks up a little as the boat comes to a slow float, swelling with the tide like a buoy. We're out in the middle of the ocean or what feels like it. The thought of land is just a blurry mirage no longer on the horizon. Lighter hues of aqua and turquoise emerge around *Salty Stel*. We all notice we're hovering over a shallower depth. Sandy rivets become clearer as the bottom is only about thirty feet down. The boat glides over a shallower reef before Brodie kills the engine.

I lean over the chrome railing and see a giant sandbar in front of us. Naturally, the boat spins as it floats without being anchored. Coming half circle, I see the unique view in front of me. A large white sandbar sits before us out of the literal blue. On one side, the shallow sandbar radiates shades of gold as it butts up to the dark open ocean where the depth drastically drops. On the other side, the sandbar's edge cascades more gradually as bommies, or giant circles of reef, scatter the ocean floor. The water's so clear, it looks like you could reach out and grab a fistful of sand at the bottom. In fact I do reach out a little to dip my hand.

"I can't get over how clear it is," I echo my thoughts.

"Ten metres like it was two. Bloody beautiful," Brodie joyfully remarks, standing and peering over the rail, admiring the water visibility, "vis." He walks over towards the rear of the boat, and stands next to the twin engines. Donnie and Shayno plank him. The three of them suss out the world below like doctors surveying a surgical patient. Brodie says, out of the corner of his mouth, "Whaddaya boys reckon?"

They all smile at each other before exclaiming in total unison, "Day for it!"

Brodie walks past us, and climbs up on the gunwale. The threshold is only about six inches wide. Holding onto the roof shade, he shuffles sideways as he skillfully maneuvers to the bow of the boat, barefoot. The bow opens up to a nice, flat laying area, the perfect spot for sunbathing. I haven't made my way over there yet, as it requires a shimmying, side step dance along the fringe line of the rail. Brodie opens a compartment and lowers the anchor. Small vibrations from the little mechanism sound off from the bow.

The boat starts rocking slightly as all the bodies onboard busy themselves stripping off clothes, finding hats, and sunscreening each other's backs and shoulders. Stella paces around, wanting to be involved in any and all activities. Today under my boating clothes, I wear my cute green and white daisy one-piece suit. It's slightly lower cut in the chest, but actually lifts the "girls" nicely. It's made out of thicker, water cloth material so it hugs everything in the right places, while hopefully keeping everything secure. I'd hate to slip a nip out here. Just as I'm about to undress, Brodie walks up behind me.

"Neens, do ya think ya can take the dronie up real quick? Suss out the fishies 'n our conditions?" he asks over my shoulder. I can feel and hear his smile as he tries to butter me up. "I hate to ask, but I've neva had a remote pilot on board before."

"Sure thing, cap'n," I nod, replying lightly in a shrug.

He smirks in response as I unzip my backpack. Happy to launch The Khal, I feel a touch of relief at the idea of prolonging something that's bound to be out of my comfort zone. I mean the first night I ever hung out with this crew they all skinny dipped like it was a casual Taco Tuesday. I've been a little worried about this trip. Don't get me wrong, I've been eagerly awaiting it, counting down the days even, but I also worry about Brodie and the gang pushing me past my limits. *There ain't no pansies in this crew.* I bite my lip, and decide to focus on the present task at hand, prepping The Khal for lift off. I double check my status and see all systems are a go. Tilting my head up for my departure scan, I realize a little too late that the roof shade inhibits my options for a clear takeoff. The opening by the swim deck is chock full of the crew changing into their dive suits and putting on their fins. I scan the boat and deem the bow is the best spot at present. I'm a little nervous, not about the lift off, but about the eventual landing.

After scanning through endless forums and tips for droning off a boat, I learned you normally don't lift off from the front in case the boat glides forward into the drone before it has a chance to get up in the air. Or if there's wind, you don't want to launch the drone, only to have it blow back directly into you or the vessel. I either have to launch from the back swim step, lean out over the side - but I don't think my arms are long enough for that - or lift from the bow. The back has lots of bodies so I won't have adequate clearance. I glance back at the empty bow. It's so wide and open. I look around and judge the air. It's very calm and still at the moment. My hair doesn't even lightly sway around my face. I make the call and decide bow it is. But how do I get there carrying all this stuff?

"Whatchya thinkin', Neens?" Mel asks, watching my face.

She has a pool of sunscreen in both palms of her hands, as she's smack dab in the middle of her application.

"I'm trying to figure out the best way to get up there..." I mutter, gesturing to the bow with my chin.

"Oy," Mel bellows to Brodie, "Neens needs help. She's worried about fallin' ovaboard with the dronie in hand."

I roll my eyes at her, but I guess that's the gist of it.

Brodie walks up and clicks his tongue, thinking. He purses his lips slightly.

"I'm just worried with my leg I won't be able to catch my balance if I fall," I explain.

"Why don't ya give it a red hot go 'n see what happens first," he replies encouragingly, gesturing to the railing. Not wanting to lose my drone so soon into the trip, I make a dismal face. He watches me. "Go on, I'll be here in case, 'n if yar that worried, I'll hold the dronie for ya."

I walk over to the railing, and hand Brodie the drone and controller. Not feeling as dexterous nor as confident as he, I reach up and pull myself up onto the gunwale. I plant my bare feet soundly on the gritty barrier that mirrors the chrome railing along the upper perimeter. He hands me the controller, and tries to hand me the drone, but I shake my head vehemently. *Baby steps, Nina*. Slowly at first, I sidestep, carefully positioning my feet so I don't stumble. I skirt along the cockpit until I reach the bow and jump down, wobbling a bit as I regain my balance as I land on the slightly rocking, slippery surface. Happy I didn't fall overboard with my controller, I spin around, grinning. Brodie walks up to the cockpit and extends my drone to me over the glass windshield.

"See, no biggie," he says casually.

"I think it's safe to say The Khal might be swimming right now if I tried that no handed," I tell Brodie. "But thanks."

Now the rest should be a piece of cake, assuming a gust of wind doesn't invade my calm surroundings right this second. I reach over, start The Khal and his props whirl quickly to life like a fan, shooting a micro current of wind in my face. Just as quickly as it fires up, it's already flying up through the air. *One part down, one to go.*

"Well that went better than I thought it would," I exclaim proudly, feeling relieved, while keeping the drone in my line of sight. "First boat launch is a success!"

Brodie eyes me with surprise.

"Wait, but ya seemed so calm," he says, then the realization dawns on him. He says loudly in an accusatory tone, "Ya mean to tell me the dronie coulda what? Flew into my boat?!"

"Brodie! Ya gotta get in already, mate," Donnie yells from the water.

Brodie ignores him, while I stifle a giggle.

"Well, that was a possibility…" I respond to his accusation, then playfully exaggerate, "and I do still have to land it, so…" I fall forward, laughing as his face drops, then I straighten up. "No really, I didn't even think about it. I knew it would be fine. And it will be, assuming the wind stays away, but I'm not super worried about it."

"I guess I'll just have to trust ya then," he scoffs playfully.

I focus on the display screen to observe the camera's perspective. It's early morning so the sun isn't too bright yet, minimizing the glare. A bird's eye view never ever gets old. It's breathtaking to see such a different outlook that I don't think I'd ever get to experience unless I was flying in a jumper plane. I "ooh" and "ahh" as I maneuver the drone around the sandbar. The water vis is next level, allowing me to make out great detail even from the display monitor. Interest peaked from hearing the sounds escaping my lips, Brodie joins me, hovering over my shoulder.

"It just neva gets old, does it?" he exclaims, mirroring my thoughts as he shakes his head in awe, smiling.

"I was literally just thinking the same thing. I think the only thing that could be better would be to be in a chopper or something," I say dreamily. "Now *that* would be crazy amazing."

Mel jumps over from the railing, and planks my other side. She leans down, spewing off positive remarks at the framed imagery. Donnie and Shayno swim over below us, wondering why we haven't jumped in and joined them already.

"Sorry, lads, Neens took the dronie up," Mel informs them.

They nod and tread lightly near the hull, looking up, trying to find it in the vast sky.

The Khal is up relatively high, about one hundred meters, when I notice a darker hue entering the frame. Being a photographer, my eyes are insanely attuned to color variations. The moment colors change or differ from their surrounding tones, my eyes dart directly to it, allowing me to pick up on movements in a fraction of a second, especially from the air. I start to descend to get a closer look at this large shape.

"Look here," I shout, pointing to the section on the monitor, alerting the others.

I press record because if my hunch pans out, I'll want this footage. I lower The Khal a bit closer, but am still at least sixty meters up when I see the shape's form very clearly. Suddenly, a whale breaches the surface, powerfully releasing its breath through its blowhole. Misty air shoots up and sprays a good twenty feet high. I screech in delight. My little audience starts yelling in excitement, though they're not as surprised as I am. Based on the amount of wildlife we encounter on the daily out here, I gather they see whales on a regular basis. Still, they can't deny how powerful a whale's presence is to behold in person. Mel and the ladies scan the horizon.

"To our left," I direct them. "It's coming up pretty close to the boat."

Just as they turn their heads, the giant whale's fluke emerges, looking like a postcard, only about ten meters from the back of the boat.

"I don't know what's goin' on with whales, but every time there's a boat, they seem to gravitate right towards 'em," Donnie says.

"Maybe it's their way of sayin' 'hey there!'" Jaz cries out. She lifts her hand and waves in the whale's direction. Over her shoulder she asks me, "Getting footage of this? I'll buy it off ya for my research."

I nod, not really listening. Giddy with delight, I click down on the shutter button. I already can't wait to see these and upload them tonight.

*Holy cow!*

"I've never seen one before," I admit, at a loss for words.

"Like eva?" Shayno asks me, shocked.

"Nope," I confirm, shaking my head and biting my lips tight.

"Wow," Jaz says, "we see one almost every time we come out, 'n during the season, even from shore."

My eyebrows shoot up to my hairline. *That often?!* The gang laughs, and starts snickering about America. *Here it comes - the grand debate.* The crew has formed a habit of discussing the pros and cons of "Straya" verses America. Clearly as the only Yank here, the conversation always heavily leans towards pro Australia. I gotta say, there are a lot of pros...

I notice a smaller shape materialize next to the whale. My heart melts as a calf appears. The detail of the calf clarifies as it rises to the surface level, about to breach.

"Wait for it guys," I bellow. "Here it comes... right... now!"

The small calf breaches and the gang roars in cheers. We all collectively fawn over seeing a baby. It's so much smaller than its gigantic mama. Good thing we just anchored. I learn that you have to wait a while before starting the engine when closely crossing paths with whales. So many get hit by boat propellers each year and either wind up washing ashore or becoming the buffet for all the local tiger sharks. You'd never want to run over one, but they might be swimming only inches below the surface. Luckily for the whales, we just parked it here, so no worries on us leaving any time soon. Trying not to interfere with nature as much as possible, I keep the drone a good distance from the whales and just observe them from afar, watching them eloquently do their thing. Looking from the drone's vantage point, I see both whales submerge below to an unseeable depth, and just as quickly as they appeared, they melt away. *How can something so large vanish without a trace?*

I steer The Khal around, scanning the surrounding water, but a quick glance at the remaining battery life urges me to bring it back towards my direction. I want plenty of battery life in case it takes a few tries to land. As I fly to the boat, I see some larger fish swimming close to port side. Brodie points to them on the screen, and shares the details to the guys in the water. They sound excited. I hear the words "mahi mahi."

"Alright, boys 'n girls, let's suit up then," Brodie commands us.

Everyone jumps to, and I'm left on the bow on my own. I bring The Khal close and stop it, leaving it to hover, midair. The boat slightly rocks and I plant my feet in a sturdy stance, preparing to hand catch the drone. I slowly and gradually steer it to about two feet in front of me. One bad rock of the tide and I'm plowing right into the propellers, most definitely shredding my fingers. I surmise that dwelling on it might cause a hesitation on my part, so I commit to mind over matter and decide to trust my instincts, allowing muscle memory to perform the task for me. I take a deep breath and confidently reach up, snatching the body out of the sky. Quickly, I slam down the control stick to perform a force landing. The props die in seconds. I turn around and see Brodie applying white zinc to his face. His eyes open briefly and I catch his attention. I hold up the drone in my hand. He freezes, with streaks of white paste smeared all over his cheeks, and raises one eyebrow as he scoffs. I shrug, smiling with an attitude that reads, *see told ya so* as I gesture to the drone. Shaking his head, he rubs in his sunscreen. Mel walks over to the cockpit and stands on her tiptoes towards the bow.

"Oy, Neens, give him here," she commands, motioning me to hand her the drone with her outstretched arms.

I do as she says then make my way around the side, back to the main deck. This time it's a little easier. I shakily land on the vinyl with a soundless *thunk*, laughing at my own lack of grace as my hair explodes around my face.

Margot, clad in a skimpy black bikini top and thong bottoms, saunters closer and bends over right in front of Brodie specifically, while looking for a dive belt in the cabinet. Brodie leans over her, and pulls out a bin full of suits and weighted belts, some newer looking and some older. He fishes around and finds a black one with a couple of bars attached. Before handing it to her, he removes one weight bar. She smiles, and walks towards the back of the boat, strapping it on. She's so skin and bones the extra slack could loop around her another time or two.

I peel off my tank top, standing only in my one-piece. I hear Mom's voice telling me to stand up straight and to suck it in. While I acknowledge I'm not as chunky as I used to be, I'm definitely not skinny, and parading around in any bathing suit - bikini or one piece - makes me a bit uneasy. You can attribute this to the low self-esteem I've carried around like a backpack since I was in high school. I was heavy and girls can be downright cruel.

Mel's blessed with thin genetics, but she doesn't look anorexic like Margot. She strips down to her bikini, a notch more modest than her sister's, but still pretty cheeky. I honestly pass no judgement. I know it's the style these days. I just personally prefer to leave some things to the imagination. Plus, honestly, who's to say that if I was built like a bean pole, like Mel, I wouldn't entertain the style myself? *Never say never, folks.*

"I always love that one," she compliments me on my suit, smiling.

Brodie walks over, and hands Mel a dive belt. He's already suited up and carries his speargun in his right hand. The sight of the gun dries up all the saliva in my mouth. He catches me staring at it like it's a rattlesnake and marches over, holding it out to me.

"Here," he offers. I refuse, closing my fists while looking down at it, adamantly shaking my head. Brodie sighs. "Neens, ya can't be afraid of it if ya know how to use it." He flicks the safety switch on and off repeatedly. "Rememba?"

"How can I forget?" I whisper, and reach for his arm as he shows me again. "Stop that, it could go off."

"Yeah, if it was loaded. See?" he kindly informs me, showing me the spear's not cocked in the rubber sling.

He smirks in amusement at my abhorrent expression. He runs through another impromptu lesson on speargun safety, including tips, and concludes with how to generally use one correctly.

"Wow, Neens, didn't realise yar gonna spear with the lads," Mel surprisingly states, coming up behind us.

"Just wanted to teach her some basics, Mel," Brodie explains lightly.

For a second I think he's going to blab, but again he doesn't say anything more. She walks off, stretching the mask's band as she pulls it on and around her head. Now that I'm not distracted by the speargun, I look down at Brodie and emit a loud laugh. He's wearing what we at home call Happy Flaps. It's like a spring wetsuit, but instead of the bottom turning into shorts or full pants, it cuts down in a "V" shape and hugs the crotch, like a wetsuit leotard. For diving, this is usually worn on top of wetsuit bottoms as a two piece set, but Brodie is wearing it over his boardies. Donnie and Shayno walk over all wet, dressed in the same fashion. The Happy Flaps hug all the wrong places. I do my best to avoid staring at their bulges, but there are seconds where I can't help myself. They all look ridiculous, and I imagine it must feel slightly uncomfortable as well. They catch my darting eyes and I flush deeply. The color in my cheeks rises rapidly.

Margot, looking like she'll blow away in the breeze, comes and stands next to me. The stark contrast between the two of us must be amusing. She's tall, obviously leggy, fair colored with a touch of sunshine gold, and incredibly skinny with mousy platinum hair. In fact, she looks like a tall Viking queen. Then there's me, who stands at least a foot beneath her with dark features, an unruly mane, a stockier build and a nice strong tan, compliments of my latino blood.

Margot pulls on two diving fins, dons herself a mask and snorkel, and falls blindly off the side of the railing into the water. Mel follows suit. The guys and Jaz jump off the back swim deck. Stella barks after them as they splash through the water, coming up for air. Brodie and I stand alone near the console. He walks towards the dashboard and checks his phone one last time. *Who is he planning on texting out here?* Jordan maybe? He grabs his speargun, pulls down his mask, and heads for the railing.

"Wait, what about me?" I cry out, before he jumps overboard. He halts and pulls up his mask, resting it on his forehead. His skin looks all squishy and funny looking, the tight rubber blocking blood flow in various places on his face. Trying not to laugh, I stand there, expecting a response. "Well?"

"Well, what? As I recall, last time ya nearly put my head on a spike for assumin' ya'd want to join in," he explains respectfully, without major judgement. "This time, I just figured ya'd wait up here."

I pause for a second.

"Well this time I want to come... I think," I say questionably, then nod confidently. "No, I for sure want to go."

He stops and stares at me for a moment, trying to make up his mind about something. After a beat, he walks over and grabs a dive belt from the bin before standing a foot in front of me.

"Yar sure, Neens? Don't feel pressured by the crew, eh."

I shake my head quickly back and forth.

"No, I'm tired of being afraid," I whisper, feeling incredibly vulnerable by admitting this. "I don't want to be that person anymore... I need to do this, Brodie, for me."

Brodie doesn't say anything as I look at the others laughing at each other as they adjust their masks. Suddenly I feel his arms as they reach around my waist, pulling the weight belt around me. He fastens it. The added weight feels a little odd at first.

"Yull get used to it," he assures me, nodding towards the bars.

I look overboard and tense slightly with nerves as I see nothing but open, endless water all around us. An open door for any predators to wander right through if they want a lunchtime snack. *Nina, don't overthink it. You're doing this.*

Brodie tugs on my belt, jostling me, to make sure it's secure. I glance down to inspect it and am startled when Brodie lightly tips my chin up to meet his eyes. Peering directly into my gaze, I see his green eyes closely for the first time. He usually wears sunglasses. His irises are like a dark, mossy river with little flecks of yellow splashed through, condensing around the pupil. My breathing catches just slightly. We stand just inches apart.

"I'll be right by yar side. The whole time. Cross my heart," he says quietly and sincerely.

He steps back and I clear my throat.

"OK, let's do this then," I exclaim, smiling at him as I pull the diving fins on.

He walks over to the edge, drops his gun in the water. It lands with a splash and floats on the surface. Brodie tips his body overboard, disappearing into the dreamy blue. I peer over the edge. It's not even deep blue. I remind myself it's only thirty feet deep on this side of the sandbar.

*You can see the bottom for heaven's sake, Nina.*

Taking a deep breath, I quickly exhale.

"Here goes nothing," I declare, glancing back at Stella, and close my eyes as I fall backwards.

Cascading water envelopes me as I fall into its weightless embrace. I quickly come up for air. I rub some spit inside my mask, hoping this trick will keep it from fogging up right away. I dunk it back underwater and stretch it over my large head, positioning it where it feels most comfortable. Next, I look down and adjust my suit so it hopefully covers all the right places. *If not, cheap thrills.* I notice the water temp is a little brisk today, but in a refreshing way.

Brodie keeps his promise and treads a couple of feet nearby. Wearing snorkels prohibits real conversation so he hand signals for me to follow him. I bob under the water as I swim after him along the surface. Growing up, I've snorkeled before in Hawai'i, but never have I ever seen anything so clear before. It's an entire new world down here. Brodie motions for me to take a deep breath and descend. I inhale largely through my snorkel hose, hold my breath and dive down, kicking thoroughly to keep up.

As I outstretch my arms to swim, I feel my suit slide down, revealing more of my chest. Maybe this suit wasn't the best option, but it's too late now to do anything about it. I've aways been told by my sisters that besides my ankles, my round and enviable breasts are my best features. Swimming, I can feel them floating like buoys, jostling with and against the water. It's kind of an unnerving sensation. I wonder if men notice things like this... more specifically if the men I'm swimming with will notice mine. Hoping I go unnoticed, I swim down to a bommie, and tropical fish in all sizes and colors flurry around. It's like something out of *Finding Nemo*, but way better because it's real. The weight from the belt helps immensely. You don't have to burn as much energy holding yourself under.

Donnie and Shayno float a few feet to our right, with Jaz close behind them. None of them are armed with a speargun, but instead wear gloves. Mel comes up to my side and gives me two big thumbs up. I can see her large square teeth beam at me through the bubbles.

I'm beginning to run out of air and start to panic. It's a good fifteen feet back to the surface. The pressure builds and my head feels like it's ready to pop like a balloon. I hastily kick my way up, barely reaching the surface before I come crashing through, gasping for air. I wheeze a little, trying to expel excess water from my lungs. I lift up my mask, taking deep breaths. Foot wide circles of air bubbles rise to the surface next to me. Mel suddenly pops up, followed by Brodie.

"Ya alright, Love?" she asks me.

Her hair's all disheveled, tangled in knots around her mask.

"Yep, sorry, I just need a minute," I admit. "I'm not used to the pressure."

"Yull adjust to it ova time. Just rememba to swallow a bunch as ya go down," Brodie suggests. He opens his mouth and bites down on the snorkel again before gesturing to the boat and over pronouncing, "Do ya wanna go in?"

*Do I?* It's so beautiful out here. I answer by pulling my mask back down, and inserting the snorkel back into my mouth. I give them both a thumbs up and dive down, kicking hard. The two follow close in my wake. I don't push myself this time and instead only dive down about ten feet. Brodie continues swimming down a little further, but is never out of considerable reach.

I love the weightless feeling that comes with being totally submerged under water. All the tension from excess weight and stress just vanishes, and everything seems to move better. My joints pop as I swim around, welcoming the low impact exercise and flexibility. My leg and knee certainly feel best under water.

Mel and I watch as Brodie eyes a good sized blue and white fish. He follows the direction of it, aiming his spear. Removing the safety, he pulls the trigger. A giant band *popping* sound travels through the water as his spear hurtles like a javelin, piercing the fish directly through the cheek. The fish jerks and continues swimming, slowing down as it thrashes about. Brodie uses the reel on his gun and cranks it, reeling in his catch. When the fish is at arms' length, he takes out his knife, strapped around his calf, and stabs the fish in the head, putting it out of its misery. This all happens within thirty seconds and already my lungs are crying for some air. As I swim back to the top, I look down and see Brodie swimming up in my wake, the fish dangling in his hand as he holds it by the gills. We both emerge at the surface around the same time. Swimming closer to me, he shows me his prize. The fish looks way bigger than it did when it was alive and swimming from a few meters away. In context next to Brodie, it looks a good couple of feet long. I inspect the site of trauma closely.

"Bullseye," I whistle.

"Dinna, baby," Brodie squeals happily.

He swims over to the back of the boat, setting the fish and his gun down on the swim step, and climbs in effortlessly. He opens the esky and tosses the fish in for safe keeping. Before I can ask if he's coming back in, Shayno pops out of the water holding what looks like a giant lobster but full of colorful blue patterns. I swear everything is healthier and bigger here in the land of Oz.

"Yew!" Brodie cries out giddily. "Nice one, Shayno. I got us a Blue Bone."

Shayno yells a positive affirmation Brodie's way, and swims to the side of the boat. He hoists the crayfish up to Brodie. Brodie puts that on ice as well. He informs me that icing a crayfish puts them to sleep which is a more humane way of killing them.

"D have any luck?" he asks Shayno.

"Dunno, but there's heaps of cray unda that one big bommie straight below," Shayno replies.

Brodie grabs his gun, gives Stella a kiss, and jumps back overboard. He adjusts his mask. Shayno drops under, disappearing back down to the bommie. Re-centering my mask, biting on my mouth piece, I follow Shayno as he swims in the opposite direction to the other side of the boat. I realize I'm swimming towards the drop off zone. Endless blue and an unseen bottom await us. It's slightly sketchier and daunting being on this side, not going to lie. I feel like something large and predatorily can just materialize out of the darkness at any moment. I follow the guys anyway. I feel safer knowing I'm not alone. I notice when Brodie swims, his arms tighten and relax methodically. As he angles upwards I can see his abs and ribcage stretch.

Mel and Margot swim up beside us. The sisters swim like mermaids, not even using their arms, just their long limber legs as they kick their feet in unison. I wish I could swim that confidently and comfortably. *Maybe one day.* Mel swims over to me and taps my shoulder and points to Brodie, then moves her finger over, directing my attention to something separate in the distance. Brodie looks down the barrel of his gun, clearly targeting his prey.

The water's transparent and infinite, but I still can't see a thing. Out of the blue, a couple of bright shapes glide by, glinting silver as they catch a ray of light. Spooked, I grip Mel's arm tightly. She doesn't seem to mind. The silver passes in and out of visibility, but seems large and fast. I pray hard it's not a shark.

The giant band *popping* noise goes off again. I look out and see Brodie's spear fly through the ocean, piercing a gray shape in the far distance. Grabbing the circular reel, he reels in his catch for the second time today. It's a good sized mahi mahi. He pulls it in with serious effort. The beautiful creature thrashes and fights, way more than the Blue Bone did. When it approaches Brodie's outstretched arms, Brodie drops the gun, which floats nearby. He scrambles for the knife tucked away in its sheath, but the bull bucks and fights fiercely. It's almost the same length as Brodie, and puts up quite a fight. Knife in hand, it takes Brodie a few tries trying to brain it, but the buck resists, slipping out of grasp. Margot swims over and wraps her arms around it, trying to get a good hold. This allows Brodie to more easily reach for the head, and he stabs the fish through the brain, instantly putting it out of its misery. A light trail of blood pours out of the knife wound, leaving what looks like pink powder spewing in its wake.

Breathing through my snorkel, I catch another flash of silver out of the corner of my eye. Just as I see it, it's gone. Nudging Mel, I point to the direction but find it empty and void. She holds up her hands gesturing *what?*

*Flash!* There it is again, only this time, it's not a fish. Panic sets in. My blood suddenly feels like it's two hundred degrees and boiling, while the water around me feels icy like the Arctic Circle. I break out in goosebumps and latch on forcefully to Mel, shouting "shark!" through my snorkel. She looks at me, trying to make out what I'm saying. While muffled underwater, if you project and enunciate clearly, you can manage to communicate basic messages.

"SHARK!" I push out, with all my might.

Mel looks to where I'm pointing, her eyes slightly widening in her mask. A large reef shark circles us. I manage to peel my eyes away briefly to notice Brodie's aware of it as well. He swims in circles to stay facing the shark the entire time, holding his prize in one hand and his knife in the other. Knowing Brodie's love and affinity for the ocean, I'm confident he would only use the knife as a last defense. The shark glides towards Brodie a little closer to investigate the bleeding mahi. Brodie appears calm and collected. I'm amazed how long he's capable of holding his breath. The shark now approaches him within two meters. About to pass out from fear, I detach myself from Mel's arm, deciding to make a break for it. I swim as fast as I physically can towards the boat. I hear shrieking behind me and turn to see the shark switch directions towards me.

*Is this how I die? Is this what gets me after all that's happened. Am I ever going to see my family again? Javi.*

Racing through a mixture of bubbles and blurry unclear shapes, I pray with all my might I can kick harder and faster. The swim step is within reach. I don't let my momentum slow, and I barrel into the step. I hoist myself up like lightning, bruising my hip on the chrome hinges, and lay flat on the swim deck, panting my brains out. I hastily lift my dangling feet up out of the water. Eyes closed, I lay here wheezing for air as my heartbeat pounds fiercely in my head. Bright red light from the sun filters through my eyelids, followed by a clouded darkness. I peep one eye open and see Stella looming over my face. She bends down and covers me with kisses, lapping up the salt water on my face and ears. Exhausted and defeated, I reach up and pet her face. At least I have all my limbs. That shark was headed directly at me and Mel. *Mel?!*

Jolting upright, I stand, pulling off my fins, and run to the side of the boat, peering over. A cluster of the guys' heads pressed together catches my eye about twenty feet away, but no sign of Mel. I scour the surface for my friend when she abruptly pops up on the back swim step and climbs her way on deck. My shoulders hunch in relief. Mel clamors over to me, pulling off her mask with a suction popping sound. She has a giant red ring around her cheeks and forehead.

Her hair falls like a rats nest around her face. I grab her and envelope her into a giant hug.

"I don't reckon I've eva seen anyone swim like that before, Neens. Bravo," she chortles, impressed and not the least bit concerned.

Breaking away, I try to disentangle the mask from my hair, but it's no use, so I leave it hanging there on the side of my face. A stray strand of wet curl is embedded in the plastic fastener.

"The others?" I bellow, full of concern. "Are they alright?"

"Yeah, that was wild, eh?" she says, wiping the drips off her nose. She sits down and unfastens the dive belt. It drops with a *thunk* on the floor. "That shark wanted a piece of the pie for bloody sure."

"What happened?" I beseech her.

"Ah, well it started gettin' a little hot out there, 'n the shark got a little too close," Mel describes animatedly, but casually, "but Brodie shoved his fin out towards its face 'n it swam off, spooked."

The crowd of heads swims towards the step. Shayno jumps up on deck, followed by Margot and Donnie. Brodie hangs back, treading and carrying the giant dorado. Donnie turns back towards the step, holding the gaff with Shayno beside him. Brodie grunts as he pulls the giant fish closer, and using the gaff, the guys pull it onto the boat together. Struggling to heave the cumbersome fish, their grips slip and they almost lose hold. Luckily Shayno recovers it in time and they manage to lay it flat on deck. Brodie effortlessly climbs up and rips off his fins and mask. He sets his gun out of the way and walks over to the mahi mahi, shaking his head in disbelief as he catches his breath.

"The tail, mates," he instructs, picking up the head.

"Quick, Neens, grab yar camera," Mel says.

In my bathing suit, I run over to the cabinet and quickly snatch my camera from my backpack. I hastily run back just as the three boys outstretch the mahi mahi's burdensome body in front of them. Holy hell it's massive. I snap a couple pics and switch to video as well. Brodie recounts the shark incident, saying he thought for a second he was going to have to give up the mahi to the interested party. His tone implies only slight nervousness, nothing remotely close to my reaction.

"It's boilin' out there today, cobbers," he shouts joyfully.

Donnie and Shayno drag and position the mahi so its head hangs over the swim step above the water.

"Wanna hop back in the drink?" Donnie asks Brodie.

"Just for a quick rinse," he responds. Slimy, bloody fish scales cover their hands and wetsuit tops, along with light traces of watered down blood. Looking down at the large fish, Brodie cackles in disbelief. "I reckon we've got plenty of meat for the week."

"'N it's not even arvo yet," Shayno adds, impressed.

They all laugh.

"Can I help ya with that, Nina?" Jaz asks, eyeing my hairline.

My eyes search around my face, and I catch the clear plastic mask hanging in my peripheral. I laugh, completely having forgotten it was even there.

"That would be awesome, thanks so much," I chuckle.

As Brodie and the guys bleed the fish, meaning they cut it at the gills and hang it overboard so the blood drains effectively into the sea, Jaz and Mel both sit on either side of me, working on my mask and snorkel extraction.

"Ya could always go with dreads, ya know," Mel pokes fun at the tedious task.

"Ha! Ya defo have heaps of hair," Jaz points out, a little overwhelmed.

While they both have soft touches, my scalp starts to itch and feel raw after so many little picks and pulls.

"We may have to cut out this last part," Mel says slowly and pitifully.

"Dun wuckas, Nina, we'll have this sorted in two shakes," Jaz interjects, in a more reassuring tone.

I reach back to feel the knotted section of hair. A small coarse ball rolls around in my fingers. I deem it irreparable, but luckily it's towards my ends. Sending up an apology to Ria, I forcefully grab the tangled mess and tightly grip the mask with my other hand and pull them apart, wincing only slightly as the hair tears away. Jaz and Mel recoil at the sight, and Margot looks over at me in horror as I hold up the dead hair. I then rip that from the mask and toss the small casualty overboard. It disappears instantly. Triumphantly, I turn my attention back to the fish festivities. *Fishtivities?* I laugh to myself. *Good one, Nina.* Thoroughly bled, the mahi bull sits on the filet table. Donnie walks over to the cabinet behind me, looking for the knife.

I attempt to tidy up my chaotic curls. Glancing over at the water, I debate if I should dip again to smooth out my hair, but no one's out there, and there's a bleeding fish a few feet from me, so I decide to hold off. Bending over, I thoroughly shake my hair out, then flip my head upright. Turning back around, I find Donnie checking me out. He playfully wiggles both eyebrows up and down in admiration.

"Lookin' good, Chica," he blatantly teases. The giant teddy bear smirks at me as I laugh nervously, unsure how to respond. Before returning to the boys, he winks at me. "Ya got a rippa body, no need to hide it."

*Okay, Donnie, thanks for the vote of confidence and the life advice.*

Even with the head gone, the mahi's body is still too big to fit inside the esky as one piece, so the guys decide to chop it in half and filet it back at Brodie's. They wedge the two halves on ice and shut the lid.

"Jaz!" Brodie hollers. "Anchors up."

"I reckon she's the only one who's allowed to muck around with his precious cargo," Mel says, leaning into me.

I barely hear Mel because a large splashing sound catches my attention and I instantly freeze. *Oh gosh, did it come back?* Scanning the water for a fin or dark shadow, I see the large mahi head floating by the boat. My posture relaxes in ease. Mel snorts, and tells me that if you have the option, you always return the spare bits of fish back to the ocean, that way the other creatures can feast off the carcass and the sustainable cycle continues.

Dripping wet, Jaz makes her way to the bow and stows the anchor. The boat starts to rock slightly as we secure cabinets, and stash stow away items. I sit down on the warm bench seat. The roof shade blocks a lot of heat from beating down on the deck, but depending on the sun's location and the time of day, a small section of the vinyl seats are exposed to the hot sun. The warmth is a welcome delight. Even though it's warm for winter, it still is winter and the water becomes a tad chilly after a while. Overall, I must be adapting because the air temps are still in the low eighties at midday and I'm finding the water chilly in the mid to high sixties. When I first arrived, I thought it couldn't be possible to feel cold ever again, but nowadays, I occasionally find myself with goosebumps, reaching for a sweater. The heat from the warm seat clings to my back and legs, traveling up my skin, blanketing me like a hug. I sigh in bliss. My eyes shut, reveling the warmth before I dry and find it overbearing. It's a perfect dry desert day out here on the water.

Brodie takes command at the wheel, Stella by his side per usual, and everyone else takes their seats. He fires up the engine, does one last once over and we're off again. Since we've already caught our fair share of meat, instead of more fishing Brodie chooses to head back towards land. Wearing his black baseball cap, sunnies, and shirt, he sits in his captain's chair with ease, his bare feet resting on the chrome pegs under his seat. He turns on the music. U2's "Sunday Bloody Sunday" blares through the air. I smile. Brodie didn't chintz on the sound system and I appreciate the fact that he cranks it at a higher decibel right off the bat.

The crew sits lazily about as the events of the last couple of hours catch up. I see Donnie stifling a big yawn as he looks out to sea, while Shayno somehow manages to wedge in a cat nap. We see more whale spouts in the distance, but they're headed in another direction and are good distance away.

"Someone text Jordo as soon as ya can 'n let him know to meet up at Lucky's," Brodie calls over his shoulder.

Margot whips her mobile out and her spider fingers immediately begin typing.

"K, sent it," she yells. "Hopefully it'll go through in a tick."

I laugh at the thought of having cell reception out here in the middle of the ocean when it's spotty back on land.

Forty minutes go by, but it feels like we're just getting started. I could sit here all day with the mist in my face. Sighing contentedly, I spot small clusters of land in the distance. As we approach, the ocean floor takes shape and becomes lighter in color, indicating we're nearing shallower waters. Bits of darker spots, bommies and reef, fly underneath us as we jettison over them. The sandy bottom becomes increasingly clear. Thousands of greens, yellows, and blues litter the shallows as we speed across the mixture of shapes. It's dead calm and glassy, an absolute "banger of a day" as the crew would say. The boat slows a little. Standing and steering, Brodie leans over the railing, clearly eyeing something in the water.

"Look starboard!" he shouts with urgency.

The whole crew jumps up, scrambling to the right side of the boat. The engine quietly hums as we idle.

"Woah!" cries Margot. "She's huge!"

Mel points over and about twenty feet away I see a large dark spot. After a couple of seconds, I realize it's moving in a forward trajectory; it's alive.

"Tiga?" Donnie mutters to Jaz, which she instantly confirms.

*TIGER?!*

"Bloody beauty, she is," Brodie says, motioning for Jaz. "Here, take ova the wheel for a sec." Jaz switches him places. Brodie grabs his shirt and pulls it up over his head, looking excited. "Get in front of her, Jazzy. Take a wide birth, mind."

"Nina, ya might wanna get The Khal ready," Shayno suggests.

"What?" I mumble in confusion, but am already unpacking it.

Since we're moving slowly, I'm going to have to lift off from the back. There's enough room this time; I think I can manage it. Walking to the stern, Mel kindly offers her hand as the launch pad. Within minutes, I hit the lift off button, toggle the stick and away he flies, hovering overhead.

"A little more towards the right, Jaz," Brodie instructs over his shoulder, "but don't crowd her, eh." He looks down at Stella. "Stay here, Stel, ya hear? No shark bait for my girl."

He jumps overboard wearing just his fins and mask. Stella, on his heels, paces around the boat looking for her dad. Running to the back swim step, she halts, obeying his command.

I watch as Brodie dives under. The water's barely a consideration with the vis being so high and glassy. Positioning the drone above, I can see the scene very clearly. Brodie keeps his distance, but swims back alongside the magnificent creature. Judging her length against his, she must be a good ten to twelve feet because she easily doubles him. Jaz keeps a watchful eye as we follow alongside them from a safe distance.

"See how he's sussing her out, seein' if she's agro or not," Donnie informs me.

Aren't all sharks aggressive to a certain extent?

Jaz tells Shayno to scan the water nearby to make sure other sharks don't sneak up without warning. I glance around my screen and don't see any incoming threats.

"Most of the time, they're chill, but ya never know the sitch down there, so best to be on the safe side, eh," Margot informs me, perking up with the opportunity to educate me.

*He's playing with fire.*

It dawns on me: there is a massive tiger shark only meters from me. *I think we need a bigger boat.*

I peer down at my screen and lock on Brodie, pulling in a little closer. Now he swims parallel with the unpredictable, striped animal. All it would take is one swift and quick behavioral change and Brodie could be toast, *well dinner*. Oscillating my gaze around our surroundings, I see there's nothing for miles, no hospital for hours. Anyone seriously injured - or bit - out here wouldn't stand a chance.

I lower the drone a little more and follow the unfolding scene below as they swim side by side, only meters apart. She is one of the most beautiful and most graceful creatures I've ever seen. Shaking from excitement and nerves, I realize my remote controller vibrates in my hands. I take a deep breath to steady myself and focus on my composition. Thankfully the drone operates on a separate stabilizer and holds its steady position. The shark sways its tail back and forth, looking like a voluptuous dancing woman, propelled by the movement of her hips, while her "hands" remain small at her side.

"She's gorgeous," Margot exclaims, with a hint of jealousy.

Everyone stands in awe, pointing and sharing their two cents when we notice the shark swims farther away, leaving Brodie swimming in its wake. Jaz kills the engine as Brodie turns around and swims back to us. Stella greets him with gleeful kisses as he boards the back swim deck. Beaming from ear to ear, he pulses with adrenaline and excitement.

"Did ya cobbers see that?!" he yells, pulling off his fins.

As he galavants around the boat in pure delight, all of us cheer and yell, reiterating how incredible it was. Donnie opens the esky and digs out Coca Colas. He passes them to everyone, and raises his can.

"That deserves a fizzy, mate," he cheers.

"Here, here," we collectively chant.

Running a towel through his wet hair and face, Brodie grabs his hat and sunnies. He squats next to Stella, and rubs her ears.

"See, Dad's back," he says. "I owe ya a swim, girl."

He stands and takes a giant swig of the cola followed by a crisp, "ahh." He laughs his head off, screaming a little in disbelief at how close he got to the tiger. Donnie belches loudly and we all laugh, finishing our sodas. Still amped, but slightly calmer, Brodie assumes the wheel again as we take our usual places and cruise along the shallows as small little mirages of land make their appearance.

# 12

The afternoon sun beats down on the water. The glare refracts into a thousand tiny, shiny diamonds. It's breathtaking in its magical raw form. We slow down as we maneuver through a cluster of small islands. Brodie commands the boat with ease and we make our way around one. The view opens up, revealing a picturesque sandy island. Pale turquoises and celestial blues slowly lap along the golden shoreline. The somewhat substantially sized island is big enough to run around, out of sight, as bushes, small trees and sand dunes litter the coastline.

"This, Nina, is Lucky's," Jaz announces proudly, leaning over.

I've never been on a "private" island before, and the thought leaves me speechless. This is all ours. An adult playground.

*How cool is this?!*

As Brodie slows down, I notice a beached SeaDoo about a hundred feet down the shore. A figure lying down on the sand sits up and I recognize it as Jordan.

"Oy!" yells Brodie, grinning when we approach closer.

Jordan waves hello. Brodie kills the engine and angles the boat so the stern faces the beach. We float about twenty feet from shore for a couple of minutes while he lowers the anchor. All settles. Mel and I jump off the step, landing in about four feet of water. The water feels exceptionally great, a little warmer here than when we were out at sea; it pushes into the low seventies. I can't help myself from checking out my surroundings, looking for more moving dark spots. I see a tiny one, but it's only a turtle.

"Relax, Neens, ya'd see it comin' in these waters," Mel assures me, noticing my anxious expression.

She looks up to the sky, enjoying the sun, then playfully splashes me to distract me. It works. The feeling of the water on my arm invites me to fall back, pull up my feet and float in the shallows without a care in the world. Brodie does a backflip off the roof shade, landing a few feet away, followed by Shayno. I bob up and down in the wake of the rippling splash, while Mel shouts as the flying water hits her right in the eyes. Stella jumps off the swim deck and doggie paddles towards shore. Her little hairy paws hit sand and she shakes furiously a couple of times before running down the beach.

Jordan runs over to us, kicking up tons of water as he steam piles into the crew. As we all hang and chat in the shallows, Shayno places a smaller esky on the swim deck for easy access and passes out tinnies to everyone, popping tops as he disperses them. Having had more drinks in the last two weeks than I've had in my whole life combined, I take one. I'm not a huge drinker, but it's ice cold and feels amazing, counteracting the blazing sun. I dig my toes into the sand and relax, sipping my drink; it's not the best taste in the world, but maybe I can learn to like it.

Mel nudges my elbow and rolls her eyes, gesturing to her sister. Margot lounges on the sand on her stomach. Straightening her long legs, she props herself up on her elbows. We watch as she unties her bikini to avoid tan lines, while stealthily peeking to see if the boys are checking her out. *At least she's trying, Nina.* Though Mel and I both snort at her efforts, I wish I had a fraction of her confidence. Donnie certainly eyes her, I note, as his stare fixates on her. Apparently he loves to admire the female physique. She does look like a beached mermaid or a mythic Viking queen poised at the water's edge. Sadly for Donnie's sake, I don't think he's the one she's interested in. I don't get why. He's very handsome. I look around at the men in front of me; they're all really good looking. Any girl would be lucky to be with any one of them, more because they all have amazing personalities to go with their hot bods, well jury's still out on Jordan - about his personality, not his bod - I muse.

*So why don't you be one of the lucky ones then, Nina.*

As if testing me, Jordan wanders over to me, clearly enjoying himself. I sneak a peek at his abs and toned arms, and notice that his blonde chest hair accentuates this rugged quality about him. *He's practically drool worthy.* He stands next to me so our shoulders lightly rub against each other. I move slightly away, using the current as an excuse for inches of separation.

Back home, I often felt overlooked by guys. The constant rejection and feeling like I wasn't good enough led me to close myself off to the possibility of someone being interested. After years of this practice, to make matters worse, any attention I do receive, I run from because I don't know how to handle it. Thus, the conundrum of my dating life, or lack thereof; it's become a vicious cycle. Today is another perfect example. Here's this cute, attractive guy who seems interested, and here I am shriveling inside at the thought of us literally rubbing elbows. The skin on skin contact absorbs my sole focus while I try to come off like I don't even notice. I want this, but I won't let myself have it.

*Stop overthinking it, Nina.*

My sisters would roll their eyes at me right now. Selena and Maria both know I'm a terrible flirt and have zero confidence with any romantic prospects. Trying to prove them and myself wrong, I stand up a little straighter, setting my shoulders back in a nice, upright posture. I smile a little too big to be genuine, but Jordan doesn't know me well enough to know the difference. Tipping the drink back, I take a big swig of liquid courage and finish off the can. I can definitely feel myself getting a little buzzed. I giggle more than necessary and laugh louder at the jokes being tossed around. I look around and see it's happening with everyone. Already overly jovial from a terrific day, our crew now erupts, busting a gut in mutual hysterics as we recount the morning. Jaz and Shayno run hand in hand up the beach, giggling. Everyone besides Brodie whistles and hollers after them, teasing.

"Those two are toeier than a roman sandal," Donnie snorts. "I mean, he's all ova her like a rash."

I snort at these expressions, not fully understanding the first one, but getting the gist of his meaning just fine. Within a minute, the love birds run around a large sand dune and disappear from view and, I hope, earshot.

"Alright, show's ova," Brodie says in a protective tone, rolling his eyes as they disappear.

The rest of us snicker and laugh while floating in the warm shallow water, lapping up the relaxing afternoon. The sun is well past its high noon intensity, already beginning its interminable, long kiss goodnight as it passes the promise of the day. Mel and I float in the shallows, enjoying the perfect weather. My bum scrapes along the sandy bottom as the small ebbing of the tide ushers me closer to shore. The guys stand a little deeper, chatting, making crude remarks over another round of beers.

Jaz and Shayno reappear down the beach and walk up towards the group. They both seem lighter in the way they carry themselves. They smile at the crew unapologetically. The group starts to make snide comments, but one stern look from Brodie stifles them all. Mel and I rejoin the rest of our friends. We all stand together in a wide, rough circle.

"Nina, wanna hop on the ski 'n go for a quickie?" Jordan asks, turning towards me.

All eyes land on me. I don't want to be rude. I barely know him and honestly the last time I sat behind him on a moving vehicle, it didn't go so well... I reach involuntarily at my mostly healed forearm. Yet considering my failed attempt with Big Al, it does sound amazing to get on a SeaDoo. And what's the worst that could happen? I fall off? If I do, its straight into the water which will cushion the blow.

Barry Manilow's "Ready to Take A Chance Again" sounds off in my head. I immediately try to shake off the imaginary tune; it didn't fare too well for Gloria Mundy for the first half of *Foul Play*... but thinking of Selena and Ria's imaginary commentary again, I find myself nodding yes. Tipsy, my shoulders over exaggerate my shrug of acceptance.

"Sure," I loosely say, somewhere in between a response and a question. Jordan claps in anticipation before swimming back towards the ski. I gulp in surprise, hollering, "Wait, right now?"

"Yep!" he calls back over his shoulder.

Jaz glances with interest at Brodie briefly, but he looks unbothered, a smile still on his face.

"Stellaaaa," he calls out, scanning the beach, looking for her.

Sure enough, she comes running around the bend.

"Nina, c'mon," Jordan shouts, without looking back.

"Here, take this," I tell Mel, handing her my empty can.

"Have fuuun," she says playfully, encouraging me with a hint of suggestion.

That stops me in my tracks for a brief moment, but then I continue and approach the ski and Jordan. He opens the seat compartment and grabs a thin lifejacket, handing it to me. It must be more for regulations than actual safety or maybe it works. I don't know, but I put it on. It fits snuggly, especially around the hips, and smashes my boobs against my chest, like a constricting corset. Jordan closes the seat over the open compartment, then pushes the ski back off the sand a few feet. He hops on and gestures for me to climb on behind him. Without anything or a hand to hold onto, I clamor up the side clumsily, falling off once in the process. I wince as my knee hits the hard siding as I fall again.

Out of my peripheral, I see Brodie flinch. He looks like he's about to start towards the ski, but I manage to climb aboard simultaneously so he holds back. Panting from my failed efforts, I attempt to balance while standing on the moving craft. I tipsily wobble towards the seat. Finally in the right angle, I swing one leg over the black vinyl seat and plop down behind Jordan. I adjust my position to leave a couple of inches of space between us. I look over and see Mel motioning me to scoot forward to bridge the gap, her giant eyes widening in a non-verbal conversation. Donnie, Jaz, and Shayno watch, holding their beers in hand, clearly enjoying the little show. I search for Brodie, but he's gone. He was just there a minute ago. *Where'd he go?*

I scan around the shallows and find Stella lounging under a little bush on shore and Brodie sitting next to Margot, the two of them chatting. She glows, overjoyed with his attentions.

Jordan starts the engine, and I awkwardly grab ahold of his torso and pull myself closer so I won't fall off the seat. Not having anything to support my back, combined with a speedy forward momentum, I latch on tightly, holding on for dear life.

The crew hollers as we jet away around the island out of view. Stella sprints along the beach, trailing us. I hear a faint whistle and she obediently stops, turning back. Jordan steers us out towards sea and we do a few loops and circles. He's definitely showing off a bit. I can't deny how much fun I'm having. He stops messing around and continues straight for a few minutes. I close my eyes, enjoying the total emergence with nature. I laugh in enjoyment, and even work up the courage to lessen my grip around his waist, eventually having enough confidence to barely hold on. It's so liberating being literally right above the water. Looking down you can see so many shapes and colors as we pass just inches above, leaving a giant trail of white wash in our wake.

We drive for a few more minutes. I admire the other smaller islands as we zig zag around and in between them. There's a tiny island of sand on our right. Jordan directs us straight to the beach until the ski hits the bottom with a light *thud*. I didn't realize we were stopping. *Dang*, I was just enjoying myself. Turning off the ski, Jordan jumps off and sheds his vest. He then jogs up the beach a few yards, plopping himself down on the dry fluffy sand. He looks around, admiring the view. Lying there, he motions for me to join him. Still on the SeaDoo, I stand, wobbling again as I manage to jump off the back into the couple feet of water. It's way easier to get off this thing than on it.

Walking towards shore, I take my vest off, immediately feeling the physical relief. I take a deep breath until my lungs burn, reveling as they expand openly. I sit down beside Jordan and hug my legs with my arms. My bare skin burns from the heat of the sand. My boat blown hair shoots out like Medusa's wild mane, the sun bleached pieces catching my eye. Grabbing my hair tie from my wrist, I reach up and tie my curly catastrophe into a large, messy top knot. My neck instantly cools ten degrees and I feel much better.

We sit together in the blazing sun for a while, not speaking a word. Honestly, I don't have much to say other than another comment on the amazing view. I wait for him to engage, but he doesn't seem too interested in making conversation... The charged awkwardness grows worse by the minute.

A little wave of water lightly greets my toes and the cool temp feels amazingly welcome. I gaze around. How lucky am I? White, fluffy sand beaches, extraordinarily clear waters. Maybe that's why the crew secretly calls this place Lucky's, though I wish I had better company and I yearn for The Great Khal. Drooling at the thought of droning, I glance around at the wondrous locale. I could get some unreal shots of the island clusters. I turn to scan the view to my right and discover Jordan waiting for me with a fixed stare. His eyes burn into my profile as he holds his gaze far past the point of discomfort. My genuine smile shifts to a more polite and cordial one. Seeing a stick protruding from the sand, I reach down and grab it, trying to find anything else to focus on. I don't really know him that well, so I try and think of something neutral to say. With the stick, I playfully write random words in cursive on the sand.

"So I heard your dad's okay and that it was a big misunderstanding," I say brightly. "You must be so relieved." He nods, looking at my moving hands, but doesn't reply. *Okay...* I try again. "Have you always lived here?"

He nods again, then resumes his gawking. Another awkward silence ensues. I glance at him, but my smile falters slightly. I don't know if I can hold up this charade much longer or maintain his heavy eye contact.

"So how long have you known Brodie?" I endeavor again. When he doesn't immediately answer, I nervously laugh. "Sorry for the twenty questions, it's just I don't really know that much about you..."

He smiles, finally responding, "Best mates since we were four."

*Okay, that's a long time.* I knew it was since they were younger, but four years old is *young*.

"Cool," I state over enthusiastically, trying to come off extra friendly to get some conversation started.

When he doesn't elaborate or contribute further, I sit up straighter and look at my hands resting on my knees. Back to silence we go. I hug my knees tightly in nervousness before standing upright and walking over to a small plant a few feet away. I see some type of natural, flowering pink bud and lean over to take a closer look. It's beautiful. I'm about to ask if we can go back to the others when I hear the light swishing of damp boardies closing in on me. Jordan looks at the bush only for a brief second, finding it disinteresting. I reach out to touch the micro flower, and he leans over and grabs my hand, softly caressing my mount of Venus. His touch brings back memories of the massage from the wedding. *This guy is handsy.* I quickly pull my hand back, moving it straight to my face to wipe a stray strand of hair out of my eyes. I give him a sheepish smile in return and a nervous laugh.

"Nina, yar a hottie," he says blankly.

"Oh... thanks," I say quietly, turning and walking back towards the ski.

Here I go again, avoiding attentions. I can't put my finger on it, but something about being with him doesn't feel right. Jordan doesn't give up that easily and he trails behind on my heel. Maybe if I indicate I'm ready to ride again, he'll get the message. I pick up my wet life vest, and put my arms through the holes. It's pretty frosty from the water and cold windchill of riding. The wet material immediately drops my body temp to the point where I break out in goosebumps. Fumbling with the zipper, it catches on something a quarter of the way up, a few inches below my naval.

Just having put his vest on, Jordan walks over directly in front of me, and pushes my hands out of the way, taking control of the small plastic tab. I should bat his hands away. I am more than capable of zipping my own vest, but my arms remain frozen, much to my chagrin. With force, Jordan tries to dislodge the zipper, and in doing so practically lifts me off my feet. Smashing against the tight restraint of the thin vest, my squished boobs lie directly beneath his fingers, skin on skin. Jiggling slightly as he vigorously tugs on the zipper, my chest rubs against the freezing material, prickling in goosies. I can't tell if Jordan's staring at the zipper or the round swells of my cleavage, but regardless, I feel extremely uncomfortable and incredibly vulnerable. I breathe deeply, trying to calm my nerves, but that seems to only exaggerate the swelling of my protruding bust line, exposing more centimeters of skin. Finally back in command of my motor functions, I try to butt in and regain control of the situation, but he pushes my hands away.

"Fuckin' zippa," he mutters to himself, shaking his head.

He finally frees it, and rethreads it, gliding it up over my stomach. His finger stops right at the hemline of my low cut suit, perfectly framing my breasts for his benefit. His Adam apple bobs up and down as he licks his lips. His fingers linger on the zipper's little tail. Slowly and sensually, he pulls the zipper back down until the vest hangs open.

Frozen like a statue, unable to move, I edge out in a raspy whisper, "What are you doing?"

He looks at the fullness of my bosom admiringly, and then straight into my eyes. Breathing heavily through his nose, his fingers stroke my breasts and slowly outline them in exploration as he lowers his hands to my hips. Despite feeling petrified, I shift in my stance and try to extricate myself from his touch. From what I've heard, if I was even remotely interested, this whole scene should turn me on, but instead I want to vomit. *Wake up, Nina!*

"Nina, I want you," he exhales loudly.

Leaning in, he kisses me ardently, rubbing his thumbs over my hardened nipples. My body feels like an ice sculpture, almost foreign to me. I don't kiss back. Part of my demobilized brain ignites finally and I manage to position my hand on his chest, and as politely as possible, attempt to resist further advances.

*Sorry, buddy, but that's not happening. I barely know you.*

He pulls back a little, reprieving my lips from his warm invasive touch. I catch my breath for a second before his lips come crashing down again with lustful strength. He pulls down on my head, holding it against his, pinning me against his moving mouth. He's a bigger guy, easily twice my size, and very strong. He doesn't flinch from my resistant pushes. His tongue drives my lips apart, forcing its way down my throat. About to gag, I shove back harder against his chest, trying to escape.

"Stop," I mutter. He ignores my plea and continues inhaling me. He finally removes his tongue and intensely kisses my chin, sucking and groping his way down my neck. Stepping back, I whisper coldly, but firmly, "Please, stop."

Ignoring me, his hand cups my right breast and crudely squeezes it, clearly wanting more. He thrusts his hips at mine, full of suggestion. I recoil with force and serious intention, and withdraw a few paces back, shouting "woah" while trying to regain my composure. Confused, Jordans frowns. A look of wounded pride emerges on his face. I try not to make this more awkward than necessary. I'm just starting to fit in, and I don't want to stir anything up with the crew, especially given he's Brodie's best mate. I force a rigid smile and step back towards him.

"I'm sorry," I whisper, trying to break it to him gently. "I just like to take things slow."

*What are you doing, Nina?! Tell him off!*

While he's extremely attractive, and a make out session on a private beach does sound rather exciting, I can't help how I feel, and I feel violated, not romanced. Clearly, I'm not ready for what he has in mind. I don't want to hurt his ego and cause tension, but I don't want to lead him on any further then I apparently already have. I quickly zip up my vest to the very top to make my message crystal clear.

He smiles and grabs my hand, kissing it. I pull it out of his grasp before he tries anything more. We walk back towards the ski where I realize we have to cozy up the whole way back to the others. I get on first this time, and he jumps up and sits down quickly in a huff. It's hard to gauge whether he's chapped or just ready to go back. I sit farther away, clearly making an effort to not lead him on.

After a a few minutes out at sea, he stops the ski and turns around, appearing his normal, unbruised self.

"Wanna drive?" he asks me eagerly.

"I'm not the best driver, Jordan," I state, laughing nervously.

He waives that off and before I can say another word, he stands up and grabs me by the hands, pulling me up with him too. We stand facing each other and he begins to swap places with me, urging me to scoot forward and take the wheel. I do as he says. I just want to get back as quickly as possible, and I have a feeling he won't take "no" for an answer. He uses my waist as an anchor as he shimmies around me. Finally in front, I sit down and take the handlebars in my hands. Jordan's body mashes against mine from behind.

Very eager to get back to the comfort of the crew, thinking particularly of Mel and Brodie, my safe havens in this new place, I stare at the ski's controls, unsure where to start. Jordan's long, tan arms come around me and he places his hands on top of my fingers. He arrogantly instructs me where the gas and brakes are located and how to start the motor, aiming the handles in the proper direction back. I have a decent sense of direction, but out here even I get confused. As I reach to throttle the gas, Jordan pulls his body so close to mine, his head rests in the crook of my chin and shoulder. I feel his hot, ragged breath in my ear. He lowers his hands back around my waist.

I start up the ski and steer back to where I hope lies base camp, riding like hell. I think it's still a few minutes away. Without my consent or immediate knowledge, Jordan reaches up and slowly unzips my vest, part way down. I feel a cold, stiff hand resting right below my boob, his fingers moving up slowly, filling me up.

"No, go slow, remember?" I remind him, literally trying to shake him off while I navigate, but his grip only tightens.

I can't let go of the ski or we might crash. I'm literally helpless. Shivering in compromising discomfort, my nipples harden more about the same time I feel something else harden against my lower back. I almost throw up in my mouth.

"Let's have a quick little naughty, eh, warm ya right up," he suggests, running his tongue down my neck.

"Jordan, that's enough," I state angrily, in built-up disgust.

"I know ya want it, Nina," he breathes into my neck, and squeezes me again, suggestively thrusting his hips back and forth on my tailbone.

I could cry and just about do. I look around and see a bunch of little islands, but they all look the same to me. Sadly, my options are limited. Short of jumping off the ski and swimming back, *but in which direction and for how long,* I'm stuck here with this horny effing pig. I pull back as far as the throttle will go. Barely acknowledging what's happening below my neck, I just want to get back to the boat ASAP so this whole nightmare can end. His hands tighten around my breasts, using them like a tether as he squeezes them every time he braces against an incoming wave and *thunk* of the ski on water. The feeling is unbearable.

We must have been gone only about thirty minutes or so, despite it feeling like a small eternity. Relief instantly floods my system as the sight of my friends comes into view. Jordan immediately drops his hands and leans back. I find it baffling and downright enraging that he has the sense to not flaunt that behavior in public, but has the audacity to do it behind closed doors without question or remorse.

I do my best to steer us towards the beach as everyone swims in the shallows.

"Oy!" Mel yells, as she sees us approaching.

Jordan instructs me to steer straight for the beach. Parking, I immediately jump off, stripping off the vest. I thrust it into his handsy palms and run towards Mel.

"How'd it go?" she asks, drawing out the "o" sound at the end, clearly eager for details.

"I'll tell ya later," I answer flatly, stifling a sob. *I just want my mom.*

"Okay, fine, lata then," she says quietly, clearly picking up on my mood as she worriedly glances back at me.

Jordan joins Donnie and Shayno, who smile and snicker and look back and forth between me and Jordan. Brodie, Jaz and Margot also pile around them.

"I don't kiss 'n tell," I overhear Jordan say proudly.

*Shoot me in the face.*

I reach up to smack my forehead in frustration, but think better of it. Gosh, what is Jordan saying about me to the others? They're all going to get the wrong idea. If I tell them the truth what would Brodie and the rest of them do or think? They're all best mates since school and I'm just a "blow in." I swallow audibly. Brodie stands there stiffly, while Margot glances at him, looking exceptionally happy regarding Jordan's retelling of our "romantic pash." Reassuring Mel that I'm okay, I nod and laugh nervously and we make our way back in the huddle.

"Pack it in, guys, we're headin' back," Brodie exclaims, suddenly hopping up on the boat.

The others whine a little in protest, but know better than to challenge the captain. We all swim back and climb aboard. Jaz and I are last to climb up the swim step.

"Nina, wanna ride the ski back?" Jordan eagerly asks.

As nice as I can muster, I smile politely, and reply truthfully, with conviction, "No, thanks, it made me a little sick."

Not waiting for a reply, I walk past Brodie, who cleans up, and I plop down on my seat. I draw my legs into my body, hugging myself. A single tear rolls down my cheek, but I wipe it away quickly before anyone notices. While the crew gets ready to jet, I brood internally. Mad mostly at Jordan and more at myself, I decide I want to forget about the whole thing and not let it bother me so I can enjoy the rest of the day. I'm determined to leave this in the past.

*One little hiccup, Nina, the rest has been bliss.*

Sensing something's up, Stella jumps on my lap and rests her head on my knee. I lean down and kiss the top of her forehead, pulling her in for a hug. I close my eyes for a minute, happy to escape in her embrace. I look up and see Brodie watching me, but he quickly looks away.

"Ready?" he calls out.

We all shout back various forms of affirmations with mine sounding most eager. I wave goodbye to Lucky's, hoping to never see it again. I feel less tense and more like my normal self with each passing minute as we put distance between us, the islands, and Jordan.

# 13

We make it back to the launching ramp. Brodie has been particularly withdrawn since we left Lucky's. I notice that the crew's overall spirit feels more deflated, the high of the day well behind us. Everyone unloads off the boat, but Stella and I hang back. Besides Brodie and me, all the others live on the other side of town so they carpool here and there for the most part.

"See ya tonight for the usual?" Donnie yells from his truck towards Brodie.

"Defo!" Brodie says.

Jaz lingers behind the rest of them. She passes her brother and leans up to give him a quick peck on the cheek.

"Thanks, brotha, for another banga," she says gratefully, hopping out. "Yar the best. See ya at the house lata, eh."

"Yep, sounds good," he answers in a clipped tone, strapping down some loose items and organizing his fins, masks and snorkels in their respective compartments.

Having no tolerance for Brodie's attitude, Jaz waits, staring at him with raised brows. He notices and pauses before glancing up at his sister. His cool demeanor melts and he offers her a sweet little smile as she runs to catch her ride. We wave goodbye to each other as they load up their cars and leave. I stand up and look around to see how I can contribute.

"Can I help with anything?" I ask, feeling useless, and right now I could use something to keep my mind off certain feelings and events.

"Nope, all good here, Nina," he says, not meeting my eyes as he shakes his head.

*Nina?* He rarely uses my full name anymore, especially when it's just the two of us.

*Cool*, Brooding Brodie has returned. *Hmm*, this thing with Jordan doesn't bother him, does it? I was really hoping to move past it and not have to tell him what really happened. While I should shout Jordan's indiscretions from the rooftops, the last thing I want is there to be this giant, awkward elephant in the room with my new group of friends and Brodie, especially considering the fact that the two of us are finally on better terms, after what, a whole two minutes? Besides, I don't think Brodie's jealous, he certainly has no reason to be. Maybe I can give him a simple explanation without going into detail.

"Look," I say, walking towards him, forcing him to meet my eyes, "I just want to say what happened with Jordan, it's—."

"None of my business, I know," he states matter-of-factly. "It's all good, Nina, ya do whateva ya wanna do."

"But, it wasn't like that," I whine in frustration.

"Oh, I reckon I got a good idea of what it was like," he sneers in my face. Mad at his little outburst, I want to tell him about Jordan's piggish ways when he says more calmly, "Besides, Jordo's my best mate."

*Ughhh*, and that's why I can't say anything. While I would out Jordan in a heartbeat, I don't, because doing so would affect Brodie. I don't want to be the cause of any rifts between life long friends and I don't even know how long I'm going to be in Australia. Brodie doesn't deserve to be put through that. I could care less about Jordan's feelings, but not Brodie's, so I hold my tongue. Instead, I pivot.

"Well I don't want it to come between us, seeing as how we're..." I struggle, trying to find the right word, "friends, I guess?"

"Yep, we're friends, Nina," he clarifies, while struggling to untangle some line. "Glad we're on the same page, eh."

"So we're okay then?" I ask hopefully, wanting it to go back to how it was before.

"We're aces," he quips with such shortness that I can tell we're far from it.

He hops onto the deck, and sighs deeply, rubbing his head in frustration. I stand, leaning on the rail, looking out at the still water around me. I wish I never climbed aboard that stupid SeaDoo. I absentmindedly rub my knee, thinking about my two failed attempts to even get on the thing. That should have been my first red flag. I sigh. *It is what it is.* You can't rewind the clock. I pinch my eyebrows together in frustration of that sad truth and lift my leg up on the seat to heave myself over onto the dock.

Seeing my pained expression, Brodie leans closer and extends a hand out to help me. I accept the small gesture as a peace offering and take his hand in mine, which brightens my mood instantly. He carefully hands me my backpack as I collect myself on the dock. Brodie aptly hurtles over the railing and runs off to get the ute, his keys jingling in his pocket. I hang back with Stella as he handles the boat. After he secures it in place, he tells me to drive the ute forward a few feet. I attentively do so until he hollers at me to stop. He opens the door and ushers me over, sliding in, then punches the ute in gear and we're off towards home.

We drive for a few minutes, neither of us talking. Brodie focuses on the highway in front of us, while I stare out the window at the endless fields of red earth. We're now only a few kilometers from Mick's and still we sit in silence. I can feel tension lingering in the air around us. Music plays from the stereo, but I can barely make out the song it's so low. I need music right now to assuage the atmosphere, and I need it loud. It's my turn for a peace offering.

"May I?" I ask, reaching towards the dial, but waiting.

Growing up in a family with loud opinions and a general lack of respect regarding someone else's music, I'm always ultra considerate of anyone's radio.

"'Course ya can," he mutters, simpering at my mindfulness.

He seems to relax a little as I crank the volume and roll my window down. "Clouds" by BØRNS moodily plays. I don't know this song, and don't even really listen to the lyrics, but zone out at the passing bush that leaves a muddled streak of dark greens and browns as we zoom by. Without realizing it, the music fades into The XX's "Intro." The sounds of rubber tire treads lull across the asphalt, and I stick out my hand and let it dance through the wind, clearing my mind in the process. The moon rises in the distance. I can barely make out the tiny, crescent shape. In tandem, the sun has begun its lengthy descent, but there's still plenty of bright light left in the sky.

"And just like that the world turns and it'll be a new day," I sigh, looking out the window, feeling lighter and more hopeful as I let the thought sink in.

I turn and see Brodie smiling as he drives.

"Quite the optimist," he says casually.

"It's been a wonderful... full day," I exhale in thoughtfulness, before chuckling. "I still can't believe you swam with a bloody tiger shark. Sometimes I think you're just asking for it." The thought of sharks and Brodie reminds me of something I've been wanting to ask him for a while now. I turn to fully face him as he drives. "Hey, I have something serious I want to ask you."

He waits.

Playfully, I let the suspense build a little and wait a beat.

"Are you named after Chief Brodie," I ask puckishly. "You know, the main character from *Jaws*?"

"No," he clarifies in a laugh, adamantly shaking his head. "I'm not. That's a hard no in fact!"

"Oh, that's one of my favorite films."

"Really? I hate that movie."

My eyebrows shoot up to my hairline.

"Wait, *what*?!" I shout. "How could you possibly hate *Jaws*? It's a cinematic masterpiece, it's like hating *Indiana Jones* or something!"

He shrugs, clearly enjoying our difference of opinion.

"It vilifies sharks, 'n I happen to love 'em," he explains simply.

*Hmm.* I sit back quietly. While the movie is groundbreaking in terms of its creative endeavors, it undoubtedly paints sharks in a terrible light. After today I can see why he holds them in such a special place in his heart, the reef shark not withstanding. They're special and remarkable, and ultimately they're the embodiment of nature.

"Ya see, that flick glorifies shark huntin'," he says, like he's reading my mind, "'n seein' what ya've seen today, bein' within metres of something so pure 'n raw of Mother Earth, how could anyone wanna hunt one purely for sport or revenge?"

I'm at a loss for words, simply because what he says is true.

We ride in silence for a minute. Brodie has his left hand on the wheel and the other resting on the door frame, half out the open window.

"That's why I love it out here," he whispers in reverence. "Sure, we're away from nearly everythin', but I'm the lucky bastard who gets to swim with sharks on my day off." He smiles to himself, deep in reflection. I sit back quietly, enjoying listening to someone's perspective on nature and the world. He swallows. "It's all innaconnected, Nina. The sun, the moon, the tides... the fish 'n the sharks, they're all a part of somethin' so much bigga than us. A neva endin' cycle of life, 'n I find that bloody beautiful."

He nods, content with his view of the world, and I must admit it's an incredible view. I've always had a deep love and respect for nature and the environment. Papi, like his ancestors, passed down a deep appreciation for the land and all that it offers in terms of life fulfillment and its priceless teachings. While I thought I was very much in tune with the earth, it's nothing compared to living every day truly in *tune* with nature. Dana Scully's line from an episode of the *The X-Files* comes to mind.

I whisper, as I recall the proper words, "'Respect nature, for it has no respect for you.'"

"Exactly," he replies, looking at me in satisfaction.

"I can't take credit for that one," I chuckle softly, "but I want you to know I understand what you mean. I hear you... About nature, I mean."

He glances at me out of the corner of his eye, still facing the road, and nudges me softly. We both sit quietly while he drives. There's not too many people in this world that I can sit with in utter silence and feel totally at peace. There's no pressure to speak or make conversation. We each can just be. That's a rare thing in life. I only have it with a handful of people, and Brodie's one of them. *Funny considering the road it took us to get here.* The thought warms my heart. My shoulders begin to shake as a laugh emerges and Brodie looks at me with an inquisitive eye.

"What's so funny?" he asks curiously.

We pass the turnoff to Mick's and continue straight towards Brodie's house. I guess he's not dropping me off first. His property is only the next one over.

"Nothing, really," I reply. "I was just thinking about when we first met, I couldn't really stand you. I thought you were arrogant and a tad indifferent."

"Me?!" he quips, and jabs my side. "I reckon ya've got that backwards."

"Wait, let me finish," I press on as I dodge his hand. "Anyway, we didn't really get off on the best foot, and now here we are sitting in comfortable silence with one another." He looks at me, smiling, starting to understand, then returns his eyes to the road. He turns off the highway towards the beach as I explain. "How many people do you know can sit with you and not pressure you for something in return, like awkward conversation? It's like sitting in silence is taboo these days."

"Ah, yeah, nah, I get it."

"I appreciate that about you," I say, as he pulls down a long dirt driveway. "That's rare."

Stella perks up, sensing we're close to home. I see a house in the distance. This is my first time to Brodie's. I'd be lying if I didn't admit I'm eager to see how he lives. Suddenly, he reaches for the volume dial and cranks the volume so high I can barely hear my own voice. "Ordinary World," the version by Red, screams from the vibrating speakers. The heavy guitar sections deafen the cab. *What happened to David Bowie??*

I laugh as Brodie leans over, crowding me as he drives.

"*I won't cry for yesterday, there's an ordinary world,*" he bellows, placing his mouth right next to my ear. "Is this quiet enough for ya, Neens?" he jokingly shouts. Stella tries to worm her way in between us. She showers Brodie with kisses as he sings. Laughing hysterically, I playfully push him away, shaking my head. We approach his house, but he leans in more, while continuing to sing obnoxiously. "*And as I try to make my way to the ordinary world, I will learn to survive.*"

He leans back in his seat as he pulls up alongside the house and parks. He turns off the car, but leaves the key in the ignition so the music doesn't stop. Tears form at the corner of my eyes as I double over, belly laughing. Brodie cranks the dial even louder, almost maxing it out. He swings open the ute's door, jumping out.

That's another beautiful thing about being out here in the middle of nowhere; you can do whatever the hell you want. No noise limits, no nosy Mrs. Kravitz living next door. It's one of the most liberating feelings in the world.

I follow Brodie's lead, barreling out of the ute and we run around with Stella, screaming the lyrics at the top of our lungs. It's just the cathartic release I need.

The song ends, and a forgettable ballad begins. I reach the front porch steps and fall over, lying halfway on the top step while my feet rest on the dirt walkway. The last heat of the day hits my face as I extend my arms to prop up my head. The edges of the wooden steps grind into my forearms and backside, but I don't even care. I exhale deeply, letting go of any underlying tensions, and push the feeling of Jordan's hands on my chest far away. Stella lies beside me as I stare up at the sky. Big, billowy clouds form overhead. They're not angry or gray. Brodie approaches, leaning over me. His amused face takes up most of my view. He holds out his arms, gesturing me to take them.

"Come on, Sunshine," he says. "Need yar help."

Happy to finally contribute, I reach out. He pulls me up stoutly onto my feet. Instructing me to wait by the shed, Brodie shuffles the trailer and boat. He hollers at me to climb on board - but only if I feel capable and to take it slow to avoid incident - and carry any items to the back swim step to be unloaded and cleaned. I do so without so much as a hiccup. After moving all of the looser and easier items such as the bags and snacks, I *carefully* handle the spearguns, then walk over to the giant esky. I grab the lid with both hands and push, using all my strength, but it doesn't budge.

"Ughhh" I squeeze out, the pressure building on my knee.

"We don't unload this big fella, just the fish," Brodie laughs, looking at the heavy esky. "I'll rinse 'n drain it lata once the ice's melted." As I rub my knee, massaging the thick scar under my fingers, he notices, and gestures to it. "How's it doin'?"

I'm surprised to hear him bring up anything related to my accident. I glance down at the site of my injury. The scar's faded some but still looks angry as a large, reddish purple jagged line. Seeing so much sun everyday, I'm paranoid about it burning and scarring so I sunscreen the crap out of it. Some would see the scar as a disfigurement, a sad reminder of lost vanity, but for me, when I see it, I think about how far I've come each day and how lucky I am to be here alive and walking.

"It flares up every once in a while," I answer in a shrug, "but most of the time it's bearable and I forget about it."

"Good."

He jumps off the edge of the swim deck, landing with a *thud* as his sandals hit the dirt. Stella waits idly by, as moral support. Brodie looks up at me. I stand about five feet over his head. It's a fun vantage point. I smile sardonically down at him, cocking my head in superiority.

"Here," he snorts, reaching up, "hand me the mahi mahi."

I open the lid of the esky and peer down at the lifeless, dull yellow body cut in two. It seems like ages ago, not hours, when I watched him spear it. I'm not the squeamish type, but I'm also not one to just reach in and grab a wild animal, especially dead ones. *Hmmm.* I hesitantly reach down and touch the scales, poking at the skin quickly. It feels slimy and stiff to the touch.

"It's dead, Neens," Brodie assures me, rolling his eyes.

I make a sour face as I reach for the tail and lift it. Holy hell, it's heavier than I thought. I flashback to this morning when it took all three muscular men to pull this beast onto the boat. I get a good grip on the tail with both hands and make another disgusted face.

"Wanna come down here 'n have me hand it ova to ya?" he offers, waiting below.

Imagining myself squashing like a bug, I don't see that as a better option. I shake my head in answer and hoist up the heavy fish from the ice chest. My biceps burn, but the chilled weight of the fish and touch of ice feels amazing against the dying heat and my current exertion. I carefully twist my torso, carrying the fish towards Brodie, when I feel it slipping from my grasp. Sensing this, Brodie urgently reaches up and grabs it before I lose it.

*Phew.*

He walks it over to the filet table, next to the deck. He lays it down with a giant *thunk,* grunting from the relief of his efforts. He positions it while searching around for his filet knife.

I refocus my efforts on the other half lying in front of me, wedged tightly in the esky. This half is the front end of the dolphinfish, so the bulk of the meat is here, meaning it's going to be harder to bench than the first piece. I reach for it, and pull it to me, dislodging it from its tight surroundings. Before realizing it, I'm holding it in a close embrace to carry the heavy weight. Abruptly, it slides all the way down the front of my bathing suit and drops back into the esky. I peer down. A rusty colored skid mark, clad of scales and watered down blood, streaks my upper trunk and chest. It's super slimy and reeks of dead fish.

"*So* nasty," I exclaim, holding my arms out in disgust.

Determined and unwilling to let this deter me from my objective, I resume my task at hand and reach again for the fish. I don't have the tail to hold onto this time, so I need a better game plan. Back by my feet, Brodie watches patiently as I make it my personal mission to extract it and finish the job.

"I can just do it, Neens," he proposes, after minutes go by, but I shut that down with one hard shake of my head. I grunt, trying to lift with the right angle of my arms. Brodie laughs, taunting me. "At this rate, we might be here all night."

Cringing slightly at the thought, I move my fingers over the dark green dorsal fin, endeavoring to clamp down on it tight like a handle. It feels almost sharp against my fingers. I reach around the other smooth side with my other hand. Mustering all of my might, I manage to lift the rest of it out of the tub.

"Brodie, I'm losing it," I warn, feeling it slipping down.

"Hold tight, just a tick longa," he assures me, standing right underneath me, waiting to catch it in case.

I angle it slightly sideways, balancing it to keep it from skidding away. Thankfully, I manage to lower it enough where Brodie can reach it. He takes it. My body bounces backwards, free. That's work, right there, and to think he normally does this alone. Stealing a glimpse of my disgusting hands, I catch the diminishing sun glisten off the clear, scaly fish oil from my fingers and palms. I wipe some sweat off my forehead with the back of my hand, and carefully climb down the steps. It's late arvo and still in the low eighties.

Finding the right angle, Brodie begins to lay out the smaller half, carving a deep gash down along bone. A giant piece of white meat peels off. Watching him, he looks like a professional butcher, clearly a man skilled and comfortable with a blade. While one hand carves, the other adeptly pulls the tip of the meat away, lifting it off cleanly. I walk over to the hose, adjacent to Brodie, and turn it on. I jump as the water hits my toes, shrinking away from the surprisingly refreshing temp.

"Straight outta the well," Brodie cries out over his shoulder.

Conservatively at first, to not splash cold water all over me, I lean over and timidly wash off the scales from my bathing suit. Quickly, I realize it's going to require some elbow grease. I pull off my denim shorts, which somehow remain untainted, and hold the hose overhead. I squeal as the water hits my head, encompassing my whole body. It's frigid!

Brodie looks up as I endeavor to brush off the bloody scales, shield the water from my eyes, and hold the hose above me, all simultaneously. Water flies everywhere. Setting the knife down, he walks over and grabs the nozzle from me. I peer up at the shape of him, my eyelids batting wildly as beads of flowing water endlessly envelop my open eyes. He signals for me to continue with the spin of a finger. Much easier with the flexibility of using both hands, I take the opportunity to wash through my hair. I feel the ends of my curls hitting my lower back as it cascades down completely straight, the water creating a silky bed of golden and brown flowing strands. I massage my hands through the top of my head thoroughly, and hastily wash away any remaining traces of sunscreen from my face. My lips stiffen from the cold. I move my way down from my neck to my chest, scrubbing hard to get the scales off my suit and skin. Some stubbornly stick and require extra attention.

I open my eyes and find Brodie staring down at me in amusement. Clad in just my bathing suit, I feel a little self-conscience as he basically watches me bathe. While it's a tad disconcerting, maybe what Donnie said earlier is true. Maybe I need to be less shy with my body and just embrace it? *I need to care less*. I breathe heavily from the icy water and speedily move my hands back and forth over my suit, giving my front a once over before I signal to Brodie. He leans over and turns the hose to a trickle, washing his fishy hands before turning it off completely.

Shivering, I stand there dripping wet, looking around for a towel or a rag or something. Suddenly, a dry towel folds around me from behind, wrapping me tight like a burrito. I sigh loudly at the present comfort, and turn to face Brodie. I manage to emit a teeth chattering thanks before he spins me towards the house and guides me inside to a warm space. Brodie doesn't leave the A/C on when he and Stella leave all day, so it takes a while for the house to cool down after a hot sunny day. However, after my unexpected well-water shower, I embrace the coziness and immediately relax.

I look around and realize Brodie's left me alone. I hear the door close shut behind me and turn to see my backpack leaning against the wall, with my crusty shorts folded neatly on top. I reach for it and unzip the main compartment, looking for something dry. That's the only downside of being a light packer... you don't really have options. Mom instilled in us girls to always carry a backup pair of undies so I unzip a pair from my hidden pocket. *Thanks, Mom.* I also pull out my damp tank top. It smells of sunscreen and musty salt water, but I deduce it's better than my sopping wet suit.

Scanning my surroundings for what I hope is a bathroom, I glance around me. The house is a bit older, but surprisingly very clean. Actually I'm not that surprised. Brodie keeps his boat and ski immaculately spotless. The ute's another story, but we can't all be tens. You can tell a bachelor lives here all on his own. There's not much to speak of regarding interior design and decor. There's only two framed pictures on the wall, one is a family shot of him, Jaz and their parents on a boat from years ago, and the other is him holding Stella when she was a tiny puppy on the beach out front. Holy cow was she an adorable little teddy bear!

Trying not to pry, I can't help but look around. I notice tan tile floors butt up to white walls. One black leather loveseat sits in the middle of the living room, and there's a small table with four chairs in the open dining room. Overall, the house boasts a wide open floor plan. The kitchen, living room, and eating area are all one large room together. The designated eating space opens to sliding glass doors adjoining the deck out front. The house is not large by any means, and most Americans would consider it on the smaller end, but as a huge advocate of tiny house living, this place feels enormous and pretty spacious to me.

Movement from outside the window catches my eye, and I look out to see Brodie hauling off the plastic wrapped fish filets to the shed, probably to load up his fish freezer.

Dripping water across his floor, I hastily tiptoe down the little hallway in search of the bathroom. I see three doorways, two of which are closed, and one which opens at the end of the hall. Must be a two bedrooms and two bathrooms layout, I note. All of a sudden, I hear the kitchen faucet spurting to life far behind me.

"Toilet's at the end of the hall in my room," Brodie hollers. "I'm gonna go hose down the boat, alright?"

Not wanting to make a total mess all the way through his house, I quickly run through his room and pounce on the bathroom rug in front of a built-in vanity. I feel kind of exposed since his bathroom is a part of the master bedroom, but I see a door for the commode and shower, and step inside, closing it behind me. I hastily shed my freezing suit, leaving it in a damp pile by my feet. Standing there stark naked, I pull out my clothes from under my armpit. A light knock on the door turns my whole body rigid like a marble statue. I freeze in suspense. I glance down and notice a shadow perforating under the door.

*It's locked, right?! Wait, I definitely did* not *lock it.*

The wood squeaks as the dark figure moves away on the other side. Wrapping the towel tightly around me, I listen closely at the door, but don't hear anything or sense anyone close. Very slowly, I open the door an inch and see the bathroom empty. What was that about, I wonder? Taking a small step out to see what's going on, I notice a stacked white shirt and flannel folded perfectly on the floor in front of me. Grateful, I grab them and change back in the commode quarters before opening the door again. I coil my towel around my hair and twirl it up, around my head. It feels awkward to scope out Brodie's room without him here, and I really need to find a place to hang my drying suit.

I walk outside and see him power washing the boat from the inside out. He notices me with my suit dangling from my fingers and points to a rack of hanging hooks above the hose. After hanging up my suit, I peer back at him. I never really realized the amount of effort and maintenance that goes into owning a boat. While everyone else reaps the benefit of enjoyment, Brodie has to spend another hour or more cleaning it up after each use, and I never hear him say a word in complaint or ask for help. I suppose he's used to it considering he does it for a living, but still.

While he finishes that chore, I head back inside. Clad in my dry outfit, I feel much improved standing in Brodie's modest white and wood kitchen. Looking around for something to do to help get dinner started and lighten his load, I open the fridge and see a wicker basket of veggies. I grab it and lay it in the sink to wash the individual tomatoes and variations of squash. Above the sink, a large, open screened window lets in a breath of fresh ocean air. Hanging chimes would be a nice little touch there.

I look out past the deck and smile as Brodie playfully laughs at Stella, squirting her with the hose as she hops around, barking at the nozzle. After she runs off, he coils up the hose and heads to the deck to prep the other half of the filet. He notices me standing in the window and turns my way, checking on me.

"Much better," I mention appreciably, adjusting the flannel's rolled sleeves.

It smells of a mixture of Brodie: salty with a manly musk scent, and laundry detergent. Blue and gray, it's very much broken in and worn, in the best way imaginable. Back home it would probably sell for at least fifty bucks at a thrift shop.

His smile lingers on me as I begin chopping up some tomatoes and squash at the counter. I don't know how Brodie usually does it, but I'm thinking veggie kabobs sound amazing with the fish. Finally locating the kabob sticks, I set them in a bowl of water then turn my attention back to the fridge to scour the rest of my marinade supplies. I'm delighted to find some teriyaki, tamari, wasabi, hot chili oil, sesame oil, sriracha, and a can of pineapple. Mom, a huge sauce connoisseur, would be proud of his collection. I pile the cut veggies, along with big chunks of sweet onion into a bowl to marinade, which back home we call "Refrigerator Door." The marinade is literally made up of everything you can find in the fridge that's sauce related, and somehow the combination always turns out delicious.

Brodie tinkers with the speaker out on the deck. While he's not busy, I request "Dosas and Mimosas" by Cherub, and he puts it on loudly for me to hear in the kitchen. He laughs when I belt out the chorus enthusiastically. Aw, this song is always so cathartic. In fact, I feel so good that I feel like I've had a metaphoric glass of wine. Music is my immediate mood enhancer. I wave the knife in the air, singing unabashedly when the chorus comes again. "*To all the bitch-ass hoes who hate me the most, yeah, I hate you too!*"

As the hour passes, Brodie cleans his butchery station, while I wash and ready the lettuce, tidying up the kitchen as I go. Brodie shuffles a reggae playlist of his, playing some Steel Pulse, Peter Tosh and Bob Marley & The Wailers classics before rolling into more contemporary songs such as "Warning (feat. Stick Figure)" by Pepper to "Music Daisy" by Jason Arcilla. I pull out the marinade and assemble my kabobs, adding in the pineapple. I line them up in an oversized dish and pour the leftover marinade all over, allowing them to soak for as long as possible before the crew arrives. We both bob our heads collectively as the catchy tune "How High?" by Damnboy! fills the air. Brodie plastic wraps each portion of meat, stacking the white fish filets into a big pile on the large outdoor table. He preserves some large chunks for dinner, and carts away the rest. He returns and throws some smaller raw pieces to Stella who gladly snatches them in the air with the clamp of her jaw.

Spearfishing is the most sustainable way to live. I've learned you take only what you need to eat, when you need it, and you discard as much of the bones and bits back to the ocean for some other creatures to feast on. Not to mention it's a lot easier than trekking out to the store, and loads more fun.

I finish my duties ahead of Brodie and walk out through the sliding door onto the covered deck and sit on the front two steps. I have no idea when the rest of the crew will show up, and ask Brodie as much.

"Wheneva they feel like it," he grins, explaining. "For my sista, it's usually about an hour afta everyone else."

His playlist must have ended because after a silent minute, The Eagles' "One of These Nights" comes on. Arranging the drinks and ice in the deck esky, Brodie hums along as I snuggle Stella on the steps.

"Like that, Lel?" I say, rubbing under her chin, then repeat my term of endearment, which rolls off the tongue. "You're such a good noodle, Lella."

"Spoiled girl," Brodie mutters, looking at us while he lays a stick of butter next to his spices, adjacent to the grill. He catches my attention and holds up a large chunk of wrapped meat. "This is Mick's. I'll put it in this esky so we don't forget lata."

Standing with bloody fishy hands, he twists on the hose and water pours, squirting out. I feel cold drops hit my toes on the steps. Naturally, I gather the toasty warm flannel tighter around my torso. Brodie washes his gut ridden hands before reaching up and grabbing his shirt, pulling it off in one quick swoop. He throws it at my face. It hits me square in the nose. I smirk as it falls into my hands. He then continues to wash his body and holds the hose over his head with his left arm, his bicep naturally flexing as he does. He closes his eyes as the water flows seamlessly from the top of his curls, down his face, and over his chest and hips.

While he's preoccupied, I take a minute to appreciate the sight in front of me. He's toned and muscular, but not in a gym rat, body building way. Instead, he's lean and chiseled from staying in great natural shape from spearfishing, swimming, and playing off the land. By no means skinny, he's positively a picture of sun kissed health. He reaches over to turn the nozzle off, and I see the indents of his abs softly accented by the porch twinkle lights. He turns towards me and I look away before he catches me eyeing him. A tad frazzled, I stand up and begin to look around his property, trying to act natural. Again, he has no close neighbors other than Mick and the crabs and occasional sea turtles. As he dries off quickly, he reminds me, pointing straight out to the ocean, that his property butts right up to the beach.

"Wanna grand tour?" he asks in a tone mixed with pride and shyness.

"Sure. Thought you'd never ask."

He leads me around his house to the detached shed. He rolls up the giant door revealing a couple of dirt bikes, a SeaDoo, the giant fish freezer, and a mess of tools and camping gear. Then he guides me on a walk around the back of his house where he has a garden full of vegetables, all of which are thriving. I quickly surmise that the ones from the fridge must have been recently plucked from this little oasis.

"How wonderful!" I exclaim, squatting down to survey the growing leaves and ripening veggies. I lightly caress a tomato leaf with my thumb, feeling the familiar little prickles against my skin. I note there are dozens of tomatoes ripening on the vine. Thinking first of my garden back in the US and then about the kangaroo's decimation of my budding one at Mick's, I sigh wistfully. "I miss getting my hands dirty."

"Anytime, feel free," he offers, with a hint of a smile in his voice.

He then leads me inside and shows me the rest of the house. His room literally consists of a three drawer walnut dresser and a simple bed with a heather gray comforter. On top, two sleeping pillows stack against the wall. I notice the barren walls, there's not even a television set. We briefly pass over the already familiar bathroom. The second bedroom is even more minimal with just a basic desk and wooden chair. The desk boasts a speargun he's clearly working on as spare parts lie next to the shaft. As I glance around quickly, before moving ahead with the tour, I notice a guitar leaning against the wall in the far corner of the room, but before I can ask about it, he ushers me onward.

Brodie motions to the third door in the hallway and explains it's the guest bathroom, but he's in the midst of renovating it himself. He laughs, telling me construction has come to a crashing halt with little downtime lately between all of our fun days spent out on the water or under the stars. I notice how all of the rooms have nice lighting, but he confides it doesn't really matter as he's pretty much outside every day.

"It's not a whole lot, but it's enough, and it's mine," he says happily, looking around at his home.

"I beg to differ. Seems you've got everything you could ever need."

"Well, now ya've seen it all, well almost all. Ya know the beach out front obviously, but there's one more place I wanna show ya," he says, sounding slightly eager. "Aside from the beach, it's my favourite part of the property."

Before he can show me, we hear Stella barking, alerting us to an incoming vehicle. A red dust trail travels quickly towards the house, confirming her alarm. We both walk to the front and see Jordan stepping off his bike, leaning it on its kickstand.

I freeze in my tracks. I completely forgot he existed for a minute there. Brodie keeps walking towards him, not noticing my sudden hesitation.

"J-Dog, mate!" Brodie cries out, clapping Jordan's back in affection as they embrace.

Jordan turns and sees me, lighting up, "Hey!"

"Hi," I reply, keeping it short, in a more clipped tone.

He walks up and kisses my cheek in greeting. My blood ices over the second his lips touch my skin. I stiffly pull back and smile politely, stealing a glimpse at Brodie. He smiles warmly at us, perhaps a trifle bit too warmly, but that could just be me imagining things. He really must of meant what he said about us being friends. For a minute there, I could easily see it maybe turning into something more, but maybe I've been reading too much into those signs and feelings as well.

Another engine looms in the distance and within a minute, a familiar charcoal ute arrives and out piles Donnie, Mel, Margot, Jaz, and Shayno. They all look recently showered and a bit more refreshed.

"Look at this," Brodie hollers towards Jaz, clearly impressed. "Arrivin' on time for a change, eh?"

She waives him off with a laugh.

Margot skips over to us, wearing a white billowy dress and roman style sandals. She eyes my flannel briefly before standing at Brodie's elbow. She reaches out and pulls him into a hug as she greets him. Much to my chagrin, she lingers before letting go.

*What do you mean, Nina? She can linger for as long as she likes. You have no say, remember.*

Jordan stares at me with desire in his eyes. I turn away abruptly, giving him the shaft as I warmly greet Donnie. Jordan circles back, and tries to put his arm around my shoulder, but I immediately pull away, leaving him looking slightly wounded. Mel runs up in her cozies and crushes me in a big hug as if it's been months of separation and not a couple of hours.

"I need to know what happened?" she mumbles in my ear.

"Later," I whisper. "Not now."

Her large eyes widen in understanding, taking the hint.

Jaz pulls me in for a hug and we all make our way to Brodie's deck. He has long bench seating so all of us can sit comfortably together at the large table directly underneath the swaying strands of twinkle lights. Jaz opens up the esky and takes out some coldies. I see there's a couple of bottles of hard liquor in there as well. She starts pouring rum and passes me a small glass.

"No, no, I already had one drink too many today," I mutter, vehemently shaking my head.

"Exactly why ya need at least two more," boasts Jordan.

The rest of the crew won't have it either and they urge me to enjoy myself. While I don't typically cave to peer pressure, I accept the drink, but make myself a compromise to only slowly sip the one, and no more. Like I said before, Aussies could easily drink *anyone* under the table.

"What are you guys doing to me?" I ask rhetorically, staring at my drink.

I look at Mel and she laughs. She knows I don't drink a lot. She raises her own glass and downs it. I shake my head at her, raise a dramatic eyebrow, and take a lady-like sip from mine. I even stick out my pinky finger for flare. She snickers in delight.

Light fades gently from the sky as night sneaks upon us, engulfing our backdrop in an embrace of violet blues. Everyone enjoys themselves and as I hear them discuss some mutual acquaintance's love life, Brodie mentions he's going to fire on the grill and prep the fish. I jump up from the table, remembering my kabobs. He eyes me, wondering what I'm up to as I disappear into the house and make my way to the kitchen fridge.

"Veggies!" I call out over my shoulder.

Shutting the fridge door tightly, I balance the dish, trying not to jostle any of the marinade onto the floor or Brodie's shirt I'm wearing. I carefully carry the platter of kabobs out to the deck and set them down next to our grill master. He looks at them in admiration before smiling largely at me, brows raised, impressed. He takes them and starts placing them next to the mahi mahi. The marinade sizzles as it hits the primed grill. I smugly raise one shoulder before rejoining the others.

Minutes later, the delicious and familiar scents of Refrigerator Door waft throughout the air. In between rotating the kabobs and waiting for the fish to grill, Brodie relaxes and takes a swig of his cold beer, glancing at the boys.

"Oy, what's that crackin' smell?" Shayno wonders, actively looking around.

"Nah, yeah, mate, it's makin' my mouth wata," Donnie agrees, sniffing the air.

Not wanting to publicly acknowledge the praise, I sit back and keep quiet, while inside I'm reveling in it. Stealing my attention away, Jaz asks about home. I tell her all about the family and how we're all very close and basically all live together with Abuela.

"Three generations all togetha?" she exclaims.

"Well, four if you include Javi who practically lives there too. Yeah, Papi's familia's from México and that's just how they've always done it and how we do it, I guess."

"Yeah, guys, she speaks Spanish," Donnie happily explains.

"Mi apellido es Esquivel. Hay una gran posibilidad de que lo haga," I reply in basic Spanish 101, laughing. The entire crew stares at me. I look at each of their surprised faces. "You guys should see your faces right now."

"So that's why ya call her Chica, then," Shayno says, looking at Donnie.

I inform them how growing up so close to México, Spanish is the second most prominent language spoken in Southern California, but then quickly realize that's not the case out here.

Brodie refocuses back on the grill. Dinner must be cooked because he readies and serves up plates for everyone. He dishes everyone a veggie kabob next to a couple of fish tacos. I notice how he doesn't grill or warm the flour tortillas. *Interesting.*

"What are these?" Jordan mouths, biting into a kabob.

"For real," Margot chimes in, " that flavor is incredible."

"Nina's doin'," Brodie announces, shooting me a nod and a smile as he hands me my plate.

As soon as my plate is set in front of me, I pick up a taco. I bite into the tortilla and immediate warmth and astonishing flavor flood my mouth. Steam rises off the freshly grilled fish. I moan, closing my eyes. Everyone laughs. Sensually biting his lip, Jordan looks at me with a different kind of hunger that makes me gag on my taco.

"This is really good. Like crazy good!" I tell Brodie truthfully, while also giving it extra flare to cover up my choking reaction. "That breadcrumb thing combined with that fresh fish is just *wow.*" Brodie looks pleased with himself, and Jordan looks like he feels overlooked. I don't really care about anything though, I'm just enjoying this taco. The fish is literally falling apart in my mouth it's so tender and flaky. "I love how the seasoning doesn't overcrowd the natural flavor of the fish."

The whole crew chuckles, and Brodie tears into his filet, clearly enjoying it too. He pulls apart a kabob and pops a few veggie bites into his mouth. He chews for a few seconds and closes his eyes before they pop wide open in pleasure.

"Bloody rippa," he moans, in between bites.

Now it's my turn to laugh.

As we all eat and drink, we sit back and recount the thrills of the day out on the water; I obviously withhold my uncomfortable exchange with Jordan. After second servings are had, the fish long gone and a few funny stories shared, I tell everyone to pull out their phones. I loaded a bunch of photos and a fun video edit from our camping trip last weekend. I airdrop the collection of photos to everyone except Jordan; I blame a faulty connection. The crew freaks out as they view each photo.

"I mean, I knew yar a photographa," Jaz says, sounding surprised, "but like, wow, Nina, these are *really* good."

"Chockers of talent, this one," Mel says, playfully petting my head with affection, like a proud mom; my freshly dried curls bounce all over as she does.

"Nah, I just capture what I see," I argue, trying to downplay it.

"Well, I could 'capture' what I see 'n it would neva look like these," Shayno chimes in, holding up his phone with one of my photos to emphasize his point.

Margot, who normally comes off too cool for school, even looks interested in them.

"So ya like use a filta or somethin'?" she snorts cynically, and condescendingly. "Everyone uses those nowadays."

"Not really," I inform her. "I just tinker with the exposure and basic settings. If I do use one it's one of my own."

"The real dealio," Jordan chimes in, leaving Margot looking like a snake ready to strike.

"Again, no filta in the world would make mine look this good," Shayno repeats, reiterating his last point.

The group erupts in laughter and collectively agrees. I haven't even shown them the video edit I made yet, but don't want to debut it on the small iPhone screen. With drone footage, I think bigger is better when it comes to its display.

"Brodie, do you have a TV or a laptop?" I ask him.

Part of me is eager for them to see it, and another part of me hopes they don't. I'm a little nervous.

"What, Nina, ya think Brodie's from the middle ages or somethin', eh?" Jordan laughs, and quips in a belittling tone.

"I don't know," I answer truthfully, thinking about his minimalistic vibe inside. "I don't think I'd be too surprised if he was."

Brodie's mouth forms a big "oooh" like he's been mortally wounded, but it's all in jest. I laugh, looking down at my hands.

"Yeah, two shakes," Brodie says, getting up, lightly touching my shoulder as he walks towards the sliding glass door.

Jordan gives me this look I can't read; it's not malicious, but not altogether friendly either.

*This guy just needs to evaporate.*

"Here's a lappy for ya," Brodie says upon his return, and places a MacBook down on the table in front of me. He leans down. "'N it's even got charge, too. Not bad for a cave man, eh?"

I purse my lips. *Touché.*

The crew chuckles at our little entente. Brodie stands behind me, while the rest of the group huddles around me, patiently waiting.

"Give me one minute, guys," I inform them. Thankfully it's a Mac, otherwise the whole process would be more of a pain and a lot slower. I queue it up. "Alright, it's no big deal, really, but here it is. Hope you guys like it."

Suddenly music, "Lovers" by Anna of the North, starts playing and a visual of crystal clear water appears. Big giant rocks from our park adventure emerge, followed by sequences of quick paced video snippets. The edits are timed to the song's beat. Everyone starts "ooh-ing" and "aww-ing" and laughing when they see themselves on screen. The compilation is a couple of minutes in length of all my shots: video clips of us in the car laughing, Jaz and me making funny faces at the camera while hiking, Mel snuggling me by the bonfire, the guys wrestling in the swimming hole, Stella sticking her face out the window, Brodie trailing Donnie's ute down the red, dusty trail. Admittedly there's not too much of Margot, but, hey, she's the one keeping to herself for the most part. Her loss. I steal a glance at her and she definitely looks a bit regretful. Shayno and Jaz laugh as they see themselves kissing behind the campfire.

"You two just smashin' yar backs out the whole time, eh," Jordan exclaims loudly.

Jaz's face flushes in embarrassment as she glances at Brodie out of the corner of her eye.

The song builds momentum before breaking out into a giant crescendo right after the midpoint of the song. *Ooh*, this is my favorite part. The song and visual build anticipation and I edit the video in a way so a long, wide drone shot of the desert highway lingers as the rhythm amps up.

"Wait for it," I tease.

Mel giggles beside me. Brodie leans in closer, and Jordan eyes him territorially. Just as the beat approaches the boiling point, it drops a heavy base line simultaneously as a topdown visual of the hammerhead shark fills the screen. Brodie screams, beaming at the screen. The crew freaks out.

"Yewww!" yell Donnie and Shayno at the same time.

"No way!" Brodie exclaims in disbelief, grabbing his head with both of his hands, as his mouth drops wide open.

The video intercuts from Brodie swimming alongside the hammerhead to the rest of us on shore literally jumping up and down. Then it transitions directly to Stella running along the beach. I add in some B-roll snippets of the water lapping up on shore, and us laughing our brains out, hanging by the car as Brodie dries off after his encounter. There's even a cool shot of me launching The Khal. In the clip, I have no idea Brodie's even filming me until I look up and laugh, then roll my eyes at him, covering the shaking lens with my hand. Watching this clip, he happily looks over at me, scrunching his nose and eyes.

"Yeah, Neens!" he hollers.

Next, the volume of the song lowers as it switches to hilarious footage of us and our actual dialogue, belting out "Tiny Dancer" on the ride home. The whole crew chimes in while watching the laptop, singing the chorus aloud. Back on screen, after a nice pano aerial shot of the utes trekking across the beach, I cut to a close-up topdown angle of the hammerhead swimming swiftly off to sea, tracking downward while following it until it's out of sight. The drone sweeps up, flying towards the sun as it fades to white as the song comes to a simultaneous end. The group erupts into giant applause and Jaz hugs me as Mel mock punches me in the shoulder, smiling.

"Yar a wizard, Chica!" Donnie cries out, swooping me in for a hug.

"Crash hot, Nina!" Shayno exclaims, shaking his head.

"Wow, that was bloody brilliant, Neens," Brodie cheers, giving me a stinging high five.

The whole group requests the video so they can watch it "ova 'n ova again," as they put it.

"This is just the thing I need for my insta," Margot states.

"Hold on a sec, GoGo, if yar gonna post it, ya ask Neens for permission first. Then ya gotta give her credit. She won't ask for it, but that's the least ya can do as it's free conny for ya," Mel declares to her sister.

"'Course," Margot replies, with the biggest fake smile. "Always do."

Mel gives me a look that says clearly the opposite.

I'm one of those people that's cursed with the invisibility stick. My photos and videos are pretty high quality if I do say so myself, and there aren't too many girl drone pilots out there in the world, but I still have a pitiful following. I decided long ago I could never keep up with the chase, and would rather chase the passion than the follower count instead. Maybe that's why I don't have that many. Besides the point, I don't do any of this for attention. I do it because it's fun and I have full creative license, and the best reason of all: *it makes me really happy*. Hopefully it brings others a fraction of the same joy it brings me; that's why I even share them publicly in the first place.

"In fact," Margot continues nonchalantly, "I might need some help to build some conny if yar around."

"Yeah, sure, sounds good," I say in agreement.

"She'll pay ya," Mel assures me, glaring at Margot, waiting for her to confirm.

"Nah, yeah," Margot reluctantly says, stalking off. "Rack off, Mel."

"I should hire you as my agent," I laugh at Mel.

"Ya couldn't afford me," she jests back.

We all sit outside on Brodie's porch for a while longer. The stars shine brightly and there's not a lick of wind.

By 11:30PM, Mel is three sheets to the wind, or a "gutful of piss" as Aussies say, and Jaz, Shayno, and Donnie support her, guiding her to the truck's backseat. They lay her flat so her feet hang off the side of the bench. The others climb in the front seat and on the other side of Mel, gently shifting her around to fit. Jordan glances at me, waiting to ask me something, but thankfully Brodie cuts in before he can.

"I'll take Nina home, J-Dog," Brodie declares. "It's only next door 'n yar off in the otha direction."

"Yeah, but then ya'd have to get back in the ute 'n take her when I'm already headin' out," he counters.

Brodie glances at me, as does Jordan, the two waiting for my opinion. Stalling, I don't know what to say. All I do know is I can't be alone with Jordan... *Think, Nina, think.*

Margot walks up to the ute, but doesn't climb in. She stalls to hear how this conversation plays out.

When my palm starts to sweat and I'm about to answer, Brodie says, "Wait, almost forgot, Old Boy Mick needs to borrow my saw for tomorrow 'n I told him I'd bring it tonight. Reckon it won't fit on the back of the bike."

I close my eyes in relief and want to hug Brodie on the spot. It's settled then. Jordan looks a little disappointed, and wishfully stares at me. I look down and uncomfortably smile. Pretending, I yawn hugely, perhaps a bit too exaggerated, covering my mouth with my bare hand. *Take the hint, buddy.*

"I'm wiped," I reiterate to Brodie, hoping Jordan will get the memo. "Can you take me home soon, please?"

Margot shuts the ute's door and instead asks Jordan for a ride. He gladly accepts as he gives me a face that reads *you're missing out.* The pair of them load up and take off on the bike, followed by Donnie and the crew. With the ute and bike well out of earshot, Brodie laughs.

"Ha, nice one, Neens. Yar a terrible liar. Anyone can tell yar not buggered. That fake yawn," he says, laughing again. "Are ya really cooked? Want me to take ya back now or can I show ya somethin' first?"

"No, I'm nowhere near tired," I answer truthfully and curiously.

I forgot he wanted to show me something earlier.

He starts walking around the corner of the house and I follow. A ladder leans against the side, leading up to the aluminum roof.

"Take it slow, Neens," Brodie suggests over his shoulder, as he begins to climb. I test the stability of the ladder. It's seems really sure footed. The moon's so bright tonight I can actually see quite a lot. "It's secure," Brodie reassures me, leaning over from the roof. "Cross my heart."

I grab one slat and then another and before I know it, I make it to the top. It looks a bit tricky crossing onto the actual roof, but Brodie's there, waiting, and takes my outstretched hand and pulls me up onto a small deck. Really it's just reinforced wooden boards lying flat in a 8'x8' square. I notice he has a blanket spread out next to a lit lantern. Stella whines from the ground below us, wanting to come up with us too.

"House, Stel," he orders, and she reluctantly listens.

Without the twinkle lights below, it's a lot darker up here. The little lantern helps, and thankfully the moonlight casts a silver glow on anything brightly colored. Following the bright shape of Brodie's shirt, I see him lie down on the blanket. He motions for me to come lie next to him. As my eyes adjust, I hesitantly walk over with my arms outstretched. I almost trip, but he catches me and we both laugh at my clumsiness. Finally, I sit and get situated.

"Lie all the way back," he instructs. Listening, I lean back, and settle into the blanket. He raises his finger, pointing up. "Look."

I inhale suddenly, gasping as I gaze up to see the entire sky, unobstructed, full of bright twinkling stars. It reminds me of our view out of the ute window as we camped, but this time without the truck's frame blocking out a good portion of the skyline. Living out here remotely, one of the best benefits is the lack of light pollution and human intrusion. It's incredibly empty and desolate and still. The desert around us feels like a giant landscape the dark night sky can swallow whole.

"You get this all to yourself, whenever you want?" I whisper, exasperated, and feel him nod.

We sit and stargaze for a while. I squeal as a shooting star flies by. Brodie chuckles at my genuine enthusiasm.

"Thought ya'd like it up here," he says simply.

Just as I really nestle in and pour my attention into the detail of the Milky Way I think about Mick.

"Mick!" I exclaim, sitting up a little. "I forgot to call him and tell him I'd be late."

"Dun worry," Brodie urges me back down, tugging on my arm. "He called a coupla hours ago. I told him about the crew 'n how much fun we were havin' 'n said ya'd be lata 'n not to wait up."

"Okay, thanks," I reply, knowing that Mick will still stay up and wait for me.

I lean back again and relax. At least he knows I'm not in some ravine on the side of the road. *Wow, that's a morbid thought, Nina.*

I shake my head a little to expunge the despairing feeling. Taking in this all encompassing view of the universe, I imagine how many uncharted areas of exploration there is and how I could easily find myself getting lost in the never ending possibility of life, awe, and beauty. If I were an astronaut, how great would it be to have God's own view of the world. What a celebration that must be. I'd definitely need music. Imagine the absolute freedom of not having any worries about how loud you're blasting your music when seated at the precipice of the world's open frontier. What song would I be listening to first?

"What are ya thinkin' ova there?" Brodie asks.

"I'm trying to decide what song I'd be blasting if I were an astronaut up there in that nebula."

A heavy silence fills the air before we both start snorting.

"And?" Brodie asks in between hysterics.

"I don't know. You asked me before I could make up my mind," I reply, trying to decide. "At this moment I'm trying to choose between U2's 'Beautiful Day' or Tash Sultana's 'Notion'. Hard to say definitively, but I think I'm leaning towards the latter. Have you ever heard the intro to that song? Yeah, I'm definitely going with 'Notion.'"

We lay in silence for a while again. With Brodie's flannel shirt on, I'm surprisingly not that cold considering it's almost midnight. I do pull the sleeves all the way down, covering my fingers.

"It's funny," I say, thinking aloud. "I always want music on. Like if I could have one magical super power, it might be to have a soundtrack playing along to my life."

"Ya must be dyin' right now then," Brodie chuckles in amusement.

"Hold up. I was going to say it's actually really nice sitting here in absolute silence. It doesn't happen often so when it does, I take it as a sign to appreciate it and listen to what it's trying to tell me. It's a different type of music... nature's song." I twist my head around, concentrating. As if on queue, a cacophony of little cricket chirps, the hooting of an owl, and the sounds of a cracking stick emit through the quiet landscape around us. Smiling, I look around. "I forget how much life there is in a desert."

As I return my attention back to the stars and minute changes above, another shooting star burns its way across the atmosphere. Small noises of mirth spew out from me like a child seeing fireworks or a magic trick for the first time, sounds full of raw excitement, astonishment and pure joy.

"Ya see the world without abandonment, like an ankle bita," Brodie says in a laugh.

Unsure if this is a compliment or a criticism, I turn and look over towards his face, trying to read it.

"Your tone implies something good, I dare say even a compliment, but ankle biter?" I ask, clarifying.

He rolls over and looks me square in the eyes and pauses for a minute. We lock eyes and stare deeply into each other's irises. His green eyes are so dark, I can just make out the whites around them. He smiles softly and looks all over my face, his eyes hovering around my forehead to my hairline, down to my mouth, up at my nose and finally back in my eyes.

"Oh, it's a good thing," he mutters softly.

Without realizing it, I find myself leaning towards him, and for a second I see it in his eyes, the wanting, as he also reciprocates, but then he hesitantly draws back and clears his throat. Brodie remains silent but sits up suddenly, looking straight towards the darkened beach.

*Okay, then...* At least I'm not the one to pull away.

"Nina," he says, drawing my name out in a slightly sober tone.

*There he goes again with the full name thing.* I twist and look up at him, nervously smiling.

"Nina, what happened with Jordo?" he asks me straight, cutting the bullshit.

I close my eyes, the smile evaporating off my face. Thank goodness he asks me now in the guise of night.

"Nothing," I mutter quickly.

"Nina, I know it's not nothing," he calls me out. "Before I bailed ya out, I could see ya freakin' out 'bout not wantin' him to take ya home." *Ugh, why does he have to be so damn perceptive sometimes?* He exhales. "Are ya gonna make me guess? Do ya fancy him, is that it?"

"No, of course not!"

"Then what is it? Do ya just really hate him then?"

"I don't think I could ever hate anyone," I mutter truthfully to myself. *A strong dislike sure, but hate... no.*

"Did somethin' happen, then?" he stumbles in frustration. "I mean, I'm runnin' outta guesses here."

Instead of answering, I stand up and blindly feel for the ladder.

"Could you maybe just take me home?" I answer, avoiding the question. "It's getting late and I don't want Mick up worrying."

He follows me, swiftly trading places so he can go first. He skillfully climbs down the steps. I follow more haltingly, but make it down and immediately set off inside to gather my things. Stella greets me at the door, wanting some attention.

*Sorry, Lell, but I need to get out of here.*

"Neens," Brodie chases after me, imploring me ardently, "don't run away from me. Tell me what happened!"

"It's fine, Brodie. Let's not make a thing of it," I beg.

"What aren't ya tellin' me?"

I grab my backpack and walk to the ute, ready to leave.

"We had a terrific day, let's not taint it, okay," I mutter, stopping at the door. "Take me home." He's so stubborn. He looks like he's going to keep pushing this. I grab his arm and give it a little squeeze and a small smile. "Please, I'm asking you to drop this. I don't want to talk about it."

His shoulders hunch in surrender, and he opens the door for me, before walking around the hood and climbing in. Thankful the ride is quick, I get in and buckle up, and he drives me home.

# 14

It's been about a week since my little confrontation with Brodie after our intimate moment of stargazing. He reaches out, trying to get in touch with me but I'm fielding his calls and text messages. I know he'll get the truth out of me if I see him.

It's midday and I lie in bed in my loose tank top and shorts. Scrolling through my Lightroom library, I sort through the photos from our day at Lucky's. Normally, these types of pics would inspire me to be creative, but today they make me a little sad. Instead I load the wedding photos and begin the tedious editing process. Mick knocks on my door with a plate full of cookies. He sets them on my nightstand, then sits down on my bed next to me. I sit up. Clearly, he wants to talk.

"What's goin' on, Sheila?" he asks gently.

I pull up my legs and hug my arms around them, feeling like I did when I was twelve years old and in trouble.

"Nothing," I answer in a shrug. "I'm fine, Mick."

"Yar friends are worried about ya. They called this mornin'."

*Ugh*. I groan and fall back on my pillows.

"By friends, do you mean Brodie?" I moan. I look at him out of the corner of my eyes and he nods. "What'd you tell him?"

"I told him I don't reckon what's goin' on with ya which is the bloody truth," Mick replies, genuinely perplexed, "but I can tell that somethin's eatin' at ya, eva since ya got home the otha night." I sit up, frowning. I hate seeing Mick distressed, especially on my account. "Sweetheart," he mutters, endearingly patting my shoulder, "ya know ya can tell me anythin'. I won't think differently of ya, *eva*."

He reminds me that I'm not alone. I nibble on the top of my thumbnail and take a deep breath.

"Promise me you won't speak a word of this to anyone," I urge. "Especially Brodie?"

"Ya have my word," he says, looking me straight in the eyes.

"Well, you know last week we went out on the boat?" I start. He nods, listening as I continue. "Well there was this guy there. The same guy from the wedding when you picked me up."

He stills, the wheels turning behind his piercing blue eyes. Despite Mick's age, he's still incredibly sharp and intuitive. Plus, he's a doctor. I bet he's sat in this same seat many times before.

"Well this guy, Jordan's his name," I say, taking a deep breath before diving in, "well he asked me to take a ride out on the ski, away from the others, and I thought, yeah why not. He's everyone's mate and he seemed nice. So we go and we wind up on this secluded little island nearby, but far enough away, and—." I stop as tears come to my eyes. *How do I describe how I feel?* "And before I realize it, Jordan, he, he—."

I stifle a sob. It all builds inside my chest, not just the uncomfortable encounter but homesickness - everything - like a dam about to break. Mick clutches me in his arms, holding on tight.

"He took advantage of ya, didn't he?" he whispers gently in my ear, the pain apparent in his voice. "I shoulda warned ya, Sweetheart."

"But how could you have known?" I console him.

I don't want him to take an infinitesimal fraction of blame.

"I'd heard some things 'bout him from a coupla mates, but just chocked it up to furphy nonsense. Knowing Brodie, 'n how he's his best mate, I chose to give him the benefit of the doubt... I'm so sorry." Mick shakes his head in anger as I slowly lean my head on his shoulder. He whispers, asking the question he hopes isn't true, "Did he...?"

I shake my head thoroughly, as I say, "No."

"Good," he says in relief, squeezing me tighter.

I sit up. My throat feels thick full of tears and snot from my crying runny nose. I look him in the eye, and wipe my own.

"I feel bad because I should be happy nothing that terrible actually happened, but I still feel... violated. Maybe he just assumed I, I," I stammer, looking for the answer and not finding one. Mick offers me a little reassuring smile as I sit up straighter. "I'm angry and mad at myself and him for putting me in that position, and I can't tell the others because he's their friend, but I see him all the time and he's relentless. I don't know what to do."

"Ya shouldda told me soona, Sheila."

"I didn't tell you because I didn't want you to worry," I mumble into his shirt.

"Aw, Sweetheart, dun eva think such a thing," he mumbles in my ear. "I can handle myself 'n the worryin'. That's life."

Sniffling, I take a giant breath and relax in relief. I feel so much better having told him. I didn't realize how badly I needed to tell someone. I didn't tell my parents or my sisters because being on a continent half a world away doesn't help the situation, and I didn't want their imaginations to run wild and cloud the reality of the situation.

Mick stands and kisses my forehead. I grab his hand, squeezing it three times.

"Thanks, Mick," I offer simply, but wholeheartedly.

"Thanks for telling me, Sheila," he replies. "Here, have a cookie."

I take Mick's cookie. It's the best medicine in the entire world.

A couple of hours pass. Mick and I sit in the living room, enjoying the lasting remnants of his peanut butter cookies. We listen to our favorite mutual record, *You Don't Mess Around With Jim*. "Tomorrow's Gonna Be A Brighter Day" appropriately plays and Jim Croce's iconic voice fills the room as I lie sideways on the recliner, my legs hanging over the edge. Mick sits on the couch, working on a crossword puzzle.

"Three letters. Initials," Mick calls out. "Clue is 'Star 'n creator of *Hamilton.*'"

"Easy! 'L, M, M' for Lin-Manuel Miranda, the musical genius," I beam, happy to know a clue.

"Figured yar generation might know that one," he grins, looking through a couple of clues. "Alrighty, 'bout halfway there. Let's see... Six letters. Clue is—."

An engine sound creeps into the room. Mick puts his crossword down and stands, looking outside.

"You expecting anyone?" I ask, sitting up.

He shakes his head, and curiously walks towards the sliding door and out onto the deck. I hear a door slam shut outside.

"Pryce," Mick says in slight surprise.

Freezing in my tracks, I look down at my current position. I'm a mess. I look around the room, trying to find an escape, but I can't get to my room without being visible from the deck. Torn between desperately wanting to run out and see Brodie's cheerful face and wanting to teleport anywhere other than here, I back up against the wall and wait, hiding.

"G'day, Mick," Brodie's voice greets him.

"Can I help ya with somethin', mate?" Mick asks cordially.

Mick swore he won't tell Brodie, and I stressed that Brodie knows nothing; Mick's tone doesn't betray my confidence. I hear the crackling of plastic or something.

"Just brought ya some more meat from the mahi we caught," Brodie's voice explains. "It's been in the freeza, so it's still good."

"Thanks," Mick says, and shuffles his feet.

Is he coming back inside?? I hear another set of footsteps come across the deck towards the road. The song winds down to the last couple of verses.

"Truth is, Mick," Brodie starts, "I came by to see if Nina's around? She still won't answer my calls, 'n honestly, I'm a bit worried." He pauses. "I know she's in there, Mick, I hear Jim Croce on the player."

"Give her space, Pryce," Mick's huskier voice suggests. "She'll come around when she's ready."

"Did something happen Mick?" Brodie asks, full of frustration from being kept in the dark. "Ya'd tell me if somethin' did, right?"

No answer.

"Thanks for the fish, mate," Mick says. "Come back anotha time, eh."

Brodie sighs heavily. I hear his footsteps and the opening of the ute door.

"Tell her I miss her, eh," I hear him say in a lower voice.

Then the truck door shuts and he drives off.

Realizing I can't hide out forever, I collect myself and decide to drive to the beach on the other side of town. I don't feel like blatantly avoiding Brodie anymore, but I'm also not going to seek him out either. Clearly I could use some work on confrontation. Sadly, I missed that gene from Mom. I call Mel, who's ecstatic and relieved to hear from me. I ask her to come meet me so we can talk. I'm hoping she can help me strategize the best way to tell Brodie when I do finally encounter him.

Sitting on the sand by the water, I wait for her to arrive. I glance at my phone. She should be here any minute. I sit on the bare sand. It's another warm one today. *Shocker.* Staring out at the ebbing tide, I watch it rise and fall, and think for a bit.

I hear a small ping, alerting me to a new text. Thinking it's Mel letting me know she's late or something, I open my messages. There's a text from an unknown number. I open it and almost drop my phone in the sand. A selfie of Jordan, shirtless, flashes up on the screen. It's a wide shot of his torso, but from farther out, showing off his naked body. He covers his genitals with his hand. I immediately shove my phone in my back pocket, trying to erase the haunting visual from my memory.

A few minutes go by. I hear sandy feet make their way towards me. Mel sits down beside me, and asks me what's going on. She's known something's been up ever since I got back from the ski. Slowly, I explain the unfolding of events to her. For the first time ever, she doesn't say anything, but sits like a statue, listening. She waits in silence as I describe the uncomfortable, nasty bits of the experience. I share in detail his hands on my breasts, the painful squeeze with every thump of the ride back, me clearly telling him "no" several times, all the way through to my confrontation with Brodie in its wake later that night. Getting it all out, it's my turn to be quiet, waiting for her reaction.

She continues to stare at the ocean before finally edging out in a snarl, "I could kill that fucker!"

"I'm aware it could have been a lot worse," I admit.

"Yeah, but it was bad enough. Ya blatantly told him no 'n he didn't mind ya... the bloody mole. I mean I know he's a root rat 'n can be a bit of a tramp, but I neva thought he'd violate a girl's consent, let alone yars," she replies sadly. "'N to think of what he told everyone right afta it happened," she exclaims furiously, her accent broadening in anger. "Him laughin' 'n ya standin' there beside him the resta the day."

"That's the worst part. He doesn't think anything's wrong, he must think I *liked* it because he's still pursuing me, but the thought of seeing him makes me want to kick him in the balls."

I laugh, releasing some tension.

"I reckon the worst of it is how he made ya feel," Mel whispers seriously, shaking her head in utter disappointment.

I immediately feel loads lighter now that she knows, my surrogate sister. I take a deep breath and lean onto Mel's shoulder affectionately. She leans back, lending me strength.

"I'm lucky I have you," I tell her sincerely. "I told you because I'm hoping you can tell me what to do. Brodie won't let it go. How am I supposed to be around him and the crew and not tell them what happened?"

She straightens out her posture and turns, looking at me before she says matter-of-factly, "Yar just gonna have to tell him, Neens, 'n to hell with Jordan."

I moan in frustration. I told Mel because she's grown up with these guys, she knows them, and she will know the best way to handle the situation. So if she says I need to be honest and outright, then I guess that's my answer. The thought of that actuality makes my stomach flip. She leans over and gives me a giant rib popping hug.

"It's all gonna be okay," she assures me.

For the first time in days I feel that it will.

Now that I'm of mind to tell him, Mel suggests I get it over with, plus, I just want to rip off the bandaid. After Mel leaves, I call Brodie but he doesn't pick up. Now that spring is officially here, he's been taking the boat out more often, chartering more tourists around. Pleased for his pocket book, but annoyed I have to wait to get this over with, I call Jaz and ask if she knows Brodie's schedule. She tells me she heard him say he's taking a family out until this evening, and has a second night fishing charter afterwards. Anxious, I glance at the clock. It's 6PM. There's a big chance he's already left for the night shift, but I decide to try anyway.

I call Mick and tell him I don't know how it's going to go, but not to wait up. He wishes me luck. I hop in the Trooper, start her up, and drive towards the marina. Brodie mentioned to me once that on working days he launches from there because he can charge more, plus he doesn't have to give away the location of his secret launching ramp.

After passing through town, I arrive at the docks and park nearby. Hastily walking though the couple rows of boat slips, I spot the familiar vessel in slip twenty-three. I didn't miss him.

*Thank you.*

Hopefully he has a break between charters, or maybe it'll force me to keep it brief and to the point. Taking a deep breath for courage, I approach the boat. "11 Minutes" by YUNGBLOOD & Halsey rages on the boat's speaker. Searching the deck, I don't see or hear anyone and my heart drops. I'd really like to do this now... Suddenly, shuffling comes from inside. Brodie scoots out backwards from the hidey-hole. He stands up and rubs down the vinyl seats, singing along to the song. Turning around quickly, he sees me and jumps a little in surprise. I raise both hands up in the air, calling back to the same gesture he played on me in the shed.

"Don't shoot, it's just me," I offer, smiling.

He smirks at me before looking down. *Good.* I'd rather this conversation start off on a lighter tone. Brodie resumes rubbing down the rest of the seats while I stand there on the deck. I wait for him to engage with me with a look of acknowledgement or something, but a couple of minutes pass by and he continues cleaning.

"Are you just going to ignore me all night?" I ask, trying to be friendly.

"I don't know, maybe," he shrugs. "Then yull know how it feels."

"Fair enough, but I would really like to talk to you. If you have time."

He stops and stands up, and stares at me for a moment, squinting his eyes in thought. Deciding to hear me out, he offers me a hand into the boat, urging me to come aboard. I accept it and climb over the chrome railing.

"Need to be anywhere tonight?" he asks.

"No," I answer, shaking my head curiously, "but, don't you?"

Without answering, he unties the boat in a flash and starts the engine, gliding us through the small harbor. We both sit in silence the entire ride while Post Malone blares through the speakers. Brodie drives for another twenty minutes before he suddenly slows and stops the boat. He kills the engine and the music immediately dies. Swiveling in his chair, he turns, folding his arms and stares at me head on.

"Now ya can't run away this time," he states with a hint of retaliation in his voice.

I open my mouth to speak, but stop. How did I practice this on the drive over? My mind's drawing a complete blank.

"Okay," I start, "so I had no right to go radio silent on you. That was rude and that's not what friends do. I want to apologize for that first."

He nods, waiting. I sit in silence for a minute, and take a deep breath while staring down at my hands.

"Nina, what aren't ya tellin' me?" he pleads in a tone that's way past the point of annoyance. I bite my lip. I hope he doesn't hate me and I hope he doesn't lose his temper. "All I want is the truth," he implores. "Along with all the details. Every single one. If ya leave out anythin', I'll chuck ya ovaboard."

I raise an eyebrow, but nod, agreeing to his terms.

*All the details? Fine then, but you'll wish you didn't.*

I dive right in and start to tell him the long story from the moment I left him on the beach at Lucky's. Due to general embarrassment, I tone down some of my choice words from my description, but I think he understands the gist of it. Like Mel, he sits in complete silence, staring out to sea, not moving a single muscle. I spare him no detail, per his request, but since I just relived it with Mel, I find myself more detached and can share it less emotionally. I come to the part of the story where Jordan and I meet up with the crew back at Lucky's.

Sitting quietly through the retelling like a gargoyle, he finally snaps to life and roars, "Why didn't ya just tell me? Right then 'n there!"

He jumps up, standing, and hits the side of the captain's chair. I've never seen him this angry.

"Because..." I blunder, searching for words, "you had just told me that he's been your best mate since *childhood* and I didn't want to cause a rift between you two."

He sighs and runs his hands through his hair, frustrated and upset with disillusionment. His curls stick up a little wild.

"Lemme worry about that," he snaps.

"I'm not sure how long I'm even going to be here in Australia," I blubber. "I couldn't stand the thought of being the one to burst the bubble on such a good thing you've all got going."

I feel tears coming on. *Damnit, Nina, hold it together.*

"That's a poor reason, Nina," he mutters, shaking his head. "He hurt ya, hurt yar spirit, 'n if Jordan does that to someone I care about then he isn't the bloke I thought he was."

"But don't you see? He doesn't even think he crossed a line." The anger builds up inside me when I think about the photo he just sent. "He's still trying to get me to fuck him for Christ's sake!"

I let out a small whimper and drop my head in my hands.

"Not after I'm through with him," Brodie counters.

"No, this is my battle, Brodie," I exclaim adamantly. "I will deal with it and fight it in my own way."

Shaking his head in frustration, he walks up to me and pulls me into a bear like embrace. He holds me tightly and I wrap both arms snugly around his body. Closing my eyes, I finally feel relief. We stand in each other's arms for what feels like forever. I open my eyes and see the sun setting, lighting the entire sky a fiery coral. We rock back and forth a little, as the swelling tide tosses the boat around, still hugging each other. I feel his lips on my head as he kisses my forehead tenderly.

"Promise me you won't do anything to Jordan?" I demand with emphasis, squeezing him.

I lift my head up on his chest and wait for him to meet my eyes. Sighing, he looks around at the ocean, before finally staring down at me and reluctantly nods.

"Cross my heart," he pledges.

With no more secrets lingering between us, tensions lighten. Enjoying the sunset to Post Malone's "Circles," we sprawl out on the bow of the boat, our backs leaning against the glass window. Enormous clouds crackle overhead, splintering the sky into a thousand fragments. The neon hues of oranges and pinks explode through the open cracks, lighting up the dimming sky into a breathtaking vista. The whole sky paints the heavens a cotton candy pink. It's a special one tonight. I badly wish I had my camera. I smile at the thought, trying to burn the view into my retina's memory for life.

"And just like that, the sun will set, the moon will rise and another day will begin anew," I mutter peacefully in a sigh.

Brodie stops and looks over at me and smiles.

"How can ya do that? Be so pozzi after everythin' ya just told me," he mutters, genuinely interested.

I look around the horizon as the sun gains its iconic shape over the water, thinking about his question.

"Because it's true. The world is a scary place. Disappointing things happen all the time, and I can't dwell on them or I'll get swallowed up in a black hole and lose myself. I realized that after my accident. The sun does come up, and I'm choosing to come up with it. It might not be perfect every day, but I don't want to be lost, and honestly, it could have been much much worse. I'm still just Nina, same as I was yesterday, no matter what he tries to do to me."

He fidgets with a rod and lowers his head, chewing on his lip as he slowly thinks about my answer. He shakes his head a little.

"Nah, yeah," he offers admirably, "but yar stronga."

I walk over to him and take his hand in mine. I give it a squeeze, finding his eyes.

"How are *you* holding up? He's your best friend."

"I'm fine cause I have to be. Yar strong cause ya choose to…" he sighs, squeezing my fingers back.

*I think that's the nicest thing anyone's ever said about me.*

"Do ya have yar suit on?" he asks, looking over at me.

I nod. I never leave the house anymore without wearing one. You never know when you're going to get wet, and being out here with the heat and the beaches, I pretty much jump in the ocean every day, so now it's just become a uniform of sorts. Tonight I wear my blue retro style, two-piece bikini.

"C'mon then," he says, nodding to the water. "Let's hop in the drink." Nervously, I bite my lip as I peer down over the side at the dark ocean below. With the sun going, the brightness and exposure are going with it. I can't really see anything and the thought freaks me out. Brodie, sensing my hesitation, walks up next to me and nudges me in support as he strips off his shirt. "C'mon, just a quick dip. We'll both feel betta, eh."

I hastily strip off my dress and toss it over the window onto the captain's seat. We walk together and climb up on the rail. He reaches over and extends his hand, waiting for me to take it. The option to choose makes it clear to me. While Jordan is forceful, superior and assuming, Brodie is gentle, patient and considerate. He encourages me to try things I don't like, but respects me and supports me if I choose not to pursue them. I look down at his hand, then at the cobalt water, and take his palm gladly in mine. I beam at him, locking in on his eyes. He raises his eyebrows gently in question and without even prompting each other, we both jump off the side of the boat in unison.

We land in the refreshing giant pool and pop up for air, both laughing, allowing any remaining agitations from earlier to drain away. Brodie realizes his boardies have come untied, so he swims back towards the swim step and perches as he reties the knot. I swim over, freaked to be alone by the bow at dusk. Brodie crouches on the step. Half submerged in water, his toned abdominal muscles tense as he stares, admiring the fallen sun and lovely view. I pause, lightly bobbing with the current, and enjoy my view. Not only is he beautiful on the inside, but his body... I can't get over how hot he is, especially in this moment.

He catches me watching him and dives back in, almost on my head, then surfaces behind me, pretending to scare me. I push him away in jest, and then the two of us stop smiling suddenly, and float, staring at one another. The water laps between us, flushing our cheeks in fuchsia from the reflection of the sky as

I feel the chemistry surge between the two of us. Then without warning, even to myself, I splash him in the face, breaking our little trance.

*What the hell was that, Nina?!*

Brodie returns the favor and we both laugh. I'm so content I don't even think about any possible creatures lurking nearby. Hopping back onto the deck, I tell Brodie we should head back. He explains the evening's already well underway, so we might as well enjoy the truly untouched stars from the water. The thought does sound rather amazing, but I'm starting to shiver. Coming off the curtails of winter, it can still get really chilly some nights. I ask him to put on some good sunset music, and while he fiddles with the stereo, I check the towel cabinet, standing in my wet bikini. The compartment's empty. *Cool, cool.* I use my dress to dry off my hair and body. After it's completely soaked, I realize I should have just changed into it.

"Novice mistake, Nina," I say to myself in annoyance. Brodie whirls around, trying to figure out my said mistake. Between chattering teeth, I explain, "Ugh, I'm stttupid. I used my dddress to ddry off and now I'm freezing in my wettt suit."

"Here, wear this," he offers kindly, handing me his blissfully dry sweatshirt.

I don't even ask if he needs it. I accept it and turn my back to him while he shakes off his wet hair. The sky's getting darker by the minute and I'm so cold I quickly untie my bikini top as I try to find the opening of the sweatshirt. The suit lands with a small squishy *thud* on the deck. *That's nice.*

Standing here topless, but thankfully facing towards the ocean, I search for the opening of the sweatshirt. My whole body convulses in goosebumps. Sensing stillness on the deck and a watchful eye, I glance over my shoulder and find Brodie staring at my bare back. He hastily looks down, hiding his embarrassment with a smile. He's the one caught in the act now. Surprisingly, I discover I don't mind so much, and dare I say I might even enjoy the feeling of his directed gaze. It feels so scandalous, so unlike me. A tantalizing excitement rises up in my belly. Taking my time, perhaps even hoping he still watches, I slowly reach up over my head to guide the sweatshirt on, before sucking in my stomach and letting it playfully fall over my torso.

*So this is what the fun's all about... hmmm.*

I leave my bikini bottoms on and pull out my long, damp hair from inside the collar. I turn around. Brodie clears his throat, leaning over to hit a switch. Little rope lights ignite, kindling along the whole boat. He walks along the gunwale to the bow. I follow suit, maintaining a sure footed grip, and shimmy over after him.

As the stars begin to make their unabated appearance, Brodie and I resume our positions side by side on top of the bow on the white squishy cushions. The tide gently rocks us back and forth. The two of us lie flat with our legs crossed at the ankles. I hold my hands over my stomach, while Brodie keeps one by his side and the other resting on his bare chest. Sarah McLachlan's "Path of Thorns" serenades us in the background from the deck speakers. It's so peaceful and quiet.

"I'm so pleased with your song choice," I admit to Brodie.

"I threw on a random nineties mix," he says, laughing.

"You know, she was the first person I ever saw live in concert," I share, enjoying her angelic voice.

The stars, fully alive now, glisten around us in all of Mother Nature's glory like she's putting on a special show for us. Paired with this gorgeous song, the atmosphere seems to be screaming with love and a fiery feeling of being alive. This feeling is second to none, and I never want it to end. We lie in pleasant silence until the song winds down.

"Hey, I meant to ask you earlier," I say quietly, leaning over. "Can we keep this whole Jordan thing just between us? I mean Mel knows, but she's sworn to secrecy."

Brodie sighs deeply, clearly thinking it's the wrong idea, but says "Nah, yeah, okay, but can I tell Stel? I need to tell someone."

Glancing around, it dawns on me, and I ask accusatorially, "Where is Stella?"

"With Jaz, dun worry," he answers, laughing at my tone. "Thought I was doin' an ovanighta, but it got postponed." He smiles. "'N sometimes I give 'er the day off."

The next Sarah song "Push" begins. I close my eyes, humming along. I *love* this one. I've always wanted to sing it to someone and really mean it. Feeling like I'm in an early 2000s JJ Abrams' show on a boat under the twinkle lights, I sing along, unable to keep quiet. "'*You stay the course, you hold the line, you keep it all together, you're the one true thing I know I can believe in.*'"

"She's good," Brodie says, sounding impressed. "I've never really listened to her before."

I smile at the thought. Something else comes to mind.

"So don't hate me," I poke his arm gently and ask, "but I saw your guitar last week at the house. Do you play?"

"Why? Do you?" he asks curiously.

"While I'm told I have some artistic talents, I'm afraid playing an instrument isn't one of them," I reply sadly, shaking my head.

Sensing my disappointment, Brodie offers, "Well ya love 'n appreciate music more than anyone I know, so I reckon it's just as well."

"Wait, you never answered my question," I realize, nudging him softly. "Do you play?"

"Possibly, when no one's around," he replies enigmatically. "No one has eva heard me play, not even Jaz."

My eyes round at this key bit of knowledge.

"I guess it'll be our little secret," I pledge, thinking about it for a few seconds. "I get it you know. I paint, or I used to anyway. I abhor the notion of anyone looking over my shoulder during the process. It drove me crazy because my family constantly had to see what I was painting. So one day, I just stopped."

Speaking about family, I think about Papi and especially Mom. I wonder how she's fairing. It's been well over six months now since I left home. *I miss you guys.*

"Whaddaya thinkin' 'bout?" Brodie asks out of the blue.

"Home," I sigh.

"Mick'll be fine, he's an Old Boy."

"No, not that home... my *home* home in America."

He uncomfortably adjusts himself next to me, and asks, "Whaddaya miss about it? Maybe tellin' me will help."

"Okay..." I say, smiling, while exploring my mixed emotions. "Well I don't really miss home as in the location or the town as much anymore. But, I miss my people." I look up at the moon thinking at least my family and I can stare at the same sun or moonrise and feel like we're all in one place. Sighing, I want to plead with the universe. "I wish I could meld both of my worlds into one." Realizing that can never happen, I exhale in frustration as Sarah continues to croon gently in the background. "I don't have many friends back home, so that's not the issue," I admit, trying to get him to understand. "In fact, I LOVE how I feel here with the crew, and I love this place, Straya, I mean. Like I genuinely don't ever want to leave, but I don't know how much longer I can go without seeing my sisters and my family."

"So tell me about 'em. Whadda they like?" he asks, sounding genuinely curious. Trying to lighten the mood, he glances up at my hair, and lightly picks up a ringlet. "Do they all have Tarzan hair like you do?"

It works. I laugh.

"Well Maria, 'Ria' as I call her, is my youngest sister. She's twenty-three. She has pretty curly hair, but I definitely inherited the most curls out of all us girls," I answer. Selena comes to mind, in which I enviously grin. "And Selena, my other younger sister, her hair's wavy, but controllable. She's super tan, tall and lanky, the total opposite of me. She got that from Papi, my dad. She's married to a great guy, Ray, and they have the most precious little boy, named Javier. We call him Javi." The mentioning of Javi leaves me feeling melancholic. "He's the one I miss most," I divulge. "We call him a cherub because he looks like a little angel with rosy cheeks. He's sweet and has these amazing blue eyes and two curly sideburns that are good five inches longer than the rest of his hair."

"So *he's* baby Tarzan?" he teases, laughing.

Thinking about Javi brings a smile to my lips.

"When I left he was still a little baby, and now apparently he's walking and babbling," I mutter. I hold my breath for a few seconds before whispering my greatest fear, "I'm worried he won't remember me."

"Ah, sure he will," Brodie says, nudging me, trying to get my mind off Javi. "Now tell me 'bout Ria 'n yar parents."

"Hmm, well Ria's fun. She's daring, and outspoken. A true individual. Come to think of it, you remind me a lot of her," I say, reflecting on that for a second. I can feel his smile. "Yeah, you're both fearless. I wish I was more like that... Ria's loyal, and she's my best friend. Selena too." *I miss my sisters.* "We're really lucky we're all so close and have stayed close." I giggle. "I guess my mom never gave us an option otherwise."

"What's so funny?" he asks, intrigued.

"If you knew my mom, you'd understand. Lucy's spastic and a teensy bit flighty, but knows exactly what she wants. She'll do whatever it takes to get it, but never in a malicious way," I clarify. "She doesn't have a mean bone in her body, but she's Irish and she's feisty and intense, and hilarious. And she always has a knack for having everything happen to her at once. It's a family inside joke in fact." I laugh out loud thinking about Mom and how she always manages to schedule the delivery guy, the WiFi man, the appliance fixer, the window washer all at the same time. You name it, it always goes down at the same moment without her ever intending it. "She's the most generous person I know," I declare, unable to hide the sadness in my voice, "and I miss her terribly."

"'N yar dad?" Brodie pushes.

"Oh, Papi, he's super easy going and mellow. He loves trying new things, and gets along with just about everyone. He works his tail off so my sisters and I can have a wonderful life. Um, he's a glass half-full kind of guy, is the best motivator... and I think his best quality is he chooses to see the good in people."

"Hmm," Brodie mutters to himself, as he points to a shooting star.

I chase the fading tail across the giant sky-scape. The song changes, and an enchanting rumble of ethereal keyboards fills the air, along with little tambourine chimes. Sheryl Crow's voice fills the speakers in "I Shall Believe," another magical vibe for this intimate setting. *Good playlist.*

Brodie rolls over towards me. We lie only six inches apart.

"Neens, don't take this the wrong way," he says cautiously, "but I've never met anyone quite like ya before." I burst into a fit of giggles and snorts. His eyes shoot wide in surprise. "Why are you laughing? I was hoping for a decent reaction, but not this."

"I'm laughing because my entire life I've never felt like I fit in anywhere, and I think you just confirmed it." I can just make out his face. He bites his lip in patience, waiting for further explanation. I stifle a small chuckle. "You couldn't understand because you have friends and a life that comes so naturally to you. I never had that back home. I never had a boyfriend, just one cringeworthy three whole minutes in college." Brodie's eyebrows shoot up. "*That's* a story for another time. Anyway, I felt like I was always waiting for something to happen but it never did... until now."

The truth dawns on me.

"Wait, ya've never had a boyfriend?" he asks, genuinely shocked.

While the subject is a tad humiliating, it is what it is.

"No," I reply honestly, while trying to downplay it. "I mean I liked some guys, some guys *a lot*, but I'm shy and I got really good at hermiting myself away. And, I don't know, no one's ever really liked me like that I guess. They take one good look and decide to pursue the leggy blonde instead." I also explain the cycle of my self-sabotaging efforts involving areas of attraction. Brodie laughs so hard his knees lift off the cushion. "You don't have to be mean about it. I know, it's embarrassing," I say a bit defensively, starting to sit up. He grabs my arm, pulling me back down, while a playful smiles rests on his lips. I turn over to him so we lie face to face. "Okay, then, tell me something about you, something I don't know."

He pauses for a minute, scrunching his face in mock agony and spits out, "My favourite colour's yellow?"

"That's not what I mean and you know it," I smirk, punching his arm as he laughs. "That's my favorite color too, by the way, like the sun."

When he doesn't elaborate, I lean in closer. I open my eyes as huge and wide as they'll go, willing him to open up with my intrusive gaze. We stare each other down until, finally, he sighs and stills.

"I'm not who everyone thinks I am," he says, his tone shy like a boy's. "Everyone thinks I'm this good guy who takes care of everythin' 'n cleans up everyone's messes when in reality, I'm tired of it. I'm tired of the rat race of life, 'n social queues, n' picking up afta people. It's exhaustin'." He pauses for a beat. "Sometimes I wanna go get lost on an island 'n neva come back. Sometimes I wanna forget it all."

Understanding him perfectly, I give him a kind smile and decide to share something I've learned since having so much time to self-reflect these past several months.

"I get it. I used to want to run away from everything. I'd feel guilty for reacting a certain way, or for feeling scared and feeling trapped by it," I say, pausing. "I felt like I was constantly boxing myself into certain categories of who I should be or what I should want or do... Well I don't know about you, but I've realized this year that I don't ever want to be described as just one thing. I feel like it's easy to polarize people *and yourself,* whether that's with politics or personalities or emotions, but it's discrediting to all of us. We're all human, we all live in the gray, so I wouldn't hassle yourself too much, Brodie. You're more than one thing, and you're still a *good* man."

He stares at me. Even in the dim light, I can see him thoughtfully searching my eyes as if he's looking for the meaning of life inside them.

"I Still Believe" forges on, and I pick up on the line that sings, *"I know it's true, no one heals me like you, and you hold the key."* The beautiful melody swirls through the air, feeling like a soundtrack to this moment.

"Truth is," Brodie whispers, "before ya crashed into that ravine, my life had been pretty miserable. Bearable, but miserable all the same 'n I didn't even see it. I forgot what it meant to actually live 'n not take my life here for granted. Ya showed me that 'n gave that back to me, Neens... you 'n yar damn optimism 'n childlike wonda."

Speechless, I roll onto my back. We sit in silence and both stare out into space. I reach out my hand and find his by his side. I slowly take hold of it and squeeze it three times. He answers by intertwining our fingers. The light tambourine "tssks" along to the beat, and I turn my head towards Brodie's.

"What are you thinking?" I ask him quietly, calling back to our night on his roof deck.

He looks at my face for a minute, his eyes softly darting all around it.

"That all those blokes musta been flamin' galahs to not see what I see," he gently says, with the utmost tenderness.

Now, I'm floored.

With his free hand, he reaches over slowly and delicately moves a wisp of hair from my eyes, tucking it softly behind my ear. I feel his breath exhale lightly on my cheek as his face is centimeters from mine. I smile at him, pouring sunshine and happiness from my soul. He glances over and beams back, reflecting the same felicity in his eyes.

*Brodie, you make my heart sing with joy.*

We both start to lean in towards each other, when suddenly, a horn goes off close by. We both jump start upright.

"Who the hell could that be?" I ask incredulously, and mildly irritated.

*We were having such a moment!*

Brodie squints, and grabbing my hand, guides me to the gunwale where we make our way to the main deck. A boat pulls up about twenty feet away. Brodie ushers me to sit in the co-pilot's chair. I feel so special, but in all fairness, Stella isn't here.

A young man stands behind the wheel and yells, "Pryce, thought I'd find ya out here, mate. Day for it!"

"Day for it, Andy," Brodie hollers back in a friendly tone.

*Andy?!*

Andy eyes me and stands up a little straighter. He smiles largely, revealing a giant gap in his two front, crooked teeth.

"G'day, Miss Nina," he says, tipping his hat to me.

I smile politely and wave lightly back, stifling a giggle.

"Don't ya dare, Neens," Brodie edges out between closed teeth, as my shoulders tremble. I try my hardest not to explode into a fit of laughter. Andy just stares at us, smiling. Trying to figure out why Andy's lingering, Brodie asks, "Can I help ya with somethin', mate?"

"I was leavin' the marina when some lady asked for ya," Andy shares. "Said she went 'n left her phone on yar boat. Reckons it fell unda a seat."

As Brodie looks around the dashboard and shelves, I get up and search under the seats, and sure enough, I find it buried in the cushion.

"Found it!" I shout, raising my arm up.

"Thanks, mate," Brodie says with a nod. "I'll bring it in lata. Nina 'n I aren't quite finished just yet."

I hand the phone to Brodie and assume my position next to him. Andy stares at us, scratching his head, and purses his lips.

"Well the lady said she's catchin' a flight tomorrow outta Perth to the Goldie 'n needs it before drivin' out in, I'd say," he explains, glancing at his watch, "a half hour or so. I'd take it back myself, but I'm headed out."

Brodie bites his lip. Clearly we have to go back now.

"Alrighty, then, that's that," he yells, starting the engine. "Thanks, mate."

Happy to be of some use, Andy grins proudly, and shouts, "Cheers, Pryce, 'n see ya around, Nina."

He steers away, leaving us in peace once more. I can't help it, I let out the biggest laugh and Brodie reaches over and playfully squeezes me, which makes me laugh harder. I try to get him back, and almost knock the phone out of his hand.

"We best go back now before she writes her review," I joke, gesturing to the cell phone, regaining some calm composure.

"Half of me wants to just toss it into the sea 'n just stay out here foreva," Brodie admits, rolling his eyes, "but we best go back."

I reach over and grab his hat off the dashboard, plant it firmly on his head, take the phone from him and sit down dutifully.

"Aye, aye, cap'n," I declare, like a well behaved movie deckhand.

"Bloody sheila," he mutters annoyed, shaking his head.

Looking around, he sighs, then punches the accelerator. The boat lurches forward towards the direction of the marina.

# 15

Now that all that annoying drama with Jordan is behind me, I feel light and back to my old self, well the self that I've become since living here in Australia. Mick senses my upbeat attitude and we enjoy a couple of fun game nights, playing cards. Aside from some intense rounds of backgammon, Texas Hold 'Em is Mick's staple and he's taught me all the tricks of the game. I grew up playing boardgames and some card games, but never really felt comfortable enough to hold my own in poker. Mick and I begin betting on who does the dishes, and now - days later - our wagers are much higher.

Getting cash from those drone gigs, I try to pay Mick back in full, though he adamantly insists I stash the money for future keeping. I argue with him that it's the least I can do for taking care of me all these months, and he always argues back with the same response: "nonsense." It's turned into this little back and forth stalemate. Before bed, I sneak into his room and leave the cash under his pillow. A couple of days go by and I find said cash back under mine. After a few times of this exchange, we decide to use the cash to raise the stakes in poker. Mick's actually quite good at it so I tend to be the loser, which is fine by me. I must admit to not harboring a more competitive spirit. Yet, I'm happy when he wins because I can talk him into pocketing the money for a future round.

Brodie and Mel catch wind of our nightly games, and they decide to join in after work one afternoon. Waiting for Mick to return from town, I show Brodie and Mel the footage from our tiger shark encounter. As they watch the screen, my phone buzzes near the kitchen sink. Walking over with a smile, I look down and my grin immediately falters. It's a message from Jordan. *Ugh, more?!* Disgusted by yet another indecent and obscene text, I roll my eyes. Ever since the almost naked pic, he's been sending me one profane text after the next. I should just block him, but I don't want to cause a scene. I look back at Brodie and Mel, and shake off the repulsive feeling.

Losing it in mirth, Brodie immediately sets a drone photo as his phone's wallpaper. The slider door swiftly opens, revealing Mick, encumbered by a heavy looking, white cardboard box. I rise from the table, with big excited eyes as I recognize the familiar USPS logo. It's finally my birthday care package, only months after the fact.

I tell them all this, and Mick and Mel both say together, "Wait, it was yar birthday?"

Brodie grins to himself while I take the box from Mick and slide it on the table in front of me. Both men rummage around in their pockets until Mick pulls out his pocket knife and hands it to me. I open the mangled box, and am delighted to see it's stuffed to the gills.

"Oh, Mom," I exclaim happily.

Thoughtful about the heat and distance, Mom managed to wedge in some of my favorite treats from home. I pull out each prize with a big grin as the others watch. There's a can of Sees Candy salted nuts, a pack of my favorite local beef jerky, our favorite family game SkyJo, a pair of Stance socks for Mick with the California flag across them, a pair of new AirPods with an iTunes gift card attached, a dress two sizes too big now from Marci, a new little portable speaker from Ria, and a framed photo of the family for my bedroom. Lying at the bottom is a giant homemade card with a large "Happy 30th" scribbled across the front. I open the card and find handwritten notes from each member of my family, including Abuela and Javi. There's even a "note" from Cosmo, saying he misses sleeping in my cubby, behind my legs each night. I read each one, getting a little teary eyed, and set it upright next to my goodies.

Mel takes the card and reads it. A giant smile spreads across her face. Mick asks if he can read it, which he does, followed by Brodie. They each grin, reading all the funny and sweet things my family wrote.

"I like the part where Ria said," Mel says, giggling, "'I love 'n miss ya more than a million Thai teas with honey boba 'n endless banana cream pies.'"

Mick laughs recalling the words "gnarly" and "dude," while Brodie points to Javi's squiggle of a signature with a chuckle.

"Yar family really loves ya, Sheila," Mick mentions sweetly.

"They 'love yar face,' Neens," Mel laughs, quoting Mom.

Brodie nods his head in agreement as he sits back in his chair and thoughtfully looks around at my bounty on the table. I can't wait to FaceTime them. With my heart bursting in happiness, I neatly pile everything back into the box and set it aside so we can resume our night of cards. I keep the can of salted nuts and pass the tin around.

Mick and Brodie resume their more serious demeanor as I begin to shuffle the deck. Brodie more than makes up for my lack of combative energy, which Mick appreciates.

"The victory will be that much sweeta, eh," Mick says appreciably, as he shuffles and deals.

I roll my eyes at the two of them. Mel laughs then promptly puts on her game face. Stella accompanies Brodie and sits perfectly at his side. We each deal at least one hand. After Brodie wins twice, and Mick three times, the two agree for a rematch the following night. It's now been a few nights of rematches and now Shayno and Donnie are in on the action. They've also raised the stakes so not only does the winner get bragging rights, but also gets to make a request from one of the losers. The arrangement is they play fifteen hands and the person to win the most hands wins. They have dubbed me the token dealer. Happy to oblige and get out of such a competitive ring, I sit in the center, commanding their attention with my shuffling. Thankfully I've always been a quick shuffler. I glance at Mel in between deals. She sits this tournament out and hangs on the barstool with a coldie in her hand, laughing and rolling her eyes at the battle about to go down in front of her. Elvis songs roar in the background, rotating through his classic '50s rock phase rather than his Vegas ballads.

Now dealing round thirteen, I shuffle the cards for the umpteenth time. Mick is in the lead with six wins, Brodie with five, Donnie with one, and Shayno with none. The boys take their cards and shuffle them around as they arrange them for their ideal hand. We go around the table and they reveal their hands, one by one. Stella sits picturesquely by my side like she wants to play too. Donnie goes first. He lays down a full house, raising his eyebrows up cockily. Hard to beat. Brodie and Mick immediately lay theirs down, losing. Shayno reveals his hand: a royal flush. The lot of us hoot and holler with excitement as Shayno finally wins a round. Stella wags her tail and gives Shayno a congratulatory lick.

"Knew ya had it in ya," Mel exclaims, raising her drink to him.

Elvis's song "Hound Dog" wails in the background, adding to the general loud and party atmosphere.

Shayno's face goes bright red with joy and attention. Brodie and Donnie both pat him on the back, chuckling in excitement. Now, there's only two more rounds to go. Brodie trails Mick by one. He'd have to win this round and next. Looking between the pair of them, I don't know who I'm rooting for more. After the usual dealing, trading, and unveiling, Brodie wins the penultimate round. Mick closes his eyes and smiles.

Here it is. It's all boils down to this. Shuffling, I inspect both Mick and Brodie's faces, both of whom are hard to read even having spent so much time with each of them.

"Whaddaya doin', Sweetheart?" Mick asks, as I shuffle the deck again.

I look closely at him. His expression seems normal - no signs of sweat or reddening veins. He doesn't even so much as tap a finger.

"Nothing, really," I nonchalantly mutter. "Just sussing you guys out to see who's more nervous."

Even at the dead giveaway of my motive, neither one of them changes their behavior or any minute facial tells. I turn and face Brodie straight on, staring right into his shining green eyes. Shayno, Donnie, and Mel guffaw at my serious posture and stare. Brodie sits up straight and leans forward, returning my gaze right back. Studying his face at such close range, I look for any sign of weakness, but honestly can't tell any difference. *He has nice skin and long dark lashes that curl up enviably.* He leans back, giving me the eye, and playfully lifts an eyebrow, smiling crookedly at me. Shaking my head, I return to the deck at hand.

"Ready, boys?" I ask, looking between the four players.

"First I want a kiss for luck, Sweetheart," Mick says, surprising me.

I smile at him, narrowing one eye, but oblige. I will do pretty much anything Mick asks of me. I walk over and plant a soft kiss on his cheek.

"Good luck, Old Man," I say confidently into his ear.

He smiles and nods, returning to his A-game posture.

"Wait, that's not fair!" cries Donnie. "I want some luck too, Chica."

I sigh, but walk over to him and quickly peck his cheek. I don't say anything though, that's reserved for just Mick. Shayno also gives me a look that screams, *where's mine?* so I make my way to him and repeat Donnie's peck. Brodie shifts in his seat. Is it a tell that he's nervous perhaps? I get self-conscious suddenly thinking back to our almost kiss last week. He sits and smiles, waiting. Not wanting to make a big deal out of anything by not kissing him, I demurely walk over and gently kiss the side of his cheek. His incoming whiskers blanch my soft skin. My face flushes as I pull back. Stella, sensing kissing is allowed, takes the opportunity to jump up and lick Brodie's face.

"Easy, girl," Brodie commands, lightly pushing her down with a smile.

I clear my throat and walk back to the table.

Mel gives me a suggestive raise of an eyebrow and mouths, "Talk lata."

The opponents all fidget with their hands, hungry to get their paws on their cards. Building the anticipation, I slowly deal.

"Any day now, Neens," Brodie says.

At that remark, I deal even slower. He rolls his eyes. Finally, I place the last card down. They all sort through their hands with the utmost seriousness. Mel stares at me and bites her lip in anticipation, trying not to giggle. As we round the circle once more for the final lap of trades and new cards, I think I'm going to lose it and join in with Mel, stifling a chuckle. Luckily, I pull myself together and clear my throat.

"Alrighty then. Final deal," I project like an announcer. "Who's it going to be? Mel, drumroll, por favor."

Mel comes up right beside me and claps her hands on her thighs, quickly imitating a drum line. I roll my tongue loudly and effectively. Everyone looks at me, startled.

"Spanish speaker," I remind them, shrugging.

"Back to it, eh," Mick directs, nudging Donnie next to him.

I roll my tongue again and stop, prompting them to begin. Mick reveals his hand: four kings and a queen. Not bad at all. Shayno follows suit with a hand of random cards, immediately folding. That leaves Donnie and Brodie. Donnie shakes his head and unveils his hand by throwing out three jacks and two queens. He laughs and folds. I look to Brodie. I can't tell if he can beat Mick's hand, but he narrows his eyes slightly and looks down at his cards. He sets them down and reveals four aces and a queen. He falls back into his chair slightly, playing it cool, while the rest of us roar in excitement. Stella barks a couple of times, picking up on the general celebratory climate of the room. Part of me is super happy for Brodie, and the other part of me is disappointed on Mick's behalf. I guess I just can't win for losing in this case. Mick, the good sportsman that he is, shakes his head and laughs, proudly clapping Brodie on the shoulder.

"A worthy opponent," he announces. "Thanks for lettin' this Old Boy have a go in the ring again, eh." He stands up and tips his hat off to Brodie, then to Shayno and Donnie. Mick smiles and heads towards the deck. "Lemme know when ya wanna collect on yar prize."

What? Brodie chose to request his winnings from Mick? I just assumed he would pick Shayno or Donnie.

Mick opens up the slider, unveiling the most wonderful night outside. Spring is here in full force and the nightly temps are inching their way back up. The gang makes their way outside onto the deck, snickering and recapping the night's highlights. Hugs and high fives later, Shayno, Donnie and Mel wish us farewell and climb into Donnie's ute and drive off. Brodie lingers behind, offering to clean up. I assure him I can handle it this time. Mick and I walk him out to his ute, where he stops in front.

"Mick, do ya mind if I collect on ya this weekend?" he asks.

Mick looks at me, and I reciprocate with a shrug, feeling just as confused.

"Alrighty, then, name yar pleasure," he tells Brodie.

"Do ya mind sparin' Nina next weekend?" Brodie asks respectfully.

Mick looks to me, silently asking permission with his eyes. I smile gently at him, and barely close my eyes in approval.

He peers back at Brodie, and sighs, "Aye, I reckon I could."

"What are we doing?" I ask Brodie, naturally curious.

"It's a surprise," he admits, before looking to Mick and adding, "but no wucka's, Mick, she'll be safe."

Mick nods and pulls me in for a side hug.

"Yeah, I reckon one weekend away won't kill me," he mutters, smiling.

"You won't make it a day without me," I jest, while squeezing his side tightly.

Brodie laughs, shaking his head at us as he gets in the driver's seat and takes off. Mick and I walk back inside, and I can't help but wish it was already next weekend... only six more days to go.

I'm set to leave with Brodie tomorrow on our unknown adventure. Mel comes over and hangs on my bed as I pack. I have the full extent of my wardrobe laid out on my bed sheet. Busy trying to switch up my attire by combining new variations, Mel drops her options in a heap and adamantly insists we go shopping in town for something new. Apparently I've exhausted all my current combos for a weekend getaway. Before I know it, I'm buckled in Nigel as we head into the main strip to visit the one and only thrift shop that also carries a section of current clothes. It's safe to say the options are very limited, but she insists I might get lucky.

We park in front of the store, Tippe Canoe's Hideaway Treasures, and make our way inside. A little bell rings as we open and close the door, announcing our presence. We have the entire place to ourselves.

"Tip, it's just Mel," she calls out.

A distant voice shouts, "Oy!"

Mel walks me over to the designated clothing area and begins rifling through the racks. She directs me to pull out anything that I'm remotely interested in because you never know until you try it on. Psychedelic Fur's "Love My Way" rocks on. The fun upbeat melody wafts through the store's sound system. I bob my head as I pull out some cute looking pieces while Mel racks up quite a collection. I see this dainty vintage tank blouse that has yellow crocheted daises all over the white airy linen. I think it would pair well with my denim shorts and my jean skirt. I add it to the top of my pile. We both come across the swim suit section. I start to gloss over it when Mel pulls out a few pairs of skimpier bikinis.

"What are you doing?" I whisper in worry.

"I love yar whole vintage, greenie vibe, Neens, but c'mon, yar goin' on an exclusive Brodie Pryce getaway. This calls for some spice, 'n I am gonna add it to ya life, Love."

She hands me the pieces. Some look like scraps of fabric, and I hold them at arm's length, shaking my head. There's a black one she thrusts upon me that I shove back into her hands, adamantly refusing.

"No black, sorry," I exclaim, standing my ground. "I love color in my life, Mel, and what the hell is that? A bandaid? Because it's about the right size for one."

Mel looks at me and blatantly rolls her eyes, pouting, "Fine, no black then."

She grabs more suits before spinning me towards the dressing "room," a little area behind a vintage rattan room divider. There's a tall mirror against the back. I get to work, stripping down to try on the various articles of clothing, saving the suits for last. Thankfully the billowy, daisy tank fits me. With vintage pieces you never know, especially being curvy, most of them don't work out. I try on a couple of the other items, and after a lot of misses, I sigh from all the effort.

"Oy, Neens, get to the suits already," Mel shouts from the other end of the store.

I audibly groan, but I've reached the end of my clothing pile, so onward I must venture. I grab my selection first. It's a ribbed yellow top, almost like a balconette bra, made of a terry cloth style material. It pairs with matching high wasted bottoms. Mel said to go for something a little more daring. The set offers less coverage in the bust than I would normally wear. I almost didn't consider it, but the color is too cute to pass up. I look at it closely before taking it off the hanger. *Is it too revealing?* Selena's voice echoes yet again, "*You can be whoever you want to be...*"

I pull on the high waisted bottoms and put on the cheery banana colored top. It fits in all the right places, pushes up in even better places, and I gotta say, makes me feel empowered and even a little sexy - *a downright first!*

"Lemme see, lemme see," Mel yells, popping up above the divider. She looks me up and down. Her big eyes go round. "Neens, I knew ya had nice knockers, but wow, ya look banga! Crash hot!"

I can't help but smile. No one's ever used the word "hot" to describe me before. I look down and see the swells of my cleavage exposed to the world, but not in an outpouring kind of way. Mel assures me it's sexy, but still tasteful. I notice I have a funny, awkward tan line.

"A few hours in the sun 'n that'll be gone," she says, gesturing to the pale lines on my skin. "Man, ya got nice tits. Wanna give me some?"

"Gladly, if I could," I reply honestly.

While Mel flaunts without a care in the world, she's about the same bust size as a high school boy.

"Alright, lemme see yar arse," she orders, motioning for me to turn around. The bottoms are high rise, perhaps a little cheekier than I'd prefer, but still provide decent coverage. The high waisted style keeps my mid-drift tucked in nice and tight. Mel claps. "Aw, Neens, ya look rippa." She sassily twerks her head. "A nice curvy piece a pie."

I laugh at her and her silliness. She holds up one of her swimsuit picks - the ultra revealing one - and demands that I try that on next. I do, and after four more thong sets, I repeatedly shake my head in refusal.

"Absolutely not. I cannot parade around in this," I explain. "It's simply not me. I wish it was, but I just can't do it."

"Brodie's loss," she mumbles, shrugging.

She picks up a baby blue set and thrusts it into my hands.

"Not another one, please," I beg. "Let's compromise with the busty, cheeky banana one please?"

I scan her eyes for a shred of compromising surrender. Shaking her head, she holds up the set again. I stare at it almost in fear, like it's a porcupine about to unleash its quills as she orders like a general.

"This is lingerie, Neens, ya know, knickers, not anotha bather," she proclaims stubbornly. "I've seen yar old, mangey tank top, 'n that's not an option I'm afraid... We're not leavin' 'til ya try it on."

"Fine," I grumble in surrender.

I yank the lingerie from the hanger and slip off the last of Mel's revealing bikinis, feeling more me already. I hold up the lacy bra. It's basically a delicate bra with gauzy, semi see-through patches, fashioned in a low cut style. It looks so small, I strain to double check the cup size on the tag, but when I put it on and clasp the back, it shockingly fits everywhere and supports everything. *Holy hell* is it busty! It makes my banana bikini top look modest in comparison.

"Ya won't be wearing this out, Neens," Mel reminds me, giggling. "Just for sleepin'... 'n otha things."

I slide on the bottoms and this time it's a full fledged thong. I'll admit it's actually more comfortable than I thought. The front also has matching lace patches along the hem that angle downward. I remind myself it's just for sleeping, unless... *er, well*.

"It's not like that," I explain, flustered. "We're just friends."

"Oh, c'mon, Brodie has been pinin' afta ya since he found ya on that beach," she declares, searching my face, trying to decipher my silence. "Ya do fancy him, no?"

Just thinking about him makes me smile. While I'm nervous about what could be, he's one of my best friends now and I can't wait to be with him, in whatever capacity that entails.

"Ya do! I can tell!" Mel confirms, studying my face. "Well, this'll help speed things along." She stands proudly over my shoulder, then leans in. "No one would eva wear this just for a friend."

She waltzes off while I change back into my normal Nina clothes. I glance down at the pile of successes, second guessing if I will actually wear them.

*To hell with it, Nina.*

Emboldened, I snatch the pile and make my way to the cashier. As Tippe rings me up, I hear a wind chime above and see a beautiful wood one with long chrome chimes hanging right next to the air vent.

"How much?" I ask Tippe, looking at it.

"Fifteen," she says.

"I'll take it," I add, glancing at her.

Brodie picks me up at four the next morning for our surprise... outing. Like a zombie, I go through the motions of waking, dressing, and readying when one's up way before their usual time. Clad in my jean shorts, my new-to-me daisy tank, and one of Mick's old denim jackets, I stumble around the house, double checking I have all my drone batteries. Mick carries my stuffed backpack in hand along with a lunchbox of snacks for the drive, however long that may be. He walks me out to the ute in his token flannel robe.

Brodie gets out and opens the passenger door for me. I see Mick smile at this. He hands Brodie my bag and snack pack, before grabbing me by both shoulders and looking me square in the face. Admittedly, I'm half asleep, but I do my best to give Mick my full attention.

"Have a rippa time, Sweetheart. Call if ya need anythin'," he tells me sincerely, as his kind eyes shine into mine. He looks at Brodie who's busy setting up my little area in the front seat. "I wouldna let ya go with anyone else, mind ya."

He pulls me towards him and kisses me on the forehead. I wrap my arms around him, giving him a giant squeeze. He lets me go and I climb in. Like a gentleman, he closes the door tight behind me, resting his hand on the open window frame.

"Take care of my girl, Pryce, or I'll pinch yar head off," he orders, smiling from Brodie to me.

"Will do, mate," Brodie assures him.

"Miss ya already, Old Man," I mutter, grabbing Mick's weathered hand, and squeeze it three times.

"I'll be seein' ya, Sweetheart," he replies sweetly.

Brodie starts the engine and Mick walks back towards the house, waving from behind. We meander down the dirt driveway before pulling out onto the paved highway. Yawning like there's no tomorrow, I nestle in my seat, and eye Brodie's sweatshirt from the floor boards. I reach down and roll it into a pillow for my head. Finally finding the sweet spot, I relax and sigh. I hear him chuckle softy and he turns up the tunes to a nice, neutral volume. Paper Kites' "On the Corner Where You Live" plays lightly through the speakers. Brodie doesn't say anything at all, but lightly hums and drives as I blissfully drift off to sleep.

# 16

Small ongoing bumps and rumbles jostle my head. I'm in the middle of a dream state, somewhere approaching reality. I see red and oranges swirl in my mind's eye, followed by more bumps.

I clearly hear the soft melody of Joshua Radin's "Cross That Line" in the cozy cab.

Slowly stepping out of my hypnopompic, cognitive state, my eyelids flicker. *Wow, it's bright.* I open them again. My vision, overexposed from sleep, blurs together trying to track focus. Blinking away the crustees in my eyes, I realize the heated sun beats down on my torso and legs. I fully wake up and prop my head up, wincing. My stiff neck feels like it's been trapped in a vice from being bent against the side of the door.

"What time is it?" I hoarsely mumble, stretching my body out as far as possible in the passenger seat, feeling little pops throughout my joints and spine as the pressure points release.

"Mornin', Sunshine," Brodie says cheerfully, with a hint of humor.

I squint, peering out the half open window. It's well past sunrise and I could really use my sunnies.

"Morning," I mutter heavy with texture, as I try to clear my throat.

"I wanted to wake ya for sunrise," Brodie informs me, "but one look at yar droolin' face 'n I didn't have the heart to wake ya."

*My drooling face.* I snort. *That's nice.*

I turn, squinting, and rummage around my backpack, digging for my honey frames. I know I packed them. They're always first on my mental checklist.

"Looking for these?" I hear him say, and turn towards him.

He holds out his hand with my sunnies in his palm.

"Thank you from the bottom of my heart," I say half facetiously, half seriously. I hastily take them and put them on, instantly relaxing as I do. "Now I have eyes again."

Realizing I'm sweating, or close to it, I take off the heavy jacket and toss it in the backseat. I roll the window all the way down, letting the cool breeze envelope my cheeks.

"Is there any coffee?" Brodie asks casually, driving.

Fumbling to open the lunchbox, I open the top and find the thermos tucked inside. I pull it out and carefully pour some of the hot steaming coffee into the small lid. I hand it to Brodie and he accepts it by taking a big sip.

"Much betta," he exclaims.

"I'm sorry, I'm the worst co-pilot in history," I offer. "You probably needed this hours ago."

"Nah, dun worry. All good," he replies, shaking his head as he takes another sip. "This's hitting the spot."

He looks down at the cup very pleased, and tilts the makeshift cup all the way back, downing the rest. I grab it from him and refill him another batch. He reaches out to take it, but I actually bring it to my lips and slowly inhale the scent of it before taking a small drink. Swallowing, I smile at him and place it back in his hand. Glancing down inside the lunchbox, I notice that aside from the coffee, there are a couple of muffins, two bags of chips, and two sandwiches for later.

"Sometimes I don't know how Mick thinks of everything," I reflect aloud, grateful.

"Can I have another pour?" Brodie asks, handing over the cup.

Even without coffee, Brodie is hyped on life. After I happily refill it, he takes a swig, then holds out the cup, offering me some. I accept and take a big sip myself.

"Glad ya woke up now 'cause there's the most heatha bay near here, n' I think it'll be a banga spot for the dronie," he teases.

"Oooh, yes, please," I say excitedly. In my most authentic Aussie accent I can muster, I jest, "Would neva wanna miss a *banga* spot."

He laughs and chuckles.

"Yar accent's gettin' betta. Ya almost sound like a loc 'n not some blow in," he muses.

This reminds me of a debate I had with Mel when I first arrived here.

"Why is it that Australians or foreigners can come to America and lose their accents, sounding more American over time, but when an American comes to Straya they're not 'allowed' to gain an Aussie accent or local quality to their voice?" I say, rambling on. "It's so unfair. I could easily walk around bumbling in an Aussie accent. It practically comes naturally to me these days, but, no, I'd get weird looks from everyone who knows I'm an American. Seems to me it's a downright double standard!"

I stop, coming up for air.

Brodie's eyebrows shoot up over his sunnies, and he balks, "Wow, was not expectin' all that this early from ya... if it makes ya feel any betta, ya can always speak any way ya like with me."

I laugh and give him a soft crooked smile in thanks.

"May I?" I ask, pulling out my iPod.

"Be my guest."

I plug in my iPod to the stereo and select John Mayer's "In the Blood." The heavy natural beat and warm strumming rhythm fill the car. I sigh contently. I look over and see Brodie thumping his finger to the bassline on the steering wheel.

"This is impossible to say definitively, but I think this is my favorite song of his," I inform Brodie, who casually stares out at the road in front.

"Why?" he asks, usually eager to listen to the thought process behind my musical statements.

I've never had to put this into words before. How do I explain this? I don't have much time to gather my thoughts, but begin anyway.

"Well, it's a song about family and about being who you want to be," I mumble. "It's about feeling the pulls of what or who makes you who you are, but then you have to make a choice about who you want to become. Are you someone who's ingrained in your blood or are you a new person in spite of it?"

We sit for a few seconds, quietly pondering.

"It's also sad realizing maybe you don't want to be like your parents, who for so long you idolize," I continue. "And then it's about making someone and something of yourself in spite of those differences. I find a lot of truth to it honestly. I mean my parents are amazing people and I'm lucky to have them as my examples, but there are qualities I would choose to carry in me and some I wouldn't... and a part of me is proud of the fact that I want to be my own person... flaws and all."

I sigh deeply, stretching out my legs, and finish passionately, "I find his confession incredibly moving and personal. John Mayer writes from the soul... Not to mention his melodies and riffs, it's like his guitar has a voice of its own. He's easily one of the most talented artists of our generation."

I take a deep breath, sighing dreamily.

"Ya got all that from one song?" Brodie jokingly mocks, looking at me, then back at the road.

"And then some too," I snort, playfully throwing the sweatshirt at him.

I know he takes music seriously, but I also like how he knows not to take me too seriously either.

A road sign approaches, indicating distances in kilometers. I don't recognize any of the destinations. About a kilometer later, we pull off the highway and veer down a dirt road towards the beach.

"I don't know about you, but I feel like hoppin' in the drink," he suggests. "Ya can also fly The Khal if ya want."

I glance around, trying to find a bush or something leafy to gauge the wind. I extend my arm out the open window. Thankfully it doesn't seem windy. The breeze has already warmed up a few degrees since I woke up. I lean my head on the door frame, enjoying the warm springtime air. My iPod rolls into John Mayer's "Belief," another excellent song of his, off my favorite JM album *Continuum*.

We continue traveling down this über bumpy path.

I cheer as we hit a big bump, yelling mid collision, "Boom!"

Brodie expertly maneuvers us through pot holes until we manage to hit sand. We drive further down to the water. I quickly find The Drums on my player and blast "Let's Go Surfing." The fun, surf tones feel just right as we drive along the sand with a panoramic view of brilliant blue shoreline. I scan the coastline and as far as the eye can see, there's not a single soul. Another pro for Straya. Brodie drives right along the water for a couple of minutes, then parks it. We climb out.

"I keep wanting to call for Stel, and then I realize she's not here," I whine, gazing around at the empty beach. "I still don't know why she couldn't come."

"Yull find out in two shakes," he teases. "Besides, she's probably gettin' a nice belly rub at the 'rents rightta 'bout now."

Brodie strips his shirt and starts to sunscreen his face. He's always diligent with the blocking. The UV rays out here are no joke. They're some of the most intense in the whole world and aren't to be trifled with. I think back to a horrible nose peeling session I had when I first arrived here. I shake off the unpleasant memory. Luckily I was able to log in a few sunbathing hours at Mick's while he went to town yesterday, so my tan lines aren't too noticeable anymore. I grab my reef friendly sunscreen, and generously apply it to the paler areas out of fear of getting too much sun too soon. I should take my tank off, but I manage to cover all the areas without revealing my suit just yet. Moving up to my face, I rub it in all over, careful to cover my ears as well. Glancing at Brodie's face, I laugh. A big white smear streaks across his nose. I reach over and gently rub it in with my pointer finger. He closes his eyes, grinning.

"There," I exclaim, wiping my fingers on my denim shorts as I go to strip down to my suit.

"Hold up," he calls out, and walks over. He gently rubs in a spot on my cheek below my eye. We both stand and smile at each other. I double check and lightly rub my fingers over my face quickly. Brodie looks me in the eyes, excited with a game plan. "Ya lift the dronie up, 'n I'm gonna hop in, alright. Meet me in the drink when yar done."

I nod and take out The Khal, turning him on and taking off straight up in the clear sky. Meanwhile Brodie dives in the water, howling and shaking his body. The water must be a little refreshing if he seems revitalized. He dives down again, and then resurfaces, shaking his head to fling off the excess water.

I look down at my monitor and realize the bay is enclosed with the most beautiful and stunning rock formations. Two clusters stack from the shore out to sea in an almost hourglass shape with the most clear sandy bottom in between. The waves don't break until further out at the reef, so the whole bay lies still. I take a crap load of photos before I command the drone higher. The greater height reveals more of the red landscape. It juxtaposes the bright aqua water in an otherworldly kind of way.

"You have to see this!" I squeal in delight, and glance at Brodie.

Running up the beach, dripping wet, he comes up behind me and peers over my shoulder. I flinch as water droplets land on my exposed shoulder. Seeing the intense environment, he cracks a giant smile from ear to ear, and shakes his head in amazement.

"I've an idea," he exclaims, and points to a certain spot on the screen. "Can ya hova it ova here 'n take it up a notch so ya can see the entire formation?"

I glance at The Khal's current height. I'm still well under the droning regulatory limits. Nodding, I maneuver The Khal to the exact spot he suggests, and snap another pic.

"Here, film this," he directs, and I hit the record button. He cautiously takes the remote from me, setting it down on the ute's hood. He grabs my arm. "Quick!"

"Wait a sec," I wail, halting as Brodie keeps pace all the way down to the water, unable to suppress his excitement. "I still have my clothes on!"

I'm out on a limb wearing my new suit and feel a little nervous about unveiling it, but I guess now is as good a time as any. Hastily, I pull my new daisy tank top over my head, sucking in my mid-section, revealing the banana yellow bikini top. I toss my tank into the ute and am about to fold my arms over my chest when I remember Mel, Donnie, and all the confidence boosting moments from the last few months. I drop my arms, and stand up proudly with straight posture, and take a deep breath and run towards the beach. Jogging, I reach up and grab my scrunchy from my messy top knot. My unruly mane - a mix of tight curly ringlets and frizzy waves - bounces around my face.

Brodie looks back and does a double take.

I gulp. *No going back now, Nina.*

Mustering all my confidence, I don't break stride and run right past his interested gaze, barreling into the spritely waters. I don't stop until I come swimming up for air. I pop up smiling. My soused hair falls straight down my back in refreshed bliss. I hear Brodie crashing into the water beside me. Laughing in delight, he jumps around before diving under. He surfaces again and shakes the water from his head.

I look around the little bay. It's some of the clearest water I've ever seen. Patches of light turquoise and cadet blues speckle the earth all the way out until a darker line encroaches, the marker of deeper depths. Twirling back around, I find Brodie checking out my new bikini. His unabashed stare is pretty unnerving, so I decide to address it head on.

"Mel got me a new suit for the trip. Like it?" I ask.

He beams appreciatively, looking me up and down. Clearly he likes it. *Damn, Mel.* She's always right when it comes to these things. Licking his lips, Brodie nervously smiles. We both end up chuckling our nerves away.

Brodie urges me to float, leading by example as he extends all his long limbs out. I make myself look like a bobbing snow angel, relaxing peacefully for a minute. I can feel my hair swirling out around my head like a drop of pigment in water. While I lie still, Brodie playfully starts swimming in circles around me. It almost feels like a choreographed dance, but he's clearly into his vision, which amuses me. We keep our current positions for about a minute or two more before he hollers for me to follow him. We both swim back to shore, and walk up the shallows onto the sand and lie down, side by side. Water streamlines from my hair, running like a small river down my back. Standing up, I flip my head over a couple of times, trying to dispel some of it. The platinum edges are getting lighter, if that's even possible. I can already feel the sun drying up the tiny water particles on my skin.

Brodie stands up, quickly rinses his hands in the ocean, and runs to the ute. He grabs a towel and dries his fingers before grabbing the drone controller to end the recording.

"Why don't you bring it down?" I holler back playfully.

I'm covered in sand, and besides, it's super entertaining to watch someone fly a drone for the first time. This is the perfect setting after all; there's no one around, or any thing for that matter, for as far as I can see. The Khal catches my attention.

It haltingly descends with lots of jerky motions as the novice pilot figures out the commanding sticks.

"It's a lot harda than it looks," he shouts in surprise.

"Just focus on the left toggle and pull it towards you," I coach. "That one controls the height." That helps immediately; the drone stills and then punches in one, quick swooping descent before coming to an abrupt halt. The blades roar in protest at the uneasy transition. I remain in my cozy position by the water. "How fast you pull also determines the speed."

He adjusts accordingly and manages to bring it down slower and with more agility than before, bringing it to a hover above the ute. Brodie stares at the drone and pushes on the toggles, but it shifts in the opposite direction of what he wants.

"Nah, more to the left, mate," he rants in protest.

Enjoying his efforts, I direct him with some basic maneuvering and he more or less guides the drone back towards him. I teach my new apprentice how to land it when he feels ready. Brodie manages to clumsily guide the drone fairly close to him, bridging the gap as he catches the undercarriage with his hand, force landing it. Smiling, he stashes it away in the shade of the Troopy.

"Did you record anything?" I ask over my shoulder, hearing him crunching down on some chips by the ute.

"Yar jokin', right?" he snorts back. "I was just tryin' to fly the bloody thing, Neens."

Happy he's willing to learn, I can't help but feel slightly relieved that Brodie's not some natural drone superstar. I swear he's good at everything he lays his hands on. Besides, droning is my thing. I'd prefer it if he sticks to being in front of the lens with me behind it; not to mention, teaching Brodie something for a change is going to be fun.

I stand and walk into the calm water and take one more dip, wiping off any stray sand from my body. I look up and find Brodie admiring the view, but his eyes perforate so deeply into my skin I feel an onslaught of panic bubbling under the surface. Unsure how to react, I smile back at him before hastily looking away. *How do I tell what he wants?* Before submerging once more, I steal a quick glance and find him holding his gaze. My intuition tells me he definitely does not want to just be friends... clearly there's an attraction between us. I just don't know if I have what it takes to encourage him, or at least open the door to let him try. I guess I'm admitting to myself for the first time that I'm interested in him, but does he know it? How do we get to the next level if I keep putting up walls? I mean I can barely handle him looking at me for more than five seconds. *I'm in uncharted territory here.*

Shaking off my anxious thoughts, I glance down at my bikini. Is the top too boobalicious? Clearly it's captured his attention, but is that all he's interested in? *Don't be silly, Nina. You know he's deeper than that.*

Rolling my eyes at myself, I self-assess my suit. Unbiasedly, it's no more revealing than the current standard all the girls wear these days, but obviously is far more exposing than my normal Nina-wear. Maybe I should take this opportunity to stretch my comfort rubber band and emerge out of my shell. *Be a newer, more confident Nina, a more empowered Nina.*

Selena's voice sounds off in my head again, repeating, *"You can be anyone you want to be."*

*No one knows who you were, Nina.*

I find myself nodding my head, feeling mad inspired from my own pep talk.

*You almost died, Nina. Stop sweating the small stuff. Who the eff cares about a couple more inches of skin.*

Right here and now, I pledge to be more daring.

*Fearless Nina, here I come.*

A little shell catches my eye in the sand, and I bend down and grab it, pulling it up for a closer view. Just as the water pulls away, I slowly forget all about the suit and the feeling of self-consciousness. I stand with my toes slightly buried in the wet sand as the water pushes the grains around with the ebbing tide.

Brodie approaches from behind. Out of my peripheral, I catch him stealing a glance at my bottoms before he walks up beside me. I laugh. *He's still a typical bloody man.*

*Be bold, Nina. Stop sitting on the sidelines and play the damn game.*

I decide to test Mel's theory. I pull a page out from Margot's book, and lie down along the shoreline, extending my shorter legs. I lean back and prop myself up on my elbows as they dig into the sand under me. I let my salty wet hair slide down my back as I lie here as casually as possible, soaking up the view in front of me. My backside's on fire from the heat of the dry sand, but what do they say? No pain, no gain.

Brodie sits down next to me, glancing at me quite a few times. He seems interested, almost like he wants to say something, but he simply raises his arms and crosses them on his bent knees.

"Thanks for bringing me here, Brodie," I say genuinely, while also testing the waters. "I'm so glad I have a friend like you."

I laugh internally at my horrible attempt, and my breasts lightly bounce up and down, rebelling against the confines of the fabric. Brodie catches a close look and clears his throat, but then looks away cooly, "surveying" the water.

"Nah, yeah, just friends, Neens," he gulps. "Like ya want."

"And you too, right?" I clarify, making my eyes round and doe-eyed.

"'Course, yeah," he spits out.

*This is hilarious. My horrible flirting/scheming is working.* If only Selena, Ria, and Mel could see me now.

He looks over at me and we lock eyes for a second. I recognize the unbridled yearning in his eye. The feeling is a little unsettling, but Nina 2.0 steps in, unfazed.

"Okay, then," I say, nodding my head, and bite my lower lip.

"Well, I reckon we should be on our way, eh," he bristles, immediately standing up. "The surprise awaits."

"Oh, I thought this might be the surprise," I add, standing up and following him back to the ute. I hold out an outstretched towel towards him. "Do you mind wiping some of the sand away? I don't want to trek half the beach with me back in the ute."

*Nina, I'm impressed.*

He nods and takes it and I turn my back to him, pulling my long wet hair forward over my shoulder. I stand there, waiting.

*I honestly didn't know I had this in me.*

Suddenly, I feel the bulk of the towel wipe across my lower back.

"Make sure you get it all," I add across my shoulder. I feel the towel sweep lower, brushing against my sandy skin moving down along my thighs until behind my knees. I turn my head back to see. "Am I good?"

I hear Brodie clear his throat, and mutter, "Yep."

Internally dying of hysterics, I put on my best neutral face as I slide my new daisy tank over my bikini. The damp yellow fabric clings to the white linen. We close up everything and board the ute, setting off down the highway.

Another hour passes on the open road. Starving, I unfold the two sandwiches wrapped in wax paper and pull out the other bag of chips. I smile at the thought of Mick's consideration and care. I offer Brodie a sanger which he gladly accepts and tears into it with a gigantic bite. While "Pure Devotion" by Turnover happily plays, Brodie digs through the esky behind the center console and grabs an ice cold carbonated water for me. It tastes heavenly. He also hands me a pack of beef jerky, my favorite road trip snack, and opens some emu jerky for himself. He tells me how he remembered me sharing this fact when I opened my birthday package.

"It's true. I swear I could live on jerky like in the Wild West - well maybe that and fish," I declare, pulling off another big bite between my teeth, chewing profusely. Brodie extends a hand out and I place a fat slab down in his fingers. He rips off a giant piece and sends his jaws into snacking overload. Picking the jerky bits out of my teeth with my tongue, I ask, "Brodie, where are we going?"

I study our surroundings. There's not much around in terms of a town or outpost. In fact there's nothing but diversely textured landscapes that contrast the barren sandy beaches. Swirls of run-off marry the coastline as the road gets windier. Giant shorelines of estuaries, where river and sea embrace, co-mingle like a curvy snake. They intertwine towards the road and suddenly, the highway banks sharp right, away from the water, going the long way around the inlets.

"Almost there," Brodie teases.

"What?" I ask in disbelief, swirling my head, but finding nothing.

"Relax, Neens, we'll be there in a a few clicks," he assures me with a chuckle.

I trust Brodie so I lean back into my seat and relax while still taking in the general spender of the surroundings. I gaze out the window for what feels like two minutes, but is in fact four songs worth of time. The speakers play "Chateau" by Angus & Julis Stone at the moment. I move my head to the beat of the song. Brodie turns right at a turnoff and we hit a red, poorly kept dirt road. The ute jostles slightly. I look over and see what looks like a long, open path leading out to nowhere. We ride for a few minutes before a small shed and hanger appear out of the mirage lining the horizon. I'm having flashbacks of when I first landed in Western Oz. *No, it can't be.*

"Brodie, where are you taking me?" I ask, in a mixture of nerves and excitement.

"It's not like that, trust me," he urges. I take a deep breath as he parks next to the hanger and pockets his keys. "Bring yar camera."

He stashes my backpack in the esky to keep my drone and batteries cool and locks up the ute. He grabs my hand and leads me behind the hanger where I stop in my tracks.

"No, you didn't?!" I exclaim, covering my open mouth with both hands.

A blue helicopter sits before my eyes. *I can't believe this.*

The pilot comes running out of the hanger. He's younger than expected, in his thirties, and a little taller than Brodie. His friendly smile encompasses his entire face, kind of like Dennis Quaid's. Brodie introduces him as Jai. Apparently he's an old school mate of Brodie's and the two merrily catch up as I walk around the chopper, taking in its enormous expanse. Its gargantuan propeller balances far and wide across the roof. It must be thirty, more like forty feet in diameter.

"Neens, ya ready to fly?" Brodie asks me, amused.

Eyes wide, mouth gaping, I can't form words. I merely nod my head. The two chuckle in response.

"First tima?" Jai asks Brodie, who nods. "Good on ya," Jai hollers in my direction. "Day for it!"

I follow them and walk up directly to the chopper. It's massive. The main cabin is like one giant fishbowl. Along the side, an expansive opening reveals a larger area with only two seats. The pilot's seat and cockpit fill out the front cab. Jai conducts his pre-flight checklist and advises us to climb in the back and strap in.

Brodie jumps in first and turns back, offering me a hand. He gets me settled and buckles me in the harness, placing a headset and mic around my head and over my ears. He does a sound test and motions a thumbs up followed by a thumbs down. Hearing his voice, I signal back a thumbs up. I'm not quite ready to talk yet. I'm taking this all in. With us both strapped in side by side, there's still plenty of room around us without nearing the cockpit. Jai jumps in, sliding in front of us to double check our buckles. He also checks the connection to the welded base on the helicopter's floor. He climbs into the pilot's seat and buckles in. He flips a bunch of switches and I hear him speaking aviator talk into the mic. I recognize some of the lingo from my commercial drone exam. He signals to us for takeoff and we both give him a visual thumbs up. I wrap the camera strap over my head.

Suddenly the chopper starts to vibrate and shake immensely as the propeller starts to fire up to life, swirling fiercely. I feel wind blowing everywhere.

*This is really happening. Eeek!*

My hair swirls around in the spinning wind. Caught up in the sheer shock of flying, I completely forgot to pull back my hair. I attempt to gather it, but strands escape my grasp and fly freely about. Brodie leans over and with strong hands and dexterous fingers, collects the stray pieces. He grabs my scrunchy from me, and hastily ties it back in a tight high ponytail.

The chopper jolts as it lifts for take off and I reach out, grabbing Brodie's hand next to me. He squeezes it in excitement and support. I feel the weight of gravity as we lift off from the ground. Before I can blink, we're decently high up in the air. My eyes must be the size of saucers as they scan the parting ground below us. The ute gets smaller and smaller as we gain elevation. Grinning from ear to ear, I look at Brodie then back down at the Troopy, now the the size of an ant.

Through the mic, Brodie informs me we're harnessed to the frame of the chopper, and if I'm feeling brave enough, can venture forward on the seat and even lean out the large opening. While this sounds a little reckless for one of Lucy's daughters, I realize it's the only true way to see and photograph the world below with totally unobstructed views. Naturally, my tendency is to forgo self-preservation when a camera's involved to get the shot, and while this situation does seem daunting, this is no exception. *Sorry, Mom.*

"Only if yar comfortable, Neens," Brodie yells.

As he checks with me, I simultaneously sit forward. Holding up my camera, I scoot out with more willingness than I thought I could possess, and lean over the exposed opening. I gulp as I hang over the edge with nothing between me and the ground besides several thousand feet and a cable. I feel a rush and a high like I've never experienced before.

The soundtrack to my life right now would be Khalid's "Hundred." It plays loudly in my head. It's got the best beat that would sum up my current mood, lyrics notwithstanding.

Stunning views of river inlets meeting the ocean mix together with blue seascapes and red, burnt rusty earth. I squeal in delight and hear Jai chuckle at my exuberance. Brodie asks him to fly over a certain spot. I feel the chopper shift direction slightly, the harness tightening harder around my torso. I look down and see a large portion of the northern coastline from two thousand feet in the air. Endless amounts of dark spots of coral reef contrast against the white sandy, blue bays as they rendezvous and tango with the harsh red terrain. The way the chopper banks, I'm almost leaning straight down towards land. I take pictures of everything. My stomach flips as Jai drops our altitude below one thousand feet and we sweep over the coastline once more. I shake my head in awe, and beam back at Brodie. I yell random shrieks of thrilling hysteria. He laughs whole heartedly, his nose scrunching as it does when he's really enjoying something. I turn and snap a photo of him with his giant headphones on. I don't think the pair of us has ever seen the other so happy. He holds up his phone and takes a photo of us with our heads together before zipping it back up in his boardies. Over my shoulder, he points to something down below. Currently at an altitude that's way higher than the drone's allowed to fly, but still close enough where I can make out shapes, we see a pod of whales breaching. I squeal again, mad with ecstasy.

We fly inland for a couple of minutes, paralleling a long, flowing river. Jai guides us over a river mouth which meets the most beautiful raging waterfall. Dewy mist sprays against the flaming rock formations. A rainbow appears in the middle as the light refracts through the minute water droplets. I shout to Brodie who's eyes round wide. He squeezes my leg in excitement and I take a couple bursts of photographs.

It's truly breathtaking how quickly the landscape changes out here. Just as we stumbled across the waterfall, we now are gaining traction above the bush. I thump Brodie's arm as a pack of wild kangaroos stampede across the territory. With the angle of the sun against our top down vantage point, their long shadows spring to life, like black silhouettes jumping across the red soil.

Jai's voice pierces through our headphones, informing us there's a giant crocodile lying on the shore of the swamp bed to our right. He drops the chopper lower to give us a better view. The croc chomps down on what looks like the remains of a wallaby or something. Living on the coast and immersing myself in ocean culture, I almost forgot that the Outback is such a large part of Straya's identity, and I haven't been able to really see it until now.

"This is amazing!" I shout through the mic.

We continue to fly around the backlands for another twenty minutes before returning to the coast. It's incredible to see how open the west coast truly is and how much coverage you gain via helicopter. Only tiny parcels of towns sparsely scatter the desert floor. We truly have God's own view today. Jai informs me that we're currently flying over the Kimberley Coast, a super remote part of the coastline. You have to get permission from the Aborigines to even access this section or even fly over it. I snap plenty of shots and videos, but I also put the camera down to soak up the experience with my own eyes.

We fly low over the water now, parallel to these giant, raw-edged cliffs that stack up against the ocean as if they guard this divine land from all intruders. Waves pummel into the sides of their unflinching jagged faces. Remarkable colors of red and orange stone, along with green bush, pop out against the clearest forms of deep turquoise water. Healthy flowing waterfalls cascade down the cliffs, stirring up colossal splashes of mist. It feels outer worldly and downright sacred. This land remains untouched and you can feel the reverence even from above.

We turn around and make the path back towards the "airport." As we approach the area, Brodie points out the beach we swam in only hours ago. It looks so small I can barely make out the hourglass formation. As Jai steers us back towards our "runway," I laugh and shake my head, taking it all in before it comes to an end. My heart thumps out of my chest, my adrenaline raging inside. We land smoothly, and Jai flips more switches, turning off the motor and propeller. You can hear the swooshing slowing overhead.

Brodie and I sit, staring at each other, coming off of this mutual high. Jai busies himself with his controls before hopping out of the pilot's door. Mentally flabbergasted from our experience, a hysterical laugh erupts from inside me. Brodie unbuckles himself and then liberates me from my harness. He laughs uncontrollably as well, and rests his forehead on mine. We both sit face to face, losing it in our mirth.

Finally, he breaks away and gently removes my headset, along with his own. The chopper lies still now, the buzzing electronics cooling off. We both hop down, away from the propellor. I immediately run to Brodie and give him a crushing hug, then give Jai the same treatment.

"That was better than Christmas morning! By *far* the best experience of my life!" I yell at them, freaking out.

Brodie asks Jai to take our photo standing in front of the helicopter and he does so happily. Brodie puts his arm around me and we take one nice picture together. After, I throw one arm up into the air, and clutch Brodie with my other as I bellow loudly. Brodie does the same and howls.

"Can't thank ya enough, mate," Brodie says, grinning ear to ear as he gives Jai a big hug.

"Think nothin' of it," Jai responds happily.

I thank our amazing pilot another thousand times and tell him what an amazing job he has getting to do this every day.

"I absolutely loved it," I repeat to him, "like I can't find the words it was so bloody awesome."

"I reckon I know how much ya appreciate it," Jai says nicely.

Brodie chuckles, informing me I was "oohing" and gasping about every two seconds.

"I had no idea," I mutter in a laugh. "I guess I got carried away in the moment."

"'N this is why I love flyin'," Jai explains, looking from Brodie to me, "'causa people like you." He beams at me, drawing out the long "u" sound at the end of the word. He looks at me. "Brodie tells me yar a photographa, eh. Think ya got some good shots?"

"More like a thousand! I can't wait to see them. They're going to be insane," I exclaim, already catching a glimpse as I scroll back through my camera at some of the images.

Brodie tells Jai he'll reach out and share some of the photos as a thank you, which I readily confirm. Jai appreciates it so much. With my insistence, I force him back into the cockpit and snap one of him clad in his gear. He thanks us for being "rippa passengas" and we wave goodbye. Brodie practically has to drag me away. I still can't shake the energetic high. On our way to the ute, my flying companion asks me if I'd prefer to turn back towards home or keep adventuring and see where the day takes us. I immediately say yes to further exploration. After that ultimate ride though, I honestly don't know what could be better, but the idea of spending more alone time with Brodie is almost as thrilling, and I don't want this feeling to end just yet. Taking one last look at the helicopter, we climb into the truck and Brodie starts the engine, turning the A/C on full blast. "Morning Light" by Dusty Boots fires up.

"Incredible! Absolutely incredible," I ramble. "I need to find better words to describe how amazing that was." Brodie just laughs and takes a long drawn out gulp of water. Shaking my head again in awe, I feel my excitement bubbling up through my hands, which shake. "Hard to believe all that beauty is around us just at our fingertips."

Brodie hands me the canteen, offering me a drink. I take it. Having no idea how parched I am, I end up guzzling the entire canister. I hand it back to him on empty, apologizing, but he doesn't even seem to notice.

"That was truly remarkable. Straya, ya bloody beaut!" he roars in awe. "I just can't get ova that view. It neva tires. I reckon every bloke should see her like that."

It dawns on me.

"Alright, break it to me gently," I request, raising my eyebrows playfully in anticipation. "How many times have you done that, 'Mr. I've Done Everything'?"

Brodie stifles a giggle, and bites his lip, scrunching his eyes.

"Yull neva guess," he muses.

He smugly looks out at the road, and presses on the gas, leading us back down the dirt road to the highway. I look at him, trying to estimate in my head.

I take a stab in the dark, and offer, "Six?"

Snorting, he shakes his head. An extra bumpy stretch of road hits the tires. He gasses it more than usual, jostling the ute playfully. I brace by arm against the dashboard as everything in the ute joggles.

"Like that, eh?" Brodie edgily jokes, driving a little faster, causing the ute to bounce wildly up and down as we encounter a large dip in the road.

My seatbelt locks as I push forward in my seat.

"Oh, yeah, baby, I love a bumpy ride!" I yell, laughing louder.

He slams on the brakes. The ute comes to a screeching halt. I sit, laughing my head off. He releases the brake, jolting the Troopy forward in bursts, like an amusement park ride, stopping and lunging forward and stopping again.

"Want more?" he jovially taunts, slowly slipping the brake.

I can feel the ute start to move forward, vibrating under his control.

"Yes!" I cry out.

"More?!" he shouts, bouncing forward.

I brace my arm on the seat, holding on, and scream even louder, "Yessss!"

Brodie revs the engine and guns it! We jostle, bags sliding towards the boot. My bag of jerky flies from the center console to the backseat. The turn to the highway approaches and he speeds towards it, shifting gears at the last minute, before turning and merging onto the paved road. He adeptly stabilizes the car and drives just above the speed limit. I fall apart in my seat, dying from hysterics.

"I think I just peed a little," I squeak out. Brodie laughs so hard, he starts to cough, wiping tears from his eyes. We drive along the coast. I look at Brodie's hand, switching gears. "Is the ute okay?"

"She'll be right. Worth it," he assures me, smiling.

We drive for a minute, collecting ourselves. I unbuckle, turn around in my seat and kneel against the backrest as I reach back to grab the jerky bag. While leaning back here, I manage to tidy up some of the dislodged items. Flipping back forward, I look down. Brodie's hummus avocado wrap flew from his bento box and crash landed on my denim shorts, leaving a nice trail of green guck all over my bottoms. I look down, frowning slightly.

"They're the only pair I brought. Cool," I admit to myself. I grab a napkin and dab the smear with some water from my canteen. I attempt to rid the green from the denim, but no dice. I return to our original conversation. "Fourteen times?"

"Ya still on that, eh?" Brodie mutters, laughing. "Negatory."

*More than fourteen times?! Ridiculous!*

I sigh, contemplating, and bite the side of my lip, narrowing my eyes.

"Hmmm, twenty-one?" I guess. "If it's more than twenty-one times, Brodie, I'm going to punch you in the face."

"Nope," he retorts, sticking out his tongue at me. "'N anything more than ten, I admit, would make me a lucky bastard." He smiles, eyes focused on the road, clearly enjoying this little game. We keep driving up the highway and if it's possible, our surroundings get more and more remote. The wild bush takes over in full force. He asks playfully, "Alright, ya really want me tell ya?"

My ears perk up at the radio. Oingo Boingo's "Just Another Day" starts. High off the buoyant energy of the afternoon, I scream, startling Brodie, who jumps in his seat.

"What's the matta?" he asks, as I crank the dial volume LOUD.

He rolls his eyes at me, relieved it's nothing serious.

"Sorry, but this is one of my favorite songs!" I giddily yell.

I roll down the windows and lean out, throwing my entire head and upper body out the window as the beat rages on. I shake my loose hair and yell to the passing landscape. Brodie pulls me back in by the waist of my shorts, laughing. I look at him and bob my head to the beat and start belting out the lyrics. I close my eyes, clearly enjoying the moment as the awesome beat rages on. I get to my favorite part of the song, and hit Brodie in the arm a few times, and excitedly tell him. I wait for the section to arrive for a couple of seconds, then turn to him, beaming.

"Here it comes," I exclaim. "Ready?"

He raises his eyebrows at me, playing along.

I close my eyes, air drum with my hands and imaginary drumsticks, then click my tongue to the changing beat, and sing loudly, *"But there's a smile on my face...*

*for everyone... and there's a golden coin that reflects the sun. There's a lonely place... that's always cold... There's a place in the stars for when you get old."*

I howl in happiness. Nothing beats a good road trip sing along. I raise up my arms and dance along, super into the moment. I don't care what I look like or what Brodie's thinking. It's just me, the melody, the guitar and this slice of time. I squeal as the song bridges into the change, dropping the beat. I push on, lowering the timbre of my voice, *"There's razors in my bed, that come out late at night, they always disappear before the morning light!"*

I sing along to the rest of it, releasing this pent up energy I didn't even know I had.

*I AM ALIVE!*

Brodie joins in and sings along too as we round out the last few chorus sections. I switch to air guitar while he plays drums on the steering wheel. The song comes to an end and I flop back in my seat.

"Yar crazy!" Brodie exclaims, joking. "I'm a bit scared for what comes on next."

Smiling ear to ear. My shuffle turns on "Roots Girl" by Eli Mac, a totally different vibe as the reggae beat starts up. While I dearly love this song, I'm still reeling from my Oingo number. I reach down and drop the dial slightly, but leave it loud enough for me to still enjoy it.

"How do ya do that?" he asks me.

"Do what?" I ask, not a clue as to what about.

"Jump from one genre to the next 'n not skip a beat?"

"I never really thought about it before," I truthfully explain. "I've always listened to music this way. Shüfflé, *shoo-flay,* I call it." I turn to him and lick my lips. "Brodie, what would you like to listen to? Any requests?" I hold up my iPod, finger on the ready to search. "Mind you, if it's post-2007, there's a good chance I might not have it. There are exceptions to the rule, but chances are slim."

Personally, I'm not a huge fan of music streaming services. I still prefer to support the artist as directly as possible. I have a whole library saved up since I was fifteen or so, back from when I used to collect discs and records, which comes in handy in times like these when cell reception is sketchy at best. For most people, it's connectivity or bust.

"Hmmm, lemme think for a sec," Brodie mutters, narrowing his eyes. Waiting, I sway to the ending little ditty of "Roots Girl." The guitar reminds me of falling rain. I briefly close my eyes in bliss. Brodie nudges me. "Nah, yeah, I got it. Can ya put on 'Chosen Armies' by Children Collide? Love that tune."

I raise my eyebrow devilishly pleased, and say, "Good choice, my lad."

Within seconds, it fills the speakers. In unison, we both bob our heads and sit listening. I put my legs up on the side of the window, hanging my boots out in the wind. I shake my feet to the beat, and Brodie drives on.

# 17

A couple of stops later, Brodie and I make our way up the coast, chilling together in harmonious quiet, listening to the wonderful Selena as she duets in "Ámame, Quiéreme." I absentmindedly sing along in Spanish as I scroll through my camera, looking at the photos from our heli adventure. I smile from ear to ear. There are so many good ones. Just wait until those back home see these. They're going to lose it. I'll just downplay the whole open cabin thing to Mom.

"Ya should sing in Spanish more often, Neens," Brodie says, driving, before glancing over at me with a hint of a smile.

I pull up some of my favorite Spanish speaking artists and play him a few songs. We wrap on "Fotografía" by Juanes featuring Nelly Furtado. As I loosely translate the song for him, he veers the ute off the highway and we hit a hard dirt pathway.

"Pull the dronie out, Neens. Trust me," he says, steering us into an empty lookout point, and I do as he says.

At first the parking area looks like all the other beautiful spots we've been passing on our drive, but once I get out of the ute and walk over to the edge, my jaw drops. Amazing fiery rock formations kiss the sea. I launch The Khal quickly and beeline straight for the water. Serendipitously, a squadron of spotted eagle rays swim near the surface. Like their cousins, the manta rays, they flap their giant wings, jumping clear out of the water. Unlike their cousins, they have longer barbed tails. Seeing the rays from the air this time, I eagerly get some amazing video footage from respectful depths and angles. The white spots on their dark, shagreen skin look like fluid art as they dance around underneath the clear surface.

Brodie shares they can reach up to more than three meters in width from wing tip to tip. He's aways full of much needed, random knowledge involving the sea, which he claims he picks up from his sister, the marine biologist. A massive manta cruises into the frame. Brodie yells "yeww" as we see its undercarriage, exposing its gills as it flips upside down in a somersault just under the surface. The rays submerge and drift off out of range, so I bring The Khal back in and we both discuss how nature is just utterly miraculous as we load back in the truck and keep driving.

We burn rubber for another two hours until the light starts to fade, going back and forth selecting different bands to accompany us on our drive. So far we've gone through favorites of Bruno Mars, The Police, The Killers, Matchbox Twenty, Amber Run, The B-52s, and Foo Fighters. We're currently bouncing between John Mayer and Coldplay. We then take it one step further, picking genres and doing band face-offs. Right now we're battling it out between Bob Marley and Maxi Priest. On a technicality of a collaborative tour, I throw in some UB40 which makes Brodie laugh.

At sunset, Brodie pulls off the road next to the beach. We watch as the neon ball of light drops quickly under the stark horizon line. We take a little sunset dip in the ocean before hitting the road for another stretch. We ride for about ten minutes when my stomach growls loudly. With all the excitement we forgot to eat and we ran out of snacks a while ago.

"Hungry?" Brodie asks the obvious, glancing at me.

I nod quickly. Now that it's been brought to my attention, I find myself getting hungrier by the minute.

"Starved," I reply. "I could just about eat my hand."

We see stationary lights in the distance as we approach some form of township.

"Cracka timin' if I do say so myself," Brodie says proudly.

Within twenty minutes, we enter the outskirts of a quaint, but charming little town. Clearly more of a tourist attraction, the locale boasts two motels and a full blown restaurant about a quarter of a mile apart. Tall palm trees cluster around the beach.

Assuming we're heading towards food, I expect Brodie to pull off at the restaurant, but he circles back and pulls up in front of the little beachfront, blue motel.

"If it's alright with ya, Neens, I'm gonna check 'n see if they have a coupla rooms," he announces. "I reckon I'm a bit cooked to drive back on through tonight."

Stepping out of the ute, I thoroughly stretch my arms and back, hearing a few *pops!* as the stagnant tension releases from my stiff vertebrae.

"Yeah, sounds good, whatever you want to do," I say in an amenable tone. "I'm just along for the ride."

Brodie stands next to the ute and pats himself off. A couple of crumbs fall off as he stretches his legs.

Trying to fully embrace the fact that I haven't sat down in a restaurant in ages, I decide I want to look a little more presentable. I glance down and see my dirty shorts. Feeling grungy, I hopelessly upend my backpack, looking for anything else to wear, when I remember I stashed my jean skirt last minute. Rejoicing, I clutch it and messily throw the discarded items back in my pack. As I lean back to the shut the backdoor, I catch a patch of blue out of my peripheral. Recognizing the lacy fabric, I see it's my blue lingerie thong wedged in the side door compartment. Scandalized, I grab it like it's about to catch fire and stuff it back deep into my bag in my secret undie pocket. *Imagine if Brodie found it first!* I glance around and find a couple of other items thrown into random crevices from when we went "off roading." I search for the bra and find it on the back floorboard, and quickly zip it up with the bottoms.

"I'm going to hang back and change really quick," I inform him, before he makes his way for the motel check-in window.

"Nah yeah, take a tick, 'n I'll check in on Mick 'n let him know we've decided to head back tomorrow," he offers.

He crosses the empty parking lot out of sight. I give my denim skirt a good shake to remove any wrinkles. Luckily the denim's thick enough it smooths out naturally. I steal a peek at the road and see no one coming.

*Cheap thrills, Nina, besides you're still wearing bikini bottoms.*

I pull off my avocado crusted shorts and toss them in the back floorboards. Unbuttoning the top of my skirt, I bend over slightly as I slip my feet through the opening, pulling it up over my knees and up my thighs. Since I'm curvier, I always have to shimmy the narrowest part of the skirt along the widest part of my legs, and while I have toned my figure some, my hips remain unchanged.

I hear a light gravel crunching noise and turn to find Brodie snorting in amusement. Frozen, I look up at him like a deer in the headlights, my skirt only pulled halfway up my cheeky butt. *That's a good look there.*

"I'm gonna take our bags inside," he chokes out, amused.

I finish hoisting the skirt up over my bum, and turn to hand him my backpack. He smiles sheepishly at me and heads off back towards the motel. Checking out our abode for the night, I notice each room opens to the outdoor common area which features a pool. However, I see the pool lacks water, the key element... Huh, I wonder what that's about. I look down and finish buttoning up my skirt before adjusting my daisy tank top. Still damp from our sunset swim, my blouse clings to my suit. I pull it away but then remind myself no one's around besides Brodie anyway. At least I don't have crusty avo smears plastered across my thighs.

Brodie returns, burying a bronze key in his pocket for safe keeping. He leans in and locks the ute's doors. Confused as to why we're not hopping in, I ask him so with a simple look.

"Reckon it's a nice night for a walk on the beach," he says.

While I observe our scenic surroundings and the dry night climate, Brodie makes his way towards the sand. Never far, he lingers for me to catch up. I trail after him until we walk side by side along the water, admiring the violet hour. He's right. It is a wonderful night. Calling back to temperatures from hot summer nights in California, I can't help but feel like it's summertime already. Then again, I only caught the tail end of summer here last year. It's warm enough now. In fact, tonight is one of the hottest nights I've experienced in this country, and it's not even the season yet. Between hastily packing up my bag in the muggy ute and now walking through thick sand trying to keep up with Brodie's wider strides, I'm starting to work up a sweat. I glance at my right leg, but it seems to be holding up without any strain.

A little before the restaurant, Brodie leads us onto the main street so we can window shop while we walk the rest of the way. It's late dusk now, the stores long closed, but it's fun to see what this small town has to offer. Dainty strands of twinkle lights sprawl across the main drag, adding to the summertime atmosphere. Most of the small shops display funny, cliché knickknacks such as glass blown crocodile figurines, and plush kangaroos and koala bears. Honestly it's not anything that I would personally buy being the minimalist I am these days, but I can easily see the appeal for most travelers wanting to commemorate a trip up country.

My stomach growls again, so we take a shortcut through an alley between a little dress shop and a tour guide kiosk. Giant pictures advertise local attractions. Nearing the end of the dark alley, we pop out on the sand only steps from the restaurant.

"I hope this place has air," I remark, fanning my clammy face. "It's a scorcher tonight."

"I'll remind ya of this in a coupla months, Neens," Brodie replies, chuckling.

As we approach the glass door, I notice the side parking lot looks more or less empty. The pandemic has pretty much kept all foreigners out, allowing Aussies to explore their own country undisturbed. While that's been really beneficial for domestic morale, the lack of foreign tourism has significantly impacted smaller businesses. I hope this isn't one of them. Brodie opens the front glass door for me and we enter the small restaurant.

*Holy cow!* It's frigid in here. Immediately, I break out into goosebumps from the extreme transition. This environment is way past the point of refreshment; I'd go as far as to say it resembles more of an arctic igloo. The thought alone turns my damp bathing suit to ice on my skin. Reigning in a shivering convulsion, I look around in front of me. Giant glass windows face the beach.

A man, in his sixties who looks like he just challenged a croc and won, walks out from what I presume is the kitchen.

"Sit anywhere ya like," he hollers.

Even the leather stools and chairs look like alligator hide, another reminder I'm in some scene where Croc Dundee should be bursting through the door any minute. Surprisingly, there's a few groups of older men, fishermen by the looks of them, sitting at a few booths around the perimeter, all drinking stubbies. They stare at us as we stand there, deciding where to sit. We both look around, scoping our options. Aside from bar seating, there's only booths, all of which are occupied, and one table in the middle of the room situated with two chairs. Brodie suggests sitting at the bar, but seeing as how I haven't sat down and eaten in a restaurant in roughly seven months, I request the table with a demure smile. Brodie glances around at the men.

"Whereva ya like, Neens," Brodie concedes with a slight touch of humor in his voice.

He walks towards our stand-alone table and I follow. I would really love looking out over the water as we eat, but don't want to hog the view. I offer to move the seats so we can both enjoy the vista, but Brodie just shrugs, assuring me that he doesn't care, so we each sit down. Much to our delight, the waiter quickly brings us our menus. I'm famished.

"Fancy a bottle of our local cleanskin?" the bloke asks.

"I have no idea what that is," I admit, looking to Brodie.

"Wine, Neens," he tells me simply, with a smile.

The server patiently waits. Brodie's gathered I'm not naturally a big drinker, but lately even I would beg to differ. Brodie shakes his head at the waiter, assuming my answer.

"Why not?" I interject jovially. Surprising Brodie, his eyebrows shoot up. I simply shrug, raising a playful eyebrow back at him as our server rushes off to fetch it. "It'll be my treat."

Brodie chuckles and looks down at his menu, while muttering under his breath, "Defo not."

"Live a little, Pryce," I say mockingly, and take a glance at the menu. "You're not driving tonight."

The waiter returns, setting down a rather large bottle of red wine on the table along with two glasses. I snort at the sheer size of the unmarked bottle. He pops the cork and pours us each a full glass before leaving. Brodie slides a glass over to me by the base with two fingers. Staring into the crimson abyss, I have always wanted to know what the big fuss is about. I hesitantly sniff the glass, and carefully take a small sip, swishing around the liquid in my mouth before swallowing. *Disgusting!* I do hear it's an acquired taste, but still I make a face.

"Whatchya doin'?" Brodie asks me, slightly entertained.

Maybe if I keep drinking, the taste will grow on me. I take another sip, bigger than before and repeat the same method, this time finishing with a nice slow lick of my lips.

"Enjoying the bouquet as they say," I answer brightly, trying to repel the squalid taste from my mouth. He snorts, so I say, "What? That's how they do it in the movies."

"Yeah, nah, maybe in flicks," he says, leaning in and laughing, "but in the real world ya just slowly savour it 'n swallow."

He demonstrates. I must admit he looks damn good sipping wine out of a thin stemmed glass, especially in his white tank top. He holds the glass by the larger cup, not the stem, which accents his long, dexterous fingers.

"Do ya always drink wine this way?" he asks curiously.

Finishing another sip, I shake my head.

"Actually tonight's my first time," I reply. "*Ever.* I was never a big drinker, remember? That is until I met you lot."

His eyes bulge for a second as I chuckle and take another sip. He grabs his glass and tips it up, swallowing the entire thing. Talk about not savoring it. He leans in, and grabs the bottle, refilling his glass and mine.

"Well, then, let's get pissed," he states with a crooked smile.

I laugh. Suddenly, I feel a heavy breeze hitting the tops of my shoulders and head. I glance around and see the air duct directly above our table. It blasts frigid air right in my direction. I try to shake off the frozen sensation, but my body breaks out into goosebumps again. Grabbing the wineglass, I take another gulp. I can definitely feel it travel through my bloodstream, warming me up in the process. I decide to go with Brodie's plan of action and chug the rest of my glass. I heartily place it down on the table, signaling for a refill.

"Whaddaya reckon?" Brodie murmurs, nodding to my empty glass.

"Honestly, it's a little strong for my beginner's palette, but surprisingly, it's not actually terrible," I confess.

"Ya come to like it... usually," he adds, taking my glass.

Red crimson liquid pours into the clear basin until it almost reaches the rim. I raise my eyebrows in nervous anticipation and wait as he sets it back in front of me. We each study the menu for a minute before the waiter returns to take our order. Brodie decides on the chicken parmigiana, "parmi," and I opt for a meat pie.

The air-conditioning seems to be pumping more and more. Despite my efforts to counteract the frozen tundra with wine, I grow colder and colder by the minute, until I sit shivering. My frozen damp bikini almost hurts against my bare skin, it's so stiff. I adjust my top, trying to get more comfortable. The waiter stares down at my chest as I mess around with my bikini strap and I hastily stop. *What are you looking at, buddy?*

Brodie stifles a chuckle and orders. I follow suit.

"Did ya get that, mate?" Brodie asks the man, double checking.

The waiter's lingering stare is interrupted as we hand him our menus, and he nods, quickly repeating the order as he makes his way to the kitchen. I take my glass and sip repeatedly. *Brrrr.* Maybe I need more wine. The rich flavor does seem to grow on me with each passing swallow. Brodie watches me with a smile in his eyes.

We sit in the quiet for a while, sharing small happy exchanges as we drink and relish the view of the moon glinting off the water. Pretty quickly, the server returns with our dinners. My meat pie looks and smells utterly divine. One glance at Brodie's parmi and my mouth waters. We each dig in, downing more wine in the process and enjoy our meals as we recap the amazing day.

"Bloody good tucker," Brodie mutters, biting into his oozing chicken.

Raving about my meat pie, I basically force him to share a bite. A giggle fit erupts as my fork misses Brodie's mouth the first time, spilling vegetables and ground beef on his lap. After I aim at my target, he nods as he chews, agreeing with my review. I sense more eyes staring our way, but chalk it up to my general loud and exuberant nature.

Feeling a little tipsy, I tell him rather than ask him, "You know what, Brodie? You know what's so great about you?"

I take a big bite of my drool worthy meat pie. I'm really going to miss these when I go back to the US... I hastily push the thought away.

"Nah, what's that, Neens?" he admits, amused, mid swallow.

I move the veggies around, gathering a good bite on my fork.

"You never shush me," I state loudly. "Not *once* have you ever told me I'm too loud." Brodie sits there patiently listening to me as he eats. I scoop my fork into my mouth and add some wine to help it down, and feel like venting. "Imagine being told your whole life you're too loud, too much." I swallow a large bite and set my fork down. "You know, when someone would tell me that or tell me to turn down my music, I used to get so mad. My spirit would be crushed. I mean I never meant to be loud. I was just born this way, I can't help it. People try so hard to change that about me." I laugh into my glass as I take a drink. Brodie looks down at his glass, and licks his lips deep in thought. I chuckle some more. "I don't know why I'm even telling you this."

Feeling very relaxed, and very much a fool for my random babble, I lift the wine to my lips and down the remaining liquid in one big go. I make several nasty faces from the overload of flavor, and push my glass away from my plate, while the waiter approaches to check on us.

"Tide's gone out," he cries, gesturing to my empty wineglass.

He reaches for the big bottle and refills my drink halfway before exiting back to the kitchen.

Brodie, oozing cool sophistication, leans back and stares at me right in the eyes.

He softly declares, in almost a whisper and in an utmost precious tone, "If ya were a melody, there's not a single beat I would change."

He smoothly tilts his head back and, with a hint of seduction, drains his glass. Stunned by his omission, I merely sip the crimson liquid in my glass for a minute straight, swirling the wine around between my lips and my mouth, all the while holding Brodie's gaze. Still not knowing how to respond to that compliment, I reach across the table for the bottle and, giggling, almost knock it over, but catch it at the last second. The old men turn their heads, watching us, which makes me chuckle even more.

"Pour me another," I demand, animated.

Brodie takes the bottle and instead of refilling my glass to the top, pours only two inches before placing the bottle out of my reach. I playfully frown at him, but accept the small amount nonetheless.

*I feel gooooood.*

If only that blasted air would stop. I feel like I'm back in the arctic snowstorm. I stare up with a quizzical brow at the vent. Suddenly, my phone chirps from Brodie's pocket; I jump in my seat.

"I thought that was on Do Not Disturb," I declare, frowning. Being out of signal sure has its perks. Slightly annoyed at the intrusion, but also curious if it's Mick, I hold out my hand across the table, waiting for Brodie to hand it over. He looks at me with a mischievous smile, raising an eyebrow, asking if I really want it. I say, mid-hiccup, "What if it's Mick?"

"I thought he doesn't text," Brodie reminds me.

Realizing this fact, I purse my lips as Brodie places the phone in my palm nonetheless. I swipe up on the home screen and see a text from Mel; it reads: *Hope you're having fun in blue* with a kissy emoji face and a crude blend of emoji fingers.

"It's just Mel," I explain, rolling my eyes.

Next, I see a couple of texts from a number I know recognize as Jordan's. The first one reads: *wanna come over tonight? - Jordo.*

Talk about a wincing buzz kill.

"Gag me," I mutter, scrolling down.

The second text in the thread reads: *You know you want it. Come on, Nina, here's a taste of me.* There's a photo of his lower abdomen panning further down, revealing *all of Jordan.* Then another text underneath the photo that reads: *Can't wait to lose myself in your big, juicy—.*

I can't read the rest. Frazzled from my first official nudie pic, I fumble to switch off the screen, and my phone drops to the concrete floor, hitting the leg of my chair. It slides across the restaurant. I must be making a face of pure surprise mingled with disgust because Brodie knits his brows and leans forward, sitting up more alert.

"What's the matta?" he asks. "What was that?"

Shaking my head, I try to pretend like everything's fine.

"Nothing. Wrong number," I mumble, trying to dispel the vulgar visual from my brain.

Brodie jumps up swiftly and picks up my phone before bringing it back and seating himself at the table again. While I normally could care less if Brodie looks through my cell, I begin to protest as he swipes up on the home screen. *Yes, I'm one of the only persons on the planet who doesn't use a password lock on my phone.* Clearly Brodie sees the texts because his mouth opens, his brows hunch tighter together, and his head starts to shake back and forth. I can see his eyes reading the messages at lightning speed.

"Ignore them, Brodie," I implore him. "Please."

His right hand balls into a fist next to his plate.

"Why that little *mole*," Brodie exhales angrily. "Does this happen often?"

Brodie's finger scrolls up, revealing the random texts of harassment I receive from Jordan on an almost daily basis. I've just learned to ignore them. Tonight's was the first full frontal photo though. *That's kind of hard to ignore.* Brodie's eyes look horrified, and ultimately, disappointed.

"I'm gonna show him a piece of my fist the second we get back," he says. "In fact, I reckon I'm good enough to drive on through."

My entire face grimaces, upset.

"What?! Absolutely not," I exclaim, reaching for my phone. "First, we've had too much to drink, and second, don't let him ruin our night. We were having such a wonderful time." When none of that deters his posture, I remind him, "Plus, you promised me, Brodie."

He shakes his head, and his shoulders heave up and down as he takes a deep breath. Briefly standing to reach the wine bottle, I grab it and fill Brodie's glass back up to the top. Looks like he lost his buzz.

*Curse you, Jordan.*

"Besides, it's my battle to fight as I see fit. Remember?" I tell him firmly as I sit back down. "I don't need you to fight for me."

I stare at him, beseeching him to accept and acknowledge that he will stay out of it.

"So I'm just to sit idly by 'n watch him be inappropriate with ya? Knowin' damn well he makes yar skin crawl," he states. "He won't stop ya know."

I respond by taking another sip of my drink.

"Nina, yar my..." he explains, looking for the right word, then continues gently, "look, I care about ya a lot." Then he frowns, sneering, "'N so what if I wanna defend ya?"

"Defend me? You want to go be a bloody man, rough him up a little, and swoop in and save the day," I half-shout back.

"What's so wrong with that?!"

He accidentally thumps his hand on his plate and it bounces up in a clatter. His parmi almost goes flying.

"Because I don't need saving, Brodie," I roar back.

He snorts, upset now, and shakes his head.

"Ah, yeah, well, ya coulda fooled me," he spits out in a snarky tone. "Who was it then who pulled ya out of the ravine, eh?"

*Shots fired.*

I narrow my eyes back at him. Why does he have to throw that in my face, and specifically when it's convenient for him? Suddenly, he reminds me of the Brodie I first met, the calloused and arrogant Brodie.

"Ya should be thankin' me," he boldly says.

"*Thanking* you?" I ask. Imaginary steam releases from my ears. "*Thanking* you?!"

"Ugh, ya give me the shits, Nina," he exclaims loudly.

I glance around the room. All eyes are on our little "show."

Searing from his little outburst, I sneer back, "Yeah, well right now you're not my favorite person either."

I'm the worst with comebacks. I could have said so many other effective remarks and that's what I say? *Really, Nina?* We sit in silence, both of us stubborn, upset, and sore. Our poor waiter must not want to get in the middle of our little spat because he's no where to be seen.

*Nina, Brodie was only trying to defend you.*

He was trying to butt in and save the day.

*His intentions are noble.*

Why did he have to get so defensive and throw that in my face?

*It's his friend, remember?*

I look at him. He's stewing on the other side of the table, thinking God know's what about me. I can see the hurt in his eyes. He manages to hide it very well. I guess after poker I should have known he has a knack for hiding feelings, well the bad ones anyway. He must be upset, I know it. Jordan's been his best mate for forever. I don't know what I would do in his shoes. Suddenly, I have the urge to hug him.

No! I need to stand my ground.

*But, he* was *incredible today.*

Fingers cupping my wine glass, I tap my pointer finger repeatedly and stare at him, narrowing my eyes in thought. I've never felt so alive and overjoyed since waking up beside him on the road this morning.

*Damn you, Brodie, for making me happy. Sometimes I want to throttle you, and other times...*

I take a drink of water. All of a sudden, I'm parched. The glass feels cold in my fingers, and little beads of condensation run down its side, dripping onto my upper thighs. I gasp as the icy water hits my tender skin. It seems that every time I slightly adjust to the blizzard temps, another freezing encounter has me breaking out into fresh goosebumps.

One of the old men grunts and jabs the bloke next to him, and nods, gesturing towards me. I shift uncomfortably in my seat. Brodie, who's face has already softened, swallows a mouthful of wine and looks back at them as the air conditioner's motor revs up. I feel the chilled air blast colder above me. The men look at me, snickering, while one of them bites his lip. Brodie looks back and forth between them and me, before looking me over. He tilts his head down slightly. A smile erupts on his face, followed by a little chuckle.

"What's so funny?" I snicker, peeved from missing the joke.

I look down at myself then back to him and the old men. I don't get what's so intriguing. He fills up my wine glass to the brim as an olive branch or a white flag of surrender. He shakes the hollow bottle, allowing the last spare drops to run out. Brodie sets aside the bottle and pushes my wineglass towards me.

"I shoulda neva said that earlier. I'm sorry," he offers. "Drink."

I smile at him, accepting his apology. Wanting to return to my more carefree state before we were so crudely interrupted, I take the glass and chug over half of the inebriant, wincing as it goes down my throat to my belly, relaxing my knotted muscles. I loosen up my shoulders, and sit up straight. I feel the warmth moving through my veins, like a live wire.

"I don't get it. What's so amusing?" I ask again, somewhat louder than necessary.

He clinks his glass with mine in a gesture of cheers. He then tilts his head back and downs his, the burgundy bouquet gone in a matter of seconds, then he takes a large gulp from my cup. He swallows, licking his full lips.

"Well, Neens, just enjoy the last of yar wine 'n dun worry 'bout the old boys," he says. "They're only taken with yar norks."

"Norks? What the hell are norks?" I whisper, leaning in towards Brodie as I glance down at my outfit, trying to pinpoint what's going on.

"Nah, yeah, those cherries," he says, gesturing towards my boobs. "I reckon they've been captivated by 'em all night."

I look down and sure enough my damp, sheer blouse highlights my yellow bikini. My frozen nipples shoot out like glass cutters. Scandalized, I cross my arms across my chest, but the friction only amplifies the situation.

*You're never going to see them again, Nina. Stop apologizing.*

True… Choosing to take back the power, I drop my arm and go so far as to sit up even straighter to exaggerate my curvy bust. Brodie's eyes widen a little.

"Cheap thrills, cheap thrills," I say, exhaling in a shrug, letting go as I feel the wine travel through my relaxing body.

I even dance a little in my seat and there's no music playing. I reach out and grab my glass, and as sexy as I can muster, seductively take a sip of wine. It's almost empty.

*Nina 2.0 is back!*

I smile, laughing at myself, then try to sensually tilt my head back. The men freeze, eyes transfixed. I even go the extra mile and reach up, slowly pulling out the scrunchy that holds my high pony. My curly, sun kissed hair falls in tresses around my face. I catch a sight of my reflection in the wine glass. Surprisingly my hair looks somewhat decent in a chic bedhead kind of way, less Tarzan lost in the jungle. When my hands drop back down, the loose strap of my tank falls off my shoulder. Biting my lip, I tip my glass up and polish off the wine. I finish my performance by slowly and sensually licking my lips clean. I blow the old men a kiss from across the room, and then resume finishing my meat pie, all without skipping a beat. *Up yours, blue boy.*

Brodie looks at me in total bewilderment. I raise my shoulders in a shrug, keep chewing and give him a sweet smile. I do admit to feeling loads better. The old geezers hastily look away from me, embarrassed that I have the courage to call them out.

Brodie aptly raises his hand for the bill. He looks at me as I casually chew and finish my last bite. We make eye contact and, in unison, snort in laughter, bending over the table towards each other, losing it. I gleefully glance at Brodie, who reciprocates my grin. I already forgive him for the whole Jordan thing. *Ahh, he really does have such a nice smile.* His white teeth are so straight too, but not too straight; secretly I love it when people have some character left to them. Snorting from mirth and feeling light and loose, I surmise I've got my buzz back.

I realize Brodie has stopped laughing. I look up at his eyes, when suddenly, I still in my chair. I take an audible, soft intake of breath. Brodie leans back in his seat, his head tilting down, while his eyes pierce through my soul. His dark lashes add a layer of intensity to his gaze. His face screams a look I've never really seen before. He has the aura of a lion who has just found his prey after roaming the African Sahara for days on an empty stomach. And he's staring directly at me... I guess that makes me the gazelle? His ogling holds a hunger I recognize from earlier at the beach... and all of a sudden I'm yearning and hungry for the exact same thing. I'm no longer cold at all, quite the opposite in fact.

We stare, holding eye contact for what feels like minutes, but must be only seconds. Both like statues, we're completely frozen in this moment. Slowly, I let out a breath I didn't realize I was holding. It's like the longer we meet each others' eyes, the more burning this yearning feeling becomes until it smolders so greatly I feel like we're going to combust.

Swiftly, but never taking his eyes off mine, Brodie takes out a few Australian notes and leaves them on the table. He stands and motions towards me. The whole thing feels like it's playing in slow motion. He softly, but thoroughly, grabs my hand and leads me out the restaurant. I don't hesitate a fraction of a second. He escorts me around the corner, away from any lingering, prying eyes, down to the alley. All noise evaporates, all other movement too. Nothing else matters. Intertwining my clammy fingers in his, he guides me past a giant wave mural. I can barely endure the yearning any longer. We make it about ten feet when he passionately thrusts me against the wall, pinning me underneath his encroaching body, and crashes his face to mine, all in welcome urgency.

Bliss. Blazing passion. Fury. Pent up tension. Relief. Mutual desire. They're all there, boiling under the surface, erupting into a fiery series of kisses. I've never felt so alive. Never having experienced anything like this before, I act purely on instinct. Before I even realize it, I'm kissing him back with so much fervency it feels like we're both trying to consume each other. Warmth floods my mouth as his tongue enters mine, playfully twisting and inviting me to return the favor. It's oozing depravity... and I love it. I feel his warm hands on the sides of my arms moving up, back and forth from behind my neck, up my cheeks, and down again to my wrists. Things are moving like quicksilver. I hear this ragged panting and realize it's coming from me.

I pull back, tilting my head up against the brick wall and laugh a little. Brodie continues kissing my neck, then moves a little downward towards my chest. He grabs both of my wrists and playfully pins them up beside my head against the wall.

"Is this okay?" he murmurs, briefly halting for a second.

Beaming with joy, I nod, giggling. I can feel the weight of his upper body press against mine. He returns his attentions to my neck, sending shivers down my spine.

Finally, Brodie pulls back so I can see him. A giant smile encompasses his entire face. *This man is beautiful.* I try to move my arms so I can step towards him, but he firmly holds them at my sides, shaking his head, emitting a tiny chuckle. His mouth and chin are blotchy red, but his green eyes shine, reflecting light off the village lights as night swallows dusk. Keeping his body completely still, he reaches out with just his head and steals a little kiss, biting my lip lightly as he pulls away. I'm about to say something, but he kisses me quickly before abruptly letting go, taking a few steps back. He keeps hold of one of my hands and leads me down the street, not looking back at me. We walk in silence all the way from the back alley towards the sand.

Being a foot shorter, my smaller stride is doing its best to keep up, and believe me, I am more than willing. Brodie squeezes my hand in reassurance, not letting go. We pass a couple of bonfires with small huddles of town folk. Laughter and campfire music waft in and out as we make our way down the beach as the moon rises. Little white glints of light dance off the water looking like myriads of diamonds in the darkness. It's absolutely breathtaking. We hastily make our way through the sand for another minute or two until the last bonfire is plenty far away. Twisting me like he's twirling me in a dance, I find myself in Brodie's arms as he pulls me into his embrace. His mouth craves mine, searching for it. Ravaging his neck, I make my way up towards his chin and then find sanctuary in his lips.

Sand flies up as we jostle our clumsy bodies across the waterfront. He walks me backwards, again like a dance until I bump into something hard against my spine. I pull back, coming up for air, and reach behind me while Brodie carries on, thoroughly acquainting himself with my collarbone. His hands twist deeply into my hair, trying to pull some of it back, but also using it as a nice handling grip. Reaching around my back to see what's behind me, I feel with my fingertips small, thin ridges stacking on top of one another. The surface feels coarse and almost hairy.

"What—?" I manage to breathlessly ask, turning to look.

Brodie pauses for a second, and exhales slowly as he explains, "Coco palm."

Apparently this part of Australia doesn't have native palm trees or coconut palms - it's a desert and way too dry - but years ago, local B&B owners planted some out front of their motels on the beach to bring in a tropical feel for the tourists. That, I assume, is where we've landed.

"Won't someone hear us?" I breathe.

"Closed," Brodie mutters, shaking his head.

He presses me further into the palm's long trunk. Even if it's slightly rigid and uncomfortable, my mind focuses on the man in front of me. His strong, warm palm cups my right breast gently. I respond by pressing my hips into his. He softly squeezes his new found friend and I moan. I can't help it. *Nina, get a hold of yourself. Or don't, and let it go.*

He laughs and does it again. Another small moan escapes my lips. I bring my hands back around to Brodie and slip them underneath his shirt, feeling the solid shapes of his pecks and abs beneath my fingers. His lean muscles pulse and tense in all the right places. I slowly move my hands up his back, applying a good deal of pressure as I try to bring him closer to me.

Meanwhile, Brodie lingers on my neck before he glances at my shirt, waiting for me to see if I want to continue. I nod thoroughly and in one swift motion, he pulls off my tank and tosses it somewhere on the sand. I tug at his shirt to reciprocate, pulling it up by the hem. He snatches it behind his neck and it disappears in the blink of an eye. Standing in just his boardies, he steps back and admires me in my bikini and skirt. I see his eyes rest their sights on my skirt. Demurely, I reach for the top button and slowly unfasten it. It frees with a light *pop!* Working downward, we both laugh at the absurd amount of buttons this skirt entails. Waiting impatiently, his chest heaves from the adrenaline as he watches me clumsily slide the rest of the denim down over my curvaceous hips, dropping it in the sand. I stand in my bikini. Brodie mirrors me in his trunks. We've seen each other like this dozens of times by now, but tonight we see each other in a whole new light.

Feeling like a depraved, wild teenager, I feel impulsive. Startling Brodie and myself, I run and holler as I make my way towards the ocean. Brodie whistles playfully behind me and chases me down the beach. Catching up, he picks me up and throws me over his shoulder like a sack of potatoes as we barrel into the water. Water splashes up, wetting my face and body. Brodie dumps me into the warm lagoon and dives in. I come up for air, laughing my head off. Brodie pops up next to me and joins in as we both stand in waist high water. He reaches out, pulls me to him and gathers me into his arms, then steps deeper into the water. Naturally, I latch my arms around his neck and hoist my legs around his torso. I hold on for dear life.

He stops when we're pretty deep; Brodie can just touch the bottom. With both my arms folded around his neck and both his folded around my waist, I pull back to examine his face. I want to remember him in this moment, to log it for the archives. Taking in every millimeter of his face, I gently trace his features with my eyes and discover he's doing the same. We both look into each other's gaze at the same moment and see nothing but radiating elation peering back. Smiling sweetly, I lean in and tenderly kiss his lips before benevolently pulling back. He returns the favor with a simple kiss then gently pulls me in for a sentimental embrace. We stand here, hugging for a while, telling each other without words how grateful and happy we are that we can just be, and now we can just be together. The water moves around us like the tide upon a jetty.

"Thanks for being my best friend, Brodie," I whisper in his ear.

He squeezes me tightly before softly kissing my cheek. Then he playfully upends me and tosses me underwater. Surfacing mid laughter, I hop up and down closer to shore until I can reach the bottom. Brodie splashes after me as I reach a shallower depth, barreling towards shore, shrieking in laughter from the chase. He catches my hand, twirling me around. He pulls me to him, determined for a kiss, this time with raw, unbridled romanticism that melts away my thoughts.

He pauses and jokes, "Not bad for a friend, eh?"

We make out for who knows how long, and just when it feels like we're about to consume one another and really cross that line, Brodie pulls back and looks me straight in the eyes with a question in his own. My heart stops for a second, but

I return his unequivocal gaze and nod in answer. To solidify my choice, I gently kiss his lips.

His fingers fumble with the neck tie of my bikini and we both laugh at the struggle. Pushing his hands out of the way, I work quickly away at the tangle. Brodie busies himself by burying his face in my chest. Groaning in pleasure, I manage to untie the blasted knot and my arms come down along with my top. Brodie appreciatively looks down for a minute then pulls my mouth towards his, letting my naked breasts smash against his bare chest. Things progress naturally, and as the sand joins the sea in perfect harmony, Brodie and I become one, unaware where one begins and the other ends.

Sitting in each other's embrace in two feet of water, my flushed cheek rests against Brodie's chest. His heart beats strong and steady and there's a weird mixture of sweat and salt water on his skin. Slowly, my heart rate normalizes as Brodie's does.

"Whaddaya reckon?" he asks me in a whisper.

"That the only thing missing from this perfect moment is a good song," I say truthfully, in a giant smile.

"Shoulda guessed," he replies, lightly snorting. He gently plays with the ends of my wet hair on my back and sighs peacefully. I feel a little shy. I was primal, definitely animalistic in some ways. Bubbling with silent mirth, my head slowly bounces against Brodie. He catches my eye. "What's so funny?"

"We behaved like animals," I answer, burying my face in his neck, losing it in hilarity.

He seems to like the thought because he nuzzles further into mine, showering me with quiet, tender kisses. Enjoying the feel of him, but also growing slowly overheated from our combined body temperatures, I roll off Brodie's lap into the shallow water. It instantly rejuvenates my skin. In the heat, my hair dries quickly, and already little curls sprout around my temple while the rest of my hair falls around my face and neck, the ends dipping in the sea.

"I almost forgot about yar lion mane for a sec," he says, smiling as he lightly grabs a mini ringlet. I shyly go to push them back, but he stops my hand. "Nah, they're bloody beautiful, Neens." He continues caressing my hair until he reaches the end, down my back. "I didn't realise how long it is."

I chuckle and dip down, dunking my head underwater. The feeling is second to none, especially being all sweaty. Sitting up tall, I let my freshly dipped hair fall in front of me like a mermaid. Glancing down at my naked body, I realize I lost my suit. I scour through the waters, hoping I can locate it, but the still pool is practically black against the moonlight.

"Whatchya lookin' for?" Brodie asks.

"My bikini..." I mutter, scanning the beach in hopes that it washed up nearby. "If I've lost it, you can be the one to explain that to Mel. She was pretty fond of it."

"Her 'n me both," he says, kissing my shoulder affectionately, before he looks around to aid in my search. "I'm sure it'll turn up, but, eh, if we can't find it, I'll take ya tomorrow 'n outfit ya a new one." He jumps up, and walks down the beach, before waltzing back, triumphantly holding up my bikini top. "See, told ya!"

I look at him, his white buttocks glowing in the darkness. He searches a little and stumbles across the bottoms. He laughs and swims back over before handing me my bikini, which I put on. We walk back up the shore.

"What about you? Where are your trunks?" I ask.

He reaches over and grabs his trunks from on top of my clothes.

"I thought ahead. Forward thinkin', Neens," he says, tapping his temple with his pointer finger.

I roll my eyes at him.

Sand scrapes against my skin in every crevice as I walk in my damp bikini back towards the motel; luckily, we managed to land directly in front of the place. I'm about to pass the coco palm. Brodie whirls me around, slowly pinning me again, but with more tenderness this time as he slowly invades my lips with his own. He pulls back, and gratifyingly pats the tree trunk.

"Thanks, mate."

I laugh at him.

Brodie makes his way towards the open communal area.

"Gosh, I hope no one saw us," I admit in wariness, passing some of the darkened rooms.

Brodie shakes his head and explains that the motel is actually being remodeled. Apparently with the lack of tourists, the owner decided now is the time to update while they're low on rentals.

"Oh, that's a relief," I say, but then realize, "but wait, if that's the case, how come we get to stay here?"

We approach a room, room seven, and Brodie digs in his pocket and fishes out a bronze key.

"Well, Neens, see that's the thing," he says, looking down at the key, "they have one room finished..."

*One* room.

I stop and scratch my head. Is this moving too fast? I mean I know what we just did, but still this seems like we're going zero to sixty in a hot second. Besides all that, Brodie's my friend. I haven't even had time to think about what tonight means, let alone share a hotel bed... I was kind of liking the idea of having a little bit of space to privately collect myself.

Brodie narrows his eyes as he watches me having my internal discussion.

"Don't ova think it, Neens," he says, raising his brow a little. "This doesn't have to mean anything. Besides, we've shared a bed before in the ute."

*Does he want it to mean something?*

But he's right. We have slept side by side and it was actually no big deal.

"Yeah, you're right," I reassure him, nodding my head and giving him a smile.

He unlocks the door and holds it open for me. I enter the room. It's pretty basic: a square room, white walls, a flat screen tv on a dresser, and a queen bed in the middle, with a nightstand on each side. Seeing the bed does give me butterflies.

I mean I think I was drunk - I'm definitely still buzzed now - before, you know, what went down at the coco palm. Suddenly, I'm finding myself extremely shy.

I see my bag sitting on one of the nightstands, and I hastily grab it and walk towards the little bathroom in the back. Thankfully Brodie does his own thing. Sitting at the foot of the bed, he digs around his bag for something. I set my pack down at the sink, and stare at myself in the mirror. My damp hair already sprouts ringlets. I grab my denim shorts and wash them in the sink to get the dried avo out. After, I hang them out to dry on the shower rod and take off my soaked clothes. Standing in my banana yellow suit, I look at myself once more in the mirror. *Do I look different after being ravaged and being the ravager?* I turn a little, and don't see any notable changes. Small little red blotches line my chest and neck, not quite a hickey, but definitely a sign of prolonged attention given by someone with scruff. I smile at the thought.

Shimmying off my damp suit, I hang that up as well on the shower head, rinse the sand off me and grab my sleep attire. I realize, aside from my lingerie, I can't find my oversized sleep shirt. In my defense, I thought I would have my own room, but I know I packed it. Frantically upending the contents of my backpack, I come to the conclusion that it must be lying somewhere in the ute, jostled and dislodged from earlier. Standing stark naked, I slide on the lingerie bottoms, which admittedly do feel super comfortable, and then I put on and clasp the balconette bra. It definitely does not leave much to the imagination. I could run out and try to look for my shirt, but Brodie has the keys to the ute, wherever they are, and short of strutting to the locked ute basically in the nude, I decide to take my chances and wrap myself up in a towel. I brush my teeth and wash my face.

Taking one final look in the mirror, I suck in my stomach, stand tall, and take a giant deep breath. I quietly open the door, trying not to draw attention to my re-entrance. Brodie's crossed feet stick out over the edge of the bed, but I can't see the rest of him. Tiptoeing, I make my way out of the bathroom. I come up to the edge of the bed and look at him. Facing my side of the bed, Brodie lies on his side, deep asleep. I stare at him for a moment. His long, dark lashes rest completely still against his sun kissed cheeks. I reach down and pull up the top sheet over his legs and torso. I creep over to turn off the lights when I see a white t-shirt sticking out of his bag. I grab it and throw it on over my skimpy outfit, knowing I'll sleep better this way. I hit the lights and the moonlight glows through the open window curtains. Back at the bed, I cautiously get in under the covers, careful not to disturb Brodie. I turn on my side and count sheep until I fall asleep, feeling the memory of the touch of the man sleeping beside me.

Soft tendrils of light enter my eyelids. I lie still as my lids flutter. Warmth floods the back of my neck and I feel a weight encapsulating me. Batting my eyes fully awake, I look down. A tan, light haired arm comes into focus, hugging me around my waist.

*Shoot. Last night.*

It all comes flooding back to me: dinner, the walk, sex on the beach... *with Brodie.* My eyes shoot open wide, and my head pounds from the flash flood of bright light. Wincing, I shut my eyes tight. *So this is what a hangover feels like.*

Brodie must still be asleep, despite his usual early bird status. Gently as ever, I lift his arm up and carefully lay it down behind my hips. In slow motion, I slide out from under the covers, pausing first to make sure my sleeping partner doesn't wake. Not hearing anything or feeling any movement, I get both legs on the ground and stand. My head sways a little as I find my footing. I stealthily make my way to the bathroom where I brush my teeth and clean up for the day. I come out feeling much improved and recharged. I sneak across the room when I hear throat clearing coming from the bed. I whirl around and see Brodie stretching himself across the mattress, his head half buried in the pillows. Squinting, he eyes me.

I smile sheepishly and wave. *Really, Nina, you're waving?*

"Mornin', Sunshine," he says happily, with a morning gravel texture in his voice as it greets the day from sleep.

"Morning," I say, clearing my throat.

Brodie sits up in bed, wipes his eyes, then looks around the room. He lets out a big yawn as he stretches his long arms up towards the ceiling. Finally, he stands and walks over to me. Unsure if he's going to come in for a hug, dare even a kiss, I freeze next to my backpack on the table. I don't know what I want him to be other than normal Brodie, my friend. The rest I can sort out later after my head stops spinning so much.

He walks right past me and reaches for his bag, grabbing his toothbrush. Sighing in relief, I tell him the bathroom's open. About fifteen minutes later, the ute is packed and we're ready to hit the road. I ask him if he feels up for the long drive back home, and he assures me he's fine; nothing a cup of coffee won't cure. I admit to feeling a little worse for wear, and he also assures me that a good brekky will do the trick along with a little power nap in the car.

After we stop at the "servo" to fill up the tank and replenish our road trip snacks, we grab breakfast. As we sit across from each other, eating an egg and toast brekky, we settle right into our old, natural rhythm. Brodie's right. I do feel loads better after eating some food and drinking a couple glasses of water.

As we make our way down the highway, I recline the passenger seat and drift off with the cool air blowing across my face from the open window. I wake up a couple of hours later. The lingering affects of my hangover are basically nonexistent. Power nap locked in, I face the rest of the day feeling my old self again. Brodie plays James Taylor, lulling me in the background, but now I feel ready to amp up the atmosphere in the ute. After all, as co-pilot I have to keep the driver fully awake and alert.

We drive for a while, listening to good, loud tunes, belting out the lyrics together during songs we mutually know and appreciate. I discover Brodie has an affinity for The Smiths, much to my pleasant surprise, so we spend time listening and discussing how such sad lyrics sound so upbeat when paired with happy melodies and tempos. This leads us to another band face-off with The Cure. We each select a favorite song and listen to them back to back. Brodie chooses "The Headmaster's Ritual," while I pick "A Letter to Elise."

"Both excellent choices," I say, smiling at him.

"They're all such sad boys," Brodie remarks.

Brodie stops a few times so I can stretch my leg or drone. Putting pedal to the metal, we're now only an hour away from home, but we both agree we're in dire need of a break. We've been driving all day. At one stop, I strip down to my suit, and catch Brodie gawking. He just smiles at me and pulls off his shirt, revealing his toned body, and I find myself admiring his physique as well. Will it always be like this between us now? *A girl can only hope.*

Trying to keep the mood light and casual, I run and jump straight into the sea. Brodie follows and we mutually keep a couple of feet of distance between us. My stomach rumbles and I roll my eyes. We ran out of car snacks a bit ago, and being so close to home, we haven't stopped until now. Looking around, there's not a man-made structure as far as the eye can see. I get out and dry off quickly, wrapping my Turkish towel around my drying midsection, eager to get back on the road. If I'm lucky, I can catch Mick for dinner.

I need a night to myself to redraw perspective and figure out what I want. Though we were semi-drunk, last night was not a mistake. I just need to figure out how fast or slow I want this to go. I also have to think about the future. Brodie seems to feel the same. Even though I clearly notice him checking me out, he doesn't push anything one way or the other. He climbs back in the ute next to me and away we go.

As we near the fringes of town, Brodie pulls off a long dirt road to his parents' home. We see Stella run up from the house at the sound of our engine. Grinning from ear to ear, Brodie parks and gets out. His fur baby rushes straight to him, her booty shaking madly with happiness as she welcomes him home.

"Dad's back, girl," Brodie coos. He pets her frantically and kisses her back as she smothers his face with licks. "Miss me much?"

Sue comes out and greets us, laughing at Stella.

"Have a terrific time, Loves?" she asks with a hearty smile, looking back and forth between us.

"Nah, yeah, it was banga," Brodie answers, scratching his head. He looks to me with a gleam in his eye as he clears his throat. "Right, Neens?"

Stella makes her way over to me and demands some serious attention. I kneel down and let her shower me with affection.

"Yeah, it was incredible," I tell Sue, petting Stella. "The helicopter ride was insane. I've never seen anything like that before."

"So, ya finally made the jump, eh," she says, eyes widening as she turns to Brodie and laughs.

"What do you mean 'finally'?" I ask, as Brodie looks at me, chuckling.

"He finally made it on an egg beater," Sue replies. "He's been talkin' about goin' up in one for years, but always hesitated. He swims with sharks, but won't do that. I guess 'til now."

In total surprise, I turn to Brodie with large eyes.

"Thanks, Mum. Thanks for watchin' my girl," I hear him mutter, hugging his mom before pulling apart. "Best get Nina back to Mick."

After hugs we're back in the ute. Just as I'm about to dig into this chopper revelation, Brodie reaches over and puts on "Which Way To Paradise" by Poolside. The song blares in the speakers, and I can't help myself. I lose my thoughts in the melody.

# 18

After my night with Brodie, time seems to slow down and speed up simultaneously. I decide to take a step back on the Brodie romantic front. Adding up the months in my head, I really don't have that much time left here. Honestly, I'm unsure if I want to start anything serious when I know it can't really last. I should have thought this through before crossing *that* line, but I can't rewind the clock. It about breaks my heart. Why couldn't this have happened at home?

Mick, delighted in hearing about the helicopter tour, invites the crew over for dinner so we can regale tales of our adventure. Mel's been hounding me for all the soppy details ever since I got back, but I tell her it'll be easier to share in person, so she comes over earlier than the others. I'm usually one to keep romantic stories to myself, but I'd really like to talk to someone about this. My sisters are always a FaceTime away, but I'd actually really like to hear Mel's thoughts since she knows Brodie. She sits at the end of my bed as I fold laundry.

"So," she squeals. "Spill yar guts, right here 'n now."

"Shhh!" I sneer.

I peek my head out of the door to make sure Mick isn't close by.

As if his ears are burning, we hear him holler, "Gonna go load up the esky in the garage if ya need anythin'."

Mel smiles broadly in delight at his timely departure. As soon as the slider closes, she claps her hands quickly together in anxious anticipation.

"I don't kiss and tell," I say demurely.

Her large round eyes grow bigger, if that's possible, and she gasps before a proud smile plasters across her face.

"I knew it!" she cries out, then looks at me seriously. "Now for real, gimme the deets. How far did it go? I wanna hear everythin' startin' from when he picked ya up that mornin'."

She lies on her stomach with both hands propping up her head. Looking like she's waiting to watch her favorite movie again for the first time, she hunkers down on the bed, getting comfy.

I tell her all about the drive, our pit stops, then I slowly build up to some of the more intimate moments at the beach right before our heli tour. Now, I sit criss-cross-apple-sauce on the bed next to her, deeply animated and invested in my storytelling. I share with her my awkward attempt at seduction by the water's edge and then the sandy rubdown by the ute. I bury my face in my hands as I laugh, recalling that cringe worthy moment.

"Mel, you would have died," I whine. "It was *so* bad."

"I reckon it bloody worked," Mel adds impressed. "It was defo that new bikini."

"Definitely," I assure her in a mock praising tone, giving her the kudos she desires. "So then it feels like something's about to happen. Again. But it doesn't. I mean at this point we've almost kissed, what? Two, three times?" I sigh before diving back in and describing the unreal helicopter tour. I pull my legs up to my chest and fold my arms around my knees, reflecting on all the small moments that keep playing over in my head like a highlight reel. "It's all these little things, with Brodie. Like, he was so sweet about strapping me in my harness, and how he wanted to take photos of us during and after, and how he remembers everything. He even brought me beef jerky." I chuckle while Mel rolls her eyes. She's very well acquainted with my love of beef jerky. I dreamily sigh. "He's just so thoughtful..."

"So then what?" she asks, highly invested.

I bring her up to speed on all the turn of events leading up to dinner.

"Then we have this romantic stroll on the beach together and end up at this beachfront restaurant."

Gripped, Mel sits on my every word as I go into detail about our frigid, but fun, wine induced dinner. I even tell her about our little spat regarding Jordan's text messages, and how by this point, Brodie and I both are very tipsy, if not drunk.

Mel's jaw actually drops as I tell her about our savage make out session in the back alley, and she applauds.

"Neens, I'm lovin' this new side of ya," she boasts. "'Bout time."

I throw a pillow at her face in loving jest. It bounces to the floor.

"So then, did ya go back to the motel, 'n... *ya know*?" she asks, lewdly acting out a dirty dance move.

"No! Actually, we wound up against a coco palm tree on the beach," I admit, as Mel actually coughs in disbelief, as I edge out, "before running naked into the sea."

My face flushes bright red and I fall to pieces, laughing into my hands. Mel grabs my shoulders, forcing me to look into her giant owl eyes.

"Nina Esquivel," she says, "good on ya! Ya've got nothin' to be ashamed of."

"Well, one thing led to another... and—."

"Ya copped a root with Brodie Pryce. Bravo, Neens," she declares in admiration. In girlish intrigue, she asks, "So how was it?" Trying to find the right words, I simply stare at her as she impatiently fidgets. She begins to guess. "Erotic? Too fast?... Or too slow? Or—."

"It was magic," I say simply. "That's the best way I can describe it. It was nothing I've ever felt before. I mean, I know I don't have much to compare it to, but for me, it was near perfect even."

I lean back on the pillows behind me, pondering about that wonderful moment in time. Then as I start to think about the next morning and every moment since, my heart drops a little, as must my face.

"Then what's the problem, Neens?" Mel asks, nudging me.

"I'm the problem, Mel," I mutter, shaking my head in frustration. I look up at the ceiling as all my mixed emotions swirl inside my head. "I never thought in my wildest dreams that anything like this would happen to me when I booked a plane ticket last February. I've come to love my life here, but I don't know when I have to go back home. And home is... *home*. How is that fair to do to Brodie, or myself for that matter? I mean, I knew I was developing feelings for him, that's undeniable, but I had no idea that it would ever get as far as it did."

"But it did, Neens."

"I know, and I feel bad that it did, but at the same time I'm also so happy that it happened because it was one of the best nights of my life."

"So whaddaya reckon yar gonna do then?"

"What would you do in this situation?"

"I'd enjoy the ride, 'n the sex," she proclaims in a giant laugh.

Half expecting that answer, I roll my eyes and reiterate, "What would you do if you were me?"

She exhales deeply and leans back on the pillows. We both stare up at the little popcorn ceiling.

"I'd say just keep it casual 'n have fun, but I know the pair of ya, 'n I reckon casual's not really realistic, so..." she clears her throat, and finally replies, "I reckon ya do what ya always do. Follow yar heart. 'N as for Brodie, let him make up his own mind, don't make it up for him."

"I just don't want any hearts to break," I confess. "Right now, it would hurt, but I think anything more might kill me if I had to leave."

"Maybe that's yar answer then," Mel says simply.

Suddenly, the muffled sound of the front slider door opens and Mick shouts, "Eh, ladies, a ute's comin' down the drive."

Sometimes I wish I could hit the pause button on my life. Mel stands up, then pulls me up next to her. I reluctantly drag behind as we make our way to the kitchen and look out the window. Thankfully, Donnie's silver ute pulls up to the house first. Jaz, Shayno and Donnie pile out and walk up the deck.

"Where's your sister? And Jordan's not coming right?" I whisper to Mel. "I think Mick might kill him, or shoot him at the very least."

As we both wave to our new arrivals, Mel edges out the side of her mouth, "Margot stayed back, watchin' a flick, 'n Jordo's for sure workin'."

Jaz opens the slider first, carrying a glass bowl of cut fruit which she gingerly places down on the counter. She turns, smiling, and brings the pair of us in for a big squeeze. As Mick greets everybody, Stella runs in through the slider, alerting us to Brodie's arrival. All seven of us crowd in the open entry way as he steps in through the open doors. Looking better than ever, downright hot even with a little stubble on his sun kissed face, he benches in a blue esky. Mick ushers him into the open kitchen. Not having met his eyes yet, I steal subtle glances as I make conversation with my gal pals.

Busy with the boys, Brodie unpacks a few fish filets from the esky. I overhear how they're from his charter catch this morning. Mick passes out drinks until everyone has their pick. Finally, as I peep the room, I find Brodie scanning over us ladies. Our eyes meet. I can't help myself. A small smile engulfs my face and he returns the favor with a tiny grin back, the lines around his eyes briefly creasing. Just as soon as our eyes lock, they're pulled apart again as we engage with who's directly in front of us; Brodie takes a sip of beer as he talks to Shayno, and I giggle at Jaz's joke. I must admit, ever since the trip, Brodie has been truly great. We've only seen each other twice, but to my relief, Brodie doesn't push anything one way or another. Ever since he dropped me at Mick's that next day, he's been back to being Friend Brodie. I can't tell if he's happy about that or disappointed. I suppose time will tell on that front.

*You can't have it both ways, Nina.*

A little nervous for tonight, I take a big swig of my icy hard seltzer. While I'm so exited to see everyone and share the photos from the Outback, it's a little awkward considering it's all about Brodie and me, which personally is a little up in the air unbeknownst to the crew.

As the night progresses, we act normally together. Other than Mel, I don't think anyone suspects anything has happened or changed between us. Brodie and Mick grill up the fish on the deck while the rest of us sit on the outdoor patio furniture as I describe the waterfalls, the spotted eagle rays, and the wild stampede of kangaroos amongst some of the other chosen highlights. Brodie chimes in occasionally to embellish some hilarious or ridiculous detail.

"How was the egg beater, Chica? Better than the dronie, eh?" Donnie asks me, popping the top of another tinnie.

"Donnie, it was like nothing I've ever seen before," I beam. "The wind in my hair, the thousand foot plus drop. I felt like a kid on Christmas morning."

"Yous shoulda seen her up there," Brodie interjects playfully. "I don't think I've ever seen anyone 'ooh' or 'aww' as much as she did. There were multiple occasions where she downright screamed in joy. Thought my eardrum was gonna burst."

The whole group laughs, myself included, until I kindly meet Brodie's gaze. Caught in the truth of the matter, I don't deny it.

"I admit, I may have been a *little* overexcited," I say playfully. I turn my attention back to Donnie. "But to answer your question, yes. It was way better than the drone."

I catch Brodie smiling to himself as he flips over the last of the fish and announces it's time to eat. Mick ushers us girls first as we all grab plates and forks, and forge a small line. Despite a diet consisting mostly of fish, it never gets stale or tiring, because honestly if you're a meat eater, nothing beats freshly caught fish straight from the ocean and hot off the grill.

After full bellies stuffed of Red Emperor, fruit and a few more drinks, I bring the laptop out and reveal the edited photos from the heli tour. I must admit, these are some of my favorite photos I've ever taken. The height alone is astonishing, not to mention the subject manner. The group has some questions about our location and the actual flying experience, so Brodie and I trade off answering as we tell the backstory behind certain images. We arrive at the last of my artistic shots. It's the single-file line of kangaroos jumping along the fiery Outback with their crisp exaggerated shadows and long tails melting into the burnt earth. The lot hollers in admiration at this one. Next, I click through the funny ones of Brodie and me in front of the chopper. The girls "aww" at the one of us standing arm in arm, clearly beaming in exhilaration from our ride. Then our audience whistles and chuckles at one of us goofing off, howling up to the propeller. My windblown hair's a giant, messy frizz ball.

"And that's all she wrote," I announce sarcastically, and the whole room snickers. "Clearly we had no fun."

Just as I'm about to close up my laptop, Brodie leans over me and grabs it.

"Not so fast, eh," he exclaims, punching in a few keys and clicks. He reaches back over and sets it down in front of us all. Mel looks at me, wondering what this is about, but I'm just as much in the dark as she is, so I shrug in response. Everyone turns their eyes back to the screen as Bodie requests, "Press play for me, Neens."

I oblige, and click the trackpad on the little "play" icon. A slideshow pops up, showing more photos. These images are raw and clearly taken with a phone. Photos appear on the screen: one of me past out in the seat of the car, with my head halfway out the window, another of me launching the drone at a lookout point. There's several scenic shots from Brodie's perspective - I note his compositions are quite good - and a cool one of the ute parked right on the sand. The whole room cracks up as a photo of us fills the screen. In it, we're decked out and suited up in our harnesses, clad with our giant headphones and mics.

Jaz leans over and mumbles to me, "Now that's cute."

I stop in my tracks, looking at the picture before it vanishes. It's just a photo, but somehow it manages to emulate exactly how we felt in that moment; we both are glowing in happiness. I glance in Brodie's direction and discover he's looking at me with one of his nose scrunching smiles.

A couple more photos flash by. There's one of me standing waist deep in the water from behind on the beach, and a pretty silhouette shot at sunset. The last one is a selfie of us both, all beach crusty with beef jerky in our hands as we lean together in the ute, making funny faces at the camera. It freezes on the screen as the slideshow ends.

Mel bumps my shoulder with hers. She looks at me thoughtfully, then gives me a look that reads: *I'm sorry, but I don't know how you're going to do this.*

I muse, *I don't quite know myself.*

As the crew readies to leave, we all share casual goodbyes. Thinking and hoping he might go in for a hug, Brodie just gives me a friendly wave and a grin as he heads out the door with Donnie and Shayno, like I might as well be his sister. Actually, even Jaz gets a big hug from him goodnight. Trying not to look too disappointed, I stand out on the deck next to Mick as we cheer everyone off.

It's been two weeks since our helicopter... weekend. The word "date" comes to mind first, but I need to stop thinking of it in those terms. I've been really trying hard to keep a platonic line drawn between myself and Brodie. I mean, not only am I going back to America in a matter of months... but I can't help but think back to his more distant behavior at Mick's. *Does he just want to be friends?* My brain keeps replaying certain events under the moonlight from our night together. *Coco palm.* I hastily shake the thought away. I really think Brodie wants more, but either way, maybe I take this as a sign to keep things on ice for the moment. It helps to stay in a group setting or at least have Mick around as a buffer, because otherwise, my every thought returns to that twinkle lit alley.

It's Saturday today, and I have a photoshoot at the beach of two newlyweds. Trying to mix business and pleasure, I invite the crew down to the same beach as the intended shoot. I tell them all to come around sunset for a bonfire, just about when I should be wrapping up with the work thing. I beg Mick to get out of the house and join us, but he says he has a dinner meetup with his old friend, Gus, again. Happy to hear the other has plans in town, we drive in together, enjoying a crossword puzzle on the way. While Mick drives, I provide the clues and we both make hilarious guesses, well mine are more ridiculous while Mick's are more educated. We manage to uncover about two-thirds of the puzzle when we pull into the dirt car park. After we each tell the other to enjoy their night, I remind Mick that Mel can give me a lift home as she's sleeping over.

"We might be late," I warn Mick, hopping out.

"Nah, doesn't matta," he assures me with a snicker. "Wake me when ya get in so I know yar home safe. I'll be seein' ya, Sweetheart."

"Okay. Later, Old Man," I agree sweetly, and turn, waving goodbye as I make my way down the little pathway to the sand.

I hear the ute's engine evaporate in the distance.

Eyeing two youthful figures standing by the water's edge, I pull out my camera from my backpack and put on my game face.

Two hours pass as if they're two minutes. After a successful shoot, I give the love birds one final wave and walk over to the crew huddled down the beach. I come over to the ladies and put my camera away.

"Well that flew by in the blink of an eye, or should I say the click of a shutter," I tell them.

I burst out laughing while the others shake their head, mocking me. Hey, I think it's pretty punny if I do say so myself.

Margot passes me a glass of red wine. The one and only memory I have involving wine flashes before my eyes. I glance to Brodie, who looks from the wine to my face and smiles like he has a secret, which in this case he does. Grinning back at Margot, I accept it with genuine thanks. She simpers back. Thrilled by her inclusion, I sit down and we all catch up on our week. About thirty minutes go by and it's starting to get chilly, well chilly for summer. I've officially adapted to high desert living. In just my billowy dress, I walk over to my backpack and unearth Mick's denim jacket. I pull it on, immediately feeling cozy as I pull it tightly around me. Brodie gets up and nudges Donnie and Shayno. The three of them collect the sticks and logs from a nearby pile and begin to build the fire while us gals watch. The men take turns igniting the kindling. After a few failed attempts, Jaz marches over and grabs it out of Brodie's outstretched hands. She squats over, and in one swift motion and exchange of her fingers and flint, the logs burst into flames. Satisfied, she jumps up with two hands on her hips. Offering her credit where credit is due, the guys nod, giving her props.

"Brodie knows I'm the better fire starta. Have been since we were grommets," she declares. "Shoulda just asked me first."

"Nah, yeah, well," he playfully smirks, "thought I'd give it a red hot go to keep ya on yar toes."

The fire really roars to life, the flames growing larger by the minute. The heat hits my face and warms it instantly. Looking around, I wonderfully realize we have the whole beach to ourselves. It's grown dark now, the deep amethyst purple enhances the night sky.

Margot asks if I want a refill. I glance down bashfully, afraid to admit that I haven't even started my first one yet. Before I reply, I quickly chug the cup, recognizing that familiar feeling of the alcohol flowing through my bloodstream. I hand her my empty canister, and say thanks. She fills it up again. While I originally only wanted one glass, I don't want to do anything that might deter her new found friendliness, so I accept the second cup.

"Easy now," Mel vivaciously warns.

I give her a quick dart of a pouting scowl and she laughs, asking Margot for a refill for herself. We sit by the fire for a bit, drinking and laughing. Suddenly, I'm in the mood for something sweet. I rummage around my bag for the supplies I've been gathering for the last week. Pulling out a bag of marshmallows, a carton of wheatmeal biscuits, and a bar of chocolate, I stand in front of the group and hold up my prizes. They all takes sips of wine and ogle the items near my shoulders.

"It's s'mores time!" I announce giddily.

"What is it with ya Yanks 'n yar s'mores?" Mel hollers in a chuckle.

"I don't know," I explain, as Donnie jumps to and grabs the mallows from me, "but I do know it's never summer without one." I lay out the spread of goodies on my towel, lining up the order of events. I want my pals to match my enthusiasm. "Come on, it'll be fun."

Shayno stands up and looks for roasting sticks. Finding a handful of them, he runs down to the water and plunges them completely under for a minute so the sticks won't burn as easily in the fire. Glancing down at the pile of marshmallows, I notice they're a mixture of pink and white ones alike. Giggling at that random fact, I hand everyone a biscuit.

"'First you take the graham,'" I instruct, quoting the iconic scene from *Sandlot*.

"We all know how this works, Neens," Mel laughs.

"'N those are biscuits," Donnie chimes in, nodding to the wheatmeal.

"Yeah, I know," I explain, rolling my eyes at them, "but you guys don't have graham crackers here. So biscuits it is." I clear my throat. "'First you take the graham.'"

I dramatically illustrate the rest, demonstrating like a flight attendant explaining how a flotation device works. The group watches in amusement.

As if my assistant, Shayno steps in to hand me my roasting stick. Jabbing two marshmallows onto the end, I hold it out onto the fire and let the flames take it from here. The fire burns bright green from the salty stick and the seaweed kindling. It's a beautiful little sight. Shayno gives everyone a stick and they all follow suit quickly. My pink mallow is really starting to inflate, crackling as the smoke billows off the top. My white mallow directly under it starts to heavily sag. I rotate, trying to get the right angle so it doesn't slide off and fry in the fire.

"Watch out, Neens," Brodie gasps, warning me as my white mallow drips beyond salvation.

"I'm losing it!" I cry out in all seriousness.

Margot and Jaz snort as they watch me battle the fire gods, but it's too late. The mallow droops into the flames with a roaring hiss. We all collectively make "ooh" sounds, mourning the loss of a fallen comrade. Meanwhile, the pink mallow, the sole survivor, flares to the size of a tennis ball.

"I never knew one could get so big," Jaz says with humor, then glances down at her crispy mallow.

"That's cause we've neva copped a root, Jaz," Donnie snidely teases, raising his eyebrow at his own innuendo.

The whole circle laughs.

Margot catches hers on fire, and she screams out a little, trying to blow it out with some huffing and puffing. She manages to stifle the fire, revealing a burnt mallow puck.

"Mel, we're gonna need a setup over here," I request.

"Yeah, nah, just the mallow for me," Margot says, interrupting me.

She waits for it to cool before trying to peel off the top layer of carcinogens.

"Neens, that bloke's gotta be done soon," Mel exclaims, nodding at my swelling marshmallow.

A little bigger than a baseball, my crackling mallow barely balances on my stick holder. The whole campfire watches as I slowly twist the stick out and away from the fiery pit to safety. Mel swiftly squishes my prized specimen until it nestles in between the chocolatey goodness. I pull out the charred twig. Delighted, I thank her for her help and skill.

"I hope it's good, Neens," Brodie chuckles.

I glance down and see his perfectly golden marshmallow sitting securely on his stick as he slowly spins it like a rotisserie chicken.

Pressing together the two biscuits, the mallow oozes out the side of the s'more and with my tongue, I lap up the excess. Biting heavily into my gummy treat, I feel the uber sticky sugar smear across my nose and chin. Mel roasts hers, and Margot acts as the designated helper to those pulling theirs off the flames. I hear the crunching around me and smile. The dried marshmallow tightens around my face.

"So does this mean it's summa then?" Jaz questions me.

"Absolutely," I yell happily, while everyone else guffaws.

I reach down and take a big drink of wine to wash down the biscuit crumbs. To my left, Shayno and Jaz playfully smear their sticky fingers all over each other before running down to the water and out of sight. Per usual, the group mumbles suggestive assumptions. Brodie just shakes his head and pops the last bite of s'more cleanly into his mouth. He jumps up and disappears behind us. I take another large sip of wine. Maybe Brodie was right that night at dinner. It does seem to get better each time you drink it. Donnie pulls out a soccer ball, and begins passing with Mel. Margot jumps in and the three of them juggle the ball back and forth without letting it drop. Alone, I watch them from my towel. Suddenly, static playback quietly distorts behind me.

"I knew we were missing something," I exclaim boldly to the universe.

*Music!* A giant hiccup shakes my frame. *Oh, no!* I hate it when I get the hiccups. I vocalize a groan, followed by another hearty hiccup.

Chuckling sounds off right behind me, and I jump, startled. I turn to see Brodie messing with the Bluetooth speaker, turning the volume up. Khruangbin's "A Calf Born in Winter" fills the air around me. I immediately try to stand, but sway a little, and almost spill my glass of wine on my white dress as I manage to heave myself up. Grinning as I listen to the magical notes flow through the airwaves, I stumble up to Brodie. Ever the picture of collected coolness, he stands with both arms folded across his chest, watching me. His expression shows a mixture of amusement and patience. I walk right up to him. I look straight up at his beautiful face, which towers over me by a good ten inches, dimly lit by the fire.

"This is one of my most coveted favorite songs in the whole wide world," I breathe.

He bites his lower lip as he smiles, looking down over the bridge of his nose at me. I hiccup again and lightly fall into his chest. I close my eyes as I inhale his familiar scent of ocean salt, sunscreen, and manly musk. A little dazed, I step back, and try to regain my composure.

"You," I mutter, pulling back a little further, "you... Brodie." I must be half drunk because I bubble up into a fit of hysterical laughter, all the while Brodie stands there with humor in his eyes. "You were right, as always. It does start to get a little better each time." I clarify. "The wine."

Throwing my head back, I polish off my glass, and proudly hold it up in the air, empty. I turn back to the fire.

"Nina, wait," he says.

I pivot slowly to find him walking right towards me. Sobering by the second, I stand still as he steps directly in front of me. Holding my breath, I wait as he raises his hand towards my face. I stare at his eyes, searching for his intention, when he softly grabs the base of my head, and angles my face up to his.

*Finally.*

As my favorite melody in the song plays softly, Brodie slowly leans in a little and just as I close my eyes, his finger wipes off a chunk of chocolate off my cheek. I jerk upright as he turns on his heels and runs off to the water. Frazzled, I let go of a deep breath and shake off the feeling of Brodie's touch on my skin.

# 19

The town's big annual festival at the marina is Sunday. The excited buzz of energy even tentacles its way to the remote parts of town. Due to the odd year the world's been having, the town has decided to go big and celebrate something fun by renting a yacht. Mick and Mel both assure me that it's always one of the best events of the year, and this year should be extra fantastic. I laugh because I feel like it's the only event of the year around here. Due to their build up of such a special occasion, I realize I need to find something appropriate and exceptional to wear, well exceptional for my standards. Mick drives me into town to hopefully find something. Mel's working today so Mick's my wingman. We pull up to Tippe's and park. We enter through the doors and the small chimes go off, alerting Tippe we're here.

"Just me, Mick, 'n Nina," Mick hollers.

"G'day, guys," Tippe yells from the back room.

I lead Mick over to the apparel section and begin to rifle through the dozens of hangers on the rack.

"So what's the dress code for this shindig?" I ask, half expecting it to be the usual casual attire, but also surmising the event must be at least a step up to have made such a lasting impression on everyone.

"Well, Sheila, for this we usually try our hardest to look our best." He smiles. "For some that's easier than othas, I reckon."

Snorting at his joke, I begin to set my sights on any and all dresses or anything a bit fancier. I pull out a couple of options that look like they'll fit, but they're black, and I hate black. I'd love to wear a pop of color. Not one for fluff and bling usually,

I can't help but feel excited. This will be the first time in over eight months that I get to dress up beyond my white sundress. Sensing my excitement, Mick grins at me, and pulls out a baby blue, more fitted dress from his side of the rack.

"This reminds me of ya," he says sweetly, handing it to me.

I hold it up high and assess it from top to bottom. I probably would have glossed over it. It's a bit fancier than I envisioned wearing, but it's undeniably beautiful. Slightly old fashioned looking, it looks like it's from the 1940s, but in excellent condition. Sadly, I doubt it will fit.

"What will you be wearing?" I ask him, peering around the dress.

"Oh, ya know, a button down, somethin' of the like," he teases, looking around the store.

Taking one more quick look through the racks, I find only two other serious contenders. Seeing all there is to see, we head back to the makeshift changing room. Mick sits comfortably in a large wingtip chair, waiting for my little fashion show to begin. Standing behind the room divider, I hold up the baby blue dress. To amuse Mick, I glance at the tag. It's my size. I calculate that it must be a newer design perfectly replicating an older fashion; I don't think they made dresses in my size in the 1940s. I pull it on with some effort and look in the mirror, already expecting disappointment. It feels snug.

My eyebrows shoot up to my forehead as I stare at the figure in the mirror in front of me. The dress fits like a glove. Aside from dainty flutter sleeves, the material is fitted up top, and tastefully "V's" down in the chest, where a bunch of old fashioned fabric buttons line single file all the way down the front. A trace of a hem gathers at my waist, accenting my curves only in the most flattering of ways. From there, the material hugs my hips and thighs before flaring out like a mermaid's tail above the knee. The large bottom ruffle travels to about mid-calf. It's sophisticated, yet still playful.

"Ready, Old Man?" I shout from behind the divider, barely able to hide the enthusiasm in my voice.

"Yep, when you are."

I step out and walk in front of him, singing, "Ta-da!" as I theatrically lift an arm up for flare. He just gawks at me. Desperately waiting for his opinion, I ask, "So, what do you think?"

"Gimme a spin," he commands, twirling his knobby finger.

I spin slowly, and feel the material of the sleeve and tail flutter as I do. I laugh at the carefree feeling and stop again, facing Mick.

"Aw, Sweetheart," he mutters, as little tears come to his eyes, "yar a vision." He stands up, shaking his head in admiration, and walks over to me before lightly kissing the side of my cheek. He gently pats me on the shoulder before shuffling over to the cash register. "Tip, we're ready to check out."

I skip back into the changing room and give myself one last look before Sunday. I don't think I've ever owned anything that makes me feel so confident and glamorous. I put my daisy tank and shorts back on, not even giving the other options a second glance, and make my way to meet Mick at the register.

Today's the day. My date and I arrive at the marina. Mick opens the ute's door for me as I slowly slide out, careful not to roll my ankle as I drop to the pavement, wearing borrowed white, pointed heels.

"I can't get over how dashing you look, Mick," I state in adoration, for what must be the twentieth time already.

Adorned in a gun metal gray, two-piece suit which he pairs with a crisp, white button-down dress shirt, Mick is the embodiment of a classy gentleman, looking like Glenn Ford straight out of *The Big Heat*. His shirt tucks into a camel leather belt, matching his leather shoes. A light blue pocket square completes his ensemble, along with the finishing touch of his gold cufflinks. I lean over and make a final adjustment to his black tie.

"Thanks, Sweetheart, but I'm not the showstoppa here," he counters lovingly.

I dare to disagree. I've never seen him look so handsome before, and suddenly, I see a flash of what he must of looked like as a young combat medic, oozing vitality in the peak of his life.

He nobly holds out his elbow, and I gladly take it as we walk arm in arm down through the dock's entry. As we walk, Mick informs me that the festivity will take place on the yacht parked at the end of the big landing, where the lookout gazebo stands tall like a beacon. I glance down at my shoes and the dock beneath them, grateful for the support of Mick's arm. After my accident, and not having worn anything remotely resembling a heel for almost a year, my feet are slightly unstable on the uneven wooden planks. I carefully watch my step as we slowly make our way down the wharf. As we approach the gazebo, I notice well dressed people gathering around the entrance, cheerfully embracing and complimenting one another as they snap some pictures with disposable cameras. I feel a few eyes lingering on us. Mick and I simply smile as quite a few townsfolk regard us with admiration and shower us in commendations. Everyone knows Mick, and they all rightly love him.

After an acquaintance takes our photo standing in front of the yacht, my spiffy date guides me over to a railing inside the gazebo, panting, a little out of breath.

"Just need to rest for a tick," he assures me, not wanting to go in just yet.

We stand side by side, leaning on the railing and look around the little harbor. A seal playfully swims around the yacht while another on a nearby dock warms itself in the last of the afternoon sun. The marina glows in hues of orange and yellow as sunset approaches, melding with the blue sky above.

I glance behind me to find the boat's entrance completely empty. All the townspeople must have carried the party onboard. Scanning the dock, I still don't see any of my friends yet. They must either already be inside or running late.

Standing up a little straighter, I adjust my posture, and pull down on my dress, smoothing out any wrinkles from the car ride. My hair falls in loose barrel curls as I look down. Mel was kind enough to blow out my Hagrid mane. I roll my eyes in amusement because it's already resisting its straight confines. I actually prefer my hair this way with a teensy bit of wave; stick straight hair feels alien to me. Embracing my old-fashioned aesthetic tonight, I chose to part my hair pre-dominantly to the right and pin back the twist of hair on the left. Mick sweetly gifted me with his wife's vintage hairpin. I reach up and check the dainty, but hearty piece, making sure it's tight and secure. It feels snug as a bug.

Only the lightest of makeup accents my face. Predisposed to a more natural look, all my efforts show in my eyes. After not having worn makeup for what feels like an eternity, I find myself feeling a little giddy every time I envision the golden amber eye shadow resting on my lids. The warm tones bring out the hint of yellow surrounding my pupils as my blue green irises pop out against the mascara and very thin black cat eyes. I pair this look with an understated, light rose lipgloss.

"Stop fidgeting," Mick mumbles with a smile, turning back around as he offers me his arm again.

He leads me towards the entrance. Trying not to trip with unsteadiness, I focus on the irregular boards underneath me. We walk a couple of yards when I feel Mick nudge me lightly. I look up. Butterflies flutter by the thousands inside my stomach and for a second, I stop walking. Time stands still.

Brodie stands tall and relaxed near the entrance looking down the dock in the other direction. Dressed in a light tan, two-piece linen suit with a white button-down tucked in at his trim waist, he drips attraction and oozes allure. He turns his head and his eyes widen in surprise as he catches sight of me. He blatantly rakes over my dress in pleasure.

Mick urges me forward and holds his hand out to Brodie as we meet. Finally pulling his eyes off me, Brodie greets Mick with a slightly distracted, yet firm handshake. He offers Mick a happy smile before returning his gaze to meet mine. The first three buttons of his shirt are left undone at the collar. The stark, fresh white cotton exposes his long, golden neck. While my mouth has gone completely dry, I notice his Adam's apple bob slightly as he swallows. He clears his throat.

"Neens, ya look..." his voice trails off as he struggles to find the words, but his admiring tone and expression say it all. I watch as his eyes dart around my face and flutter over my hair. He steps forward and gives me a polite kiss on the cheek. "Yar hair. Almost didn't recognise ya."

*Wow, he smells divine.* I gulp.

Mick grumbles a little and Brodie steps back.

"Sorry, Pryce, but my date 'n I need to find our seats," Mick says jovially. "See ya in there." He pats Brodie's shoulder as he pulls me along, and as we step onboard the ship, I look over my shoulder to find Brodie unmoved, still staring after us. Mick mutters, "Sorry 'bout that, Sweetheart, but I really need to sit."

"Don't be sorry," I reply earnestly.

While I'm a little reluctant to leave Brodie's dapper side so quickly, I do worry about the man beside me. It's unlike Mick to cut anyone off. Glancing around for a good resting place, I spot a few empty tables and chairs in the outside lounge area towards the stern. I point them out to Mick and we make our way over.

He somewhat collapses into one of the seats.

"Are you sure you're alright, Mick?" I ask with slight concern.

"I'm just runnin' outta gas, Sweetheart. I'll be right in a few."

"Fine, but let me get you a glass of water," I say in a tone that entertains no rebuttal.

With the squeeze of his shoulder, I'm off to find some. I quickly notice this yacht is pretty enormous, larger than it appears from the docks. I've never been on one before so I can't really compare it to any others, but once onboard you can really start to understand the size and scope. Maneuvering amongst a few cocktail tables and clusters of townsfolk, I wander through the lower level until I find a server dressed in all white. Thankfully they carry a tray of drinks, water being amongst them.

"May I?" I ask, gesturing to a glass, which they kindly hand me.

Having a better idea of the layout, I circumvent a congested area and find Mick already chatting with some friends from the pub. All of the seats around the table are taken. Setting the water down in front of him, I stand behind him and survey our fantastic surroundings. Amidst the big band music playing in the background, I suddenly hear my name being called. Hearing my name a second time, I look around, trying to pinpoint its location. I hear it again and it sounds like it's coming from above me. I tilt my head up and see Mel standing on tiptoes over the railing on the second level, waving her arms broadly to get my attention.

"Oy, we're up here, Neens!" she yells excitedly.

I glance at Mick, clearly the life of the party amongst his table. He urges me to go with a smile and a wave. I squeeze his arm once more and make my way through the main cabin, keeping my eyes peeled for the stair alcove to the upper deck. I can't help but notice how when I briskly walk, the sleeves and the bottom of my dress bounce lightly. It feels amazing and serves as a constant reminder of the fun occasion of getting to play dress up.

Working my way through busy crowds of people, most of whom I don't know, but know me, I get stopped several times. Politely prying myself away, I finally discover the spiral staircase and run up quickly before someone else wants to chat. I pop out in the middle of the giant upper landing. A large open area, usually for lounging, encompasses the middle of the deck, forming an empty dance floor for those who feel so inclined. This early in the evening, I think either a larger crowd or more alcohol is necessary before anyone would willingly join in. Not for the first time, I notice music playing. Scanning the floor for a band or DJ, I discover a man in headphones in front of a computer nestled next to the upper cockpit.

I hear my name again and whirl around and see Mel and Margot waving me over to their corner of the balcony. Walking over to them, I stand back and smile, admiring their outfits. Margot officially looks like a viking queen dolled up in modern fashion, while Mel rocks a backless burgundy jumpsuit on her lean frame. She stretches even taller, wearing four inch black pumps. The gorgeous sisters nod in approval as they assess my dress.

"Those shoes are perfect," admits Margot, who found them for me.

"Love the hair," says Mel, who leans in and whispers in my ear, "'n that dress is bloody aces, Neens. Yull have all of 'em wantin' to pash 'n dash ya tonight."

Unsure what that means exactly, I understand her meaning just fine. Making audible squeals of delight at my dress, she orders me to give her a little spin. Mid twirl, Jaz runs over, accompanied by Shayno and Donnie.

"N-i-i-i-ina!" Donnie practically sings my name, letting out a small groan of approval. His admiring gaze travels downward towards my backside. "That dress with those hips."

"Easy, tiger," I jest, before raking in his attire.

Built like a linebacker, Donnie tightly wears a cobalt blue jacket and white pants. He looks like a stylishly cool captain, which is appropriate considering tonight's venue. Mel talks animatedly to Jaz and I shift my attention to her. She rocks an all black jumpsuit with a plunging neckline with her chin length hair brushed back tightly into a sleek mini bun. Her crimson red lips make her teeth glow as she smiles.

Donnie already holds a stubby in one hand as he scopes the room, nodding and addressing Shayno in the process. Shayno's classy in all black, to compliment Jaz I suppose. I stifle a giggle because Shayno also has his usually untidy locks slicked back into a tight bun, mirroring his partner. My shoulders shake as I assess the pair of them.

"What's so funny?"

I whirl around and discover Brodie advancing towards me. The sight of him again all gussied up makes me weak in the knees. Looking like he was built for yachts, sailing and a life of luxury, he strides over to us, boasting an air of raw magnetism, and hands me a glass of champagne. I take it by the stem and smile in thanks, unable to break my stare.

*He's downright beautiful.*

Exhaling quickly, I gesture to Jaz, "Oh, nothing really. I just noticed how your sister and Shayno both came twinning with the same updo."

Brodie snorts into his champagne, mid sip, and wipes off his chin as he looks at the pair and chuckles in agreement. As if her ears are burning, Jaz walks up to Brodie and kisses the air around his cheeks. They both smile, always genuinely happy to see one another.

"Brotha," Jaz says, looking him over with approval.

"Sista," Brodie matches. "Nice hair."

He slips a smooth wink at me and I stifle a giggle.

Angling around to include the rest of the group, I declare a toast and raise my glass, "I don't think I've ever seen a group of better dressed individuals. To us. ¡Salud!"

With some chuckles and "cheers," we all clink glasses with one another before taking sips.

Donnie raises his beer, and adds, "To the ladies, who are utterly crash hot tonight."

He nods towards each of us women before specifically saluting his glass to me as he appreciates my fuller figure. Raising mine back in tradition, I mockingly shake my head in surrender as I take a small sip. I catch Brodie smiling as he also steals a quick glance down the contour of my dress. Men will be men, I suppose. Completely owning the double standard, I take a long minute to ogle them back. Glancing up from Brodie's lapel, I find him waiting to meet my eyes. He narrows his eyes and purses his lips lightly with an expression that says *like what ya see, eh?*

In a tone that screams *yeah, I do!* I say his name, somewhat speechless, "Brodie, I—."

The DJ's voice looms out over the deck through hidden speakers, encouraging those to grab a partner and enter the dance floor. The beat picks up and he starts to play some music actually dance worthy. Some man I've never seen before approaches Margot and asks for a turn. She takes his hand and happily saunters out onto the open space. The boys all remove their jackets, discarding them on the cocktail table, and Jaz and Shayno quickly follow Margot. I notice a few more people skip out under the twinkling lights.

Suddenly, a large, dark hand looms in front of my face. I look over and see Donnie patiently waiting for me to accept. Giggling, I reach for his grasp as he lurches us out onto the dancing arena. The DJ then segues into The BeeGee's "Stayin' Alive." My mind immediately replays the scene of Dudley Moore dancing in his heart boxers in *Foul Play* and I begin to shake my shoulders. I embrace the disco beat and let loose to the catchy rhythm. Donnie comes up next to me, rubbing his backside along my hips. This action doesn't even offend me because it's so *Donnie*. He's one giant teddy bear who's so over the top, but we love him for it anyway. From the second I met him, he's been unapologetically honest and crass, but with only good intentions at heart.

As he drops to the floor by my ankle, I'm taken aback by his flexibility for having such a large frame. Using my leg like a stripper pole, he thrusts his hips dramatically. This whole scene feels straight out of *Dirty Dancing*. Trying to get a grip on my laughter as Donnie grinds along my thighs, I notice Mel and Brodie also dance nearby, watching and roaring in amusement. They slowly push in so we're all surrounding each other. Donnie really hams it up and spins me to face him as he pulls me towards him, so we grind together. Never having done this before, I fall to pieces in hysterics. The entire gang dies laughing as Donnie just tosses me around like a rag doll in the middle of the dance floor, the bottom of my dress flaring out in all directions from all the quick changes of motion. I can barely breathe from the hilarity of our whirlwind dance.

Finally the song changes to "Despacito." Trying to breathe again after my wheeze attack, I take a second to compose myself. Reminding me of home, I always love a good latin beat. I dive right back in and kick up my dress, and as soon as the main beat drops, I quasi salsa dance and sing along. The whole group circles around me and cheers. I do a couple of spins and wind up spiraling straight into Brodie. He takes me by the hands and dances smoothly and rhythmically alongside me. After a couple of mishaps, he impressively and closely mimics my latin stepping, letting me lead. Both lost in the heat of the moment, we just smile and chuckle intimately into each other's arms as the song comes to a close. We all dance a few more songs when a slow ballad transitions in, which really dampens the mood. We were just getting started.

Slightly disappointed, we all clear out to our little corner on the deck while some of the older couples enjoy their turn in the spotlight. While the others gather around the tall cocktail table, I stand at the railing, facing the water. Sweating from exertion and having too much fun, I fan my face, trying to let the ocean breeze cool me down. Leaning over, I glance at Mick's table below and am relieved to see he still enjoys the conversation as the whole table erupts in laughter.

Out of my peripheral, I notice something to my left. I look over my shoulder and see Brodie, leaning on the railing about five feet away, a glass of champagne in his hands. He looks so foxy and downright sexy, I can feel temptation thawing my Brodie resolve. I simper in his direction and with the quick tick of my head, invite him my way. He smoothly slides over to me until his arm bumps into mine. His champagne sways a little on impact.

I reach over and take the flute from him, which he allows, uncontested. I raise it to the edge of my lips, and daintily take a long sip, trying to preserve my glossy lips.

I hand it back to him and notice a small lipgloss mark plastered on the rim of his glass. Without breaking eye contact, he slowly tilts his head back and deliberately guzzles the rest of the champagne. Like a rehearsed skit, he extends his arm out as a server walks by and aptly takes his glass. Brodie mutters a small thanks as we hold each other's stares. He shifts a little on the rail and I feel the heat from his skin sear mine. Feeling my blood pressure begin to boil, I tear away and look around the harbor view of the twinkle lights illuminating the smaller boats around us. Completely dark now, the stars begin to shine. While this feels like a scene out of a movie in its beauty, I can't help but want to look back down. I'm acutely aware of our touching arms. I try to think of anything to say to distract me.

I come up with, "It's a hot one tonight. My neck's on fire."

Brodie softly smiles, and slowly but steadily pushes the hair off my shoulder to the far side of my back, with the tips of his fingers. As he does, he leans in so closely that his lips are about to touch the top of my collarbone. I bite my lip as my skin crawls, captivated by the undeniable, electrifying chemistry surging between us. He pulls back marginally and we lock eyes once more. Feeling him lean in towards me, I naturally angle my face towards his as we press our bodies together infinitesimally.

"Neens, I..." he whispers slowly and seductively.

I look down and see his fingers are centimeters from mine. My blood pressure heightens even more as he wears an expression of smoldering tenderness. Slightly intoxicated from his spell, I stare back with giant hopeful eyes.

"Yes...?" I breathe back hoarsely.

Our hands are about to touch. Brodie gently clears his throat as his pointer finger slowly caresses the back of my hand. My heart starts to pound even faster and my hands feel clammy on the rail. I hold his gaze and it feels like it might swallow mine whole.

"Neens," Brodie murmurs, "we need to talk—."

"Nina!" cries out a loud voice behind me.

Shaking my head out of my revery, I flip around to discover Jordan standing in the midst of our little party. Brodie turns as well and upon seeing our interloper, his whole demeanor stiffens.

"I hope ya didn't wear that just for me, Nina, cause I intend to rip it right off ya," Jordan piggishly gloats with a snort.

I immediately get the feeling he's had a bit too much to drink.

I can feel Brodie about to pounce, so I reach out and grab his hand in mine just in the nick of time. I hold it behind his back and give him a little squeeze as a reminder. I see his shoulders visibly relax as he releases a deep sigh. My head snaps back to Jordan.

"I don't know how many times I can say this," I say matter-of-factly, like I'm spelling it out, "but I'm not interested, Jordan. Please stop sending me vulgar photos. Please stop harassing me. It's never going to happen. Listen to a girl when she says 'no.' I'm saying 'no' now. I'm. Not. Interested."

I turn my back to him, giving him the cold shoulder to reiterate my meaning. Slightly bruised, but more or less unfazed, he makes a crude remark about my backside. Searing in a bubbling rage, I shake my head, trying to aptly reign it in. The last thing I want is to cause a scene.

He takes another sip of beer and says to Donnie, nudging him, "Eh, once I have a go at her, I'll toss her yar way, cobber. Ya can smash yar back out to yar heart's content."

He laughs into Donnie's side, who stands there, clearly unamused with a hint of disgust in his eyes.

Revolted, I motion to walk away when Jordan steps over and snatches my upper arm forcibly. He holds it so tightly, I wince from the pinching pressure. It feels like my arm is locked in a cranking vice, the bone about to crush. He pulls my face eye level with his.

"Dun worry," he muses, "he's built like a brick shithouse, Nina. Yull thank me afta, that is if yar not too sore, eh." Cocking his head back to Donnie, he taunts him, deliberately ogling my heaving breasts. "She's all real, D-Man. Bronzer good titties. Reckon I'd know."

"Jordo, that's enough!" Brodie roars, snapping forward.

The whole crew freezes as the tension ices out the room.

Jordan blinks at Brodie, and demands broadly to our group, "Waddayareckon? I bet Brodie here wants to save her all for himself. Some pal *you* are."

"Yar loose, mate, rack off," Brodie immediately cracks, his hand balling into a fist at his side.

"'Rack off?' Alrighty, fine then, but I'm bringin' her with me," Jordan declares, pulling me towards him.

The pinch of his grip is almost unbearable and I try to pull away again.

"Jordo, I reckon it's best if ya just leave," Donnie tactfully threatens, stepping in.

Jordan looks around the circle and sees his friends' faces mirroring disappointment, scorn, and overall embarrassment on his behalf. Mustering all of my strength, I heartily resist his hold, finally thrusting my arm free. Tenderly rubbing the sore spot on my flesh, I rise up to my full 5'4" height and face him, confidently standing my ground.

"I'm not going anywhere with you," I counter firmly. "Now go home."

Reeking of whisky and some other hard alcohol mixed with beer, he peers down my top and snickers. He then looks me over for a minute, deciding something. We lock eyes and I can see the dangerous hunger clouding his expression. My pulse kicks into high gear, hitting speeds like a horse rounding the final corner at the Derby. Though nervous and scared, I don't back down.

"I shoulda taken ya when I had the chance on that island," he sniggers, advancing towards me again.

Instinctively, I take a step back towards Brodie.

Jordan catches it because he leans down, and mutters, "What? Ya wanna cop a root with him instead, is that it?" Brodie's eyes dart to me at the same time as I drop my gaze. "Wait a sec," Jordan says with broad strokes of suspicion quickly dawning into realization, "ya already have, haven't yous." I don't deny it and my silence more or less confirms his accusation. He seizes my arm again and sneers, spitting into my ear, "Why ya little dead-set mole—!"

"Jordo, we're done," Brodie bellows. "On yar bike!"

Jordan turns to Brodie with complete shock in his eyes.

"Yar just gonna throw our friendship to the wayside for this bloody bitch—," he roars, before Donnie dishes him a solid blow across the jaw.

We all gasp as Jordan falls back. Brodie pulls me to his side, not messing around. By now, several party-goers turn and stare, their interest peaked as they try to catch a glimpse of what's happening in our small corner.

"Alrighty then, so this is how it's gonna go down, eh?" Jordan mumbles, assessing his jaw as as he bounces back.

He stands up tall and combs through his greasy hair with his fingers. Like a bull cornered in an arena, Jordan readies himself for a fight. Mel and the others watch in astonishment at the unfolding of events as Donnie rolls up his shirt sleeves. Brodie nudges me out of the way, and stands in front of the railing on the opposite side of Donnie; they both flank Jordan. On the outside, Shayno idly stands next to the table, on standby.

Eyeing both of his opponents back and forth, Jordan readies to strike. It's not a question of *if* but *who*. While Brodie might be fast and slightly taller, Jordan outweighs him by a good thirty pounds. I look from Jordan to Donnie, but personally, I wouldn't go for Donnie because, simply, he's huge. Donnie taunts him, calling him a "wuss" amongst other names. Jordan acts like he's going to lash out at Donnie, but quickly pivots and lunges, barreling towards Brodie. Just when he's about to pummel his fist directly into Brodie's face, Brodie sidesteps out of the way and Jordan flies up and over the railing. A giant splash emerges from down below.

Man overboard!

Reeling from shock, we all run over to the side, peering down into the black waters. It's so dark out, we can't really see, but we hear Jordan gasp for air as he surfaces.

Adrenaline pumps through my veins, and I take a few deep breaths, trying to calm my body. Relieved it's over, I turn directly into Brodie's chest. His arms come around me like a blanketing reinforcement.

"Neens, ya alright?" Mel asks, full of concern from behind me.

"She'll be right, Mel, just give her two shakes," Brodie suggests, smoothly rubbing my back.

Feeling better, I pull away and turn to Mel's open arms. She squeezes me tightly and then we both sit down at the cocktail table next to the others. Donnie walks over and stands next to us. Tears well in my eyes when I think about him willing to go to blows on my behalf.

"Thanks, Donnie, I'm so sorry," I say directly to him with the utmost sincerity. I glance down at his hand and frown. "How is it?"

He smiles to cheer me up and shakes off the pain.

"Dun wuckas," he offers. "It'll be like it neva happened, soon as I have anotha coldie."

The whole top deck is abuzz with talk. I realize word will quickly make its way to Mick.

"I need to check on Mick," I tell them, standing up. "Be right back."

Mel motions to say something, but I see Brodie shake his head softly at her. She sits back quietly, letting me go. I make my way down to the main level and find Mick in his usual spot. Seeing him immediately brightens my mood. His face lights up in relief as soon as he sees me. Clearly he's heard some scuttle.

"Who flew ovaboard?" he asks, in mild shock and curiosity, as I sit down in the empty seat beside him.

"Jordan..."

"Ah," he exclaims, assuming the bigger picture.

"Yeah."

"You?" he asks wistfully. Shaking my head, I recap the last few minutes while Mick sits quietly, facing me. Upon finishing my story, he reaches over and grabs my hand in his, giving me a solid squeeze. "I'm sorry, Sweetheart, but sounds like ya can make peace with it at last."

"I'm just glad it's over with," I admit. Offering him a sweet smile, I squeeze his hand back three times. He offers me a bite of cake, and after I steal a few more, I feel almost back to normal. "Can I talk you into a dance? I mean you are my date after all." I raise a playful eyebrow at him. Seeing him gauging the entrance to the staircase, I interject, "We don't have to go up there. We can do it right here."

I turn back in the direction of the upper balcony and holler Mel's name loudly. A few people at the neighboring table give me the eye, but hey, I'm used to it. Mel pops over the edge and waits for me to engage. I yell up my request, and she nods, disappearing. The rest of the crew's faces pop over the ledge trying to pinpoint the commotion before they spot me. I don't give them a glance as I focus on my dance partner.

Suddenly, Jim Croce's "Tomorrow's Gonna Be a Brighter Day" floods the air. Like the honorable man that he always is, Mick extends a hand, waiting for me take it. I do and he leads me over to an open area by the stern. Smiling, he pulls me in close, tucking our hands in between us as we slowly sway along to our song. Moving back and forth, we circle in a slow dance around the little area, and as the guitar melody glides along, Mick pulls back, commanding me to twirl. I laugh as my hand spins in his as he pulls me back close. I rest my head on his collarbone and close my eyes, enjoying the moment. This man has come to mean the world to me. We rock back and forth until the song comes to an end. Once the music stops, we break apart, and Mick brings our enclosed hands up to his face as he kisses the back of mine. Laughing sweetly, we make our way back towards the table. Hearing little cheers from above, we look up and see Jaz, Shayno, Mel, Brodie, Margot and Donnie all lined up, enjoying our little moment. They all cheer on Mick with smiles and whistles.

"I think that's my cue, Sheila," Mick announces, passing the table. "I'm gonna say my goodbyes."

I'm not ready to leave my friends, but I also don't want Mick to drive back so late all on his own.

"Let me run up real quick and tell the others bye," I mention, turning towards the stairs.

"Absolutely not," he declares vehemently, pulling me back. "Yar to stay here as long as ya like. Relax. Go take a turn 'round the dance floor with yar mates. Dun worry 'bout me, I'll be right."

"But I do worry, that's life," I say with a wink. "Just give me one more dance upstairs and then I'll be ready to go home."

"If ya insist, Sweetheart," he mumbles a little begrudgingly, but with a smile. "I'll slowly make my way to the ute. Dun rush."

He waves from behind his back as he begins the shuffle through the dock. From the stairs, I see him bump into a friend and they chat.

"How's Mick?" Brodie wonders, as I approach the table.

I smile at him, pleased by his thoughtfulness to even ask.

"Neva reckoned he had those moves in him," Margot laughs.

"What a night. One minute we're jivin'," Donnie exclaims in bewilderment, "'n the next I'm throwin' a bloody punch."

The whole group stills and fidgets in their chairs, contending with the elephant in the room.

Shayno, the most taciturn of the bunch, asks in deep confusion, "So, Nina, what the bloody hell happened between the two of yous?" Eyes dart between Brodie and me, so he clarifies, "Between you 'n Jordo."

I sigh and glance at Mel first, then Brodie, but am also aware Mick's waiting for me. The entire table obviously wants to hear the backstory too, so without going into much detail, I succinctly explain the key events that led up to tonight's confrontation. After many exclamations of surprise and disdain from my audience, I put both hands on the little table and look them all in the eyes.

"Enough about Jordan," I announce with conviction. "Let's not have him ruin another second of our night."

The table hollers in agreement as I run out to the dance floor. With reckless abandonment I groove to the uplifting tempo of a remix of "Head & Heart (feat. MNEK)." I put my arms up, stretching them high into the air as I close my eyes and just lose myself completely in the music. I dance like it's just me alone on a deserted island for most of the song, but at the bridge I open my eyes and see Mel, Jaz and Margot next to me, all letting go with the same intensity. I smile at them and they all raise their arms and release a collective cathartic scream as the music heals all.

The song transitions and we all share a group hug, laughing and enjoying the natural high that only dancing freely can bring. The guys join us. No one pairs up, and instead we all move around, trading off dancing with everyone. Feeling full and grateful for our core, we all get down and move to the pulsing beat of "Lasting Lover (Tiesto Remix)" by Sigala & James Arthur. The main expanse of beats sounds off. I can't help but love this song. It's very catchy and its beat is undeniably captivating.

Brodie skirts my way as his shoulders and head bounce up and down to the mix. A major crescendo comes up and we all stall as the tempo builds. At the climax, we all jump furiously up and down, letting go of everything else. There's something about sharing an experience like this, when you're completely wrapped up in a singular moment. Brodie thumps his chest as he screams the words. He comes up and gives me one of his million dollar, Brodie nose scrunching grins. We're both feeling the high energy as the second crescendo blasts off, allowing the music to bring us together. Brodie pulls me in close by the waist, intoxicated by the same stimulant currently coursing through my bloodstream. Doped up on life, we both abandon any preconceived reservations and hesitations and just embrace this flash of time. Like in the helicopter, this feeling is second to none.

*I AM ALIVE!*

Brodie lowers his head so our eyes are only inches apart as we jump up and down together in synchronization. I can see the shared longing in his eyes. Closing mine, I wrap my forearms around his neck, and together we dissolve into the rhythm of the upbeat tempo.

The DJ changes tracks again and I break apart from him and the crew, leaving them looking a tad confused.

"That's it for me, guys," I explain in a giant smile, barely meeting Brodie's eyes as I nod my head to the exit.

The last thing I want to do is leave them, especially him, but I also can't help but feel that it's the right time to call it a night, plus I feel bad making Mick wait any longer. As I wave, the others also say they're ready to pack it up too, so we all pile out of the yacht, and giddily run and skip down the dock back to the car port. Brodie carries his linen jacket over his shoulder and my white heels, which I totally forgot about, in his other hand. As we approach the utes, Mick waves from his, then gestures there's no hurry. Donnie climbs in his truck and starts the ignition. The high beams shoot out at us as we gather in front, saying our little goodbyes. Brodie opens the door to set aside his jacket and start his engine. Music comes blasting out as it fires to life. I can just make out Maluma's "Hawai'i" because it has a really sexy latin beat. *I'm glad he's enjoying the playlist I made him.*

Besides Brodie, the crew piles in with Donnie and we exchange small waves as they pull away. The two of us are now alone. I notice Mick starts to fiddle with the radio, attempting to give us an ounce of privacy, as Brodie casually walks over to me. He stands just inches from me and I can feel the heat radiating off his person. It's like his entire being is electric and I'm a moth to a flame. I search his face as he searches mine with warmth and longing. It's been a long night with so many emotions swirling, and before we can unpack any of it, I instinctively find myself standing on my tiptoes, pulling him in for a hug.

"I'm so sorry about Jordo," I whisper in his ear, before grabbing my shoes from his hand and pulling back.

Running to the car, I leave him speechless as he stares after me. I start the ute, and Mick and I drive off down the highway. I look back in the rearview mirror and say goodnight to a piece of my heart.

Today, Saturday, is the first full day everyone's had off since the yacht party a couple of weeks back, and the crew is heading camping for the night at their favorite place. No one will tell me where we're going or explain why this place is so special. They all want me to wait and find out for myself.

Mick drives me to Brodie's to drop me off. I haven't really seen him much other than in a couple of group settings. We've both been busy with work, him especially. Honestly, it's been a relief. I miss him like crazy, but it's been a little easier on my emotional stamina to not be in close proximity to something I want but shouldn't have. I'm curious to see how it goes. We haven't had a chance to even really talk about the Jordan fallout.

When we pull up outside Brodie's, Stella comes out and greets us as her dad hops down from the boat in happy spirits. He runs to the back of the ute to unload my sleeping bag and backpack before Mick gets the chance. Brodie's been really sweet and extra attentive with Mick lately. We've both noticed him slowing down, especially since the party. Mick claims it's from not sleeping well the past few weeks, but I can't help but worry about him. He is almost eighty-seven for crying out loud, but he keeps assuring me he's fine.

"It's hell to get old, Sweetheart," he constantly tells me.

*It's hell to watch someone you love get old.*

I cast the thought aside as Brodie sets my things on the back swim deck and heads back to properly greet Mick.

"G'day, Pryce. Take care of our girl, eh?" Mick requests with a smile.

"Always," Brodie replies, and taps his hands on the weather stripping. Mick yawns and coughs into his elbow. The hacking sounds full of congestion. Brodie frowns slightly. "Ya alright, mate?"

Clearing his throat, Mick emits another cough, then reiterates that he's good, he just might be coming down with a bug.

"Want me to hang back?" I say, poking my head around Brodie's. "It's not too late."

"Nah, I'll be right, Sheila," he orders, waiving off my concern. "Just enjoy yar trip with yar mates. Ya can get back to lookin' afta me when ya come home."

"You sure?" I urge. "I'm happy to stay."

Brodie and I exchange a glance. I don't want to miss out, but I will gladly stay back if Mick needs me. I know Brodie would understand.

"Nina," Mick says, rolling his eyes at me. He *never* calls me by my name. "Go. Dun worry about the Old Man. 'N besides I'm gonna visit Gus. Rememba, he's a docta."

That does make me feel a little better. I hesitantly nod my head in acceptance. I lean in the window and give him a quick kiss on the cheek. I'll miss him even if it's just for two nights. I rest my hand on Mick's shoulder and give him three squeezes.

"I'll be seein' ya, Sweetheart," he hollers, smiling at me, as he shifts the Trooper into gear.

Brodie and I stand back as he takes off down the red dirt road. Brodie pulls me to him, enveloping me in a side hug as we watch the Trooper drive out of sight.

"He's an Old Boy, dun worry," he says, squeezing my arm lightly in reassurance.

While it immediately makes me feel better, and overall feels blissful, I gently pull away because it also hurts. *We can only just be friends.* I have to keep reminding myself. I just as easily could lean up on my tiptoes and plant a soft kiss on his cheek, but I can't. *Why can't you?*

Instead, I turn to face him, and give him a smile.

"I know, thank you," I mutter appreciatively. I turn to the boat, and pull my shoulders up to my ears eagerly. "How can I help?"

He chuckles, and with the quirk of his neck, directs me to my small tasks. Minutes later, Brodie and I load up the eskies and the boat before piling into the ute with Stella. We turn down the highway towards the launching ramp. I can't help but feel the charged silence in the ute. I feel like Brodie wants to say something but is holding back, while I clearly want to keep things light. I raise my eyebrows and ask if I can put on some tunes.

"'Course, ya don't need to ask, Neens," he replies.

I put on Lord Huron's album *Strange Trails* and discuss how somehow the band creates a feeling of frontier exploration with their use of the slide guitar, but then they meld that with some vintage surf riffs. The compilation makes you feel like you're suddenly exploring an empty island for the first time a hundred years ago. It's a really unique sound.

"I'm really excited for today," I admit dreamily, staring out at the ocean through my open window. "I can't wait to see where you lot are taking me."

"Me too," he chimes, nudging me, before his smile falters.

I feel his elbow linger on my arm. I abruptly clear my throat and turn up the music as we pull off towards the ramp. Perfect timing. As I expect Brodie to jump out and handle the launch like he always does, he turns the engine off and leans back in his seat, clearly not going anywhere. I glance around. We're completely alone. All I can hear is the tiny crashing waves along the shallows. We both sit back and listen to the lulls of the lapping water. Leaning against the headrest, I turn my head to face him, feeling the soft leather against my cheek. He faces forward, zoning out, deep in thought. I wonder if he's thinking about Jordan, missing his friend.

"You know, you can talk to me... about Jordan," I whisper. "It's okay to miss him. I just want you to know I'm here. I know that can't be easy. He's your best friend."

I swallow, feeling sorry for him. Wanting to console him somehow, I reach over and carefully take his left hand in mine. He swivels his head against the headrest and looks me softly in the eyes.

"Not anymore," he breathes.

I squeeze his hand reassuringly, to remind him he's not alone. He closes his eyes and takes a deep breath, sighing. I take the moment to study his features. His eyelids are at least four shades lighter than the rest of his face. His long, dark lashes still as if he sleeps. Tiny wrinkles line his forehead and around the corners of his eyes and mouth. The thought of the millions of smiles it took to craft such lines makes my heart burst in joy.

As if sensing my thoughts, Brodie's eyes open and he stares deeply into mine. Feeling terrible that I've been leading him on unintentionally, *well maybe with some intention*, I slowly let go of his hand, and face away, looking out my window.

A few silent seconds pass by.

"Nina," he breathes next to me.

Somehow, hearing my full name paired with his serious tone, I know what's coming and I'm not ready for it. I close my eyes for a few seconds. I can't face him. It hurts too much.

"Nina," he says again, slightly pleading, waiting for me to respond. He gently begs, "Look at me, Neens."

Mustering up an emotional shield, I twist my head over to meet his gaze.

"Brodie, please don't," I whimper, feeling the emotion sliding back in by the second.

"Why not?" he wonders, ardently searching for the answer in my eyes. "I thought if I gave ya some time 'n space ya'd come round. At first I reckoned well, we copped a root, 'n maybe ya just didn't feel the same way anymore. But then I watched ya 'n I knew ya were sussin' me out, stealing little glances at me when ya reckoned I wasn't lookin'.

"This," he urges, passionately grabbing my hand in his, sending a little jolt passing through my stomach, "this is magic. I feel that still, 'n I reckon ya feel it too."

"That's besides the point," I groan in frustration. "Brodie, I have to go back home *to America*. I'm trying to do the right thing here and not hurt either of us. Because if we do this, we can't go back, and I don't think I could take it if we had to split up. It's going to be hard enough as it is—."

"That's what I'm tryin' to tell ya, Neens, what I've *been* trying to tell ya," he stresses, sounding frustrated. "I don't care."

"That's easy to say now."

"It's easy to say because it's real. You 'n me. We're real. Look me in the eye 'n tell me ya've felt this way with anyone else?" I roll my eyes at him. He knows my history. He knows the truth. "That's what I thought. Then everythin' else, come what may."

Stella looks back and forth between us, sensing our distress.

"It's not that easy. It's not like I'm from another territory. I'm from all the way across the world," I explain, trying to get him to see the enormous complexity of the situation. The truth hits me like a ton of bricks. *Either way I'm losing a home.* I look away, unbuckling my seatbelt quickly. "I can't do this, Brodie, I'm sorry."

Needing fresh air, I hastily jump out of the ute. Trekking through sand, I stand at the water's edge. I hear his door open and shut behind me.

"What are ya so scared of, Nina?" he demands, already at my side within seconds.

Tears begin to streak down my cheeks, chilling me as the light wind hits them.

"I'm not scared." *I'm terrified.*

"Bulldust ya ain't," he immediately bellows. "See all this time, I thought, wow look at her, she's bloody fearless, nothin' scares her anymore, but it comes back to the same answer as it did when we first met." I whirl around on my toes, ready to snap back, but he continues, disbarring my feelings, "Yar the one holding yarself back. You 'n yar goddamn fears."

"I'm just tryin' to protect you," I yell incredulously.

"Well I don't need yar protection!"

I turn my back on him, stifling a sob.

Hugging myself with the wind blowing against me, I can barely hear Brodie slowly make out the words, "I just need you."

I turn to face him. He looks out in agony at the ocean.

*You're both bloody miserable now, Nina.*

I realize that in my quest to guard my heart, I'm the one who's pulverizing it. *Just follow your heart and come what may.*

Brodie looks back at me, and without any further thinking, I walk right up to him. Standing on my tiptoes, I pull his head down for a deep, simple kiss. We pull apart and rest our foreheads together, breathing in each other's air.

"You sure?" I mutter, softer than a whisper.

Instead of answering me, Brodie simply slides his arms around my waist, and pulls me in for a knee bending embrace. He kisses me in the nape of my neck as his hands travel up to my hair before tenderly drawing my face to his.

*Game over.*

# 20

This is the part where the movie usually cuts to black. After many missed opportunities and hidden feelings, the two main characters finally get together just as the story ends. Well, for Brodie and me, our story is only just beginning.

After we make out on the beach for a few minutes, I realize the crew will be arriving any second. Reluctantly, we manage to get the boat in order on the dock, stealing small affectionate glances and moments here and there. It's a marvelous feeling, turning and being able to freely kiss him just because I feel like it.

"Hey, do you mind if we keep this just to ourselves for now?" I ask him, feeling hopeful as I walk down the tiny dock. "It's just so new—."

"Cross my heart, Neens, whaddeva ya want," he pledges, taking my hand to help me over the railing.

As I land with a *thunk*, he pulls me in for a tender kiss that quickly deepens. I mutter a small moan of elation. I hear the sound of an engine growing in the distance. Someone will be here shortly. Begrudgingly, we separate as I stow away my backpack. Donnie's truck arrives and the rest of our party unloads. Running back to help Mel with the carton of drinks, I witness Jaz sprinting full send into Brodie's arm with a bone crushing hug and a shriek. I can't make out what they're talking about, but she seems really excited. Meanwhile, Shayno and Donnie greet Brodie with big hugs, high fives, and "Day for it!" Everyone seems in high spirits, today especially. As the crew settles, I see Brodie eye me as I casually walk back to the boat. Smiling, he pauses and waits for me to get to the rail before taking the crate of bevvies and offering me a hand over. I land with a small *thud* on the landing and he holds on to my hand a little longer than necessary, squeezing it before he lets go. Biting my lip, I smile and turn away, plopping down in between Mel and Jaz on the bench seat. Mel raises a quizzical brow at me.

"I'm so pumped!" Jaz bellows.

"Shhh! It's a surprise, eh," Brodie jokingly scolds in a laugh.

"Right," Jaz quips, nodding her head as she winks at him.

"Ready when yar ready, Birthday Boy," Donnie hollers at Brodie.

My eyes almost pop out of my head.

"*Birthday Boy?*" I reiterate, astonished.

Brodie's head drops and his eyes close as he sits in his captain's seat, laughing and shaking his head in mock annoyance. Stella, in the co-captain's chair, looks at him.

"It's your birthday?" I ask, dumbfounded. "*Today?*"

"What, Brodie didn't tell ya?" Mel asks, looking from him to me.

Brodie simply shrugs and smiles in embarrassment. I shake me head, but I get it. I'm not a huge fan of birthdays myself. I just feel bad, I didn't get him anything. The Birthday Boy turns on the radio and The Movement's "Take Me To The Ocean" fills the air loudly. We both start singing along.

"So much for convo," Jaz shouts, trying to be heard over the song.

"Oh, I don't mind," I yell back loudly. "I love to be out here with nothing but the music."

"Yar as bad as he is," she exclaims at a high decibel.

I see Brodie twist in his seat and smile at me. If he wasn't wearing glasses, I swear I think it was a wink. He guides us out on the open water and punches the boat in gear. We stop only once to spearfish for food for dinner, and awesomely enough, the boys catch three Red Emperors. Talk about a birthday delicacy. We start our journey again. Nudged in between Mel and Donnie, I feel the mist hit my face. I close my eyes and tilt my head back, letting the wispies swirl around my temples. I take in the feeling of embracing nature and freedom all rolled into one. Lulled by the ocean and the sound of the engine, I doze off, accepting sleep's enticing invitation. Everything goes black.

Feeling the soft pull of light and consciousness, I feel the boat slowing down and I stir.

"There she is," Donnie quietly chuckles. "Oy, Chica."

Adjusting to the light, my eyelids flutter, and I crane my neck up from Donnie's shoulder.

"How long was I out for?" I groggily ask, coming to my senses.

It couldn't have been that long. Just a little doze. Hopefully I didn't drool on him. He was nice enough to lend me his side as my pillow.

"Almost an hour," Mel says on my other side, nudging me. "Ace timing, Neens."

She jumps up as the others spring to action. Brodie cuts the engine and the boat rocks slightly with the swell of the tide. Still shaking off the ebbing pulls of slumber, I yawn largely and glance around. There's nothing but ocean all around us. A strip of land lies in the distance, but it must be a dozen miles away.

I stand up, get my footing, and walk up to Brodie who sits at his captain's chair, re-applying his regime of sunscreen and zinc.

"Mornin', Sunshine," he muses.

I glance around and see the others are all preoccupied on the bow. Clearing my throat, I reach out and rub in a white spot of sunscreen he missed on his cheek.

"*Happy Birthday to you*," I hum lightly, offering him a sweet smile. He softly grabs my hand from his face and discreetly kisses my palm. I gesture to the vast expanse of ocean surrounding us. "Brodie, where are we?"

He grins, clearly excited, but still doesn't share. The rest of the group reconvenes on the deck. We all form a sunscreening party line, making sure everyone's backs, shoulders, and necks are covered. Mel and I wear rash guards so we do most of the work. I hear laughs and can feel the excitement buzzing in the air. Mel, beaming from ear to ear, offers to braid my hair and does so quickly.

"Suit up, Neens," Brodie commands, handing me my pair of fins, weight belt, and mask and snorkel.

Somehow I'm the first one all suited up and ready to go. I stand at the back swim deck. Unsure what's so unusual about this spot, I pray it's not shark related, or sea snake related for that matter. However, not allowing fear to envelope me anymore, I take a deep breath and jump in alone. The tiny rivulets of water and bubbles explode to life around me as I pop back up above the surface, and make the necessary adjustments to my mask. Brodie appears next to me, seconds later. The others still scramble on deck, peering over the edge.

"Brodie!" cries Jaz enthusiastically, pointing over our heads.

The gang's attention shifts there and they collectively "ooh" and "ahh." I can't see what they see, but suddenly realize whatever it is is close by and sharing the same proximate space with me. Brodie's hand grabs mine and gives it a little squeeze before letting go. He throws me a thumbs up. Nodding in affirmation, we both take a deep breath and dive down, letting the weighted belts do their part. We swim in the direction of Jaz's pointed finger, and suddenly, I stop swimming in my tracks.

A massive, spotted shark swims across our path. I quickly realize this twenty-two ton gargantuan is none other than a whale shark. Thinking back on all those summers of *Shark Week*, I rack my brain for more information on these enormous beasts. You never hear about them in the news like you do tiger or white sharks, but I've never seen an animal so big in my entire life. It's easily thirty feet in length, maybe more. We must be somewhere along the Ningaloo Reef. I've seen pictures of these docile giants before, but nothing compares to being within fifteen feet of one. About the length of a school bus, it glides in front of us. It's unbelievable how these humungous animals can materialize out of the blue. I mean, I know they're down here with a billion other creatures, but when you're under water you rarely actually encounter them. Hundreds of white dots glow bright, almost like its coarse exterior is being lit by a blacklight. Its colossal four foot mouth opens up, its gill rakers on full display as it slowly passes through the water, collecting micro plankton and shrimp. I can't believe I'm swimming with the world's largest fish. *This is incredible!*

I kick my fins and begin to swim alongside it from a respectful distance. Six small pilot fish hitch a ride alongside its back. Focusing on its dark gray, gritty skin, I notice the darker patterns of streaks and striations dissolve into its white underbelly.

With my heart beating a thousand miles a minute, I smile from ear to ear and glance at Brodie. His eyebrows shoot up to his hairline. He's clearly loving this as much as I am. We watch for a few more seconds as I climb to the surface for air.

Mel swims over and we dive back under together. Mel and Brodie look so small swimming next to it, and suddenly, it feels even more gigantic seeing it scaled next to two taller humans. We admire the lazy twitch of its tail as it cruises by. It really doesn't seem to mind our watchful eye. Squealing on the inside, I'm running out of breath. I watch as the whale shark swims further away before I resurface. Popping above the water, I rip off my mask and scream into the air. Mel and Brodie also surface nearby and do the same. The others cheer us on from the boat.

"I can't believe that!" I yell to my water companions. "That was the ultimate!"

"Did ya see the size of her?" Mel exclaims, swimming back to the boat. "She had to be at least ten metres."

"I reckon so," Shayno hollers from the swim deck, helping her up. "She came right up to the surface for us so we didn't miss her."

"Bloody beauty," Donnie reiterates.

"That's one of the bigger mamas I've seen out here," Jaz states, sighing in awe.

"Now that was the best birthday gift!" I hear Brodie shout.

Everyone laughs.

Unable to get over the sheer size of such an angelic creature, I shake my head as I tread lightly, and chuckle, "I can't believe I swam with a whale shark."

"Not many people can say they've done that, Neens," Jaz chimes in, over the rail.

She holds up my camera in her hand and gestures for Brodie and me to look at her and smile. We do so, laughing. I feel like I can't smile any bigger. She leans back over as the boat lightly rocks in a slow circle. Now we're in front of the bow. I slowly start to swim towards the back swim step, but feel a little tug from behind me. I whirl around and see Brodie biting his lip, waiting for my attention. He grabs my weight belt and gently tows me closer to the hull so we're completely out of sight from our friends. As we float, he pulls me in for a soft, salty kiss.

"Now that's the best birthday gift eva," he quietly announces, and throws a nose wrinkling grin my way.

"I can't believe you didn't tell me. I owe you a present for real."

"Kiss me properly," he demands. "That's my wish."

As I'm leaning in, I feel a watchful eye. I glance up and find Stella's head poking over the bow, looking down at us. She might alert the others, so I swim back and climb onboard. Brodie, looking a little disappointed, follows suit.

"How did you know that whale shark was even going to be here?" I ask him, as we peel off our gear.

"I have a mate who operates a jumpa plane for a few Ningaloo tours, so he always gives me a heads up when he spots 'em, especially now during the off season, they're harda to find," he explains. "'N he knew we were comin' this way, so he sent me the general coordinates ova the radio."

"Must be nice to have friends in such high places," I joke, laughing at my poor attempt at a pun.

Mel rolls her eyes in amusement, and Donnie and Jaz belly chortle.

Wrapping my towel around me, I sit down on the warm seat, soaking up the high that comes from a rush of blood to the head after witnessing nature in its purest form. The whole crew settles back in their spots. Shirtless, Brodie air dries as he kicks the boat in gear.

"Beach camp here we come," he announces, and punches it.

After boating for a while, we approach land. Brodie kills the engine and we coast up towards the shore of a small little island. It's not like Lucky's where there are a cluster of tiny ones. This slice of land is slightly bigger and more substantial. Dazzling clarity highlights the small sand divots in the shallows as micro shadows meet the light. The crew stands and stretches before readying to depart the boat. About fifteen feet from shore, Brodie drops anchor. He turns around as we begin to round up some of the camping supplies.

"Alrighty then, I've only one birthday wish," Brodie shares, smiling. "Before we make camp, let's all hop in the drink togetha, eh?"

The crew erupts into cheers of confirmation and all begin to strip off coverups and clothes. Mel and I pull off our damp rash guards simultaneously. She sports one of her usual black bikinis, while I don my newer yellow suit.

"Damn ya look hot in that," she exclaims. She nods in Brodie's direction and chums, "Nice to see I was right, wasn't I?"

I shake my head playfully, refusing to divulge anything at the moment. I unpack and launch The Khal into the air, locking the focal point on me before hitting the record button. I set the controller in a safe spot where it won't be disturbed, then shimmy over the side rail towards the bow where Jaz and the boys all hover. Mel follows my lead.

"Banga, Chica, love the yellow," Donnie says approvingly.

All heads turn to me with looks of appreciation directed at my bikini. Trying to change the subject, I glance at Brodie. This time without his sunglasses on, he does wink at me. I return the favor with an uncomfortable smile, and close my eyes in embarrassment.

"Alrighty, mates," Brodie says, taking the heat off me. By now he knows I'm not particularly fond of overt attention. We all line up along the rail. I stand on his left, and on Mel's right. Brodie grasps my hand. "On my count." I reach and grab Mel's hand tight in mine. We all brace ourselves, half poised on the railing, and chuckle in anticipation. "One..." Brodie draws it out. "Two... three!"

I jump out away from the boat, stretching my arms to keep hold of both Brodie and Mel's hands. We all yell, holler and shout as we simultaneously hit the ocean with our feet. Pulling us under, the water swirls around us in a million tiny bubbles. Every single time I submerge below its surface, it feels like it's the first time I've ever experienced it. It's a reverent feeling. I find the sandy bottom with my toes, and pop up through the surface, smiling from ear to ear. I wipe the water from my face before opening my eyes. Brodie catches my attention, heavily scrunching his nose in a grin. We stare at each other for a second before the guys swim over and begin to tackle him playfully. Mel, Jaz and I jump back, laughing as they wrestle around. Stella, barking from the bow, runs back to the swim deck and jumps in, beelining directly to Brodie. She lunges on him with her paws, trying to use him as a floatation device. After he gives her a few kisses, Brodie commands Stella to either go back to the boat or swim to shore. She chooses the shore, and after shaking herself off, runs around blissfully at full speed.

Suddenly, a dark, rock-like head pops up about five feet from me. I scream and jump on Mel, then quickly realize it's a sea turtle, and immediately exhale in relief.

"Neens, always the scaredy-cat," Mel cries out in humor.

Now that I see the turtle, I feel totally comfortable. After I capture some artistic shots of its shell - the patterns look like exploding fireworks! - Mel and I swim alongside it. With zero wind, the water vis is impeccably clear. You can pretty much open your eyes underneath and see everything, even without a mask. The larger turtle suns itself near the surface and pops its head up and down repeatedly. For scale, I could maybe just get my arms around its shell if I hugged it - *which I would never do, nor touch, unless it was in serious duress*. Wow, it's gorgeous! As I make my back to the swim step, I pray the drone captured some decent footage. As I bring The Khal home, catching it in my hand above the twin engines, the crew jumps aboard, and we follow our captain's lead, carting our gear to the sandy shore. Australians really are experts on the matter of outdoor living. Everyone assumes positions, and we operate smoothly and über efficiently. Before I know it, the beach looks like we've been here for weeks. Our camp sits right on the unobstructed stretch of sandy beach with crystal clear water views.

After our efforts, we all float and chill in the shallow waters, enjoying the last heat of the day with coldies and hard seltzers as we reflect back on our whale shark encounter. The sun dips low in the sky as magic hour descends upon us. Brodie and the lads get out of our natural pool and unload the Red Emperors from the esky. They begin the process of cleaning and filleting while us gals get out and change into our sweats and look for wood and kindling to start a fire. After an impressive minute or two, Jaz ignites a flame and we pull all of our camping chairs into a loose circle around it. Everyone takes a moment to watch the sun embrace the horizon before it quickly slips out of sight. Just as soon, violet hour floods the sky and the boldest stars begin to greet us in a twinkling dance.

Brodie mans the grill. Amazing scents of buttery cooked fish fill the air and my mouth begins to water. We're eating early tonight. Good thing too. Loud wails of my empty stomach take over, growling obnoxiously, and everyone stares at me, snickering in amusement.

"Tucker'll be ready in two shakes, Neens," Brodie chuckles. "If ya can wait that long."

"I've an idea," Mel perks up. "Let's all go round 'n share a fav Brodie Pryce memory while we wait."

"Ooh, yeah. Day for it!" Jaz agrees, jumping in her seat.

Donnie holds up his cold beer, and shouts, "I'll start us off."

Everyone finds a seat around the fire, except Brodie, who relaxes by the grill, and we all nestle in the firelight, drinks in hand.

"So this was," Donnie begins, "I don't know, God, I reckon ten years ago now."

"At least mate, I'm thirty-five today," Brodie clarifies with a titter.

"Fuck me dead," Donnie realizes. "Well anyways, this was right afta I moved back from Perth, 'n I didn't have much money or anythin' really then."

"Like ya have heaps now," Mel interrupts sarcastically.

"Oy, ya gonna let a bloke tell his story, then?" Donnie counters in jest. "*Anyways,* I was out at Old Monroe's 'n got bogged. The tide was rushin' in, 'n I couldn't get out. The more I tried, the deeper my tires sank."

I glance at Brodie who looks down at his beer. His shoulders shake as he laughs quietly to himself.

"'N I'm startin' to worry 'n wonda how I'm gonna get outta this little... predicament," Donnie continues. "So just as the wata is only a few feet from the ute, *my dearest love,* I hear an engine come outta the bush. A ute pulls up beside me 'n this bloke jumps out. At this point, this guy - Brodie - is a total godsend. I explain to him I already tried all the usual tricks 'n nothin's workin'. So what does Brodie do?"

Brodie takes a swig of beer and looks into the fire with a hint of a smile, clearly reliving the memory in his mind's eye as Donnie builds the suspense.

"He bails on me," Donnie says exasperatedly. "Yep, that's right. As I'm thinkin' he's about to hook me up, he climbs in his ute 'n drives off, kicking sand up in his wake."

The whole crew gasps and laughs.

"Fair dinkum?" Jaz asks, staggered.

"Hold on, let D-Man finish, alright," Brodie defensively chuckles into his drink, then adds a bit sheepishly into his can, "but, yeah, I did."

"At this point, the panic's settin' in," Donnie presses on. "Feelin' utterly devo, I'm thinkin' I just missed my chance, there's no way in hell anotha bloke's gonna roll in, 'n I'm about to be without a lift. I'm down to one bar of battery left on my mobile."

"Ya were not even!" Brodie chides. "Every time ya tell this story, ya get one bar closer to a dead battery."

"So just when the truck's about to be taken ova by the tide," Donnie says, ignoring Brodie's remark, "I hear the engine comin' back again, 'n I look up 'n it's Brodie headed my way with anotha ute in tow. Turns out it was Jordo, 'n the two of 'em got me out. Been friends eva since."

"I can't believe ya just left him without a word," Jaz reiterates, flabbergasted by the uncharacteristic behavior.

"I only left to grab help," Brodie replies, laughing. He looks at Donnie. "Ya were so deep in sand I honestly thought ya might not be the full quid. In hindsight, I shoulda warned ya I'd be back. Though I'm not gonna lie, makin' ya sweat was a bitta fun."

"My turn, my turn," Mel commands, jumping in as the circle laughs. She clears her throat. "So one night I find myself at some dive rubbity-dub 'n a gutful of piss, 'n no one would answer their bloody mobile except our Birthday Boy here. It was what, three, four in the mornin' 'n this cobber drives clear 'cross town to pick me up 'n gimme a lift home. He sat up all night makin' sure I didn't choke on my own chunder. Even held my hair up for me when I did, tryin' not to upchuck himself. The next day, he made me the most banga hangova brekky I've eva had." She raises her frostie to Brodie and toasts, "Yar neva once threw it in my face, yar neva even mentioned it eva again. To Brodie, who's always there when ya need him."

We all aim our glasses to the sky and drink to that. Shayno pipes up.

"Hard to pick just one," he shares, "but I reckon the time we went skiin' in Middle Earth. We were playin' a round a cards the night before in a lil hidey-hole, 'n the losa had to fulfil the wager. Well, naturally I lost. So next mornin' comes, 'n it was a frigid day, mind ya, 'n I'm standin' on top of the summit in the nuddy." Everyone doubles over laughing at the hilarious picture Shayno's painting in our minds. "I'm about to ski down when I look ova 'n see Brodie ski over from behind a tree, wearin' nothin' but the pack on his back holding our clothes. I'll neva forget as we both went full send down the peak, starkers. Turned a lotta Kiwi heads."

Donnie snorts so hard, beer shoots out from his mouth onto the fire.

"I forgot about that!" he bellows, half choking.

Brodie's shoulders shake a little as the rest of us erupts into a fit of roaring laughter. After a minute or two, we all try to calm down as Jaz raises her tinnie.

"Brotha," she lovingly says, "like Shayno said, it's hard to choose just one, so instead I'm gonna propose anotha toast." She clears her throat, looks to her big brother and smiles kindly. "To the best brotha a girl could ask for. To the man who swims with hammaheads 'n bloody tigas, to the man who lives life on full throttle, to the man who gives us days like today. Thanks for showin' us the way 'n for always havin' our backs, no matta what. Cheers to ya, brotha!"

Everyone salutes Brodie enthusiastically, vocally reiterating Jaz's toast with hoots, hollers, and whistles. Then they all shift their attention to me. I realize it's my turn as I'm the last one left. Clearing my throat, I bite my lip and take a deep breath before looking at Brodie. He leans back on his little table, his arms folded comfortably across his chest as he wears an endearing expression on his face, waiting to hear my memory of choice.

"Well, um, I'm debating between the time I almost speared you with the speargun," I share, much to the shock and amusement of the group, then continue with a hint of sass, "or the time you almost handed me a venomous sea snake."

My audience laughs some more, this time aiming their attention to Brodie, who lightly chuckles.

"For real though, Brodie," I push on more sweetly, "ever since you pulled me out of that car, we've shared quite a few laughs, had some unreal experiences in and out of the water, under the stars and in the sky, but my favorite memory is the moment you and I became friends." I raise my can to the man of the hour and tilt my head in salute to him with a loving smile, encouraging the rest of the circle to do the same. "To the best dog dad around, to the man with whom I can max out the volume with, *and* to our best mate, Brodie. ¡Feliz cumple! ¡Salud!"

With a twinkle in his eye, he scrunches his nose at me in thanks, and raises his glass up before we all take a long drink. *Thank you, my lad.*

Serving up the Red Emperor, Brodie thanks everyone for their kind words. As we all pile around the fire and dig into our amazing flakey fish, the group wants to hear about the speargun incident in more detail.

I'm in the middle of my story when Brodie interrupts, "She almost killed me ya guys. I've got the hole in my boat to prove it."

"So that's what that was. Ha!" Donnie belly laughs.

The whole camp erupts into hysterics. Shaking my head, I can't help but join in at how absurd the story sounds. After our delicious dinner, things mellow out amongst the camp. It's still not super dark just yet. The playlist singing from the portable speaker is on a roll. From "Sunlight" by Spacey Jane to Beach Fossil's "Down the Line," to our current song, Whitney's "fta," it plays, lulling us by the fire. Brodie sits in a beach chair while I sit on the sand, resting against his legs with Stella curled up beside me. Everyone hangs out, quietly listening to the music. The fire crackles like a small symphony as the flames lick and evaporate into the night air. In a daze from staring into the mesmerizing flames, I barely notice Jaz walking up, carrying a cupcake with a lit candle.

Everyone sings, *"Happy birthday to you. Happy birthday to you. Happy birthday, dear Brodie. Happy birthday to you."* While I shout in excitement, the rest of the crew keeps singing in true Australian fashion, *"Hip hip hurray!"* We all cheer as Brodie stares into the small flame. He catches my eye and smiles before blowing out the candle in a single swoop. He then takes the cupcake, gently peels back the paper liner and stuffs the entire thing - cake and frosting - into his mouth as we all root him on, bursting out in applause. Our applause subsides, but we hear ongoing clapping coming from the dark in the near distance. Camp grows quiet. Stella runs off in the direction of the sound as everyone looks after her. A figure finally emerges in the flame's light.

"Many happy returns," Jordan states, walking closer to us. Shocked, we all just sit, staring at his random arrival. "Can I share a memory?"

"Jordo, what the hell ya doin' here, mate, 'n how long ya been there?" Donnie asks, standing up.

I can feel Brodie tense beside me. I reach out and take his hand in mine, squeezing it, hopefully sharing my strength for restraint.

"Oh ya know, wouldn't miss my brotha's b-day," our interloper snidely remarks, with a menacing tone lying just below the surface. "Been comin' here since we were, what? Fourteen? Since the time Brodie 'n I stole my dad's ski 'n found this place. Seems wrong to fuck that up, don't ya agree, mate?" He looks straight at Brodie, who clears his throat and exhales. Jordan looks at our intwined fingers and scoffs. "Looks like ya didn't waste any time."

"Not tonight, Jordan," I counter, annoyed.

The whole crew remains silent, holding their breath, waiting for Jordan to go off. Jordan merely laughs and looks back at Brodie.

"Ya reckon that if this blow in bitch hadn't come here, we'd still be right. But no, instead I'm cast aside, 'n for what? I didn't even get to—."

"Jordo, I'm warnin' ya," Brodie urges.

"Whatchya gonna do, mate?" Jordan eggs him on. "Toss me ovaboard again? For her? Yar gonna let her come between brothas, when she'll spread her legs, have ya at her mercy, then leave ya cold for The States as soon as she can catch a flight out." Brodie stands, looking threatening and ready to strike. Jordan pulls off his shirt, preparing for a fight. "Oh, we doin' this, mate?" Brodie doesn't answer, but his answer is clear. Jordan nods. "Okay, then."

I try to interfere, but Brodie shuts me down. He whirls around and looks me dead in the eyes. His expression says it all. He's decided. "No, Nina," he snaps, "I'm not gonna stand idly by while he talks to ya like that. Not this time."

"Ooh, whadda we have here?" Jordo says, clicking his tongue. "A lover's spat? You her knight, mate? The pussy that good? I mean I knew it might be, hoped anyway—."

Brodie lunges halfway over the fire at Jordan, hitting him square in the chest. Both bodies stagger feet away into the sand. Everyone stands, stunned, too engrossed with what's happening right in front of us to do anything else. I can make out objects and shapes from the dimming light. A dark blur sprints up and jumps on Jordan, snarling and growling ferociously. *Stella!* Her contour jumps at the pile of moving shapes.

She must nip Jordan's leg because I hear him cry out, "Fuckin' Stella!"

Poor puppy, she's just trying to defend her dad. I call for her, not wanting her to get hurt, and she immediately runs up beside me.

I see a shirtless Brodie and a shirtless Jordan dishing and receiving blows in nothing but their boardies. Grains of sand kick up everywhere in a glorified fist fight. While Jordan is denser and perhaps heftier, Brodie is taller and more agile. The scrambling pair move directly in front of us. Brodie takes a punch to the gut and doubles over, slightly wheezing. Stella barks for him, but I hold her back by the nape of her neck. Jordan stands on top of Brodie, leaning over him.

"Throwin' away our friendship," he screams in Brodie's ear, "for a fuckin' sheila?"

Donnie intercedes, telling Jordan to calm down, and lends Brodie a hand. Meanwhile, Jordan looks at me like he wants to wail on me too, and advances towards me. I stumble backwards, away from him, but he grabs my arm. I trip over a chair, and whack my face on the table. I see stars. I try to regain my composure as Mel and Jaz hover over me.

Grunting, Brodie re-emerges, barreling into Jordan. He manages to punch him square in the jaw, and as he falls back, Brodie knees him in the side. Jordan drops to the ground, gasping for air. Brodie stands tall, heavily breathing. His chest heaves up and down as his lungs crave oxygen from the exertion. Donnie and Shayno jump in to corral Jordan, while Jaz and Mel look on with utter shock.

"Why?!" Brodie shouts exasperatingly at Jordan, who's propped up between Donnie and Shayno's arms. Brodie roars in hurt, anger, and disappointment. "Why couldn't ya just let sleepin' dogs lie!?" Jordan shoots daggers at me with his piercing gaze, but Brodie continues, "Nah, mate, don't blame Nina, blame yarself. My brotha, the Jordo I know, wouldn't act this way. Whaddaya doin', mate? Hurtin' ladies, pickin' fights with *me*, yar friend. Ya've changed into this guy I don't recognise anymore, a guy I don't care to know."

"Brodie," I mumble sadly, wanting to comfort him.

Brodie looks at me clearly for the first time. I wince as I graze a tender spot on my cheek. Brodie looks back at Jordan. *Boom!* Brodie sucker punches Jordan square in the jaw, who chortles in amusement as he spits out some blood.

"I hope ya hear me, mate," Brodie shouts, his voice cracking. "I don't wanna see ya around anymore. I don't want ya anywhere near Nina or me again. Is that sinkin' into that thick skull of yars?"

"Whaddaya wanna do with him?" I hear Donnie ask Brodie.

"Keep him on the other side. We'll deal with him lata," Brodie commands, as Shayno and Donnie drag off a thrashed Jordan.

Cautiously, Brodie waits in front of me, searching my face for damage. Mel and Jaz back up, giving us space. Beads of sweat line his brow and patches of sand stick to his skin and neck.

"How's yar head?" he implores, deeply concerned as he looks me over. He lightly touches my cheek, and I wince again. "Ya okay?"

"I will be," I confess, working up a genuine smile. "Happy Birthday."

His shoulders shake as he laughs, the tension pouring out of him.

"It may be the best one yet," he jests, trying to bring light to the situation.

We all sit down around the fire, trying to decompress, but it's weird considering Jordan's still nearby. Jaz brings me a bag of ice from the esky and commands I ice my cheek. We try to resume our evening, but the elephant in the room swallows every lingering second. With a small rag, I wash off Brodie's cuts and dried, sandy blood. "I Can't Tell You Why" assuages the atmosphere from the portable speaker.

"Ya sure yar okay, Neens?" Brodie asks me for the fiftieth time.

"Yes," I sigh, rolling my eyes. "Really, it's just a bruise. You're the one I'm worried about." I grin, but feel the soreness. It's pretty tender, but I'll be damned if Jordan sours the fleeting moments of Brodie's birthday. I want to celebrate him. I clear my throat and muster up my best smile. "This might sound ridiculous, but let's pretend he never came. Let's not let him ruin your birthday. We were having such an epic day."

The rest of the crew perks up, and agrees. We all slowly sing along to the song, and enjoy discussing our Birthday Captain for a while. Jaz and Shayno eventually sneak off, and Mel and Donnie linger for a bit before heading into their tent and swag, respectively. Despite the turn of events, I'm not ready for bed just yet. I'm dying to cozy up to Brodie, especially tonight on his birthday. Finally alone, I glance back at him.

"Come here," he softly demands, with a casual jerk of his head.

I walk over and kneel down a few feet in front of him. He tilts his head, urging me to move closer. I scoot towards him until we're facing each other in front of the flickering flames.

"I don't live my life with regrets, but I actually regret having invited everyone out here today of all days," he whispers, "because all day long, all I've wanted is to be alone with ya."

"I'm right here," I assure him.

"Yar still too far I reckon." He grabs me by the sweatshirt and playfully pulls me closer until my knees are caged inside his legs. Positioned a little taller than Brodie, I softly extend both arms around his neck, aware of his sore spots. He nuzzles into the crook of my neck and softly bites my earlobe in sweet jest. He mumbles seductively into my ear, "Now 'bout that birthday wish."

I pull back and face him.

"Uh, what was it again?" I playfully pretend to forget.

He pulls back so I can see his face, demanding coyly, "Kiss me properly."

I nod slightly, mock remembering, "Ah, yes, that."

I delicately place my hands on both sides of his jawline, look into his eyes, and gently pull his lips to mine. We share the sweetest and most assiduous kiss before we pull apart. He wipes a curly wispy from my temple and smiles, radiating my inner happiness back at me. He leans in and kisses me thoroughly this time. We both forget all about our bruises. Before things get too heated, Brodie climbs down from his chair, and sits on the sand. I spin around, nestling back into him. I feel his body take a deep breath and relax.

"Finally," he whispers in content, wrapping his arms around me.

I melt into his embrace and sigh happily as the blazing fire heats my skin. Slowly, Brodie's hands move up my arms towards my neck as he gently massages my shoulders. I stifle a moan and he chuckles slightly. Leaning back, I angle my head towards his.

"It's your birthday," I mumble. "I should be the one giving you a massage, especially after the beating you just took."

He dismisses this with the click of his tongue and continues to knead my neck for a couple of minutes. Suddenly, I feel his weight shift behind me as he rises. He steps in front of me and offers me a hand. I accept it and he pulls me up. He keeps hold of my hand, intertwining our fingers, and leads us along the water's edge towards the boat. Stella trots close by, never far. We walk up to *Salty Stel* which anchors a few feet out in the water. Wearing a pair of Mel's sweatpants, I pause before Brodie picks me up and hoists me over his shoulder like a sack of potatoes. He carries me over to the back swim deck and sets me down, waiting until my feet steady themselves beneath me. He then returns to shore and grabs Stella before climbing on board. His boardies are all but a little damp.

Without saying a word, he leads me to the bow, where we lie down on the cushions and snuggle in each others' arms as we watch the stars glow in exaltation. As I sigh against Brodie's chest, I still can't get over the feeling of finally enjoying being together, both on familiar ground.

I hear waves crashing against the reef in the distance followed by smaller lapping sounds, closer along the sand. I peer up and can see endless combinations of stars and nebula swirls. It's completely breathtaking. While the stars are hypnotic and mesmerizing, I find my gaze returning to Brodie's face. With my hand, I lightly caress the stubble forming on his chin. It feels gritty, like fine sandpaper, but the feeling isn't unwelcome in the slightest. Reaching up, I lightly kiss his jawline. Feeling the rough texture against my lips, I shiver slightly in delight. Brodie pulls me up a little and bridges the gap until our tongues softly and gently intertwine. We continue to kiss for a while, making out under the stars, when Brodie asks if I would want to sleep over on the boat with him.

"Who am I to refuse the Birthday Boy," I say coyly, yet mixed with a hint of nerves.

For one, I wouldn't mind having a little barrier between us and Jordan. But more than that, despite our one unforgettable night amongst the coco palms, which sometimes feels like a fever dream, I can't help but feel the shyness trickle in; that was a moment of passion some time ago. Brodie moves some cushions around, making a bed, and unfolds a few blankets on top. The full moon lights the scene well, considering we're out in the middle of the ocean with zero light pollution. We both lie down side by side, and my bashful thoughts are instantly quelled the second Brodie rolls over and lays his lips on mine. We pick up directly where we left off.

We spend minutes without coming up for air when I feel his hand travel down my chest and cup my breast. Ever so gently, he lightly moves down, caressing the skin along my rib cage. I can't help but giggle from the ticklish sensation. I lean my head back and laugh before clamping down on my mouth with my hand. I freeze, hearing a noise from camp.

"Dun wucka's," Brodie assures me, hovering over me, beaming in joy. "They can't hear us."

I roll over on my back, laughing quietly in mirth as I hear the small stirrings of camp, indicators of our friends all around us.

"You know, hearing everyone's stories tonight got me thinking," I divulge with sincerity. "You're so lucky to be surrounded by such awesome people."

"*We're* so lucky, Neens," he amends.

"This place is so beautiful, no wonder you come here every year."

"Well, it's tradition," he shares with a laugh, before sighing wistfully.

"Cymbidium" by WMD starts to play quietly from the boat's speakers.

"I'm so sorry about Jordan," I whisper. "I wish it was different."

"Ya did nothing wrong but state yar truth," he says incredulously. "I'm the one who should be sorry."

"Don't be, please. I'm not going to let him crush my spirit. I'm more sorry that my truth lost you your best friend."

I search his eyes. The hurt, anger and loss all linger. Then he meets my gaze and they soften and fill with hope again. Little creases tease and tug the corner of his eyes.

"Nah," he breathes, "besides he's not my best mate. Hasn't been for a while."

"Well, that's good," I say, relaxing into his arms. Maybe that will help lessen the blow. "I'm sure Donnie or Shayno will be relieved to hear it."

Brodie swallows and a small smile creeps onto his face. He looks like he has a secret he desperately wants to share.

"What makes ya think it's either of them?"

*Oh... hmmm. Duh, Nina!* Realizing it must be Jaz, I say, "Your sister."

He laughs and shakes his head slightly.

"Neens, yar my best mate."

Shock, delight, and warmth flood my system.

"Me?" I whisper.

"'Course, it's you," he states sweetly and simply.

Speechless, I return his happy expression, which at this point erupts into one of his nose scrunching smiles. I lick my dry lips and lean up, propping myself on my elbow.

"Well from one best 'mate' to another," I say, leaning down towards Brodie's face, and tenderly kissing his lips.

Despite wincing, he pulls me onto his chest, and happily returns the gesture. He passionately kisses me as he positions me underneath him on our makeshift bed. He lightly takes my hand from my face and gently pins it above my head as he smiles crookedly down at me. I smile like a schoolgirl into his eyes.

"You make me very happy, Brodie, even though you hate *Jaws*," I say wholeheartedly. "Happy Birthday. I'm sorry I don't have anything to give you."

His eyes dart all around my face, like he's memorizing my features or seeing me for the first time.

"Ya've given me you," he says simply, slowly lowering his face to mine, before tickling my stomach with his endless supply of kisses.

# 21

After a slow morning, we pack up camp for another day on the water. Brodie pulls up anchor as "Apocalypse" by Cigarettes After Sex blares over the stereo, which rolls into "These Stones Will Shout" by the Raconteurs. He shifts the boat into gear and maneuvers the vessel away from the beach. Upon the noise from the engine, screams and cries come out from around the side of a big mound of sand and bush. Jordan comes raggedly running around, waving his zip-tied arms frantically. He tramples through the shallows, trying to make his way after us. Brodie looks from the purple bruise on my cheek then back at Jordan.

"If I had it my way, I'da left ya tied to a tree, Jordo," Brodie hollers loudly in his direction.

"Ya can't just leave me here?!" Jordan screams back, flabbergasted.

"Dun worry. I'll radio it in. Someone'll come 'n get ya," Brodie shouts, adding more quietly, "eventually."

With that he opens the esky and pulls out a cold water bottle. He takes a big gulp, reaches into his pocket and drops a small pocketknife down the bottle's opening, before twisting the cap back on. He hurls it towards Jordan, where it lands a few feet away from him in the water. Jordan frantically searches for it, splashing water all around. Leaving him seems like a step too far, but Brodie assures me it's not far from the mainland, and Jordan can take the opportunity to think about what he's done. Without another word, Brodie guns the motor and we're off with Donnie in tow on Jordan's ski. As the change hits the song, the heavy guitar section rages on, and no one looks back.

We ride for a while out to sea. Out of nowhere, Brodie stops the boat and rallies us all to jump in for a quick dip. We know better than to argue with the captain, and besides, maybe it'll pull us out of our collective funk. We swim for a bit, enjoying the refreshing water, when we suddenly hear the large push of air shooting high into the sky as an enormous dark shape surfaces forty feet from us.

"Oy, ova there!" Brodie shouts. "Bloody massive humpies!"

A pod of whales breaches not too far from us. We quickly pull on our masks and snorkels. I'm not going to lie, it's a little daunting knowing they're right next to us. The Pryces both squeal in delight. I'm dying to drone them, but I can't drone and swim at the same time, I'm afraid, and right now, I want to live in the actual moment.

Just as Brodie's about to plunge down closer, I yell, "Hey! What about me?"

I swim towards him, ready to follow. His eyebrows shoot up in surprise.

"Sorry, Neens, just figured ya'd rather watch from the swim step. These guys make the whale shark look smol."

"I'm tired of watching from the sidelines."

He licks his lips approvingly, and replies puckishly, "Well, then."

Brodie waits for me while I adjust my mask. I tell him to just go, but he smirks at the thought. Honestly, I'm slightly relieved. I mean I know I've been saying I won't live my life dictated by fear anymore, and I meant it, but these majestic creatures are simply massive and perhaps a little overwhelming, especially to a more inexperienced free diver like myself. They range another twenty feet longer and ten tons heavier than the whale shark. Also, they swim and breach, while whale sharks basically cruise slowly along. On the off chance they come closer, I want to have a buddy at hand. Nodding my head at Brodie, I signal I'm ready, and we both dive down into the big blue drink.

Brodie carries the GoPro in one hand and leads the way. I look around and don't even see any whales, just endless blue that gradually turns to darkness when I peer down. The cooler water of the deep feels very welcoming after a hot and busy morning. I glance around and just see endless myriads of sunlit rays piercing through the blue in millions of striations. Being underwater in the ocean is an addiction, a pleasurable rush indescribable to anyone who hasn't experienced it.

When it grabs you, it never lets go. It's peaceful and buoyant and I can feel the water filling in my metaphorical holes of whatever ails me, healing me from the inside out. In the sea, I'm just me and everything else can just be.

Brodie looks over at me and motions in a direction to my left. I look to where he's pointing but don't see anything, just boundless ocean. They were so easy to spot from above, but down here I can't make anything out. Maybe they swam further away out of sight. Suddenly, a giant dark contour with an underbelly of white appears in the distance in front of us, looming larger and larger as it gets closer. My eyes go wide. Brodie looks over and I can see his face scrunching under his mask as he looks back at me. I latch onto his arm, squealing in a mixture of amazement and nerves. I hear his muffled chuckle in response, as micro bubbles spout out from his snorkel, rising in a hundred directions to the surface.

The whales swim right up to us and adjust their path slightly to avoid hitting us. One breaches about forty feet away. As their five meter long flippers hit the surface, you can hear the giant slap even underwater, and feel the forceful buoying of the pulsing water from impact. We swim alongside them as they lounge and casually swim just below the surface. A sound like a high pitched moan, followed by a low wail, reverbs through the water as they go back and forth communicating. *It's incredible!* A calf swims alongside its mom and my heart melts at the sight.

Never in my life have I encountered, let alone shared, close swimming proximity with anything so large and overpowering. Each one is easily ten times the size of me, maybe more. I shake my head in awe. Feeling a bit bolder, I disentangle myself from Brodie's arm, grab the camera out of his hand and swim a little closer. I look down to make sure the GoPro's recording and it is. *This is going to be insane.*

I film them as they slowly pass in front of me. Up closer, I see the deeper grooves lining their skin, almost giving them a look of rubber or clay. Brodie swims up to my side and takes the camera from me. He urges me to keep swimming, this time I'm to be in the frame. Feeling like a downright mermaid with my giant flounder, I swim like one, pulling my legs together and making big sweeping motions with my long dive fins. I've noticed my lungs have conditioned more from all the free diving these past few months. I can hold my breath for much longer than I originally could.

After inhaling a giant breath, I keep swimming as Brodie follows, filming alongside me, briefly going up for air before he descends deeper down. From the lower depth, he rises, spinning gradually as he swims towards the surface. The vis is so clear, you can see everything. Mel and Jaz swim over beside me and Donnie sees the camera in Brodie's hand and does too. This feeling is second to none. It's similar to how we felt during our dancing stint, but on an entirely higher level. Even underwater and being speechless, we each feel it surge between us.

With so many gentle giants surrounding me, I feel incredibly dwarfed, but they swim with such elegance and grace, it's a humbling feeling. Nothing like Mother Nature to make you feel small in the world. Without the camera, I'm truly able to enjoy the moment which is a rare and liberating feeling for me, enhancing this once in a lifetime experience.

I see the mama whale about to breach and I decide to swim to the surface to see it from above the water. As I tread at the top, I dip my face under, watching in utter astonishment as the whale gains momentum before bursting through the surface. I quickly raise my head up and see fifty feet of pure whale twirl into the open sky before slamming back down, creating shock waves in the water.

*Thank you, Mother Earth. You've outdone yourself yet again.*

Pinching myself to make sure I'm awake, I take the camera back from Brodie and set my sights on Mel and Jaz. I signal to the camera so Mel dives down further, her hair billowing and flowing behind her. I frame my shots and video. She looks back and smiles as she mirrors the whale's position behind her. They swim fluidly in unison. After getting lots of footage, I swim up to the surface and stay there, watching one whale's fin flap down on the water's surface over and over like he's clapping at us or waving goodbye. They begin to slowly move faster than we can keep up and naturally part ways with us. Part of me feels sad because I never want this experience to end, and another part of me is so grateful that I got as much time with them as I did. Gliding on Cloud Nine, the crew treads back towards the boat. As my head bobs above and below the surface, I hear shouts and screams of joy, some muffled underwater and others sounding clear as day. Floating close by the swim-step, but on the port side of the boat, I pull my mask up, resting it on top of my head. I let out an ear piercing shriek, bellowing at the top of my lungs. It's the only way I can begin to articulate my current high on life right now. Everything feels so visceral: the water swooshing between my legs as I tread, the slight breeze on my face, the taste of salt on my lips.

"Is this real life?!" I shout.

Brodie surfaces a few feet away and also yanks up his mask, and swims over right beside me. He clutches my neck, pulling me closer, and plants a passionate kiss on my lips. I still for a millisecond. What about the others? *Who the hell cares, Nina!* Giggling, we break apart as I try to tread and kiss at the same time. We turn around and see Mel, Donnie, Shayno and Jaz peering over the railing, all with giddy expressions to some degree. Even Stella sticks her face out through an opening in the railing, and I swear she's smiling.

"'Bout time, ya galahs," Donnie yells playfully. "Good on ya."

Jaz makes an "aww" face, beaming at us.

I blush and let myself submerge under water. I pop back up and hear them all laughing, especially Brodie. We both climb onboard and they cheer. *Oh, gosh.*

After our "outing," they surprisingly don't really heckle us and or make it too weird, to my relief, and instead recap our incredible encounter.

"Ya seemed so smol next to her," Brodie laughs at Donnie.

"That's a first I reckon," Donnie muses suggestively.

The gang chuckles at him as I stow away my backpack. "Saltwater" by Geowulf plays like a soundtrack over us. The catchy, sunny tune embodies our current climate of happy smiles, sunscreen, salt mist, and an excitement in the ocean air around us. Before we take off, Brodie double checks for the pod. We see spouts blowing off in the far distance in the path where the humpies were headed. Brodie fires the engine and we set course in the opposite direction towards home.

Unofficially officially together, Brodie and I try to spend most of our free time in each other's company. Lately, it hasn't been easy as we're each busy with work and friends. I really enjoy my life here and just because I'm with Brodie doesn't mean I want that to change necessarily. I still want to be with my friends, spend time with Mick, and work when I can. We both have an unspoken agreement that we're not quite ready for any labels or anything like that just yet. Maybe it's because we both want to hold onto it ourselves and keep it special for the time being. It's really new and fresh, and I don't think either of us wants to push that feeling away, plus I've always been a more private person when it comes to any sort of romance. We are what we are: Brodie and Nina; Nina, and Brodie.

I haven't even told my sisters what's happened between us. Somehow saying it aloud to them will only bring about the discussion of the future, and for now, I'm pushing that topic clear out of my mind. I want to enjoy the moment and be present. Now, it's just a bonus when Brodie and I are alone. It's a lot like it was before when we would hang out, only now he'll steal a quick kiss here and there when I'm least expecting it. In turn, when we go for drives, I'll reach over and either hold his hand or lean over to tenderly kiss his neck as he keeps his eyes on the road, smiling.

My favorite moments are when Brodie looks at me. We could be at Mick's playing cards, on the boat with the crew, or anywhere really, and Brodie gives me his happiest Brodie scrunch. I used to think this was a quirk of his, but I've come to realize he only does it when he looks at me. It's his Nina face.

After a nice arvo out on the water with the crew, Shayno announces that his cousin just got a new place in Perth and wants us to come stay for a few days for New Years.

"Hells yeah!" the whole crew shouts in agreement.

I never made it to Perth so I'm super excited. I've heard amazing things about the coastal city. The rest of the crew reiterates how no one's travelled, like really travelled, since before isolation, "iso," hit. Plus it'll be New Years. With it being summertime down here, I completely forgot about all the "winter" holidays.

"Cracka, I'll let her know," Shayno gleefully says. "She mentioned we can come down that Wednesday. Ya guys keen?"

We all look at each other, nodding.

"Yeah, Shayno, lemme check my iso schedule... oh wait, yeah, nah, got nothin'," Mel jokes.

The others laugh and say that day works for them as well. It dawns on me I have an elopement shoot I'm doing for Tippe's niece that Wednesday night...

"Dang, I have that thing with Fiona," I say aloud, frowning at Mel.

"Ugh, right, but Neens, ya gotta come," she whines.

"We'll fly down Thursday," Brodie states matter-of-factly.

I look at him, asking him with a face that reads: *you sure?*

"Besides, I've a charta that arvo too," he explains. "Then we'll meet up for the rest of the weekend, eh."

Everyone else nods excitedly, including Mel, who claps her hands together happily. After the boys get the boat on the trailer, we all hug and say our goodbyes.

"See ya, cobbers," Brodie shouts, hastily piling into the ute.

He shuts the door quickly, sliding in beside me. He normally waits and is the last to leave, but today he shifts the ute in gear and pushes his foot down on the gas. He seems really eager to get back. We wave as we pass the others getting into their cars, and head down the highway.

We're only about a mile away from home when I realize Mick's gone tonight, visiting Gus. Prepping for the turn off to Mick's, Brodie takes his foot off the gas ahead of time, preserving his brakes. I scoot closer to him and lean over to kiss his neck.

"You know," I say flirtatiously, in between kisses, "Mick's away at his friend's for the night."

Brodie emits a small sound of elation, and plays along, "Is that right?"

I feel the truck maintain its current speed.

"And I've been thinking," I breathe seductively into his neck, and see him shiver ever so slightly, "I really don't want to be alone tonight."

Brodie bites his lip, keeping his eyes on the road.

"Yeah, nah, we can't have that now, can we?" he agrees, in mock seriousness.

I move down to his collarbone, kissing it thoroughly and skim my closed lips along the bone from his neck to his shoulder and back. He lets out a tiny whistle and scrunches his nose slightly as we pass the turn off and maintain due course straight to his place. Continuing my efforts, I slide my hand under his shirt, and glide it up slowly across his taught stomach, playfully twisting the small sprouting patch of chest hair with my fingers. Stella sits in the backseat with her head out the window.

We turn down Brodie's red dirt road and drive to the house. Brodie pulls us up in front and turns off the ignition. I readily shift my weight onto his lap, placing my arms around his neck. He giggles as he lightly holds me around my waist, then stills, patiently allowing me to continue with my little game. I grip the back of his head, getting a fistful of short curls in my hands as I pull his face to mine. After a few minutes we come up for air. He looks me in the eyes, his face just inches from my own.

"Ya sure ya want me?" he asks, slightly joking.

"I'll have you any way I can, Brodie Pryce," I whisper, nodding my head and smiling from my soul.

"Yull stay the night with me?" he reiterates.

I roll my eyes, and start to pull myself off his lap. He grips me with his strong arms, pinning me in place. Playfully, I look away. Trying to meet my eyes directly, Brodie mirrors my movements as I shake my head back and forth in jest. He follows my gaze until our eyes finally lock.

"I mean it, Nina, I'm yars, howeva ya want," he whispers, leaning towards my ear as he squeezes me. Then he begins singing. "*We can take it slow if you want to, we can have a good time if you want to, we can get, we can get down if you want to, buy another round if you want to, do it in the wickedest style if you want to. We'll do everything that you want to... As long as I'm with you.*"

I feel a giant bubble of laughter emerging from my stomach and I let myself go to pieces. I do love that song.

"Bravo," I say, entertained and impressed by his musical pun.

"Especially the part 'do it in the wickedest style,' eh," he says, cocking an eyebrow, looking hopeful. "What can I say? Imma bloody bloke afta all."

"Ya never know," I tease, pecking his cheek as I open the door and jump out with Stella on my heels.

Turning to close the door, I wink at him. He sits behind the wheel, smiling after me as I make my way into the house to turn on the air. After we unload the boat and clean everything, I head back inside. The A/C should be kicking in by now. As I'm glancing through the kitchen cupboards trying to decide what to make for dinner, I vaguely hear Brodie shuffling vehicles out front. I bob my head to the sound of "Vale" by Maribou State, scanning the refrigerator, when Brodie's hands slide around my waist.

"Just trying to figure out dinner," I explain, smiling.

"Not so fast," Brodie exclaims, whirling me around to face him. "Close yar eyes." I do so squinting in surprise and confusion. It's hard to consciously keep your eyelids shut, and I can feel them dance slightly from the effort. "Ugh, uh, no peekin', Neens, it's a surprise, eh."

I feel a piece of fabric - a shirt of his by the smell of it - softly fold around my eyes and head.

"Brodie, what are you doing?" I chuckle, but don't protest.

"Nope, Stel, ya gotta stay here, I'm afraid," he tells her.

*Why can't Stella come?*

Blindly, he leads me outside, carefully down the front steps as he guides me into, what I feel, is the Trooper. Laughing, I settle into the seat, surrendering to his request. I hear the door shut, confirming my suspicions. Suddenly, I hear and feel his door open and he starts the engine. Without sight, my other senses enhance so I deeply feel every little bump and rock we hit on the road.

"Brodie, where are you taking me?" I ask completely bewildered, but he just chuckles. "If you're thinking about kidnapping me, I think it's too late. I'd already have Stockholm Syndrome."

He doesn't say anything, but I feel the wheels hit hard ground, briefly followed by more uneven ground. We jostle for a minute or two more. I brace myself as Brodie turns the ute in a giant half circle. The ute shifts in reverse and I smell the ocean. I hear the door open and close as he jumps out. He busies himself with something for a minute then returns and opens my door. He carefully helps me out of the car and unties my blindfold. The shirt falls to the ground, revealing the SeaDoo floating in the shallows.

"It's no biggie, but..." Brodie shrugs, gesturing to the ski.

My face erupts into the biggest smile, my eyes rounding huge.

"You know I've been dying to ride one of these. Why now? Why tonight?"

I don't really care what the reason is, I'm just stoked this is finally happening. After my failed attempt with Big Al, then my mishap with Jordan, I've yet to get on a ski for fun, until now. I peel off my clothes. It's pushing high temps this arvo. Brodie also sheds off his shirt and hands me a thin life vest. A memory of my past encounter with Jordan flashes in my mind, but I shake the thought away just as quickly. I pull it on, guiding my hands and arms through the holes, and adjust it over my shoulders. I leave it unzipped at the moment.

*New memory to erase the old, Nina.*

As if reading my mind, Brodie walks up and stands in front of me. He slowly grasps my life vest with both hands and gently pulls me to him. He hesitates before my face, only inches from me and waits, his expression endearingly patient. I know what he's doing. He's asking my permission, a clear acknowledgement and nod to my previous unhappy encounter. He wants me to know he's different and in doing so is showing me. He's giving me the choice to decide this time. Without question, I lean forward, bridging the gap between us, and accept his invitation wholeheartedly with a grin and a quick smooch on the cheek. Like I said before, while Jordan is forceful and a brute, Brodie's strength comes from being sweet, caring, thoughtful, and, above all, respectfully gentle. There's no question of a comparison between the two. Brodie is, and always will be, an infinitely better man. I smile at the thought.

He reaches down and lightly zips my vest, steadily pulling the zipper all the way to the top in one swift motion.

"Alrighty, then," he says eagerly.

He locks the ute and places the key on top of the back tire, and then helps me up onto the ski. He jumps up and graciously moves around me and sits down. I grab his torso with ease, pulling myself closer to him. I hug his back and bury my face into his vest when he starts the engine. Both of my hands latch on tightly around his waist, and I smile into his back, feeling my heart ignite, buzzing from enthusiasm.

"Waddayareckon'?" Brodie asks, twisting his head back to me.

He has his phone out, scrolling through his music.

*Hmmm. What am I feeling?*

"Um, 'Kiss You All Over.' Exile," I answer, chuckling.

"Nice one, Neens," he snorts. "I'll add a bitta Yacht Rock too."

The song starts and he cranks the volume. In jest of my musical pun, I lean forward and plant a couple of quick kisses along his neck and shoulders as we wade towards deeper depths. The sun is already dropping low in the sky. We probably only have an hour or so before sunset. Brodie places both hands on the steering handles and punches the ski forward, moving fast. We leave a trail of mist in our wake as we head along the coast. We ride for about twenty minutes, not speaking. I occasionally squeal with delight as we see a turtle or ray, and even tense when Brodie slows down to admire another bloody sea snake, but shockingly he just watches and doesn't try to jump off to get a closer look. Our speed drops to a cruising pace as we glide along the shallows to a remote part of the coast I haven't seen yet.

"'Slow Ride' please," I lean up, requesting it in his ear.

He nods and within seconds, sounds of The Lulu Raes fill our airwaves. The ski has decent speakers, especially when maneuvering at slower speeds.

This moment feels like something out of a movie. There are nooks and crannies, almost like caves, in the rocky coastline as they embrace the water's edge. Brodie informs me that you can only access this spot via the water, so it's private and remote. Seeing a smaller alcove, I assume he's going to steer us there, but he kills the engine instead. He twists in his seat so he's facing me and he bites his lip.

"Finally, all bloody alone at last," he sighs in appreciation. He scoots me closer to him, pulling my legs up over his, so I'm basically straddling his lap. He tilts his head up and smothers me in a passionate kiss, before he breaks away for a second. "Just makin' up for lost time."

I lean forward as he leans back, and we collectively recline on the seat. My life vest bunches around my neck in slight discomfort and annoyance. I pull it down, but it slides right back up. Over the impediment, I hastily unzip my vest, and Brodie does the same. We each pull them off quickly, laughing. Brodie grabs mine and tosses them both on the steering handles to hang.

Things get a little heated between us and quickly. We're practically consuming one another's lips, breath, necks and chests. *I wonder how long these lustful feelings will last?* Sometimes it feels like we're depraved teenagers... I don't stop to linger on this thought for too long. My arms move lower down Brodie's back as I suggestively pull his hips towards me. He reaches for my hands and stills them, chuckling.

"I can't do this," he stammers.

I freeze. *What?! Is he rejecting me?*

This fear must cross my face because he promptly explains, "Nah, Neens, it's not like that. Of course, I want ya. More than ya reckon, but this isn't how I imagined spendin' our first real time togetha."

I raise both eyebrows, trying to understand.

"What happened to 'wickedest style if you want to'?" I jest, mocking his earlier comment.

"I do. I just want to savour it is all."

"But it's not our first time together," I point out blatantly. "*Coco palm.*"

"Nah, yeah, but this'll be our first time *togetha* togetha..."

His voice trails off. I can start to see where he's coming from. Honestly, it's really sweet on his behalf. Before was a night of long overdue passion when we didn't know where we stood, but now, while we've done our fair share of kissing and then some, we've never fully slept together since we "declared" ourselves.

"That's sweet," I sigh into his mouth, going in for another kiss. *Maybe my actions will dissuade him*. "But you know, we *have* been *together* together, so I don't see what the big deal is."

I never thought I'd make love on a jet ski, but now that we aren't, I find myself remiss of the lost opportunity. As my hand trails lower, he grabs it, and stops me with a laugh.

"Neens, please, let's at least wait til we're on dry land," he asks, hopeful for a compromise.

"Fine. Who am I to stop you from being romantic?" I mutter, pulling back. "But promise me we'll revisit the ski idea at a later date?"

"Cross my heart, Sunshine," he pledges, laughing.

"Well, okay, then," I amend, sitting up straight as he straightens as well. "You're going to still touch me, right?"

He narrows his eyes at me and starts the ski. We both put our vests back on, but leave them unzipped as Brodie leads us into the tiny alcove not far away. We have to pass through a naturally chiseled archway and once through, the cove opens up to a tiny sandy beach, all blanketed in shade. The last remnants of light shoot out in sun rays though the tunnel opening.

Brodie turns off the SeaDoo and we coast onto the sand, beaching ourselves. Like a respectful gentleman, he hops down and extends a hand out to me, offering me assistance down. I land with a small *thud* in the sand. Slowly, Brodie walks up to me and gently, almost like in slow motion, takes my neck in his hands and softly pulls my lips to his. I close my eyes, just enjoying the sweet and innocent sensation.

"I neva said I wasn't keen to pash," he laughs.

"Pash?"

"Passionately kiss as they say," Brodie educates me in a dramatic tone.

Man, these Aussies and their abbreviations. Just when I think I'm getting them wired, new ones sprout up like weeds.

It's bloody warm out, so Brodie hoists me up in an embrace and runs, carrying me out into the crystal clear lagoon. With our arms wrapped around each other, we barrel into the calm waters. Emerging above, we laugh as we shake off the salty liquid from our eyes. Our current pose reminds me of our first night together. It seems like so long ago, but also like it was yesterday. Smiling, I give Brodie a squeeze and look out as the sun drops towards the horizon. My head leans on his and we both blissfully watch the magic happening right before our eyes. The light's perfectly framed in the center of the arch. Brodie suddenly breaks apart and runs through the shallows to the ski where he opens up the hatch door and pulls out my camera. He must of stashed it in there, knowing I'd want it, which I do. *He really does think of everything*. I meet him back on the sand and start by taking pics of the dying light coming through the tunnel. I sneak a couple of close ups of Brodie when he's not looking, but he catches wind and begins making silly poses. He plucks the camera out of my grasp and demands to take some portraits of me.

"You're asking the wrong girl," I chuckle.

"Ah, come on, Neens, ya just need practice is all."

"For real, Brodie, I'm the worst. I prefer being *behind* the camera for a reason."

He walks over to me, and looking the part of the photographer, directs me to lay down on the beach with the ocean behind me. Doing as he commands, I lie down on my stomach, propping myself up by my elbows. He places my forearms across one another and pulls my curly hair to one side, while also grabbing a piece of it so it falls over my collarbone. I must admit, he's taking the part seriously. I stifle a giggle, but play along. My banana suit rides up my butt a little. I go to adjust it.

"Leave it," he says. "Yar perfect."

I roll my eyes at him and relent.

"You're not gonna ask me to take my top off are you, Mr. Photographer?" I ask innocently, mocking the cultural stereotype.

"Only if ya want," he chortles, "but I think yar banga just how yar are, suit 'n all."

"Good, cause I wouldn't," I reply, satisfied by his answer.

He snaps some photos as I laugh and look around the alcove.

"Eh, this is great fun," he realizes, looking at the camera.

I motion for him to show me some, and he kneels down beside me and scrolls through the thumbnails on screen. Expecting to hate them, I unknowingly gasp. I must admit I look good, but more than that—.

"Whaddayareckon'?" he asks. "Ya look—."

"Happy."

Wow, the girl in the photo is beaming. She's healthy, elated, and loved, not only by her new found friends here, but also by herself - *most importantly herself*. I don't think I've ever seen myself look so blatantly fulfilled. The time of day and shade make my salty, bleached brown hair stand out against my tan arms. The light pieces accent my celadon eyes, making them pop. Giving myself a mini once-over, I smile in reflection. I've been swimming with whale sharks and humpback whales and most importantly have had some of the best moments of my life lately. Being so far from home, rallying myself after my accident, I'm stronger than I thought, braver than I thought. I hum contently to myself.

Brodie beckons me to get up as he balances my camera on the seat of the ski, and hits the timer button. I rush to his side and grab his torso with my arm, taking a nice photo. He repeats the motion and runs quickly to my side as the countdown sounds off. I smile, and just before the shutter goes off, Brodie kisses me on the cheek, and I laugh closing my eyes. *Click!* We do one more, and this time, both of us go in for a kiss. The light wind kicks up my curly wispies, swirling them around my face. The shutter goes off again, but Brodie doesn't pull away and instead only deepens his kiss. Too worried about my camera falling into the water, I run over and grab it and lock it back up safely in the stow-away cabinet. It seems to be getting darker by the minute now that the sun's disappearing for the evening. I sigh. I guess that's our cue. I look around, taking in all of these incredible surroundings before clamoring onto the ski. Brodie pushes it off the beach before climbing onto the seat himself.

Out of the alcove, there's still plenty of residual light left overflowing in the sky, churning together pinks and oranges. We jet off back towards home. Halfway back to the ute, Brodie slows the ski and offers me a chance to drive. I jump at the chance. I remember really liking this part of it. He brushes me up on the basics and I steer us towards the beach. Admittedly, it takes us longer than if Brodie was driving, but he doesn't seem to care at all. With each passing minute, I gain more confidence as a ski driver and accelerate a little more. I feel Brodie squeeze my waist, holding on, and I let out a giant ear piercing scream, grinning ear to ear.

*This is marvelous!*

The sea is extra calm and glassy tonight so the ski smoothly carves along the surface. The ute waits for us only a few dozen feet away now. Brodie taps my leg, signaling me to slow down a little. I do, shaking my head in awe at the sheer fun of being so close to the water. Brodie reaches over my shoulder and kills the engine to a lulling idle. It's much quieter now as we glide towards shore.

"Okay, that was the coolest thing ever! I can see why you always want to drive," I say, chuckling. "It's addicting!"

He snorts in amusement and jumps off in the shallows, running to get the ute started. The tide must be dropping because the entire trailer sits dry on the sand now. Brodie backs up the trailer a few feet directly in front of me. He leans out the window and instructs me to steer it onto the platform. I do it with such precision it connects without a hitch. I'm not going to lie, I'm kind of impressed with myself. I climb into the ute and we drive the minute drive back to Brodie's.

After greeting Stella, Brodie suggests I take a hot shower while he deals with the ski. Standing under the shower head, I relax and let the water flow down my head and face. The shampoo and conditioner smells of coconut. I think back to our time at the coco palm and feel slightly excited about what tonight may bring.

Barely rinsing out my hair, I have this theory about tropics and curly hair, and have tested it now with ample success. Back in The States, I normally wash my hair every couple of days and then put some product in after to help with the frizz. But out here, in the more coastal environment and being in the ocean every day, I rarely shampoo it. The buildup of salt actually completely eliminates all frizz, and I'm left with the best version of my hair I could ever imagine. I still rinse it and comb it out in the water, but the salt spray and ocean are the best things that's ever happened to me.

Stepping out of the shower, I realize I don't have many options in the clothing department, and I left my pack in the ute. Really not wanting to put my wet bathing suit back on without letting it dry a little first, I wrap the towel around me and crack open the door, trying to figure out what to do. I step out and bump into my backpack. Shaking my head, I smile. I should have known. Brodie must have placed it directly in front of the door for me, knowing I'd need something to change into. I grab it and push the door closed behind me. I unzip the top compartment, feeling a little hopeless. Rooting around my camera and my small Stasher Bag of toiletries, I realize that's the one drawback to being a light packer... if the opportunity arises for the need to look cute, you're more than likely S.O.L as Mick would say - *shit outta luck.* I reach back into the separate compartment and find a ball of fabric. I pull it out and unfold it, revealing my white, billowy sundress. *That'll do.* I shimmy it over my head and it falls nicely over my curvaceous hips. I don't have a bra, but decide to just go with it. Honestly, it feels amazing to be "free" and airy in this heat, and the fabric is tight enough against my well endowed chest, so it mostly holds the ladies in place.

I open some bathroom drawers, trying to find a brush.

"Whaddaya doin', Neens?" I hear Brodie say in amusement, behind me.

I freeze, caught in the act.

"Just invading your privacy, looking for a brush. You know, to tame the wild beast," I retort playfully.

He snorts and comes up directly behind me, and reaches over my side, opening the top drawer. I don't know why I didn't look there first. *Duh.* He grabs a blue brush and hands it to me. He pauses, holding me with both hands lightly at my hips and leans in. He closes his eyes as he smells my wet hair by my temple.

"Mmm, coconuts. Smells betta on ya," he says with a crooked smile.

He sees my wadded up bikini on the counter and grabs it to hang in it on the outside line to dry.

"Thanks, I'll be out in just a sec."

"Dun worry, no rush," he mentions, walking off.

I brush out my hair thoroughly and then flip it over a couple of times so it hopefully doesn't dry weird and frizzy on top. Having curly hair is like playing a game of craps every day. *Life's always a gamble.* Standing up straight, I look at myself in the mirror and smile. I'm right where I want to be. Feeling refreshed, I tidy up the bathroom and make my way to the living room; it's empty. Where's Brodie? And Stella?

All natural light is gone and the house seems a touch darker than usual with only the living room corner lamp on. I wander into the kitchen and see the front slider door open wide. I hear music playing lightly, and as I get closer, it gets louder. Gerry Rafferty's voice fills the air, singing "Right Down the Line." I love this song. It easily brings in the good vibes. I walk through the open doorway and stop in my tracks.

The porch table dons an assortment of mottlecah, a local wildflower. Its fuchsia coloring pops out against the wooden table as its yellow pointed pistons dust the tops of its bottlebrush looking blooms. A cousin to eucalyptus, its green leaves look picturesque lying along the center of the tablescape. To make it all even more romantic, little white candles flicker flames of light, sporadically dispersed through the greenery. I always laugh in movies or tv shows when a character just happens to have a hundred candles on hand, but here, there's a realistic amount of four. Two settings of black plates and white linen napkins are placed across from each other, along with a bottle of some alcoholic beverage and two glasses. Beaming, I look at it in awe, soaking it all in. Best part of all is Brodie sits facing me, clearly waiting for my arrival.

"There's our girl," he says to Stel, while looking at me.

"Brodie," I mutter simply, in awe.

Clearly pleased with my reaction, he gets up and walks over to me. I notice he wears a buttoned up Spooner with actual khaki shorts. I don't think I've ever seen him in real attire before other than his fancy linen suit. Kissing me softly on the cheek first, he takes my hand and guides me over to my chair. Being a gentleman, he pushes my chair in for me as I sit. He takes his seat across from me.

Suddenly, I'm taken aback by the aroma. It's absolutely mouth watering. Overwhelmed by all of the incredible visuals, my head almost sways from the amazing sensory overload. I bite my lower lip in happiness, glowing at Brodie. He returns my radiant countenance with one of the biggest Nina face scrunches I've ever seen. Laughing in mirth, I don't even know what to say. Brodie picks up the bottle and pops the cork. His eyes grow big as small bubbles overflow.

"Champagne!" I lick my lips. "It's—."

"Yar favourite. I rememba," he says confidently, pouring us each a full glass. "I almost went with wine because, ya know, but I wanted tonight to be different."

He must be really excited about tonight. Shaking in felicitous mirth, I accept my glass wholeheartedly and take a deep sip. I close my eyes as the sweet flavor and bubbles slide down my throat. I glance over at Stella, who lies on the top deck step with her head lying between her two paws. Taking a moment, I look around at our view around Brodie's property. Brodie must catch me, because I see him do it as well out of my peripheral. The evening is gorgeous and utterly still. You can only hear some little birds chirping in the distance. It's so still and quiet I swear you can hear the stars twinkle as they dip into the ocean. Due to the candlelight, our surroundings are darker than usual, allowing us to revel in the heaven's spectacular illumination.

"Gosh, this view's..." I raise my shoulders, looking for the right word.

"Bloody beautiful."

I turn to find him only staring at me. *Is he even real?* At times, he's like a character out of a work of fiction. I smile into my shoulder, the feeling of admiration still new and bizarre. I take another sip of champagne.

"Brodie, I never knew you to be the overly romantic type. I mean you always think of everything in the most sweet and thoughtful way, but this..." I say happily, gesturing to his efforts around me.

"I suppose ya bring out a different side is all," he replies, smiling as he tops off our drinks.

I narrow my eyes, showing him I'm pleased to hear that. I feel his foot under the table and I gently nudge it. He taps mine back.

"What do we owe to this special occasion?" I ask, completely curious.

He leans back in his chair. His eyebrows narrow slightly, contemplating his response as he sips some more from his champagne. Just as his mouth opens to answer, a timer rings off on his phone. I'm a little surprised he even used one; he never does. He must be really serious about his fish tonight. He stands up and casually goes to the grill and lifts the lid. Out wafts the most drool worthy smell. I make my way to help, when he orders me to stay seated.

"Sit back 'n enjoy yarself, Neens."

It feels so strange to just chill idly by, but he insists on it. I watch him as he grabs and preps our plates.

"I don't know when you had time to do all this, Brodie," I muse. "I mean, truly, I'm impressed."

"I was ready just in case," he pleasantly shrugs. "I reckon I had hope is all. I learnt that from you."

He sets down a plate in front of me. It's full of grilled white fish, freshly toasted veggies, and a side salad. It looks like something out of a cooking magazine. He even places a small flower on the corner of my plate as a beautiful garnish. I grin up at him then reset my sights back on this incredible meal. After giving Stella her fish dinner, Brodie rejoins the table with his own plate. He nods, signaling me to dig in, and I do. I take a bite of fish and moan in delight at the mouth watering flavor. Oh my goodness, it's incredibly tender.

"I marinated it with Refrigerator Door. It's been in the fridge since yestaday," he says proudly, taking his own bite. He moans a little. "Wow, even I gotta admit, that tucker's ripper. That flava is bloody aces."

"Right?" I say, pleased. "Okay, this is out of this world good."

We both sit and revel in the amazing, decadent flavors. He laughs as I try to pinpoint the specific ingredients of his concoction. I swear Brodie could be a chef somewhere and even suggest it. He laughs and says where on earth could he work with us being so remote out here.

"Besides, I'd neva leave here," he adds. "It's home."

I wouldn't either. But I know I have to at some point. The thought makes my food catch in my throat.

I must frown slightly, because Brodie asks, "What's the matta?"

Shaking my head, I fake cough to hide any concern.

"Went down the wrong pipe is all," I mutter, taking another sip of champagne to wash it down.

As we finish dinner, we discuss topics of music, our upcoming work, Mick, and our mutual friends. Brodie's in the middle of telling me how he and Mel's families grew up close friends and neighbors. He and Mel were always friendly in that regard, but it was him and Margot who got close.

I start to laugh.

"I thought you two were a couple when I first saw you together," I tease. "You know, at the ice cream shop."

"Actually, I'm pretty sure ya saw us at the pub before that." Squinting, I look back, racking through my internal memory reel. He leans in, cockily smiling. "She was the leggy blonde givin' ya the eye, sittin' at the booth the first night I saw ya with Old Mick at the pub."

"Can I tell you a secret?" I whisper, leaning closer to him. He nods excitedly like we're in school as I hunch my shoulders towards him and snort. "I used to call Margot 'Leggy Blonde' before I knew who she was."

I go to pieces laughing at myself and Brodie chimes in with me. Reigning myself in, I can't help but want to know the answer to the lingering question I've always had regarding Margot. It's none of my business, but honestly, I'm so curious. I can't tell if I'd be bothered or indifferent if my suspicions are confirmed. I take the opportunity to ask.

"So were you ever together?" I ask bluntly, just coming out with it.

He narrows his eyes at me, and demurely smirks. The anticipation is killing me. My eyes loom larger as I wait. Chuckling, he leans back, and shakes his head.

"Nah, neva," he explains. "Though I reckon she tried. A few times, too."

Hmm, that's surprising and fascinating. Funny to think he would be interested in me when he had the Viking Queen banging down his doorstep.

*Nina, you're "banger." Give yourself more credit.*

"What, leggy blondes aren't your type?" I say lightheartedly, yet still intrigued.

"Yeah, nah, I prefer brunettes, preferably short ones with giant Tarzan hair who hate spiders 'n have a knack for gettin' pissed afta a drink or two." I throw my rolled napkin at his head which he dodges easily, and he laughs. "Keen on dessert?"

"Wait, dessert?" I reply, stupefied.

He stands up, bends down to blow out the candles, and takes my hand. I look back at the table, not wanting to leave the mess, but he interrupts me.

"Dun worry, it'll still be here when we get back."

He whistles for Stel to follow us as we head to the ute, climb in, and take off. After wondering for a good while where in the world he's taking me now, we pull up to the little car port, in front of the ice cream shoppe, and park. I turn to open my passenger door.

"Ugh, ugh," he mutters quickly, running to open the door for me. "Two shakes."

I nod at him in thanks as he ushers me out like a gentleman.

We begin to walk side by side when Brodie reaches down and freely takes my hand in his, interlacing our fingers together. I've never publicly held hands before, so the simple act feels oddly bold, yet sweet and sends happy somersaults in my stomach. After weeks of keeping our "thing" to ourselves, it feels rather unsettling, yet liberating to make ourselves known to our little town. News will get back to Mick sooner rather than later depending on who sees us. The gossip pipeline travels at light speed around here. I suppose it's time to tell him face to face, rather than leave him to his assumptions or hear it second hand. I think he can tell something's been going on between us, but he doesn't pry, and ultimately I know he just wants me to be happy.

With Stella on our heels, we get in line. This is by far the busiest I've seen the stand thus far. Pushing well into October, the summer season is well underway so the temperatures grow warmer by the day. Without realizing it, I lean into Brodie's side. He lets go of my hand as he wraps an arm around me. I catch a couple of curious glances from some older women. Brodie notices me noticing them and he squeezes my shoulder. I lean into the crook of his arm and look up at him, feeling puckish.

"They're probably shocked to see the elusive bachelor Brodie Pryce holding the American girl in his arms," I tease. "Wait, unless you do this often. Do you? Am I just a flavor of the week? Pun intended."

He snorts, shaking his head as we move up the line.

"So what's yar fancy this time, eh?" he muses, changing the subject. "Is it that bizarre combo ya ordered last time or a classy cone?"

I study the menu board which stands at my side.

"Hmmm," I hum to myself, trying to decide, "a shaved ice does sound amazing right now, but so does a cone..."

With my fingers, I play innie-minnie-miny-moe, going back and forth between the two. Brodie looks over at me and raises his eyebrows.

"Are ya playin' a carpet grubber's game?" he whispers in my ear, sounding surprised.

I shrug. I don't get what's so weird about that, but apparently he finds it funny.

"Dang it, I've lost track. Thanks," I mutter sarcastically, as we move closer to the ordering window. Having finally come to a conclusion, I state proudly, "I think I want a good old fashioned vanilla cone."

"'N I wanna chokkie."

"We make a swirl, you and I," I chuckle, feeling punny for the second time in ten minutes. *I think that's a first for me.*

He squeezes my arm in jest, and the person in front of us finishes their order and steps out of the way. We walk to the front window, standing side by side, about a foot apart. Andy faces us through the opening. He sees me and his eyes light up, clearly very excited. I give him a friendly smile which makes his eyes open wider.

"Nina!" he hollers.

Brodie stifles a snort, and I stealthily kick him with my foot.

"Hi, Andy, how are you?" I greet him. "It's been a while."

"Oy, Miss Nina, I'm banga, but not as banga as ya look tonight," he exclaims, blatantly looking me up and down.

"Aw, Andy, stop being so nice," I reply with grace, taken aback at the compliment and uncomfortable with the ogling.

Brodie puts his arm around me and looks Andy straight in the face. Andy notices Brodie's hand placement around my waist and his countenance darkens slightly. I lean in the window and order my vanilla cone and Brodie's chocolate one. Andy insists mine is on the house, before asking full price for Brodie's. Now it's my turn to stifle a giggle. Andy retreats, filling our cones to the brim with frozen soft serve - well mine's to the brim, the chocolate one is definitely smaller. He hands me mine first, which dons a cherry on top, then gives Brodie his. I lightly jab Brodie's side, and turn to him, making eyes from him to the tip jar. He sighs and leaves a couple bucks.

"Thanks again, Andy," I say loudly, turning to leave. "It's by far the best cone around. Take care, and have a good one."

I part with a happy grin and he seems very pleased with the attention, restoring the chipper look to his face as he waves me goodbye. I meet up with Brodie a couple of feet away, with Stella walking next to him.

"Don't say a word," I warn him playfully. He just chortles as he licks away at his cone. I guffaw, biting off the top part of my ice cream. "The kid is easily half my age, and just that, a *kid*."

"Can't blame the bloke," Brodie says, with a mouth full of ice cream as he appreciatively stares in my direction.

"I just don't get it. Being invisible for so long, I came here and now I get all sorts of looks and stares," I explain, completely baffled.

I shake my head and skip off along the dock towards the beach with Stel in tow. Brodie runs to catch up. As we walk along the shoreline, side by side, we eat our ice cream in the quiet peace along the tiny waves. Little marina lights glow around us, brightening our way. We circle back and wander along the harbor, admiring the smaller boats and charters. A seal swims by below us, and Stella pops her head through the slits in the railing and cocks her head at it. They have a stare down.

As we stand, leaning on the banister, Brodie tells me about his work, how it's slower than normal due to the lack of tourists, but how he's also thankful for the work he's had, considering. He explains how luckily 2019 was one of his best years to date, and how naturally, he's a saver being a simpleton; it doesn't take much to live on when he either grows or catches his food and spends all of his time out on the water.

"When work is living, it's a bit easier," he admits. "My home, the boat, 'n petrol are really the main concerns." He laughs. "Oh, 'n coldies. They've always gotta be on the list, specially for the lads.

"So thanks be to God that I was somewhat prepared for this year. I'm not sayin' I'm rich, cause that's far from the truth, but I've got everythin' I need 'n want right here. I can still live with the freedom to choose how I want to live at the moment."

He stills for a minute, donning an abashed expression. "Honestly though, I'm grateful for this pandemic. That's a terrible thing to say with so many sick 'n what not... but it gave me you."

While I lose my thought in Brodie's sweet confession, the light catches his face. His nose and chin are covered in chocolate smears. I hold in a laugh and turn him to fully face me. Going back to his statement, I understand exactly what he means about not needing more, about simple pleasures and experiences bringing life fulfillment rather than things. I stand on my tiptoes and reach up, gently kissing the tip of his nose with my lips. Yummy chocolate floods my tastebuds. I reach up and aptly wipe off the dark smear on his chin with my finger then put my finger in my mouth, carefully licking the chocolate off. I pull back and take another bite from my vanilla cone.

"That's not fair," he whines. "Whadda 'bout me?"

"What about you?"

Grabbing my hand, he guides my cone towards his mouth. When it gets within an inch of it, I jab it forward, smashing it onto his face. He takes a step back, smirking with white liquid plastered all over his nose, mouth, and chin. I crack up, laughing. I lost about half of my cone, but that was so worth it. In fact, now I have my favorite part, the crunchy tail end of cone mixing with the last bit of ice cream, all to be eaten in one or two swift bites. I look up and see Brodie scarfing the rest of his cone quickly as he stands hunched over, trying not to get vanilla and melted chocolate all over himself. Chewing my final bite of ice cream, I stick out my tongue at him. He hastily walks up and pulls me into a jaw shattering kiss, the melted ice cream blending together in a literal swirl. Kissing a sticky mouth feels so funny and weird as I taste the vanilla and remnants of his chocolate ice cream. We pull apart as a figure walks past us. Snorting in hilarity, I bend down and let Stella shower me in kisses while she also licks off any stray sticky sugar from my face. Miraculously, I manage to keep my white dress clean.

We pass a public outdoor shower near the beach and Brodie takes the opportunity to wash off his hands and face. Dripping, he walks over and shakes off like a dog. Stel and I stand, watching him in amusement. Shaking his hands as a last ditch effort, he wipes them on his dry khakis. He resumes his position next to me and we walk side by side back towards the carpark, looking out at the water, and enjoying the natural rhythm of the ocean.

"All I want in this life is my girl, 'n my *otha* girl," he says with ease, clasping my hand in his as he gestures to Stella, "'n to be out on the wata, under the sun, listening to some good tunes."

"Then we want the same thing," I whisper sincerely.

We both smile at that happy and important truth.

The shaved ice shop comes into view. A thought from earlier comes creeping back in.

"So you dodged this earlier," I say, "which I just now realized, but I have to know, did you do this often? This whole dating thing?"

He sighs deeply and spots a bench. He sits and I join him. *Oh gosh, this is worthy of a sit down chat?* As he pulls me closer, Stella jumps up and lays her head on the other side of Brodie, closing her eyes in bliss. I rest my head on his shoulder and smile down at her sweet face.

He looks back and forth between us and breathes, "My girls."

The thought makes my heart swell.

I lightly poke him in the ribs.

"Come on, tell me. No mater how bad it is," I demand softly.

"Nah, it's not like that," Brodie replies, sighing. "Well maybe it was. I'm not gonna lie, Neens, I've had my fair share of moments with the ladies." We sit in silence for a beat. I can hear the faint lapping sounds of the water in front of us. "Do ya wanna hear more?"

As Brodie fidgets, I can tell he'd rather leave it alone.

"Only if you want to tell me," I respond earnestly.

Knowing Brodie and how amazing he is, not only his looks and physicality but also his personality and his soul, I'd be a fool to think he's been a monk all his life. I tell him just as much.

He laughs and leans his head on mine.

"Most were only dalliances," he says. "I don't even reckon any of 'em eva understood me, let alone my soul."

My head lightly moves up and down on his chest as he breathes steadily. With my finger, I lightly caress the skin along his jawline, feeling his freshly shaved chin. When on earth did he manage to squeeze in a shave??

"I'm sorry for that, they missed out big time," I mutter apologetically.

"I'm not," he replies, with conviction. "I don't reckon I was ready... 'n besides it all led me here, to you."

I grin. It's true. One way or another, it doesn't matter.

"And that's why I don't need to know anything more. The rest is history," I kindly suggest. "Let's leave it there."

We smile at each other before I playfully nudge him and jump up, running with Stella back towards the car. Chuckling, Brodie jogs after us.

We drive back home, meandering along the highway. The headlights shine on the paved road. There are no street lights or manmade structures out here, so at night, driving is literally driving in the dark. I lean my head on the window, being lulled by the passing asphalt, rolling underneath us. "Our House" by Crosby, Stills, Nash & Young cozily plays through the speakers. I stifle a yawn, and feel Brodie's hand, resting on my leg. We pull up to his house and I slowly clamor out towards the porch. Brodie matches my stride, and gently pulls me by my outstretched arm. We pass the fragments of our wonderful dinner and head straight inside. Brodie offers Stella a bone and she runs off with it happily. The house is dimly lit. Neither one of us says a word as Brodie leads me straight to his room. Without signal or discussion, we both take a slow pace. I queue up some Norah Jones on the player, and her sultry voice creates a nice background ambiance.

Brodie sits on the edge of his bed, waiting for me with a sentimental smile as I pull off my boots. I make my way to him and carefully place my arms around his neck. His hands come up to my sides and I feel their heat through the billowy fabric of my dress. Leaning down, we affectionately meet in a kiss. My hair falls in tendrils like a waterfall around his face and cheeks. I pull most of it back to one side of my neck. He thoughtfully kisses me in the most innocent manner before lifting me onto his lap. He lips touch the nape of my neck as I inhale, breathing in his scent. Very slowly, we fall back onto the mattress, with me lying on top of him.

Using his hands, he inches the hem of my dress upward above my hips. He leans up and thoughtfully lifts his shirt, peeling it off. I delightfully rake in his toned stomach. Looking at me, he waits with a question in his eyes. I nod willingly and smile with my eyes.

Our last time together was full of built up tension and downright lust. This time is different. We move together tenderly, showing our mutual deep affection for one another. Unthinking, we flow in one smooth rhythm, as two halves make a whole, and surrender to each other completely.

After our breathing slows and normalizes, we lie in silence, our legs intertwined. I trace over his chest with my finger and wonder if I've lost him to the pull of sleep. Carefully, I kiss the crook of his neck and angle my face up so I can see his face clearly. His eyes are closed, but I can tell he's awake. The house is completely quiet.

"You make me the happiest, Brodie," I reveal, in a shy whisper.

I kiss his lips delicately as if he were a statue about to crumble, then rest my head back over his heart. I can feel him grinning from ear to ear in the dark.

"'N ya me, my Nina," he whispers back, his voice a little hoarse.

# 22

The oven timer sounds off. I scramble up from the recliner and rush to grab the potatoes before they burn. Clutching an oven mitt, I pull them out just in time.

"Everythin' alright back there?" Mick hollers from the couch.

"Yep! Perfectly crispy," I yell.

I want tonight to go well. Tonight is the night I tell Mick about my relationship with Brodie. Suddenly, I'm more nervous about his reaction than anyone else's, probably because he knows us both very well, and he seems to find a flaw regarding any man that breathes in my direction.

I scoop the rosemary potatoes into a dish and place it on the counter, letting it cool for a minute. I glance at the table. Another platter of grilled asparagus sits in the middle. I check the oven again to examine the roast; it's Mick's personal favorites for dinner tonight. As I do, I notice he still has that lingering cough. I ask him what Gus, a doctor, thinks about it. Maybe he can take some medication for it, but he dismisses it with a wave of a hand.

"He reckons there's nothin' to do but just wait. It'll run its course," he mumbles with a tone of finality.

Frowning slightly at that advice, I respect Mick's mindset. He can be very stubborn when it comes to his own self-regard, even with me. He's been so happy ever since our long weekend apart, and I've missed him a lot. Lately, I've been feeling like there's an internal clock ticking away on my time here with my visa expiring sooner rather than later. My family, back in The States, informs me that Covid regulations are still being enforced and while California is slowly opening up by the day, it's still not normal living whatsoever. Meanwhile, here, life seems completely unaffected. I'm making good money and more than anything, I'm happy.

I check the roast again; it's ready. As if on call, I hear Brodie's ute pull up. The engine dies as I hear the truck's door open, followed by a bark. Mick stands up and advances towards the door to welcome the duo.

"Sweetheart, why don't ya queue up Sade?" he calls back over his shoulder to me.

*Ooh*, sure thing. Sade is a gift to this earth. She always sets the tone. I rush over to the player and hunt for her record *Diamond Life*; it's never very far. *Found it!* I pull the vinyl out of the sleeve and place it on the player, dropping the needle. Smooth and sexy sounds of "Smooth Operator" fill the air, maybe a little too atmospheric for tonight's spotlight of events, but who am I to ever turn down Sade. I stroll back to the kitchen. Brodie and Mick shake hands, smiling in normal greeting. Stel makes a beeline for me and gives me one lick before tilting her head up and assiduously sniffing the air, probably catching wafts of the roast. I look up and see Mick and Brodie both grinning at me.

"Pryce brought it," Mick mentions, holding up a bottle. "That was mighty kind of ya."

"I was at the Bottle-O 'n saw it, reckonin' as how much Nina loves it 'n all," Brodie says, waiving it off.

Mick grins fondly at him and struts to the cabinet to fetch some flutes. Brodie walks up to me and leans down, sweetly planting a little kiss on my cheek in greeting. *He smells good*. He smells fresh of a shower. Smiling, I hand him the dish of potatoes. As Mick walks past us, Brodie turns and heads towards the table. Taking a page out of Brodie's book, I have some fresh, perky wildflowers sitting in a vase in the middle of the table. I don't want Mick to freak out too much, so I decide simpler is better; less is more.

Remembering I have some videos and photos of the whales to show the boys, I run back to my room and retrieve my laptop. I set it down on the table and put on a slideshow for them. As I pull out the fragrant entrée, Brodie reminisces about our experience.

Humming along to my favorite track on the album, "Your Love Is King," I cut into the roast to make sure it's properly cooked and tender. Steam rises as the meat unfolds. *Heavenly!* As I cut it up into thin slices for the table, I overhear Brodie telling Mick about how they caught three Red Emperors.

"That's the best eatin' fish in the wata, whadda delight," Mick hollers.

"Nah, yeah hands down," Brodie continues, "but my favourite part of the trip was divin'. Mick, ya shoulda seen her."

"I've already told him several times," I chuckle, chiming in. "He's probably sick of hearing about the whales."

"Nah, the humpies were rippa, no doubt," Brodie grins too, but shakes his head, looking at Mick, "but it was Neens that was the star of the show." Surprised, I wait for his reasoning. Mick quiets too as Brodie explains enthusiastically, "She was unafraid. These guys were massive." He taps Mick on the arm. "Ya reckon what they're like, but she just went at 'em. But the best was afta, seein' her face when we hopped on the deck, it was like pure joy if I'd eva seen it."

Brodie beams at me in memory. Mick looks from Brodie to me, and gives me a wink. With that, I bring the roast over and set it down next to the other dishes. Mick takes a deep whiff, inhaling the yummy smells.

"Aw, Sheila, ya spoil me," he mutters affectionately, reaching for the serving spoon.

"I got it," I playfully snicker, lightly batting his hand away.

"Nah, ya take care of everythin' all the time, Sweetheart," Mick sweetly pushes my hand back over. "Lemme at least do this part."

I nod, happy he feels up to it.

"Oh, the bubbles," Brodie mentions, grabbing the champagne bottle, and carrying it to the sink where he opens it with a light *pop!* He brings it back and fills three flutes to the top. We each dig into our meals as I sit in between my two guys. Stella lies down on the floor next to us. I grab a couple of slices of roast and place them on a spare plate I have at the ready.

"Who's that for?" Mick asks.

"Lella, of course," I explain, speaking in my dog timbre.

She sits assertively, waiting for her goods, licking her chops. I tell her to shake and she offers me her paw instantly. Proud, I place the plate down in front of her and she hastily gobbles up the meat.

Brodie laughs and nudges Mick, with a glance to Stella, "Yar not the only one who's spoiled, eh."

We spend the rest of our pleasant dinner enjoying the backside of *Diamond Life*. Leaning back in his chair, Brodie taps his finger lightly on his flute, then looks at me with a face that reads: *now's a good a time as any.*

I clear my throat and sit up a little, and gaze into Mick's eyes. His blue eyes radiate love back at me and already I feel more confident. Knowing Mick, I don't have to worry about a thing. I grab his hand with my left one and squeeze it three times, taking a small breath.

"Old Man, I've something to tell you," I say.

Brodie sits up straight as well and grabs my right hand in his. Mick looks at our hands and back at the pair of us. A crooked smile creeps up on his face.

"Yar gettin' hitched?" he guesses.

We both snort, and I lower my head down towards the table, dying at the absurd possibility. I turn to see Brodie biting his lip with raised eyebrows in surprise and amusement.

Reeling my laughter back in, I start, "No, but what we're trying to say is—."

"Mick, Nina 'n I are togetha," Brodie finishes for me. "She's my partna. We've decided to give it a red hot go, with yar blessin' o'course."

*My partner.* Hearing the word sounds so peculiar, yet so right. I've noticed the Aussies use that word above the American default "boyfriend" and "girlfriend." Somehow it holds more meaning or gravitas. I glance at Brodie, surprised. We've never discussed labels, but I guess we're at that point, and honestly, I find the notion rather exciting.

Mick takes a deep breath, looking back and forth between us.

"As long as ya take care of my girl, ya have it," he says.

"Cross my heart," Brodie promises him, turning to me with his scrunching smiley expression.

I move to clear the dishes, but Brodie softly nudges me back, ordering me to stay put while he does them instead. As he's in the kitchen with the water running, Mick grabs my hand, seeking my full attention.

"I can tell yar happy," he mutters. I beam, nodding at him in confirmation. He looks at Brodie and slightly sighs before refocusing his gaze back on me. "I wouldna trust anyone else with ya, Sweetheart." He squeezes my hand tightly three times. I reach over and kiss him lightly on the cheek. His approval means the world to me, and I know Brodie recognizes that. Mick holds up the deck of cards to Brodie. "Well then, fancy a round?"

I roll my eyes at them, but Brodie instantly hollers back, holding up a soapy plate, "Yeah, Old Boy, gimme two shakes."

While we wait for Brodie, I open up my computer again. We scroll through the dozens of images which highlight different parts of our trip: Stella leaning over the rail of the boat with her wind blown hair pushed back, the boys pitching the tents, the ladies and me all huddled together around the fire, Brodie smiling as he holds his birthday cupcake, about to blow out the candle. I note that one's one of my personal favorites. I pause a fraction of a second longer on that photo because it makes me happy. We both decided to pretend the incident with Jordan was another time, separate from such a wonderful trip. I glance sideways at Brodie, who now stands behind me. He's grinning at the screen. Finally we come to the whale shots. Brodie hollers. An image fills the screen of the humpback whales breaching the surface, spinning at such high velocity the water forms a swirl around them. More shots slide through the screen of Mel swimming like a mermaid, Brodie smiling ear to ear, and then a couple shots of of me swimming beside the magnificent beasts. I glance back at Brodie who mouths the word "hot." I flip to another photo of me swimming down as the smaller calf swims towards me. My legs look extra long with the diving fins on. In the photo, it looks like the calf and I are about to kiss, but it's just the perspective; still it's an amazing shot.

"What a banga shot," Mick exclaims, shaking his head in awe. "By far, my fav."

"Maybe I should take up photography, eh?" Brodie jests smugly.

"Yeah, you can be my second shooter," I reply in a laugh.

He grins and chuckles at my response. My favorite picture is next. Mick clicks his tongue in appreciation. It's the photo Jaz snapped of Brodie and me with our diving masks resting on our foreheads right after we've come up from the whale shark. We both radiate elation. In the photo, I'm looking at the camera while Brodie only has eyes for me.

"What a crackin' picture!" Mick cries out.

I feel Brodie's hand squeeze my shoulder.

"Wait until you see the video," I declare, queuing it up.

"Simple Song" by The Shins begins to play as a bokeh filled sunrise lights up the frame and wide aerial shots flood the screen, showcasing the breaching whales. Mick and Brodie both roar in awe as the video bounces back and forth between underwater footage of us diving with the creatures and the drone shots. The water's so clear, you can really see the context and scale of their giant sizes. As the video ends, Mick yawns deeply. I glance at the clock, it is getting late, especially for him, who hasn't been sleeping well.

"Well, Sweetheart, ya neva cease to amaze me," Mick says proudly, clasping my shoulder as he stands. "I'm off to hit the hay."

He leans down and kisses my cheek. He walks over to Brodie and pats him on the back before going in for a firm handshake. They both nod to each other and bid goodnight.

"Sleep tight, Old Man," I sweetly holler at Mick, as he shuffles down the hall.

He continues walking, but lifts his hand in a little wave, and closes his bedroom door behind him.

"See, that was easy," Brodie says, looking at me.

"Yeah, I'm just glad he *knows* knows," I agree. Brodie tilts his head in question, shifting closer to me. As I close down my computer, I laugh. "Well, I suppose if he thought we were getting married, he must of had his suspicions, but he never came out and said so."

"Uh, huh," he says, clearly not really listening anymore.

I look over at him. His eyes burn a hole in mine. I don't move a muscle as he reaches all the way over to me and brushes his lips on mine. He breaks away and stands up, saying he has to be up super early for a morning charter.

"Wish ya were comin' home with me," he sighs wistfully.

While the thought sounds wonderful, and I do love all the time I can soak up with him, I don't want things to move too quickly. I love where we're at right now, and I love being here at home with Mick. Thankfully, I get the best of both worlds at the moment.

With the click of a tongue, Stella is ready by the door. As Brodie opens the slider, I lean back and give him a little wave.

"G'night," he replies, bracing both hands on the sides of the open doorway. Leaning through the opening, he coyly adds, "Partna."

Biting his lower lip, he scrunches his nose in a full Nina face and turns away, walking to the ute.

Glowing from tonight and Mick's reception, I get up, tidy a couple of items left on the table, and close down the house for the night. I peek into Mick's room and he's sound asleep, breathing deeply under his covers. *Thank you.* I really hope he can catch up on some shut eye.

Opening my door, I make my way towards slumber city.

A week flies past. Brodie's been super busy chartering locals, pent up with border lockdowns. During one of the weekend charters, the family hires me to photograph and document their day trip. I get to spend the day on the boat observing Brodie as an official captain, and get paid to boot. I laugh at the thought. Originally going to charter his boat myself, at the time I thought Big Al couldn't have been more wrong about Brodie being a people pleasing captain. Now looking back, how could I have been so wrong? I smile at what a difference some time makes.

The morning on the water goes extremely well, so well in fact, that the family generously tips the pair of us. It's perfect timing for our Perth trip next weekend.

"Maybe I should I bring ya with me more often," Brodie suggests, smiling as he hands me my earnings.

We tidy up the boat while Two Door Cinema Club's *Tourist History* shuffles in the background. Mick's arriving soon with Stella. Brodie surprised him and asked if he wanted to join us on the boat after work. I can't wait to get all my favorite Aussies together on the water. I asked Mel to come, but she's working and can't "chuck a sickie," especially with Perth so close. All of a sudden, I hear a bark coming from the car port. Stella sprints along the dock with Mick far behind her. We both grin at the sight of them.

"Thanks again for this. I know it means a lot to him," I say gratefully, turning to Brodie, adding in a sentimental tone, "and to me."

I stand on my tippy-toes and softly kiss his cheek. He humbly accepts the thanks with a smile and a nudge. I look back at Mick and decide to go accompany him across the dock to the boat. Hopefully my concern for the uneven planks might be masked by my excitement to see him. I jump out and happily jog over to greet him. Tucking my arm in his, we walk together back to *Salty Stel* and board. Brodie offers Mick a hand and he climbs on easier than I could have imagined. Brodie offers him the co-pilot chair. *A real honor, Old Man.* Mick settles in his cushy seat and asks how the morning went.

"Ask Nina," Brodie tells him, grinning.

Mick looks confused and I tell him all about our prosperous trip.

"Well, I'm just glad they're appreciatin' ya, Sweetheart," Mick snorts.

"Alrighty then, ready?" Brodie checks, untying the ropes.

We both nod in confirmation and he ignites the engine and backs us out. At the edge of the marina, Brodie punches *Salty Stel* into higher gear. While always very safe, Brodie is also known for racing a little, enjoying himself, and on occasion, living life on the edge when the parameters allow. He's never dangerous or stupid when captaining, but today he opts for a smoother, mellower ride for Mick's sake.

Clad in a blue Spooner and trunks, Mick wears deck shoes and a fishing hat. Growing up and residing on the water, Mick feels right at home; it's just been a while since he's been able to make it out here. He looks back and forth between me, who sits behind him, and the horizon ahead, smiling and laughing at the amazing sensation of being on the open water. I completely understand; it's mesmerizing and honestly there's no other feeling quite like it.

Putting the boat on auto pilot for a minute, Brodie unearths my camera. He hands it to me, knowing I must be itching to take photos, and I am. I snap some pics of Mick enjoying the ride. His joy and satisfaction make my heart swell with happiness.

A pod of dolphins swim along with us, down the sides of the bow through the wake of the boat. They're gorgeous. Brodie slows down and they swim past us as he turns the engine off.

I have Brodie take a photo of me standing next to Mick with my arm around him as we both smile. I want a memento of this afternoon. Brodie then walks to the side compartment and pulls out a couple of fishing rods. Mick spins in his chair and lights up at the sight of them. Brodie walks over and hands him one and digs into his little tackle box. He pulls out two colorful lurers and readies Mick's pole. Mick gladly takes command of it, and balancing himself, stands at the starboard rail.

Brodie hands one to me and I laugh, accepting it.

"I've never done this before," I explain. I then remember trout fishing with Papi. "Well that's not true, but I think I was eight the last time."

Mick already has his line cast, letting the line drag for a bit as we drift slowly. Brodie informs us the FishFinder shows good signs below. I bust a gut laughing as I attempt to cast my line. I look at Mick then at Brodie, dying at my one failed attempt after the next. My lure drops maybe five feet away each time. I hear the shutter button *click!* and turn around to find Brodie taking photos of us fishing together.

"Mate, look back," he yells at Mick.

Mick turns and we both beam broadly, poles in hand. Brodie sets my camera down on the seat and comes up behind me, tentatively hovering around me. I like how he doesn't try and grab the rod from my hands, cast it himself, and hand it back to me to simply reel in a fish. I guess we're both in agreement that that would be a disservice to me, that it would feel like a half-assed attempt. To his credit, he wants to give me the chance to do it all on my own.

*I wouldn't mind a few pointers though.*

I give him a look that screams I need assistance. Bending down, he instructs me on how to hold the spool of line in my thumb, when to let go, and a better casting motion. He backs up and waits for me to try again. Taking his advice, I pull my arm back and cast the line high and wide, releasing as much line in the process. This time, the lurer hits the water about twenty feet away. Mick, Brodie, and I collectively holler in delight at the difference. By this time, Mick is already on his fourth cast.

"Hook up!" he suddenly yells, his pole bending.

Stella senses the action and stands dutifully at Mick's side. Brodie jumps up, happy to help if need be, but again, waiting to be asked. He stands right next to Mick, bending over the rail, overlooking the water. Mick grunts as the catch pulls the rod around with mighty strength. When the fish ascends, Mick hastily reels in the line, then surprisingly firmly holds it while the fish tires itself. The process repeats over and over again.

"I see colour!" Brodie finally yells in excitement.

Curious, I glance down, and sure enough, a sliver of silver shimmers around, skirting all over the place around the boat. Mick and I are constantly working around each other to not tangle our lines. Since I'm more in the way, I decide to reel mine in.

Working up a sweat, Mick has the thing by the tail. He reels it in close enough for Brodie to reach down and gaff it. Brodie starts screaming in astonishment. He pulls up a pretty good sized wahoo. Mick stands back in awe. The tension from the exertion drains from his back and shoulders as he slightly slumps back.

"Must be forty kilos at least," Brodie cries out. He brains it quickly and it flops down for good, leaving a bloody mess on the deck. Stella sniffs the creature intensely. Mick stares at it, shaking his head, still not believing he caught a wahoo. Brodie leans in and gives him a crushing high five. "Way to go, Old Boy!"

I look down at the fish. Its huge body lies lifelessly along the deck. I peer down and see the stripes along its long body. It's beautiful. It definitely seems a worthy catch. In fact, I hope the fight doesn't wipe out Mick too much. I don't think anyone was expecting that, especially on the first couple of goes.

I grab my camera off the seat, and catch Brodie's attention, gesturing to it in my hands. He's already on it. Winded, Mick leans down to overlook his fresh catch. Brodie grunts as he hoists up the heavy and awkward elongated body, holding it out in front of Mick. Mick grabs it by the head as he and Brodie smile at me. *Click!* That's one for the books. Delighted I squeal and set my camera down. Brodie manhandles the catch, then stands and extends the rod to Mick for another cast.

"I think I'll call it," Mick says in humor, shaking his head as he breathes heavily. "I'm knackered."

He grunts as he settles himself back into his chair. Smiling, I cast my line. Brodie grabs Mick's rod and casts out next to me. He elbows me playfully as we stand together, holding our poles; clearly he's happy to have me fishing alongside him. Stella stands right in between us.

"All we're missing is music," I tease.

"Not for long," he replies, setting his pole in a rod rocket.

He asks Mick what sounds good and Mick requests some Johnny Cash. "Flesh and Blood" starts to play. Brodie rushes back and grabs his pole, and we fish together, enjoying our time with Mick on the water. About a half hour goes by, and I'm ready to call it. Suddenly, my rod arches sharply, and I feel a sharp pull on the line. I yell out, unsure of what to do. I'm always watching the crew fish and it looks simple in theory, but now with the situation directly in my hands, I freeze, feeling overwhelmed. Instinctively, I start to spin the reel.

"Hold on a sec, Neens," Brodie says, leaning in, "let him swim or yull lose him."

I nod in understanding and brace my arms on the pole. It's bloody work. I feel muscles tensing in all parts of my arms and shoulders as I do what I can to handle this excited fish on the line. I have to duck under Brodie's pole. While Mick chuckles watching us both fight the good fight, I find myself grunting from the sheer strength required to keep up. This is exhausting. I start to get the hang of it, reeling in when it feels right and knowing when to pull back so the line doesn't snap. Brodie then turns to me and guides me on my wrangling struggle. I see a flash and shriek in excitement.

"It's huge!" Brodie wails, shrieking. "A tuna!"

Mick gets up and shuffles to the edge, peering over, wanting in on the commotion. Stella also barks for good measure. Brodie gets the gaff ready and lifts it in the air, ready to strike.

"I don't think I can do this much longer," I warn, my depleted arms ready to give way any second.

"Hold on, any sec now," Brodie says, following the furious trajectory of the fish. He points with his free hand. "Hoist it up if ya reckon ya can."

Gathering all the remaining strength I can muster, I pull up on the rod, praying for it to be over, but also hoping I don't lose it at the last second. Brodie spears it in the cheek and takes over, pulling it up on the deck and removing the hook. Stella's at his heel for support. I feel my remaining strength ooze from my body as it relaxes in relief. Using whatever adrenaline I have left, I clasp the hook onto the pole and set it aside. Brodie stands, besides himself, holding the giant tuna, grinning from ear to ear. I walk over to the pair and stare at the mighty fish in amazement. I closely look at its gleaming, lifeless eye. There's actually a lot more detail in its eyes than I ever thought. Mick stands behind me and clasps me lightly on the shoulder.

"Mighty proud of ya, Sheila," he says.

I half hug him, still zoning out from the whirlwind. Grunting, Brodie hands me the large animal. I take it, wincing from the sheer weight.

"Got it, Neens?" he asks, double checking.

Hoping so, and feeling like I have a good grip on it, I nod. He slowly releases it in my arms, and I almost drop it, but catch myself before I do. He tells me to look up, and I tilt my head up to see Mick holding my camera, peering through the viewfinder.

"Cheers, Sweetheart," he says happily.

Trying to balance, I smile as best as I can, and stand there, proudly holding my catch. Brodie jumps in beside me and grabs the tail. The relief of weight already makes me feel more stable. We both grin and look at the camera as Mick snaps some more photos. We part and Brodie takes over again, sliding it next to Mick's wahoo. He cuts them and bleeds them over the back swim step as Mick watches me practice casting some more. Once Brodie finishes with the blood bath, he washes off the deck and joins me again. He recasts and waits to see if anything bites. Just as I'm about to make a joke about the fisherman who doesn't hook up, his pole bends.

"Hook up! On! On!" he yells, squealing like an excited schoolgirl. "It's boilin'!"

He works with ease, clearly comfortable. His rod and reel are like an extension of his hand. Brodie's fish comes swimming towards the surface. Decently sized, but nothing crazy, he hauls the small tuna onto the boat. He quickly unhooks it from the mouth and it flops around on the deck, clearly very lively. He grabs it and quickly shows it to us before tossing it back in the drink.

"I reckon that does it for one arvo," Brodie announces.

"Wait, you don't want to reel one more in?" I ask.

"Yeah, nah, I'll be right," he replies, shaking his head. "We've got our fair share. We only take what we need, nothin' more, 'n I'd say we're good for 'boutta week."

Mick offers to help Brodie fit the two fish in the esky. Brodie chops the wahoo into two halves and hands them to Mick, who deposits them on ice. We decide to head back to the marina. The wind picks up slightly so I'm more than fine with that decision. Elated with all of our success, Mick happily agrees. We spend the hour ride back listening to some Yacht Rock. The classics roll, shuffling songs from The Eagles, Gilbert O'Sullivan, Bread, and Hall & Oates to name a few.

Before heading towards the harbor, Brodie pulls up to a little alcove, stopping the engine close to shore, and offers Mick a chance to dip in the water. I know it's been ages since Mick's been in the ocean. He swam with me months ago at Recovery Campus, but I know the whole process of traipsing through the sand is tiring for an eighty-six year old, especially one who's been pretty breathless on the daily. His eyes light up at the mention of swimming, and Brodie takes that as a yes, so he drops anchor.

There's still plenty of sunshine with a couple of hours left until sunset. I strip off my nasty fishing shirt to my green, flower one-piece suit underneath. Mick pulls off his Spooner, and kicks off his deck shoes. He lays his hat on his pile of clothes on the seat. Slowly, he shuffles to the back swim step. Brodie and I both give him a hand, more so he doesn't slip, and we help ease him into the water. Mick falls back, sending little splashes up around him. Brodie and I both follow him in and we all exclaim at how amazing it feels, especially after our fishing escapades. It's been a warm day today, so the shallows are particularly cozy feeling, like a bath. Mick moves his arms around him, keeping him afloat, and I see all his wrinkly, paper crepe skin sagging along his bony frame. He gives us one of the biggest smiles I've ever seen.

"Ah ya beauty, you," Mick declares, looking all around him at the gorgeous cove we have all to ourselves.

He leans back and floats on his back, going perfectly still, looking peacefully serene. Brodie and I both mimic him and the three of us enjoy the peaceful feeling as "You Make Loving Fun" by Fleetwood Mac dreamily plays from the boat. I close my eyes and sigh in bliss. This is a slice of heaven.

We pull up to dock the boat and I offer to stay behind and help Brodie clean up, but he waives it off, reiterating that he's good. He says, more importantly, I should go home with Mick and get him fed after such a big afternoon. We help Mick off the boat, and not wanting him to trip, I walk beside him back up to the ute. I realize I didn't really give Brodie a proper goodbye or thank him, although Mick thanked him plenty for the both of us. I accompany Mick to the Troopy with Stella, then tell her to go back to her dad and she listens, taking off back to the dock.

After getting home and fixing Mick some spaghetti, he showers and climbs in bed, completely "cooked" and wiped out. I tell him a few times to let me know if he needs anything, and he assures me he'll just be catching up on some lost sleep and not to disturb him.

Reeling from the day, I wonder if Brodie's finished with cleaning the boat and filleting all the fish. That's always a beastly job. Standing in front of the kitchen windowsill, I look out to the ocean across the way. I reflect on the amazing day we all had from start to finish, with the back half being the best by far. The memory of Mick swimming, reeling in that big wahoo makes me well up inside, about to overflow in joy. Brodie was spectacular today. I see what Big Al meant at the time. In general, he thinks of everything, and as a captain that only expounds tenfold. Whether it being gear, suggestions, snacks or an extra hand, he's super thoughtful and accommodating without coming off commandeering or as a know-it-all. *I should have made more of an effort to thank him.*

Before even realizing it, I grab the keys to the ute and scribble a note for Mick on the counter, just in case he wakes up and wonders where I am. I dash out the slider, and within minutes, am pulling up to Brodie's house. I park out front and see Stella run over. I glance in the house but don't see any other movement. I get out of the ute and walk towards the boat. It looks freshly sprayed down, with water droplets everywhere. I then walk to the shed, but don't see him. I open up the freezer and see all these fresh filets lined inside. Where can he be? Pacing around the yard, I finally see him coming around the corner from the outside shower. He sees me and stops.

"Neens, I told ya, ya don't need to help, I got it covered," he explains, but is clearly happy to see me nonetheless.

I run up to him and pull him into a big embrace, squeezing my arms around his wet torso. Tilting my chin up, I passionately kiss him. After a long minute, I pull back.

"That's for today," I say dreamily. "Thank you."

I break away and run back to the ute, climb in and drive off back home to Mick's. In my rearview mirror, I see Brodie standing there, staring after me.

# 23

The week seems to dredge by slowly despite it being full; not only is the Perth trip coming up, but Christmas is this week. I think I'm finally ready to break the news about Brodie and me to my family. There's only one problem: none of us can agree on a day, night, or time to FaceTime. I really want Brodie to be there. He's only video called them a couple of times with me, and that was before, when we were just friends. Like Mick, I think Ria catches onto something going on between us, but she hasn't voiced her suspicions to Mom or anyone else yet. Well, if she did, they're all hiding it, and hiding anything isn't what my family does well.

When Brodie's around, he lets me piggy back off his WiFi instead of trekking into town, but today he's working, and Mick needs to go check on the post. I decide to join him for lunch and to video chat with Ria.

Sitting at Lotte's while Mick talks it up with the postie, I FaceTime dial my sister. I'm thinking I can gauge what she does or doesn't know if I bait her, and then see when it works to chat with the whole family at once. As I sit in my cozy chair, Common King's "One Day" plays from my phone as I wait. Ria picks up on the second ring and laughs immediately. Selena stands next to her. This is like striking gold, the two of them together.

I turn down the music, but Ria chuckles, "No, I actually miss there being music on in the house 24/7. Leave it for a minute."

The music plays, but Selena instantly nags me to turn it off with a playful eye roll. Pausing it, I put in my headphones. I don't want to bore Lotte with my family catch up, plus we can all be a little... loud.

"Hey, hey!" Selena cries out, with a giant smile.

Going from talking every single day to maybe once a week is like a crime in my family, but a crime we're still adjusting to, so we all get thrilled to see each other when we can. This last FaceTime drought is the longest one yet. It's been weeks. They both reach out to the camera, giving me "air hugs."

"I miss you guys so much," I whine, giggling at them.

I ask about their last couple of weeks and Ria fills me in on the salon. After endless months of Covid drama, hairstylists are finally allowed to open back up. It's been a ridiculous roller coaster of openings and shutdowns without warning. She's thrilled to be back, despite trying to enforce strict Covid guidelines, where in the OC, everyone basically sticks it to The Man. Yet, she's making great money because most clients haven't colored or cut their hair in over nine months now.

Selena butts in and gives me some good Javi updates and tells me how her life is pretty much one endless loop of "baby land." She shows me a photo of him dressed up as a Dodger baseball player for Halloween, smiling in Papi's arms, who also wears a matching jersey. They both share highlights from their tiny Thanksgiving before asking me how I'm doing. Realizing I haven't talked to them in a while, I dive right in with some of my favorite recent memories.

"It was Brodie's birthday a few weeks ago so the whole crew went camping. You guys would've died," I dish. "We had our own island for the night." Ria's mouth practically drops open to the floor in shock and jealousy, while Selena's eyebrows shoot up. "Yeah, and it was as banger as you're thinking too. We swam with humpback whales, and a baby calf to boot! It was the coolest thing I think I've ever done. I sent you some photos and videos. Did you guys see them?"

I look at them accusatorially.

"Papi beamed them to the TV. Looked rad, Neens," Ria assures me.

"It was, and there's more too. Brodie took Mick and me on a special afternoon boat ride, and it was just magical," I reminisce, sighing dreamily as I notice Selena's eyes narrow slightly. "Mick hooked this giant wahoo and Brodie got me to fish, can you believe it? I caught this massive tuna!" I hold out my hands to demonstrate the general enormity of it. "The best part though was Brodie took us to this secluded alcove and Mick jumped in and swam with us. I don't think I've ever seen the Old Man so happy." I pause. "Brodie's so sweet with him."

"I'm hearing a lot of 'Brodie this' and 'Brodie that,' Nina," Selena says suspiciously, cocking her head.

I'm not the best liar in the slightest, but I'm not giving in just yet. I really wanted Brodie to be here and the rest of my family.

"Well, I'm with him a lot," I retort lamely.

"Sounds like it," she states. *Wait, is she baiting me now?* She presses further. "Do you like him?" I try to act nonchalantly, but I look away. "Yeah, you do, I can tell," she yells excitedly into the phone, feeling proud. "Even from across the ocean, I can tell."

Ria jumps up and down in her chair. The two of them look at each other.

"So what if I do?" I counter.

"I don't think I've ever heard you say that before," Ria squeals.

"Shhh, you're going to wake Mom," I warn them, "and I really don't want to talk about this with her right now."

"Just watch out, Neens, before you cross that line," Selena says, sobering slightly. "I mean flirting is one thing, anything more and it would be downright masochistic." I look at her, puzzled, so does Ria. She explains, "I mean you're coming home soon, I guess I don't see the point in starting something that can't last."

I definitely frown; this is not the support I was hoping to find.

Ria mimics my expression, and shaking her head, suggests, "No, go for it, hunnay."

"But you've already been there almost ten months, Nina," Selena counters. "Your visa is bound to run out soon, so again, why start something when you're just going to hop on a flight home? We all know long distance is the death of any relationship."

*Ouch.* You can always count on Selena for the hard truth.

"Listen, Neens," Ria softly chimes in, "this is a big deal if you like him. I say go for it. You never know where it might lead. Who knows, you guys might realize you're better off just friends."

*That, we most certainly, are not.*

Feeling slightly deflated by the conflicting and pointless advice, I see Mick shuffle in. I light up at the sight of him, my own personal ball of cheerfulness.

"Is he there now?" Selena asks guardedly, seeing my face; she adjusts her top.

I wave him over, disconnecting my headphones.

"We're almost done, but want to say hi to Marci and Ria?" I ask him.

He lights up some more, and comes over, leaning down into the frame over my shoulder. Ria and Selena's faces brighten when they see it's Mick.

"G'day, sheilas," he hollers to the laptop. "Havin' fun catching up with my Sweetheart are ya?"

"I could just listen to him all day," Ria mutters under her breath.

"Hi there, Mick, you're looking good," Selena says. "Nina was just telling us all about your fishing trip."

His smile broadens, and he says, "Nah, yeah, it was a beaut of a day. I reckon maybe the last for me on the wata." I scoff at his comment, so do my sisters and he laughs, bending down over my ear. "Headin' to the rubbity. I'll order ya yar usual?"

"Yep," I reply with a nod, before looking at him. "I'll wrap up soon and meet you there."

He looks back to the screen and bids farewell, "Well aren't the three of ya a sight for sore eyes. Ya've made this Old Boy's day."

They cry out goodbyes to Mick and he waves, leaving us. Selena glances at her phone and says she has to run too. She was just having Ria wax her mustache and chin hairs, but she needs to get going home to lend Ray a hand. We firm up our Christmas FaceTime time and she blows kisses at me, and I to her, and she leaves the frame. Not wishing to return to our Brodie conversation, I ask Ria how Mom and Papi are doing. She tells me that tensions have been running high at home with Christmas coming up. Half of the family wants to gather, despite Covid, while the other half isn't comfortable with Abuela being so high risk with her age. Happy I'm not around to deal with that, I sit back and listen to her vent. While in the middle of telling me about Mom's saga of coffee makers - she's now on the third machine since quarantine began - a text notification pops up at the top of my screen. It's from Brodie. I jump at it, smiling broadly. It's so unlike him to text me. Normally he either calls or just comes over to talk to me face to face. I have an Australian phone plan, but not many of my friends text, they're definitely callers.

Before it disappears, I quickly read the preview on the screen. The text reads: *Can't wait for Friday. xx*

Since I'm in the middle of FaceTime, I'll respond later. I don't want to be distracted from the my limited sister time.

"See, that's him, isn't it?" Ria smirks as I glance up. I shrug, not giving a definitive answer. She smiles broadly. "Don't listen to Selena, Neens. Just follow your heart, hunnay."

With that, we wrap up our call, say our "I love you's" and log off.

Trying to brush off Selena's "advice" and ignore the fact that my visa countdown is approaching, I make my way to the pub to soak up as much Mick time as I can.

So today is Christmas. If I didn't have the calendar reminding me, I'd swear it was just another day out here in Western Oz. The temps are hitting all time highs and it's been absolutely beautiful on the water. Even growing up in Southern California for Christmas, there would be signs of Christmas trees or jolly Santas amidst blankets of fake snow, but here, there's nothing. It feels so forced. I'm learning Aussies have their own way of celebrating, and especially up here in the bush, it's pretty mellow. Celebrating more for my family's sake, Mick and I go over to Brodie's for an early breakfast so I can use the WiFi and video call home.

After many holiday well wishes, my mom laughs that we're in tank tops and bathing suits over here, while they're sipping hot coco in sweaters. I can see remnants of shredded wrapping paper litter the floor after a full day of present giving. I was doing okay before this, but I have to admit, it's really difficult being away from my family on Christmas. Now that I'm seeing our traditions through a computer screen - the whole family wearing matching pajamas and spending the day watching old family home videos on the couch - *I miss them and I miss that desperately*. This is the first time I'm away for Christmas, and I can tell Mom is struggling with it too.

Mom and Papi tell me that they didn't want to send another care package, considering the last one took almost three months to get here, so instead they sent me a digital gift card for some new music, and deposited money into my bank account for the upcoming Perth trip. Thankful to Selena and her reminder, I had a new Reyn Spooner delivered to Papi, and a new cooking pan to Mom. They unwrap them on screen, exclaiming they love their gifts and appreciate the thought, despite the distance. After Mick and Brodie exchange pleasantries, we painfully hang up. The screen cuts to black.

"How ya doing, Sheila?" Mick asks me.

"I miss them... a lot," I confess, trying to keep my tears from welling.

He nods, while Brodie gives me a supportive smile.

Trying not to dwell in homesickness, I take a deep breath and bat the wetness away from my eyes. I choose to focus on my two guys in front of me. Now it's my turn for their gifts. Giddy, I run to my backpack and unearth two presents, each wrapped in butcher block with my doodles drawn on them to jazz them up a little. Suns cover Brodie's paper, while hearts scatter across Mick's. They each smile and open their gifts.

"Ah, Sheila," Mick exclaims, opening an enlarged framed photo of the two of us, fishing side by side. "I love it."

Brodie smiles as he unwraps the wind chime I found some time ago at Tippe's. He lifts it and the chimes hang in the air, already making beautiful warm tones as they sway in the breeze through the open door.

"I was thinking they can go above the windowsill in the kitchen," I suggest excitedly.

Smiling in thanks, he leans over and gives me a quick kiss before hopping up. Within minutes the chimes are hanging above the sill.

"Thanks, Neens, they're aces," Brodie says, grinning.

"Nature's music is some of the best," I say happily, as we listen to them.

Mick hands me a small parcel. Surprised, I immediately nudge it back in his hand.

"You've already done too much for me, Old Man," I explain, trying to reason with him.

Brodie snorts.

"Bulldust," Mick declares, and thrusts the package in my hands, despite my protests.

Slowly, I unwrap it and discover it's a tiny black box. Hesitantly, yet eagerly, I open it. Wedged in the little cushion is a dainty opal ring, set in pure gold. It sparkles brightly. It's not big by any means, but two tiny aquamarine gemstones line the sides. Speechless, I look to him and smile with my whole heart.

"I don't talk 'bout her much, but I'd reckon she'd want ya to have it," Mick sweetly says. "We neva had a daughta, but if we did, I reckon we both woulda hoped she was like you, Sweetheart."

Brodie remains quiet, wearing a sentimental expression on his face as he watches our exchange. With tears in my eyes, I slide the ring on my ring finger. It fits snugly just right. Still not having the words, I lean over to Mick and give him a bone crushing squeeze.

"Thank you. I love it, almost as much as I love you," I tell my dearest friend with the utmost respect and gratitude. "I'll cherish it forever."

"Good," Mick simply says.

I clear my throat, and Brodie sits up a little.

"I don't think I can top that," he mutters.

"Nope, probably not," I jest, but it's the truth.

He and Mick both laugh. Brodie bounces up and runs into his second bedroom before waltzing out, carrying a box that's easily taller than me. My eyebrows shoot up to my hairline. *What could that possibly be?* He walks it over and deposits the long and narrow box in my lap.

"Sorry it's not wrapped, I didn't wanna waste the paper," he confesses, with a sheepish grin.

"I'm glad you didn't," I assure him. "Brodie, what is this?"

He nods, gesturing me to open it. I catch Mick's attention and he looks thrilled. Grabbing the top of the cardboard box, I rip open the re-taped opening. Staring down into the dark hole, I still don't have any notion as to what awaits me. Reaching down with my hand, I feel something rubbery with my fingertips. Gripping something that feels like a handle, I pull out my prize, revealing long, black diving fins.

"Flip 'em ova," Brodie commands me, clearly excited.

Already freaking out that I now have my own personal diving fins, I do as he says and squeal in delight. Along the top face of each fin, a custom visual of my hammerhead photograph is printed in white, and in fine detail.

"From her drone shot," Brodie explains to Mick.

"This is so cool," I exclaim, and rush over to give him a hug. "Thank you, thank you!"

Clearly happy I'm happy, Brodie grabs me around the waist and gives me a little squeeze.

"Happy Chrissie, my Neens," he whispers into my ear.

"Feliz Navidad," I reply wholeheartedly.

I hold out my fin, admiring my two gifts as my new ring glints next to the hammerhead. Gazing between two of my favorite people, my heart alights with a joyful fire. While I'm super grateful for their presents, I have the two best gifts standing in front of me.

Wednesday comes and goes without a hitch. I photograph Fiona's small elopement, and by small, I mean literally her and her new wife at the county hall, and a small intimate party at our local watering hole. Mick picks me up after it wraps up, and we head home. We spend the ride back going over the handful of necessities I need for tomorrow's trip. I've never been an early packer, if anything, the exact opposite.

"You're sure you don't want me to stay?" I ask for the tenth time, turning to him as he drives.

"Would ya stop askin' me, Sheila. I'll be right, dun worry," he repeats for the tenth time.

"I know, I just worry about you," I say, slouching back in my seat. "I can't help it, that's life."

"I reckon ya do, but, Sweetheart," he replies, taking my hand in his, "ya gotta live yar life 'n not hold back on my account. Please go 'n have a cracka time. I'll be right here when ya get home."

Nodding my head, I know he's right. I squeeze his hand three times as he returns the squeezes right back. He holds my hand until we're home.

It's about 9AM. Mick and I wait on the deck with my backpack. We hear an engine pull down the road and I see Brodie's white ute heading down the path. It pulls up to the front of the house, and Brodie jumps out.

"Is there more, or this it?" he asks, jogging up and grabbing my bag. I shrug, and he laughs, shaking his head. "Shoulda reckoned."

"Come here, Sheila," Mick commands me, standing as he opens his arms.

I walk up to him, letting him pull me into a giant embrace. His grasp feels so solid and safe, despite his bony frame that comes with aging well into your eighties. I take one big squeeze, but not too tight, and take a big whiff by his neck, savoring the unique scent of his cologne.

"That should carry me through the weekend, Old Man," I jest.

"I'm always with ya," he whispers, and kisses me on the cheek affectionately.

He escorts me to Brodie's ute and opens the door for me, making sure I get in nice and tidy before closing it. Brodie walks by and gives him a soft clap on the shoulder. Mick smiles at him and returns the gesture. Brodie climbs in the ute and starts it as Mick leans in my window.

"Take care of our girl, Pryce," he commands, like always.

"Always, mate. Cross my heart," Brodie replies, chuckling.

"I'll be seein' ya, Sweetheart," he says endearingly to me. "Happy New Year, yous."

With that, Mick lightly taps on the weatherstripping and gives my arm a little squeeze in farewell. Brodie shifts the ute into gear and we're off. I wave my hand out the window as we drive down the road and see Mick waving back in the rearview mirror. Feeling slightly worried, I must frown slightly, because I feel Brodie's hand on my leg. He gives me a tiny squeeze.

"He'll be right, Neens. It's only for a few days," he says, kindly comforting me.

I look over and give him a big reassuring smile.

Mick's voice echoes in my head, "*Ya gotta live yar life.*"

I sit up, and reach over to raise the volume. Cosmo's Midnight's "Yesteryear" floods the ute, and suddenly, I'm lost in the positive, happy vibes as we begin our adventure.

# 24

Wheels down, touch down. Brodie and I land in Perth. It's such a big city, well the biggest on the west coast. Back in March, I was supposed to come and stay for a couple of days before heading back to Sydney.

Brodie and I stumble out of our small four man plane. Brodie has a pilot friend who was flying down and offered to give us a lift. As we walk across the separate, tiny tarmac, I look around and survey the city skyline. It's the largest city I've seen in almost a year, and honestly blows me away in its enormity. Since my brief tour across Australia, I've learned cities aren't really my thing. I tell Brodie as much, and he agrees, but does say, out of all the cities, this one is way more laid back than most. Regardless, I'm just super excited for a change of scenery, and I especially love exploring places I've never been before.

Brodie, "Mister I've Done/Been/Seen Everything," is thrilled to show me the sights and introduce me to some of his favorite spots to eat and drink. He tells me about a few of them as we exit the hanger. Apparently, Brodie told our friends we can't meet up with them until tonight, and it's only 1PM now.

"I just want to soak up some solo Neen time before, ya know, we get swept up in the mob," he explains, grabbing my hand as we walk down the street.

We hop in an Uber and wind up in line for the spotted red and white ferry from Fremantle "Freo" to Rottnest Island "Rotto." Due to the lack of tourists, the island won't be that crowded, which is how I always prefer experiencing places, so I'm extra excited. Brodie and I stand at the rail, side by side, as we scour the ocean looking for whale spouts during the twenty-five minute ferry ride. Brodie manages to find four while I see zero. He has a knack for locating any and all wildlife, like he's tuned in on their frequency or something. He playfully nudges me because every time he points to the spout, by the time I look, the whale goes under and doesn't resurface. He laughs at the timing of it, and when I roll my eyes, he reaches over and pulls me into a playful side hug, squeezing so I can't escape. This always makes me feel better and is my kryptonite when I'm even remotely annoyed.

I tap my fingers, feeling slightly antsy. Before we left home, Brodie informed me that you can't really drone downtown and not at all on the island, which is kind of a bummer. I was really looking forward to droning some new terrain, but they're way more regulated down here so The Khal sits on my dresser at Mick's. Even though light and travel friendly, I didn't want to cart him around all weekend long when I most likely can't even use him. It feels strange without him in my arsenal on my back whilst sightseeing, like I'm missing a hand or something. Brodie tries to spin it as a good thing, urging me to make the most of focusing on my camera. He's right, so I embrace it.

We approach land and unload in no time. For a little island, Brodie assures me there are tons of things to do and it's one of his favorite things about visiting Perth. We rent e-bikes and ride them along the boardwalk that lines the jaw-dropping coastline. With fat tires, the bikes make it through some of the sandier areas of the paths and trails. It's amazing! Brodie brought a portable speaker, which he clips on the back of his bike. We pedal, listening to Iration's "Guava Lane" before rolling into the rest of the album. *Coastin*'s become one of our favorite mutual records to listen to together.

As I follow Brodie, I look around and see white sand beaches with the most gorgeous blue and green shallows. Crystal clear waters highlight the reefs underneath. Smaller sand dunes with some bushes pepper the sand. There's a path lined in weathered wood fencing that splits off into little entrances and stairways, leading down to the coves and bays. Occasionally, I see these brown little creatures scurrying around, behind bushes, looking like cuter and bigger versions of our Californian beach squirrels. After we pass a picturesque white lighthouse and more beautiful coves, we eye a little lagoon. I inhale quickly at the sight.

"Reckoned ya might fancy this spot," Brodie states proudly.

We're at Henrietta's Point, which boasts a real life shipwreck called The Shark. You can see it from shore. Parts of it shoot above the surface from where it succumbed to the shallows. My mouth hangs open and I immediately reach for my drone, realizing I don't have it. I grimace at the loss. If I can see it from the shore, imagine... *Damn regulations.*

"This wreck's a good intro for ya, Neens, not as sharky or nearly as deep as most," he says, handing me my mask.

"Yeah," I snort at him, replying flippantly, "because I happen to come across shipwrecks all the time."

He rolls his eyes at me. Another pro for Straya apparently.

I look around and there's no one around as far as I can see. There's not one footprint on the entire beach. The entire bay is lined in bright cream sand that butts up to these amazing rock formations, almost limestone in texture. One of those furry creatures scampers out from the nearby bushes, hopping up to me. I grab my camera to snap a picture. Brodie comes up to my side and squats low, urging me to squat too. He informs me that I'm meeting the island's namesake, the local quokkas. Originally, in the late 1600s when the Dutch were exploring Straya, they came across this island and thought the quokkas were large rats, thus originally naming the island "Rotte nest," derived from the Dutch word *rattennest,* meaning "rat's nest." I hum in amusement as he tells me they're considered the world's happiest animal. I look at it and see exactly why. Hopping onto my towel, the quokka looks at me straight in the eyes and appears to be smiling at me, even showing its little teeth. I gasp in amazement.

"Whatever?! It's straight up smiling at us," I exclaim to Brodie, over my shoulder, who squats right behind me.

"Like I said, it's kinda their thing," he explains, laughing. The quokka leans in, intrigued by the lens. Brodie shuffles a little closer. "Ya know, if ya wanna be cool, ya gotta snap a quick photo with it."

"Really, you can do that?" I ask with raised eyebrows.

"Nah, yeah, these guys are used to it. There's heaps of 'em online."

I try and take a selfie, but my arms are too short for my camera, so Brodie graciously takes it and holds it out in front of us. Entranced by the glass lens, the quokka follows the camera. Brodie clicks down on the shutter and we review it on the screen. It's perfect and hilarious. The little quokka looks like he's posing with us, fully smiling.

Laughing, Brodie strips his shirt and hands me a dive mask. I steal a quick, satisfying glance at his athletic torso as I put away my camera. I eagerly strip to my yellow, high waisted suit, jumping at the chance to see a shipwreck with my own two eyes, not just on some screen from a movie or Instagram reel. I race to the ocean, with Brodie hot on my tracks. Giggling, I dive down into the water and then surface, readjusting my mask for optimum sight. I wait for Brodie to lead the way. Always the more experienced diver should embark first. I don't want to be put in an easily preventable situation. Just like Brodie respects my domain in the sky, I respect his under the sea.

The tide is high at the moment, so most of the wreck is submerged. We swim closer to it. Only meters away, I see how the panels and frame have rusted over time. Brilliant orange and burnt yellow algae form along the contour; it appears as if it's glowing as it spews off the frame in tiny tendrils. It's a small wreck, not large by any means, but it's so beautiful, forming its own little ecosystem. We swim, exploring the wreck for a while before I slowly make my way back to the shallows. Popping my mask off, the feeling of the water hitting my bare face feels like a contact high, a feeling second to none. I dunk a couple of times before sitting down along the water's edge.

"That was banga, Neens," Brodie shouts from deeper out. "Ya looked like a total fox down there with yar hair flowin' all around ya, like a mermaid."

I snort. He swims for a couple more minutes before swimming closer in. Tanned to his year long tropical, golden brown, Brodie walks in hip high water, the top band of his boardies showing. His lean, brawny arms sway at his sides. I stare at his muscles as he shuffles across the sandy bottom towards me, flexing as he wipes some running water off his face with his hand. I bite my lip in appreciation. *Talk about a fox. He's downright sexy. And he's mine.* As he checks out our surroundings in this amazingly private bay, I only have eyes for him.

The thought makes me bubble up in excitement. He catches me eyeing him, and squints with humor in his eyes.

"Waddayareckon?" he asks me casually, tossing his mask a few feet away before lying down next to me.

"Honestly?" I ask, relieved we're not making eye contact. "That you're downright sexy."

At this, his whole body quivers as he erupts into a fit of laughter.

"I reckon I wasn't expectin' that," he says, rolling towards me.

He pulls me down next to him, hovering over me, as he encompasses most of my view. I see half of his body is covered in sand. He stares down at me, searching my face. I raise my hand up and lightly caress his cheek with my sandy fingers.

"What are *you* thinking?" I ask, breaking his intrinsic gaze.

He looks me right in the eyes with a hint of a smile.

"That yar downright spunky," he shares. With care and practice, he moves a stray curl away from my eyes. I crease my brows. In America "spunky" means lively, peppy or energetic. I get the feeling it means something different here. He leans in closer and plants a soft kiss on my neck. "It means yar a downright hottie, Neens."

"Oh," I say, slightly embarrassed and taken aback, but pleased.

It's still pretty bizarre to hear a guy, let alone a very attractive one such as Brodie, refer to me as hot. He kisses me again, more seductively this time, along my neck, whilst whispering things like "my spunky Neens" along my jaw. I laugh as he does. The soft murmurings tickle my skin. I reach my sandy hand behind his head and guide his lips to mine, not willing to wait any longer. We pash for a few minutes. His arm lightly enfolds around me, while he holds my torso with his other hand, as the tips of his fingers lightly trace the shape of my breast. Funny to think a few months ago I couldn't handle attention, let alone a touch, without going into ballistic hyperdrive; now his hand placement feels so right, I barely even notice it. He kisses me on the tip of my nose before breaking away and standing. He sighs and extends both hands to me.

"Don't wanna, but I gotta share ya," he relents.

I reach up and grab his hands. Both covered in sand, he pulls me to my feet and we both take a quick dip to rinse off before biking back towards the ferry. As we board, I turn and give Rotto one last look.

As we reach the mainland, I ask, "Where are we meeting the crew?"

"We're not, just yet. They're actually seein' some flick for anotha hour or two, so I still got ya to myself 'til then, eh."

My stomach rumbles loudly, and I chuckle.

"Food might be nice," I mention.

"Yep, 'n I've just the place."

We Uber to Leederville, where we're staying. Apparently it's a fun, upbeat borough for younger people. Our thirty minute ride feels short as I take in the city sights. As we pass restaurant after restaurant, I'm now starving and could almost eat my hand, but Brodie assures me his pick is worth the wait. Suddenly, we get dropped off on the corner, out in front of this amazing, happening restaurant. I look up and see white printing on the little overhang. It's called Pinchós, a bar de tapas. I turn to Brodie and light up, actually jumping a little.

"I know it's not authentic Mexican," he shares in a smile, "but it's the best I could do."

More than delightfully surprised, I turn and give him a giant smile. With the tick of a head and the click of his tongue, he leads me towards the entrance. A hostess gives him the eye as we approach her.

"How can I help ya?" she asks, overly friendly.

"G'day," he states, leaning in. "Brodie for two."

She glances at me and I give her a sheepish grin back. Her smile falters slightly. She checks the list and nods, and guides us through the restaurant. As we enter, the smells already make my mouth water. The hostess leads us to a little table in the corner against the glass window that overlooks the street. We sit across from each other. The hostess points to the QR code on the table so we can pull up our online menus. She mutters the word "Covid" as she walks off. Shuffling in my chair, I look around. Giant hanging light pendants hang from the open beam ceilings. A beautiful bar, full of all types of alcohol, lines the wall. It's very swanky, and feels very Spanish European.

"Brodie, I don't know what to say. This place looks and smells divine," I mutter, dumbfounded. "If the food is half as good as the ambiance, I'm sure it'll be amazing."

Clearly pleased with his selection, he chuckles softly and unfolds the napkin on his lap. Brodie scans the code on his phone and the menu pops up. He hands it to me and I scroll down. At first glance, I pick up on familiar dishes that have me reminiscing of home and Abuela.

"Albondigas?" I say in wonder. "Paella, quesadillas, chorizo?"

Each word just amplifies my excitement.

"So I made the right call, eh?" he smiles.

"¡Claro que sí!" I reply, nodding my head enthusiastically. "I don't even know where to start. It all reminds me of home and Abuela."

He looks a little smug.

"Well, I reckon ya miss 'em 'n the food," he explains, shrugging.

A waiter walks up, asking if we'd like to start with any drinks or tapás.

Detecting a thick accent, I say, "Estoy tan emocionada de estar aquí. Soy del sur de California y hace años que no como comida española o mexicana. ¿Recomendaciones?"

The waiter looks excited to hear his native tongue, while Brodie looks slightly taken aback. I guess he's never really heard me speak more than a phrase or two before. The waiter, Jaime, suggests the calamari along with the albondigas for starters. As for drinks, if we're in the mood for something refreshing, he loves the Rambla or there's the Pisco Sour, a house specialty. Biting my lip at all of the options, I look to Brodie, who narrows his eyes thoughtfully.

"How do you say 'all of it' in Spanish?" he asks.

"Really?" I lean forward, thrilled. I turn to Jaime. "¡Todo porfa!"

Delighted, he runs off to get our drinks going. I lean forward towards Brodie and actually squeal a little. While Brodie is always more than generous and not a penny pincher at all, I've never known him to be so frivolous and carefree - although, we've never really been in a setting until now where the action would present itself. I make a face of slight surprise at him. He leans back a little, relaxing and looks at me affectionately.

"I reckon it's our first official date out in the public eye, eh," he reveals.

I look around at all the people, then peer through the glass window to see a bunch walking around the sidewalks. Smiling, I nod, realizing what he says is actually true.

"What about that night at the diner?" I ask inquisitively, raising an eyebrow.

"Yeah, nah, doesn't count. Besides that was the night we did the naughty," he explains wickedly. "We weren't *togetha* togetha then."

Super entertained by his outlook on the start of our relationship, I sit back, watching him.

Jaime sets down two beautiful glasses that look like works of art. The Rambla, I presume, is a berry colored blended drink, full to the brim in an hour glass shaped tumbler, with sprigs of mint shooting out the top, along with a white and black striped paper straw. The other, the Pisco Sour, is in a wide mouthed flute glass with a thin stem. About an inch of whipped egg white foam layers the top. A pretty, russet leaf design is stamped into the foam. My eyes loom large between the two.

"Rambla on over here," I joke.

I sing the beginning notes of Led Zeppelin's "Ramble On" as I slide the glass closer to me. Brodie's shoulders shake as he laughs at my musical pun. I take a large sip from the straw and close my eyes. It tastes amazing. Flavors of blueberry paired with a hint of lemon fill my tastebuds, followed by the bite of alcohol. I offer Brodie a sip and he takes one, licking his lips as he swallows.

"There's a lot of gin 'n Triple Sec in there," he says appreciatively. He hands it back to me and I grab it, taking another long sip. It's ice cold and super refreshing. "Look out, Neens," he warns mockingly, playfully raising his eyebrows quickly up and down. "We can't have ya pissed rotten by the time we meet up with the crew."

"Yeah, yeah," I reply sarcastically, as I down another sip. Swallowing, I nod to his drink. "How's that?"

"Honestly, I'm tryin' to find the words to describe it. Here," he says, offering it to me, urging me to find out for myself.

I bring the wide glass to my lips and hesitantly take a little drink. I feel the whipped egg whites on my upper lip as I swoosh it around in my mouth. My eyes shoot up in surprise. He's right. I don't even know how to begin to describe the flavor.

"Is that jasmine or peach?" I lick my lips, deliberating. "Or both?"

"But then there's the lemon 'n mint thrown in there, I reckon."

"I don't think I've ever tasted anything quite like it," I say with a smile, licking my lips as I revel in the fusion of flavors.

I take another bigger sip before handing it back to my date, giggling as I do. As I feel the temperature of my reddening cheeks with the back of my fingers, I hear him mutter the words "two pot screamer" under his breath, full of amusement.

Jaime returns, setting down our tapás in between us. The calamari looks utterly crunchy and tender. I can barely see the bowl of albondigas because my eyes well up in delightful tears.

"Everythin' alright, Neens?" Brodie asks.

"Mom and Abuela make the most amazing pot of albondigas," I explain, smiling longingly, then gaze at the meatballs. "It reminds me of them is all."

"I reckon ya miss 'em heaps. Sorry if it's—."

"No, no," I shake my head, hurriedly. "I'm really happy Brodie. And while I miss them terribly, there's no where I'd rather be than right here with you."

I take my spoon and break up a meatball. The steam rises off it. Spooning some broth, I scoop up a piece and bring the spoon straight to my lips. *Wow!* It's amazing, and super different.

"Does it compare?" he asks curiously.

"Not really, see this is more of a Spanish style albondigas than Mexican, so it's completely different, which is a good thing," I explain, holding up a spoonful towards him. "Come on, you've got to try some. It's delicious!"

He leans forward and cleans the spoon dry, nodding his head, agreeing with my review.

"Just wait until you try my mom's," I say, my voice catching at the end.

I realize for that to happen either one or both of us would have to be back in America. Though neither of us is afraid to discuss the future, it's not something that we willingly chat about at length because for any type of decision to be made, it would have to be forced on us by my visa's termination. Ignoring the elephant in the room, I grab a calamari and dip it into the reddish sauce before biting down onto its tender filet. The flavor melts away any previous thoughts. Brodie dives in too, and together, we lose our minds in its perfection. Before we know it, the plate is empty. The bowl of albondigas sits empty on the table as well.

"Clearly yous didn't enjoy that at all," Jaime jests, clearing our plates. He waits to take our order. Both of us are already getting full off our tapás and drinks, which are nearly gone, so we just order the Pintxos de Pollo to share. Scribbling on his notepad, Jaime nods. "El pollo es muy increiblé."

Before walking off, he halts and asks us if we want another round of drinks. I hesitate. If I get a second one now, I'll be pretty much done for the night, and I know we're meeting up with the crew for our big night out on New Years Eve. It's better to pace myself. Brodie watches me as I have my internal debate.

"Just a mojito for me, mate," he announces, "but we'll defo have the flan for lata."

"Un mojito y El Tocino de Cielo," Jaime repeats with a grin, stepping away.

"Wait til ya try the flan, Neens," Brodie exclaims, leaning forward very enthusiastically. "It's somethin' special I reckon. It's so cracka that even ova a year lata, I rememba it."

"Wow. Well in that case, I'm sold already," I say. Picking up on his little clue, I ask, "So what brought you here last time?"

I take another gulp of my melting drink. *It really is so delicious.*

He quirks his mouth to the side, fidgeting.

"Nothin' important really," he answers politely, maybe too politely, and with a hint of nervousness.

I pinch my lips shut, trying to hide my amusement. I can tell he doesn't really want to say, which I find intriguing and also entertaining.

"You know, Brodie," I say innocently, making a doe-eyed expression, "it's okay that you had a life before me. I'm not stupid you know." Caught in some semblance of the truth, I see his shoulders drop slightly. I want to dig a little deeper, maybe to pry some information out of him. *I am in fact only human.* I mutter slowly, "Was the reason for this trip perhaps a... girl?"

In his eyes, I see his answer. *Bingo.*

"Look, Neens, it wasn't that big of a thing, her 'n me," he sighs, "'n it ended a while ago... well before ya blew into town."

"Brodie," I say gently, reaching my hand out towards his, and leaning a little closer to him from across the table, "it's okay. You have history. Like I've told you before, I don't really care because it led you here to me. You don't have to tell me more if you don't want to. I trust you."

He bridges the gap and takes my hand in his, squeezing it in thanks. He grabs the rest of his drink and downs it, foam and all. He beams at me, donning a foam mustache, and then out of nowhere, leans over the table and kisses me. He leaves foamy bits all over my mouth before dropping back to his seat. Laughing, I lap up the foam with my tongue. It tastes so good.

Jaime returns with our dinner and Brodie's mojito, and sets the large plate in the middle of the table, along with two smaller ones. The Spanish style plate is full of three large, grilled chicken skewers over crispy eggplant with melted feta and honey. A romesco sauce is drizzled all over with pine nuts sprinkled on top, and a few pieces of flatbreads on the side, garnished with grilled lemon wedges. Brodie stares at it, smiling wide. Before we dig in, I grab my camera out of my bag behind my chair and take a quick pic of the meal, and another one of the platter in front of a thrilled Brodie. Brodie, in turn, asks for the camera and then flags Jaime down to snap a picture of the both of us at the table, holding up our drinks in front of us.

After, we grab our forks and spoons and gather some helpings onto our individual plates. We each begin to taste the superlative combination of flavors. I take a large bite of my chicken, straight off the skewer, and close my eyes as the tender meat practically melts in my mouth. I moan a little. Brodie does the same as he chews. We eat in silence, just admiring the view and jovial atmosphere around us. It's never awkward with him and I know he feels the same. We can just be. Looking out the window while I eat, I notice the light is fading outside, casting a long, orange tint across the little intersection.

"Sunset here is beautiful," I remark. "Different, but still beautiful."

Personally, I still prefer the wild Outback compared to this busy city life, but it's refreshing and welcoming to get out and experience something different for a couple days. This is the most amount of people I've seen collectively in more than nine months.

"I reckon what ya mean," Brodie agrees.

Stuffed, I set my fork down and wipe the corners of my mouth with my black napkin.

"I hope I have room for flan," I say, leaning back in my chair.

"Make some, then," he advises, chuckling, before taking another bite of the eggplant.

The plate is almost clear. He sets his fork down, finished, looking very much satisfied. I notice he still has about a third of his mojito left, and he grabs it and finishes it off in one full swoop. He looks at me with a broad smile. I can tell he's starting to get a little buzzed. Buzzed Brodie always makes for a fun time, especially when he loosens up after another drink.

Jaime comes and clears our plates, while dropping off the flan in front of us. The rectangle plate boasts a perfectly round flan with an accompanying strawberry and mint salad, topped with passionfruit and honeycomb. My mouth literally falls open.

"It's so pretty I don't want to eat it," I say.

Taking his spoon, Brodie jabs the flan and breaks the mold. Its gelatinous form jiggles as he scoops away a piece.

"Trust me, ya do," he says, taking a bite, and closing his eyes. "Aces, absolute aces. Here, try this, Neens."

He grabs a generous portion of flan in his spoon, and tries to feed me across the table, like a baby. I've never thought the act of feeding someone in public is very romantic or enticing. Laughing, I grab the spoon out of his hand and try the flan, wiping the utensil clean with my lips. I give him back his empty spoon as my eyes pop open at the sensation of the tasty dessert on my tastebuds. It literally melts in your mouth. Creamy tastes of caramel, infused with coconut, flood my senses. I moan audibly as I close my eyes in mirth. Brodie snorts and digs in some more, urging me to get my share or he'll eat it all. I take a couple more bites, mixing it with the honeycomb and strawberry, but I'm really starting to feel full at this point. I take one more big bite for memory's sake and savor every second as it swirls around in my mouth before I swallow. I set down my spoon, defeated, but incredibly satiated. Brodie practically licks the plate clean. Jaime brings us our check. My date pulls out a wad of Australian dollars - his money from our recent charter - and leaves a generous tip for Jaime after he pays. Jaime bids us adiós and we gather our bags, heading out onto the street.

According to Brodie, Shayno's cousin's flat is only about a five minute walk from here. We walk hand in hand towards our stay until my sweaty palms can't take it anymore. Brodie laughs as I pull away. His phone chirps, indicating a text alert and he pulls it out of his bag's front pocket. Startling me because I rarely see him on the phone, I wonder if it's one of our pals. After checking it, he quickly slides it back into his duffle. That's another thing I appreciate and admire about Brodie, he maintains a healthy and balanced relationship with his "dog and bone" as Aussie's call it; I agree, it's an apt name for a cellphone.

Brodie relays the text to me, paraphrasing, "Alrighty, the flick is ova, so they're headin' back to the flat to change. Banga timin', eh, Neens?" He looks at a street sign. "We should be there in two shakes of a lamb's tail."

Along for the ride, I'm just happy to be here.

I see a group of people approaching the same intersection as us and I realize one of the pretty, leggy chicks is Mel. She sees me at the same time, and hollers my name loudly, before running across the street and barreling right into me in a giant, rib cracking hug. The rest of the crew - Shayno, Donnie and Jaz - also realizes it's us and follow suit, hollering out in pleasant surprise. Jaz and Brodie exchange a big squeeze and Donnie envelopes me in a generous hug as well. Shayno offers me and Brodie high fives and Mel locks Brodie into a sizable side hug. Everyone is very happy to be reunited in a fresh place with some nightlife and culture. Clapping Brodie on the back, Donnie offers to take both of our bags. Walking without anything, it feels incredibly liberating to travel without any additional weight. I relish the feeling, however fleeting.

"Ya carry this thing all the time, Chica?" Donnie remarks, shocked by the weight of my camera backpack.

I laugh and shrug. *It's usually heavier.* We walk for a couple more minutes before Shayno and Jaz lead us to a two story building. At the sidewalk, there's a tall, front wooden gate that Shayno opens with the twist of a knob. The door opens to a small courtyard. We all pile into the little entryway as Shayno opens another door that leads into the actual flat. We enter through the living room. A nice white kitchen lines the back wall, mirroring a large set of stairs up to a second floor, a loft by the looks of it. I notice there's a hallway leading to a back room behind the kitchen.

"Maddie's out for the night, 'n won't be back 'til tomorrow," Shayno informs us.

I don't know anything about Shayno's cousin, but now I at least know her name. Looking around, clearly Maddie has style. She has plants everywhere, which I like, and she has abstract paintings all over her chartreuse painted walls.

"Maddie has a nice place," I declare.

"Only the best for Maddie," Jaz mutters under her breath, but I hear her just fine.

*Hmmm*, does Jaz have a beef with her or something? Funny, I thought Jaz loves everyone.

Donnie guides us upstairs to the loft. One queen bed fills the room with an adjacent dresser. Mel announces she and I will be sharing the bed while Brodie and Donnie will crash on the couches downstairs. I look to Brodie and stifle a giggle. He doesn't look too pleased, but doesn't buck it either. Donnie sets all of our bags down on top of the dresser, out of the way. Mel then tells us, since Shayno is Maddie's cousin, he and Jaz get the privilege of her private bedroom downstairs. As she talks, Mel grabs clothes from her bag and starts to change, without a thought or care to any modesty. Feeling energized by my little buzz a la Rambla and the reunion with the gang, I'm ready for whatever the night brings. Over her skinny frame, Mel effortlessly slides on a white, crushed velvet jumpsuit. She looks like she just stepped out of a catalogue. I tell her so and she eats up the praise. Donnie throws her some serious looks of appreciation and admiration.

Strapping on her stilettos, Mel announces we're to get ready for a night out at The Reveley, a "cracka rooftop bar."

When I apparently don't look impressed enough, Mel says, "Tons of music, Neens, *loud* music."

Naturally when it comes to music, I perk up even more and she looks satisfied. As Brodie and Donnie change their shirts in the corner of the room, Mel opens up my bag and rifles through it, looking for something.

"What are you doing?" I ask curiously, lightly laughing.

I'm honestly not offended from the lack of privacy.

Not finding what she's looking for, she moans in frustration.

"I was hopin' ya came with some new outfit, a top maybe, but nah, ya didn't," she wistfully explains. "So besides the Tarzan rat's nest, I've gotta dress ya as well." Brodie chuckles, and gives me a face that reads: *yikes, good luck with that*. The boys escape downstairs as Mel energetically rummages through her own bag, and beams proudly. "Which is why I planned ahead."

She holds up a sunshine yellow dress, a very short dress by the looks of it. In fact, the more I inspect it, the more non-Nina it becomes, aside from the color. She offers it to me, but I just stare at it like it has rows of ridged teeth. She thrusts it into my hands, ordering me to strip and put it on. Not wanting to challenge her in this setting, I take off my clothes, revealing my banana bikini.

"Really, Neens," she mutters, mid eye roll. "What happened to the," she lowers her voice, and whispers, "lingerie?" Sighing, I grab my bag and reach in, unzipping the hidden compartment. I pull out the bra and thong. She applauds. "Yar not a total lost cause yet."

I hear laughter from below. Stripping quickly, I'm still not totally comfortable with complete nudity, even in front of Mel, and there's no door. However, I know she won't give me a choice, so I just relent. I slide the thong on quickly and clasp the bra hastily. Adjusting the bra so it covers all the right places, I hear footsteps on the stairs and freeze. Jaz pops up, sporting a gold glitter mini dress. I relax, seeing it's just her, and finalize the position of the bra to get maximum coverage as possible, which isn't much with this thing. I hold out Mel's "dress" in front of me. It looks like a glorified jammie top. Not wanting to disappoint her, I pull the dress up over my head. The fabric falls loosely over my face, blocking my view. The bust is going to be a tight squeeze, I can already tell.

"What makes you think I can fit into one of *your* dresses, Mel?" I mumble through the fabric.

"'Cause I bought it for ya, ya galah," she replies, snorting.

"What? You didn't need to do that," I argue, touched.

"Nah, yeah, I did," she counters immediately, with a hint of pride. "'N I even got it from a modern vintage shop today. Totally yar style."

I pull the fabric down, and surprisingly it all slides right into place. It is pretty snug in the top, but nothing like a corset. I hear Jaz and Mel both gasp in appreciation. I peer down. The entire dress is banana yellow. One-inch straps come straight down over my shoulders to a very fitted bust. From there, the yellow fabric billows out, stopping only a few inches down my thigh. The bottom hem is lined with a fuzzy strip, like a small boa of mini feathers. Basically I'm wearing a baby-doll bustier. I turn, rotating for the girls, and my boobs jiggle, all perky from the bra balconette combo.

"Wow, Nina, ya got crash hot titties, eh," Jaz exclaims, eyeing me, before glancing down at her own B-cup.

"Yar a fox, Neens," Mel declares, squinting in thought. She bites her thumb and refers to Jaz. "Whaddaya think, do we lose the bra? I don't reckon she needs it."

"Nah, yeah, I think we pull it," Jaz agrees, eyeing my bust line.

Reaching back, I unclasp the bra and strategically wedge it out from under the dress, stuffing it back into my pack. The ladies are right. The dress is so tightly fitted, a bra isn't necessary. Mel twirls her hand, ordering me to spin, and I do.

"Yar heatha," they speak in unison.

Taking their word for it, I glance at my boots. It's not really the baby-doll look, but they're all I have. Sliding one on my foot, Mel butts in, thrusting white block heels in my arms.

"You really think of everything," I say, seriously impressed.

"With you, someone's gotta, but yar lucky," she replies, "I happened to pack these."

She reaches up to work on her hair, but I push her hands out of the way. I quickly do this really cool, side waterfall braid Ria taught me. It's easy and looks top notch. Mel stairs in her tiny compact mirror, nodding in approval.

"You have to let me return the favor every now and again," I joke.

"If I'dda known ya were keen, I'dda had ya do it — wait, why don't ya do this to yarself, eh?" she asks accusatorially.

"Because I can't do it on myself. Tarzan, remember," I retort. "But, believe me, I wish I could."

Tying to figure out what to do with my mane, I check out Jaz's hair, which she wears crimped and flowing. I tell her how much I adore her whole retro heist movie vibe.

"Oy, ya ladies ready or what?" Shayno calls up from below.

"Yeah, be there in two shakes, babe," Jaz hollers back.

She sits down and offers to do my makeup quickly. She, like Mel, knows I don't wear tons of it and goes for a more natural look, similarly to how I wore it to the town yacht party. My hair is another story after our day swimming and biking. I settle with a high bun, pulling most of it back. Mel leans forward and pulls out a couple of shorter tendrils around my temples. They both sit back, looking very pleased with their hasty makeover. I stand, eager to see who I've become at their behest. I feel so tall with the extra three inches of block heel, but now my dress feels super short. Is it too short? Oh well. Short of sewing on a ruffle, it is what it is. Looking like Charlie's Angels with Mel and Jaz flanking me, I giggle. Both tower over me. Mel looks stunning in her white velvet, paired with pink stilettos, and Jaz with her gold sequences and aqua boots.

I follow my compadres down the stairs to see the guys waiting, bored, on the sofa. Donnie and Shayno hear our heels on the wood and turn, smiling. Seeing them twist our way, Brodie gets up and looks everyone over, before his eyes rest on me as I step down to ground level. Brodie's mouth visibly drops. I pause on the last step.

Shayno and Donnie look floored as their gaze travels over the three of us. Donnie quickly snaps a picture of us. I glance around, uncomfortable with the attention. I clear my throat, which breaks their trance. Mel storms towards the door, yelling we've gotta get there before the line gets too long. The rest of them, minus Brodie, follow her out into the courtyard to order an Uber. Brodie, still as a statue, blatantly looks me over, head to tow.

"Girls did it," I mention lamely, shrugging. He just stares, so I mutter nervously, "Say something, damn you."

His face breaks out into the most genuine, jaw breaking smile.

"Sorry, it's just…" he searches for the right word, "wow, Neens. Ya look…?"

"Different?"

I step down to his level. I realize with these heels on, he doesn't tower over me as much as usual.

"We betta go, or I might rip that right off ya 'n to hell with The Reveley," he explains with a growl, holding out his elbow, offering me to take it.

I slide my hand through the crook of his arm and we walk out to join our party in the street.

After a little socially distanced line outside, we finally make it to the rooftop bar at The Reveley, which under normal New Year's Eve circumstances would be untouchable; however under domestic lockdown, the smaller crowds work in our favor.

Mel grabs my arm on one side and Jaz on the other as we make our entrance. I glance around. It's absolutely gorgeous. The restaurant sits below, while the upper roof deck functions as the dance floor and bar. The location sits right on the water in downtown. Lights from the city swirl around like bokeh in the background, glinting off the water from the bay. Having left my camera and bag behind tonight, I take a mental snapshot. I think it's the first time in months I've ever felt so physically carefree and light for hours on end. I glance back at Brodie, who stands tall in a light aqua button-down and straight-leg denim jeans, flanked by Shayno and Donnie, who also dress up a little for our big night on the town.

We find a cocktail table and a few barstools and make ourselves comfortable. The boys take drink orders. Brodie leans in and asks me what I want. *Hmmm.*

"Sex on the Beach," I answer unabashedly.

Mel and Jaz laugh their heads off. Brodie snorts, shaking his head slightly, and catches up with the boys at the bar. What can I say other than it's one of my favorite drinks from back home?

The boys return a few minutes later, passing our drinks around. Taking a sip, I close my eyes; sure enough it's wonderfully sweet and reminds me of a tropical vacation. Feeling really good, I start to loosen up and sway to the beat of the music. Some DJ stands on the side of the stage, jockeying vinyl records. I nudge Mel, telling her how amazing it is to see a dying art in action, when she tells me to finish my drink. I down it and she grabs my hand, along with Jaz's and pulls us out onto the dance floor, shouting in excitement. Feeling the beat, I don't resist, but actually embrace the dance. In fact, I start feeling so breezy and carefree that I close my eyes and move my hands in the air to the tempo. I let out a loud holler. It's enrapturing and enthralling. I open my eyes and see Mel and Jaz grinning back at me, clearly enjoying themselves too.

Suddenly, Donnie makes his way out to us. After the last time we shared the dance floor on the yacht, I throw him a wary grin. He shakes his body to the rhythm and dances right in between us "sexy sheilas." Us ladies share a look, and feeling puckish, all dance alongside him, encouraging him on. As always in jest, he dances practically on top of us, with some new hot moves if I do say so myself. I have flashbacks to a few weeks ago of him grinding along my thigh. Again, I'm surprised for his robust and vigorous build, he moves so fluidly and provocatively. I have to admit, he's a super fun dance partner, and find myself digging his sensuous rhythm. I glance back at the table and see Brodie and Shayno watching us, laughing their heads off as they drink their coldies. Since I can't wink, at least not smoothly, I nod quickly to Brodie.

Donnie and I go head to head, busting a move. Mel and Jaz hoot and yell on the sidelines. I suddenly see a hand come over Donnie's shoulder, pulling him back, revealing it's Brodie. He grabs me with eyes that scream *come hither* and pulls me up against him as we grind to the music. That aqua shirt really showcases his vitality, along with the dark washed denim and sneakers. Brodie oozes cool. I don't think I've ever seen him wear jeans before, and I gulp as his whole look right now is really turning me on. He pulls me towards him, and leans in flirtatiously.

"Hold up," he demands.

He steps back ever so slightly and looks up, gesturing to my top knot. Stilling me, he reaches over my head, and lightly untwists the scrunchie, letting my hair cascade down my backside. Satisfied, he pumps me back and forth dramatically as we sway to the beat of the music. We're both really feeling the moment, completely wrapped up in losing ourselves to the rhythm. Sweaty, I can feel the heated electricity pour from Brodie's fingertips into me. The beat morphs into a sultrier, yet bass heavy mix. In my peripheral, I see the others enjoying themselves, but I don't even really care. All I care about is Brodie in front of me in this euphoria, us both buzzed and high on life. Squealing as he dips me, I come back up, dying laughing. I place my hands on his clammy chest and stare into his eyes. Panting from the exertion, we dance in cadence as the beat picks back up. Desire surges in me. *I want him.*

"No need to smash yar backs out," Donnie yells at us.

I chuckle. I guess we are getting a little carried away. I break away and dance with Mel. She pulls me into a sweaty side hug as we jump in sync to the new hardcore beat. Jaz and Brodie dance side by side, grinning from ear to ear. After a couple more mixes, we head back to the table, parched. Mel hands me a tall glass of water and commands I drink it on the spot. Then she yells she's ordering another round of drinks, and takes off in the direction of the bar. She has the eyes for the bartender, I can tell. She returns, asking for help and I jump up, following her. Upon closer inspection, the bartender is a total cutie. I raise a thick eyebrow Mel's way, which she pretends not to see. He leans over, looking very friendly at the pair of us.

"Skip, this is Neens, my bestie," Mel shouts over the music.

She kisses me scrumptiously on the cheek.

Skip raises his eyebrows at us, then leans down.

"Whaddaya doin' afta, maybe we can cop a root, the three of us, eh?" he whispers, in between our heads.

Shocked and scandalized, I double over, laughing. Apparently Skip thinks it's hilarious and I see him eyeing my busty cleavage. I stop, sobering slightly. *Oh, he's serious then.* He sets down my drink and a Moscow mule, and I grab them, running off to the table. I set them down, roaring in hysterics. I tell the crew about the preposterous offer. They all blanche in surprise, then hilariously bust a gut, laughing. Brodie eyes Skip, but thankfully doesn't do anything else about it. I hate it when guys are so blatantly territorial. I finish off another drink and start to walk back to Mel to see if she needs help when I almost trip over my heels. A small hiccup escapes me. I hold my breath, wishing with all my might that they'll go away quickly. When I hiccup, it sounds like a rooster croaking. I inherited this less than desirable trait from Papi.

"Reckon we lost her, eh," Brodie says, chuckling to our friends as he clutches me by my waist.

"No," I slur. "I'm right here, silly."

"Yep, defo," Shayno says, guffawing.

We all go out on the dance floor one more time. Apparently it's close to midnight. The DJ amps up the crowd, prepping us for the iconic midnight countdown to reign in the New Year. I think this is the latest I've been up in months. I used to be a night owl, but after continuous days in the sun here in Straya, I started mimicking the sun's patterns of early bedtimes and early risings.

"Two minutes," the MC warns the crowd. The dance floor erupts in energy, gearing up. The DJ matches the vibe of the room by queuing up some hardcore EDM track. Immediately, we all start jumping madly to the quick tempo. The MC builds the anticipation. "Sixty seconds." I glance around at my friends, happy to be here with each of them to end the weirdest year of all time. "Goodbye 2020, ya fucker," the MC roars, "'n g'day 2021 in ten, nine, eight..." He countdowns. "Three, two... one!"

The whole floor screams and whistles Happy New Year wishes, while everyone grabs their respective partners for the customary kiss. Big bellowing pops of fireworks explode over the marina around us. The whole city celebrates. Brodie takes my face in his. It's so loud I can't hear him, but I see his mouth yell, "Happy

New Year, Neens!" before he pulls me to him. I happily give him a healthy, hearty, and lustful kiss.

Dragging Brodie around the dance floor, I try to seductively dance around him. I think it's working. He won't take his eyes off me. I can't tell if he's into it or just making sure he's around to catch me if I fall. It's beginning to feel like I'm on the Teacups ride at Disneyland. Twirling, I spin towards Jaz and Shayno, who make out in the middle of the many moving bodies. Twisting around Mel, I see she's pash and dashing with Skip. *Good for her.* Donnie's also dancing with some pretty chick across the room. I spin back towards Brodie and crash against him. He leans in and takes my breath away as he fervently and excitedly kisses me.

"Let's get out of here," I murmur in his ear, spending some ample time around his jawline.

Chuckling, Brodie steps away, holding my hand, and pulls me across the dance floor. He leans down and tells Shayno and his sister we're heading back, and the two smile happily at us. I hear him tell Donnie to to keep an eye on Mel and to make sure she gets back to the flat safely. With his arm around my waist, we exit The Reveley. It's kind of a blur, but somehow, we wind up at the flat. Brodie guides me inside, propping me up with his arm. I laugh as he steers me up the darkened stairs. I almost face plant, but he catches me and eventually we make it to the top. He sits me down on the edge of the bed, and bends down, undoing the zipper of my heeled boots. I hear them fall with a chunky *thud* to the floor, one by one. I moan at the amazing feeling of being barefoot again and the immediate relief on my knee. With my thumb, I rub it briefly.

He carefully massages my incision site for a minute as I lie back on the bed and emit a loud groan of ecstasy. *That feels incredible.* I tell him so and he continues for another minute or two. Suddenly, my dress is itchy.

"Itchy," I mumble, trying to pull it off by the hem, but failing.

I close my eyes and hear Brodie rummaging through a bag. The flat's pretty dimly lit so I don't know how he's finding anything. He returns and I open my eyes. My lids feel like leaded weights. My thoughtful beau slowly lifts my dress up and over my head, and quickly slides his tank top in its place, pulling it down over my stomach. He then squats in front of me, holding a wipe. Gently and with great tenderness, he wipes away my makeup. I hear him chuckle.

"There she is," he reveals endearingly. "There's my Nina."

I look at him. About to fall over from exhaustion, I don't care, I *want* him. I pull him by the collar of his shirt towards me, wanting to pick up where we left off on the dance floor. I manage to steal a kiss or two, but he pulls back, giggling.

"But I want you," I whine.

"I reckon so, 'n I you, but I reckon yar gonna pass out in a tick."

"Come here," I try again, pulling him towards me. "Ya know, you're my favorite person. I mean it. Out of all of them, it's you."

Now I hear his chuckle deepen. He leans me back on the bed and scoots me up so my head's on the pillow. He places my feet under the covers, pulling back the comforter so I won't get too hot. Tucking me in, he leans down close to me.

"I like you a lot, Brodie, like maybe more than a lot," I whisper, trying to stifle a hiccup.

He bites his lip, amused. "Do ya now?"

I close my eyes and yawn.

"I love you, I think," I faintly say.

I feel his lips touch mine briefly before I swim down into oblivion.

# 25

My eyelids flutter as light sneaks its way underneath into my irises. I bat them a couple of times and look around. *Where am I?* White walls and ceiling fill my view. I hesitantly move and feel a body next to me. I twist ever so slightly and see Mel passed out, asleep with her mouth open, just barely, exposing her large square teeth. I tilt my head up a little and look over at the other side of the bed and find Donnie wedged in, snoring next to Mel. How the hell did three grown people sleep on a queen mattress? As quietly as possible, I sit up, wincing as my head begins to pulse and pound in a deep throb. I try not to jostle Mel too much, but she wakes. Her eyes open in slits, and she frowns.

"Too early," she croaks, and twists around, pulling my pillow over her head.

She takes the opportunity to stretch out and take over the available space. As I stand, memories flood in bits and pieces from last night. I remember dancing on the rooftop with Brodie and the crew, having a terrific time, but getting from The Reveley back here to the flat is a little foggy... I'm pretty sure Brodie had to carry me back halfway. I grab my water canteen and chug the entire canister. I admit it helps me feel loads better. *They do say drinking too much after the age of thirty is a bitch, Nina.*

I grab my bikini from my bag and hastily change into it under my baggy tank top. I slide off the tank and replace it with my white flowing sundress. There's a framed photo hanging on the wall and I use the glass's reflection to assess my hair. *Hmm, not my best look.* Stray curls shoot out all over in every direction. The underneath actually looks decent, but the top layer is frizz central. After trying a couple of styles out, I grab the top pieces and pull the strands into a loose side braid, sweeping from one side of my head to the other like a loose natural headband. All my lighter highlights pull forward, forming a neat pattern, while the rest of my hair falls down my back in a mess of ringlets. It's not the best braid, but it's adventure ready, and honestly, it pairs really well with my dress. Snatching my sandals and bag, I put on my sunnies and tiptoe across the room and down the stairs. About to burst, I need to find the bathroom right now.

With blankets and pillows stacked neatly on the couch, Brodie sits quietly talking to some raven haired woman, who sits on the sofa across from him. With her back to me, I don't recognize her, but I can tell by Brodie's expression and posture he's very much engaged and clearly well acquainted. Brodie looks up and sees me descending the stairs. His face lights up into a radiant smile. I point to the bathroom and make a bee-line for it. After finishing my quick morning routine and feeling much improved, I walk back out to the living area towards the kitchen. Brodie jumps up from the couch and walks in my direction.

"G'mornin', Sunshine," he says, passing me to the fridge, and squeezes my arm affectionately. "Sleep alright?"

"Morning," I say, smiling back. "Yeah, I slept like a log. Feel better than I thought I would. The back end of the night is pretty hazy."

Brodie chuckles as he pours himself some orange juice. He asks me if I'd like a glass with a look, but I shake my head.

The woman stands up and turns to greet me. She towers over me by a good six inches, and actually looks like she could rival Margot as Viking Queen, only less Nordic and more southern European with dark features. Looking down at me with the most beautiful, whiskey colored eyes, she smiles. Her smile is magnetic, or maybe it's her incredibly white teeth. She extends a long arm out, and I take her hand, shaking it politely.

"G'day, I'm Maddie," she says enthusiastically.

"Hey, I'm Nina," I reply back, just as energetically. "Thanks so much for letting us crash here. You have the coolest flat."

"Thanks," Maddie laughs, friendly, and looks from me to Brodie. "Do I detect a Yank accent?"

Standing by my side with a glass of water in hand, he looks to me, with the crook of a smile sneaking up.

"Guilty," I say nervously, eyeing her paintings on the wall. "So are they yours?"

She smiles at the one closest to us and shakes her head.

"Madds is an art curator at a local gallery down the street," Brodie butts in, explaining.

"That's awesome," I say, grinning.

"Nina here is our resident photographa," Brodie shares, looking from me to Maddie. "A bloody cracka one at that."

"Well, I don't know about all that," I say shyly. "I just love to drone. It's an amazing perspective."

"Aerial photographa. Interesting," she exclaims, her smile widening. "I'd love to see yar work. We're always on the hunt for upcomin' talent, especially female artists."

My eyes pop open, which makes Brodie chuckle.

"Yeah, I mean that would be terrific," I stammer. "I'll have Brodie send you my link?"

"Brilliant," she states, satisfied.

Jaz comes barreling down the hall, bumping into me. She smiles politely at Maddie, then loops her arm through mine and tugs me towards the door.

"Let's pop down to coffee 'n donuts," she demands.

I look back, eager to talk further with Maddie.

"I reckon ya just go with her, Neens," Brodie suggests.

Jaz turns and sticks her tongue out at her brother. Before I know it, I'm being hauled out the door.

As soon as we're on the street, Jaz erupts, "Oh, God, Neens, sorry I didn't rescue ya soona."

We walk side by side down the sidewalk. I glance at her, confused.

"Wow, it's bright out here," I say, adjusting my glasses, then look back at Jaz. "Wait, what do you mean, rescue? Maddie seems super sweet. I can see why Brodie likes her."

She snorts, but doesn't explain further. I grab her arm gently, forcing her to stop.

"Sorry, I shouldn't have meddled," she mutters, looking at me. "She can be very nice, just watch yar back, Neens, she's not all she's cracked up to be."

With that said, she walks briskly down the street to the corner.

"So we actually are going for coffee and donuts," I say, standing outside of a little breakfast cafe.

"'Course. Gotta commit to the ruse, eh."

Dozens of different types of donuts line the window. Jaz nudges me inside and we wait in the two person line. I'm starving, but am also borderline nauseous after last night. We wait, and when its our turn, we order our coffees - a flat white for Jaz, and an iced latte for me - along with a box of a dozen donuts. I throw in a few extra coffees as well for the others. Jaz selects an assortment of donuts, that as a Yank, I need to try. Apparently I don't really know what a donut is until I've had an Aussie one. Thinking about back home and all the hype over donut shops over the last decade or so, I snort to myself. I suppose tastes will tell.

We walk a little slower back to the flat, sipping our coffees and enjoying the early morning sun, that for the first time in my life physically hurts my head. Each passing sip of coffee feels like an injection of life into my body. I hold a tray of drinks in one hand, while Jaz holds tight to the box of donuts. I glance at her through my sunnies. She seems perfectly normal with me. I wonder what that was about back there?

"I'm trying not to pry," I say, feeling curious beyond my control, "but what's the deal between you and Maddie?"

She takes another sip, but I don't let her off that easy. I press her with a *tell me now* stare.

"I told Shayno stayin' with her was a bad idea," she moans.

"Why?"

"Ya didn't hear this from me, but she's Brodie's ex. She was the one who broke his heart."

*Oh!* My interest peaks. *I did not see that coming.*

"They seem so friendly with each other," I admit. "How long ago was this?"

"I'd ratha ya had this convo with my brotha," Jaz says, smiling pathetically.

"OK, but you can't just drop that and not expect me to have questions. I'm only human here."

"Ugh, fine. It happened a few months before ya blew into town," she blurts out, mid eye roll and head shake. "Bottom line was my brotha's too good for her, but he's always been too good for all of 'em." She looks at me with an encouraging smile. "'Til now."

Jaz bounces into my shoulder, playfully nudging me. We both smile. I take a big sip of my quickly disappearing latte until I obnoxiously slurp every last drop.

"If this latte is any indication, I think those donuts are going to be wonderful," I say, much to her delight.

"Just ya wait, Neens," she teases, as we round the corner of the flat.

So Maddie's his ex... suddenly, I'm a touch anxious.

The door hangs open and we walk into the little courtyard entryway. The rest of the gang sits on the patio furniture, absorbing the heat of the sun like lizards after a bad rainstorm. Hearing us enter, they perk up a little, wincing as they open their eyes. Brodie seems totally normal as he sits up with a pleasant grin for us. He must not have partied as hard as the rest of us. In fact, the memory of him escorting me back here flashes through my mind.

Mel groans at the sight of Jaz's donuts. She looks a little worse for wear in the corner chair. I beeline directly to her and lean over, handing her a warm paper cup of coffee. She puts both hands around it.

"Yar too good to me," she croaks.

"Just drink," I kindly instruct her.

I whirl around and pass out the rest of the coffees to the boys.

"Thanks, Chica, yar givin' me life," Donnie mutters, before taking a sip and sighing in delight.

"I figured you guys might need it," I chuckle. "I certainly did."

I brought Maddie a coffee too, thinking she'd be here, so I set it down on the micro table. I hand Brodie his, but he pulls me down carefully to sit on his lap.

"That was nice of ya, Neens," he whispers into my ear, before taking a swig of his own cup.

"Neens," Jaz coos, turning to us as she holds the box of donuts. They're all lined up perfectly in two rows. "Ya get first dibs."

"Go for the crumb one," Brodie mutters under his breath.

Jaz hushes him, saying I get to decide for myself. After she goes over all of the options such as avocado chocolate, turkey maple bacon, and a couple of other weird combinations, I naturally settle on the crumb as it looks to be the most basic option. I take a bite and cinnamon swirls around my tastebuds. I'm not quite sure if it has America beat, but regardless, Jaz doesn't need to know. She eagerly awaits my review.

"Delicious!" I say with a mouthful. "Amazing. You were right."

Brodie reaches around me and grabs the chocolate avocado one. Smiling smugly, Jaz whirls around and offers them to the rest of the gang. Mel waives them off vehemently. We all finish off our breakfast going over the events of last night, laughing at each other's versions of how we each got home as the others fill in the gaps with reality.

"Whaddaya rememba, Neens?" Mel asks, in between sips of coffee.

I pinch my lips, trying to bring some clarity to my hazy memory of the back half of the evening.

"Well, I remember us having the best time at the club, dancing, drinking," I say, as the crew hollers. "Then I remember more drinking and that's when things start to blur..." I glance at Brodie, who sits with an amused expression on his face as he listens. "Um, I think Brodie and I left, but then I have no idea how we got back here." I laugh as a flashback fills my mind's eye. "Oh wait! I do remember Brodie carrying me over his shoulder at some point."

I can feel Brodie's body shake in laughter under mine.

"Bloody oath," he chimes in. "I had to, afta ya kept runnin' loose into the street ova 'n ova. Almost got hit by a parked car." Everyone laughs and I bury my face in my hands. He smiles. "Let's just say it was a long way home, then ya finally passed out, completely knackered on my shoulda, but when we got back, ya fired right up again, keen on doin' all sorts a things." Donnie's brow raises suggestively, while I moan in embarrassment. Brodie teases him, "Sorry, mate, I can't share the deets."

Having no recollection of any of this, I turn and laugh into Brodie's chest, not wanting to make eye contact with anyone just yet. I can feel him smile as he locks his arms around me.

Mel stands and says she's going to take a quick shower for the day and suggests the rest of us get ready too. Everyone steps to, while Brodie and I stay on our little seat, unmoving.

"What did I say?" I ask him hesitantly. "Or do?" When he doesn't answer, I pull back. Eye level, I look straight into his face. "Was it that bad?"

"It was the best night of my life," he says simply, squeezing me a little. Feeling scandalized, my eyes pop out of my head, but he reassures me, "But not for the reason yar thinkin'."

I relax slightly. *But why then?* I mean to ask him when a head pops out of the doorway. It's Maddie, *his ex.* That fact isn't lost on me. However, so far, she's only ever been kind to me. I decide right here and now to give her the benefit of the doubt.

"Sorry to interrupt," she mutters, hastily pulling back inside.

I go to tell her to wait, but she's already gone.

Standing up, I reach down and offer Brodie a hand up, like he usually does with me. Smiling at the reverse gesture, he takes it, but instead of rising, he pulls me down for a sweet, soft kiss. We part and go inside.

The common area of the flat's pretty empty as everyone's either changing in the loft or in the bedroom. Maddie wipes down the counter in the kitchen, wearing a black fitted dress and freshly blown out hair. Seeing her close up, I scope out her features. Beautiful by anyone's standards, she stands tall as a model, thin as one too, with mid-length, mousy hair, a straight nose and bright sherry eyes. I bring over her coffee and set it next to her with a peaceful smile.

"That's for you," I offer pleasantly. She takes it with a polite grin, and I add, "Sorry if it's cold."

"That's so nice, Nina," she replies. "Thank you."

I can't tell if Brodie seems slightly nervous or not as he grins at the pair of us. I suppose without Jaz's omission, I'd still be in the dark about their past relationship. I decide it doesn't really matter, because I'm with Brodie. I trust him more than anyone in my life; Maddie had her chance and she blew it.

"Need to get ready?" Maddie asks me after a sip, assessing me to a certain degree.

Glancing over my attire - my white billowy sundress, my trusty go-to sandals, and my part-up, part-down hair style - I shrug.

"Nope, this is pretty much it," I state, a little unapologetically.

"Just how I like ya," Brodie says, winking at me. "I've already got yar pack." With that, he looks to Maddie. "Alrighty then, Nina 'n I are gonna sneak out. Tell Shayno or Jaz to call 'n we'll meet up with ya guys then."

I smile sheepishly in goodbye, giggling as Brodie ushers me out of the flat. He hands me an AirPod, and I pop it in my right ear. He then tenderly takes my hand in his and we slow our pace slightly, waiting for our friends. We share the music as "The Wolves & The Ravens" by Rogue Valley rolls into "Wake Me" by The Bleachers. They play like a soundtrack as we meander through the idyllic streets, admiring the neat architecture. We only make it a few blocks when Jaz calls. The crew's behind us, trying to catch up. The song has now transitioned from the wonderfully upbeat "Portugal" by Walk the Moon into Jadu Heart's "I'm A Kid." We both break apart and start to dance a little on the street, grooving as we walk, laughing at each other as we unabashedly sing along. We're both really feeling the laid back beat. Suddenly, we hear "Oy!"

Caught in the act, we both turn to a few raised eyebrows and smiles from our familiar prying eyes. The whole group erupts into laughter. Maddie looks at the pair of us like we're speaking in tongues, but we take out our headphones and fall into stride with the gang.

As I'm walking with Mel and Jaz, I see Brodie drop behind us. My backpack jostles slightly on my back as Brodie turns on my clipped speaker. I hear the familiar sound of the little, but powerful amp powering on. Brodie grabs my phone out of the side pocket and thumbs through my music library.

"I dedicate this one to Neens," he declares with a smile.

"You Are a Tourist" by Death Cab For Cutie blares through the mighty speaker. Everyone chuckles at the song selection.

"It is fitting, Pryce," Mel jokes, "I'll give ya that, considering she plays it all the bloody time."

"That insane intro always gets me!" I share with a giant grin.

"We know, Neens, ya tell us that every time too," Mel laughs.

Unsure where we're headed, I'm just so excited to be with some of my favorite people exploring the city on a hot summer day, with music to boot. We walk for a few more minutes before we turn down a street and see tons of little independently owned shops, cafes and restaurants. The whole vibe feels retro meets freshly restored. The energy swirling in the air is full of youthful vitality and I am here for it. Giving my neck a workout from twisting around to not miss a single sight, I feel overwhelmed trying to take it all in. It all looks so cute! Mel points and guides us to a little glass storefront, squealing. It's a vintage thrift shop, but filled with nice, quality clothes and goods. We all pile in the smaller space. The 1975's "This Must Be My Dream" blares through the tiny space. Brodie beelines for the flannels with Shayno, Donnie checks out the hat collection, and us ladies wander towards the racks of women's clothes. Mel pulls out a handful of items, thrilled at the options, while I look through the Large section. Coming up empty handed, I walk over to the "flannos" and men's section; they have a great assortment of Hawaiian style shirts, Spooners specifically. It's nice to see they carry them around the world. I see one that looks like Mick. It's light blue, with white and blue sail boats all over.

"I didn't realise Brodie wears those," notes Maddie, coming up behind my shoulder.

"Actually, it's for Mick, the man I live with," I explain.

Brodie approaches us with a blue flannel in hand, which I instantly like. He sees me eyeing it with approval.

"Gotta stock up, I reckon," he mutters playfully, leaning in. "Someone keeps stealin' all my good ones."

Smirking, I hold up my pick.

"For Old Boy?" Brodie mutters appreciably. "Looks like him."

Mel yells my name from the back corner. She wants me to come review her fashion show. I hurry up to the register and pay quickly, folding the shirt into my backpack. Without my drone, I feel like I have a whole suitcase at my disposal. I make my way to the changing room where I give my opinion on Mel's options.

"It's too hard to choose. They all look amazing on you," I tell her honestly. "I wish you could give me a few inches of your legs. I wouldn't mind being a couple inches taller. Everything might fit better then."

"Yar no help," she grunts, changing behind the curtain.

She pops out and settles on the top, and gets in line behind Brodie, who pays for the flannel.

Donnie sports a new fedora and heads outside with Jaz and Shayno. I follow them. They tell me all about this cafe restaurant that offers old school, video arcade games. I guess that's where we're headed, which sounds fun to me. While Perth is surrounded by beautiful beaches, we're not as interested considering we're spoiled with untouched, uncrowded stunning coastline all the time.

All together on the sidewalk, we walk by a few more cute looking stores before we stumble across a plant shop. I practically skip directly towards it. The others are concerned about a wait at the restaurant, so they go ahead to flag down a big enough table.

"I'll be really quick," I yell to their disappearing figures.

Brodie hangs back with me and we both enter the shop.

Dozens of plants hang at the entrance. For a second it feels like we're stepping into an oasis, encompassed by so much greenery. *It's breathtaking.* Several tables stand in the middle of the store, displaying cute knick knacks, home goods, pots and books. It feels like a groovy 70s jungle in here with orange wavy stripes painted on the back wall. I gasp in bliss. Brodie chuckles as he watches me taking it all in.

"Now I know where to bring ya first, next go around," he muses.

"Brodie, I..." my voice trails off as I pass by several large plants. Feeling hopeless, I mutter, "I wish I could cart half of these back to Mick's, but since we flew..." There's the most amazing yellow pots, kind of mid-century, Gainey style, that I literally almost drool over. "See, if I had my tiny house, this groovy pot would be perfect." Brodie hears all about my obsession with tiny homes on the daily, and normally he just listens as a sounding board, but today he seems quite interested.

I see a sea foam blue ribbed pot, and squeal. "Ooh, then I'd pair it with one of these."

My index finger, on hyperdrive, points to a few interior house plants that would look amazing in those pots. Picking up fun flower power dishcloths and a matching cup set, my mouth hangs open in awe.

"Okay, this store is rad," I declare. "I wish we had one back home."

"Maybe they ship," Brodie wonders aloud.

Before I know it, he's up at the counter, talking to the employee. I see him gesture to me, then back to the woman. Then I see them both looking at the woman's computer screen.

Distracted by locally crafted ceramic plates, I pick up the small salad plate and feel the uneven ridges. Everything in this store was hand selected with care, I can just tell. I make my way across the small shop, stopping to test the tropical candle scents along the way. It's the perfect blend of home, plants, and kitchen, all in either retro or plant themes. *It's you as a store, Nina.*

Brodie walks back over to me and tells me that we need to get back to lunch as they found a table and are ordering soon. Sadly, I can't fit anything back with me, so I leave empty handed. Dragging my feet, I give the store one last look before I drudge forward, praising it all the way to the restaurant, until we find the others and sit down, and order.

Everyone drinks a cold stubby while I sip an ice cold Schweppes lemonade. After a hearty meal, we go head to head, playing pinball in the arcade. After Brodie and Jaz battle it out sibling style, Jaz and Shayno break away for a few minutes, all goo-goo eyed at each other, much to the crew's entertainment. As we play, I find Maddie watching Brodie constantly. It's not threatening as much as it is annoying. I mean, I guess she would be curious about him, but come on, she's not his girlfriend. He doesn't seem to notice, so I pretend not to either.

Donnie drops his head in defeat as Brodie hollers in joy. Shayno, the reigning champ, is no longer here to sweep everyone. Brodie quickly ticks his head to me, telling me it's my turn. I roll up my imaginary sleeves and Mel laughs. With a beer in hand, she stands at my side.

"Yeww, Neens," she yells.

I go first. Papi has always been a mega pinball fan so I grew up playing at our local pizza parlor. Suffice to say, I can hold my own. I play for a while, racking up combination points, before my first ball drops. Impressed a little with myself at my high score after such a long absence from the game, I step back, feeling a little smug.

"Top that," I counter, as Brodie snidely makes his way and slings back the ball puncher.

The ball sling shots up to the top before looping back and dropping down, starting the game. He plays for a while, but his first ball drops way sooner than mine did. He only manages to get a little over half of my score before stepping back in defeat. Ever the sportsman, he graciously applauds my win as Mel and Donnie cheer. Jaz and Shayno return and we collectively decide to go to the river and rent a little Duffy style boat.

After a few hours putzing around the river that runs through the city, we stop by at the little local sanctuary to feed the koalas and kangaroos.

"Now I can officially say that I've been to Australia," I joke, holding a docile koala as it feeds from my hand.

"Nah, yeah, Neens, cause swimmin' with humpies, tigas 'n whale sharks wasn't True Blue enough," jests Mel.

Maddie gawks and asks if I really did all of those things.

I answer with the nod and a sheepish smile.

"That's heatha," she says, sounding genuine.

As I delicately hand off the koala to its caretaker, I ask the zoologist a few questions on how to help this dying breed so future generations can enjoy these iconic classics. He recommends a few organizations to either donate or volunteer, or he says simply, spread the word.

The sun seems to dip in the sky slightly as dusk settles upon us. We leave the ecology center and make our way back towards Maddie's flat. Instead of doubling down on a nightclub, we decide to keep it mellow and choose a nice bar to grab some drinks. Us ladies pile into a booth in the corner, while the guys order appetizers and drinks. Maddie wants to swap drinks so she hops out, following Brodie. They stand together at the bar, talking for a couple of minutes. I can't tell what about. She refers back to me as they smile close to one another. She pats his arm affectionately as she leans in to tell him something. Not the naturally jealous type, I try really hard to suppress any type of unhealthy curiosity. The pair look quite cozy from an onlooker's point of view.

*Maybe you're just reading too much into it, Nina.* Yeah, maybe I am.

I know Brodie... *cares* for me. Maybe you really can be friends with your ex. Besides, Maddie will come and go. I have to believe that. I choose to believe in Brodie and my heart. Mel raises an eyebrow from them to me, while Jaz furrows hers slightly. As Maddie saunters back to the table, I take a deep breath and smile at her as she sits down across from me. Suddenly, Jaz and Mel both get up to use the restroom, so it's just me and Maddie. Using her elbows, she leans on the table, lightly crossing her forearms, as she stares at the guys.

"Lucky dog," she states without preamble. Unsure how to respond or to who she's referring, I just smile politely. "For reals, Nina. B's one of the bloody good ones. Believe me, I know."

"I already do," I announce in friendly confidence.

"See that's why he's the lucky one. He finally found someone who realises it before it's too late. I should be jelly of ya, but for some reason I'm not," she confesses.

"Why, you don't even know me?"

"I've seen the two of ya today, 'n I've neva seen him happier, even when he was with me," she states, officially confirming their history for the first time aloud. "Sorry to be the one to tell ya," she adds, almost as an afterthought. "Brodie told me he never told ya about me. That's fair after what I did to him."

"I already knew," I say simply, not wanting to rehash their past. "Jaz."

"'N it doesn't botha ya, him 'n me?" she murmurs, raising her eyebrows in surprise.

"No," I say nicely and truthfully, and take a deep breath, "not really, because there's no more you and him. There's only me and Brodie, and that's all that matters to me."

She leans back in the booth at a loss for words just as Brodie and the other two walk over and join us. Brodie looks back and forth between Maddie and me, sensing something past between us, but doesn't pry. I greet him with a warm smile, and we enjoy the rest of our drinks with the crew.

After our pit stop, we all walk back in a loosely knitted group to the flat, listening to "Don't Stop the Dance" by Bryan Ferry. Maddie walks next to Shayno, with Jaz holding his hand. Donnie and Brodie walk side by side a few feet behind Mel and me, who walk arm in arm. We chat about the day, random little comments that we've been dying to share with each other throughout the hustle and bustle. I ask Mel about Skip from last night, and she snorts, saying she doesn't remember anything.

Only a handful of blocks away, they all decide they want some special dessert across the borough. Donnie runs up and offers Mel a piggy back ride, which she gladly accepts. She hops on and the pair goes zooming off. My knee aches from all the walking so I tell them I'm going straight to the flat, but to enjoy the treat. I holler at Brodie to join them, but he shakes his head as the others depart. I slow my pace, waiting for my beau to catch up. He does so in seconds, and naturally without thinking, I loop my hands through his outstretched elbow and hug his arm as we walk. Laying my head on his arm, we enjoy the peaceful night underneath the twinkle lights and lit shop windows as we go by.

"Neens," he says, clearing his throat, "look, there's somethin' I've been meanin' to tell ya—."

"I already know, about Maddie, you mean?"

"How?" he asks, surprised. He looks around the little park we're passing through, then realizes. "My sista."

"She didn't mean to. Honestly. She even said I should have this conversation with you, not her," I say in Jaz's defense. "I was beginning to wonder though why you never mentioned her."

"Nina, I—."

"Brodie, it doesn't matter, and that's what I told her tonight when she told me herself. There is no her and you, there's only you and me, only *us*. I'll admit, it wasn't the best feeling finding out after the fact, but I realized tonight that I don't care. I have to believe in you, have faith in you, because after this year, there's only a handful of truths I know in the world to be real, and you're one of my truths."

I stop walking, under quaint street lamps, and turn to look him directly in the eyes. "I trust you. More than anyone else in this world, I trust you with my heart, Brodie."

He scours my irises with his own as they glint off the warm street lights around us. I can feel and see his eyes brim with gratitude and happiness. He pulls me by the waist, close to him and rests his forehead on mine.

"For the record, for me too," he whispers. "There's only you."

Smiling, we walk hand in hand until we wind down the street to a little bench. Glancing around to the emptiness around us, he sits down and pulls me towards him so I stand in between his legs with my arms around his neck. We share a sweet, little kiss. He gently pulls my hair loose from my smaller upper bun, and it falls in spewing waves around his face.

"Betta," he mentions under his breath, smiling at my curls, before returning to our kiss, which quickly deepens. I giggle as I tear apart before readjusting myself on his lap. I use one of his legs like a little seat, twisting into his side as I snuggle him. We both sit, basking in each others' features, memorizing the other one's face. As our eyes lock, he breathes, "Neens, I love you."

I close my eyes in pure elation. He's been showing me acts of love for almost as long as I've known him, but hearing him say it aloud brings a whole new weightlessness of happiness over my heart.

"I was hoping so," I reply quietly, smiling.

"I've wanted to tell ya that pretty much since we slept in the ute side by side that first night under the stars, but I didn't wanna scare ya off. Rememba when ya fixed me up in Mick's shed, blowin' on my bloody arm? I knew it then 'n it scared the bejeezus outta me. Ya forget, I met ya when ya first came here, 'n I've seen how much ya've grown, changed yarself with the help of no one, save you. Even at the start, I was drawn to ya. In fact, I fought like hell to find something wrong with ya."

"I could help you out there," I joke, caked in a self-deprecating tone.

He smiles, looking over my face once more. His eyes shift slowly over my head, around my temples to my hair, and back to my pupils.

"From yar frizzy Tarzan hair to yar well endowed curves, I was hook, line 'n sinka. Again, I tried to find something wrong with ya, knowin' ya'd have to go back to The States at some point, but then I gotta know ya, know yar quirks, observe yar strength 'n courage... then ya became by best mate, 'n well, that was it for me, Neens."

It's my turn to crinkle my nose at him. While he's said it once before, hearing him say it again makes my stomach flutter in mirth.

"Ya blew into my life literally with a crashin' bang, 'n eva since, my world's been tumbled upside down," he confesses in a whisper.

"Brodie, I..." I'm speechless. He leans down and lightly kisses my lips before pulling back like a gentleman. "I think I've always loved you," I whisper back. "Even when you annoyed the hell out of me, I think I loved you then."

His face erupts into the biggest Nina scrunchy face I've ever seen. We beam at each other from ear to ear for what feels like minutes, but must be only seconds. Butterflies rise in my stomach along with something else, something more primal. I return his kiss, but mine's full of passion, love, and long rooted lust. As if he can read my mind, he pulls us both up. Kissing me quickly and deeply, he playfully bites my lower lip. We can't get to the flat fast enough.

As we enter the front patio, Brodie kisses me with so much fervency I feel like we're going to combust. Trying to find the hide-a-key, we're both laughing while inhaling each other. Finally, I locate it and we get the door open before shutting it quickly behind us with the kick of a boot. The flat's pitch black. I slowly begin to undress Brodie as we climb our way to the loft, snorting and chuckling as we bump into furniture on our way.

"How long do we have?" I murmur.

"Twenty, maybe thirty at least," he exhales, pulling my dress over my arms and tossing it. Clad in just his trunks and my bikini, we blindly make it to the bed. Brodie struggles with my bikini knot, so I nudge his fingers out of the way and quickly untangle it. Freeing myself, I lie back on the bed and see Brodie hover on top of me. I reach up to untie his boardies, when he stops me. "Nah, I want ya slowly, Neens."

"You can have me."

Smiling, he shakes his head and teases me with a slow simple kiss, forcing me to relax and savor it. Making my skin crawl in elation, he slowly and tenderly kisses and caresses my neck and chest. Wrapping my arms around him thoughtfully, I draw him to me and together we make love with a newfound fire in our hearts.

# 26

Having slept like a rock, I wake without fully knowing where I am. My lids flutter open and I find myself wedged in next to Brodie in the loft. I feel Brodie's diaphragm swell underneath my hand as his body awakens to the new day. I shift my head to look at his face.

"Mornin', Sunshine," I say, echoing his usual term of endearment.

Smiling, he leans over and kisses me, morning breath and all. The sun peaks through the upstairs window and lightly touches our faces, turning everything a golden tint that only sunrise can bring.

"I've slept in," Brodie guffaws.

"A good night's sleep will do that to you."

"That 'n other things," he playfully retorts, kissing my shoulder.

As we lie listening to the morning's still peace, I can't remember a time when I felt happier. It's so quiet up here, like we're all alone in the world.

"Will the others be up?" I ask, motioning to move, but Brodie pins me back at his side.

"I'm always first up with the sun, but even now I reckon it'll be a while still," he explains.

I sit up and put my denim shorts on over my high wasted bottoms on the off chance someone is up and about this morning. I stand up and stretch fastidiously. Poor Mel. I hope she wasn't too bothered by Brodie taking over her side of the bed last night. I glance over the railing and see her drooling on the couch pillow below. Donnie snores next to her on the makeshift bed. I walk over and find my bikini top and turn, tying the strap around my neck, then slide on my crochet daisy tank.

I pack my backpack pretty quickly. I leave my toothbrush out near the top for easy access. In fact, I should probably do the bathroom trip while everyone's asleep. I tiptoe down and close the door quietly behind me.

Afterwards, heading back up to the loft, I find Brodie still in bed. That's unusual. I slide back in beside him and place one of my AirPods in his right ear, and the left one in mine. I select "Never My Love" by The Association. With his eyes closed, he smiles against the pillow. As the vocals come in, his sleepy eyes open and we just stare into each others' souls, letting the lyrics speak for us. It's such a sweet little song, and after last night, it holds new meaning. It ends softly as the morning light pours onto Brodie's face.

"Well, then," he muses, reluctantly hauling himself out of bed.

He pulls on a pair of boardies, and gently kisses the nape of my neck before bending over and picking up my white sundress off the floor. With a quiet chuckle, he tosses it to me. We start to hear lower mumblings below. We grab our packs and head down to the kitchen to make coffee for the crew before we embark on our last fun filled day.

Tired from a full weekend, the gang slowly rallies their belongings as we wait for our ride to the airport. Ready, I sit on the couch, waiting. I realize I haven't checked in on Mick or my phone in a couple of days. I miss him and can't wait to see him. Glancing at my screen, I find only one missed call and voicemail from him, which came in last night. I hold it up to my ear and listen.

*"Sheila, hope yar havin' a cracka time down there with yar mates. Just checkin' in to say I miss ya 'n I can't wait to see ya tomorrow. Sending three squeezes. I'll be seein' ya, Sweetheart."*

"What time do we fly out?" I ask Brodie, who sits beside me.

Now that I've heard Mick's voice, I wish I could blink myself back right now, and skip the whole jumper plane ride.

"Zac said eleven," Brodie clarifies. "Ya ready to go home?"

"'Wild horses couldn't keep me away,'" I quote with a smile.

We bid farewell to Perth, and a few hours later, we're driving in the ute back to Mick's, listening to The Goo Goo Doll's "Name." We just picked up Stella from Brodie's parents' house. She sits in between us, showering us both with non-stop welcoming kisses, clearly thrilled at our homecoming. A beaming smile encompasses my face the second I see the familiar turnoff to home ahead.

"Ya've missed him heaps, huh?" Brodie observes.

Nodding my head happily, we turn down the long, little road.

Pulling up to the front of the house, Brodie parks it. Getting out, I skip to the front door as he gets out and grabs my backpack. I reach to open the slider, but it feels hot to the touch. Pulling it open with a giant yank, I feel warm air greet me in the face. It's mid-afternoon; usually the air's on by this time.

"Mick," I call out, but don't hear anything. I cry out his name a few more times, but only silence greets me. Now I'm starting to worry. Brodie approaches my side and sees me frowning. "He should be here," I explain, the concern in my voice clear as day. "He knew when we'd be coming back."

"Lemme go look. I'll turn on the air," he offers, going inside.

I wait with Stella on the deck. A few minutes go by and Brodie doesn't return, so I open the slider.

"Nina, keep Stella outside," Brodie commands gravely.

A lump rises in my throat, I've never heard Brodie use that solemn tone before. I instruct Stella to remain outside as I re-enter the house. With deep caution, I walk towards where Brodie's voice came from, the back bedroom. With each passing step, my heart pounds louder and louder. Already knowing the answer before being told, I brace myself.

Brodie blanches, leaning over Mick's bed.

"Stay there, Nina," he says authoritatively, hearing me approach. "Don't come in here. Please."

Mick's back faces me. He's in his pajamas with the covers tucked up around him. I can't see his face or anything else. He looks like he's sleeping.

"Mick?" I ask, in nothing more than a whisper.

Brodie closes his eyes, deep in pain.

"He's gone," he breathes, barely audibly.

Suddenly, I can feel my heart break into a thousand pieces. I feel like I'm standing in a pile of melting quicksand. My air passage narrows and I can't breathe. It feels like a giant black hole is opening inside my heart, wrenching it apart to swallow me hole. My eyelids rapidly flutter and my whole body starts to shake.

"You sure?" I squeak, as if I just got the wind knocked out of me.

Brodie bites down on his lip and solemnly nods. He looks at me warily.

Feeling like I've left my body, I turn around and go to my room, shuffle to the farthest corner and lean back on the wall, sliding down to the floor. The biggest sob overtakes me, and all of a sudden, I'm weeping. Tears I didn't even know I was capable of making, burst out of me, as if my whole body is coming unglued. Gutturally crying from this dark well inside, my shoulders shake as I bawl thinking about Mick.

*No more three squeezes.* I squeeze his imaginary hand in mine, telling him how much I love him each time.

Dazed, I must sit here for hours because somewhere outside myself, I register footsteps, deep murmurs of conversation and the usual after beats of death. Brodie checks on me a couple of times in between handling everything, but thankfully he leaves me to myself. The light fades as I sit in the dark, wallowing. I hear a light knock at the door and Brodie walks in. He squats down in front of me, looking at me like I'm an injured animal. He rubs me on the back and carefully ushers me to stand. Once I'm up, I walk out the door. I pause in front of Mick's bedroom, and Brodie informs me that they've already left and taken his body. Gulping, I nod my head and look around. I'm surrounded by Mick everywhere I turn. Everything's exactly as he left it. The more I look around, the more I well up in tears of sadness and loneliness.

"Do ya wanna pack a few things?" Brodie says gently. "I don't want ya to be by yarself here tonight."

Feeling outside myself, I nod and walk towards the door. Stella sits on the deck. When she sees me, she cautiously approaches, as if she knows what's happened and how I feel inside. With raw eyes and a running nose, I sit on the top step and put my arms around her and go to pieces in her embrace. She softly licks the side of my face, trying to heal me with her love. There's something about letting yourself go to pieces with an animal that can never compare to another human being. They seem to absorb all the negative energy while only outpouring comfort and support. Feeling lighter for a second, I stand and Brodie delicately helps me into the ute with Stella in tow. We head away from my heart and my home that will never quite feel like home again.

It's been a few days since Mick's passing. Brodie's been a saint, making sure I go through the basic daily motions when all I want is to curl up in a ball and shut out the world. Every time I think about wanting to run home and hug Mick's sturdy frame, I burst into tears all over again. I don't even really feel like listening to music other than Amber Run's "Haze" because it perfectly sums up my mood and feelings. Sometimes I leave the song to play on repeat for hours in the background, forming a musical haze in an emotional one.

Brodie must have told my family because they keep messaging me and trying to FaceTime, but I don't feel like talking to them. I know the second I do, I'll want to jump on a flight *home* home, and I can't honestly deal with the emotional rollercoaster of leaving Brodie at the moment.

Brodie receives tons of calls on his and my behalf. Dinners keep getting dropped off by our close knit community. Mel and our friends check in several times, but I don't really feel like engaging. I have everyone here, yet I feel utterly alone. Mick is, *was*, such a big part of my life here; I'm trying to figure out what that means now that he's gone. It's been three days, and I lie in Brodie's bed in the same pair of his oversized sweats and tank top. Stella curls up behind my legs in my cubby. Brodie lies facing me, gently brushing my hairline with his soft fingertips.

"I'm sorry, Neens," he whispers sincerely. "Tell me what I can do."

*Bring him back.* But that's impossible, I know.

"Mick wouldn't want ya goin' on this way, on his behalf," Brodie says, in a mixture of kindness and agony. "I know it." Nodding my head, I know he speaks truly. This is the last thing Mick would want, but I can't turn my feelings off or change them at the flick of a switch. Brodie forges on, trying to be positive. "Nah, I reckon he wouldn't want ya to be sad for a minute. 'N he'd tell ya to throw on some Jim Croce 'n celebrate the bloody brilliant life he led."

Talking myself into it, I nod rapidly and take a deep breath. I even go as far as to sit up. I make my way slowly into the bathroom. I catch sight of myself in the vanity mirror and barely recognize the person staring back at me. Dark purple patches encircle a forlorn set of eyes, enhancing a pale wretched face. Suddenly, I feel like showering... *in the ocean.* Without a word, I slowly make my way to the kitchen and grab the keys hanging in their usual spot by the door. Brodie doesn't follow, but gives me my space. Within minutes, I'm on the sand, wrenching open the ute's door. In one continuous motion, I peel off all my clothes and dive straight into the incoming tide. I stay under water as long as my lungs allow, just floating weightlessly, listening to the endless void. I can feel the water cradle my heart for a minute, healing it like only nature can do. I emerge, feeling much refreshed, having regained a piece of myself that was lost, anchor-less at sea.

Parking in front of Brodie's, I make my way inside. Mel must have come over because when I walk into the kitchen, she rushes over and hugs me, telling me how relieved she is to see me up and active. She steers me to a chair at Brodie's table and rushes off to find a brush. She stands behind me and graciously brushes my hair out. Brodie stands with a coffee cup in his hand, watching us, deep in thought. At first touch of the bristles on my scalp, I close my eyes, enjoying the simple pleasure. My whole body deflates in comfort. Mel brushes it in silence until it's smoothed and detangled. She aptly plaits it for me, before leaning down and planting a loving little kiss on my cheek.

"Do we have any food?" I ask. Much to Brodie's relief, he jumps on my request and quickly scrambles two eggs. I scarf them down in less than a minute. "Can you take me back, to... to," I stutter, closing my eyes, barely able to say his name aloud, "Mick's?"

"Is that wise, Neens?" Mel says. "Maybe it's too soon."

"No, I need to do this," I declare, shaking my head. "And just sitting here isn't making me feel better. The only way forward is... forward." I turn to Brodie. "You were right. He wouldn't want this. The last thing he wanted was for me to be unhappy. So I'm going to pack up some of my things and then the three of us are going to throw Mick one last party."

Mel and Brodie both smile and agree wholeheartedly. The three of us, and Stella, pile in the ute and head back to Mick's.

Mick's doctor friend, Gus, ends up getting ahold of me and drops some serious news. Apparently, Mick had been suffering from some advanced stage of cancer, well past the point of treatment. He didn't want anyone, least of all me, to know about it. His instructions were clear. He was to die in his own bed and be cremated. Unfortunately, the nearest mortuary is a ways away so I won't have Mick's ashes to spread for another week or so, so instead we plan a wake in his honor. We invite those near and dear to celebrate him at our favorite pub.

Wearing my Yacht Party blue dress, Mick's favorite, I stand in the middle of the pub, full of people. All of my friends show up in support and to pay their last respects. They huddle back in a corner booth. Johnny Cash's "Sunday Morning Coming Down" plays throughout the room. It hits extra hard because that was Mick's favorite song and we lost him on a Sunday. *He would have appreciated that fitting detail.* Framed photos from the walls at home now line the bar top. The one I gave him for Christmas, the one of us fishing together, sits in the center next to a smaller one of him and Brodie holding his massive wahoo. Taking a deep breath, I blot my eyes, and face the guests in front.

A few coldies later, everyone begins to share stories about Mick. I really enjoy listening about parts of his life that sound like lifetimes ago. Sadly, as it is with funerals and wakes, the person who would love it most isn't here to soak it in and enjoy it.

I graciously thank everyone before sitting down amongst my friends, who greet me with a large hug and a glass of wine.

"I know for most people, he was an eighty-six year old man. Yes, he lived a long life, but for me, he was my best friend," I stop, my voice catching in my throat. "He took me in when I had no one. He gave me a house, no, more than that, he gave me a home, and he made me feel special and loved. To Mick. I don't know how to thank you. I'll be seeing you, Old Man."

I raise my wine glass and the table erupts into a giant cheer.

"To the Old Boy," Brodie reiterates in warmth.

We all toast to that.

It's official. I've received word from the Australian office of immigration. My visa is officially terminating. I'm to depart the country in six week's time, not a day longer.

It's only been two weeks since losing Mick, and I feel somewhat back on my feet, emotionally. This news blows for a multitude of reasons, the chief one being separated from half of my heart. I don't even want to tell Brodie yet, but I know I must. I decide to tell him this afternoon when he gets back from his charter. Glancing at the clock, that should actually be any minute. *Oh gosh.* My stomach twists in knots just thinking about it.

Suddenly, a dusty trail kicks up in the air, along with the low hum of a motor approaching. I see a white van coming down the drive. It's one I don't recognize. As far as I know, Brodie's not expecting anyone. Maybe it's one of Mick' friends from town, dropping in to check on me. Slightly hesitating, since I'm completely alone out here in the middle of nowhere, I glance around and grab my phone as the van parks right in front of the deck and the driver pops out. It's a man in his thirties.

"Brodie Pryce?" he asks.

"No," I explain, shaking my head, "but this is his home."

"Oh, banga," he replies, relieved. "Ya never know out here in the bush."

He walks around and opens the back of his van.

"Can I help you with something?" I offer lamely, full of curiosity as to what's in the trunk, but also taking a wide berth in case I need to bolt.

To my utter astonishment, the man roughly disappears into a mini jungle of greenery. He resurfaces and pulls out a tall Audrey ficus tree. Standing with a look of confusion, I watch as he lines up a few more large indoor plants, then hauls out five medium sized cardboard boxes. I direct him to set them on the deck while I walk inside and grab a knife from the kitchen. Unboxing one, I free the heavy item from all the wrapping paper and see a shade of retro yellow flash before my eyes. Based on the shape and color, I recognize the object instantly as the planter from the shop in Perth. A smile blooms on my face. Distracted by the delivery, I barely notice Brodie pull up. He jumps out with Stella, who alerts us to our visitor with a sounding bark.

"Brodie?" the delivery man asks.

Brodie nods, grinning at what's unfolding in front of him. I look at him, completely flabbergasted.

"Where should I put these?" the guy asks him, gesturing to the plants.

Pleased, Brodie instructs the man, turning to me, "Wherever the lady tells ya."

Giddy with excitement, I lead the guy into the living room and pick out a couple of spots near the windows. I decide to put the larger fig species in the corner of the bedroom, and then the larger palm in the yellow pot in the corner of the living room, with the big, beautiful cactus stacked in front.

Admiring our fresh arrangement, I hum along to Bread's "Make it with You," which plays from the kitchen. The delivery man shakes Brodie's hand and heads out the door as Brodie thanks him profusely.

"Brodie, what's all this?" I demand, in complete surprise, now that we're alone.

"Open the rest, Neens."

I cut open the other cardboard and unearth the white ridged pot and the cute sea foam one. I decide to put the cactus in the white one and the blue one in the bedroom with the fig. Brodie carefully places the plants inside their respective pots.

"What could these possibly be?" I murmur, opening the remaining two boxes. Full of smaller individually packaged items, I dislodge a wad of tightly packed bubble wrap and unravel it to discover it's a cute groovy drinking glass. Two minutes later, I find it's the entire set of glasses, along with the matching dishtowels. The other box reveals the full set of handmade ceramic dinner plates. Shocked, I can't mask my delight. "What brought this on?"

He shrugs and comes up, wrapping me into a hug from behind. We sway slightly as he rocks me.

"Day for it," he jokes. "Nah, that day in Perth, ya were so tickled, 'n the lady said her brotha was comin' up here on a campin' trip, so I offered to pay him to deliver 'n he went for it. So I did too." I hold up the cute flower power orange and yellow glasses, smiling. He asks sheepishly, "Did I do right?"

"You did more than right," I reply instantly, nodding, then twist my head so I can lean into him.

"I don't know," he murmurs, and shrugs, "but it seemed like good timin' with everythin' goin' on the past coupla weeks."

The visa countdown looms in my head. I set down the glassware and whirl around to face my friend and lover. I lovingly hold his face in my hands and channel all my happiness from my eyes into his.

"Most days I don't know what I did to deserve you," I say from the depths of my soul, "so thank you. I love it all, but mostly I love you." As if that's all he wanted to hear, he leans in and we kiss softly and simply. I take a deep breath. Now is a good a time as any. "And speaking of timing, I got some news today." I pause. "From the office of immigration."

His brows furrow in nerves as he nods and gulps, gearing up for my answer, "How long?"

I take a deep breath and spit out, "Forty-one days."

I feel his grip tighten, and he says, "Okay, then."

"'*Okay, then?*'" I repeat back to him.

"Whaddaya want me to say, Neens?" he retorts, holding up both hands. "The answer is obvious. I don't want ya to go. I'm scared as hell."

I'm not used to hearing Brodie admit feelings of fear, and honestly, I don't like it, but oddly I feel calm.

"Why haven't you told me that before?"

"Told ya, what? That if ya go, I'm scared yull neva come back. That yull meet some bloody Yank 'n forget about me."

I actually laugh out loud.

"Brodie, that will never happen. You know how I feel about you—."

"Yeah, but that could change after months apart."

"Hey, who's the scaredy-cat now?" I say, trying to lighten the mood. I reach out and take both of his hands in mine. "No matter how many sunrises and sunsets we have to endure alone, I know in my deepest heart of hearts that I'll never quit loving you. You're my sunshine. I have faith in us."

"So do I, but that doesn't mean it's not gonna be bloody miserable."

I reach out, and pull him towards me, enveloping him in a hug.

"I'm scared too," I whisper in his ear, my heart tightening. "I'd rather take on a sea snake."

He laughs in my neck and pulls back, kissing me simply, and says, "Well, it's not tomorrow, 'n when it is, we'll figure it out."

Feeling a little better, I unwrap each individual dish and set up the kitchen. Already the space has such a homey feel.

"I'm thinkin' we hang a coupla of yar drone shots here," Brodie says, motioning to the large empty wall in the living room. Motioning to the opposite wall, where two small frames of Brodie with his family and puppy Stella hang side by side, he says, "'N ova here, I've just the thing."

As I tidy up the boxes, he heads down the hallway and returns with his drill and a larger, light wood frame. Minutes later, he stands back and crosses his arms, smiling at the print. He glances over at me. I notice the photo for the first time. Stunned, tears well in my eyes. I was feeling okay until now. I look over the 11"x14" picture from top to bottom. It's from the yacht party on the dock. Mick and I are all dolled up, standing arm in arm, holding hands, happy by each other's sides. Frozen in that heartwarming moment of time, my eyes fill to the brim before they pool up and over, lightly sliding down my cheeks. *I completely forgot we even posed for that.*

"Brodie," I choke out, "where did you get that?"

"I have my ways," he says thoughtfully, walking over to me. "I reckoned ya'd want it."

I hiccup slightly as I stifle a sob, and nod my head up and down, heavily confirming his generous thought. I try not to come to pieces over his most precious gift.

"Ya looked banga that night," he continues softly, "but more than that, ya both look so full a joy."

He puts his arm around me and gently squeezes me as we both gaze at the photo.

"I just want to talk to him one more time," I admit.

"Ya will," Brodie assures me tenderly. "Yull hear him 'n see him in all the little things 'n that'll be his way of checkin' in on ya."

"How are you even real?" I mumble into his side.

"Neens, yar my family, 'n Mick's yars. He'll always be with ya, 'n I'll always be takin' care of his girl," he preciously says into my hair, as he kisses my Tarzan mane.

I stand up straighter and look around our cozy space. Brodie's doing everything he can to show me this is still my home. I look at him, my heart about to burst in gratitude. He's right, we'll figure out our future, because one way or another, we'll have each other.

He smiles and walks up to our new plants, slightly adjusting them. The house looks so much more lived in with some greenery. I tell Brodie this and he agrees wholeheartedly with a little chuckle.

"This is yar home, Neens. Now let's make some dinna 'n pop some wine," he advises, making his way to the kitchen.

After we share a glass, we sit out on the deck, enjoying the warm night air under the little twinkle lights. Using our new beautiful plates, we revel in the last couple bites of our fish and grilled veggies as we eat in pleasant silence. I set my fork down, announcing I'm full to the dinner gods. I'm going to miss this. *You're not gone yet, Nina.* I can't help but think about my impending departure. Six weeks is not that far away.

"Do you know anyone in immigration?" I ask. "Or anybody else who could maybe help?" He shakes his head, and I take a deep breath. "Mick did, but I don't know who it was. I can try to find out."

I tilt my head back, and down the last bit of white wine.

Elvis's "Can't Help Falling In Love" croons from the deck speakers. Brodie appears at my side with an outstretched hand, politely waiting for me to accept. I do so gladly, and he takes me lightly in his arms as we slow dance under the lights and violet night sky. I sigh in bliss as we sway together to the sweet classic tune.

We dance peacefully for a minute when Brodie says against my head, in barely more than a whisper, "Ya know, I can think of an obvious way to keep ya here." He pauses, and when I don't respond, he declares softly, "Marry me. Be my partna for life."

I still just for a second before smiling into his shoulder. We've never openly discussed this before. I think we both have known this is the eventual outcome, but the key word being *eventual.*

"I don't want you marrying me for a green card," I sigh.

"Come on, Neens, ya know that's not the only reason," he retorts, snorting.

"I know that, Brodie," I say honestly, nodding into his chest. I pull back a little. He watches me with a mixture of patience and longing. I look him in the eyes. "And while the answer is yes, it will always be yes, marriage is just not something I want to step into right now, especially because of all this. I want to take this at my own pace, not be rushing into anything because of an... eviction. And while I'm not a fan of weddings, I am a fan of marriage, and I think I want you to at least meet my family first.

"Either way," I explain, harkening back to the sad truth, "I have to say goodbye to my home. Either I leave my home here - you, my friends, my *life,* risking who I've become - or I have to say goodbye to my family. And that home is still... home." I emit a deep sigh. "It's an impossible choice."

Brodie quietly looks around as we dance, before he says, "What if it wasn't a choice? What if I come with you?"

"No, that's the last thing I want. Aside from a nightmare immigration policy, I couldn't bear it if you left all of this," I say, gesturing to his property, his life. "No, your family's here. Stella's here. Your job. Your friends. That would destroy me to see you give it all up just for me. I won't let you."

"While I admit, it wouldn't be without its challenges, I would gladly do it for you," he stresses. "For us."

"I know that, I truly do, but I don't want that. I don't even want to leave. In a perfect world, we would stay here and go back and forth, and right now, for the foreseeable future, that's not possible with how the world is." I laugh. "Our timing kind of sucks."

"Nah, I reckon we'll just have to get creative is all."

"Love Me Tender" lulls us now and Brodie pulls me in tighter as he sings the lyrics in my ear. I hold onto him for dear life, nuzzling into the crook of his neck as I listen to the poignant words: "*You have made my life complete and I love you so. Love me tender. Love me true. All my dreams fulfilled. For my darlin' I love you, and I always will. Love me tender. Love me long. Take me to your heart. For it's there that I belong, and we'll never part.*"

It's been a week since the visa news. Five weeks to go. I've decided I owe it to Mick to pack up his things before I leave. I ask Brodie for help. I don't think I can do it without him. I haven't been able to bring myself to see the house until now. We park out front, and Brodie hops out with Stella in tow. I climb out, slowly looking around, trying to discover any infinitesimal changes. Brodie unlocks the front door and enters, opening up the slider to allow some fresh air in. Stella runs around, sniffing. Craning my head through the opening, I peer in, scanning the all too familiar room, while assessing my emotional stamina. Cautiously, I take a step inside. Reflecting Mick's absence, the house seems dark and gloomy. I take a deep breath. *You can do this, Nina*. Making my way around, I open every curtain and blind, trying to allow as much daylight inside. Immediately, the house feels more familiar. By the couch, I notice Mick's crossword puzzle next to the armrest of his chair. A pen sits on top. Sacredly, I pick up the crossword and sit down. *Hold it together, Nina*.

Just as I can feel my tether weakening, I hear Brodie gently ask behind me, "Should we start in here?"

Jumping a little, I pop up and clear my throat. Gazing around the room, I can see and feel Mick everywhere. I glance from the records we listened to daily to the old fashioned television where we would watch our syndicated reruns of *Jeopardy!*.

"I'm not ready to say goodbye to this," I declare, with a lump the size of a golfball wedged in my vocal cords. "This is home."

Brodie sighs and suggests we start in the kitchen first. As he runs to the ute to grab the boxes, I find myself returning to the turn table, running my hands along the album covers. I don't even realize I've turned on the player, because suddenly the discernible sounds of Jim Croce ooze from the crackling speakers. The sound of his guitar stops me in my tracks.

*"I'm right here, Sweetheart."*

I snap my eyes open and turn my head around. I swear I heard Mick clear as day, as if he was standing right next to me.

*Hi, Old Man. I miss you*. I send up three squeezes: *I. Love. You.*

Brodie's back in the kitchen so I turn up the volume and head that way, wiping my eyes dry. Before we know it, we've packed the whole house with only Mick's bedroom left. Flashing briefly to the afternoon where Brodie found him, I turn and look at Brodie. He stares at the bed with a forlorn expression. This must be so hard on him. I reach over and take his hand in mine and give him three squeezes, which he returns.

"I never did find out what happened to his family," I say.

"He neva told ya?" he asks, with a touch of surprise.

"No," I reply, shaking my head. "I figured it was his story and if he didn't want to share that part of his life, I didn't want to be the one to push him."

"Well, it's a sad story, that's why," Brodie sighs. "Both his wife and son died in a bad wreck, turns out not far from yar crash." My eyes round large. *Mick, why didn't you tell me?* "I reckon that's why he was so attentive to ya in hospital. He was alone, having lost his family to a car accident, 'n ya were alone havin' survived one. Plus, he's Mick, he probably didn't want ya worryin'."

Brodie and I both go quiet for some time, performing the somber task of packing up a life. We don't really speak much unless it's a question of to keep or not. He motions to Mick's dresser. Before diving in, I queue up John Denver's greatest hits on the player. Returning, I find Mick's bottle of cologne on the vanity. I pick it up and lightly twist off the cap and raise the nozzle to my nose. I close my eyes and deeply inhale the scent of him, trying to memorize the smell.

Meanwhile, Brodie carefully piles the socks, Levis and pants on the bed. He opens up the top drawer and pulls out Mick's Franklin, his old school calendar book. It was one of Mick's most cherished possessions as it kept a small diary of his daily appointments and reminders. Seeing it makes my heart swell. Brodie also hands me a wad of rolled up Australian dollars in a tightly coiled rubber band. It's all the winnings from our games of backgammon and poker.

"Put those on top will you?" I ask, going through the upper rack of his jackets.

I instantly reach out for his most frequently worn leather jacket. It's aged and broken in perfectly. I hold it up, smiling fondly at it.

"Neens, there's an empty closet in our second room," Brodie kindly offers. "Why don't ya pick out yar favs 'n keep 'em in there."

I already have Mick's denim jacket that I basically took over. It would be nice to have the pair of them stay together with me.

"OK, thanks. And if you see anything you want, I'm sure Mick would want you to have it. And I want you to too. It would be nice to still see the things he treasured the most."

Brodie doesn't agree or respond and I turn to look at him. He sits on the edge of the bed with an envelope in his hand. He looks at me, startled.

"It's for you," he explains, holding it out to me. "Says yar name on top. It fell out of his Franklin."

Carefully, I take the letter. My name is written in Mick's unmistakable, curly script. I lightly rub my name with the tip of my finger.

"I need a minute," I say quietly, and walk out of the room to the outside deck where I sit on the top step.

Taking a deep breath, I turn the envelope over. It's not sealed so I open the flap and pull out the yellow papers folded inside. Just seeing his scrolling cursive makes my eyes flood with water. It reads:

*My Dearest Sweetheart,*

*If you're reading this, then you know I'm no longer here. At least my old dying body isn't. There's so much I want to tell ya, but I don't know where to start. You've made me the happiest Old Boy this past year, and for that, I can't thank ya enough. From your enormous talent to your big heart, I'm so very proud of you. I know it'll be hard on you, but ya have so many mates to lean on, especially Brodie. Take care of him the way ya took care of me. I wouldn't have left ya without knowing you'd be loved by a good man. He's got a strong handshake, a good poker face, but more than that he knows how to take care of my girl. Tell him I'm forever indebted to him, will ya?*

*Sheila, I never want ya to worry. That's why I kept my cancer a secret. I'm sorry for that, but know I didn't want ya in any pain. Ya deserve the world and I wish I had it to give ya, so I want you to have what's left of me and my world. At the bottom of my dresser drawer is the deed to my land and property. It's yours. The house, the Trooper, all of it. Underneath is my will; I had my lawyer add your name to it. It's not much, but knowing I can give you something allows me to be at peace with the world when I go.*

*Know that I'm always beside ya, always showin' ya the way. Sending ya a big kiss on the cheek, and three hearty squeezes, I love ya from the bottom of my heart.*

*Forever yours, and always with you, Your Mick*

*P.S. I'll be seein' ya, Sweetheart*

I didn't know it was possible to cry any harder, but I lower the letter down in my lap and raise my head to the heavens and weep. Even from the grave, Mick's looking out for me. He's made sure I'll never be without a home. After collecting myself, I sit, staring out at the red terrain of Mick's land. *My land*.

Stella rushes to my side and plants endless kisses on my cheeks, wiping up the salty remnants of tears. Brodie walks over and sits down next to me, waiting for me to speak first. I merely hand him the letter and he reads it carefully for a couple of minutes before he takes me by the shoulder and pulls me in for a warm, supportive hug. He exhales, a little lost for words. He looks down the road towards his own property next door.

"I found the deed and his last living will like he wrote. It's got your name all over it," he explains. He clicks his tongue and blows out through his open mouth to the sky. "Agh, Mick, still takin' care of yar girl I see, ya bloody lej." He laughs in mad respect then looks around us in awe. I follow his gaze as it wanders over the pathway leading towards the beach, the house, the small shed, and the ute. "Out of all this, you were his greatest joy 'n his most cherished treasure, 'n I'm so thankful yar mine too. Whether ya marry me tomorrow or ten years from now or neva, if that's what ya want, whether an entire ocean separates us or not, yar mine 'n I'm yars, Nina, 'n I'm never lettin' ya go."

I close my eyes as he wraps his arm around me, and I sway into his side. He kisses my forehead softly and sweetly before abruptly running into the house. He returns with the land deed in his hand.

"This, this changes everythin'," he emphasizes, holding it up to the sky.

# 27

I stand in front of Perth Airport with my backpack and small duffle at my feet. I look around at the city. After saying my goodbyes, and trying to sew up any loose ends, I find myself back here against my will.

I scan the giant letters that read: DEPARTURES.

I gulp down a lump in my throat. Honestly, it's bittersweet. While I'm devastated to uproot my happy life here, I can't deny the fact that I'm super excited to reunite with my family again. I'm set to message them when I touch down in Sydney for my connecting flight.

"Neens," yells Mel, as she charges down the sidewalk, barreling into me in a bone crushing embrace. We stand for a while in each other's arms. Through tears, she says, "I'm not gonna cry."

"It's not goodbye, it's just bye for now, Mel," I reply, trying to be cheerful and optimistic as I find myself a little misty eyed. I lean in and whisper in her ear, "Thank you for being you. I'll miss you something fierce, my friend. Talk soon?"

"Promise?" she stresses.

I nod, smiling, as I pull back, squeezing her arms as I let go.

Knowing my friends will still have each other gives me joy. The entire crew spent the whole day on the boat yesterday, soaking up each other's jovial company until the last minute. A thousand hugs later, Brodie, Mel and I flew down to Perth this morning. I insisted they didn't need to come with me, but they rather insisted they did. They even tried to follow me to Sydney, but with the current lockdowns, I put my foot down. I don't want them to risk getting locked out of the western territory just to prolong the inevitable.

I look back to a sniffling Mel. Now it's my turn to ask for a promise.

"Take care of him for me," I request, gesturing to Brodie, who stands a couple of feet away. "Make sure he stays out of trouble, will you?"

He shakes his head, and exhales playfully through his nose. Mel promises she will with a laugh.

"It's the otha way 'round, Neens," Brodie replies. "I'll be the one keepin' Mel in line, eh." Mel stands back and Brodie glances at his phone. "It's time."

I nod my head, trying to talk myself into having the courage to leave them. I have no idea when I'll see them again. Even though every fiber in my being is telling me to stay, I don't have a choice or say in the matter. Brodie walks up to me and leans his forehead against mine, taking both of my hands in his. I breathe in his salty, manly, musky goodness.

"Take care of our plants," I demand softly. "Take care of yourself. And give Lel all the belly rubs for me."

"Cross my heart," he breathes back.

"Thanks for saving my life, Brodie Pryce," I mutter, "in more ways than one."

"Ya saved yarself, 'n me along with ya," he retorts, in a laugh, taking a deep breath. He pauses for a beat. "I love ya, Nina. Even when I'm not with ya, 'n ya can't hear my voice, know I'm thinkin it from here."

"Me too, Brodie, I love you more than you know," I whisper through tears. Trying to repair the sad mood, I attempt a joke. "You won't even miss me I'll be back so fast."

I can tell he's trying to put on a brave face as he smiles.

"Hopefully, 'n until then, Sunshine" he mutters, amorously pulling me in for one last farewell kiss.

My stomach flutters again as if a hundred butterflies take flight, and I feel the electric current surge from my heart up through my lips into his. I know he feels it too. Unwilling to part, but knowing it must happen, I rip the bandaid off and break away. Brodie hands me my backpack and with one final wave at my best friends, I turn and enter the departure gate, not looking back.

Over twenty hours later, my face sweaty from wearing a KN-95 mask the entire time, I feel relief flood my system as wheels touch down. I look through the tiny window around the hazy sky, unable to distinguish the horizon, and stifle a depressing dry sob. I walk off the plane and step into the airport. A giant sign reads: Welcome to Los Angeles.

*Nothing about this feels welcoming.*

I look around me as I make my way to the arrival gate. A flurry of people busy themselves in every direction while everyone's glued to their phones. It's cantankerously loud. I haven't seen this many bodies in over a year, even in Sydney. With my backpack and duffle in hand, I quickly exit the terminal and stand on the sidewalk, waiting for my ride. Honks emit everywhere like a domino affect as people are too uptight and impatient to wait their turn. I see Papi's white van circle the congested carousel before it pulls over. A black BMW honks behind him so I run over as quickly as possible, popping open the side door. Jumping in, I close it hastily behind me, and Papi hightails it out. Cheers of happiness erupt from Mom and Papi as I settle in the bench seat. Mom climbs over from the passenger seat to mine and gives me a proper greeting and hug. We hold on, squeezing the life out of one another.

"Mama!" I exclaim into her shoulder.

I can feel myself getting emotional, like a five year old soaking up the feeling of finally hugging their mom after a long week away, only the week was one whole year. It feels so easy and so good to be hugging her. Papi watches from the rear view mirror, smiling from ear to ear.

"Mija, it's good to have you home," he announces.

I lean forward and plant a big kiss on his cheek before settling back into my seat. Mom returns to hers up front. They bombard me with a million and one questions and I do my best to answer them, but honestly I feel overwhelmed at the moment.

"Sorry, I'm just cooked after my journey," I say, trying to hide the real reason, which is I feel like I'm being stretched emotionally and my rubber band is about to snap.

"Of course," Mom reiterates.

"Where's Ria?" I ask, unable to mask my disappointment.

"She had to work," Mom says.

"¿Tienes hambre?" Papi asks.

After nothing but cheap airport food, I'd kill for a good meal, but really just want to get home. My stomach growls in resistance.

"Yeah, I'm starving," I admit.

"What do you want, Neens?" Mom asks. "Sky's the limit."

Hmm, what does sound good? Red Emperor? The mere thought stops my heart for a second, and I push it hastily away with a wince.

"Um, honestly, I'm good with anything easy. I'd kill for a bowl of Abuela's rice," I reply, laughing a little.

"It's waiting for you at home, Sweetie," she proudly says.

Papi asks if pizza sounds good to bridge the gap and I nod, agreeing. I don't really care, as long as it's quick. I just want to get in my bed. Thankfully, we quickly find one of Papi's favorite chains and park. I climb out of the van first and wait for mis padres to catch up. I look around at my surroundings. We're in industrial city and to my utter and expected disappointment, there's nothing but smog, a disgusting stench in the air, and not a tree or beach in sight.

It's chilly here. I rub my arms with my hands, and adjust my top, pulling it tightly around my torso. Wearing one of Brodie's flannels over my trusty tank, paired with my denim shorts, it wasn't the best move coming hot off a plane straight into a California winter. Mom approaches me with a wild expression in her eyes as she looks me up and down.

"What's up? Why're you sussing me out?" I ask her, in a joking tone.

"Honestly, Nina, I barely recognize you. You look..." she replies with a hint of amazement, and her voice trails as she eyes me up and down. "Let's just say Australia agreed with you, honey."

I look myself over. I guess from Mom's perspective, when she last saw me, I weighed a good thirty pounds heavier, had darker hair and my skin tone was a solid four shades lighter.

She hands me my mask and we put them on as we enter the pizza parlor and find a booth in the corner. Papi and Mom inform me Covid regulations are up in the air. Honestly, it's all really confusing. Papi walks to the register and orders a large pepperoni pizza for us though the glass partition. As we sit waiting in the stuffy parlor, I find the heater on full blast directly above me. I've grown accustomed to warmth living in the Australian desert, but nothing is worse than fake heat. Suddenly I'm a thousand degrees. I reach back and pull Brodie's flannel off. I fold it neatly and carefully tuck it on my lap. Having it here is like having a piece of him with me. I sit back in the seat and patiently wait, looking around.

"It's so funny," I try to explain, "seeing all of this Covid stuff. We don't have any of that back—," *home;* I amend my word choice for their sake and offer, "back in Straya."

"Really?" Papi asks, interested.

Nodding, I explain to them the typical day to day of general lockdowns, but reiterate, "We're just so isolated up there, I completely forgot Covid even existed until I went to get on the plane."

Mom can't stop staring. She reaches over and grabs a stray curl.

"For real, Nina, I can't get over it," she gushes. "From your hair, to your outfit - you even sound a little like them - to your physique. You even look a little toned."

I lean forward, and smile in response, "Must be from all the diving."

I hear Justin Bieber's "Peaches" faintly playing throughout the restaurant. I nod my head up and down to the music. Papi laughs at the familiar sight. The server arrives and places our bubbling pizza in the center of our formica table. I close my eyes, inhaling the cheesy goodness.

"I haven't had pizza since I was last here, in America," I say.

Mom's eyes shoot out of her head.

"What did you eat Down Under?" she asks, amused and very much intrigued.

"Oh, ya know, fish," I explain in a shrug, reaching for a slice of pizza. "Tons and tons of fish. Brodie brings home a fresh catch about every single day, and lots of grilled veggies from his garden. There's also heaps of meat pies from the local pub, and the occasional burger, but mostly some sort of fish."

I bite into the pizza and it practically melts in my mouth. I moan a little at the all too familiar flavor. I stand up to grab a ranch dressing so I can dip my crust into it.

"Mask!" Mom hollers, and tosses me my reusable one.

"See, when I hear 'mask' I automatically think of a diving mask," I chuckle, trying to strap it on my ears over my curly mane.

I note the take-on, take-off process is just as annoying as my familiar mask and snorkel. I go to the counter where they inform me they don't do sauces at the moment, blaming Covid. I return to my seat and tell my parents with a snort.

"I don't get it," Mom whines, while rolling her eyes. "Now due to the pandemic, apparently you can't have ranch dressing anymore. Customer service is out the window, and forget about on-time shipping and deliveries, and no more reusable cups. It's like everyone is using the pandemic as an excuse to implement all these rules they've been dying to enforce to save a buck, and act like bitties in the process."

"Because customer service was so great beforehand," I laugh.

I stifle the largest yawn. Mom and Papi finish their slices and we grab the rest of the pizza to-go and take it with us in the car. We're about forty minutes from home. I take in the sights to my left and right as we drive along the congested freeway. Racing cars zip around us, hauling butt to save a few minutes down the road, tailing other cars and bullying them into moving out of their way until they do.

"There's people everywhere," I note. "I forgot how many houses there are here." I can't help but frown. "They're literally stacked on top of each other."

"I'm glad we got you home," Mom says, sounding slightly concerned for the tenth time in the past hour.

I unbuckle and reach over Papi's shoulder and fiddle with the radio tuner, finding K-Earth 101. Some Neil Young plays through the lackluster sound system, so I turn up the volume and lean back. Mom instantly reaches over and dims the music so low I can't even hear it anymore.

*Okay... I did not miss that.*

Taking a deep sigh, I lean my head back on the headrest, wishing I could blink myself to my bed like in *I Dream of Jeannie.* It's a long forty minutes back to my childhood house. I close my eyes, hoping that my dreams will transport me back home, back to Brodie. Thankfully, I nod off against the constricting seatbelt.

My parents wake me as we pull up to the house, informing me that they had to move my belongings back to their house from next door. With Covid shutdowns and tight income, Selena and Ray are renting out my room to their friend. Walking straight into the house with both of my bags in hand, I beeline straight for Cosmo, our family Weiner dog. Super excited, he runs over to me as fast as his two inch legs will carry him. He jumps up on his hind paws and scratches at my legs, urging me to grab him and pull him up for snuggles. He starts to whimper in happiness as we cuddle and embrace. His course, wiry hair rubs against my face as he flips out in happiness like a fish out of water. I set him down, and he follows me as if he's my second shadow. I head straight to my "new" room, discard the bags on the floor without looking around, and walk directly to the bathroom where I jump in the shower and wash off all the skanky travel grime and germs. My body, accustomed to Western Australian time, is all out of whack. I haven't slept in almost two days, other than small snippets during the long flight, but those naps are never very comfortable, nor very deep. It sounds silly, but I can't bear to wash my hair yet. I still have Indian Ocean sea salt clinging to my curls and I just can't part with that right now. It's a small way of holding onto home.

I scrub my body, get out and towel dry off before sliding on one of Brodie's oversized shirts. Thinking of Brodie, I need to message him and let him know I arrived safely. With my phone plan up in the air at the moment, I'm using iMessage only when I can connect to WiFi, and now is the first time I've had it since boarding the plane in Sydney.

I clumsily type out a short text that reads: *Made it. Back in bed safe and sound. Missing you. xx*

Half asleep, I stumble to my room, shut the door behind me, plug in my phone and plop down on my bed, face first. Pulling the cold pillows under my cheek, I position myself, trying to get comfortable on my little twin bed. I hear the door creak open behind me. I turn over and see Papi and Mom standing in the doorframe. Mom walks over with Cosmo in her arm. I can hear the light jingle of his dog tag as she drops him on my blanket. Nestling in against my side, he finds his sweet spot.

"Somebody missed you," Mom quietly mutters.

"Let her sleep, Luce," Papi mutters. "Te quiero, Mija."

"Happy you're home where you belong, honey," Mom whispers, kissing my cheek.

I mumble my "I love you's" before rolling back over and making small adjustments to Cosmo's nine pound presence. For a dog so tiny, he's like your own personal space heater, which is a welcome gift on this brisk night in early March. I instinctively reach out my hand to the empty space beside me, imagining the soft touch of Brodie. My heart swells in longing. I wonder what he's doing at this very moment. Imagining him lying on the warm sand, smiling at me in my mind's eye, I drift off to a deep rolling sleep.

Light flutters. I hear the sounds of murmuring voices coming down the hall. *Where am I?*

I reach over and find the cool bedsheet empty, and it all comes flooding back. I'm back home. *In America.* Wincing slightly from the crushing blow of homesickness, I sit up as my eyes adjust to the bright light outside. Twisting my head, I turn to fully take stock of my well lit room. I can tell Mom put care into making it feel like a lived-in room, except half of my things sit in boxes in the corner, while my knick knacks and plants all huddle together on top of my credenza. All appears to be in tact. Scratch that, I notice there's four fewer plants. It's funny how being gone for a longer length of time makes you realize what you can and can't live without. As I look around the room, I actually laugh. I've had the best year of my life without any of these things.

Rising slowly, I stretch out my body. I don't even know what time it is, but I feel much recharged and refreshed. Standing, I walk over to my closet and open the door. Curious, I rake my hands through the many hanging options, realizing that for the most part, save an article or two, I never want to wear any of these again. They just don't feel like me anymore, and that's okay. I start to pull the shirts, jackets, and dresses off the hangers until I have a decent sized pile on the ground next to me. Starting to feel a little chilly, I rummage through my duffle bag on the ground, and carefully unearth Mick's flannel robe. A feeling of grief passes over me like a wave, but doesn't linger for too long. I open the door and walk down the hallway into the open kitchen.

"There she is!" exclaims Mom, from behind the stove.

"Neens!" cries Ria excitedly, as she runs from the couch and plows into me, almost knocking me over.

We hug for a minute before she pulls back, her eyes going round as she looks over my face and hair.

"See what I was saying?" Mom says.

"Neens, your curls," Ria exclaims, holding up some of my hair. "They look so happy. What's your secret?"

"Just the salt water from swimming every day, I guess."

"You don't have any product in?" she asks, in disbelief. Shaking my head, I just smile, and walk to the fridge where I find the bottle of apple juice. I bring it over to the counter and pour myself a glass. She keeps staring. "It's so light. I can't get over it... So, you happy to be home or do you miss it?"

*Of course I miss it. If I could get on a plane today and go back, I would.*

Swallowing a large sip, I take the small opportunity to gather my thoughts and response without hurting any feelings. I decide to go with the truth.

"It's really good to see you," I say, smiling sincerely. "I've missed you guys so so much."

After twenty plus hours sitting awkwardly cramped in the airplane, my knee is a teensy bit sore today. Instinctively, I rub it, massaging it gently. I notice Mom and Ria both look down. I realize they haven't seen me since the accident. They both frown as my hand pulls back, revealing the long faded, but still slightly purple, jagged line like a zipper across my knee and leg.

"Your scar," Ria gasps, unable to stifle her shock.

Mom drops the knife on the cutting board and bends down to better assess it. Their critical eye has me feeling a little self-conscious.

"Baby, I didn't realize it would be this bad. I mean I knew it based on what you told us and the recovery time, but it's another thing to see it," Mom babbles. "We should go see a plastic surgeon about that scar."

"It's fine, really," I shrug, pulling the robe tighter around me. "I'm just thankful to be alive and to be walking. The scar doesn't bother me, in fact I like it. It's a good reminder."

"Were you scared?" Ria asks, genuinely curious.

"More than you could ever know," I explain. "I thought that was it and that I would never see you guys again, but then I realized afterwards that dying actually wasn't the scary part. It was realizing there was so much more I wanted to do with my life." Crickets. They just stare at me. "So I put in the work to get back on my feet, as you guys heard. It wasn't easy in the beginning, but I had help. I didn't have to do it alone."

I exhale deeply thinking about Mick, my biggest support through the heaviest point in my life. I just want to talk to him again, even for a minute. I fold my arms and rub the sleeve of his trusty flannel.

"*I'm right here, Sweetheart,*" his voice echoes in my head.

"I'm sorry again about Mick, Sweetie," Mom says sympathetically. "I meant to tell you that earlier."

"Yeah, Neens, I'm so sorry," Ria chimes in.

I smile in thanks just as the front door opens and Selena and Javi trot in. Javi mumbles gibberish words and waddles into the kitchen. Selena walks over to me and envelopes me into a big hug. She pulls back, remarks about my improved state of appearance, then orders Javi to give me a hug.

"Come give Tia Nina a hug, Jav," she repeats. He looks at me, and rushes to her side, hugging her leg in shyness. "He does that with everyone. It's a phase." Whether that's true or not, I was half expecting this outcome. I hoped it would be different, but it is what it is. I give him a big, open mouth grin, trying to get him to warm up to me as I notice Selena looking me over. She says nicely, "Nice robe, did he give it you before you left?"

For whatever reason, Brodie has become the elephant in the room ever since I opened the car door yesterday. I'm a little unsure whether it's because they don't want me to miss him to ease my own pain, or they hope I'll forget about him so I won't want to go back. Either way, both of those notions aren't happening.

"Thanks," I divulge, "it was Mick's."

Seeing both of my sisters together makes my heart fill with happiness. Mom must feel it too, because she looks at each one of us, beaming.

"Finally, all my girls back together again," she exclaims.

We all giggle.

I start for my room and inform them I'm going to change. Naturally, I reach back for my duffle and pull out my white billowy sundress. I don't care if it's late winter here, I want to feel normal, feel like me. Moving forward, I don't want to lose even a remote part of who I've become. I reach for my bikini, then think about the sixty-two degree water and close my eyes in defeat. Settling on a pair of undies, I shimmy on my dress. I don't even know where a bra is these days, other than my blue one. Still slightly cold, I pull out the only other flannel I brought back with me - Brodie's favorite.

I smile, remembering him gifting it to me the night before leaving. He handed it to me, all rolled up tight, and said sweetly, *"It'll be my way of keepin' ya warm 'til I can wrap both my arms around ya again."*

My heart aches thinking about him, wishing we could be here together or there together. Either way, as long as we're together. I turn on shuffle on my iPod and Sheryl Crow's "I Still Believe" plays. A wave of mirth and nostalgia flashes over me as I remember our almost kiss on his boat under the stars.

I walk quickly back into the kitchen and grab a few trash bags amidst the wandering eyes from my mom and sisters, and return to my room. I reach down and begin smashing my old clothes inside the bags. I go through my entire closet in ten minutes. I drag the haul to the living room, and line them up at the door.

"What on earth are you doing, Nina? You can't throw all that away," Mom declares.

"Of course not, Mama, that would be incredibly wasteful," I retort, shaking my head. "No, I'm taking them to Good Will."

"But that's your entire closet!" she screeches, her eyebrows shooting up past her hairline.

Ignoring her and my sisters' shocked faces, I walk back to my room, grab my backpack, and head out the door.

"I'll be back in a bit," I holler over my shoulder.

I load up the trunk and start Gloria, feeling good to be headed back in the right direction.

# 28

June gloom finally dissipates with each passing day. After a beautiful and warm few months here, these past few weeks have been literally covered in fog. My sparse room requires minimal attention. Having less keeps me looking for more to see and experience outside.

Adjusting to the new normal of drone work and photography gigs, I officially pay off my lingering medical and insurance deductibles. I check my email daily, waiting to hear back from my Australian lawyer who's handling my land case as it transitions into my name. I should be hearing back from him any minute really. I smile at my little secret, having never told my family about Mick's final will and his most generous and precious gift. I know I should, but I'm waiting to get word in writing that it's officially mine before I do. In the meantime, I adjust to my new daily routine. I go to the beach usually in the morning, drone for fun, but after the stunning vistas and water clarity of Australia, it's a little lackluster here. Then I usually drone for a local real estate agent or builder before heading back home to edit my footage.

Brodie and I try to keep in touch as often as the brutal time change and our work schedules permit. Naturally, we send each other songs to exhibit our current moods and feelings. I find myself listening to our favorite mutual record, and discover the song "Zen Island" literally feels written for me, but instead of the "island" it's Australia. Brodie FaceTimes me every few days, usually before he goes to bed at night. He shares with me all about his day, and gives me little updates about the crew. He constantly tells me he misses me. Mel also calls to chat every other week. But it's not the same as being with them on the regular. It's really hard!

*I miss them. I miss my life.*

Lying in bed, my computer lights up beside me as I see an incoming video message from Brodie come in. My stomach flips in happiness, and I hit the green button on the screen. Brodie's handsome face fills my view and I immediately burst into the biggest smile. I notice he lies in bed too.

"Hey," I say, relieved to see him.

"Mornin', Sunshine," he greets me with a grin.

Despite the terrible fifteen hour difference, he always manages to stay in tune with my timetable. We chat for a while as he tells me about his recent fishing trip with the boys. They actually ended up diving down to the bommies and hand catching some hefty crayfish. They had a tasty cookout with the rest of the crew. I hear Stella bark in the background. *Lel, I miss you!* He asks about home, and I tell him more of the same. I'm just droning, trying to save money, but also trying not to go insane living back with the whole family.

"Basically these chats are giving me life," I confide. "I don't know how much longer I can do this. I miss you so damn much."

"Hey," he says, stifling a frown, "I know it's hard, Neens, but know I'm right there with ya, all the time."

He punches something into his phone. Seconds later, I get a text alert. I glance at it and it's a link to Sarah McLachlan's "Push."

"I've been listenin' to her a lot lately, missin' ya. Hit play on my count," he instructs. Relishing anything we can do "together," even all the way across the world, makes us feel better instantly. He counts from three and we each play the song, listening to its beautiful lyrics. As the chorus approaches, he shares, "This pretty much says it all."

Sarah's heavenly voice bellows, *"You stay the course, you hold the line, you keep it all together. You're the one true thing I know I can believe in. You're all the things that I desire, you save me, you complete me. You're the one true thing I know I can believe."*

We listen to the rest of the song in reflection and as it fades out, I look to Brodie with tears welling in my eyes.

"You know, for half my life, I've wanted to sing those lyrics with conviction, to have my own person to actually dedicate them to," I confess. "I always hoped someone would want to sing those words and have those feelings about me and I with them."

"Then it's meant to be, Neens."

I hear my name being yelled down the hallway. I groan, not wanting to greet the household or the day just yet. Footsteps storm down the long hall in the direction of my room. It's only a matter of time.

"I should go," I say reluctantly, realizing he needs to sleep.

He sighs, not wanting to hang up. We both say our goodbyes and our "I love you's" and sign off.

*Back to reality.*

I find distraction key for my mental health with family obligations and even meet up with a couple of friends as we socially distance on the beach. I find myself zoning out, politely replying when prompted to as everyone discusses babies and mundane married home life. I just can't connect. I know my family feels like I'm slipping away, but it's the opposite. I've learned that I just want different things and that's okay. Before my family was my everything, because it was all I had. Now since discovering myself and freedom, I choose how I enjoy my time. I've gone back to painting, have taken up ukulele, and even started printing my drone shots to sell. But there's always that nagging feeling of knowing I could have so much more that makes me happy. It's only waiting for me on the other side of the world. While disheartening as it is to want to willingly leave my family, they all have their own lives, their dreams they're working towards, and now I finally have mine. I just need them to accept it.

Sitting in the back patio during one of our family breakfasts, a *ping* alert notifies me of an incoming email. Impatiently waiting for *the* email, I glance down. My breath intakes as I see the man's name appear in bold in my inbox. I excuse myself and head to my room, barely able to contain myself. Standing, I read the message and open the link to the documents. The paper and land deed has all been transferred to my name. *It's official, I'm a homeowner.* My lawyer also informs me that he's mailing physical copies to my new address and to my current American address. He ends the email with a giant: *CONGRATULATIONS!*

Giddy, I click over and dial up Brodie on FaceTime audio. It rings loudly four or five times to the point where disappointment starts to creep in. *Please pick up.* There's no one else I want to share this with than him right now. He doesn't pick up as the dial tone rings indefinitely. Reluctantly, I hang up. Skipping, I head back outside with the biggest smile plastered on my face. The entire table looks up at me, clearly expecting me to explain my buoyant mood.

"Okay, so I've been wanting to tell you guys for a while now, but was waiting on the technicalities," I tease. "Well, I just got word that I'm officially a homeowner!"

Gasps of surprise and confusion erupt from my family. Ria squeals while Mom looks like she's forcing her excitement.

"When did you buy a house?" Papi asks me, floored.

"No, I didn't it," I explain through a big grin. "Mick left me everything. His house, his land by the water, even his ute. He gave it all to me."

Selena's mouth drops open and Mom sits, stunned. Ray raises his beer to me, and congratulates me, genuinely happy for me.

"What does that mean?" Mom finally asks.

"I don't exactly know because I still don't have a visa, but I have a beachfront house!" I confess, in merriment.

No one really says anything. Javi screams "agua," demanding his sippy cup.

Starting to feel annoyed by their lack of enthusiasm and support, I remark, slightly bitter, "I thought you guys would be happier for me."

"Happy to see my daughter move across the world?" Mom spits out.

The whole table, including Javi, sits in silence.

"Well, I think it'll be really cool to have a place in Australia to go visit, you know, when we can again," Ria pipes up, trying to think of the positives.

"Can you sell it?" Mom asks eagerly.

"I would never do that," I snap back quickly. "It's my home."

"Your home?" she repeats, bewildered.

"Oh, boy," I hear Ray mutter under his breath, as he leans back in his chair.

Mom nudges Papi, sitting next to her.

"Mija, your home is here," he says kindly, perking up.

"And it's there. I don't know why you're making feel like I have to choose," I cry out in frustration. "It doesn't mean I love you any less. Why can't you see this is what I want?"

"I knew the second you got with Brodie you wouldn't be the same," Mom bellows.

"I don't want to be!" I plead, clearly angry.

"Brodie—," she sneers, trying to blame him.

"Brodie has nothing to do with this," I roar back at her. My chest heaves. I'm close to tears. "I want to make this crystal clear, to everybody." I make eye contact with each of them at the table. "Brodie is the love of my life, but that's besides the point. I found myself in Straya. I've never been happier in my entire life than when I was there, even before Brodie came into the picture. That didn't mean I didn't miss you, and it didn't mean that I didn't love you the same. It just meant that for the first time, I felt like I was working towards something worth fighting for, for *me*. If you truly want what's best for me, you'll support me and have my back, no matter what. No one is abandoning anyone. You should want that for me.

"And back to the topic of Brodie, he's not going anywhere. So you better get used to talking about him, hearing about him, and me wanting to be with him. Maybe not today," I add, laughing, "in fact, I don't even know when, but we *will* be together. No one is going to change that."

Mom's face reflects a mixture of hurt, shock, and surrender. She stands and storms off without a word.

"Of course we love you, mi amor," Papi says, sighing, "nothing will ever change that. Selfishly, your mom and I want you here with us, but ultimately we want you to be happy." He stands and grabs a few empty plates. As he walks inside, he stops to peck my cheek. "She'll come around."

I take a deep breath after my monologue as the rest of the table sits in silence. Selena stands and urges that Javi's nap time is coming so they better leave.

"I really am happy for you, Neens," she says, squeezing my arm in parting.

I walk out to the front yard and sit on the little step in front of the gate and try to call Brodie again, but he won't answer.

*I really need to talk to you.*

Feeling alone, I grab my keys, fire up Gloria, and take off for an evening cruise, blasting George Michael's "Waiting for That Day."

I pack up my backpack to "Lonely As I Am" by Creature Canyon. I'm headed to the beach to photograph a brand's new line for a local sunscreen company. As I go to make my morning coffee in the kitchen, I notice Mom's particular absence. She must still be upset with me from yesterday. I open the fridge to grab the oat milk when I see a small post-it note stuck to the bottle. It reads in Mom's scratchy scrawl: *I do want you to be happy, xo.*

My heart lightens as if a twenty pound weight has been plucked from my shoulders. I grab my pack, the small paper bag of sunscreen products and head to SanO. After an hour or so of different product shots along the shoreline, I click down one last time on the shutter button. I grab all of the canisters and wedge them, along with my camera, back in my backpack. The sun blares in full force today at a warm seventy-two degrees, well, warm by beach cities' standards in SoCal. Enjoying the sun on my skin, I work in just my yellow bikini top and my denim shorts. I do a little rock dance through some tide pools, dredge across the sand towards Gloria, and hunt for sea glass, when I finally glance up and see Brodie.

*Brodie?!*

*I must be dreaming.* I shake my head to dispel the mirage, but discover Brodie still stands in front of me, leaning casually against my Land Cruiser. With arms folded across his chest, he rests against my open tailgate in his usual white shirt and boardies combo.

I stop dead in my tracks, staggered. My arms go limp at my sides. Shaking in joy and biting my lip in complete disbelief, my face erupts into the biggest smile, engulfing every square centimeter of my countenance. Without saying a word, without breaking eye contact, he walks towards me.

"What are you doing here?" I manage to whisper.

He's only a foot away. Instead of answering, he pulls me towards him and tilts my head back, pulling my mouth to his. We kiss passionately for a minute before we break away, wrapping our arms around each other and nuzzling into the crooks of each other's necks. We fit together like a puzzle. Unspoken greetings and feelings flow from him to me, and me to him as it suddenly feels like no time has passed since our goodbye. We both shake in happy tears that we're finally together. I reach up and kiss him tenderly, enjoying the sweet, familiar taste of him. Finally, I pull back, completely exasperated. I run my fingers through his cropped curls.

"How? How are you here? How did you find me?" I ask him, completely bewildered.

He cups my face in both of his tanned hands, as he searches my eyes, assessing any minute changes in my features. Mirroring him, I'm happy to see he's exactly the same as I remembered. He lightly pulls a stray curl away from my eye, and chuckles.

"I'll tell ya lata. Right now, I just wanna love ya."

A single tear rolls down my cheek.

"Brodie, you don't know how happy I am to see you, to touch you," I choke out.

He closes his eyes as I reach up and caress his face.

"Nah, yeah, I reckon I do," he breathes, "'cause it's the same for me, my Neens." We both touch our foreheads together, enjoying each other's simple presence for what feels like forever. We break apart. Brodie takes my backpack from me and carries it to the truck. He sits back on the tailgate, and says appreciably, "Ya know, ya never told me what a beauty she is. Neens, my partna, the hottie in the blue ute."

Laughing, I go and stand in between his legs so we're on the same level.

"I've been trying to call you, you know," I tell him.

"Yeah, sorry, been a bit busy, eh," he replies, smirking.

"Brodie, for real. How?" I ask again.

He stills for a second and looks out to the water, watching a couple of long boarders hang ten.

"Well, I just couldn't take it anymore. This was about the second after ya flew off, mind ya, so I applied for a temporary work visa for the hell of it, 'n shockingly, they said yeah," he explains. "As for today, I Ubered to yar house 'n yar mum happened to be outside when I pulled up." My eyes spring wide, but he continues before I have a chance to say anything. "At first I reckon she thought I was some rando bloke, but the second I said 'G'day' she knew who I was. I'll give her some credit, she stayed calm 'n collected, then offered to take me to coffee. Before ya say anythin', she told me ya were sleepin' 'n best not to wake ya."

I frown at this a little. I would happily have woken up to Brodie any time of the day or night.

"Nah, it's okay, Neens," he reassures me, and chuckles. "Besides there was somethin' I wanted to chat with her 'bout anyway. So we're sittin' down at brekky 'n she just dives right in. Felt like I was being interrogated or somethin' wild. Ya weren't exaggeratin' 'bout her."

"Oh, gosh," I mumble into his laughing chest, knowing exactly how my mom can be.

"Truly though, Lucy's fantastic. She's got a zest for life, like you," he says kindly, rubbing my shoulders. "Basically I reckon she wanted to suss me out, getta feel for me, 'n she seemed super keen on my intentions."

"What did you say?" I ask, stepping back.

"The truth o'course, the reason why I'm here."

"Which is?" I ask him, completely stunned, still not over the fact that he is in fact here. "I mean don't get me wrong, I'm over the moon you're here, but I just thought we'd have to wait until the travel ban lifted."

"What can I say? I reckon yar worth the prods 'n pokes 'n fourteen days of iso," he jests, playfully jabbing my side. He beams. "Yar mom told me about Mick's place. Congratulations, neighba."

"'Neighba,' 'partna,' I like how that sounds," I flirt, mimicking him, giving him a little smooch on his neck.

I can feel his face break out into a grin. He holds me around the belt loops of my shorts, but his hands inch up slowly as he nuzzles my neck.

"How 'bout Wifey?" he whispers.

I go completely still, then stand back so I can fully look him in the face. Stunned, I stare at him for a minute.

"Wifey?" I repeat, dumbfounded.

His happy-go lucky demeanor melts into one of tenderness and love, as he says, "I know we talked before, but it's been months now of agony. I understand ya wantin' to take this at yar own pace, but I want it all with ya, 'n I don't wanna wait any longa."

"Brodie, I—."

"Make me the happiest bloke on the planet, 'n say yes, say yull come home," he continues. "Whether that's here or there, I don't care... 'cause yar my home, Nina."

Thoughtfully and carefully, I lick my lips, forming my answer, and swallow.

"Brodie, I know I said I wasn't ready for that, and I wasn't, but all I know is I need to follow my heart, and my heart points homeward," I explain, sorting out my feelings aloud. "I miss our friends, and Stella, and I miss our life, but I don't want to marry you for those reasons." I grip the back of his neck heartily in my hands. "Like you said, you're my home. You're my partner, my best friend. You love me for me, you celebrate me, you *see* me. So for those reasons, yes, I will add 'Wifey' to my name."

His gaze burns a whole in mine as his entire face blossoms into the biggest scrunchy Nina face I've ever seen. Slowly, he leans in and waits for me to meet him halfway, which I gladly do.

"Wifey, eh?" he mutters in delight, and pulls me in for the kiss that sets my soul on fire.

# Prologue

Back in Straya, Brodie and I pick up where our life together paused. The printout of my Fiancé Visa sits framed by the entryway. It's our own little triumph, our daily reminder of a thankful life.

After a full day on the boat with the crew, we all pile in at our house. *Our* house; it still sounds funny to refer to it publicly as that. As I walk back to the bedroom to grab a jacket, I pass by our living room wall. A few of my drone prints hang largely next to the potted plants. On the other wall, aside from the beloved photo of Mick and me, and the other two of Brodie, we now have framed prints of us with our friends on the boat, and one of us with my family from when we were in The States. I smile at that one.

Ultimately, my family accepted my decision to emigrate here, and once they did, they have been nothing but supportive and enthusiastic. They're planning on coming out for a big trip once traveling eases up. Meanwhile, Brodie and I are slowly renovating Mick's house. We're not changing anything major, more like updating some of the plumbing and getting it ready for when the family visits. I'm also using it as my art studio whenever I feel inspired or want my own space. It's my little home away from home, a place I go to reflect and feel Mick with me.

Back at our house, I look out at the deck, quaintly lit by the twinkle lights and the dancing stars beyond, and I find myself beaming. The crew laughs as Brodie tells them more stories from America. Stubbies in hand, fresh fish on the grill, an imaginary ring on my finger where Mick's ring will go when the time's right - *life is more than good*.

"Settle on a date yet?" Donnie asks, biting into some chips.

"No," I say, as Brodie snorts. "It's not going to be like that."

"Nah, yeah," Mel interrupts, and chuckles. "Watch, one day we'll be out on some island or sandbar or somethin' 'n Neens will say 'I do.' No fuss, no thrills."

"Sounds dreamy," I genuinely admit with a hint of sass, as Brodie mutters at the same time, "Works for me."

He playfully raises his eyebrows at me as he suggestively bites his lip. For just a split second, I wish we were alone. Thankfully, now, there's all the time in the world for that.

Laughing, I reach over and crank the volume to Iration's "Coastin'." Brodie smiles and gives me a wink as he pulls the fish off the grill and tosses a chunk into Stella's open jaw. Shayno tries to hand Donnie his plate, but he's too distracted by his phone to take it. Jaz calls him out.

"Oy, I'm just gettin' ordained ova here, alright," he quips.

We all roar with laughter. I look around at all the illustrious faces I call home, before settling my gaze on Brodie, my true north.

As "Coastin'" plays on the speaker, I happily listen to the lyrics and realize that truer words have never been spoken: "*Nothin' in the world can ever take this from me. Alive with the feelin' that your lovin' gives me.*"

Our story is only just beginning.

# Acknowledgments

Thank you. Some days, I can't believe I wrote a novel, so thank you, thank you for reading it. I want to thank Mama, Daddio, Ricki, Mar, Prez, Jav, Grandma, Rach & Ryann for encouraging me to share this story. I want to celebrate those who find themselves on the outside. It's an easy place to get lost, and a lonely place to be. My hope is Nina inspires you to own your quirks, and embrace all you have to offer the world. *Don't be afraid.*

To all the bands who wrote such instrumental music in my life and the songs I've particularly included, I can't thank you enough. You're the glue keeping me grounded, fulfilled, and inspired. Honestly, I don't think I would make it in life without music. Please check out the playlist *True Blue at Heart* on Spotify for a list of all the tracks in chronological order.

To all the other female drone pilots out there, keep up the terrific work and fight the good fight to be seen...

To Stella, my muse, my puppy, my little Noodle, thanks for always being my second shadow.

A large part of this story wouldn't be present if not for my grandpa, Jack. As amazing as Mick is, he's a fraction of the man Grandpa was, so this one's for you, Grandpa. I'm sending you three big squeezes.

Lastly, there wouldn't even be a book without my biggest source of inspiration: Australia. I hope one day to swim in your waters, eat from your seas, and enjoy some laughs with your people. *Thank you.*

It's been an honor, I mean a real honor.

Tori Hernandez is a licensed remote pilot. Based in Southern California, you can find her droning the coastline, cruising in her FJ62 Land Cruiser usually with her trusty sidekick, Stella. Just listen for the music; she's always blasting her tunes. You can follow along on her traveling adventures on Instagram @lifeofacaliforniakid.

Printed in Great Britain
by Amazon

85826306R00284